KU-034-937

PRAISE FOR W.E.B. GRIFFIN AND HIS *NEW YORK TIMES* BESTSELLING SERIES...

THE CORPS

His acclaimed epic series of life and loyalty in the U.S. Marine Corps.

"GRIFFIN HAS CREATED A BRILLIANT STORY... not only worthwhile, it's a public service."
— *The Washington Times*

"GREAT READING. Griffin has done a superb job of mingling fact and fiction... His characters come to life."
— *The Sunday Oklahoman*

"LOTS OF ACTION and a love for the U.S. military and its men. Griffin delivers!"
— *The Dallas Morning News*

"THE CORPS combines the best elements of military history and the war story—the telling detail and political tangle of one mated to the energy and sweep of the other."
— *Publishers Weekly*

"THIS MAN HAS REALLY DONE HIS HOMEWORK ... I confess to impatiently awaiting the appearance of succeeding books in the series."
— *The Washington Post*

"PACKED WITH ALL THE LOVE, ACTION, AND EXCITEMENT GRIFFIN FANS HAVE COME TO EXPECT!"
— *Forecast*

Turn the page for more reviews of W.E.B. Griffin's bestsellers...

BROTHERHOOD OF WAR

His all-time classic series—a sweeping military epic of the United States Army that became a *New York Times* best-selling phenomenon.

"EXTREMELY WELL-DONE . . . FIRST-RATE!"
> —*The Washington Post*

"AN AMERICAN EPIC."
—Tom Clancy, bestselling author of *Clear and Present Danger* and *Without Remorse*

"ABSORBING . . . Fascinating descriptions of weapons, tactics, Army life, and battle."
> —*The New York Times*

"A MAJOR WORK . . . MAGNIFICENT . . . POWERFUL . . . If books about warriors and the women who love them were given medals for authenticity, insight, and honesty, *Brotherhood of War* would be covered with them."
> —William Bradford Huie, author of *The Klansman* and *The Execution of Private Slovik*

"A CRACKLING GOOD STORY. It gets into the hearts and minds of those who by choice or circumstances are called upon to fight our nation's wars."
> —William R. Corson, Lt. Col. (Ret.) U.S.M.C., author of *The Betrayal* and *The Armies of Ignorance*

"Griffin has captured the rhythms of army life and speech, its rewards and deprivations . . . ABSORBING!"
> —*Publishers Weekly*

BADGE OF HONOR

W.E.B. Griffin's bestselling saga of a major city police force—a gripping and realistic look at today's men in blue.

"DAMN EFFECTIVE . . . He captivates you with characters the way few authors can."

—Tom Clancy

"TOUGH, AUTHENTIC . . . POLICE DRAMA AT ITS BEST . . . Readers will feel as if they are part of the investigation, and the true-to-life characters will soon feel like old friends. EXCELLENT READING."

—Dale Brown, bestselling author of
Chains of Command

"NOT SINCE JOSEPH WAMBAUGH have we been treated to a police story of the caliber that Griffin gives us. He creates a story about real people in a real world doing things that are AS REAL AS TODAY'S HEADLINES."

—Harold Coyle, bestselling author of
Team Yankee and
Sword Point

"GRITTY, FAST-PACED . . . AUTHENTIC."

—Richard Herman, Jr.,
author of *The Warbirds*

"GRIFFIN'S BOOKS HAVE HOOKED ME . . . There is no one better!"

—*Chattanooga News-Free Press*

HONOR BOUND

W. E. B. GRIFFIN

PAN BOOKS

This edition published 2000 by Pan Books
an imprint of Macmillan Publishers Ltd
25 Eccleston Place, London SW1W 9NF
Basingstoke and Oxford
Associated companies throughout the world
www.macmillan.co.uk

This title first published in Great Britain 1995 by
SEVERN HOUSE PUBLISHERS LTD of
9–15 High Street, Sutton, Surrey SM1 1DF
by arrangement with The Berkley Publishing Group.

ISBN 0 330 39687 0

British Library Cataloguing in Publication Data
A catalogue record for this book is available
from the British Library.

Typeset by Hewer Text Composition Services, Edinburgh.
Printed and bound in Great Britain by
Mackays of Chatham plc, Chatham, Kent.

I would like to thank Mr. William W. Duffy II, of the United States Embassy in Buenos Aires, and Colonel José Manuel Menéndez, Cavalry, Argentine Army, Retired, who both went well beyond the call of duty in helping me in many ways as I was writing this book.

W.E.B. Griffin
Buenos Aires 10 August 1993

I

Three Grumman F4F Wildcats approached Henderson Field from
the west in a shallow descent from 15,000 feet.

These three single-engine fighters represented one hundred percent of the aircraft available to Marine Fighter Squadron VMF-
221—which put them at thirteen planes short of the sixteen they
were authorized. The Cactus Air Force, and ultimately the United
States Marine Corps, obviously had to do something.

The remaining pilots of VMF-221 had heard two fairly credible
rumors about what they would do.

According to the most pleasant rumor, any day now they would
return to Henderson and find the taxiways and sandbag revetments
crowded with sixteen glistening, new, well-maintained Wildcats
of a Marine fighter squadron flown in from an aircraft carrier to
replace VMF-221.

To those who desperately wished to believe this rumor, it didn't
make much sense to send replacement aircraft and pilots to a
squadron that had already suffered a loss of two hundred twenty
percent of its original aircraft and seventy percent of its original
complement of pilots. The only sensible solution was to bring in
a fresh squadron.

The other theory attempted to account for the reason why
VMF-221 had neither received enough aircraft and pilots to replace operational losses, nor had been relieved and replaced by a
fresh Marine Fighter Squadron. According to this rumor, the plan
was to replace all Marine aircraft with planes, pilots, and maintenance personnel of the U.S. Army Air Corps.

It was almost a matter of faith among Marines on Guadalcanal
that somewhere in the rear areas was a vast cornucopia of U.S.
Army Air Corps matériel and personnel perfectly suited for service on the island; all that had to be done to start this wealth

flowing to Guadalcanal was for the Army brass—in particular
General Douglas MacArthur—to belatedly recognize that the
Army and the Marine Corps were on the same side in this war.

Those who were looking for proof of the Army Air Corps'
matériel wealth and their ability to send some of it to Guadalcanal
seemed to find it whenever Boeing B-17 "Flying Fortresses"—
huge four-engine bombers with an eight-man crew—appeared at
Henderson Field. The squadron of Bell P-40 fighters stationed at
the field offered further proof . . . to those looking for it.

True, the B-17s didn't hit Japanese warships with any notable
consistency, and the P-40s had arrived without the proper oxygen
systems and thus couldn't operate above 12,000 feet. But that did
nothing to dissuade the *We Will Be Relieved By The Army Air
Corps* theorists of VMF-221. The B-17s bristled with .50-caliber
Browning machine-gun turrets, carried 500-pound bombs, and
were larger than any planes the Marines or Navy had, while the
Bell fighters mounted a through-the-propeller hub cannon larger
than any weapon in the Marine Corps arsenal and were more
effective in a ground-support role than the Wildcats.

As soon as the big brass came to their senses and realized how
the Cactus Air Force was hanging on to Henderson Field by their
fingernails (just as perilously as the Marine Corps was holding
on to Guadalcanal itself), a finger would be snapped and a vast
aerial armada of Army Air Corps aircraft would appear. Or so
went the rumor.

The leader of the three-plane flight of VMF-221 Wildcats was
unconvinced by both theories. He was First Lieutenant Cletus
Howell Frade, USMCR, a lanky—hundred fifty-five pounds, just
over six feet tall—dark-haired twenty-two-year-old.

Lieutenant Colonel Clyde W. Dawkins, USMC, Commanding
Officer, Marine Air Group 21, had told him (and Frade believed
him) that the Corps was not only fully aware that the First Marine
Division and MAG-21 were indeed hanging on to Guadalcanal
by their teeth, but was doing everything humanly possible to get
them reinforced. With a little luck, it might be possible to find
some planes somewhere, and an aircraft carrier to ferry them
within flying distance of Guadalcanal. In the meantime, they
would have to fight with what they had. It was not the first time
in the history of the Marine Corps, Dawkins had reminded him,
that Marines had been out on a limb fighting a nasty war in some
miserable location without adequate supplies. And it would not
be the last.

This information had led Cletus Frade to strongly suspect that he would not be going home from Guadalcanal in one piece. Or alive. The odds were against it. So far he had been lucky. Very lucky. But luck inevitably runs out. The odds increase to a point where, following the laws of probability, you lose.

He tried to avoid such thoughts, but that was impossible. So he tried to keep in mind what his uncle Jim had told him over and over: *"There's no point worrying about things you can't control."* Uncle Jim had raised him; but before that he'd been a Marine in France in World War I. So whenever Clete started to think about the growing probability that he would either be killed or badly injured, he tried to force his mind off the subject by imagining more attractive things.

Sometimes conjuring up the meal he intended to eat when he got home to New Orleans worked. But most often he turned to his memories of undraped female bodies. Recently, however, when he forced his mind off the unpleasant possibilities, he found himself turning more to food than to women. He supposed this was because he was undernourished and debilitated by the climate, like every other Marine on the 'Canal.

He weighed right at one-eighty when, fresh from Pensacola, he joined VMF-221—in time for the Battle of Midway. On 10 August, three days after the 1st Marine Division invaded the island, he was down to one-seventy. That was the day he flew a Wildcat off the ferry-carrier USS *Long Island* onto the airfield the Japanese had started and the Marines had made marginally operational. This had since become famous—or infamous—as Henderson Field (named after a Marine aviator who'd died at Midway).

He was now down to one fifty-five. His ribs showed under skin that was dotted and pocked with the festering bites of tropical insects. When he brushed his teeth, the brush came away bloody; and his tongue could move both his incisors and some of his other teeth.

Every one of the original F4Fs was gone—some shot down in daily combat, some crashed on landing or takeoff, and some destroyed by Japanese naval artillery bombardment, or by Japanese bombers or Zeroes strafing the field. Sixteen of the original nineteen pilots were also gone—some lost in combat, some killed or injured in aircraft accidents, and three killed by Japanese twelve-inch naval artillery shells—while they were cowering like rats in holes in the sandy soil. And gone, too, were all but three of the replacement aircraft, and many of their pilots.

It was difficult to believe that he would be luckier than the others. It was much more likely that the name Frade, Cletus H., 1/LT would appear on some After Action Report followed by the letters KIA, or MIA, or WIA (*K*illed *I*n *A*ction, *M*issing *I*n *A*ction, *W*ounded *I*n *A*ction).

When Henderson Field appeared below, Clete reached up and pulled his goggles down over his eyes, then looked out his open cockpit to his right, at his wingman, who three days before had reported aboard VMF-221 as a replacement pilot. The new man's eyes were on him.

Clete made two gestures: He tapped his own goggles to order the new guy to put his goggles on. After that he pointed downward, then made a circular motion, signaling that they were to make a circular descent to the airfield. The new guy, with an exaggerated bobbing of his head, signaled that he understood his orders.

Clete then looked to the left and repeated the circular descent signal to the pilot of the F4F flying twenty-five feet off his wingtip, and who already had his goggles in place. There was another exaggerated nodding of the head to signal his readiness to comply with his orders.

Clete took a final look at his instruments. Everything was in the green. He was sure that he had taken a couple of hits—indeed, there were fresh eruptions in the aluminum skin of his right wing—but apparently nothing important had been hit.

He pushed the nose of the Wildcat down and to the right, retarded the throttle, adjusted the prop, and began his descent.

A thousand feet indicated off the deck, he put the F4F into a much sharper turn, simultaneously pulled back on his stick, and released the cog that held his wheels in place. The forces of gravity came into play, pulling the wheels from the retracted position. The manual crank one was supposed to use for this spun rapidly and more than a little dangerously, but the wheels came down. The forces-of-gravity technique was specifically prohibited by U.S. Navy Bureau of Aeronautics regulations, but BuAir regulations seemed irrelevant on the 'Canal.

He leveled off, headed out to sea, turned, and made a straight-in, shallow approach to Henderson. Several B-17s were parked near the Pagoda—the control tower—and three F4Fs were on the taxiway by the threshold of the runway, waiting to take off.

The moment his wheels touched down, he knew he was in trouble. The Wildcat veered sharply to the right, taken over by forces far too strong for him to overcome using his rudder.

Time seemed to move very slowly as adrenaline started to pump.

Either my right wheel is gone, or the strut is not fully lowered.

No. I would already have started to cartwheel.

I'm going off the runway, that's for sure.

What I've probably got is a punctured tire.

The choice is to stick with it and see what happens—which means I will either run into a revetment or a parked airplane. If I don't cartwheel first. Or to take my chances putting the nose in the ground—which means I will turn over.

He cut the master switch, released the wheels lock, and shoved the stick forward.

For a moment, nothing happened.

Then came a screech of tortured metal as the propeller bit into the earth. And he felt himself being thrown against his shoulder harness with a force infinitely stronger than an arrested landing on an aircraft carrier.

And then the F4F flipped over on its back, and there was a horrifying screech of tearing metal as it slid across the field.

And then, with a lurch that threw him against the side of the cockpit, the airplane stopped.

He tried to move and couldn't.

You've got to get out of here. Dead switch or not, this thing is going to blow up.

He managed to put his hands on the shoulder and seat-belt buckle, and to lift it. He fell out of the airplane onto the ground.

My God, I can't move! What did I do, break my back?

I can smell avgas!

Worse, he could see it leaking from a ruptured tank.

I don't want to go this way!

He managed to start crawling. Every breath hurt, and he was convinced he had broken a rib, several ribs. He couldn't use his left arm. There was no pain, it just didn't work.

He crawled toward the tail, pushing himself with his feet.

God, don't let me burn!

And then hands, strong hands, were clutching the thin material of his Suit, Flying, Cotton, Tropical.

He was dragged across the ground.

More than one guy has to be doing that. Two.

There was the whoosh of gasoline igniting.

Whoever was dragging him stopped doing that, and suddenly someone was lying on top of him. The weight hurt his ribs.

After a moment, a voice said: "I don't think it's going to blow up."

Some of the weight pressing him into the ground came off. Then the rest of it.

"You all right, Lieutenant?" a voice asked.

"I don't know," Clete replied, truthfully.

He tried to roll over, to get his face out of the dirt.

Strong hands pressed him back.

"I think you better wait until the Corpsmen show up before you try to move," a voice said—a suggestion that was in fact an order.

God, he thinks my neck is broken! Or my back! Is that why I don't feel any pain, except when I breathe?

He heard the sound of a jeep engine approaching, and then the particular squeal of a jeep's brakes.

And then there were hands, fingers probing him.

"You with us, Lieutenant?" a gruff but surprisingly gentle voice inquired.

"Yeah."

"It looks like you bent your airplane," the voice said. "Can you move your legs?"

Clete moved them.

"How about your arms?"

"I know I can move the right one," Clete said, and demonstrated.

"I'm going to roll you on your back. If it starts to hurt, yell."

It hurt, but he didn't feel much real pain.

He found himself staring up into the face of a rough-hewn Navy Corpsman, who looked far younger than Clete imagined from hearing his voice.

The Corpsman was manipulating his left arm.

"Any pain?"

"It feels like it's asleep."

The Corpsman pinched his upper arm painfully.

"Hey!"

"How about here?" The Corpsman chuckled, and painfully pinched the skin on the back of his hand.

Clete said, "Shit."

"It looks like you had a good landing, Lieutenant," the Corpsman said.

"What?" Clete asked incredulously.

"I thought you guys say any landing you can walk away from is a good one."

"I didn't walk away," Clete argued. "Somebody dragged me."

"Close enough," the Corpsman said. "What we're going to do now is put you on a stretcher, haul you to the hospital, and let a doctor have a look at you."

Lieutenant Colonel Clyde W. Dawkins, USMC, walked up to the hospital bed of First Lieutenant Cletus H. Frade, USMCR. Dawkins was commanding officer of Marine Air Group 21. He was a tall, thin, sharp-featured man in the middle stage of male-pattern baldness, and he was wearing khakis, sweat-stained at the armpits and down the back. Over his arm he carried a Suit, Flying, Cotton, Tropical; a T-shirt; and a pair of skivvy shorts.

"I have been led to believe, Lieutenant Frade," he said, handing Clete the clothing, "that you have once again disgraced the United Marine Corps. I am here to rectify that situation."

This was intended as a joke, but was not received that way. Frade's face showed embarrassment, even humiliation.

"Clete, for Christ's sake, that was a joke," Dawkins went on hastily. "Believe me, you are not the first aviator who . . . had a small bowel problem . . . going through something like you just went through. Including your beloved MAG commander."

"I used to think that 'shitting your pants' was just a figure of speech," Clete said.

"Now you know it's not," Dawkins said. "I'm just surprised this was your first time."

"Sorry about the airplane, Skipper," Clete said, wanting to get off the subject.

"What happened?"

"It veered to the right on touchdown. I probably had a flat; I don't think the strut collapsed."

"Feinberg told me he saw you taking hits from the tail gunner of the Betty . . ." Dawkins said, referring to a Japanese bomber aircraft.

Feinberg? Who the hell is Feinberg? Oh, the New Guy.

". . . just before her wing came off," Dawkins went on. "How many does that make, Clete?"

"I thought I felt something," Clete said, sitting up on the cot to demonstrate with his hands the relative positions of the aircraft. "I took her from above and to the left, and was pulling up . . ."

He was naked under the sheet, and Dawkins noticed the ulcerated insect bites and the ugly blue-black of his left arm and shoulder.

He must have really slammed into the side of the cockpit, Dawkins thought. *I'm surprised nothing was broken.*

"How many does that make, Clete?" Dawkins asked again.

Clete shrugged.

"Don't tell me you don't know," Dawkins chided.

"Six. The Betty was confirmed?" Dawkins nodded. "Then seven," Clete finished.

"Seven is enough to be a certified hero," Dawkins said.

"Sir?"

"There was a radio overnight," Dawkins said. "Right from Eighth and Eye.* Your name has apparently been added to the roster of certified heroes."

"Sir, I don't under—"

"The War Bond Tour, Clete," Dawkins explained. "A dozen certified heroes have been chosen to tour the West Coast to inspire civilians to buy War Bonds, or maybe to rush to the recruiting office. Maybe both. Anyway, you're on it."

Don't get your hopes up. At the last minute something will happen and they'll change their minds.

"I thought you had to have a medal to get that."

"Your DFC, your second, has come through."

"When would I go?"

"The radio said 'will proceed immediately.' So if you feel up to it, you can be on this afternoon's R4D to Espíritu Santo." The R4D was the Navy/Marine Corps version of the Douglas DC-3 (C-47) transport aircraft.

"No shit?" Clete blurted.

"A particularly inappropriate vulgarism, wouldn't you say, Mr. Frade, under the circumstances?"

Frade blushed. This made him look even younger than his twenty-two years.

"Frade, you're one hell of a pilot and a good Marine. I'm going to miss you around here."

Frade blushed even deeper.

*Headquarters, USMC, is located at Eighth and "I" Streets in Washington, D C.

"Can I ask a favor?" Dawkins asked.

"Yes, Sir. Of course."

"Stop by the office. Say, at 1400. Precisely, as a matter of fact, at 1400. The R4D leaves at 1430. I'd be grateful if you would mail a letter for me, to my wife, when you get to the States."

"Yes, Sir, of course. 1400."

I did not tell him, Dawkins thought, *that there will also be a small ceremony waiting for him then, during which the Commanding General of the First Marine Division will pin the Distinguished Flying Cross (Second Award) on his chest. Like most good Marine officers, he is made uncomfortable by such events. He just might not show up. And I do want him to mail the letter to my wife.*

"I'm glad you walked away from that one, Clete," Dawkins said, offering him his hand.

"I'm sorry I wrecked the airplane, Colonel."

"What the hell, Clete, when we run out of airplanes, maybe they'll call the war off."

[TWO]
Headquarters, Sixth Army
Stalingrad, USSR
3 October 1942

Oberstleutnant Wilhelm von Stearner waited patiently just inside the closed office door until the tall, taciturn, fifty-two-year-old commander of the Sixth Army, General Friedrich von Paulus, raised his eyes from the documents on his desk and indicated without speaking that he was prepared to hear what von Stearner had on his mind. He then came to attention.

"Herr General, Brigadeführer von Neibermann asks for a moment of your time. He says it's quite important."

Waffen-SS Brigadeführer Luther von Neibermann was Political Adviser to the Sixth Army. Like many—perhaps most—military commanders, von Paulus did not like political advisers. They got in the way of military operations, for one thing. For another, they had their own lines of communication to Berlin, over which they offered their own opinions of the conduct of the operations they were involved in. Von Paulus did not consider himself above criticism, but criticism from someone who was not a professional soldier was hard to swallow.

Waffen-SS Brigadeführer Luther von Neibermann's rank was honorary. Before the war he was in the Foreign Ministry, where he had early on been smart enough to align himself with the National Socialists. In von Paulus's opinion, he had risen higher in the Foreign Ministry hierarchy than he had any right to, based on his intelligence and his suitability. He was a short, paunchy, bald man of forty-two, who looked ludicrous in his black uniform with the death's-head insignia. Von Paulus loathed him, and what he stood for; but he was of course careful not to let his feelings show.

More than one senior officer's military career had ended when unsupported and unjustified accusations of defeatism had been leveled by a political adviser. Von Paulus was determined that wasn't going to happen to him.

"Did he say what's on his mind?" von Paulus asked.

"He said it was a sensitive matter of importance."

"Ask the Brigadeführer to come in, please."

Von Stearner turned and opened the door.

"The General will see you now, Herr Brigadeführer," he announced.

Von Neibermann marched in, crossed over to von Paulus's desk, and clicked his heels, then gave the stiff-armed Nazi salute and the now ritual greeting, "Heil Hitler!"

Von Paulus touched his forehead with a gesture that might have been a salute, muttered something that might have been "Heil Hitler," and then met von Neibermann's eyes.

"How may I be of service, Herr Brigadeführer?"

"Herr General, it is with deep regret that I must inform you of the death in battle of Standartenführer von Zainer."

Von Paulus was genuinely sorry to hear this. He knew von Zainer. He had never quite understood why a man of good family, with a strong military heritage, had elected to transfer to the Waffen-SS—even though that was the path to more rapid promotion than he would have found in the Panzertruppen. All the same, von Zainer had been a good, even outstanding soldier, first in Poland, then in France, and now here.

"I am very sorry to hear that," von Paulus said. "Are you familiar with the circumstances?"

"The Standartenführer was making an aerial reconnaissance, Herr General. His Storch was shot down." The Fieseler Storch was a single-engine, two-place observation aircraft, the German equivalent of the Piper Cub.

"The fortunes of war," von Paulus said.

It was typical of von Zainer to personally conduct his own reconnaissance, with the risk that entailed, although such actions were officially frowned upon for senior officers (a Waffen-SS Standartenführer held a rank equivalent to an Oberst, or colonel). But von Zainer probably had his reasons, von Paulus decided. And now he was dead, so criticism was out of place.

"He had Captain Duarte with him, Herr General."

Von Paulus's raised eyebrows told von Neibermann that the name meant nothing to him.

"The Argentine, Herr General," von Neibermann explained. "Hauptmann Jorge Alejandro Duarte."

Von Paulus, now remembering, was genuinely sorry to hear this too. The young Argentine Cavalry captain had been an extraordinarily nice-looking young man; and during the few minutes of the Argentine's courtesy call, von Paulus had realized that Duarte did not view his attachment as an observer as a vacation from his duties at his embassy in Berlin but as a learning experience for a professional officer.

"I don't quite understand," von Paulus said.

"Captain Duarte volunteered to fly the mission, Herr General."

Von Paulus now remembered Hauptmann Duarte telling him—with the enthusiasm of a young, energetic officer—that he had asked for and been granted a detail to the Aviación Militar branch of the Argentinean Army. In his words: "Aircraft are the cavalry of the future."

He was not supposed to do that, von Paulus thought. *He was an Argentine. Argentina is neutral. Taking an active role was a violation of the Geneva Convention.*

Not that the Russians would have paid any attention to his neutral status if they'd been able to lay their hands on him. That was probably his rationale for doing what he should not be doing.

"Have we recovered the bodies?" von Paulus asked.

"Von Zainer's men recovered them within minutes, Herr General," von Neibermann said admiringly. "The Storch went down in the Volga."

If the Russians had found the bodies and had recognized an Argentinean uniform, there might have been complications, von Paulus thought. And then he wondered, *Is that what's bothering von Neibermann?*

"Be so good, Herr Brigadeführer, to inform me of the time of the burial service. I would like to attend."

"Herr General, there are political ramifications of this unfortunate incident."

"You mean because he was flying the airplane when he should not have been?"

"I mean because he died fighting communism."

"I don't quite follow you, Herr Brigadeführer."

"I think the body should not be buried here," von Neibermann said. "It should be escorted to Berlin, and turned over to the Argentinean Ambassador. I would not be at all surprised if they wished to repatriate it."

Von Paulus said nothing. He waited, his face impassive, for von Neibermann to continue.

"There is enormous propaganda potential in this incident, Herr General," von Neibermann said. "This brave officer's unfortunate death at the hands of the communists could well serve to maintain—indeed, to buttress—Argentine sympathy for our cause."

"What exactly do you think I should do, von Neibermann?"

"I believe Captain Duarte's remains should be transported to Berlin immediately, by air. I have been informed that your permission, Herr General, is required for space on a transport aircraft."

"The transport aircraft are being used to evacuate our badly wounded," von Paulus said, thinking aloud. "And officer couriers."

"I respectfully submit, Herr General, that this is an extraordinary circumstance."

"Very well," von Paulus said, and raised his voice: "Von Stearner!"

Oberstleutnant von Stearner appeared almost immediately.

"Arrange for a priority for Brigadeführer von Neibermann to transport a body to Berlin . . ."

"For the body and myself," von Neibermann added. "I think under the circumstances that is appropriate."

And it will give you a chance to go to Berlin, won't it? And regale the Austrian Corporal and his henchmen with tales of your bravery at Stalingrad? Perhaps with a little luck, you might not have to come back.

"Do it, please, Willi," von Paulus said.

"Jawohl, Herr General," von Stearner said.

[THREE]
Headquarters, Company "A"
76th Parachute Engineer Battalion
82nd Airborne Division
Fort Bragg, North Carolina
1345 5 October 1942

Captain John R. McGuire, commanding Able Company of the
Seventy-sixth, had not been told why it had been deemed necessary to demolish and remove from the site the World War I
power-generating station. The stocky, muscular, twenty-four-
year-old graduate of West Point had been informed only that his
company was charged with the mission.

The station was situated in a remote corner of the enormous
Fort Bragg reservation on what was now a 105- and 155-mm
artillery impact area. It consisted of several sturdy brick buildings,
now gutted, and a 150-foot brick chimney. The rusting hulks of
half a dozen World War I Ford-built tanks were scattered around
it, as if protecting it. Most of these were half buried in the ground,
and were also now showing scars where they had been hit by
artillery.

The mission could be regarded in two ways: As a dirty, unnecessary job dreamed up by some jackass at Division Headquarters. In an artillery impact area, it would be just a matter of
time until the chimney and the buildings around it were reduced
to rubble. Or as an opportunity to give his men some realistic,
hands-on training in demolitions and using bulldozers and other
heavy equipment.

Captain McGuire elected to see the mission in the latter regard.
He thus received permission from Battalion to delay the prescribed company training for five days, successfully arguing that
it would benefit the men of his company more not only to practice
their skills, but to become familiar with how other specialists
performed their duties.

In other words, the entire company would watch the second
platoon rig explosive charges on the chimney and the gutted
buildings (these would be designed to knock the chimney down
and reduce the massive brickwork to large chunks). Then the
entire company would watch the first platoon, using air-hammers,
reduce the large chunks of masonry to sizes which the third pla-

toon would then load onto trucks and haul away. During all of
these operations, everyone would lend a hand, wherever possible;
they'd all get their hands dirty. Finally, everyone would get a
chance to watch the company's bulldozers scrape the area and
turn it back into bare ground.

Since Captain McGuire thought of himself as something of an
expert in the skills required for this project, he had given it a
good deal of thought. In his judgment, it would take two days to
lay the initial demolition charges. Using the available engineer
manuals, he had precisely calculated the explosive needed to top-
ple the chimney and shatter the brickwork of the surrounding
buildings.

It would then take another two days, using both explosives and
air-hammers, to reduce the chunks to manageable sizes, and a
final day to load everything up, truck it off, and bulldoze the site.

He had kept this information to himself. In his view, the best
way for his platoon-leading lieutenants to learn how to do something was to do it themselves—using the available manuals as a
guide, of course.

Because Second Lieutenant Anthony J. Pelosi commanded his
second platoon, he was charged with toppling the tower. After
Pelosi surveyed the site, he came up with an Explosives Requirement that, in Captain McGuire's judgment, was woefully insuf-
ficient for the task.

Even so, McGuire decided to let Pelosi fail. When Pelosi blew
his charges and the chimney and the buildings still stood, he
would learn the painful and humiliating truth that he didn't know
nearly as much about demolitions as he thought he did.

Pelosi's overconfidence was perhaps understandable. Very soon
after he arrived in Able Company, Pelosi informed McGuire that
in Chicago, where he came from, his family operated a firm called
Pelosi & Sons Salvage Company; his father was one of the sons.
McGuire instantly concluded that the firm was connected with
used auto parts or something of that nature; but that did not turn
out to be the case. Rather, the business involved the salvage of
bridges, water tanks, and other steel-framed structures. The first
step in the salvage process, Lieutenant Pelosi went on to explain,
was knocking the structure down. This was normally accomplished by explosives.

While he was not arrogant about it—Pelosi was really a nice
kid, who had the makings of a good officer—he was nonetheless
unable to conceal his conviction that he knew more about explo-

sives and demolition than anyone he'd met in the Army.

After Pelosi gave him his Explosives Requirement list, his more than a little annoying aura of self-confidence inspired McGuire to go back and recalculate the explosives necessary for the job. Recalculation confirmed McGuire's belief that all Pelosi's charges were going to do was make a lot of noise.

Captain McGuire's major problem with Pelosi, however, was not his misplaced self-confidence, but his application for transfer. McGuire was trying to be philosophical about it.

For one thing, he told himself, no officer is indispensable. Losses of officers, either through routine transfers or eventually in combat, were inevitable; and as commanding officer, he should be prepared to deal with them. For another, when a young, full-of-piss-and-vinegar second lieutenant, fresh from both Officer Candidate School and the Parachute School at Fort Benning (in other words, he had *volunteered* for both OCS and Airborne), saw a notice on the Bulletin Board soliciting volunteers for an unspecified military intelligence assignment—volunteers who were parachute-qualified officers fluent in one or more of a dozen listed foreign languages—it was to be expected that he would volunteer.

Lieutenant Pelosi was not quite old enough to vote; and, Captain McGuire was quite sure, he had not yet lost either his boyish enthusiasm or his boyish taste for adventure. He almost certainly saw himself parachuting behind enemy lines, Thompson submachine gun in hand, à la Alan Ladd or Tyrone Power in the movies. On the ground, when he was not blowing up Mussolini's headquarters, he'd spend his time in the arms of some large-breasted Italian beauty. (He was fluent in Italian; where else could they send him?)

If real life actually worked that way, McGuire thought, he would have been happy to see Pelosi go. But McGuire had been around the Army long enough—his father, also a West Pointer, had just been promoted to Brigadier General—to view somewhat suspiciously the recruitment of parachute-qualified officers with foreign language skills.

Military Intelligence, for example, needed people to read the *Osservatore,* the Vatican newspaper, to see if there was anything there that could remotely be of interest to the U.S. Army. After receiving permission to recruit volunteers, Military Intelligence had decided to recruit from the Airborne Forces, since a selection process eliminating all but the most intelligent and highly motivated officers had already been performed.

Captain McGuire did not believe that Military Intelligence would be crippled if Second Lieutenant Pelosi did not join its ranks. Able Company, however, needed him. He possessed a quality of leadership that McGuire to a large degree found missing in his other lieutenants.

McGuire was therefore determined to retain at all costs the services of Second Lieutenant Pelosi in Able Company.

First he tried to counsel the young officer, suggesting to him that he could make a greater contribution to the war effort right here in Able Company than he could reading the Vatican newspaper behind a desk someplace. When that failed (Pelosi was polite but adamant), McGuire wrote what he frankly thought was a masterful 1st Indorsement to Pelosi's application for transfer, outlining his present value to Able Company and his potential usefulness in the future, and recommending that for the good of the service, the application should not be favorably considered.

He then led the Battalion Sergeant Major to understand that he would not be heartbroken if Lieutenant Pelosi's application for transfer became lost.

Next, he tried, and failed, to have the battalion commander declare Pelosi as essential, and thus ineligible for transfer.

"The only thing you can do is talk him out of it, Red," the battalion commander said. "There's nothing I can do to keep the application from going forward."

That had been more than a month ago, long enough for Captain McGuire to begin to hope that Pelosi's application would never reemerge from the maw of Army administration—like so many other documents inserted into it.

But this morning it had finally surfaced.

And now there was one last hope . . . because it actually looked like MI had sort of shot themselves in the foot: When Pelosi saw what they'd done, he could, after consideration, withdraw his application for transfer. An officer could change his mind about a volunteer assignment. People decided every day, for example, that they'd rather not jump out of airplanes anymore. Since parachute duty was voluntary, they could quit. This MI assignment was also voluntary; Pelosi could change his mind about it.

When the charges Pelosi had been laying all morning (in half the time McGuire felt was necessary to do a proper job) failed to do more than make noise, a chastened, humiliated Second Lieutenant Pelosi might be willing to listen to reason. Instead of jumping all over his ass, McGuire was going to be kind and understanding.

When McGuire's jeep reached the power station, he found the company scattered over a small rise two hundred yards from the chimney, some on the ground, some sitting on trucks and three-quarter-ton dozers, scrapers, and the flatbed tractors that had carried them to the site.

When they saw the company commander's jeep, some of the noncoms started moving among the men, to get them up and at least looking interested.

McGuire turned toward the chimney and saw Second Lieutenant Pelosi coming out of one of the gutted buildings. He signaled for his driver to head for the chimney.

When he drove up, Second Lieutenant Anthony J. Pelosi saluted crisply, smiled, and said, "Good afternoon, Sir. I'm glad you could come out. I'm just about ready to blow this sonofabitch."

McGuire returned the salute.

"I'm glad you waited until I came out here, Pelosi," McGuire said, more than a little annoyed.

Pelosi picked up on the sarcasm.

"Sir," he said, a little uneasily. "The Captain did not say he wished to be here when I blew it."

No, I didn't, McGuire realized. *It never entered my mind that you would come close to having your charges in place before fifteen or sixteen hundred.*

"No problem, Lieutenant. I'm here now. You say your charges are laid?"

"All I have to do is hook up the detonator, Sir. This was my final look-around."

"Well, let me have a look," McGuire said.

He gestured for his driver to take the jeep over to where the company waited for the show to start, then walked around the site, following the electrical cord to the various places Pelosi had laid his charges.

They were in much the same places he would have chosen himself, the difference being that he would have used at least twice as much explosive.

"You're sure you're using enough explosive?"

"Yes, Sir. If anything, I used a little more than I had to."

That, Lieutenant, is the voice of ignorance speaking.

He noticed more wire on the ground and followed it with his

eyes. The first pair disappeared under one of the derelict World War I tanks.

"Would you care to explain that to me, Lieutenant?"

Pelosi looked uncomfortable.

"Sir, it was my understanding that the Captain wanted this to be a familiarization exercise for the men."

"And?"

"Since I had a little extra stuff, and the time, I had some of the noncoms lay charges under those old tanks. I figured they would like to see something blow they had laid themselves."

"You didn't use all the stuff—the explosives—you asked for?"

"No, Sir," Pelosi said, and pointed to several canvas satchels. "Even after rigging the tanks, that was left over."

Pelosi, you are about to make a three-star horse's ass of yourself in front of the entire company. All they are going to see is a couple of puffs of smoke. I really hate to see that happen, but it's too late to do anything about it.

"Pelosi, you're sure about what you've done? The men expect to see that chimney come down."

"It'll come down, Sir. That's not my first chimney."

OK. A dose of humiliation is often just what a second lieutenant needs.

"I'll give you a hand with your excess explosives," McGuire said, and bent to pick up one of the canvas satchels. He started toward the rise where the company was waiting. Pelosi picked up the other satchel, caught up with him, and fell in step.

"You'll remember, Tony," McGuire began conversationally, "that I was suspicious of it when we talked about you volunteering for the Military Intelligence assignment?"

"Yes, Sir."

"There is no greater joy in a man's life, Pelosi, than being able to say, ''I told you so.'''

"Sir?"

"Your orders are in," McGuire said, and, taking them from the lower right pocket of his field jacket, handed Pelosi a quarter-inch-thick stack of mimeograph paper.

HEADQUARTERS
82nd Airborne Division
Fort Bragg, N.C.

5 October 1942

SPECIAL ORDERS:
NUMBER 207:

EXTRACT

****

56. 2nd Lt PELOSI, Anthony J 0-459967, CE,
USAR, is relieved from Co ''A'' 76th Para Eng
Bn, 82nd A/B Div this sta, and transferred to
WP 4201st Army Detachment, National
Institutes of Health Building, Washington
D.C. AUTH: TWX Hq War Department, Subj:
''Transfer of Officer'' dtd 10 Oct 42. Off auth
US Govt Rail Tvl. No Delay En Route Leave Is
Auth. Off is not auth shipment of household
goods or personal automobile, and is not
authorized to be accompanied by dependents.
Approp: S99-99999910.

****

BY COMMAND OF MAJOR GENERAL RIDGWAY:

OFFICIAL:

Charles M. Scott, Jr.,
1st Lieutenant, AGC
Acting Adjutant

"The National Institutes of *Health?*" Lieutenant Pelosi asked
wonderingly.

"Well, I told you it was going to turn out to be something like that," McGuire said. "But maybe, Pelosi, just maybe, I could go to the Colonel and see if he could get you out of this."

"You think he could?" Lieutenant Pelosi asked.

"Well, it wouldn't hurt to ask. I'll have the company clerk type up a letter for you, saying that you've changed your mind."

Lieutenant Pelosi looked at Captain McGuire but said nothing.

They were approaching the small rise. A network of wires leading from the chimney, the buildings, and the tanks came together at a waist-high wall of sandbags. Two noncoms were behind it, guarding a canvas-cased detonator.

"You mean you want to go to the Army detachment at the National Institutes of *Health?*" McGuire asked incredulously.

"What I want to do now, Sir, is take down that chimney," Pelosi said, walking toward the firing pit. "I don't like leaving primed charges laying around any longer than I have to."

If I don't get him to change his mind now, that's the end of it. He'll be so humiliated that he'll be willing to go to the National Institutes of Health as a ward boy.

The two noncoms came to attention.

"You two join the company on the hill," McGuire ordered, and waited until they had gone.

"You didn't need them anymore, did you, Pelosi?"

"I just wanted to know where the detonator was, Sir. I didn't want one of the men to start doing this himself."

He took the detonator and began to hook wires to it.

"Pelosi, I don't like to see an officer, any officer, but especially one I like and in whom I see a good deal of potential, embarrassed in front of his men."

"Sir?"

"The charges you laid, Lieutenant," McGuire said sternly, "are wholly inadequate. When you twist that handle, all you're going to get is a large bang and a puff of smoke. Now, what I'm going to do is call this off and lay them properly."

Pelosi met his eyes.

"Sir, with respect, when I blow this, the chimney will come down. If it doesn't, I'll withdraw my application for transfer."

Better to have him here, even humiliated, than to humiliate him by relaying his charges and then see him go.

"You have a deal, Lieutenant," McGuire said.

"With your permission, Sir?"

McGuire nodded.

"Fire in the Hole!" Pelosi shouted, in a surprisingly loud voice, repeated the shout twice, and then twisted the handle of the detonator.

McGuire looked at the chimney. As he expected, there was a dull explosion, a faint suggestion of fire, and a small cloud of smoke.

He looked at Pelosi. His face bore a look neither of surprise nor embarrassment, but of satisfaction.

McGuire turned back toward the chimney. As he watched, as if in slow motion, the 150-foot-tall brick chimney shuddered, then seemed to fall in on itself, settling toward the ground erect, in an almost gentle motion.

There were shouts from the men on the rise, and then applause.

McGuire saw now a large cloud of dust at the base of the chimney as it seemed to disintegrate in front of his eyes.

Pelosi had meanwhile connected a second set of wires to the generator. McGuire watched as he twisted the handle. There was now a rumbling roar from the crashing bricks, over which nothing could be heard, and the dust cloud at the base was thick, and nothing could be seen through it.

McGuire wondered if the second set of charges had gone off. But after a moment, he judged that they had, for the cloud at the base of the chimney had grown. Pelosi was already connecting a third set of wires to the detonator.

He waited the forty-five seconds or so necessary for most of the dust cloud on the ground to disperse enough to show everybody that the walls of the buildings were down, shattered into six-foot segments, and lying on their sides. Then he twisted the handle again.

This time there was a series of small explosions. After each, one of the World War I tanks flew into the air, one of them at least fifty feet.

McGuire met Pelosi's eyes as another burst of cheers and applause came from the company on the rise.

"The First Sergeant can collect this gear and get the company back to the Post. You can ride with me, and collect your gear, at the BOQ," Captain McGuire said. "I'll see about getting you a ride into Fayetteville. With a little bit of luck, you might be able to get a berth on the 7:05 to Washington."

II

[ONE]
Schloss Wachtstein
Pomerania
8 October 1942

"You are talking treason, you realize," Generalmajor Graf Karl-Friedrich von Wachtstein said softly, without emotion. The short, slight, nearly bald fifty-four-year-old very carefully placed his crystal cognac snifter on the heavy table in his library, then leaned back in his chair, raised his eyes to Generalmajor Dieter von Haas, and waited for his old friend to reply.

"I am talking about saving Germany, Karl," von Haas said.

"The Austrian Corporal is protected by a regiment, each of whose members devoutly believes he is the salvation of Germany."

"He will destroy Germany, and you know it."

"You are not the first to come to me, Dieter," von Wachtstein said.

"I am ashamed that I was not."

"I told them all the same thing: I believe any attempt to assassinate Hitler is doomed to failure."

"So is Freddy von Paulus's mission at Stalingrad," von Haas interrupted.

"And that in the unlikely happenstance that such an attempt did succeed," von Wachtstein went on, ignoring him, "we might not—Germany might not—be at all better off. His successor would be Hermann Goering. We would exchange a psychopath for a drug addict. And upon the death of Herr Schicklgruber, the slime around him . . . and I include the entire inner circle . . . would immediately put into operation their own plans to get rid of Hermann. There would be chaos."

"Wouldn't anything be better than what we have now, Karl?" von Haas asked.

"I'm not at all sure," von Wachtstein said.

"I thank you for hearing me out, Karl."

"I have not turned you down," von Wachtstein said.

"That's what it sounded like."

"I have a condition . . . a price."

Von Haas could not quite mask his astonishment. And obviously to find time to carefully consider his reply, he leaned forward and picked up the bottle of Rémy Martin and poured from it carefully into his glass.

"There would be, of course," von Haas began carefully, "a substantial realignment of the General Staff. I feel sure . . ."

"My God, Dieter!" von Wachtstein flared. "Have we grown so far apart that you really believed I was thinking of a promotion?"

Von Haas met his eyes.

"Karl!" he said, and shrugged his shoulders helplessly.

"I have given two sons to this war," von Wachtstein said. "I am thinking of the third. I am thinking of the family. This insanity will pass. I want a von Wachtstein around when it does."

"Peter," von Haas said.

"Peter," von Wachtstein repeated, nodding his head. "I have been thinking about honor. As strange and alien a concept as that has become. I have concluded that Peter has made all the contribution to this war, save giving his life, that honor demands."

"The Knight's Cross of the Iron Cross," von Haas said.

"From the hands of the Austrian Corporal himself," von Wachtstein said. "He was in Spain with the Condor Legion, in Poland, Russia, and France. He has been five times shot down, and twice wounded."

"What do you want for him?"

"I want him out of the war and out of Germany."

"I don't quite understand."

"I want him assigned to some procurement mission, or some embassy as a military attaché. To some neutral country. Not Italy or Hungary or Japan. He speaks Spanish. Somewhere in Latin America."

"That will be difficult to arrange," von Haas said, thinking aloud.

"Dieter, if you don't have anyone high up in the Foreign Ministry, your coup doesn't have a chance. And I am not as important to your plans as you have suggested I am."

"I will see what can be arranged, Karl."

"You will arrange it, or this conversation never took place."

"Where is he now?"

"He commands a Jaeger squadron near Berlin. Focke-Wulf 190s."

"Oberstleutnant?"—First Lieutenant.

"Hauptmann"—Captain.

"He's young to be a Hauptmann."

"He was eighteen when he went to Spain as a Feldwebel"—a sergeant.

"After," von Haas chuckled, "he was sent down from Marburg,* I recall."

"You and I, Dieter, came very close to being sent down from Marburg," von Wachtstein said.

"They were better times, weren't they?" von Haas said. He looked at his watch. "It's a long drive to Berlin. I'd better be going."

Von Wachtstein stood up.

"Understand, Dieter, that my desires for Peter are not wishful thinking. Your telling me that you're sorry, you tried, but it couldn't be arranged will not be enough."

"I understand," von Haas said, and put out his hand.

"What do they say in Spanish? 'Vaya con Dios'? Vaya con Dios, Dieter. Go with God."

Von Haas met his eyes, nodded, and turned and walked out of the room.

[TWO]
The Hollywood Roosevelt Hotel
Los Angeles, California
12 October 1942

When Lieutenant Cletus Howell Frade, USMCR, stepped out of the tub onto a bath mat, the telephone was ringing.

He walked quickly, naked and dripping, into the bedroom to answer it, wondering both who it could be and how long the telephone had been ringing. It had been a long time since he'd had access to either unlimited hot water or privacy; he'd been in the shower for a long time.

He picked up the telephone on the bedside table.

---

*Philip's University, in Marburg an der Lahn, in Hesse. It was to Marburg that the Russian and East European royalty sent their children to be educated, and at Marburg that Roentgen discovered the X ray.

"Hello?"

"¿El Teniente Frade?"

"Sí, yo soy el Teniente Frade."

"Yo soy Graham, Teniente, Coronel A. F. Graham."

"Yes, Sir?"

"Are you alone, Lieutenant?" Graham asked, in Spanish.

"Sí, mi Coronel."

"I'd like a word with you. Have you been drinking?"

"Not yet, mi Coronel."

Hell of a question, Clete thought, *and a reply that was a little too flip for a lieutenant talking to a colonel.*

"See if you can hold off for half an hour or so," Colonel Graham said, a chuckle in his voice. "I should be there by then. Nine twenty-one, right?"

"Yes, Sir."

The telephone went dead. Clete put the handset back in the cradle and walked toward the bedroom.

Jesus, did he speak Spanish to me?

I'll be damned if he didn't. That entire conversation was in Spanish. Pretty good Spanish at that. What the hell was that all about?

Clete dried himself slowly and carefully, partly to take advantage of the stack of thick, soft towels the hotel had so graciously provided for his comfort, and partly because his long exposure to soap and hot water had softened and loosened the scabs—perhaps twenty-five of them—on his legs and chest.

An incredible number of insects lived on Guadalcanal, and each variety there became addicted to Cletus's blood. Sometimes, it seemed as if they fought among themselves for the privilege of taking their dinner from him and leaving behind a wide variety of irritations. These ranged from small sting marks to thumbnail-size suppurating ulcers.

After he finished drying, Clete walked on the balls of his feet from the bathroom to the wood-and-canvas rack beside the chest of drawers that supported his suitcase. He took from it his toilet kit—once a gleaming brown leather affair, now looking like something a mechanic was about to discard. From this he took a jar of gray paste. Despite the assurances of the Medical Corps, U.S. Navy, that the stuff was the very latest miracle medicine to soothe what the doctors somewhat euphemistically called "minor skin irritations," he suspected that it was Vaseline.

He returned to the bathroom and with a practiced skill applied just enough of the greasy substance to protect each "minor skin irritation" without leaving enough residue to leave greasy spots on his clothing. He then returned to his toilet kit, carried it back into the bathroom, and shaved—in the process slicing the top off several "minor skin irritations." He dealt with these new wounds by applying small pieces of toilet paper to his face. When he examined himself in the mirror, he concluded that if he was going to look like a properly turned out officer of the U.S. Marine Corps, he'd need a haircut.

He went back into the bedroom and dug into a large brown Kraft paper bag, taking from it a brand-new T-shirt and cotton boxer shorts.

The Public Affairs Officer Escort had taken Clete and the other "heroes" to the Officers' Sales Store almost directly from the Martin Mariner that had flown them from Espíritu Santo to Pearl Harbor. There, the Escort Officer suggested that they might wish to acquire new linen. Clete Frade bought six sets of underwear, six khaki shirts, six pairs of cotton socks, and two field scarves, which was what the Corps called neckties. And then, because the very idea that anyone would sleep in anything but his underwear or his birthday suit seemed absurd, he bought two sets of what their label identified as "Pajamas, Men's, Cotton, Summer."

Since there was no room in his one suitcase for his new acquisitions, he carried them in the paper bag the rest of the way—on a Pan American Clipper from Pearl Harbor to San Diego, and then on a chartered Greyhound bus from 'Diego to Los Angeles.

The new T-shirt was usable as is, and he put it on, but the boxer shorts reflected the Naval Service's fascination with fastening small tags to garments with open staples. He sat down on the bed and removed eight of them—he counted—from various places on his shorts. He had just pulled the shorts on when there was a knock at the door.

It was a bellman, carrying a freshly pressed uniform. Clete went to the bedside table, opened the drawer where he had placed his wallet, his watch, and his Zippo lighter and cigarettes, and found a dollar bill. He gave it to the bellman, then hung the uniform on the closet door. When he turned, he noticed for the first time on the bedside table on the other side of the bed, an eight-by-ten-inch official-looking envelope. It wasn't his, and he was sure that it hadn't been there when he'd gone into the bathroom for his shower.

He picked it up. It contained something other than paper, something relatively heavy. He opened the flap and dumped the contents on the bed. Insignia spilled out: two sets of first lieutenant's silver bars and a new set of gold Naval Aviator's wings—and bars of ribbons, representing his decorations. There was the Distinguished Flying Cross, with its oak-leaf cluster signifying the second award; the Purple Heart Medal with its oak-leaf cluster; and the ribbons representing the *I-Was-There* medals: National Defense, and Pacific Theatre of Operations, the latter with two Battle Stars. The ribbons were mounted together.

The Public Affairs people again, Clete thought. *The Corps doesn't want its about-to-go-on-display heroes running around with single ribbons pinned unevenly, one at a time, to their chests; they should be mounted together. And God knows, I have never polished my first john's bars from the day I got them. And my wings of gold are really a disgrace, when viewed from the perspective of some Corps press agent; they're scratched, bent, and dirty.*

I wonder if this stuff is a gift from the Corps, or whether they will deduct the cost from my next pay.

Clete dropped the brand-new set of glistening gold wings on the bed, then picked up the telephone.

"Room Service," he ordered when the operator came on the line.

"Room Service," a male voice said.

"This is Lieutenant Frade in nine twenty-one," he said. "I would like a bottle of sour-mash bourbon, Jack Daniel's if you have it, ice, water, and peanuts or potato chips, something to nibble on."

His voice was soft, yet with something of a nasal twang. Most people he'd met in the Corps thought he was a Southerner, a Johnny Reb, but some with a more discerning ear heard Texas. Both were right. Clete Frade had been raised in New Orleans and in the cattle country (now cattle and oil) around Midland, Texas. He'd spent his first two years of college at Texas A&M, and then, when his grandfather had insisted, finished up (Bachelor of Arts) at Tulane.

"Lieutenant," Room Service said, hesitantly, "you understand that only the room is complimentary?"

"I didn't even know that," Clete said. "But if you're asking if I expect to pay for the bourbon, yes, of course I do."

And I damned sure can afford it. There's four months' pay in Sullivan's boots.

Sullivan was—had been—First Lieutenant Francis Xavier Sullivan, of Cleveland, Ohio, and the 167th Fighter Squadron, U.S.

Army Air Corps. The Corps and the Navy had flown Grumman Wildcats off Henderson Field and Fighter One on the 'Canal. The Army Air Corps, those poor bastards, had flown Bell P-39s and P-40s. The story was, and Clete believed it, that the P-39s and P-40s had been offered to, and rejected by, both the English and the Russians before they had been given to the Army Air Corps and sent to the 'Canal. They were both essentially the same airplane, a weird one, with the engine mounted amidships behind the pilot. The one good thing they had was either a 20- or a 30-mm cannon that fired through the propeller hub. But they were not as fast or as maneuverable as the Wildcat, which meant they were not even in the same league as the Japanese Zero. And in a logistical foul-up that surprised Clete not at all, they had been sent to the 'Canal with the wrong oxygen-charging apparatus, so they could not be flown over 12,000 feet.

The pilots flying them fought, in other words, with one hand tied behind them. And one by one they were shot down, Francis Xavier Sullivan among them.

Clete and F.X. made a deal. If Clete didn't come back, F.X. could have Clete's two bottles of Jack Daniel's sour-mash bourbon; and if F.X. didn't come back, Clete could have F.X.'s Half Wellington boots, which, conveniently, fit him perfectly. The second part of the deal was that each had promised the other—presuming, of course, that one of them came through—that he would visit the other's family and tell them a bullshit story about how the fallen hero had died—"quickly, without pain, he really didn't know what hit him."

F.X. went in while supporting the Marine Raiders on Edson's Ridge. He got his P-40 on the ground in more or less one piece, and he was alive when it caught fire. The Raiders heard him screaming until finally, mercifully, the sonofabitch blew up.

Clete went to F.X.'s tent while F.X.'s Executive Officer was inventorying his personal gear. About the only thing that wasn't worn out, or covered with green mold, was the boots. F.X. had spent a lot of time caring for his boots. They would, he claimed, get him laid a lot when they were given a rest leave in Australia. F.X. had heard that from a fellow who'd flown with the Eagle Squadron of the Royal Air Force before the United States had gotten into the war; women liked men who wore boots.

Clete was tempted not to claim the boots, but decided in the end that a deal was a deal. F.X. damned sure would have claimed the Jack Daniel's.

While he waited for the bourbon, he pinned the new insignia to his new shirt and freshly pressed tunic. The new shirt, being new, was not stiff with starch. Before long, he knew, it would look limp and floppy, not shipshape.

Is there a regulation someplace that orders shirts to be washed and starched before wear? I wouldn't be a damned bit surprised.

There was a knock at the door. When he opened it, a different bellman pushed in a tray on wheels; the tray held a bottle of Jack Daniel's, a battered silver bowl full of ice, a silver pitcher that presumably contained water, and two glass bowls, one filled with mixed nuts and the other with pretzels. There was also a newspaper, which Clete thought was a nice touch.

He took the bill from the bellman and signed it. When he turned back to the bellman, he was holding the newspaper open, so that it was ready to read when Clete took it.

"Welcome home, Lieutenant," the bellman said, meaning it.

"Thank you," Clete said. "It's good to be home."

"You're here," the bellman said, pointing at the photograph on the front page of the *Los Angeles Times*. It showed a dozen Marines standing by the Greyhound bus in front of the hotel. The headline above them read:

Guadalcanal Heroes Receive
Key to City From Mayor

Clete looked at his photograph.

My God, I look like a cadaver! Do I really look that bad, or is it just the photograph?

"Thank you," Clete said.

The bullshit begins.

After he joined the other returning pilots back on Espíritu Santo—in the absence of more deserving heroes, he decided, he was apparently a last-minute addition to the roster—and they were waiting for further air transportation, via Pearl Harbor, T.H., to U.S. Navy Base, San Diego, California, there was a lot of talk, naturally, about why they were being sent home.

No one believed that their pleasure, or comfort, or even physical well-being had anything to do with it. The Marine Corps did not act that way. It was certainly not a reward for a job well done, either.

All they'd been told, probably all that anyone knew, was that the orders came as a radio message from Eighth & I.

It wasn't until they were actually given their orders at Espíritu (a twenty-copy stack of mimeographed paper), minutes before they boarded the Martin Mariner, that the words "War Bond Tour" came up. And these gave Clete little more information than Dawkins had already told him:

The following officers, the orders read, *are detached from indicated organizations and temporarily attached to the USMC Public Affairs Office, Federal Building, Los Angeles, Cal., for the purpose of participating in a War Bond Tour.*

That 1/Lt Frade, C. H., USMCR was detached from VMF-229 was sort of a joke, for little—if anything—of Marine Fighter Squadron Number 229 remained to be detached from. After Clete wrecked his Wildcat, VMF-229 was down to two airplanes and four pilots. There were almost no mechanics, or clerks, or cooks either. As more of VMF-229's Wildcats and their pilots had been shot down, crashed, or simply disappeared than had been replaced, the mechanics and clerks had been transferred to other squadrons.

What, exactly, a baker's dozen of battered fighter pilots who resembled not at all the handsome Marine aviators of the movies and recruiting posters could possibly have to do with a War Bond Tour was something of a mystery, until one of them realized that they all had one thing in common besides membership in the Cactus Air Force and their surprising presence among the living. They each—he polled the jury to make sure—had shot down at least five Japanese aircraft. They were all aces. Two were double aces, and one was working hard on being a triple.

"They're putting us on fucking display, is what they're doing!" one of them announced in disgust.

There were groans. Some of these were genuine, Clete thought—including his own. And some of them were *pro forma.* There was really nothing wrong with being identified as a hero. For one thing, as one said with a certain fascination in his voice, it would probably get them laid. Clete Frade had absolutely nothing against getting laid, but he was uncomfortable with the notion of considering himself a hero. In his mind, what he'd done was only what he had been ordered to do.

He had not volunteered to fly at Midway, where he shot down his first Japanese shortly before being shot down himself and earning his first Purple Heart. And he had not volunteered to go to Guadalcanal. He was sent there, and he flew off Henderson and Fighter One because he was ordered to. So far as he was concerned, with one exception, he owed his seven victories to luck. He could just as easily have been killed. He was not a hero.

On the chartered Greyhound bus from San Diego to Los Angeles, a public relations major stood in the aisle and delivered a little speech, the straight scoop about what was going on, Clete Frade realized then.

"What this is all about, gentlemen," the major said, "is civilian morale. The powers that be have decided that civilian morale needs a shot in the arm. You may have noticed that so far in this war, we haven't done very well: The Japanese took Wake Island away from the Marine Corps, and the Philippines away from the Army. In other words, we have had our ass kicked—with two exceptions.

"The two exceptions, the only times we have at least hurt the Japanese a little, were Lieutenant Colonel Jimmy Doolittle's B-25 raid on Tokyo and the Corps' invasion of Guadalcanal. From what I've heard, we almost got pushed back into the sea at Guadalcanal, and that fight, as you all well know, is by no means over. But at least it looks to the public as if the Armed Forces, especially the Marine Corps, have finally done something right.

"So what has this got to do with you? You're Marine officers. You will carry out the orders you are given cheerfully and to the best of your ability. Your orders in this instance are to comply with whatever orders we feather merchants in Public Affairs give you. Generally speaking, this will mean being where you are told to be, sober, in the proper uniform, and wearing a smile. This will, it is hoped, convince the civilian populace that after some initial setbacks, the Marines finally have the situation under control. This, in turn, may encourage people to buy War Bonds, and it may even convince some of our innocent youth to rush to the recruiting station so they can share in the glory.

"An effort will be made to have someone from Public Affairs present whenever you are interviewed by the press. Keep in mind that the purpose of this operation is to bolster civilian morale. I don't want to hear that any of you have been telling the press about what went wrong on Guadalcanal, and that certainly means you are not at liberty to say anything unflattering about the Navy, or the Army, or indeed the Corps.

"The tour will last two weeks, and possibly three. When it is over, you will be given a fifteen-day delay en route to your new assignments. The tour will start on Monday, which will give you an opportunity to get your uniforms in shape. Tonight you are free. Which does not mean you are at liberty to get drunk and chase skirts. Use the time to call home, if you like, to have a good meal, and—repeating myself—to have your uniforms pressed and your shoes shined. Sometime early tomorrow morning, you will be informed where you are to gather for specific instruction in what will be expected of you.''

After the bus delivered them to the Hollywood Roosevelt Hotel, and the senior officer among them had received the Key To The City from the Mayor, they were assigned to rooms. Clete Frade's first priority then was a long, hot shower.

''Is there anything else I can get for you, Lieutenant?'' the bellman asked.

''How about a large-breasted, sex-starved blonde?'' Clete asked with a smile.

From the look on the bellman's face it was evident that he thought Clete meant it.

''Just kidding,'' Clete said.

''Lieutenant,'' the bellman said, ''I don't think you're going to have any trouble finding women.''

''I hope not,'' Clete said.

Clete went back to the bedside table, took another dollar, and gave it to the bellman.

Then he made himself a drink—carefully—savoring that luxury too. Just a little water and one large ice cube, which he twirled around the glass with his finger. He took a sip.

Then he put the glass down and got dressed. He was not pleased with his reflection in the mirror. His shirt collar was not only limp, it was too large. The tunic, for which he paid so much money, hung loosely on him. He looked like a stranger, wearing somebody else's uniform.

How the hell much weight did I lose over there?

The new set of shiny gold Naval Aviator's wings displeased him. In a moment, he decided that was because they added to the illusion that whoever was looking back at him from the mirror was not Clete Frade.

He took the tunic off and replaced the new wings with his old ones. Then he put the tunic back on and looked at his reflection again.

Better, he thought. *Much better. They are a connection with reality, with the past.*

Finally, he sat down on the bed, reached inside Francis Xavier Sullivan's left Half Wellington boot, and pulled out the wad of twenty-dollar bills he had been paid in Pearl Harbor. They were folded in half. He took three of these, put them in his trousers pocket, then flattened out the stack that remained and put them in the left lower pocket of his tunic. After that, he pulled the boots on and walked around the room until they settled around his feet.

He picked up his drink and raised it.

"Francis Xavier, old pal. Thank you," he said aloud, and took a healthy sip of the bourbon.

He started for the window, intending to push the drape aside to see what was outside. Before he reached it, there was a double knock at the door. He turned and went to it and opened it.

A Marine officer stood there. He was a short, trim, tanned, barrel-chested, bald-headed, bird colonel wearing a pencil-line mustache. He carried an expensive, if somewhat battered, civilian briefcase. There was something vaguely *Latino* about him.

Hell, yes, he spoke to me in Spanish. I'll bet three-to-five that Colonel A. F. Graham's first name is either Alejandro or Antonio. And the "F" is for "Francisco."

"Buenas noches, mi Coronel," Clete said.

"May I come in?" Colonel A. F. Graham asked in Spanish.

"Yes, Sir."

Clete stood out of the way, let Colonel Graham into the room, and closed the door.

"I thought I asked you to hold off on the drink until we had a chance to talk," Graham said, still in Spanish.

"With all respect, Sir, the operative word was 'asked.' "

"Then I shall have to remember to choose my words carefully when dealing with you," Graham said, smiling.

"May I offer you a drink, Colonel?"

"Yes, thank you. Bourbon?"

"Yes, Sir."

Clete made the drink and handed it to Colonel Graham.

"For the record, Sir, this is my first," Clete said.

"Good," Graham said.

"I have no intention of disgracing the Corps on this War Bond Tour, Colonel."

"I'm sure you don't," Graham said.

"Why are we speaking Spanish, Sir? May I ask?"

"I wanted to confirm that you spoke Spanish, and that it wasn't pure Mex-Tex Spanish."

"I can speak pretty good Mex-Tex, Colonel."

Is that what he wants? This War Bond tour is going to Texas, the Southwest, and the Corps's looking for somebody who speaks

Spanish to give patriotic speeches to the Mexican-Americans? Good God!

"Sir," Clete said in English, "my Spanish isn't all that good and I am a lousy public speaker."

Graham looked at him for a moment in confusion, and then, understanding, he smiled.

"Very nice. Jack Daniel's?" he said, now in English.

"Yes, Sir."

"Actually your linguistic ability has nothing to do with the War Bond Tour," Graham said, and took a sip of his drink. "And for that matter, neither do I."

"Sir, I don't understand . . ."

"Adding you to the War Bond Tour roster seemed a convenient way of bringing you back from Guadalcanal without raising any awkward questions. Conveniently for me, you turned out to be a bona fide hero."

What the hell is he talking about?

"I don't consider myself any kind of a hero, Sir."

"In my experience, few bona fide heroes do," Graham said matter-of-factly, meeting his eyes. "What it is, Frade—why I asked you to hold off on the whiskey—is that I wanted to have a talk with you, to ask you a couple of important questions. And I wanted you to be sober when I did."

"A talk about what, Sir?"

"Let me ask the important question first, to save your time and mine," Graham said. "Would you be willing to undertake a mission involving great personal risk?"

"Excuse me?"

"The nature of which I am not at liberty to discuss right now," Graham went on, "beyond saying that it's outside the continental limits of the United States and is considered of great importance to the war effort."

This man is absolutely serious. What the hell is this all about?

"Colonel, Sir, with respect, I have no idea what you're asking of me."

"Then I'll repeat the question: Are you willing to undertake a mission involving great personal risk outside the continental limits of the United States?"

He didn't say "overseas." He said "outside the continental limits of the United States."

Oh!

"Has this something to do with my father?" Clete asked.

"You weren't listening, Lieutenant," Graham said. "I said I was not at liberty to discuss the nature of this operation."

Sure, it has to do with my father. I could see that in your face, and the only possible thing about me that would interest an intelligence type like you is my father—and that's certainly what you are, Colonel, an intelligence type. And Argentina is "outside the continental limits of the United States," as opposed to "overseas."

"Colonel, are you aware that I hardly know my father, that I wouldn't recognize him if he walked into this room?"

"Yes, I am," Graham said. "But that's the last question on that subject I'm going to answer. Or let you ask."

"Until I volunteer for this mission of yours, you mean?"

Graham nodded.

"Colonel, I just got home from Guadalcanal."

Graham nodded. "I told you, I arranged that. To save me a trip over there to have this conversation."

"This—*mission.* It's that important?"

Graham nodded, then said, "It's that important."

"Do I have to decide right now?"

"That would make things more convenient for both of us."

"And what if I say yes now, hear what you have to say, and then change my mind?"

"I wondered if that possibility would occur to you. The answer, frankly, is that there's really nothing I can do but appeal to your patriotism."

"Isn't patriotism supposed to be the last refuge of the scoundrel?" Clete asked, smiling.

"I've heard that said," Graham replied, smiling back at him. "I'm not sure if I believe it. I'm an Aggie—just as you were once, for a while. We Aggies take words like 'patriotism' and 'honor' seriously." (An Aggie is an alumnus of the Texas Agricultural and Mechanical Institute.)

"At least some of us do," Clete said. He met Graham's eyes for a moment, then said, evenly, "OK."

Graham nodded, then walked to the chest of drawers and laid his briefcase on it. He opened the briefcase, took out a form, closed the briefcase, laid the form on it, then took a fountain pen from his shirt pocket and extended it to Frade.

"Would you please sign this?"

Clete walked to the chest of drawers, then bent over Graham's briefcase and read the form.

The United States of America
Office of Strategic Services
Washington, D.C.

*Acknowledgment of Penalties Provided by the United
States Code for the Unauthorized Disclosure of National
Security Information*

The undersigned acknowledges that the unauthorized disclosure of any information made available to him by any
officer of the Office of Strategic Services will result in his
prosecution under applicable provisions of the United
States Code (including, where applicable, The Rules for the
Governance of the Naval Services and/or The Manual For
Courts-Martial, 1917) and that the penalties provided by
law provide on conviction for the death penalty, or such
other punishment as the court may decide.

                                    Cletus Howell Frade

Executed at Los Angeles, California,
              this 12th day of October 1942

Witness:

A.F. Graham
Colonel, USMCR

*He knew I was going to sign this, didn't he? My name and the
date are already typed in on the form,* Clete thought, and then,
This is a little melodramatic, isn't it? And then, *What the hell is
the Office of Strategic Services?*

After a moment's hesitation, he asked that aloud.

"What's the Office of Strategic Services?"

"Sign that, Lieutenant, or don't sign it," Graham said, and now
there was a tone of annoyance in his voice. "Make up your
mind."

Clete scrawled his name on the form. Graham retrieved the
form and his pen and signed his name as witness, then put the
form into his briefcase.

"OK, Lieutenant Frade, now you can ask questions," he said.

"What is the Office of Strategic Services?"

"An agency of the federal government which reports directly
to the President. It performs what are somewhat euphemistically
known as strategic services for the government."

"In other words, you're not going to tell me."

"You will be told what you have the need to know."

"What does the Office of Strategic Services want from me?"

"As you guessed, it wants you to go to Argentina. You will
command a three-man team with the mission of taking out a merchant vessel—a merchant vessel of a neutral country, which we
have determined is replenishing German submarines operating off
the coast of South America. These submarines are doing considerable damage to shipping down there. We have to lessen that.
But additionally, if you can find the time, we'd like you to dream
up other ways to make things difficult for the Germans, the Italians, and the Japanese in Argentina."

"I don't know anything about . . . sabotage . . . that sort of
thing."

"The other members of your team do," Graham interrupted.

"So the only reason I can think of that you want me for something like this is because of my father. You know my father is
an Argentine . . . Argentinean, right?"

"Of course. And you're right."

"Did you hear what I said a minute ago, that I wouldn't recognize my father if he walked into this room?"

"We know that too. Actually, we know more about you, Frade,
than you probably know yourself. For example, are you aware
that you hold Argentine citizenship?"

"I've always been told that Americans can't hold dual citizenship."

"So far as our government is concerned, we can't. So far as the Argentine government is concerned, you were born there, therefore you are an Argentine citizen."

"I haven't been there since I was an infant," Clete said.

"Yes, we know," Colonel Graham said, a touch of impatience in his voice.

He turned to his briefcase and came out with a five-by-seven-inch photograph and handed it to Clete.

"El Coronel Jorge Guillermo Frade," Graham said, pronouncing it "Frah-day." "He looks rather like you, or vice versa, wouldn't you say?"

Clete examined the photograph. It showed a tall, solid-looking man with a full mustache. He was wearing a rather ornate, somewhat Germanic uniform, and stepping into the backseat of an open Mercedes-Benz sedan. In the background, against a row of Doric columns, was a rank of soldiers armed with rifles standing at what the Marine Corps would call "Parade Rest." Their uniforms, too, looked Germanic, and they were wearing German helmets.

Christ, he does look like me. Or, as Colonel Graham puts it, vice versa.

Well, it looks as if I will finally get to meet my father.

Do I want to? I don't feel a thing looking at this picture. He's a stranger. And he certainly has made it pretty goddamned plain that he doesn't give a damn for me. I'm the result of a youthful indiscretion, as far as he's concerned. Maybe, probably, even an embarrassment.

I wonder how he will react when I show up down there.

"Excuse me, Señor. I'm sure you don't remember me, but I happen to be what they call the fruit of your loins."

"That was taken last summer," Graham said after a moment.

"Where?" Clete asked. "In Berlin?"

"No." Graham chuckled. "That's Buenos Aires. On Independence Day. *Their* Independence Day—July ninth. They make just about as much of a fuss over theirs as we do over ours."

"I wasn't aware he was in the Army," Clete said.

"He's retired. They—people of a certain class and influence—wear uniforms on suitable occasions. This was taken before the traditional Independence Day Mass at the Metropolitan Cathedral. José de San Martín, *El Libertador,* is buried there. Do you recognize the insignia? Your father's a colonel of cavalry. And like

Generalleutnant Hasso von Manteuffel of the Wehrmacht and our own Major General George S. Patton, he's a graduate of the French Cavalry School at Saint-Cyr. And the German Kriegsschule.''

Clete looked at Colonel Graham and saw amusement in his eyes.

"And whose side is he on in this war?'' Clete asked.

"Argentina, as you probably know, is trying to sit this war out as a neutral. Generally speaking, their Navy, which was trained by the English, is pro-Allies. The Army, which is trained by the Germans, is generally pro-Axis. We don't know exactly where your father stands. If, 'in addition to your other duties,' you could tilt him toward our side, that would be nice.''

"Is that the real reason you want me to go down there? To try to work on my father?''

"No. As I said, if you could tilt your father toward us, that would be a bonus. But you're being sent down there to take out the 'neutral' submarine replenishment vessel. What we're hoping—your father is a very powerful man down there—is that the BIS . . .''

"The what?''

"The Bureau of Internal Security, which is sort of their FBI, except that it's under the Ministry of Defense. They're very good, I understand, trained by the Germans. What we're hoping is that once the BIS find out your father is el Coronel Frade, they may elect to be a little less enthusiastic, a little less efficient in investigating you, than they would ordinarily be.''

"How are they going to know he's my father? Are you going to tell them?''

"They'll find out. I told you, they're very good.''

"When does all this start to happen? I was promised a leave. I want to go to Texas. . . .''

"I understand,'' he said. "We know about your uncle, too. That must have been tough. . . .''

"Sir, do I get a leave or don't I?''

"Yes, of course. There will be time for you to visit both Midland and New Orleans.''

"Thank you,'' Clete said.

Graham looked into Clete's eyes for a moment, then nodded. He looked at his watch.

"We have a compartment on the Chicago Limited,'' he said.

"We have an hour and a half to make it. I think you'd better start packing."

"I just take off? What about the War Bond Tour? Won't they miss me?"

"They will be told that you're on emergency leave because of an illness in your family," Graham said. "Do you suppose I could have another drink, while you pack?"

[THREE]
Office of the Director
Office of Strategic Services
National Institutes of Health Building
Washington, D.C.
15 October 1942

"You wanted to see me, Colonel?" Colonel A. F. Graham asked as he stood in the door. He was in civilian clothing.

"Come on in, Alex," Colonel William J. Donovan, a stocky, well-tailored man in his fifties, replied. As Graham walked into the office, Donovan added, "Actually, I wanted to see you three days ago, and then the day before yesterday, and yest—"

"I was on the West Coast," Graham said. "I sent you a memo."

"Carefully timed to arrive after you left," Donovan said. He was smiling, but there was a tone of rebuke in his voice.

"Amazing town, this Washington," Graham said. "It only takes a couple of months for an honest man to become as devious as any lifelong bureaucrat."

"Tell me something, Alex," Donovan asked; he was clearly enjoying the exchange. "How did you manage to run the country's second-largest railroad without knowing how to delegate responsibility?"

"The third or fourth largest, actually. Depending on how you count—by trackage or by income. The Pennsylvania and the New York Central make more money; and the Union Pacific, the Sante Fe, and the Chicago and Northwestern all have more trackage."

Donovan smiled tolerantly at him. Unlike most of the upper echelon of the OSS, Colonel A. (for Alejandro) F. (for Fredrico) Graham was not awed by Colonel William R. Donovan, Director of the Office of Strategic Services—and World I Hero, spectacularly successful Wall Street lawyer, and intimate, longtime friend of his Harvard classmate, Franklin Delano Roosevelt, President of the United States.

Probably because Graham was himself a World War I hero, Donovan often reflected. And had an even greater income from running his railroad than he himself had. And had a loathing for politicians, even those who made it to the White House.

Donovan was pleased when he was able to recruit Graham for the OSS and to steal him from the President (Roosevelt was talking about making Graham "Transportation Czar"; the theft annoyed the President, but he got over it). There were a number of reasons why he was truly valuable; high among these was his reputation for not backing down from a position he believed to be the right one.

"But to answer your question, Colonel," Graham went on. "By knowing what things should be delegated, and what things the boss should do himself."

"We even have an Assistant Director for Recruitment around here. Did you know that?"

"Actually, he's a *Deputy* Assistant Director," Graham said. "He works for me. Did you ever really read the manning table?"

"No," Donovan said, and laughed. "I have an Assistant Director named Graham who does that sort of thing for me. Whenever he comes to work."

"I thought it was important, Bill," Graham said. "That's why I went myself."

"Your memo said your trip was in connection with the Argentina problem," Donovan said, his tone making it a question.

Graham nodded.

"Then let me clear the air. There will be no violation of Argentine neutrality by United States Naval or Army Air Corps forces. I took that all the way to the top. The State Department won."

"The top" meant the President of the United States.

"I thought that's what would happen," Graham said. "That's why I went recruiting in California. We need more assets down there."

Donovan nodded his agreement and then asked, "Any luck?"

"A very interesting young Marine. Young fellow named Frade."

"The Marine Corps . . . no, Holcomb himself . . . has been complaining that we're taking too many of his officers." Thomas

Holcomb was then Major General Commandant of the U.S. Marine Corps.

"You'll have to deal with Holcomb. This one we need."

"Why?"

"This one—he flew at Midway, and they just gave him a second DFC—not only comes with a large set of balls, he speaks Spanish fluently. And his father is very interesting."

"Who's his father?"

"El Coronel Jorge Guillermo Frade."

"And who is el Coronel Jorge Guillermo Frade?"

"He is the *éminence grise* of the G.O.U."

"It's not nice, Alex, to force your boss to confess his ignorance."

"It stands for Grupo de Oficiales Unidos," Graham explained. "They are planning a coup against the President of Argentina. With a little bit of luck they'll succeed."

"This fellow's father? The Argentine colonel?"

Graham nodded.

"The last briefing I had," Donovan said, "claimed that the Argentinean military, to a man, supported the Axis. Or at least the Germans."

"Then you weren't listening closely. The 'Argentines are Pro-Axis' business is simply not so. Just because they wear German helmets doesn't mean they're all Nazis. There's a good deal of pro-British sentiment among much of the officer corps, and the bureaucracy."

" 'Pro-British'? As differentiated from 'Pro-Allies'? Or 'Pro-American'?"

"They don't particularly like us; they like to think they should be the dominant power in this hemisphere. And we've never had a presence down there the way the British have. And they're a practical people, Bill. After Dunkirk, noble sentiment aside, who would you have bet would win the war in Europe? After Pearl Harbor, or especially after Singapore and the Philippines fell to the Japanese—patriotism aside—who would you have bet on to win the war in the Pacific?"

"The question of the moral right and wrong is not in the equation, so far as they're concerned?"

"As it is in ours, you mean? We violated every description of neutrality I've ever heard when we had the U.S. Navy looking for German submarines in the North Atlantic, long before we were in the war."

"You disapprove of what we did, Alex?"

"No. The point I'm making here is that the Argentine government has taken greater pains to be neutral than we ever did—even the one now in place, under Castilló, who *is* a fascist."

"Then you weren't at the briefing where I heard that they're closing their eyes to the Germans' refueling and replenishing their submarines in the River Plate."

"I set up that briefing for you," Graham said. "I hoped you would pay attention when Major Kellerman made the point that the German submarines are being supplied by neutral—not German—vessels," Graham countered. "And not by the Argentines."

"That's splitting hairs," Donovan said.

Graham met Donovan's eyes and shrugged. Then he said, "If it were not for those U-boats, Bill, Brazil almost certainly would still be neutral."*

"The trouble with that," Donovan countered, "is the feeling in Argentina that whatever Brazil does, Argentina should take the other side."

"That's only among some people in Argentina," Graham argued. "I still have hopes that we can get Argentina to see the light."

"What we don't want down there is a war between Brazil and Argentina. That strikes me as a real possibility. They don't like each other, and I'm afraid that one of your Argentine *coronels* is going to decide that if they get in a war with Brazil, Germany will have to help them."

"I think Germany likes things just as they are. They're getting Argentine beef, leather, wool, other foodstuffs," Graham said. "And they have their hands full in Africa and Russia. And I really don't think Argentina wants to pick a fight with Brazil. They know that we can supply Brazil a lot easier than Germany can supply them."

"You hope," Donovan said.

"I think they know, Bill. From what I have seen, they have pretty good intelligence."

---

*In January 1942, Brazil broke diplomatic relations with Germany, Italy, and Japan Within weeks, German submarines began attacking Brazilian shipping. The United States immediately started to equip the one-year-old Brazilian Air Force with North American B-25 Mitchell bombers, Consolidated Catalinas, Lockheed Hudsons, and PV-1 Venturas for antisubmarine warfare In August 1942, following a major submarine effort against Brazilian shipping (seventeen ships were lost), Brazil declared war on Germany and Italy.

"So I heard at the briefing," Donovan said.

"What we will see now," Graham went on, "is whether they are wise enough to close their eyes to our blowing up one—or more—of the neutral ships who are replenishing the German submarines. Which *we* have to do before the Brazilians start seriously thinking about doing it themselves. They *know* we would have to support them if they got into a war with Argentina; that certainly has a certain appeal to some of their *coronels.*"

Donovan nodded his agreement again.

"What I don't understand, Alex," he said, "is why you're devoting so much of your time and effort to this."

"It's my mission," Graham said, and then added, "Unless something has happened to change that?"

"I simply meant that Newton-Haddle has no doubt that his team down there will have no trouble in putting the German ship out of action."

" 'His' team?" Graham asked, and now there was ice in his voice.

"Newton-Haddle told me he trained them personally," Donovan said. "That's all I meant."

Colonel Baxter F. Newton-Haddle, U.S. Army Reserve, was the OSS's Assistant Director For Training, and ran the Country Club (the OSS operated a training school in Virginia at a requisitioned country club). He was a wealthy Philadelphia socialite, the archetypal WASP, as Donovan privately thought of him. Donovan was also aware that Graham, who had seen combat with the Marines in France in World War I, thought he was a strutting peacock.

Graham's face showed that Donovan's explanation hadn't mollified him.

"It may be replenishment ships, plural," he went on. "That wouldn't surprise me. Even if they take out the ship now in the River Plate . . ."

"When they take it out, not *if,"* Donovan interrupted, with a smile he hoped would remove the tension. "Think positively, Alex."

". . . there is little question in my mind," Graham went on as if he had not heard a word, "that the Germans will send another to replace it—or several others."

"OK," Donovan said. "And you think one team isn't enough? Your mission, Alex, your decision."

That satisfied him, Donovan thought, judging from the look on

Graham's face. And then he developed the thought: *If the bad blood between Newton-Haddle and Graham gets out of hand, and I have to choose between them, I need Graham more than I need Newton-Haddle.*

"Thank you," Graham said. "Frankly, I wasn't sure where I stood."

"Your mission, Alex," Donovan repeated. "Just tell me about it."

"When I get the second team down there, the primary mission of both teams will remain the interruption of the replenishment of German submarines and any merchant raiders which may still be active there. I think we have to make two points to the Argentines: First, there is a limit to our patience; we won't let them look the other way while the Germans replenish their warships in their waters. And second, we are willing, and capable, of playing hardball ourselves."

"Who's on the second team besides the son of Colonel What-sisname?"

"Frade," Graham furnished. "The second man is a second lieutenant I found in the 82nd Airborne Division. His family is in the industrial demolitions business in Chicago. I watched his father demolish a grain elevator next to my right-of-way in Wisconsin. Great big brick sonofabitch, eight stories high and a quarter of a mile long. He dropped it in on itself without getting so much as a loose brick on my tracks. If this kid is half as good as his father, he's just what I need."

"A second lieutenant?"

"And scarcely old enough to vote," Graham said. "The third man on the team will be a Spanish Jew with German connections whose family was in Dachau . . . murdered there, it looks like. I found him in the Army's Counterintelligence Corps at Camp Holabird in Baltimore. He's an electrical engineer, and according to Dave Sarnoff at RCA, a pretty good one."

"When do you plan to send these people to Argentina?"

"As soon as the explosives kid, his name is Pelosi, and Ettinger the Jewish chap have gone through a quickie course at the Country Club. And after we take care of their papers and make their cover stories credible."

"Which are?" Donovan asked.

"Ettinger is well-educated, multilingual; and he's been through the CIC training program. I want to talk to him myself—I haven't done that yet. But I think he will fit unobtrusively into the Bank

of Boston, if I can convince Nestor that he can't use him for
anything else until the replenishment-ship problem is solved."

"Jasper Nestor's the Station Chief in Buenos Aires," Donovan
thought out loud. "He may have other ideas where to use this
fellow."

"And this is my mission," Graham said sharply. "Which I
have been led to believe is the most important thing we have
going down there right now. I hope Nestor understands that."

"I'm sure he does. Nestor is a good man," Donovan said.
Then, suddenly and perversely unable to resist the temptation to
needle Graham, he added: "Colonel Newton-Haddle thinks very
highly of him."

*Good God, why did I say that? The last thing I want to do is
antagonize him!*

Graham's eyes, ice cold, locked on Donovan's for a moment.
Then, his eyes still cold, he flashed Donovan a gloriously insin-
cere smile.

"What is it they say, Bill, about birds of a feather?"

Donovan laughed, hoping it sounded more genuinely hearty
than it felt.

"And the explosives expert? What about his cover?"

"Frade's family is in the oil business. Howell Petroleum.
Mostly in West Texas and Louisiana, but with interests in Venezuela, including one conveniently known as Howell Petroleum
(Venezuela). Conveniently, it sends two or three tankers a month
to Argentina. Argentina would like to buy more oil. Howell Petroleum (Venezuela) is going to accommodate them. This will
require the opening of an office in Buenos Aires to make sure the
petroleum is not diverted. Meanwhile, the Germans are desperate
for petroleum, especially for refined product, and don't seem to
care what it costs. Money talks. And especially loudly in Argentina, or so I'm told. So it's credible to establish an office down
there to make sure that Howell oil is consumed within Argentina.
And that gives a credible cover to the Marine—his middle name
is Howell—and to Pelosi, as well. He's been around enough tank
farms and refineries—if only to demolish them—to look like he
knows what he's doing."

Donovan nodded.

"That should work," he said. "Tell me more about your plans
for the Marine vis-à-vis his father."

"That's a wild card. The boy was born there. But he was with
his mother when she died in the United States. He was an infant

then and stayed here. He was raised by an uncle and aunt, and later lived with his grandfather, Cletus Marcus Howell . . ."

"I know the name," Donovan interrupted.

". . . in New Orleans. The grandfather loathes and despises the father, and very possibly has poisoned the son against him. In any event, they don't know each other. We'll just have to see what happens when they get together."

"Best case?"

"El Coronel is overcome by emotion at being united with his long-lost American son, and tilts our way, bringing the Grupo de Oficiales Unidos with him."

"Worst?"

"He hasn't been in touch with his son since he was in diapers. The child may be something el Coronel wishes never happened, and he won't be at all happy to have his son show up down there."

"But you think we should play the card?"

"Absolutely. I don't like to think about the consequences in South America if we found ourselves involved in a war against Argentina. If somebody asked me, I wish Brazil had remained neutral."

"You're talking about J. Edgar Hoover's major intelligence triumph," Donovan said.

J. Edgar Hoover, the enormously politically powerful director of the Federal Bureau of Investigation, claimed sole authority for all United States intelligence and counterintelligence activity in Latin and South America. While not publicly challenging Hoover's position or authority, President Franklin Roosevelt had nonetheless authorized Donovan's OSS to operate in South America.

"You're not suggesting Hoover thinks we would be served by a war between Brazil and Argentina?" Graham asked, surprised.

"Of course not. Whatever Edgar is, he's no fool."

"Best scenario," Graham went on, "Argentina sees the light and joins the Allies. Next best, Argentina remains neutral, leaning toward us. Next best, Argentina remains neutral, leaning the other way. Worst, Argentina gets in a war with Brazil and becomes a *de facto* if not *de jure* member of the Axis powers. Anything we can do to keep the worst scenario from coming into being seems to me to be worth the effort. The Frade father-son card isn't much, but you play what you have. Sometimes you get lucky."

"I agree," Donovan said. "But be careful, Alex," he said.

"And keep me posted. Personally, not with one of your memorandums."

"Right," Graham said. He raised his eyebrows, asking, *Is that all?*

"It's always a pleasure to see you, Alex," Donovan said drolly. "We really should do this more often."

Graham laughed. "The very next time I'm in town," he said, and then walked out of Donovan's office.

III

[ONE]
The Country Club
Fairfax County, Virginia
1115 16 October 1942

The brick pillars which just over a year before had supported the country club's crest and the legend "Private Club—Members Only" remained; but the sign with the club's name had been taken down. Twenty yards down the macadam road, just barely visible from the highway, two new signs, each painted on a four-by-eight-foot sheet of plywood, one on each side of the road, announced that this was a U.S. Government Reservation and trespassers would be prosecuted. Eighty yards farther down the road, a guard shack had been built. On either side of the road, a twelve-foot hurricane fence, topped with coiled barbed wire, disappeared into groves of trees.

The guardhouse was manned by two men in blue, vaguely police-type uniforms. They had badges pinned to zipper jackets, and were armed with Smith & Wesson .357 Magnum revolvers.

When Graham's 1942 Plymouth station wagon came down the road, one of the guards stepped out of the shack and waved it, unnecessarily (a striped pole barrier hung across the road), to a stop. As Graham rolled down his window, the guard leaned over and looked in the car.

Graham offered the guard a small leather wallet, holding it open. It contained an identification card with a photo on it. The guard knew Graham by sight, but the security Standing Operating Procedure dictated that no one would be passed through without proper identification, not even an Assistant Director of the OSS.

"Good morning, Colonel," the guard said.

"Morning," Graham replied, then nodded his head toward Staff Sergeant David G. Ettinger, Army of the United States, who was sitting beside him. "The Sergeant is with me."

"Yes, Sir," the guard said; he didn't seem at all surprised that an Army sergeant was wearing a well-cut civilian suit. "Sergeant, may I see some identification? Dog tags?''

Ettinger, a tall, dark-eyed, sharp-featured man, with very light brown hair, reached into the pocket of his tunic and came out with a small, folding leather wallet much like the one Graham had shown the guard. The guard took it, said, "Just a moment, please," and went into the guard shack.

"I've heard about this place," Ettinger said.

There was a faint accent, but not readily identifiable. In New York City, it would go unnoticed, Graham observed when he first met Ettinger.

"From what I've heard," Graham said, "you will quickly learn to loathe it."

"I've heard that, too," Ettinger said.

"Perhaps our security here isn't as tight as we like to think," Graham said. "I'm sure it couldn't be that there are loose lips at the Counterintelligence Corps Center."

"What they told us in training was that there are loose lips everywhere, Sir," Ettinger said.

Graham smiled. In the eighteen hours since he met Ettinger, he had come to like him. He had a droll sense of humor . . . not unlike his own. And he quickly became convinced (good things as well as bad often come in threes) that he was right in choosing Ettinger to round out the Argentine Team. It could have gone the other way. Ettinger could have been as fluent in Spanish as Graham himself, as knowledgeable about radio as David Sarnoff himself, and wholly unsuitable for the Argentine Team.

The guard returned to the car with a clipboard and a visitor's badge: a plastic-covered, striped card hanging from a dog-tag chain.

"Sergeant, would you sign this?" the guard asked. "It's a receipt for the visitor's badge. Wear it at all times when you're on the reservation."

He handed the clipboard across Graham to Ettinger, who looked carefully at what he was being asked to sign before signing it and handing it back. When the guard passed him the visitor's badge, he looped the chain around his neck.

The guard inside the shack pressed a lever, and the striped steel pole barrier rose into the air.

"Thank you," Graham said to the guard by the car and drove onto the reservation.

"I had something like this when I was in kindergarten," Ettinger said, examining the visitor's badge.

Graham chuckled. "Where was that?"

"Madrid," Ettinger said.

"They called it a 'kindergarten'?"

"It was run by Germans," Ettinger said simply.

Graham turned a curve on the narrow road and a large field-stone and brick building, the Club House, came into view.

"And how did the members of this place react when it was placed in public service?" Ettinger asked.

"There were howls of protest that it was too much of a sacrifice to ask for the war effort," Graham said. "Except from the finance committee, who saw their patriotic sacrifice as a means to fill up the treasury. I hate to think what this place is costing the taxpayer."

"It's rather beautiful, isn't it?"

"I'm sorry to tell you, David, but you won't be living here. Just over the hill—out of sight of this, of course—they've built standard barracks for the trainees."

"For some reason, I am not surprised."

Graham stopped the Plymouth in front of the main entrance and opened his door.

"Leave your bag. If they don't offer to take you to the barracks, I will. But come with me now, please. I want you to meet the man who runs the place."

Another security guard in a police-type uniform sat at a desk just inside the door to the lobby. He rose to his feet as soon as he saw Graham, but did not make it quite to the door before Graham opened it himself.

"Good morning, Colonel," the guard said.

"Good morning."

"Colonel, the Colonel would like to see you."

The Colonel, the other colonel, was the Deputy Assistant Director for Training, Colonel Baxter F. Newton-Haddle.

"As his peers played golf and polo," Colonel Donovan had announced in a stage whisper, just before he introduced Graham to him, "Newton-Haddle played soldier. I think the greatest disappointment of his life was when Georgie Patton told him he was too old to come on active duty. But he's that rare bird for us, the round peg in the round hole."

Their reserve colonelcies, Graham often thought, were the only things he and Newton-Haddle had in common. He had kept his reserve commission after the First War, too, and worked his way up in the Marine Corps Reserve, as Newton-Haddle had in the Army.

But for him it was a serious business, not a game. From what he had seen of Newton-Haddle, Donovan had been right about him. Newton-Haddle loved to "play soldier." Graham did not think the war was a game, an activity to be enjoyed.

Graham led Ettinger up a wide flight of marble stairs to the second floor. Newton-Haddle's secretary, who was one of the very few women at the Country Club (he brought her with him from his office at the First Philadelphia Trust Company), rose from behind her desk when she saw Graham.

"Colonel Newton-Haddle expects you, Colonel. Go right in." When she saw Ettinger start to follow Graham, she quickly added, "Colonel, I think the Colonel would rather see you alone for a moment."

Graham ignored her and went to the door. It opened on a spacious, paneled room with windows overlooking the South Course.

"You wanted to see me, Newt?"

Newton-Haddle, a lithe and trim sixty-year-old who looked at least fifteen years younger than his age, was wearing Army-green trousers and a tieless, open-collared khaki shirt adorned with colonel's eagles and parachutist's wings. He stepped quickly from behind his desk and strode toward Graham with his hand extended.

Bounded, Graham noticed, *like a gazelle. Not walked.*

"Alex," he said, "you look fit."

"Appearances are deceptive," Graham said.

"I tried to call you before," Newton-Haddle said. "Your secretary told me you were coming down."

"Newt, this is Mr. Ettinger," Graham said. "I think he's going to be quite valuable."

"*Sergeant* Ettinger, isn't it?" Newton-Haddle said, nodding at Ettinger, and not offering his hand.

"He's a CIC Special Agent," Graham said. "They're called 'Mister,' right?"

"But now he belongs to us, Alex," Newton-Haddle said. "So he's no longer a CIC agent, right?"

"I've arranged for him to keep his credentials until he actually leaves for Argentina, Newt," Graham said, with an edge in his voice. "I thought they might come in handy."

"I don't mean to sound argumentative, Alex," Newton-Haddle

said argumentatively, "but here we operate on a military basis. We use our ranks."

"That's one of the reasons I'm here, Newt," Graham said. "I wanted to talk to you about that."

"About how I run the training school?"

"About David's training here," Graham said.

"Oh."

"I rather doubt that there will be time for him to complete the entire course. I want to get this team down there as soon as possible."

"Of course. We all do. But certainly you don't want him sent down there half-trained, inadequately trained?"

"He's had the CIC training. What he needs from you, in whatever time is available . . ."

"How much time are we talking about, Alex?"

"Documents is working on his papers. He needs a visa, which the Bank of Boston has to arrange for via the Argentine Consulate in Boston. Since we want as few eyebrows raised as possible, we can't push too hard for that. Still, I don't think he will be here for more than ten days or two weeks, and I think we had better operate on the ten-day idea."

"There's not much I can do for him—nothing personal, Sergeant—in ten days."

"Run him through as much explosives training as time permits, and if there is any time left over, work on his swimming, and maybe even infiltration techniques. Explosives first."

"Whatever you think is best for him, of course," Newton-Haddle said. "We'll do our best for him. Sergeant, I wonder if you'd be good enough to wait outside for a moment while I have a word with Colonel Graham?"

"Certainly, Sir," Ettinger said, and left the office, closing the door behind him.

"What's on your mind, Newt," Graham said, "that you didn't want the *sergeant* to hear?"

"Alex, we're friends, right?" Newton-Haddle asked. He waited until Graham nodded. "And so I may speak with candor?"

"Please do."

"It's always difficult when one feels one must—when duty requires that one must—point out to a friend where one feels the friend, so to speak, is going off half-cocked."

"We're friends, Newt. Have a shot at it."

"I see a great deal of potential in the men of your team, a

potential I would really hate to see disappear down the toilet.
Even Pelosi . . .''

"Even Pelosi?" Graham asked.

"His knowledge of explosives is extraordinary . . ."

"He cut his teeth, so to speak, on a stick of dynamite," Graham
said. "That's why I picked him."

"I would like to keep him here as an instructor, at least for the
time being."

"He's going to Argentina, Newt, sorry. But now that you've
brought up Pelosi, and his extraordinary skill, can I suggest that
you get him to teach Ettinger as much as he can while they're
here?"

"By the time Pelosi reaches Argentina," Newton-Haddle said,
ignoring the suggestion, "the problem there will be solved. The
team down there will have taken out the ship. I trained them
myself, and they're good."

"I'm sure they are, and I hope—of course I hope—that they
can take out that damned ship long before the backup team gets
to Argentina. But we can't bank on that happening. We need a
second team down there as soon as we can get them there. A
little redundancy never hurts, Newt. And I have been charged
with taking out the replenishment vessel. He goes, sorry."

"There is, of course, a good deal to what you say," Newton-
Haddle said charmingly. "There always is. It is always better to
err on the side of caution."

"I'm glad you understand," Graham said.

"Which brings us to Lieutenant Frade," Newton-Haddle said.

Graham's patience with Newton-Haddle was about exhausted.

"If you're going to bring up again my refusal to send him
through here, Newt, save your breath. He needs a rest-and-
recuperation leave, not your version of Parris Island recruit training."

"He's the asset it would really be criminal to flush away."

"Get to the point, please, Newt. I have to get back to Washington."

"I think we should give more thought to the use of this one-
of-a-kind asset than we have so far."

"I discussed the use of this one-of-a-kind asset with Colonel
Donovan yesterday," Graham said. "He seems to find that the
use I came up with is satisfactory."

"How would you feel about a meeting between you, Bill, myself—and possibly even Jasper Nestor—to look into Lieutenant

Frade's potential worth a little more deeply? I'm sure Nestor could be here in forty-eight hours if the Bank of Boston called him home for an 'emergency consultation' or some such. That would justify getting him a seat on the Pan American Clipper from Buenos Aires . . ."

"By 'Bill' are you by any chance referring to Colonel Donovan, Colonel Newton-Haddle?" Graham asked icily.

"No disrespect was intended. This is just a conversation between friends."

"To answer your question, Colonel," Graham went on, "I have no interest in discussing this mission with either you or Mr. Nestor, other than to inform you what will be required of you. Now is that clear enough, or should I get on the telephone and ask Colonel Donovan to personally make the point that operations are not your concern?"

"Now, Alex, there's no point in flying off the handle . . ."

"Do you take my point, Colonel, or should I get Colonel Donovan on the phone?"

"I take your point," Newton-Haddle said after a moment.

"Colonel, I am now going to take Mr. Ettinger to meet Lieutenant Pelosi. I am going to inform Lieutenant Pelosi that he is to devote the rest of the time he is here—however long that might be—to imparting to Mr. Ettinger as much as possible of his knowledge of explosives and demolition techniques. I am going to tell him that you will help him in any way you can, and I want you there when I tell him."

"If you wish."

"I don't know how it is in the paratroopers, Colonel, but in the Marine Corps, the proper response when given an order is to respond with the words 'Yes, Sir.' "

After a long moment, Colonel Baxter F. Newton-Haddle said, "Yes, Sir."

[TWO]
Big Foot Ranch
RFD #2, Box 131
Midland, Texas
1115 21 October 1942

First Lieutenant Cletus Howell Frade, USMCR, put his arm around the stocky, short-haired blond woman standing beside him at the grave and hugged her. Then he said, his voice breaking, "Christ, Martha, I'm sorry."

Clete was wearing a brand-new Stetson, dark-brown worsted woolen work pants, somewhat battered Western boots, and a heavy sheepskin coat. The woman, who was in a fur-collared trench coat, turned and smiled up at him and put her hand to his cheek.

"He was too damned young, but he had a good life, honey," she said. "And he was so damned proud of you!"

The tombstone, an eight-foot-wide, five-foot-high block of Vermont marble, read HOWELL in the center. Below, to the left, in slightly smaller letters, it read,

JAMES FITZHUGH HOWELL
Gunnery Sergeant USMCR WWI
March 3, 1895–August 11, 1942

To the right had been chiseled,

MARTHA WILLIAMSON HOWELL
June 11, 1899–

"We got to the 'Canal on the tenth of August," Clete said. "We flew off an escort carrier as soon as they got the field operational. I didn't even get the damned notification until the twentieth."

"You wrote me, honey," Martha Howell said.

"If I'd been in the States, I probably could have got an emergency leave," Clete said. "But not from the 'Canal."

"Honey, don't apologize for something you couldn't control," Martha said. "And there was nothing you could have done. He just keeled over in the bar of the Petroleum Club, and that was it."

"Goddamn!"

Martha moved out from under his arm, walked to the pole-and-chain fence surrounding the small cemetery, and pointed to one of the poles.

"You know what that is, Clete?"

"Looks like drill pipe," he said.

"It is. I was going to use cast iron, but the cast iron place in New Orleans is out of business for the duration, so I had them cut up some pipe, and weld some chain to it to keep the cattle off. I thought I'd get the cast iron after the war, but now I'm not so sure. What's wrong with drill pipe? And chain. God knows, in his life he wrapped enough chain around drilling strings."

"Looks fine to me the way it is," Clete said.

"That's good, for there's room in here too for you and yours, whenever that happens," Martha said.

His eyebrows went up, and she saw it.

"He left you the ranch, Clete," Martha said. "Less mineral rights. You get some of those, too, but he wanted you to have the ranch."

"Jesus! What about the girls?"

The girls, both students at Rice University in Houston, were Martha and Jim's daughters. For all practical purposes, they were Clete's sisters.

"He asked them first, and it was all right with them. They don't want to live out here in the sticks. I get what they call 'lifetime use.' It's all pretty complicated. You better find time when you see your grandfather to have him, or one of his lawyers, explain it to you. There's a provision in there that if you 'die without issue,' it reverts to the girls. Or their 'issue,' I forget which. Do we have to talk about this now?"

Clete shook his head no.

Then he said, "I'm surprised."

"I don't see why you should be. You weren't only his nephew. The way things happened, you were the son I could never give him."

He looked at her, then back at the tombstone.

"Seen enough?" Martha asked. "It's as cold as a witch's teat out here."

"Why, Miss Martha, how you talk!"

She walked to the pipe-and-chain fence and stepped over the chain, then slipped behind the wheel of a 1940 Cadillac coupe. Clete followed her and got in the passenger side.

"There should be a bottle in the glove compartment," Martha said as she started the engine. "I think I'd like a little taste about now."

He opened the glove compartment. Inside was a quart of Jack Daniel's, unopened, a leather-bound flask, and a Smith & Wesson .357 revolver in a holster. He shook the flask, heard it gurgle, unscrewed the top, and handed it to Martha. She put it to her lips and took a healthy swallow, then handed it back to him. He took a healthy swallow.

"Are you going to have time to go to Houston before you go where you're going?" Martha asked. "The girls will want to see you."

"I don't know," he said. "Probably. I'll know for sure when Colonel Graham tells me when he wants me in New Orleans."

"What are you going to do in New Orleans?"

"Except have the Old Man find fault with the way I blink my eyes, you mean?"

The Old Man was Cletus Marcus Howell, Martha's father-in-law and Clete's grandfather.

"He's not that bad, Clete."

He laughed.

"You didn't say what you're going to do in New Orleans."

"Mine not to reason why, Ma'am, mine but to ride into the Valley of Death, or wherever it is. You keep forgetting, Ma'am, that I'm just a lousy first lieutenant, and they don't bother to tell me a hell of a lot. Just do it."

She chuckled.

He purposefully changed the subject. "Jim's pistol is in the glove compartment. Did you know that?"

"That's my pistol," Martha said. "His guns are in town. They had to inventory them when they probated the will. You got them, too, of course, except for the .250-3000 Savage. Beth killed her first deer with that, and he thought she should have it."

They rode in silence for several minutes down the dirt road—really no more than tracks in the land leading down from the highest spot on the ranch toward the ranch house, which was built in a small valley to get it out of the wind.

"Your car is in town," Martha said, breaking the silence, "up on blocks. But if you're going somewhere where you can have a car, maybe you'd better get it running."

"I thought I would go into town anyway, to have a drink at the Petroleum Club. Is somebody at the house?"

"Juanita's there. I just hope she doesn't find out you're here and didn't stop by there first to see her."

"It was after midnight when I got to Midland," Clete said.

"Well, we'll fix you some lunch, so that you'll have something in your stomach before you hit the P-Club bar, and you go see Juanita. Before you go to the P-Club."

"You don't want to go with me?"

"I don't think I could handle that, not yet, honey," Martha said.

"I'm not sure if I'll be able to either," Clete said. "But I think I should go."

"Just go easy at the bar, honey. All the booze in the world isn't going to bring him back."

"Yes, Ma'am," Clete said.

He turned on the seat to look at her.

I really love this woman. She is not biologically my mother; but that's what she is in fact. She took me in when I was eighteen months old and she was for all practical purposes just a bride. I was her husband's sister's motherless child, and she still raised me as her own. I must have been four or five before I understood that I had another mother, a dead mother.

"Martha," Clete said. "I don't know if I ever told you before, I don't know why I didn't, but I love you."

She turned to look at him quickly.

"Clete, honey, that's nice. That's real nice. But you didn't have to say it. I know."

She returned her attention to the road for a moment, then said, "I think I could use another little taste, honey. Or did you drink it all?"

[THREE]
The Petroleum Club
Midland, Texas
1615 21 October 1942

The very black, very dignified bartender in the very white jacket handed Clete Howell a Jack Daniel's and water. He was still feeling the pulls he'd taken in Aunt Martha's car and really didn't want the drink; but it occurred to him that if Uncle Jim happened to be peering over the edge of his cloud looking down, he would like to see him having what he himself drank in his club.

"Were you here when it happened, William?" Clete asked.

"Yes, Sir, Mr. Clete. I was."

Clete looked at him, waiting for him to go on.

"There's not much to tell, Mr. Clete," the bartender said. "He hadn't been in here long. He was sitting right where you are, with Mr. Dennison. He said he had a headache, that it must be the new hat . . ."

"This hat," Clete said, touching his new Stetson.

"Yes, Sir. I thought that might be it. And he took it off and laid it on the bar and said he was going to the gentlemen's, and when he got to the door . . . I was watching . . . he just . . . he just fell down."

"Miss Martha told me it was a cerebral hemorrhage," Clete said.

"Yes, Sir. Well, Mr. Dennison and I run over there, and Dr. Sayre was out in the lounge with Mrs. Dennison, and he came running, and I went back to the bar to call an ambulance, and I was still on the phone when Dr. Sayre said he was gone."

"A good way to go, wouldn't you say, William?" Clete said.

"Yes, Sir. I thought about that. What he was talking about to Mr. Dennison was that a hole had come in that morning flowing a thousand barrels. It was a wildcat they put down with their own money. I had a one-twenty-eighth interest in the hole. It was a happy time."

"Thank you, William."

"We're going to miss Mr. Jim around here, Mr. Clete, for a long time."

"Yeah," Clete said.

William went to the end of the bar and picked up a towel and started to polish a whiskey sour glass. The telephone under the bar rang. He picked it up, then returned, carrying the handset on a very long coiled cord to Clete.

"There's a gentleman in the lobby asking to see you, Mr. Clete."

"You have a name?"

"No, Sir. He's on the phone."

Clete held out his hand for it.

"Hello?"

"Clete, I'm sorry to intrude on your leave, but I have to talk to you."

Christ, it's Colonel Graham. I thought he'd send me a telegram, or call.

"Yes, Sir."

"Do you think you could possibly squeeze in a few minutes for me in your busy schedule?"

"Yes, Sir. Of course. I'm just a little surprised you're here."

"I'm an amazing man. I thought you understood that. Would you tell this fellow to let me in, please?"

"Let me speak to him, Sir."

*   *   *

Clete picked up his glass and walked out of the bar into the lounge. It was furnished with tables and red-leather-upholstered captain's chairs, for ladies and for business conversations. The tables were arranged far enough apart to make it difficult to hear what was said at the adjoining tables.

He picked out one of the tables and stood beside it until he saw Graham entering the room, then signaled to him with his raised glass.

Graham was in somewhat mussed civilian clothing, and looked in unabashed curiosity around the room as he walked to Frade.

"Good afternoon, Sir," Clete said.

Graham smiled at him. "Howdy, Tex," he said. "Have you got a cowboy hat to go with that outfit?"

"As a matter of fact, I do. A brand-new Stetson, by the way. A family heirloom, so to speak."

"Why don't we sit down?" Graham asked, and sat down.

Clete set his glass on the table and sat down across from him. Another very black barman in a very white jacket appeared almost immediately.

"I'll have whatever Mr. Frade is drinking," Graham said. He turned and smiled at Frade. "Very nice place," he said.

"You have any trouble finding it?"

"No. I called your aunt from the airport—I'm on my way to California again, and the pilot said he could refuel here just as well as someplace else. So I told him to stop here."

"What are you in?" Clete interrupted, in a pilot-Pavlovian reflex.

"A TBF"—a torpedo bomber—"on its way to San Diego," Graham said. "Anyway, your aunt Martha said you would either be at her house or here; and she gave me the number. So I called the house and a very nice lady told me I'd just missed you and that you were coming here."

"Juanita," Frade said.

"We had a nice little chat about you," Graham said. "You apparently learned your Spanish from her?"

Frade nodded. "She was my aunt Martha's nurse when she was a child in East Texas. And then she came out here when my aunt was married and started all over again with me."

The waiter delivered Graham's drink.

Graham took an appreciative sip, waited until the waiter was out of earshot, then asked, "How are you feeling?"

"I'm all right, thank you."

"No signs of malaria? Sometimes it shows up . . ."

Clete shook his head. "I feel fine. I can't eat as much as I thought I would when I got home. . . ."

"The stomach actually shrinks on a diet like you had on Guadalcanal," Graham said.

"And I don't seem to be able to handle as much of this as I used to be able to," Clete said, holding up his glass.

"The ideal OSS agent would be a tea-total," Graham said, smiling. "Maybe that's a good thing."

"I wondered when you were going to get around to that," Clete said, returning the smile.

"A number of things have happened," Graham said. "Is there any reason you couldn't be in New Orleans on the first of November? That's ten days, and the first is a Sunday."

"No, Sir. No problem. Where do I go in New Orleans?"

"I know from experience that the chow and the bunks at 3470 St. Charles Avenue are a little better than average," Graham replied. "Anything against you staying there?"

It was the address of Cletus Marcus Howell's mansion.

"I didn't know you were familiar with those accommodations, Sir."

"Your grandfather was more than hospitable when I went to see him."

"I didn't know you'd been to see him."

"And more than cooperative. He's quite a fellow."

Now that he had a moment to think about it, Clete was not surprised that Colonel Graham had gotten along well with the old man. Strong men like other strong men. And if he liked you, the old man could be the personification of Southern charm and hospitality.

But that raised the question of why Graham had gone to see the old man.

"I'm on my way to Australia, and I wanted to talk to you before you go to Argentina."

"Yes, Sir."

Graham saw the look of surprise on Clete's face, and decided an explanation would not hurt.

"There are some people in the Pacific, believe it or not, who are not convinced that the OSS can be useful. One of them happens to be General MacArthur. I'm going down there to try to change his mind."

"Really?"

"We also serve, we who try to charm and reason," Graham said.

Clete chuckled.

"The other two men on your team," Graham said, turning to the business at hand, "are both soldiers."

"Yes, Sir?"

"They are Second Lieutenant Anthony J. Pelosi, who was in the 82nd Airborne, and Staff Sergeant David G. Ettinger, who has been a Special Agent in the Counterintelligence Corps. People in the CIC often don't wear uniforms; or if they do, they wear them without rank insignia. They're called 'Mister.' Did you know that?"

"No, Sir."

"Ettinger is Spanish, and a Jew. Most of his family—they had a German, primarily Berlin, branch—has been murdered by the Nazis. He's been working with the Immigration and Naturalization Service, trying to make sure that Spanish and German Jewish immigrants and refugees are what they say they are."

"Sir?"

"That they haven't been sent to the United States by the Abwehr or Sicherheitsdienst—German military intelligence and Secret Service, respectively."

"Do they try to do that?" Clete asked, fascinated.

"Not often, but enough to make it necessary to spend a lot of man-hours on the problem. People who should know tell me Ettinger was very good at what he was doing. Pelosi is from Chicago, and is really knowledgeable about explosives; his family is in the demolitions business. Even Colonel Baxter F. Newton-Haddle seems awed by his expertise."

"Sir, I don't know who Colonel . . ."

"Colonel Baxter F. Newton-Haddle is Deputy Director for Training," Graham explained. "He runs the Country Club, our training center in Virginia. Both Pelosi and Ettinger are there— or were there until this morning, when I sent them on leave."

"I don't know about the 'Country Club' either, Sir."

"You went through Parris Island as an enlisted man, didn't you? And before Parris Island, when you were at Texas A and M, you spent a summer at Fort Benning, right?"

"Yes, Sir."

"So you haven't missed anything by not going to the Country Club, except Colonel Newton-Haddle's welcoming speech. During that he customarily brandishes his dagger and tells the incoming class he will turn them into efficient killers . . . or they'll die trying."

"Really?" Clete smiled.

"I shouldn't mock him. He renders a service. But you didn't need it, so you didn't go there. Anyway, Ettinger will be in New Orleans on Monday, November two, and Pelosi the following day. They will travel separately, for obvious reasons. And a team will come down from Washington to brief you. Ettinger will go to Buenos Aires, via Miami, on Wednesday, November four. His cover will be a job at the Bank of Boston, where the Buenos Aires station chief is a vice-president.

"His name is Jasper F. Nestor. We do the best we can to compartmentalize—" Graham interrupted himself. "Can you remember that name? Jasper F. Nestor?"

"Jasper F. Nestor," Clete repeated. "Yes, Sir."

"As I said, we try to compartmentalize as much as we can. Ettinger obviously has to know who Nestor is, but he has been told, and I'm telling you now, that Pelosi doesn't have the need to know that name."

"Yes, Sir."

"Jasper may or may not, it's his decision, put you in touch with the commanding officer of the team that's already down there. But you won't meet the other members of that team. Get the idea?"

"Yes, Sir."

"Pelosi's cover, and yours, will be Howell Petroleum. This subject will be gone into in greater detail in New Orleans. But, in shorthand, the Argentines want more Howell Petroleum. The U.S. government wants to make sure they consume that petroleum and don't sell it to the Germans. Conveniently, on your medical release from the Marine Corps . . ." He paused, then added: "You did not serve on Guadalcanal, by the way. Your heart murmur was discovered while you were in flight school."

"My heart murmur?"

"Your heart murmur," Graham confirmed. "Conveniently, anyhow, you were available to go to Buenos Aires to make sure the oil goes where it is supposed to go. You will very visibly occupy yourself with that, by the way. The BIS . . . you remember what that is?"

"Bureau of Internal Security."

Graham nodded, and continued, ". . . will certainly be watching you. You and Pelosi will apply for Argentine visas at their consulate in New Orleans, and then fly down there. Pelosi has some other training, how to sink a ship, to go through first. But the sooner we can get you down there, the better.''

"Yes, Sir."

"It is entirely likely that by the time you reach there, the team already in place will have taken care of the 'neutral' replenishment ship. But the Germans will certainly replace it, and that will have to be dealt with. As long as the Germans keep sending ships in, we are going to take them out."

"Yes, Sir. But . . ."

"But what?"

"Colonel, I don't . . . Colonel, from what you tell me, both Ettinger and Pelosi know how to do this sort of thing. I don't know anything about it."

"I wondered when you would consider that."

"I started thinking about it on the train to Chicago," Clete said. "And I haven't stopped."

"Why you, in other words?"

Clete nodded. "Because of my father?"

"Certainly because of your father," Graham said. "But that's not the only reason. Clete, by now you must have learned there's no way to tell beforehand how a man is going to behave in combat."

He waited until he saw acceptance of the premise on Clete's face.

"And that the way you stay alive in combat is by making on-the-spot decisions what to do when unexpected things come up, things that were not covered in your training. You stay alive by thinking on your feet. You've proved you can do that."

"But I still don't know anything about taking out ships."

"You've proved that you can think on your feet. You would be qualified for this job if your father didn't exist."

"I feel like I'm going to find myself up to my ass in alligators," Clete blurted.

"You will be," Graham said, smiling. "But you'll be all right. If I didn't think you would, I wouldn't be sending you down there.

"You might want to consider taking your car with you," Graham said, changing the subject. "You'd be expected, I think, to do that."

"How do you know about my car?''

"Your grandfather told me," Graham said. "I told you, he's been very helpful."

"How would I get it down there?"

The idea of sending his car—a Buick convertible, as it happened—anywhere by ship, in wartime, came as a shock. The car belonged to another life, a life that ended when he went into the Corps.

"I would recommend E.L.M.A.," Graham said matter-of-factly. "It stands for Empresa Líneas Marítimas Argentinas. They have direct service between New Orleans and Buenos Aires."

He saw the look of surprise or confusion on Clete's face, and added: "Argentina is neutral. Both we and the Germans scrupulously observe that neutrality. We don't sink Argentinean flagged ships, and neither do they."

"And who's going to pay for shipping my car?" Clete asked as that thought passed through his mind.

"Howell Petroleum. We will reimburse them, of course. And we will reimburse them for your Howell Petroleum salaries and living allowances. Technically, you're supposed to turn back to the government any excess over your military pay and allowances, but I don't know of anyone in the OSS who has actually done that."

"If my grandfather thinks we're going down there to kill Argentines, I'm sure he'd be willing to underwrite all costs," Clete said.

"I did get the feeling that he's not overly fond of your father," Graham said.

Clete looked at him and smiled.

"I really hope, Clete, that you won't have to kill anyone," Graham went on. "Killing people makes things sticky. And no matter what, just make sure of the main thing—if it comes down to your team having to do it—make sure that Pelosi and Ettinger keep the replenishment ship—ships—from replenishing German submarines."

"How am I going to know where those ships even are? Where will I get the explosives?"

"The briefing team will cover most of that, and Nestor will be helpful, once you're there."

Clete shook his head and shrugged.

"Colonel, I really hope you know what you're doing."

"I believe we do. I'm sure you'll live up to our expectations. Actually, telling you that was the main reason I wanted to see you before you go down there, the reason I ordered the refueling stop here.''

"That sounds suspiciously like a pep talk."

"I hope so. That's what it's supposed to be," Graham said. "And now that that's done, I'd better get going."

He stood up and put out his hand. Clete got belatedly to his feet.

"One more thing, to answer the question I suspect has been running through your mind: No, you would not be more useful flying for the Corps. This is more important."

"Yes, Sir."

"Good luck, son," Colonel Graham said, shook his hand, and walked out of the lounge. Clete watched him go, and was surprised when he reappeared almost immediately.

"I'm going to need a ride to the airport," Graham said, somewhat sheepishly. "Can you call a cab for me?"

"I've got a car," Clete said. "I'll take you."

[FOUR]
35 Beerenstrasse
Berlin/Zehlendorf
1530 29 October 1942

Hauptmann Freiherr—Captain Baron—Hans-Peter von Wachtstein swore when he saw a Feldgendarmerie (Military Police) roadblock barring access to the Avus, a four-lane superhighway leading into Berlin. The line of cars they were holding up was long. This translated to mean they were not only checking the vehicles to ensure the trip was authorized, but also the people in the cars to make sure they had proper documents. The check would take twenty minutes, perhaps longer.

Von Wachtstein—his friends called him "Peter"—was a blond, blue-eyed, compact young man of twenty-four who was the commanding officer of Jagdstaffel 232 (Fighter Squadron 232). Peter slowed and started to pull to the left to enter the line of waiting cars, then changed his mind.

"I am, after all, on official business," he said aloud.

He drove the Horche convertible sedan along the line of parked cars. A Feldgendarmerie Feldwebel, holding a stop sign on a short pole, stepped imperiously into the roadway and signaled for him to stop. He held up the sign and waved his free hand, palm out.

Von Wachtstein applied the brakes as he rolled down the window. The Horche started to skid on the icy cobblestones of the entrance road. The Feldgendarmerie Feldwebel jumped out of the way. The Horche finally came to a rest, cocked on the road.

Peter immediately opened the door and stepped out; the one thing he didn't need was an annoyed Feldgendarmerie Feldwebel. That could keep him out here all afternoon.

"Are you all right?" Peter asked, hoping he sounded genuinely concerned.

The Feldwebel was annoyed, but he saw that he was dealing with an officer (and Peter was sure he had taken into account that the car was a Horche, and probably that the Knight's Cross of the Iron Cross was hanging around his neck). He managed a tight smile as he saluted.

"The one thing wrong with a Horche is that they are as unmanageable on ice as a cow," Peter said, returning the salute with a smile. He reached into the inside pocket of his leather jacket and extended both his identity card and the teletype from the Oberkommando der Luftwaffe (General Headquarters, Air Force), which ordered Hauptmann von Wachtstein to present himself as soon as the press of his duties permitted, but no longer than forty-eight hours from the time the message had been sent, to the office of the Chief of Protocol.

"A magnificent vehicle, Herr Hauptmann," the Feldwebel said. "Is it yours?"

"My father's," Peter said.

"And your father is?"

"Generalmajor Graf von Wachtstein."

That wasn't exactly true. The car had been Karl's. Peter had been using it ever since word came that the eldest of the three von Wachtstein sons had laid down his life for the Führer and the Fatherland in some unknown Russian village. But Karl, his father's namesake, had been only an Oberstleutnant (a lieutenant colonel); and Feldgendarmerie Feldwebels could be counted upon to be far more impressed with a Generalmajor than an Oberstleutnant.

"Thank you, Herr Hauptmann," the Feldwebel said, returning Peter's identity card and the yellowish sheet of teletype paper. He turned and blew a small brass whistle. Peter had seen and heard them before; they reminded him of children's whistles.

"Pass the Herr Hauptmann," the Feldwebel called loudly, then turned back to Peter and saluted. "Drive carefully," he said. "All Berlin is a sheet of ice."

"Thank you for your courtesy," Peter said, and stepped back into the Horche.

The encounter made him feel a little better. Among people like the Feldwebel, there was still something left of their old attitude toward their betters, a certain respect.

Driving reasonably carefully, it took him fifteen minutes to reach Sven Hedin Strasse in Zehlendorf, where he stopped the car and looked across the small park there—its grass had been raped to build a bomb shelter—toward the house, actually a small mansion, at 35 Beerenstrasse.

Now that he was in Berlin, it was clearly his duty to turn off Sven Hedin Strasse onto Onkel Tom Allee and drive the three or four kilometers to Luftwaffe Headquarters and present himself to the Chief of Protocol for whatever nonsense that idiot had in mind.

On the other hand, the teletype had said "no later than forty-eight hours" from the date-time seal on the message, and that gave him until 10:05 tomorrow morning. He'd been a soldier long enough to learn that one never reported in more than five minutes before the specified time.

Furthermore, the house at 35 Beerenstrasse was occupied by a lady he'd recently met. The lady was a film actress at the UFA studios. She and some other women, a small band, and a juggler, of all things, visited the small field in the country where Jagdstaffel 232 was based in order to entertain the troops. Afterward, Hauptmann von Wachtstein considered it his duty to ask the troupe to dinner in the officers' mess. The lady's husband, who identified himself as a member of Propaganda Minister Goebbels's staff in the Propaganda Ministry, sat on one side of him, and the lady on the other.

The lady's husband was an overfed, pompous little man, obviously some fifteen or twenty years older than his wife, who would probably have been still selling stamps in some rural post office had he not had the wisdom to join the National Socialist Party before the Austrian Corporal came to power.

The moment he saw the lady, a tall, graceful blonde with a splendid bosom, Peter sensed that she found him attractive. Proof came at dinner, when her knee, then her shoe, and ultimately her shoeless foot came looking for him under the table.

He of course asked her for the privilege of the first dance after dinner. Though the dance was brief, it gave her opportunity to rub her bosom against him and to suggest that he come see her the next time he came to Berlin.

"Alois is very often out of town on Propaganda Ministry business," she told him.

Of course, it was possible that she may have had more to drink than she should have (she liked his cognac very much). Or, for that matter, she might simply have been teasing him. So Peter approached her invitation with understandable caution.

One of the great shocks of his life occurred a year before, when he learned that what appeared to be an unquestioned invitation in the eyes and attitude of a stunning redhead was really nothing more than a desire for him to betray interest in her. That way she could complain to her husband and remind him that she was still attractive.

He put the Horche in gear, turned toward Onkel Tom Allee, and then made two left turns back toward Beerenstrasse.

The door was opened by a gray-haired woman. She was not in uniform, but she was clearly a servant.

"I am Hauptmann Freiherr von Wachtstein," Peter announced. "Is Frau Nussl at home?"

Nussl was her husband's name. Professionally, the lady was known as Lillian Hart.

"I will see," the gray-haired woman announced, and closed the door in his face.

Frau Nussl appeared three minutes later.

"God, I was afraid you'd do this," she greeted him.

Peter was prepared. He'd learned from the painful mistake with the redhead.

"I'm visiting Berlin on official business, Frau Nussl," he announced formally, and thrust a paper-wrapped parcel at her. "I hope you will accept this as a small token of the gratitude of the officers and men of Jagdstaffel 232 for your kindness in visiting us."

Laughing, she took the parcel and said, "Come back at five, or five-fifteen," then closed the door in his face.

Peter, sensing that his face was flushed, returned to the Horche and headed again for Onkel Tom Strasse.

What I will do tonight, after I see the Protocol idiot, is go to the Hotel Adlon. The Knight's Cross is usually enough to motivate some patriotic fräulein there to visit your room for its view.

The way my luck is running, there will be no rooms in the

Adlon. Maybe the Hotel am Zoo. The one thing I will not do is be back at 35 Beerenstrasse at five or five-fifteen.

"Is that the only uniform you have with you, von Wachtstein?" Oberst Howze asked, annoyance in his voice.

"Herr Oberst, I regret that it is. The teletype said nothing about uniforms."

"You are having luncheon at the Foreign Ministry tomorrow," Howze said. "That uniform is inappropriate. Something will have to be done."

"Herr Oberst, if I may?" Oberstleutnant Huber said.

Oberst Howze nodded.

"May I suggest, Herr Oberst, that under the circumstances, his uniform may be very appropriate. It is the uniform worn by officers who are flying every day against the enemy. In that sense, it may be viewed as a token of respect for the late Hauptmann Duarte; that we are taking a man from the lines, so to speak, as a token of our respect."

Oberst Howze grunted.

"At least get your trousers pressed and get rid of those boots," Howze said to Peter.

"Yes, Sir. Herr Oberst, may I inquire?"

"All I know, von Wachtstein, is that if you pass muster at luncheon tomorrow, you will be traveling to Argentina as the Assistant Military Attaché for Air. And escorting the body of an Argentine who killed himself at Stalingrad, flying a Storch."

"Sir . . ."

Howze held up his hand impatiently to stop him.

"It will all be explained to you tomorrow, von Wachtstein," he said, and added to Oberstleutnant Huber, "Go with him. Make sure he has at least decent shoes. He can't have luncheon at the Foreign Ministry in flight boots!"

At almost exactly five o'clock, after failing to obtain an explanation from Oberstleutnant Huber either about the luncheon or about Argentina, Peter went back to the Horche, dropped a new pair of low quarter shoes from the Officers' Sales Store onto the passenger seat, and drove out of the Oberkommando der Luftwaffe complex.

The more he thought about it, the chances of his finding a room at either the Adlon or the Hotel am Zoo seemed remote. If he'd had a couple of days to telephone ahead, it might have been different. That left taking a room in one of the smaller hotels around the Zoo, or off the Kurfürstendamm. They catered these days to a warm-sheets clientele; but that would be all right, in a pinch. Or he could go to the bar of one of the better hotels, and with luck he might find a patriotic fräulein with an apartment. Or as a last resort he could take her to a small hotel. But that would not solve the problem of the pressed trousers.

There was, of course, always Frau Nussl. She had said to come back.

Her maid! Certainly her maid could press my pants!

He drove back down Onkel Tom Allee and ultimately to 35 Beerenstrasse.

This time Frau Nussl herself opened the door to him.

"I couldn't have you in with Frau Leiss here," Frau Nussl greeted him.

"I understand," Peter said.

"The cognac is marvelous!" Frau Nussl said. "I started without you, the minute she was out of the door."

"I have a friend in Paris who sends it to me," Peter replied idly, and then asked, "Your maid is gone, I take it?"

"You seem disappointed," Frau Nussl said.

"I have to have my trousers pressed," Peter said.

"Really?"

"Really. Is there a cleaner's shop nearby?"

"It's probably closed," she said. "But there's an iron somewhere. All we have to do is find it. Can you do it yourself?"

"Sure."

"It's probably in one of the closets upstairs, it and the board," she said. "Let's go see. One of those lovely bottles of cognac is already up there."

There was, in fact, a small but completely equipped linen closet. Peter set up the folding ironing board and plugged the iron in.

Frau Nussl handed him a snifter generously served with cognac.

"I'd offer to do that for you, but I honestly don't know how," she said.

"Is there a robe or something I could borrow? You lose the crease unless you let them cool for fifteen or twenty minutes."

"*That* I can arrange," she said, and went down the corridor.

Peter took a healthy swallow of the cognac and felt it warm his body.

Argentina? Assistant Military Attaché for Air? Accompanying a body? What the hell is going on?

Frau Nussl returned with a heavy silk robe.

"It's Alois's. Almost unworn," she said. "When he puts it on, it drags on the floor."

"It'll do fine," Peter said. "It won't take me long. Thank you."

He closed the door, took his trousers off, and laid them on the board while he waited for the iron to grow warm.

The door opened.

"I wondered," Frau Nussl said, "what you would look like without your pants."

Frau Nussl had changed into a dressing robe.

"Oh, really?"

"And I thought you just might be idly curious to see what I looked like without mine," Frau Nussl went on, flicking the opening of her gown back and forth to give him, however briefly, that opportunity.

"Won't that wait?" she asked. "Isn't there something I could do to get you to put that off for a while?"

"You just did it," Peter said, and unplugged the iron.

IV

The Diplomatic Reception Room
The Foreign Ministry of the German Reich
Berlin
1205 30 October 1942

"There he is," Wilhelm von Ruppersdorf, Deputy Foreign Minister for South American Affairs, said softly to the three men sitting with him at a small table, and rose to his feet.

The others followed suit. Hauptmann Hans-Peter von Wachtstein looked toward the door. A uniformed guard was leading a tall, dark-haired, and dark-skinned man in a business suit across the marble-floored reception area toward them.

Von Ruppersdorf took a few steps forward, smiled, and put out his hand.

"Buenas tardes, mi Coronel," he said.

Von Ruppersdorf's Spanish, Peter had learned three quarters of an hour before, was impeccable. He had served for three years at the Embassy in Buenos Aires, he informed Peter then.

The tall, dark-skinned man smiled, showing a handsome set of teeth, and shook von Ruppersdorf's hand.

"Colonel Perón, may I present Brigadeführer von Neibermann, Oberst Susser, and Hauptmann Freiherr von Wachtstein?" von Ruppersdorf said. "Gentlemen, Colonel Juan Domingo Perón, of the Argentine Embassy."

Perón shook hands with each of them in turn. He seemed to look askance at Peter, which Peter felt was understandable.

Despite my new shoes and pressed pants, compared to these three, I look like a bum.

Von Ruppersdorf was wearing a morning coat, Brigadeführer von Neibermann was wearing an SS dress uniform, complete to dagger suspended from a silver brocade belt, and Colonel Susser was in the prescribed Luftwaffe walking-out uniform. Peter was wearing a leather uniform jacket which showed signs of having spent some time in a cockpit.

Another usher appeared, carrying five glasses of champagne on a tray. One by one the men took a glass.

"The late Captain Jorge Alejandro Duarte," Brigadeführer von Neibermann said, raising his glass.

He mispronounced every other syllable, Peter noticed, despite the coaching he'd been given by von Ruppersdorf before they came into the reception room.

"Hear, hear," Colonel Susser said.

"A tragic loss," von Ruppersdorf said.

"El Capitán Duarte," Peter said, raising his glass and then taking a sip.

Not bad, Peter thought. *German Sekt, of course, not as good as French champagne, but the Foreign Ministry of the German Reich certainly could not serve French champagne in its reception room.*

He was more than a little hung over and as dry as a bone, and had to resist the temptation to drain his glass and hold it up for another. He sensed Colonel Juan Domingo Perón's eyes on him.

"I would like to apologize for my appearance, mi Coronel," Peter said. "When I was summoned to Berlin, I had no idea it was to take lunch with a distinguished foreign statesman."

"I'm not a 'distinguished statesman,' Captain," Perón said with a smile. "Like you, I am a soldier. I am here to learn something about your social services. And if I was looking closely at you, it was to see if that is indeed the Knight's Cross of the Iron Cross."

"Hauptmann Freiherr von Wachtstein received that decoration from the hands of the Führer himself," Brigadeführer von Neibermann gushed.

"Where did you learn your Spanish, Captain?" Colonel Perón asked Peter, ignoring von Neibermann. "You speak it extraordinarily well."

"In school, mi Coronel," Peter replied, "and then I served in Spain."

"With the Condor Legion," Brigadeführer von Neibermann furnished.

"You will have no trouble making yourself understood in Argentina, Captain," Perón said.

"You think the Freiherr would be suitable, then, for the sad

duty of escorting the remains of Captain Duarte, mi Coronel?"
von Ruppersdorf asked.

"I should think that Captain Duarte's family—we are acquainted—would be honored that such a distinguished officer
would be spared from his duties for the task," Perón said.

"It is a token of the respect of the government of the German
Reich for Captain Duarte," von Ruppersdorf said. "His loss is
deeply regretted."

"We feel that Captain Duarte fell for the Fatherland," Brigadeführer von Neibermann said solemnly. "That he was one of
us."

Perón looked at him. Peter saw the sudden hardness in his eyes.
That was going a bit too far, Herr Brigadeführer.

"Did I understand you to say that you know Captain Duarte's
family, Colonel Perón?" von Ruppersdorf asked quickly.

"I am *acquainted* with his parents," Perón said. "His uncle,
Colonel Jorge Guillermo Frade, is an old friend. We shared a
room at the School of Cavalry as lieutenants, and we were at
Command College together."

"I see," von Ruppersdorf said. "Then this is a personal loss
for you, too, isn't it?"

"Yes, it is," Perón said simply.

"Would you like another glass of champagne, Colonel?" von
Ruppersdorf asked. "Or shall we go into lunch?"

"Two glasses of champagne, except when I am in the company
of a beautiful woman, gives me a headache," Perón said.

"The same thing happens to me," Peter was astonished to hear
himself blurt, "the morning after I have been with a beautiful
woman."

Perón looked at him, astonished. And just at the point where
Peter had become convinced that he had really put his foot in his
mouth, Colonel Perón laughed. Heartily.

"Are you sure you have no Argentine blood, Captain von
Wachtstein?" he asked.

"No, Sir," Peter said. "I am a pure-blooded Pomeranian, two-
legged variety."

Perón laughed again, delightedly, and touched Peter's arm.

"You will fit right in in Buenos Aires, Captain," Perón said.

[TWO]
1420 Avenue Alvear
Buenos Aires, Argentina
1430 31 October 1942

The chauffeur of the 1941 Buick Roadmaster station wagon, a heavyset man in his forties, glanced at the man in the front seat beside him and saw that wherever his attention was, it was not on the Avenue Alvear.

"Mi Coronel," he said, "the gates are closed."

Jorge Guillermo Frade, who was wearing a gray linen suit and a soft straw snap-brim hat, looked out the window and saw that was indeed the case. The twenty-foot-high double cast iron gates in front of his sister's house were unquestionably closed. He also glanced around and realized that Enrico, on seeing that the gates were closed, had elected to stop right where he was, in the middle of the Avenue Alvear, to wait until the problem was solved for him. At least four cars behind him were blowing their horns.

"Make the turn, Enrico," Frade said softly. "Pull as far onto the sidewalk as you can, so as not to block traffic, and then leave the car, enter through the small gate, and either open the driveway gates or have someone open them for you."

"Sí, mi Coronel."

Enrico is not stupid, Frade thought. *It is simply that he has not mastered—never will be able to master—Buenos Aires traffic. He can alone and without difficulty maneuver a troop, a squadron, the entire regiment of the Husare di Pueyrredón at the gallop in a thunderstorm, but a closed gate, one that he cannot leap over or go around, is simply beyond his understanding. As is the notion that it is not acceptable behavior to simply stop in the middle of a busy street because you don't know what to do next.*

Enrico made the turn, sounded the horn to warn pedestrians on the sidewalk, and stopped the Buick with its nose no more than six inches from the massive gate. He applied the parking brake, turned off the engine, and stepped out of the car.

As soon as he was out, Frade slid across the seat, turned on the ignition, and started the engine. He saw Enrico enter the courtyard inside the fence and move immediately to the gate. There was an enormous brass padlock and a chain holding the gate closed. Enrico threw up his hands in disgust, then trotted toward the twenty-foot-high double doors of the mansion.

Maybe they're not here? Is it possible they would have gone off to their estancia without telling anyone? After Jorge was killed, anything is possible. So what will I do? It's three hundred kilometers out there!

He saw Enrico banging the cast iron clapper on the door.

If there is a clapper, use that. Doorbells sometimes do not work.

The door was opened by Alberto, Beatrice and Homer's butler. Enrico pointed indignantly toward the closed gates and the Buick sitting outside them. Alberto looked stricken, then disappeared into the house, leaving the door open.

A moment later, one of the other servants appeared, this one in an apron. He was armed with an enormous key for the enormous padlock.

His name is Roberto . . . Ricardo . . . and he is Alberto's nephew, Frade remembered. *Or a second cousin, something like that.*

Between the two of them, they got the gates open, and Frade drove inside.

When he left the car, Alberto was standing there.

"My apologies, mi Coronel," he said. "We did not know you were coming, and we are not receiving."

"It's all right," Frade said. "My sister is at home?"

"I have told the Señora you are here. You will be received in the library, mi Coronel."

Frade walked into the house. There was a huge foyer, furnished with heavy, leather-upholstered furniture, tables along the walls, and a fountain, not presently in use, in the center. The floor was marble.

He walked into the library, which was carpeted and quite dark. Alberto followed him in, turning on lights and opening the curtains on two windows which looked out onto the garden.

"May I take your hat, mi Coronel?" Alberto asked. "And may I bring you something?"

Frade handed him the hat.

"I would like a drink," he said. "I know where it is. Would you get me some ice? And some agua mineral con gas?"

While Alberto left to fetch ice and soda water, Frade went to what appeared to be—and had once been—an ancient chest of drawers and tugged on one of the pulls. The entire front opened to him, after which he slid out a tray that held half a dozen bottles of spirits and as many large, squat crystal glasses. He took a bottle of Dewar's scotch and poured three fingers' worth in a glass.

He looked at it a moment, then took a healthy swallow, grimacing slightly as the whiskey passed down his throat. Then he refilled the glass to a depth of two fingers and waited for Alberto to bring the ice and soda.

When his sister and her husband walked into the library, he was sitting in a chair apparently taking his first sip of a drink. No one spoke. He rose as Beatrice came toward him, took two steps toward her, and kissed her on the cheek. A real kiss—he could taste her face powder.

Beatrice is still a handsome woman, Frade thought. *She looks ghastly right now, but even so, she seems much younger than Humberto... and they are what? Forty-six. Beatrice is actually six months older than Humberto, now that I think about it.*

"People mean well," Humberto Valdez Duarte, his brother-in-law, a tall, slender man, said as he put out his hand. "But they—we closed the gate, hoping they would think we were gone away, or take the suggestion that we are not receiving."

"I understand," Frade said.

"What is that you're drinking, Jorge?" Beatrice asked, then went on without giving him a chance to reply. "Will you have something to eat?"

"The scotch is fine, thank you," he said.

"We went to eight o'clock mass," Beatrice said.

"Did you?"

"At Our Lady of Pilar,"* Humberto said, evenly, but looking at Frade.

Christ, I know what's coming.

"And then afterward, we went to Recoleta," Beatrice went on.

There is a dreamy quality to her voice, and to the way she behaves. I hope to God she doesn't become addicted to whatever she's taking.

"We visited the Duarte tomb," Beatrice went on, "and of course ours. I left flowers on Mommy's casket and Daddy's."

"I haven't been there in almost a year," Frade said, thinking aloud.

---

*The Basílica of Our Lady of Pilar (completed 1732), on Recoleta Square, is considered to be the most beautiful church in Buenos Aires. It is adjacent to the Recoleta Cemetery, which dates to 1822 and contains the remains of the most prominent Argentine families, interred in magnificent marble tombs (many of these tombs have as many as five subterranean levels, each holding three levels of caskets on open shelves, access to which is by stairways leading down from the ground floor).

"Humberto said I shouldn't ask you, because you wouldn't know," Beatrice said, "but I have been wondering, Jorge, do you think there was a mass when they buried our Jorge?"

"I don't know about a mass, Beatrice, but I'm sure there was a priest. They have chaplains in the German Army, as we do. Beatrice . . ."

"And I would really like to know, Jorge," Beatrice said, looking at him, "whether you think—after this horrible war, of course—there are chances of our bringing him home, to put him to rest in Recoleta, with the Duartes?"

"Actually, Beatrice, that's why I'm here," Frade said.

"Excuse me?"

I don't think she will understand what I have to tell her. Thank God Humberto is here.

"There has been a radio message, Beatrice. Do you remember Juan Domingo Perón? El Coronel Juan Domingo Perón?"

She considered that a full fifteen seconds before shaking her head no. There was confusion all over her face.

"He and I were lieutenants together. And then we were at the Command College. He's in Germany, studying welfare and retirement, and social services for the poor."

Beatrice laughed brightly.

"Whatever are you talking about, Jorge?"

"It appears that the Germans are arranging to send Jorge home, Beatrice," Frade said. "Perón was called to the Foreign Ministry and introduced to—actually, he was asked to approve of—the German officer who will escort the remains."

"The Germans are sending Jorge home?" Beatrice asked.

"Odd, that you were told and not me," Humberto said.

Frade was genuinely fond of his brother-in-law—despite his penchant for taking offense when none was intended. He was annoyed with him now, but kept that from his voice when he replied.

"I'm sure there will be a formal notification. Probably by the German ambassador. But Perón knew Jorge was my nephew, and he sent unofficial word to me through our military attaché. By radio. The mail service is nonexistent these days. Rather than telephoning, someone from the Defense Ministry took it all the way out to Estancia San Pedro y San Pablo. As soon as I received it, I brought it here."

"When are they sending Jorge home?" Beatrice asked.

"I don't know that yet, Bea," Frade said gently. "I'm sure as soon as the details are known, you will be informed."

"We can have a mass, a high requiem mass, at Our Lady of Pilar," Beatrice said. "I'll have to tell the Bishop."

"There will be time for that, mi amor," Humberto said.

"And Jorge, there are still those lovely cedar caskets at San Pedro y San Pablo? Aren't there?"

Years and years before, their father somehow came onto a stock of cedar. He had a cabinet maker at the estancia turn it into caskets. It was not, Frade thought, the only odd thing the old man did after he turned sixty. But at least half a dozen cedar caskets remained stored in the rafters of the old carriage house. All that had to be done to them was to outfit the interior.

"Yes, there are," Frade said.

"That will make it nice," Beatrice said. "We will put Jorge in with the Duartes, but in a casket from Estancia San Pedro y San Pablo."

God, she's out of her mind. If she had had more than the one child, she would be far better off.

"Yes," Frade agreed, "that would be nice."

"I must talk to the Bishop and see what is involved," Beatrice said.

"Beatrice, it'll wait until tomorrow," Humberto said.

"Nonsense," she said. "I've known him since he went into the seminary. He'll have time for me."

She walked out of the room.

When he was sure she was out of earshot, Frade asked, "What is she taking?"

Humberto shrugged helplessly.

"I don't know. Something the doctor gives her."

"She is not herself," Frade said.

"Of course she's not herself," Humberto snapped. "She's lost her only child in a war he had no business being involved in."

"That's not what I mean, Humberto," Frade said.

"When she doesn't take her pills, she weeps. For hours, she weeps," Humberto said.

"She is your wife," Frade said.

"Meaning what?" Humberto snapped.

"Meaning that while I am concerned to see her drugged that way, it is not really any of my business."

"The doctor comes every day," Humberto said. "I can only presume he knows what he is doing. And of course it's your business. She's your sister. You love her."

"I wept when I heard what happened to Jorge," Frade said. "I have some small idea of what you are going through."

Tears welled in Humberto's eyes.

"Why don't you make yourself a drink?" Frade asked.

"Yes," Humberto agreed quickly. "Will you have another?"

Frade shook his head no, and murmured, "No, gracias."

When Duarte was at the chest-of-drawers bar, with his back to Frade, he said, "Jorge, I want you to know how much I appreciate everything you have done. I don't know how we would have managed without you."

"I have done nothing," Frade said.

"But you have, dear Jorge," Humberto said, turning and walking to Frade and handing him a drink. "And we both know it."

Frade put his arm around Humberto's shoulders and hugged him.

"And what of your boy?" Humberto asked. "I realize I do not have the right to ask, but . . ."

"My latest information is that he has entered the Marine Corps . . ."

"The what?"

"The Marine Corps. They are soldiers, an elite force. He will be trained as a pilot. Presumably, he will soon go to the war. As I understand it, the Marine Corps is fighting the Japanese in the Pacific."

"I will pray for him," Humberto said. "Now, after what has happened to my Jorge, I will pray very hard for your boy."

With a masterful effort, Colonel Jorge Guillermo Frade controlled his voice and replied, "Thank you, dear Humberto."

[THREE]
3470 St. Charles Avenue
New Orleans, Louisiana
1615 1 November 1942

It was growing dark enough for people to turn their headlights on, and it was raining hard, the drops drumming on the convertible's roof. It hadn't been raining long enough, though, for the rain to clean the road grime from the windshield, and it was streaked.

As he drove down St. Charles Avenue past the Tulane University campus, Clete noticed a couple walking slowly through the rain, sharing the man's raincoat. He had done that himself, more than a few times, when he was at Tulane.

They're in love, he thought, *or at least in lust.*

He'd noticed similar couples on the Rice University campus in Houston. And he'd admired a spectacular brunette in Beth's sorority house, when he was taking tea with the house mother—a "ceremony" that gave Beth and Marjorie the chance to show off their brother, the Marine Aviator Hero fresh home from Guadalcanal.

He even went back to his hotel and put his uniform on for that. Protesting, of course, and telling himself at the time that he was doing it only to indulge Beth and Marjorie, who actually wept when they saw him standing in the foyer of the sorority house. They were going to miss their father at least as much as he did, he told himself then. And since there was little else he could do for them, putting on his uniform so they could display their Brother the Hero seemed not so much of a sacrifice.

When the brunette proved to be fascinated with Marine Green and Wings of Gold, it seemed for a moment to be a case of casting bread upon the water. But he didn't pursue it. For one thing, he wanted to spend as much time alone with the girls as he could; and for another, they had enough trouble without being labeled as the sisters of that awful fellow who took Whatsername out and tried to jump Whatsername's bones in the backseat of his Buick.

Perhaps he'd have a chance in New Orleans to make a few telephone calls and do something about his celibacy. It was a very long time since he'd even been close to a woman. On the 'Canal, he thought a good bit about a nurse he'd "met" in San Diego ... that is to say, he walked into the hospital cafeteria and the nurse who thirty minutes before had drawn his blood asked him to share her table. She was also a brunette, deeply tanned, and magnificently bosomed. Her uniform was very tightly fitted; and if you looked—and he had—you could see a heavenly swell at the V neck of her whites.

There hadn't been time to pursue that—he'd boarded the *Long Island* the next morning.

He hadn't even gotten close to a woman at Pearl Harbor.

He switched on the turn signal, waited for a St. Charles Street trolley to clatter past in the opposite direction, and headed up St. Charles. Then he turned off the street onto the drive of a very large, very white, ornately decorated three-story frame mansion.

No car was parked under the portico, which probably meant that his grandfather, Cletus Marcus Howell, was not yet home from the office. He glanced at his watch; he'd probably be home any minute. That meant he would be greatly annoyed when he drove up and found another car occupying the space where he intended to park the car and get into his house without getting rained upon.

Clete stopped under the portico and stared unhappily at the garage, a hundred yards behind the house. The three doors of the former carriage house were closed. Unless things had changed, they were closed and locked. He couldn't get inside even if he drove there. All he would do was get wet.

"To hell with it!" he said aloud, then turned off the key and opened the door. He reached across the seat and picked up his Stetson, put it on, and got out. He was wearing khaki trousers and boots and a faded, nearly white shirt frayed at the neck. The sheepskin coat was in the backseat. After a moment, he remembered that, and reached in and got it.

The Buick would eventually go into the carriage house. Despite the best efforts of New Orleans' best exterminators, there were rats in there, and he didn't want them eating the jacket. Or gnawing through the Buick's roof to get at the sheepskin.

Was all that concern about the old man's convenience the normal behavior of a Southern gentleman? Or am I still afraid of him?

He was almost to the mahogany-and-beveled-glass door when it swung open to him.

"Welcome home, Mr. Cletus," Jean-Jacques Jouvier greeted him enthusiastically. The old man's silver-haired, very-light-skinned Negro butler was wearing a gray linen jacket, which meant it was not yet five. At five, Jean-Jacques would change into a black jacket.

"J.J., it's good to see you," Clete said, and wrapped his arm around his shoulders. This seemed to make J.J. uncomfortable, which was surprising, until Clete looked past him into the downstairs foyer and noticed Cletus Marcus Howell, Esquire, standing there with his hands locked together in front of him.

"Welcome home, my boy," Cletus Marcus Howell said.

Cletus Marcus Howell was tall, pale, slender, and sharp-featured. He wore a superbly tailored dark-blue, faintly pin-striped three-piece suit, with a golden watch chain looped across his stomach.

"Let me have your things, Mr. Cletus," Jean-Jacques said. Clete handed the Stetson and the sheepskin jacket to him, then started toward his grandfather.

"Grandfather," Clete said.

"You could have telephoned," the old man said as Clete approached.

"I hoped to be here before you came home from the office."

"I telephoned to Beth," the old man said. "She told me when you left Houston. I arranged to be here for your arrival."

Clete put out his hand, and the old man took it. And then, in an unusual display of emotion, took it in both his hands.

"You don't look as bad as Martha and Beth said you did," the old man said. "Both used the same term, 'cadaver.' "

"How is your health, Grandfather?" Clete asked, aware that the old man was still holding on to his hand.

"I am well, thank you," the old man said, and then, as if suddenly aware of his unseemly display of emotion, let Clete's hand go. "Why don't we go into the sitting room and ask Jean-Jacques to make us a drink."

He didn't wait for a reply. He turned on his heel and marched across the foyer through an open double sliding door to the sitting room. It was a formal sitting room, furnished sometime before the War of Rebellion and unchanged since . . . with one exception: over the fireplace, the oil painting, from life, of Bartholomew Fitzhugh Howell (1805–1890), who had built the house in 1850, had been replaced by an oil painting of equal size, painted from a photograph, of Eleanor Patricia Howell Frade (1898–1922), who had been both born in the house and buried from it.

Clete followed him. The old man walked to a cigar humidor on a marble-topped cherry table, opened it, and took from it a long, thin, nearly black cigar.

"Will you have a cigar, Cletus?"

"Yes, thank you."

"Would you like me to clip it for you?"

"Yes, thank you."

The old man took from the table an old-fashioned cigar cutter—something like a pair of scissors—walked to the fireplace, carefully clipped the cigar's end, let the end drop into the ashes of the fire, and then walked to Clete and handed it to him.

"You will excuse my fingers," he said.

"Certainly."

"It was cold, the radio said it was going to rain, and you always like a fire, so I asked Jean-Jacques to have the houseman lay one.''

"That was very thoughtful of you,'' Clete said.

Jean-Jacques produced a flaming wooden match. Clete set his cigar alight while the old man repeated the end-clipping business over the fireplace with another cigar from the humidor. Jean-Jacques went to him and produced a fresh flaming match. When the old man's cigar was satisfactorily ignited, he asked,

"What may I bring you gentlemen?''

"Ask Mr. Cletus, Jean-Jacques,'' the old man replied. "He is the returning prodigal; we should indulge him.''

"Oh, I don't see how you could call Mr. Cletus a prodigal, Mr. Howell,'' Jean-Jacques said.

"You have not been in contact with a certain Colonel Graham, Jean-Jacques,'' the old man said. "Prodigal is the word. You're familiar with the Scripture, Jean-Jacques?''

" 'There is more joy in heaven . . .'?''

"Precisely,'' the old man said. "Cletus?''

"What I really would like, J.J.—''

"I wish you would not call him that,'' the old man interrupted. "It's disrespectful. I've told you that.''

"Mister Howell, Mister Cletus can call me anything he wants to call me, unless it's dirty.''

"Not under my roof he can't,'' the old man said.

"Jean-Jacques, could you fix me a Sazerac?''

"I certainly can, it will be my pleasure. And Mr. Howell, what for you?''

"I'll have the same, please, Jean-Jacques.''

"And will you be taking dinner here, Mr. Howell?''

"That has not been decided, Jean-Jacques,'' the old man said.

"Yes, Sir,'' the butler said, nodded his head in what could have been a bow, turned, and walked out of the room.

The old man watched him go, then turned to Clete.

"One of your men is here,'' he said. "The Jew. I understand there is a certain secrecy involved, and I didn't want Jean-Jacques to hear me tell you.''

"His name is Ettinger, Grandfather. Staff Sergeant Ettinger. He lost most of his family to the Nazis.''

If Cletus Marcus Howell sensed reproof in Clete's voice, he gave no sign.

"Then there should be no question in *his* mind, wouldn't you agree, about the morality of going down there and doing whatever

Colonel Graham wants you to do to the Argentines?"

"The Germans killed his family, Grandfather, not the Argentines."

"The Argentines are allied, *de facto* if not *de jure*, with the Germans. Two peas from the same pod. Certainly, you must be aware of that."

Clete didn't reply.

"Anyway, *Staff Sergeant* Ettinger is in the Monteleone. He arrived yesterday, and telephoned. I told him you were due today or tomorrow, and would contact him. Then I called one of the Monteleones, Jerry, I think, and told him I would be obliged if he would see that Staff Sergeant Ettinger is made comfortable."

"That was gracious of you, thank you."

"Simple courtesy," the old man said. "I was going to suggest, now that you're here, that we take him to dinner. Would that be awkward? If it would, we could have him here."

"Why would it be awkward?"

"As I understand it, there is a line drawn between officers and enlisted men."

"Well, I've never paid much attention to that line. And I would guess that Ettinger will be in civilian clothing."

"We could take him to Arnaud's," the old man said. "It's right around the corner from the Monteleone, and it has a certain reputation."

In other words, unless absolutely necessary, no Jews in the house. Not even Jews who are bound for Argentina to kill Argentineans.

"Arnaud's would be fine. It's been a long time."

"When we have our drink, you can call him," the old man said. "Do I correctly infer that you are no longer wearing your uniform?"

"Yes. I have a new draft card, identifying me as someone who has been honorably discharged for physical reasons."

"Have you your uniform?"

"It's in the car. *They* are in the car."

"Your dress uniform among them?"

"Yes."

"And your decorations?"

"Yes. Why do you ask?"

"I thought I would have your portrait made," the old man said. "In uniform. I thought it could be hung in the upstairs sitting room beside that of your uncle James."

"I'm not sure there would be time."

"I don't mean to *sit* for a portrait," the old man said impatiently. "That's unnecessary. They can work from photographs. Your mother's portrait was prepared from snapshots."

"Yes, I know."

"When you know something of your schedule, we'll make time for a photographer. It will only take half an hour or so."

"If you'd like."

Jean-Jacques returned, carrying a silver tray on which were four squat glasses, two dark with Sazeracs, two of water, and two small silver bowls holding cashews and potato chips.

Clete and the old man took the Sazeracs. Jean-Jacques set the tray down on a table.

"Just a moment, please, Jean-Jacques," the old man said. Then he turned toward the oil portrait of the pretty young woman in a ball gown hanging over the fireplace.

"If I may," Cletus Marcus Howell said, raising his glass toward the portrait. "To your mother. May her blessed, tortured soul rest in God's peace."

"Mother," Clete said, raising his glass.

"And may your father receive his just deserts here on earth," the old man added.

Clete said nothing. He sometimes felt a little disloyal that he couldn't share the old man's passionate loathing for his father. Based on his grandfather's frequent recounting, over the years, of that chapter of Howell family history, he understood the old man's hatred: He held el Coronel Frade accountable for the death of his only daughter. But Clete's mother died when he was an infant, and he had no memories of his father.

That's about to change. I'll certainly meet him in Buenos Aires. And he probably won't have horns and foul breath. But he is obviously a sonofabitch of the first water. I've never known the old man to lie. And Uncle Jim and Aunt Martha have silently condemned him as long as I can remember. Both believed, and practiced, the principle that unless you can say something nice about someone, you say nothing. Anytime I asked them about my father, they answered with evasion and a quick change of subject.

If nothing else, it should be interesting to finally see the man— how does the Bible put it?—from whose loins I have sprung.

Been spranged?

He smiled, just faintly, at his play on words.

Clete saw in the old man's eyes that he had seen the smile,

and hoped it wouldn't trigger anything unpleasant. The old man looked at him intently for a moment, then turned to the butler.

"Jean-Jacques, would you please call the Monteleone and see if you can get Mr. Ettinger on the line for Mr. Cletus?"

Clete took a healthy sip of his Sazerac.

It is true, he thought, *that the only place you can get one of these is here. Strange but true. You can take all the ingredients with you, right down to Peychaux's Bitters—as I did to Pensacola—but when you make one, it's just not a Sazerac.*

He looked up at his mother's portrait and had a thought that disturbed him a little: *Jesus, she looks just like the brunette in Beth's sorority house, the one I think I could have jumped.*

"I have Mr. Ettinger for you, Mr. Cletus," Jean-Jacques said, handing him the telephone.

"Ettinger?"

"Yes, Sir."

"This is Clete Howell."

"Yes, Sir. I was told that you would be arriving about now."

"Is there anyone else there?"

"No, Sir. There was a telegram several hours ago, saying that the . . . people from Virginia . . . will be here tomorrow morning. And I was told that Lieutenant Pelosi will be on the Crescent City Limited tomorrow. He'll be coming here. I don't know about the others."

"Have you made plans for dinner?"

"No, Sir."

"Good, then you can have it with my grandfather and me. Would eight be convenient?"

"Sir, I don't want to impose."

"You won't be. Can you be in the lobby at eight, or maybe outside, if it's not raining?"

"Yes, Sir."

"You have civvies?"

"Yes, Sir."

"Wear them," Clete said.

"I was told to, Sir."

"And one more thing, Ettinger . . . *David* . . . from here on out, we will dispense with the military courtesy."

"Yes, S— All right," Ettinger said.

Clete thought he heard a chuckle.

"Eight o'clock," he said, and hung up.

Cletus Marcus Howell nodded his approval.

"Jean-Jacques, would you please tell Samuel we will need the car at seven-forty? And then call Arnaud's and tell them I will require a private dining room, for three, at about eight?"

"Yes, Sir," Jean-Jacques said.

"And finally, Mr. Cletus has left his luggage in his car. Would you bring it in and unpack it for him, please? And, as soon as you can, see to having his dress uniform pressed, or cleaned, or whatever it takes?"

"Mr. Cletus's car is in the carriage house, Mr. Howell," Jean-Jacques said. "His luggage is in his room. Antoinette's already taking care of his laundry, and she heard what you said about painting Mr. Cletus's picture, so she's already working on the uniform."

"Thank you."

"Can you think of anything else, Cletus?"

"I think I would like another Sazerac, Jean-Jacques, if you could find the time."

"If you fill yourself with Sazeracs, Cletus, you won't be able to appreciate either the wine or the food at Arnaud's."

"Grandfather, I am prepared to pay that price."

"You might as well fetch two, please, Jean-Jacques," the old man said.

"Yes, Sir," Jean-Jacques said. He turned and started out of the room. When his face was no longer visible to the old man, he smiled and winked at the young one.

[FOUR]
Schloss Wachtstein
Pomerania
1515 1 November 1942

Generalmajor Graf Karl-Friedrich von Wachtstein, wearing a leather overcoat over his shoulders, walked into the library and found his son slumped in an armchair facing the fireplace, a cognac snifter in his hand.

"It's a little early for that, isn't it, Peter?" he asked, tossing the overcoat and then his brimmed uniform cap onto a library table.

Hauptmann Hans-Peter von Wachtstein turned and looked at his father but didn't reply or stand up. After a moment, he said,

"I've just come from turning over my staffel."

"You're celebrating, then? Peter, I really wish you hadn't started drinking," the Graf said.

"I'm all right, Poppa. A little maudlin, perhaps, but sober. I was just telling myself I should be celebrating. But it doesn't feel that way."

"My father once told me that the best duty in the service is as a Hauptmann, in command of a company. In your case, a staffel. Giving up such a command is always difficult. Perhaps you should consider that it was inevitable . . ."

"Inevitable?"

"You would have had to turn it over when your majority comes through; and that should be, I would think, any day now. With a little luck, before you go to Argentina."

"I had the most disturbing feeling, as a matter of fact," Peter said, "particularly afterward, when we all had a cognac in the bar, that it was a funeral, or a wake, that we were all seeing each other for the last time."

"I've had a bad day, a bad week, myself," Graf von Wachtstein said.

"I brought Karl's car out here," Peter said, changing the subject. "I didn't know what to do with it. I thought perhaps you might want to use it."

The Graf picked up the bottle of cognac and found a glass.

"Now that I think about it," Generalmajor von Wachtstein said, "one of these might be in order." He raised the glass. "To your new assignment."

"Thank you. Did you hear what I said about the Horche?"

"I might as well use it, I suppose," the Graf said. "Otherwise it will be taken for the greater good of the German Reich. Ferrying some Nazi peasant's mistress to the opera, for example."

Peter grunted. "You must have had a bad week."

"The Luftwaffe has not been able to—will not be able to—provide von Paulus's troops at Stalingrad with a tenth of the supplies he needs. But when this is brought to the attention of the Austrian Corporal, he replies, in effect, 'Nonsense, Goering has given me his word, the supplies will be delivered.' "

"And you were the bearer of those bad tidings?"

"No. Fortunately not. Unser Führer is made uncomfortable by people like me. I have been reliably informed that he has said that the Prussian officer class are defeatists to the last aristocrat."

Peter laughed. "Aren't you? Aren't we? There's no way we can win this war, Poppa."

"I really hope you are careful to whom you make such observations."

"I'm talking to you, Poppa. The war was lost when we were unable to invade England," Peter said. "Perhaps before that, when we were unable to destroy the Royal Air Force."

"I think we should change the subject," Graf von Wachtstein said. "Have they told you when you're going?"

"They are having trouble with the corpse," Peter said. "Or the casket for the corpse. They have to line it with lead, which apparently comes in sheets. But the Foreign Ministry can't seem to find any lead in sheets. They are working on the problem; I have been told to hold myself in readiness."

"And are you ready?"

"There is of course a rather detailed list of the uniforms a military attaché is required to have. I have been given the necessary priorities for such uniforms. Unfortunately, priority or no priority, there does not seem to be the material available in Berlin. The Foreign Ministry is working on the problem."

"Perhaps you could have them made in Buenos Aires. It is a major city; there are military tailors, I'm sure. And God knows, they have woolen material. We buy it from them by the shipload. I wouldn't be at all surprised if someone were making woolens dyed to Luftwaffe specifications there."

"Dress-uniform specifications?" Peter asked. It struck him as unlikely.

"If I were a Luftwaffe procurement officer," Generalmajor von Wachtstein said, "I think I would make sure that when unser grosse Hermann wanted yet another dress uniform, the material would be available." Unser grosse Hermann—Our Big Hermann—was Reichsmarschall Hermann Goering, Commander of the Luftwaffe, and a man who was more than generously large.

Peter chuckled.

"Buttons and insignia might be a problem," Generalmajor von Wachtstein went on, in his usual thorough manner. "Make sure you take that sort of thing with you. Including major's insignia."

"Jawohl, Poppa."

"Don't mock me, Peter, please. These details are important. The last thing we want is to have you sent back here because the military attaché decides you are unsuitable for the assignment."

"Sorry," Peter said, genuinely contrite. "I'm sure there will be tailors. Oberst Perón painted a fascinating picture of Buenos Aires for me."

"Who?"

"*Argentine* Oberst Juan Domingo Perón. He's attached to their embassy over here studying our welfare programs. He's a friend of the family of the Duarte fellow. I met him at the Foreign Ministry, and I've had dinner with him. He called me up."

Generalmajor von Wachtstein nodded, then dismissed the Argentine officer as unimportant.

"Peter, we have to talk about money," he said.

"A delicate subject, Poppa. One the son is glad the father brought up first. From what I'm told, Buenos Aires is a very expensive place to live. It was put to me that I would have difficulty making ends meet, and that it was hoped I could somehow augment my pay."

"That's not what I'm talking about," his father said. "But tell me about it. Would that be permitted?"

"I think encouraged," Peter said.

"Did you have the feeling there would be a limit on how much money you could take to Argentina?"

"I had the feeling that the more you'd be willing to give me, the better they would like it."

"Pay attention to me," the Graf said sharply.

"Sir?" Peter responded, surprised at his father's tone, and baffled by his question.

"There is money, Peter. A substantial amount here, most of it in English pounds and Swiss francs, and an even more substantial amount in Switzerland, in a bank. Actually, in two banks."

Peter was now genuinely surprised. Simple possession of currency of the Allied powers or neutral countries was a serious offense. Maintaining bank accounts out of Germany was even more stringently forbidden.

"This war will pass," the Graf said, now sure that he had his son's attention. "This government will pass. We, you and I, will pass. What is important is that the family must not die, or that we, the family, don't lose our lands. We have been on these lands for more than five hundred years. My duty—our duty—is to see that we do not lose them. If we lose the war, and I agree we cannot win it, we will lose our lands . . . unless there is money. Not German money, which will be devalued and useless, but the currency of the victors, or a neutral power. Do you understand what I'm saying?"

"Yes, Sir."

"First, the money in Switzerland. The accounts there are numbered. I am going to give you the numbers. You must memorize the numbers. When you are settled in Argentina, I want you to have the money transferred there from Switzerland, secretly, and put somewhere safe, where we will have access to it after the war."

"How will I do that?"

"Von Lutzenberger will probably be able to help, but we can't bank on that."

"Ambassador von Lutzenberger?" Peter asked. Someone had given him the name of the German Ambassador to Argentina during the last couple of days, but he hadn't expected to hear it from his father.

"He's a friend," his father said. "But you would do well to consider him your last reserve, Peter, not to be used until you are sure you can't deal with a situation by yourself, without help."

"But he knows about your money?"

His father nodded, then corrected him. "Not my money, Peter. Von Wachtstein money. Money that has come down to us from our family, with the expectation that it will be used wisely and for the family."

Peter nodded, accepting the correction.

"A good man. We were at Marburg together. And he has as much to risk as we do. But keep in mind, Peter, that a situation may come where he will have to make a sacrifice for the common good, and you might be that sacrifice."

"How is it you never told me about any of this?"

"Because your possession of the knowledge would place you in jeopardy. If they found out you knew about it, you would be as culpable as I am. Your Knight's Cross notwithstanding, you would wind up in a concentration camp."

Peter blurted what came into his mind: "But what if you had died? What would have happened to the money then?"

"Dieter von Haas and I have an arrangement. If anything happened to me, he would have told you. If anything happens to him, I will inform Frau von Haas of the similar arrangements he has made."

Peter looked at his father for a long moment.

"I'm not good at memorizing numbers," he said. "I never have been."

"Then write the numbers down, make them look like telephone

numbers or something. And then, to be sure, construct a simple code," the Graf von Wachtstein said, a touch of impatience in his voice. "One or two digits up from the actual numbers. Something like that."

"Yes," Peter said simply.

"About the cash here," the Graf went on. "Do you think you will be searched when you leave the country?"

Peter thought about that for a moment.

"No," he said. "The body will be accompanied by an honor guard as far as the Spanish border. I don't think anyone will search me. And the moment I cross the border, I will have diplomatic status."

He looked at his father.

When I leave here, he thought with a sudden chilled certainty, *I will never see him again.*

"I think it would be best if you took the money with you when you return to Berlin tomorrow. They may solve the problem of sheet lead for the casket, and you might not be able to come back here. And I wouldn't want to be seen passing anything to you at the train station. Do you have someplace safe to keep it? Where are you staying in Berlin?"

"With a friend, in Zehlendorf."

"Better than a hotel," the Graf said. "Well, I'll write the numbers down for you, and while you're copying them into a code, I'll get the money. And then we'll see about finding something to eat."

"You know what I would like for supper, Poppa?" Peter said. "I'd like to go into the gasthaus in the village and have sausage and potatoes and beer."

Generalmajor Graf Karl-Friedrich von Wachtstein looked at his son. His left eyebrow rose.

"Yes, Peter, I think I would too," he said after a moment.

V

[ONE]
The Vieux Carré
New Orleans, Louisiana
1955 1 November 1942

It was still raining when the 1938 Durham-bodied Cadillac pulled to the curb across the street from the Monteleone Hotel in the Vieux Carré. Clete wiped his hand on the window to clear the condensation.

"There he is. He even looks like the picture Graham showed me," Clete said.

He started to open the door. His grandfather stopped him. He had a microphone in his hand.

"Samuel, the gentleman we are meeting is standing to the left of the . . ."

Clete took the microphone from him.

"Samuel, pull up in front of the hotel. Don't get out of the car. I'll call to him."

"Have it your way," the old man said, then leaned across Clete to look out the window he had cleared. "He doesn't look like a Jew."

"What does a Jew look like?"

"Not like that," the old man said.

Samuel found a place in the flow of traffic and drove the thirty yards to the marquee of the Monteleone. Clete opened the door and called to Ettinger. Ettinger was visibly surprised to see the car, but after a moment came quickly across the sidewalk.

"We're only going around the corner, but why get wet?" Clete said, offering his hand. "David, I'm glad to meet you." Then he turned to the old man. "Grandfather, may I present *Mr.* David Ettinger? David, this is my grandfather, Mr. Cletus Marcus Howell."

"How do you do?" the old man said.

"How do you do?" Ettinger said, offering his hand.

With a just-perceptible hesitation, the old man took it. Briefly.

Then he picked up the microphone again. "Arnaud's, Samuel," he ordered. "After you have found a place to park the car, go into the kitchen and tell them I would be obliged if they gave you something to eat."

Clete saw Ettinger's eyebrow rise, and smiled at him.

A waiter greeted them at the door to Arnaud's and led them through the crowded main dining area to a small private dining room. The waiter pulled aside the curtain on the doorway and bowed them in.

The table had been set. There was an impressive array of crystal, silver, and starched napkins. A menu was at each place.

"I took the liberty, Mr. Howell," the waiter said, removing the cover from a plate in the center of the table, "to have a few hors d'oeuvres prepared for you, while you decide."

"The last time you did that," the old man said, "the remoulade sauce was disgraceful."

"Indeed it was. The saucier was shot at dawn the next morning. We showed him no mercy, although he pleaded he was the sole support of his old mother. Can I bring you something from the bar?"

Clete saw Ettinger smiling; the smile vanished when Ettinger noticed the old man turning toward him.

"Mr. Ettinger?" the old man asked.

"Not for me, thank you, Sir. I wouldn't want to anesthetize my tongue before eating in a place like this."

The old man flashed Clete a triumphant smile.

"Then may I suggest we have a quick look at the menu to see whether fish, fowl, or good red meat?"

"May I ask that you order for me?" Ettinger said.

"I would be happy to translate the menu for you," the old man said. "They do it in French only to humiliate their patrons."

"I speak French, if your ordering for me would be an imposition," Ettinger said.

"No imposition at all," the old man said. "What would you recommend tonight, Harold?"

"I hesitate to recommend anything. You have been coming in here for thirty years, and I have yet to bring you anything that met your approval."

"In that case, we will try to wash these hors d'oeuvres down with a bottle of Moët, the '39, if there's any left. And you will then go to the kitchen and tell the chef that we are hungry enough to eat anything that hasn't fallen on the floor."

"There was some shrimp-and-oyster bisque a while back that didn't smell too badly."

"We place ourselves in your somewhat less than knowledgeable hands," the old man said.

"I am overwhelmed," the waiter said. "It is, in any case, good to see you, Mr. Frade. Didn't I hear you were in the Marines?"

"It's good to see you too. I was in the Marines. I was just discharged."

"Then welcome home."

"Thank you."

The waiter left.

The old man turned to Ettinger. "For reasons I can't imagine, that man fancies himself the best waiter here; and by inference, the best in New Orleans."

"It's probably his table-side manner," Ettinger said.

The old man actually chuckled.

"The problem with Argentina, Mr. Ettinger," Cletus Marcus Howell proclaimed, "is that it is a theocracy."

He was leaning back in his chair, cradling a brandy snifter in his hand. The dinner had gone well. The food, as Clete knew it would be, had been superb.

The shrimp-and-oyster bisque was followed by Filet de Boeuf à la Venison, a dish Ettinger had never previously encountered. When he admitted this, he thus offered the old man the opportunity to display his culinary knowledge as to its preparation.

Ettinger seemed not only genuinely interested, but also showed himself to be quite familiar with the subtleties of haute cuisine. He mentioned to the old man, for instance, that the Moroccans made a similar dish; they substituted mutton for the beef, however, while marinating it and otherwise cooking it like venison.

He also showed a genuine and knowledgeable enthusiasm for the wine. By the time the brandy was served, the old man was almost beaming. And Clete was amusing himself with what was surely his grandfather's current opinion of Staff Sergeant Ettinger: *Jew or not, that fellow is a gentleman.*

He was even daring to hope that the old man was in such a good mood he would not mention his daughter. Clete now realized, resignedly, that that was not to be.

"A theocracy, Sir?" Ettinger asked.

"A government which is controlled by a religion," the old man explained.

"Such as Spain," Ettinger said.

"Precisely. And, as in Spain, that religion is Roman Catholicism," the old man said. "Now, don't misunderstand me. There is not a prejudiced bone in my body, and I have tried to pass my tolerance for other people's religious convictions on to my son, and especially my grandson. As a matter of fact, I have a number of Roman Catholic friends, including, to put a point on it, the Archbishop of New Orleans. Weather permitting, for twenty-odd years, every other Thursday, I took his money at the Metairie Country Club."

"You are speaking of theocracy," Ettinger said.

"Indeed. You are, I understand, Spanish?"

"I am now an American citizen," Ettinger said carefully. "I formerly held German citizenship. I am of Spanish heritage."

"You know Spain?"

"I lived there."

"Then you will feel right at home in Argentina. The most outrageous things are done there in the name of Christianity, which of course there means Roman Catholicism."

"I see."

"It doesn't happen here," the old man said. "Archbishop Noonan is as fine a gentleman as they come. But, of course, that is because our Constitution wisely forbids a state religion."

"I understand."

"The Roman Catholic theocracy in Argentina murdered my daughter, Cletus's mother," the old man said.

"Grandfather, do we have to get into this?"

"I think I should," the old man said.

"You are embarrassing our guest," Clete said.

"I don't see why he should be embarrassed. He's a Jew, as I understand it. To him this is a neutral matter. Why should he be embarrassed if I tell him what he will find when you reach Argentina?" He sat up and leaned across the table. "Am I embarrassing you, Mr. Ettinger?"

"No, Sir."

"My daughter married an Argentinean, Mr. Ettinger. Cletus's father is an Argentinean. Did you know that?"

"Colonel Graham mentioned something about Lieutenant Frade having been born there, Sir."

"Jorge Guillermo Frade is his name," the old man said. He

pronounced it in Spanish—Horgay Goool-yermo Frah-day—each
syllable reflecting his loathing. "Hor-gay Goool-yermo Frah-day
is, among other things, a cattleman."

"Is that so?" Ettinger asked.

"I really wish you would stop this, Grandfather," Clete said.

"Mr. Ettinger and the other fellow who's going with you," the
old man said, "the Italian, have a right to know this story, Cletus.
Please don't interrupt me again."

Clete sensed Ettinger's eyes on him, and looked at him. The
eyes seemed to say, *I understand. Let him finish. There's no way
he can be stopped.* Clete saw also in Ettinger's eyes both sympathy for him, and pity for the old man.

"As I was saying, Mr. Ettinger," the old man went on. "Hor-
gay Goool-yermo Frah-day is a cattleman. My son James Fitzhugh Howell, Cletus's uncle, was a cattleman. When Hor-gay
Goool-yermo Frah-day heaved onto the scene, he was courting
the lady who later became Mrs. Howell. Her family are cattlemen.
Hor-gay Goool-yermo Frah-day came to this country to do business with my daughter-in-law's father. She wasn't yet then my
daughter-in-law, but I presume you're following me?"

"Yes, Sir."

"My son was at the Williamson ranch—my daughter-in-law's
maiden name was Williamson—when Hor-gay Goool-yermo
Frah-day came there to buy some breeding stock from Mr.
Williamson. Handsome fella, charming. I'll give him that, Hor-
gay Goool-yermo Frah-day is handsome and charming. Spoke
fluent English, with just enough of an accent to make the ladies
flush. Like Charles Boyer, if you take my meaning."

" 'Come wiss me to zee Casbah,' " Ettinger replied, in a very
creditable mimicry of one of the actor's most famous lines.

"Exactly, exactly!" the old man said, and then went on. "And
they were about the same age, so my son asked Hor-gay Goool-
yermo Frah-day to come to New Orleans, to see the city. He
came, and I opened my house to him. And I was the one, may
God forgive me, who introduced him to my daughter. She wasn't
even through college, had a year to go at Rice. And Hor-gay
Goool-yermo Frah-day just swept that child off her feet.

"When he came to me and asked for her hand, I told him she
was too young, and that I could not in good conscience offer my
blessing until she'd finished her education."

"I understand your position," Ettinger said. "Any father
would feel that way."

"My wife, may she rest in peace, had passed on when my daughter was fourteen. They called it 'consumption' then; now they call it 'tuberculosis.' "

"So you were both father and mother to your children," Ettinger said.

"You could say that, Mr. Ettinger, yes," the old man went on. "And so did Hor-gay Goool-yermo Frah-day understand my position. Or so he said. So he went back to Argentina, and I thought—*I've* never believed that absence makes the heart grow fonder. And I concluded that would be the end of it. Hor-gay Goool-yermo Frah-day would find some suitable young woman down there, and my daughter would find some suitable suitor here.

"Well, I'm an oilman, Mr. Ettinger . . . Did Cletus mention that?"

"Colonel Graham did, Sir."

"I thought perhaps he might have," the old man said. "Anyway, I'm an oilman, and the first thing oilmen learn is that the more you know about people you're going to deal with, the better off you are. So I had a friend of mine with the foreign department of the National City Bank of New York City—when we first went into Venezuela, he was very helpful, and together we did all right down there—make some discreet inquiries about this fellow Hor-gay Goool-yermo Frah-day down in Argentina. He reported back to me that he came from a fine family, which was highly regarded down there, and that they were, economically speaking, quite comfortable. To put a point on that, they have an *estancia,* what we call a ranch, that's just slightly larger than the State of Rhode Island."

"Very impressive," Ettinger said.

"The next thing I know, a couple of months later, I get a telephone call from a fellow staying at the Roosevelt Hotel. Says he's a friend of the family of Hor-gay Goool-yermo Frah-day, and could we have lunch. I forget his name, but he was a gentleman. Charming fellow. I was halfway through having lunch with him—I had him out to the Metairie Country Club—before I realized that what *he* was doing was checking *me* out, to see if my daughter was suitable for Hor-gay Goool-yermo Frah-day, not some Yankee gold digger after Hor-gay Goool-yermo Frah-day's daddy's money.

"Well, I didn't take offense, because I understood. There was nothing wrong with doing that. But I called him on it, and told him we could probably save some time by me letting him know I was dead set against any marriage, but just to put my cards faceup on the table, I wasn't exactly walking around with holes in my shoes either.

"Then he told me—he was my kind of man, that fellow; I wish to God I could remember his name—that they weren't exactly thrilled down there either that Hor-gay Goool-yermo Frah-day was determined to marry a foreigner, but there wasn't much that could be done about it.

"So I told him sure there was, all that had to happen was to have Hor-gay Goool-yermo Frah-day's daddy tell him, and mean it, that if he married the foreign girl he could go find himself a job someplace, 'because the money tree would be cut off at the roots.' I remember using those exact words.

"And then he told me that Hor-gay Goool-yermo Frah-day's daddy was about to pass on. Had kidney trouble, as I recall, and once the daddy was gone, there would be no control over him. And then we sat there in the bar drinking Sazeracs . . .

"I'll tell you a secret about New Orleans, Mr. Ettinger. If you're ever doing business in this town and the fellow offers you a Sazerac, turn him down. They sneak up on people; you could sell them the Mississippi River after they've had four of them."

"I'll remember that," Ettinger said. "Thank you."

"Anyway, I believed what this fellow was saying, so we sat there trying to salvage something from a bad situation. Well, after a while, it didn't look too bad. Hor-gay Goool-yermo Frah-day couldn't marry while his father was dying. And they have some sort of Roman Catholic rule that the period of mourning is one year. So we had whatever time it took for Hor-gay Goool-yermo Frah-day's daddy to die, plus a year, during which time he would work at his end, and I would work here, to simply kill the whole idea of the two of them marrying. When I drove him back to his hotel, I remember feeling a little better about the whole thing. With a little bit of luck, Hor-gay Goool-yermo Frah-day's daddy would last a lot longer than anyone thought.

"Two weeks later he died. When my daughter heard about it, she wanted to go down there; and I had a hell of a time convincing her that before she could do that, the daddy would be a long time in his grave, and that it was unseemly, anyhow. They weren't formally engaged.

"A month after he put his daddy in the ground, Hor-gay Goool-yermo Frah-day showed up here with an engagement ring in his

pocket. And then I realized that I had lost, my precious daughter
was going to marry Hor-gay Goool-yermo Frah-day whether or
not I liked it, and there was nothing I could do about it but put
on a smile and act like I liked it.

"The first time this theocracy business came up was when my
daughter came to me and said she wanted me to know she was
going to take instruction in the Roman Catholic Church. Now, as
I told you, I have nothing whatever against the Roman Catholic
Church. The Archbishop here is a close personal friend. But I
asked her why she wanted to do that—she was raised Episcopal,
and theologically, there's not a hell of a difference between the
two. And she said that for her marriage to be recognized down
there, she had to get married in a Roman Catholic Church, and
she couldn't do that unless she was confirmed into the Roman
Catholic Church, and that her Episcopalian confirmation didn't
count.

"So I called my friend the Archbishop, and he told me that
was so, she couldn't get married unless she was confirmed as a
Catholic, but that I shouldn't get so upset, it wasn't as if she was
going to become a Holy Roller or a Jew . . . no offense, Mr. Ettinger . . ."

"None taken, Mr. Howell," Ettinger said.

". . . certainly none was intended. And the Archbishop said he
would personally take care of my daughter, and that if I liked, he
would perform the marriage himself, to let her new in-laws understand that our family was held in a certain regard by the Roman Catholic Church here."

"That was very gracious of him," Ettinger said.

"So that's the way it happened. A month before the official
one-year mourning period was up, Hor-gay Goool-yermo Frah-
day showed up in New Orleans. I put him up in an apartment we
have here in the Quarter . . . Cletus used to take girls there when
he was at Tulane; he thought I didn't know, and I never said
anything; did the same thing myself when I was in college . . .
and we started making arrangements for the marriage.

"It was one hell of a wedding, I'll tell you that. Hor-gay
Goool-yermo Frah-day must have a hundred and two kinfolk, and
I think every one of them showed up, all the way from Argentina.
They were married by the Archbishop in what they call a High
Nuptial Mass in the Cathedral of St. Louis, which is also right
here in the Quarter.

"I gave her away, and she was a most beautiful bride, Mr.

Ettinger, so beautiful and so happy. I even went along with that dowry custom of theirs, not that Hor-gay Goool-yermo Frah-day needed it. I gave her twenty-four-point-five percent of Howell Petroleum (Venezuela). . . . Am I going too fast for you, Mr. Ettinger?''

"I didn't quite understand that last. I don't mean to seem too inquisitive.''

"Not at all. I think it's important, with you going down there, that you understand the situation as fully as possible. I owned one hundred percent of Howell Petroleum (Venezuela). I wanted to keep control, of course, so I had to have fifty-one percent. I had two children. That left forty-nine percent for them. Half of forty-nine percent is twenty-four-point-five percent. You understand?''

"Yes, Sir.''

"At the time I thought it would give my daughter a little walking-around money, so she wouldn't have to go to Hor-gay Goool-yermo Frah-day every time she wanted a dress or a pair of shoes. So they got married and went on their honeymoon. To Europe. All over Europe. But no matter where they were, or what they were doing, my daughter wrote me a letter, two, three times a week.

"And then, before they left Europe—they were in Venice; I still have the letter—she wrote that she was in the family way, and that she wanted me to come down to Argentina and visit them, just as soon as she got her feet on the ground.

"Hor-gay Goool-yermo Frah-day didn't invite me, you understand, my daughter did. So I went down there several months later. Went supercargo on one of our tankers. She was eight months along when I got there. She looked terrible. She was all alone in their house in Buenos Aires. Hor-gay Goool-yermo Frah-day was out at the estancia, and sent his regrets, and would be in town in a couple of days. That poor child was lonely. Hardly any of the servants could speak any English, and she didn't speak a hell of a lot of Spanish. But I was concerned about the way she looked, so I called the Ambassador, and he recommended a good American doctor to me . . . his name was Kennedy, he'd trained at Massachusetts General, and he was down there teaching Argentine doctors at the medical school of the University of Buenos Aires . . . and I took my daughter to see him.

"And I was right. She was a sick girl. The details are unimportant, but she was a sick girl; he took me aside and told me if she got through this confinement, she should never have another child. He told me he wasn't sure how that pregnancy was going to turn out, either. Well, he was wrong about that, of course. Cletus has been as healthy as a horse all his life. But he was right about my daughter. She damned near died in childbirth.

"Anyway, when Hor-gay Goool-yermo Frah-day finally could get away from his estancia and come to Buenos Aires, I not only pulled him aside for a little chat, but I took him to see Doctor Kennedy. He didn't want to go, I could tell that; he didn't say anything, but I could tell he thought I was putting my nose in where it had no business. And Dr. Kennedy told him what he told me, that if my daughter managed to pull through this confinement, she should never try to have another child. It would kill her.

"So I stayed down there until the day came. She had . . . she had a terrible time, and we damned near lost her. She was in the hospital over a month. And I was there when they baptized Cletus into the Roman Catholic Church. They make a big thing of it down there. They did it in a place called the Basilica of Our Lady of Pilar. Their Archbishop did it.

"And then when I was sure my daughter was all right, a week or two after that, I came home. It was a pity, of course, I thought, that they could have only the one child . . . one child tends to get spoiled. But at least they had that, and with a little bit of luck, she could get her health back.

"Nine months after that, I got another letter. She was in the family way again. I decided against going down there . . . God only knows what I would have said to Hor-gay Goool-yermo Frah-day for doing that to her, knowing what was at stake. But I telephoned Dr. Kennedy—telephoning down there in those days wasn't as easy as it is now—and asked him to see her. And two days after that I got a cable from Kennedy, saying that Hor-gay Goool-yermo Frah-day had told him his services would not be required."

"Why?" Ettinger asked. "Did he say?"

"I think Hor-gay Goool-yermo Frah-day was telling me to keep my nose out of his business," the old man said. "So I didn't know what the hell to do. So I went down there again, and when I saw her, she looked even worse than I imagined she would. So I had a real man-to-man talk with Hor-gay Goool-yermo Frah-day, and he finally gave in, and I took my daughter to Dr. Kennedy. And he said—and I was there when he said it, and I know damned well that Hor-gay Goool-yermo Frah-day understood what he said—that it was his advice, considering the clear threat to the mother's life, that the pregnancy be terminated.''

"I understand," Ettinger said.

"And Hor-gay Goool-yermo Frah-day said that he would have to talk that over with his wife and his priest, and that he would let us know what had been decided.''

"Abortion is against the teachings of the Roman Catholic Church," Ettinger said.

"Yeah. It is. That's what he said. But he said that under the circumstances, he was willing to let my daughter come to the United States to have the baby. Our medicine was better than their medicine, and he knew it. So we got on a ship and came here. She was sick all the way, never got out of her bed. Lost a lot of weight. Had no strength. I radioed ahead and we had an ambulance waiting on the dock when we got to Miami. I put her in a hospital in Miami and telephoned down there and told him she was in pretty bad shape. I suggested he get on a ship and come to Miami. He said he couldn't get away right then—that's what he said, he couldn't get away—and would I please keep him posted.

"Well, they fixed her up in Miami well enough so we could put her on a train and bring her here, and I put her in the hospital again here. They fixed her up well enough so I could take her to the house, and I found nurses and whatever else she needed. She was even able to get out of bed for my son's, James Fitzhugh Howell's, wedding. We took her to Texas on a train, and she got all dressed up and watched him get married.

"Hor-gay Goool-yermo Frah-day wrote that he would do whatever he could to be in New Orleans when the baby was born. My daughter really wanted him to come. He got here five days after my daughter's funeral, Hor-gay Goool-yermo Frah-day did. He was all upset about that. He said that his wife should be buried in their family tomb in Buenos Aires, not in what he called 'unconsecrated ground' here. I buried her, with her baby in her arms, in our family plot. I told him she was going to stay buried where she was buried, where she belonged. And then finally he got around to asking about Cletus . . . asked when could he take him back to Argentina, and could I recommend a nurse to care for the child on the trip. I told Hor-gay Goool-yermo Frah-day that my son and his wife were caring for my grandson in Texas, and that if he went near him, my son was going to kill him.''

"And what was his reaction to that?''

"I had the feeling that Hor-gay Goool-yermo Frah-day was relieved, that the whole unfortunate business of his marriage to the foreigner from North America was over. He wouldn't have to concern himself with raising a child, he could spend all of his time on his estancia, and he could get married again to some Argentine woman without having to worry about a child."

"That's a tragic story," Ettinger said.

"I don't like to air the family linen in public, Mr. Ettinger . . ." the old man said.

The family linen, maybe not, Clete thought, *but I've never known you to pass up an opportunity to proclaim what an unmitigated sonofabitch Hor-gay Goool-yermo Frah-day is. I wonder if it has ever occurred to you that it's damned embarrassing for me.*

Probably not. You expect me to hate him as much as you do—after all, he killed my mother. And since the child cannot choose his father, it's obviously nothing for me to be embarrassed or ashamed about.

But it is, damn it, it is. And there's no way I have ever been able to stop you.

". . . but I thought, since you are going down there, a little insight into the way their minds work might be useful to you. They're all, pardon the French, sonsofbitches. The man my daughter married is not some anomaly. I, for one, haven't been surprised at all that the Argentines are on the side of the Germans in this war against us."

"I appreciate your sharing this with me, Mr. Howell," Ettinger said.

"I thought it was my duty," the old man said. "And now, Mr. Ettinger, unless you've made other plans, I was going to suggest you ride out to the house with us. I've got a bottle of cognac out there, much too good for Cletus, that I think you might appreciate."

"I hate to impose, Mr. Howell."

"Nonsense. No trouble at all. We'll have a little cognac and a cigar, and whenever you feel you should, I'll have Samuel drive you back to the Monteleone."

"Thank you very much, Sir. I'd like that."

"If you'll excuse me, I'd like to wash my hands," the old man said, and stood up. "If the waiter should get lost and come in here, Cletus, will you ask him to have Samuel bring the car around?"

"Yes, Sir," Clete said. He waited until the old man had gone, then said, "David, I'm sorry you had to sit through that. There was no stopping him."

"Actually, it was a fascinating story," Ettinger said. "And no, you couldn't have stopped him. He's like my mother."

"Your mother? Where is she?"

"In New York. She and I got out. She hates like he does. When I told her I was going to Argentina, she was disappointed. She had visions of me blowing up the Brandenburg Gate with Adolf Hitler on it."

"You told your mother you were going to Argentina?" Clete asked incredulously, angrily. "Jesus Christ, Ettinger, what the hell were you thinking about?"

Ettinger looked both shocked and distinctly uncomfortable.

I guess I sounded like a Marine officer, and he didn't expect that. Well, that's what I am.

"I presume you signed the same form that I did, which made it pretty clear it's a General Court-martial offense to have diarrhea of the mouth about what we're doing?" Clete went on coldly.

"I felt relatively sure that whatever I told my mother, she would not rush to the telephone to pass it on to the Abwehr."

"Don't be flip with me, Sergeant!" Clete said coldly. "Exactly how much did you tell your mother?"

"Just that I was going to Argentina, Sir."

That's right, Sergeant, you call me "Sir."

"To do what?"

"She knew what I've been doing here . . ."

"You told her what you were doing for the CIC? She and who else?"

"Just my mother, Sir. I had to tell her something. I couldn't just suddenly vanish. And what I told her seemed to be the best story I could come up with. The subject of what I was supposed to tell my mother never came up at the Country Club . . ."

"You should have been able to figure that out without a diagram. You were supposed to tell her nothing! Damn it, Sergeant, you were in the CIC! You certainly should have known better than to tell anyone, much less a civilian . . ."

"Sir, I don't mean to be insolent, but your grandfather seems . . ."

"What my grandfather knows or doesn't know is not the subject here. What you told your mother is."

"Yes, Sir. I led her to believe that I would be doing the same thing there that I'd been doing here. Making sure that the refugees are in fact refugees. I told her that when I had an address, I would send it to her, but that she shouldn't expect to hear from me for a while."

"I can't believe you told her where we're going!"

"Sir, I thought it would put her mind at rest," Ettinger said.

"You did?" Clete asked sarcastically.

"Mother knows that Argentina is neutral," Ettinger explained. "And her memories of Argentina seem to begin and end with the Teatro Colón:"—Buenos Aires' opera house—"Spanish-speaking people with exquisite manners."

"She's been there?" Clete asked, wondering why he was surprised.

Ettinger nodded. "So have I. But I was a kid, and I can't remember a thing. My grandfather took us there."

"And how much did you tell your grandfather?"

"My grandfather died in a concentration camp, Sir."

"What's that, an attempt to invoke my sympathy?" Clete snapped, and was immediately ashamed of himself. "Sorry, Ettinger. Colonel Graham told me about your family. I was out of line."

Ettinger met his eyes. After a moment, he said, "So, apparently, was I. What happens now?"

"I don't know what the hell to do about this, frankly."

"If it would make it any easier for you, I'll report my . . . indiscretion to the people from the Country Club tomorrow."

" 'Indiscretion'?" Clete snapped. "I'd call it stupidity. Incredible stupidity."

"Yes, Sir. I can see from your standpoint that it would be."

"And from your standpoint?"

"I had to tell her something, Lieutenant. That was the best I could come up with."

"Incredible stupidity," Clete repeated.

Ettinger stood up.

"Where are you going?" Clete demanded.

"Back to the hotel, Sir. Under the circumstances, it would be awkward with your grandfather. I'll make a report . . ."

"If a report is made, Sergeant, I'll make it," Clete thought aloud, and then added, "The damage, if any, has already been done."

"Sir, I don't think there will be any damage. I made the point to my mother that this assignment, including our destination, was classified. She won't say anything to anybody."

"We don't know that, do we?"

"No, Sir. We don't."

If I turn him in for this, it will really screw things up. Colonel Graham feels that getting us down there as soon as possible is damned important. If they have to scrounge around for a replacement for Ettinger—and that would obviously be difficult—God only knows how long a delay there would be.

Or this fellow Pelosi and I will get sent down there by ourselves.

I need him. It's as simple as that.

"We never had this conversation, Ettinger," Clete said. "You understand me?"

"Yes, Sir. Thank you."

"Don't misunderstand me. I'm not being a nice guy. I just think turning you in would do more damage to this mission than taking you with us."

"I understand."

"I wonder if you do," Clete said. "But the subject is closed. The conversation never occurred. Clear?"

"Yes, Sir."

"Besides," Clete said, smiling. It took more than a little effort. "If you were missing when my grandfather finishes his piss call, I would have to explain your absence. My grandfather, as you may have noticed, is a difficult man."

"I repeat, Lieutenant, thank you. I really want to go on this mission. It's much more important than what I've been doing."

"Try to keep that in mind," Clete said. "Now let's change the subject."

Ettinger nodded, then smiled.

"My grandfather was not unlike yours. A difficult man."

I don't really give a damn about your grandfather, Ettinger.

"Really?"

"He believed what he wanted to believe, and the facts be damned. He chose to believe that despite what was going on, *he* was perfectly safe in Berlin. What was happening to the Jews there was happening only to the Slavic Jews, not to good German Jews like him. After all, he had won the Iron Cross as an infantry officer in France in the First World War."

"That didn't do him any good?"

"No. They took him away. He died 'of pneumonia' in a place called Sachsenhausen."

"You hate the Germans? In the way my grandfather hates the Argentines?"

"No. I understand that the flesh is weak. If you hate weak people, you hate everybody. If you're asking if I'm motivated to go to Argentina, yes, I think I can do—we can do—some good down there."

"Blowing up 'neutral' ships?"

"That, certainly. And perhaps doing something about keeping the Argentine equivalent of the Nazis from taking over the country. The Nazis took over Germany because nobody fought back."

Cletus Marcus Howell pushed open the curtain and came back into the small room. His eyes passed back and forth between them as if he sensed something was wrong.

"Have you asked for the car?" he demanded after a moment's hesitation.

"No, but I will bet it's been waiting outside for the last half hour while you bored David with our family linen."

"I don't think I bored Mr. Ettinger, did I, Mr. Ettinger?"

"Not at all, Sir."

"Sometimes, Cletus, I don't understand you at all," the old man said. "Shall we go?"

[TWO]
The Gulf, Mobile & Ohio Railway Terminal
Canal Street
New Orleans, Louisiana
1030 2 November 1942

Second Lieutenant Anthony J. Pelosi, CE, AUS, late of the 82nd Airborne Division, had been thinking—especially for the last couple of hours—that Captain McGuire was right after all: Applying for this OSS shit was a mistake; where he belonged was with the 82nd Airborne.

In another couple of weeks, he would have made first lieutenant (promotion was automatic after six months' time in grade), and as a first lieutenant he could not be ranked out of command of his platoon. He would have been the permanent—*not* the temporary—commanding officer of an Engineer platoon in the 82nd Airborne Division . . . and *not* where he was, masquerading as a goddamned civilian.

When Colonel Baxter F. Newton-Haddle called him in for what he called a "pre-mission briefing," he told him he was to report for duty in New Orleans in civilian clothing. He asked him if that was going to pose any problem. Pelosi said, "No, Sir."

Tony Pelosi liked and admired Colonel Newton-Haddle. For one thing, the Colonel was also a paratrooper. Paratroopers are special people. In the briefing Colonel Newton-Haddle gave when they first came to the Country Club, he told them about what the people in OSS did—like making night jumps into France and Italy and connecting up with the resistance and showing them how to blow up bridges and tunnels. Doing those kinds of things would maybe make being in the OSS OK. But what he was about to do now was go into some goddamned South American neutral country where a bunch of taco eaters in big hats sat around in the shade playing guitars.

Colonel Newton-Haddle didn't tell him much about what he was supposed to do in Argentina, except they had to "take out" a ship, some kind of a freighter that was supplying German submarines. He explained that the ship would be neutral. By "take out" Colonel Newton-Haddle obviously meant "blow up," or at least put a hole in it large enough to sink it.

That bothered Tony Pelosi. It wasn't a warship, but a civilian freighter. If there were people on it, they would be civilians; and if they were on the ship when he set off his charges—as sure as Christ made little apples—some of them would get hurt, get killed. German sailors were one thing, civilian merchant seamen another.

When he was in OCS, he'd studied the Geneva Convention long enough to know that if they were caught trying to blow a hole in a civilian merchant ship, they would not be treated like prisoners of war, but like criminals, maybe even pirates. If they were caught after they blew it up, and civilians had been killed, they might be put on trial in some taco eaters' court for murder.

This wasn't what he had had in mind when he volunteered for the OSS. Parachuting into France to show the French underground how to blow up the Nazi submarine pens at St. Lazaire was one thing; sneaking into some South American neutral country pretending to be a civilian and blowing up a civilian ship was different.

Anyway, when Colonel Newton-Haddle asked him if civilian clothing was going to pose a problem, he said "No, Sir," because he didn't think it would be. But when he got home, went to his

room and locked the door so nobody in the family would see him
and ask what he was doing, and tried to put on his civilian clothes,
none of them fit.

The first thing he thought was that the goddamned dry cleaners
had shrunk them. That had happened before. But not even his
shirts fit, and the dry cleaner couldn't have fucked them up, because his shirts had been washed and ironed in the house by the
maid.

After a while, though, what happened finally hit him: All the
physical training he'd gone through, first basic training, then Officer Candidate School, and then jump school had really changed
his body. He had real muscles now. That was why his jackets
were too tight at the shoulders and he couldn't even button his
shirt collars.

It didn't matter as long as he could wear his uniform. Colonel
Newton-Haddle not only told him that he could wear his uniform
at home, because that would keep people from asking questions
about how come he wasn't, but that he should. And there wasn't
a hell of a lot wrong with wearing the parachute wings and jump
boots; that went with being an officer of the 82nd Airborne Division. He wore his uniform the two times he went out with his
brothers, Angelo, Frank, and Dominic. And if it weren't for Dominic, he knew damned well he could have gotten laid. But you
don't try to get laid when you're out with a brother who is a
priest and who is out drinking with you only because of a special
dispensation from the pastor of his parish, because he told him
you were going overseas.

Colonel Newton-Haddle had also told him he should explain
to his family that he was going on temporary duty with a special
engineer unit, and gave him an address in Washington where they
could write to him. But he was not to tell them anything about
going to Argentina; that was classified. So he hadn't. An order is
an order.

So what he did was wear his uniform all the time he was home.
And then, along with his uniforms, he packed a sports shirt, a
pair of pants, a two-tone (yellow sleeves and collar, blue body)
zipper jacket with "Pelosi & Sons Salvage Company" lettered
on the back, and a pair of shoes. They got him a compartment
on the Crescent City Limited, and he decided to just wait until
he was almost in New Orleans to change into the civilian stuff.
The OSS gave him a check for two hundred dollars to buy civilian
clothing; he'd do that in New Orleans. And he'd ask what he

should do with his uniforms; he didn't think they'd want him to take them down to South America.

Two things went wrong with that plan. First of all, he wasn't all alone in the compartment. He thought he would have it all to himself, but when he got on the train there was already a guy in it. He was an expediter for the Western Electric Company, whatever the fuck that meant. So Tony had to come up with a bullshit story about having just been discharged from the 82nd Airborne because of a bad back he got jumping. Even when he showed the guy the draft card Colonel Newton-Haddle gave him that said he was an honorably discharged veteran, he didn't think the Western Union guy believed him. And he sure gave him a funny look when he started changing out of his uniform and putting on the Cicero Softball League jacket.

He really hated taking off his uniform, especially the jump boots. You had to earn jump boots, and he really liked the way they felt, as well as the way they looked (he'd polished them so you could actually see your face reflected in the shine of the toes). He wondered when the hell he would ever be able to put them on again.

And then his goddamned civilian shoes were too small. He couldn't figure that out. As far as he knew, there were no muscles in the feet, so they shouldn't have grown the way his back and arms and neck had. But he could barely get the goddamned things on his feet; and when he did, it hurt him even to walk around the compartment. And when he walked three cars down to the dining car to have breakfast, his feet hurt him so much he didn't believe it.

When he got back to the compartment, he took off his shoes. And when they pulled into the train station in New Orleans, he took his socks off and put the shoes back on without them.

Fuck how it looks. If I wear the socks, I'll never make it all the way down the platform and into the station.

Halfway down the platform, Tony saw Staff Sergeant Ettinger waiting for him, just inside the station at the end of the platform. Ettinger was wearing a three-piece suit, and he was talking to a tall guy wearing a cowboy hat, boots, and a sheepskin coat.

The shit-kicker probably asked him a question or something.

When Ettinger saw him, he smiled and waved, and Tony walked up to him.

"What do you say, Ettinger?" Tony said.

"Nice trip, Tony?"

"It was all right."

Tony saw the cowboy looking at his bare ankles.

Fuck you, Tex! Anybody wearing beat-up boots like yours is in no position to say anything about anybody else.

"Tony, this is . . . *Mr.* Frade," Ettinger said.

Mr. Frade? This cowboy is Lieutenant Frade? A Marine officer?

"Good morning, Sir," Lieutenant Pelosi said.

" 'Morning," Clete replied. "Pelosi, from here on in, you can belay the 'Sir' business."

"Excuse me?"

"We're supposed to be civilians. Civilians don't say 'Sir.' I'm Clete. He's David. What's your first name?"

"Anthony, Sir," Tony said. Then, "Sorry."

"That all your luggage, Anthony?"

"Yes, S— Yeah."

"We're parked out in front," Clete said, then laughed. "What did you do, Anthony, forget your socks?"

"My shoes are too small."

"Well, then, we better stop on the way to the hotel and find you some that fit," Clete said. "Our mentors, who got here at seven this morning, are already convinced that David and I are retarded; if you showed up in bare feet, that would be too much for them."

Ettinger laughed.

Tony Pelosi had no idea what a "mentor" was, but he was goddamned if he was going to ask.

[THREE]
The Franco-Spanish Border
1525 3 November 1942

Train Number 1218 of the Société Nationale des Chemins de Fer Français (Paris–Barcelona–Madrid) would be late crossing the border, but there was nothing the officials of the French National Railroad could do about it. It had been requested of them by the representative of the German Rail Coordination Bureau: (a) that a goods wagon then sitting in Paris (number furnished herewith), a Grande Compagnie Internationale des Wagons-Lits sleeping car with crew, and a first-class passenger car be attached to Number

1218; and (b) that Number 1218's schedule be "adjusted" to permit a fifteen- to thirty-minute ceremony at the Spanish border; and (c) that officials of the Spanish National Railroad be informed of the change of schedule.

At 1455, fifteen minutes before Number 1218 was due, the gate (an arrangement of timbers and barbed wire) across the tracks on the Spanish side of the border was moved aside by Spanish Border Police. A moment later a tiny yard engine pushed a passenger car of the Spanish National Railroad across what everybody called "No-Man's-Land" to the similar gate across the tracks on the French side of the border.

After a minute's conversation between French and Spanish officials, the French gate was opened and the yard engine pushed the Spanish passenger car approximately 300 meters farther into the Border Station, where it stopped. About forty rifle-armed members of the Guardia Nacional, all wearing their distinctive stiff black leather hats, debarked from the passenger car and formed two ranks on the platform. A moment after that, two officers of the Guardia Nacional came down from the passenger car, together with four more enlisted men, two of whom carried flags on poles.

One of the flags was that of Spain. The other was unusual. But it was finally identified by one of the French customs officials as the flag of Argentina. The men carrying the flags arranged themselves before the members of the Guardia Nacional, and the two Guardia Nacional enlisted men who had gotten off the train last took up places beside them.

At 1505, five minutes early, Number 1218 moved into the station, on a track parallel to the one where the Spanish National Railways car had stopped. The members of a small Luftwaffe band, equipped primarily with trumpets and drums, descended from the passenger car and formed up quickly under the direction of their bandmaster. They were followed by a mixed detachment of Luftwaffe, Waffen-SS, and Wehrmacht troops, three of each under the command of a Luftwaffe captain. They formed up and were marched back to the goods wagon, from which four of their number removed two sawhorses.

They set up the sawhorses on the platform between the Guardia Nacional and the band. The sawhorses were then covered with a pleated black material which concealed them. They then returned to the goods wagon, from which they removed a very heavy casket, across which the flag of Argentina was draped diagonally.

The flag had three broad stripes running horizontally, first light blue, then white, then again light blue. In the center of the white central stripe was the face of maybe the sun-god. It was golden and smiling. Radiating from it were red streaks, which were probably intended to represent sunbeams.

In the opinion of most of the French Railway officials, it was not a very *civilized* flag. Perhaps the sort of thing one might expect of some far-off former colony which now imagined itself to be a nation, but not *civilized*. Provincial people like that never knew when to stop; they could be counted on, so to speak, to try to gild the lily.

The casket-carrying detachment arranged themselves around the casket, four men to a side, one man at the head. The Luftwaffe captain placed himself at the foot of the casket, ordered "Vorwärts!" and somewhat awkwardly (it was extraordinarily heavy), the casket was carried down the platform and installed on the sawhorses.

As soon as this was accomplished, officers and enlisted personnel of the Wehrmacht, the Luftwaffe, and the Waffen-SS began to debark from the passenger and Wagons-Lits cars—enlisted and officers from the former, and from the latter officers only, including a Luftwaffe Oberst, an Oberstleutnant from the Wehrmacht, a Waffen-SS Obersturmbannführer (the Waffen-SS equivalent of an Oberstleutnant, or lieutenant colonel), a Luftwaffe Hauptmann, and then a tall, thin, olive-skinned man wearing a uniform no one could recall ever seeing before.

It was decided that he must have something to do with the casket covered with the smiling sun-god flag, and that he therefore must be an Argentinean. It was also noticed that the Luftwaffe Hauptmann in his dress uniform had the Knight's Cross of the Iron Cross hanging around his neck. One didn't see too many of those.

The officers and men who had debarked from the passenger car formed a double rank facing the Guardia Nacional. Two photographers in Wehrmacht uniforms, one still and one motion picture, and a Wehrmacht lieutenant armed with a clipboard now appeared.

At this point, two more uniformed officers descended from the Spanish National Railways car that had been pushed backward into the border station. One was a coronel, the other a teniente. They were photographed and filmed as they walked across the platform and exchanged military salutes and then handshakes with the German officers and with the one who was probably an Argentinean.

All the officers then formed in a line, facing the flag-covered casket. The Luftwaffe colonel looked at the officer commanding the mixed detachment of German Armed Forces personnel. He in turn looked at the bandmaster, who raised his drum major's baton.

"Achtung!" the officer commanding the mixed detachment barked, and everybody came to attention, including the members of the Guardia Nacional.

The bandleader moved his drum major's baton downward in a violent motion. The strains of "Deutschland, Deutschland, Über Alles" erupted from the band. The officers in the rank, except the Wehrmacht Oberstleutnant and the Luftwaffe captain with the Knight's Cross of the Iron Cross, extended their arms in the locked-elbow, fingers-together, flat salute of the Third Reich. The Oberstleutnant and the Hauptmann rendered the old-fashioned hand salute.

The German national anthem was followed by those of Spain and Argentina. And most of the French Railway officials agreed that the Argentinean anthem, like the sun-god flag, was a bit overdone.

When the music was finished, the casket was carried back to the goods wagon and placed aboard, with the photographers recording the event for posterity. The Spanish personnel returned to their passenger car and boarded it, and it immediately moved back across the border.

The German military personnel, except the officers, reboarded the first-class car. The officers entered the railroad station, where refreshments had been laid out for them. Number 1218 then backed out of the station to the yard, where the first-class passenger car was detached for subsequent attachment to Number 1219 (Madrid–Barcelona–Paris), which was due at the border crossing at 1615. Number 1218 then returned to the place where it had originally stopped, and the word was given first to the Feldgendarmerie and then to the French Immigration et Douane and Sûreté Nationale personnel that they might now commence their routine immigration, customs, and security checks of Number 1218's passengers.

A few minutes later, the Luftwaffe captain with the Knight's Cross of the Iron Cross came out of the station alone. He had with him not only his cognac snifter, but a bottle of cognac. He boarded the Wagons-Lits car.

At 1550, only twenty-five minutes behind schedule, the conductor signaled Number 1218's engineer that he could proceed through No-Man's-Land to Spanish customs. They were only five minutes behind the regular schedule. The ceremony had not taken as long as they had planned for. They probably wouldn't have been late at all, perhaps even a few minutes early, had not the Sûreté Nationale grown suspicious of some travel documents and checked them out. They discovered four more Jews trying to reach Spain on forged travel documents and passports.

[FOUR]

So far as he could recall, el Coronel Alejandro Manuel Portez-Halle of the Office of Liaison of the Royal Army to the Foreign Ministry had never heard the name of el Coronel Juan Domingo Perón of the Argentinean Army, until three days before when this rather absurd business of the Germans sending a body home to Argentina came up.

This was both surprising and rather embarrassing—he had spent enough time in Argentina over the years to learn at least the names of the more important Argentinean officers. On the other hand, the Foreign Ministry seemed to know a great deal about el Coronel Juan Domingo Perón, including the fact that he was quite close to el Coronel Jorge Guillermo Frade. Portez-Halle had come to know Frade rather well when he'd been in Argentina. He'd even spent some time on Frade's estancia, San Pedro y San Pablo, shooting partridge and wood pigeon. In the evenings, over cigars and surprisingly first-rate Argentinean brandy, they'd shared stories of their days as junior officers.

Frade was important because of his connection with the Grupo de Oficiales Unidos. According to the latest word from the Spanish Embassy in Buenos Aires, these men were about to stage a coup d'état. And Frade was reported to be the brains behind the plot, and certainly the financier.

Colonel Juan Domingo Perón, Portez-Halle had been told, was attached to the Argentinean Embassy in Berlin and would be accompanying the young Argentinean's body to Lisbon, where it would be put aboard an Argentinean merchant vessel for repatriation. The dead officer was the nephew of el Coronel Jorge Guillermo Frade. Which probably explained why the Germans were going to all the fuss they were making. They knew who Frade was, too.

The Foreign Ministry originally intended to send an official of suitable rank—say, a deputy minister—to represent El Caudillo (General Francisco Franco, the Spanish dictator) at the border. But after Portez-Halle had brought up the Perón–Frade–Portez-Halle connection, it was obvious that he should go. He would, he said, take El Coronel Perón into his home during the layover in Madrid. And have a dinner for him. Considering the importance of Perón's connection to Frade, it was suggested that El Caudillo himself might come to dinner. Or drop by to show his respect.

There had not been time, of course, to issue a formal invitation to el Coronel Perón, but Portez-Halle had not considered that a major problem. He would seek him out at the border, identify himself as a friend of Jorge Guillermo Frade, and make the invitation there.

At that point the plans went awry.

"I'm not going any further than the border," Perón told him. "And if it wasn't for the insistence of the Germans, I wouldn't have come this far. But I thank you for your most gracious offer of hospitality."

"Oh, I'm sorry, I'd looked forward to it."

"It's simply impossible," Perón replied, "but I'll tell you what you could do."

"Tell me."

"The young Luftwaffe officer, the captain?" Perón went on, just perceptibly nodding his head toward a blond-headed young German around whose neck, Portez-Halle noticed, hung the Knight's Cross of the Iron Cross.

"Yes. That's Baron von Wachtstein. He's escorting the remains. He's a very nice young man. I'm sure he would be most grateful for a hot meal and a warm bed in Madrid. They just took his fighter squadron away from him, and he's very unhappy about that. I don't think he should be left alone in Madrid; he takes a drink sometimes when he perhaps should not, if you take my meaning."

"It will be my pleasure," Portez-Halle said.

"I would be in your debt," Perón said.

Once the Paris–Barcelona–Madrid train cleared Spanish customs, changed engines, and got underway, Colonel Portez-Halle went into his luggage, took out a small leather box, and told el

Teniente Savorra that he was going to look in on the young
German officer.

As he walked into the Wagons-Lits sleeping car, he wondered
idly what had been the peculiarly Teutonic logic behind the decision to send the Wagons-Lits on to Barcelona and Madrid with
a lowly captain as its sole passenger. They could more easily have
detached the car at the border and sent it back to Paris with all
the other German officers. It would make more sense to have one
junior officer change cars than ten or fifteen officers, including a
German and an Argentinean full colonel. Colonel Portez-Halle
had long ago decided he would never understand how the German
mind worked. But it was sometimes interesting to try.

He next wondered if he was going to have to knock at each of
the doors in the Wagons-Lits car until he found the young officer.
But this didn't happen. He faintly heard an obscenity, and knowing that would have been impossible through a closed door, he
walked down the corridor until he came to an open one. And
there was the young officer, attired in his underwear.

"Guten Tag, Herr Hauptmann," Colonel Portez-Halle said.

"Buenas tardes, mi Coronel," Hauptmann Freiherr Hans-Peter
von Wachtstein replied, visibly surprised, as he started to rise.

"Yo soy el Coronel Portez-Halle."

"A sus órdenes, mi Coronel. Yo soy el Capitán von Wachtstein."

"You speak Spanish very well, Captain."

"Gracias, mi Coronel."

"I thought perhaps you might like a small taste of brandy."

"You're very gracious," Peter said. "I was just changing out
of my uniform. You'll have to excuse me. I didn't really expect
visitors."

"Colonel Perón asked me to look after you."

"Then you are both very gracious," Peter said.

"An old friend of the family, I gathered?" Portez-Halle asked
as he walked into the compartment, laid the small leather case on
the seat, and started to open it.

"No, Sir," Peter said. "I met the Colonel when I got involved
in all this . . ." He gestured vaguely in the direction of the goods
wagon.

"Then I must have misunderstood," Portez-Halle said. He took
two small crystal glasses from the case, then a flat-sided crystal
flask.

"Are you familiar with our brandy?"

"At one time I was so fond of it, Sir, that it was said I grew too familiar with it."

Portez-Halle glanced at him and smiled. The Argentinean was right; this was a nice young man, and his behavior suggested that he was accustomed to dealing with senior officers. He could also smell cognac on his breath. Perón had been right about that too. Alcohol had ruined the career of more than one fine young officer of Portez-Halle's acquaintance.

"You served with the Condor Legion, I gather?"

"Yes, Sir."

The least I can do for someone who risked his life to spare Spain from the communists is take him into my home overnight and keep him from temptation.

Portez-Halle poured brandy into both glasses, handed one to Peter, then raised the other.

"Por Capitán Duarte. Que Dios lo tenga en la gloria." (Freely: "May he rest in peace.")

"El Capitán Duarte," Peter said politely.

"You knew him well?" Portez-Halle asked.

"I never knew him at all. All I know about him is that he was shot down at Stalingrad flying a Fieseler Storch that he should not have been flying in the first place, and that he was apparently well-connected."

"Why do you say that?"

"They're sending his body home, they relieved me of my command of a fighter staffel to go with it, and you saw that business at the border. They did just about the same thing when we left Berlin."

"Colonel Perón suggested that you yourself are 'well-connected.'"

"My father is Generalmajor Graf von Wachtstein, if that's what you mean."

"Why do I have the feeling, Captain, that you are not particularly pleased with the assignment?"

"I am an officer. I go where I am sent, and do what I'm told to do."

"That doesn't answer my question."

"Just before you came, mi Coronel, I was asking myself the same question. I concluded that only a fool would be unhappy with this assignment. I'm going to a neutral country where it is highly unlikely that I will be asked to lay down my life for the Fatherland."

"And did you decide whether or not you were such a fool?" Portez-Halle asked with a smile.

"I am not a fool," Peter said.

"You'll be staying in Argentina?"

"You caught me in the midst of my metamorphosis between soldier and diplomat," Peter said. "I was, more than symbolically, changing into civilian clothing to go with my new diplomatic passport. I am being assigned to the German Embassy in Buenos Aires as the assistant military attaché for air."

"An important stepping-stone in a career," Portez-Halle said. "I was once an assistant military attaché. In Warsaw, 1933-34. It was said that it would round out my experience."

"That has been mentioned to me," Peter said.

"What is your schedule in Madrid?"

"I change trains to Lisbon."

"Is someone meeting you?"

"I was told someone from our Embassy will meet the train, arrange for the casket to be taken care of overnight, get me a hotel for the night, and then put both of us aboard the Lisbon train in the morning."

"It would give me great pleasure, Hauptmann von Wachtstein, if you would permit me to have you as my guest at my home while you are in Madrid."

"That's very gracious, but unnecessary, Sir."

"It would be my pleasure."

And, Portez-Halle had a sudden pleasant inspiration, *I will send a letter with you to Jorge Guillermo Frade. You will meet him, of course; but he would be likely to dismiss you as unimportant. I will write dear old Jorge that our mutual friend el Coronel Juan Domingo Perón considers von Wachtstein to be a charming young officer—and I agree—and that he was chosen to accompany the remains both because of his distinguished war record and because his father is a major general.*

Frade will like that. And it will let him know that I did my best to pay our most sincere respects to the late Captain Duarte—both personally and as the special representative of El Caudillo.

"Well then, Sir, thank you very much."

VI

[ONE]
The Office of the Ambassador
The Embassy of the German Reich
Avenida Córdoba
Buenos Aires, Argentina
1615 7 November 1942

Ambassador von Lutzenberger would have been hard-pressed to decide which of the two men now standing before his desk he disliked more. One of them at a time was pressing enough, and the two of them together would almost certainly ruin his dinner.

Anton von Gradny-Sawz, First Secretary of the Embassy of the German Reich to the Republic of Argentina, was a tall, almost handsome, somewhat overweight forty-five-year-old with a full head of luxuriant reddish-brown hair. He was sure he owed this to his Hungarian heritage. As he sometimes put it, flashing one of his charming smiles, he was a German with roots in Hungary who happened to be born in Ostmark—as Austria was called after it was absorbed into Germany after the *Anschluss* of 1938. He would often add that a Gradny-Sawz had been nervously treading the marble-floored corridors of one embassy or another for almost two hundred years.

Oberst Karl-Heinz Grüner, the Military Attaché, was a tall, ascetic-looking man who appeared older than his thirty-nine years . . . and who loathed Gradny-Sawz both personally and professionally. *Die grosse Wienerwurst* (the Big Vienna Sausage), as he and von Lutzenberger both thought of him, not only had an exaggerated opinion of his own professional skill and importance but also tended to interfere with Oberst Grüner's sub rosa function in the Embassy as the representative of the Abwehr—the Intelligence Department of the German Armed Forces High Command.

His Excellency, Manfred Alois Graf von Lutzenberger, Ambassador of the German Reich to the Republic of Argentina, was a slight, very thin, fifty-three-year-old who wore what was left of his thinning hair plastered across his skull. Von Lutzenbergers, he often thought when he had to deal with Gradny-Sawz, had been treading *without* nervousness the marble-floored corridors of one embassy or another since 1660, when Friedrich Graf von Lutzenberger had arranged Prussia's full independence from Polish suzerainty for Friedrich Wilhelm, the Great Elector. That was nearly *three* hundred years ago. When, in other words, Gradny-Sawz's ancestors in Hungary were just learning how to ride horses using saddles, and Grüner's antecedents were sleeping with their milch cows in some stone-and-thatch cottage in a remote meadow in the Bavarian Alps.

"Your Excellency, there has been a cable from the Foreign Ministry vis-à-vis the Duarte remains," Gradny-Sawz began. "I thought Oberst Grüner should be brought into this as soon as possible."

"That's the Argentinean boy who was killed at Stalingrad?" von Lutzenberger asked.

"Yes. His remains are to be placed aboard the *General Belgrano* of the Líneas Marítimos de Argentina y Europa at Lisbon. They are being accompanied by a Hauptmann von Wachtstein of the Luftwaffe. The *Belgrano* is scheduled to sail from Lisbon for Buenos Aires at 0700, Lisbon time, November 8."

"Have you a first name on von Wachtstein?"

"I have it here somewhere," Gradny-Sawz said, and began to search in his pockets for a notebook.

"I don't have his first name at hand, Sir," Grüner said. "But he is the son of Generalmajor Graf von Wachtstein."

"How did you come by that information?"

"In a cable informing me that he is being assigned to me as my Deputy for Air," Grüner said.

"Hans-Peter are his Christian names, Your Excellency," Gradny-Sawz announced, reading from his leather-bound notebook. "He has been awarded, personally, from the hands of the Führer, the Knight's Cross of the Iron Cross."

"How interesting," the ambassador said. "I'm sure there is a reason why it was impossible to consult with me—or, for that matter, you, Grüner—before this gentleman was assigned to us."

Both Grüner and Gradny-Sawz smiled uneasily, but said nothing. Ambassador von Lutzenberger frequently complained that the Foreign Ministry did not consult with him as often as was necessary.

Well, they swallowed that whole, von Lutzenberger thought, a trifle smugly. *I asked who von Wachtstein was; when told, I was annoyed that no one informed me about his assignment here. Therefore, they don't have any idea that his father and I are connected.*

"There is a question of protocol, Your Excellency, that I thought you should resolve," Gradny-Sawz said.

"Which is?"

"On the one hand, Hauptmann Duarte was the only son of Humberto Valdez Duarte, the banker. Under those circumstances, one would think that as First Secretary, I would deal with the family, as I did when we learned of Captain Duarte's tragic death. On the other hand, Captain Jorge Duarte's mother—Beatrice Frade de Duarte—is the sister of Oberst Jorge Guillermo Frade; I think it reasonable to presume he was named for him. Under those circumstances, considering Frade's importance, perhaps Grüner would be the man to handle things."

Ambassador von Lutzenberger focused on Gradny-Sawz's motives in raising the question, rather than on the question itself, the answer to which seemed self-evident. The more important an indigenous official was, the more senior the Embassy official should be. In the diplomatic hierarchy, a first secretary was far senior to a military attaché.

And Gradny-Sawz certainly knew this.

So why was he raising the question? In terms of real power, so far as von Lutzenberger was concerned, the two were about equal, and thus equally dangerous. In addition to being his man in Argentina, Grüner was a close personal friend of Admiral Wilhelm Canaris, the head of the Abwehr. One did not cross Canaris, or his friends, without good reason.

Gradny-Sawz's influence, above and beyond that which went with his rank in the Foreign Ministry, came from his early and close ties to the inner circle of the Nazi party. The National Socialists had been desperate early on for the support of the aristocracy. It lent them, they believed, a respectability they would otherwise not have had. Gradny-Sawz's early support of the Nazis had been a clever career move. He had nothing, really, to lose by announcing his conviction that Adolf Hitler and his National Socialists were the one hope of *das deutsche Volk,* and that Austria should "return" to the German fatherland.

He could have been discharged from the Austrian Foreign Ministry, of course—and certainly should have been—for bad judgment, or disloyalty. But he was only a minor functionary at the time, and he didn't need a job. The Gradny-Sawz estates in Hungary were extensive; and in those days he had dual citizenship; he might even have been able to buy his way into the Hungarian Foreign Service.

But he bet on the right horse. The National Socialists came to power; and in 1938 Austria became Ostmark. And the Nazis rewarded their friends: Gradny-Sawz was "absorbed" into the German Foreign Ministry and assigned to the Embassy in Paris as Third Secretary for Commercial Affairs. In 1941, he was assigned to Buenos Aires as First Secretary.

A colleague in the Foreign Ministry took von Lutzenberger aside during a visit to Buenos Aires and warned him that Gradny-Sawz had friends at the highest levels in the Sicherheitsdienst—the German Secret Service—and it could be presumed that he was reporting to them whenever Embassy personnel—the Ambassador included—strayed from his notion of the correct National Socialist path.

Gradny-Sawz reveled in high-level social intercourse.

Ordinarily, Die grosse Wienerwurst would be doing whatever he could to make sure Grüner did not usurp this privilege. He would not be asking me whether I think Grüner should be brought into the matter. The question then becomes, why?

Because he is afraid that something is going to go wrong. What, I have no idea, for what can possibly go wrong with a funeral, however grotesquely medieval it will be here in Catholic Argentina?

Perhaps he is concerned that he will somehow offend Colonel Frade. Or a member of his family. And he wants to see that Grüner is the one who will be in hot water if it does. Or else he wants to be able to say, if something goes wrong, that I ordered him to deal with the Duartes and/or Colonel Frade.

Gradny-Sawz, I know, belongs to the School of Diplomatic Practice that holds that one cannot endanger one's diplomatic career if one avoids any situation of conflict, however unimportant.

"Quite right, Gradny-Sawz," the ambassador said. "It is a delicate matter. Give me the details, and I will contact Frade myself. Have him to lunch, perhaps. And then I will decide which of you should carry out our role in Hauptmann Duarte's funeral."

He could tell from the look on Gradny-Sawz's face that that was not the response he was looking for.

What did you want me to say? What are you after?

"While I have you both here," Ambassador von Lutzenberger said. "It seems that three American—*North* American—nationals, employed by the Radio Corporation of America, have disappeared. This has been reported to the Argentinean authorities, specifically to the police commander of the Distrito Federal."

(The Federal District, somewhat similar in character to the District of Columbia, lies within the Province of Buenos Aires, and includes the city of Buenos Aires.)

"Oh, really?" Gradny-Sawz said, somewhat smugly.

"It is being bandied about that certain individuals connected with our embassy have knowledge of this matter. These allegations have also come to the attention of the Federal Police."

"I heard the same story," Gradny-Sawz said. "In fact, I have the feeling that the Americans will not be heard from again."

"Tell me what rumors you have heard," the Ambassador said.

"Your Excellency will understand that these are only rumors," Gradny-Sawz said, visibly enjoying himself, "for I, of course, have no personal information about this incident."

"What did you hear, Anton?" the Ambassador pursued, hoping that neither impatience nor disgust was evident in his voice.

"I *heard,* Your Excellency, that these three Yankees were suspected of certain activities involving neutral shipping—"

"Suspected by the Argentine authorities, you mean?" von Lutzenberger interrupted.

"Yes, Sir. They were suspected of attempting to interfere with neutral shipping, specifically with a Swedish merchant vessel, the *Sundsvall,* which was anchored in the Bahía Samborombón while conducting repairs to one of its engines."

(The Río de la Plata, which empties into the South Atlantic Ocean, separates Argentina from Uruguay. The mouth of the river, which is defined as a line between Punta Norte del Cabo San Antonio, Argentina, and Punta del Este, Uruguay, is approximately 160 miles wide. The Bay of Samborombón lies just inside this line.)

"Where exactly in the Bay?" von Lutzenberger asked.

"Approximately thirty kilometers east of Pipinas, Your Excellency," Gradny-Sawz said. "The Americans, or so the story goes, were about to attempt to sabotage the *Sundsvall*—to blow a hole in her hull. To this end, they acquired a small motorboat. Their activities came to the attention of the Argentinean Navy, and a patrol boat was sent to locate them. The Americans refused orders to heave to, and a warning shot was fired. Unfortunately, the gunner's aim was off, and the warning shot hit their vessel and sank it."

"But there has been no official report of this incident?"

"I would ascribe that, Your Excellency, to Argentinean pride. It would be embarrassing for them to publicly acknowledge that their gunnery is not what it should be. And unfortunately, there were no survivors."

"You're sure of that?" von Lutzenberger asked.

"My sources inform me, Your Excellency, that a search of the area was made and no survivors were found. I doubt if there will be."

Von Lutzenberger grunted.

"And do your sources confirm what the First Secretary has told me, Herr Oberst?"

"Yes, Sir. The details are essentially the same."

"And do you both confirm that no one can connect these unfortunate events with anyone at the embassy?"

"I very much doubt if anything like that will happen, Your Excellency," Gradny-Sawz said.

"Herr Oberst?"

"I think that the Argentineans and the Americans will both try to forget this incident as quickly as possible."

"And, Herr Oberst, did your sources tell you whether these three unfortunates might be employed by the American Federal Bureau of Investigation or their Office of Strategic Services?"

"It seems, Your Excellency," Grüner said, "that they were connected with the OSS."

Von Lutzenberger looked at Gradny-Sawz, who nodded.

"Pity," von Lutzenberger said. "If we could have tied them to the 'Legal Affairs Office' of the U.S. Embassy, we could almost certainly have had several people expelled as persona non grata. And what of the ship? The *Sundsvall?*"

"I believe that once her engines were repaired, she sailed the following morning."

"And her master made no report of this incident?"

"Her master probably decided the less he had to with the Argentinean authorities, the better," Gradny-Sawz said.

"Then she won't be coming back?"

"She is to be replaced, Sir," Grüner replied. "She was in these waters for almost two months; her stores were nearly exhausted."

"The Bay of Samborombon is quite wide and quite empty. I

would like to know how these Americans located the ship," von Lutzenberger said. "Do you think someone in the Argentinean Navy, or elsewhere in the government, told them?"

"I don't think that's possible," Gradny-Sawz said, almost indignantly.

"Anything is possible, my dear Anton," von Lutzenberger said. "Since we know that people in the Argentinean military services and their government will confide in you matters they perhaps should not, I think we have to presume, don't you, that there are people in the same places who talk to Americans about things they probably should not talk about."

"There are even, my dear Gradny-Sawz," Colonel Grüner said, "some Argentineans, in and out of the government, who hope for an Anglo-American victory."

Gradny-Sawz gave him a cold look, but did not reply.

"If there's nothing else, gentlemen?" von Lutzenberger asked, looked at the two of them, and then added, "Thank you for your time."

[TWO]
The Monteleone Hotel
New Orleans, Louisiana
0730 9 November 1942

Second Lieutenant Anthony J. Pelosi, CE, AUS, late of the 82nd Airborne Division, was shaving when he heard the knock at his hotel room door. He was taking special care. Today, officers of the U.S. Navy were going to teach him something about ships— and about blowing them up, or at least sinking them. He suspected they would know that he was an Army officer, even if he was in civilian clothing. All the same, he wanted to look like an officer and a gentleman.

He was still smarting about how he looked when he first arrived—no goddamned socks, and a goddamned zipper jacket, for Christ's sake! Especially when Sergeant Ettinger was wearing a suit that made him look like a banker. And Lieutenant Frade— after showing up at the railroad station in his cowboy suit— looked like an advertisement in *Esquire* magazine.

Tony, who was naked, wrapped a towel around his waist, then walked to the door and opened it. He stood behind it so no one would see him wearing only a towel.

"This is for you, Sir," a bellman said, and handed him a twine-wrapped paper package that looked like something you would get back from a Chinese laundry.

"Just a minute," Tony said, then went to the bed and slid his hand between the mattress and the box spring and pulled out his wallet. He took a dollar bill from the wallet and gave it to the bellman.

After he closed the door, he carried the package to the bed and sat down, making sure that he didn't sit on his new tweed sports coat and gray flannel pants that he had laid out to wear. Though it was not what he originally picked out, he liked the clothing more now than when he first bought it. Lieutenant Frade "suggested" then that he buy what he did. He was the commanding officer of the team, so Tony went along. Now he was glad he did.

For the first time, Tony saw a sheet of hotel notepaper stuck inside the twine on the package. He took it out and unfolded it:

Pelosi, put this stuff on, and meet me in the dining room at 7:45. A.

A. stood for Adams, one of the three mentors sent down from Virginia. Tony now understood that the word meant something like teacher or counselor; it was just like the OSS to use a word that nobody understood. Adams was somewhere in his thirties, a slight, bright-eyed man who had been an assistant professor of engineering at the University of Idaho. When Tony asked him how he'd wound up in the OSS, Adams replied, "That's not really any of your business, is it, Pelosi?"

Tony opened the drawer in the bedside table, took out his pocket-knife, cut the twine, and unwrapped the package. It contained a pair of blue dungarees, a canvas jacket with a corduroy collar, a navy-blue woolen turtleneck sweater, a woolen knit cap, long-john underwear, heavy woolen socks, and a pair of work shoes. Each item of clothing was marked somewhere with "USN." It was, Tony realized, the Navy equivalent of Army fatigue clothing.

And then he realized it was Navy enlisted men's work clothing. He'd heard somewhere that in the Navy, officers didn't wear work clothing, because it was below the dignity of a Navy officer to get his hands dirty.

How the hell am I going to look like an officer and a gentleman if I have to wear this Navy enlisted man's shit?

He didn't like what he saw in the mirror when he had put on the clothing. And when he walked into the Monteleone Hotel dining room in the Navy fatigues, he got a dirty look from the headwaiter.

No wonder! I look like I've been sent to unstop the fucking toilet, for Christ's sake, not sit down and have my breakfast.

He looked around the dining room and saw Adams sitting at a table with three sailors. There was a full lieutenant, a chief petty officer, and a bo'sun's mate first class. They were all wearing regular blue uniforms. Two tables away, he saw Lieutenant Frade with a couple of mentors. He had on a blue, brass-buttoned blazer, a crisp white shirt, and a striped necktie.

Lieutenant Frade saw him, smiled as if he thought Tony wearing a sailor's work uniform was the funniest thing he had seen all week, and winked at Tony and gave him a thumbs-up sign. Tony pretended he didn't see him and walked to Mr. Adams's table.

"Mr. Pelosi," Adams made the introductions, "this is Lieutenant Greene, Chief Norton, and Bo'sun Leech. Gentlemen, this is Mr. Pelosi."

The sailors looked at him with frank curiosity.

Lieutenant Greene shook his hand without speaking. Chief Norton said, "What do you say, Pelosi?" And Bo'sun Leech grunted and tried to squash his hand when he shook it.

There was little conversation at breakfast. Adams and the Navy men—all of whom were at least ten years older than he was, and all of whom, he was sure, thought he looked as funny as Lieutenant Frade did—had already eaten their breakfasts. They waited impatiently for him to order and then eat his.

Two vehicles were waiting outside: a Navy-gray truck, sort of a panel truck, but with windows and seats in the back, and Frade's Buick convertible. Frade and his mentors got into the Buick and drove off.

"Why don't you sit in the back, Pelosi?" Lieutenant Greene suggested.

Bo'sun Leech came in the back with him. Lieutenant Greene went behind the wheel, and Chief Norton got in the front beside him.

That pretty well sets up the pecking order, putting me on the bottom, Tony thought. *I wonder if Lieutenant Greene knows I'm an officer.*

They drove out of town, east, across a long, narrow two-lane bridge set on pilings. Tony saw signs saying they were on U.S. Highway 98.

Chief Norton turned around and looked at him.

"Adams said you know something about explosives, Pelosi. That right?"

I've probably forgotten more about explosives than you ever knew, pal!

"I know a little bit about explosives," Pelosi replied.

"You ever use explosives to cut steel?"

Not more than five or six hundred times.

"A couple of times."

"I generally found when I'm teaching somebody who has a little experience with explosives that the best way is to get him to forget what he thinks he knows and let me start from scratch. Think you could handle that?"

"Why not?"

"This isn't the first time we've done this," Chief Norton said. "Usually we have a lot more time, a couple of days more, anyway."

[THREE]
**The Consulate of the Republic of Argentina
Suite 1103
The Bank of New Orleans Building
New Orleans, Louisiana
0900 10 November 1942**

"Buenos días," Clete said to the redhead in the office of the Argentine Consulate.

"Good morning," the redhead said in English. "Can I help you?"

She's not an Argentinean, Clete Frade realized, which surprised him. He'd assumed that anyone who worked in the Argentine Consulate would be an Argentinean. But when he considered that, he realized there was no reason that should be so. It was obviously cheaper to hire a local than bring someone up from Argentina. It reminded him that what he knew about consulates and embassies—and for that matter, Argentina—could be written inside a matchbook with a grease pencil.

"I've come to apply for visas," he said, and smiled at her. He set his briefcase on her desk, opened it, and took out the forms and handed them to her.

"There's two applications," she said.

"Well, the sad truth is that my friend, who's going with me, right now thinks he's about to die," Clete said with a smile. "He was out on Bourbon Street all night, and most of the morning, too. I hoped he wouldn't have to come himself."

"I'll have to ask Señor Galle about that," she said. "Which one is he?"

"Pelosi," Clete said. "I'm Frade."

She examined Pelosi's visa application carefully.

"Seems to be all right," she said. "Do you have his passport?"

"Yes, Ma'am," Clete said, and handed it to her.

"I'll have to ask Señor Galle about it," the redhead said.

She went farther into the office, and a minute or so later a well-dressed, smiling man in his late thirties or early forties came into the outer room.

"Good morning," he said. His English was very faintly accented. "Miss O'Rourke gives me to believe that Bourbon Street has claimed yet another victim. My name is Galle."

He offered his hand.

"Frade," Clete said, taking it. "Clete Frade."

"I'm pleased to meet you," Galle said, looking at him carefully.

That look, Clete thought, *went beyond idle curiosity.*

"May I ask why you're traveling to Argentina?" Galle asked as he picked up the visa applications.

"It's on the application, Señor," Clete said, switching to Spanish. "Our company is opening an office in Buenos Aires."

"And your company is?" Galle asked, in English.

"Howell Petroleum," Clete said. "Actually a subsidiary. Howell Petroleum (Venezuela)."

"Oh, yes. I know them," Galle said. "And I see that your name is Howell. Is there a connection?"

"My grandfather founded the company."

"I'm not always this inquisitive," Galle said. "But we're cooperating with your government in a rather delicate area. It would seem that your government has discovered that a number of young men have decided they would much rather enjoy the delights of Buenos Aires than those of, say, Fort Benning."

"Really?"

"Our policy is that we inform young men of a certain age that while we would be pleased to grant them a visa to visit Argentina, there will be a delay of a week or so while we confer with your

Department of Justice. A number of young men, upon hearing that, have decided to change their travel plans."

"Both Mr. Pelosi and I have done our service," Clete said.

"You would not be offended if I asked to see your discharge papers?" Galle asked.

"Right here in my briefcase," Clete said. "Mine and Señor Pelosi's. And I do have my brand-new draft card, which shows my classification. Medically discharged."

"That should do it," Galle said, finally switching to Spanish himself. "You speak Spanish very well, Señor."

"Thank you," Clete said.

After carefully examining the discharge documents and Clete's draft card, Galle handed them back to him with a smile.

"No offense, Señor Frade?"

"Absolutely none. I hope you catch a couple of draft dodgers."

Galle bent over the desk and scrawled an initial on one of the visa applications—Clete could not see which one—and then started to do the same thing on the other.

"Oh, this is interesting," Galle said, straightening and looking directly at Clete. "You're an Argentinean, Mr. Frade."

"No," Clete said. "I was born there, but I'm an American citizen. My mother was an American."

"Under our laws, you're an Argentinean; citizenship comes with birth in Argentina."

"Is that going to pose any problem?" Clete asked.

"No. But it's probably fortunate that you have done your military service. You were a Marine, I see?"

"That's right."

"We have, as you do, compulsory military service," Galle said. "And we, like you, have our share of young men who would rather not serve their country. If you hadn't done your service, then perhaps it could have been awkward. But since you have, I'm sure there will be no problem. But may I suggest you take your discharge documents with you? You'll probably never need them, but if the question came up somehow . . ."

"Thank you for the advice," Clete said. "I will. And I'll tell Pelosi."

Galle put his initials on Clete's application and then on Pelosi's.

"Now, if you would be so kind as to give Miss O'Rourke twenty dollars—visas are ten dollars each—I think we can finish this up."

Clete handed the redhead the money. She opened a drawer in her desk and took from it a small metal box. It was unlocked. She put the money in a tray, then removed the tray. From the bottom of the box she took a rubber stamp and a stamp pad, and with great care stamped each of the passports. As she finished she handed them to Galle, who signed the visas with a flourish.

Then he returned the passports to Clete.

"Have a nice voyage. When did you say you were leaving?"

"In the next several days. Whenever we can get seats on Pan American."

"One final bit of advice," Galle said. "Take summer clothing. Our seasons are reversed, you know. It is now summer in Buenos Aires, and sometimes the weather, the humidity, you understand, is not very pleasant."

"Thank you," Clete said, putting out his hand. "Thank you for your courtesy and the advice."

"Have a good time in Buenos Aires," Galle said. "I wish I was going with you. You're not married, I gather?"

"No, Sir."

"I think what I miss most, here, are the women of Buenos Aires," Galle said, smiled, added, "Bon voyage," and walked away.

Thirty minutes later, Galle left his office, walked out of the business district and across Canal Street into the Vieux Carré, then went on to a building on St. Peter's Street. He let himself into a small apartment which he had rented at an exorbitant price under a name that was not his own. The landlord believed he was a Mexican-American named López from San Antonio who visited New Orleans frequently on business—and to see a woman. Once a month, at least, Galle took pains to see that the landlord noticed him entering the apartment with a woman.

Galle doubted that the FBI or the New Orleans police were even aware of the apartment. And if they were, he doubted that they either tapped the telephone or intercepted his mail. To make sure, however, he sent mail to the apartment. When it arrived, he saw no indication that it was tampered with.

He had the operator connect him, station-to-station, with a number in Silver Spring, Maryland. He doubted the FBI knew of the existence of that apartment or that telephone number either, and he thought the odds were remote indeed that they had tapped that line.

He gave the woman who answered the names of Cletus Howell Frade and Anthony J. Pelosi, and asked her to inform the appropriate functionary that he had just issued visas for their residence in Argentina and that in his judgment they should be watched on their arrival to make sure they were indeed in Buenos Aires to open a local office of Howell Petroleum (Venezuela). As an afterthought, he asked the woman to add that Cletus Howell Frade had been born in Argentina, and that the security forces might be interested to learn who were his relatives, if any, in Argentina.

[FOUR]
Office of the Managing Director
Sociedad Mercantil de Importación de Productos
Petrolíferos
21st Floor, Edificio Kavanagh
Calle Florida 1065
Buenos Aires, Argentina
0930 18 November 1942

Enrico Mallín, the Managing Director of SMIPP (pronounced "smeep"), was six feet two inches tall, weighed one hundred ninety-five pounds, had a full head of dark-brown hair, a full, immaculately trimmed mustache, and was forty-two years old. He was educated at the Belgrano Day School, operated by two English expatriate brothers named Green; the University of Buenos Aires; and the London School of Economics. After that, he embarked on what he referred to as "postgraduate schooling" in the United States. In 1938 he spent six months in Louisiana, Oklahoma, and Texas learning what he could about the operation of the American petroleum industry. There was no question in his mind that the Americans knew more about doing business imaginatively, efficiently, and profitably than anyone else, including the Dutch Shell people and British Petroleum, who were supposed to be the best in the world.

He spent a month actually working as a roughneck on a rig in East Texas, and wound up in Tulsa, learning something about seismological data. Argentina wasn't quite ready to develop its own production. . . . Although there was certainly oil in the country, it was not now economically feasible to search for it, much less produce it. But someday these things would change, and when they did, Mallín would be ready.

He also returned from the United States with a number of "barbaric Yankee habits," as his wife (née Pamela Holworth-Talley, whom he met at the Victoria & Albert Hall in London when she was nineteen and he was twenty-two) only half jokingly referred to them. In the States, for instance, he acquired a taste for sour-mash bourbon whiskey, jalapeño peppers, chili con carne (which he insisted on not only making himself, but forcing upon civilized people), and the really outrageous habit of rising in the middle of the night to go to work.

In the middle of the night—which, so far as Pamela was concerned, was somewhere between five-thirty and quarter to six in the morning—Enrico (whom Pamela called "Henry") would rise quietly from their bed in the master's suite of the large, Italian-style mansion on the corner of Calle Arcos and Virrey del Piño in Belgrano. He would then have a quick shower and a shave, dress, back his Rolls-Royce drop-head coupe out of the garage, exchange an early-morning wave with the policeman on guard at the Mexican Ambassador's house across the street, and drive downtown to the Edificio Kavanagh. The Kavanagh Building, built in 1937 (in the style now called Art Deco), was in 1942 Buenos Aires' first and only skyscraper.

Sometimes, if he was hungry, or for other good reasons, he would drive the drop-head Rolls into the courtyard of the apartment building at 2910 Avenue Canning in Palermo, where he maintained an apartment (4D; two bedrooms, a sitting room, and a kitchen with a nice view of the gardens) for Teresa, his twenty-one-year-old mistress. Teresa could be counted on to provide him with coffee or whatever else he needed. But most of the time he drove directly downtown to the Edificio Kavanagh.

There he would turn into the driveway to the underground parking garage, sound the horn, and wait until the uniformed attendant emerged from his cubicle and opened the gate. He would roll down the window and hand the attendant a coin. The attendant would touch the brim of his cap, smile, and murmur, "Gracias, Señor Mallín."

Enrico would have much preferred to deal with the attendant on a monthly basis. That way he would find the gate already open when he arrived, and his secretary could deliver an envelope to the attendant once a month. The arrangement would save him at least a minute a day, but this was Argentina.

He would then park the Rolls in space number one of the seven reserved near the elevator for employees of Sociedad Mercantil de Importación de Productos Petrolíferos, enter the elevator, exchange greetings with the operator, and ride to the twenty-first floor. Although office hours did not begin until nine, and the first employees would not begin to arrive until half past eight, once he reached his offices, one of the ornately carved mahogany double doors would be open, waiting for him.

The night man worked for Sociedad Mercantil de Importación de Productos Petrolíferos, not for the Edificio Kavanagh. He could be counted on to have the door open in anticipation of Mallín's arrival. He could also be counted on to have a kettle of water simmering in the small kitchen in Señor Mallín's private office, and to have checked with the Communications Department to make sure that all communications Señor Mallín would possibly be interested in were neatly laid out on the conference table in Señor Mallín's office.

Enrico would brew his own tea (Hornyman's Special) in a china teapot, remove his jacket and loosen his tie while he was waiting for it to steep, and then begin his day by reading the material from the Communications Department.

Very little of this was addressed to him personally. And very little of what he read required any action on his part. He made the odd note now and again to query one of his Division Chiefs, but the basic purpose of his spending an hour or two reading the communications was simply to get an idea of what was going on.

One piece of wisdom he brought home from America—an insight that was ignored at the London School of Economics—was the leadership philosophy he acquired from a marvelous curmudgeonly character of an American oilman, Cletus Marcus Howell. Howell told him—actually proclaimed—that if you have to look over the shoulder of the people you've hired to make sure they do what you tell them to do, you've hired the wrong people.

The philosophy was simplistic, of course, but in practice it worked. And in the case of Cletus Marcus Howell, in that wonderful American expression, he put his money where his mouth was in his relationship with Sociedad Mercantil de Importación de Productos Petrolíferos. SMIPP had represented both Howell Petroleum and Howell Petroleum (Venezuela) in Argentina for many years. There were twice-annual visits (annual now, because of the war) by Howell's accountants to have a look at the books. But aside from that, Howell (or his people) rarely asked questions and never offered any criticism of the way Mallín was running things.

They offered, of course, constructive suggestions, but these were precisely that: both constructive and suggestions. Generally speaking, when other SMIPP clients offered "constructive suggestions," they were actually criticizing. And "suggestions" was a euphemism for orders.

Over the years, Mallín had taken more care handling the Howell accounts than any others, simply because he knew he had a free rein, and it would have been terribly awkward and embarrassing if he was caught doing something unwise. Or stupid. Mallín took a little private pleasure in knowing that in his case, Cletus Marcus Howell was sure he had hired the right man.

Mallín almost casually glanced at the material laid out on his conference table, then poured himself a cup of tea, adding sugar and lemon. He then went to the window and slowly sipped it, gazing out at the boats on the River Plate as he did. As long as the office was his (he inherited it, so to speak, on his father's death three years before), the view fascinated, almost hypnotized, him. He privately acknowledged that looking out the window was one of the reasons he came to the office so early. If others wanted to believe he spent every moment reading the mail, no harm was done.

Now that he was here, he regretted not stopping in to have a coffee with Teresa. There was something wonderfully erotic about letting himself into her apartment, walking quietly to the bedroom, and watching her sleeping. Especially now, in the summer, when he could often find her without a sheet covering her, and with a flimsy nightdress more often than not riding high on her legs. When she was sleeping, there was a strange and entirely delightful warmth about her, and a slight musky smell. Teresa kept an apple on her bedside table. She wouldn't let him kiss her on the mouth until she'd taken a bite or two. Then her mouth tasted of apples.

Tomorrow, Mallín decided. *I will visit Teresa tomorrow.*

He turned from the window and went to his desk and consulted his schedule for the week. He had an appointment at eleven o'clock tomorrow.

There will be time for Teresa before I have to meet with Schneider. And if I run a little late, Schneider will just have to wait.

He glanced at the paper spread out on the conference table and sighed.

I better stop thinking about Teresa and do my reading. What the devil is that? A cable. I don't remember seeing that before. I've told that idiot again and again to put the cables on top!

He walked around his desk to the conference table and picked up a pale-pink envelope and tore it open.

```
WESTERN UNION NEW ORLEANS 1115AM NOV 19
1942
FROM HOWELL PETROLEUM NEW ORLEANS
VIA MACKAY RADIO

ENRICO MALLÍN
SMIPP
KAVANAGH BUILDING
CALLE FLORIDA 165
BUENOS AIRES ARGENTINA

FOR REASONS MY GRANDSON WILL EXPLAIN IN
PERSON HOWELL VENEZUELA OPENING BUENOS
AIRES OFFICE STOP CLETUS HOWELL FRADE
AND ANTHONY J PELOSI COMMA TANK FARM
ENGINEER COMMA DEPARTING MIAMI
PANAMERICAN FLIGHT ONE SEVEN ONE
NOVEMBER TWENTY STOP APPRECIATE YOUR
ARRANGING HOTEL ETCETERA UNTIL
PERMANENT ARRANGEMENTS CAN BE MADE STOP
REGARDS CLETUS MARCUS HOWELL END
```

The old man is opening a Buenos Aires office? And sending his grandson down here to do it? What in the devil is that all about?

The first thing that came to his mind was that SMIPP had somehow failed to meet the old man's expectations. Had something gone wrong? . . . He couldn't imagine what. . . . But was he about to lose Howell Petroleum as a client?

Almost immediately, he realized that couldn't possibly be the case. Their relatively simple business relationship had gone on long enough to work effortlessly; all the little problems that inevitably occur had been resolved.

In their own bottoms, or hired bottoms, Howell (Venezuela)

shipped Venezuela crude to Buenos Aires. This was most often (and now almost always, with the war) off-loaded directly into the tanks of the refinery that was to process it. Since there was an import tax, the government determined precisely how much crude there was. The government inspectors were kept honest during off-loading by the presence of representatives of the refiner (who wanted to make sure the inspectors had not been paid by SMIPP to report a greater tonnage than was the case) and of SMIPP (who wanted to make sure the inspectors had not been paid off by the refiner to report the off-loading of a lesser amount of crude than was the case).

Within forty-eight hours of off-loading, the refiners paid SMIPP for the crude. And within twenty-four hours of receipt of their check, SMIPP paid into Howell (Venezuela)'s account at the Bank of Boston the amount they were due: gross receipts less taxes, stevedoring, and, of course, SMIPP's commission.

Handling of Refined Products (cased motor oil and lubricants) from Howell Petroleum (which Mallín thought of as Howell USA) was a bit more complicated. But this was still done in much the same way. There was, of course, a greater problem with pilferage: Refined products were shipped as regular cargo aboard freighters that were not owned or controlled by Howell, and the crews of these freighters had discovered that oil products floated (even in cans and cases), and that some of the operators of boats on the River Plate would make gifts to seamen in proportion to the number of cases of refined products they found bobbing around in the river.

But over the years, even that problem had been minimized by the payment of bonuses to ship's masters and crews for their special care of Howell Refined Products. It was impossible, of course, to keep a half-dozen cases of motor oil from falling over the side when a boat operated by one's wife's cousin showed up to wave hello. But large-scale theft was really a thing of the past.

After the Refined Products were counted by a government inspector to make sure the government took its tax bite, they were unloaded into bonded warehouses, with a SMIPP representative watching. And when they were sold by SMIPP, it was on a Collect On Delivery basis at the bonded warehouses. A SMIPP representative was there to collect the check before he authorized release of the merchandise. Within twenty-four hours, SMIPP deposited a check to Howell USA's account at the Bank of Boston representing the total amount the wholesaler had paid, less taxes, stevedoring, SMIPP's commission, and the value of goods spoiled in transport.

Mallín generally succeeded in keeping the value of goods spoiled in transport (including goods actually damaged, say, when a cargo net ripped; goods "fallen" overboard; and bonuses paid to ship's crews) below one point five percent of net to Howell.

On reflection, Enrico could not imagine anything in his operation that could displease the old man.

So what is this all about? And why the grandson? He's nothing but a boy!

Mallín had met the grandson. In 1938. He was then a student in New Orleans, a tall, rather well-set-up young man who suffered from acne. The old man, Mallín recalled, doted on him. The boy's mother was dead, and the father had vanished when the boy was an infant (Mallín did not know the man's name).

If the boy was then—what, seventeen, eighteen years old?— what is he now? Twenty-one or twenty-two; twenty-three at most. If you are dissatisfied with someone, you don't send a twenty-odd-year-old to conduct an investigation.

Maybe that was why the other expert was coming. But if that was the case, why send the boy?

As a matter of courtesy to me? Highly unlikely. The old man is the antithesis of subtle.

Then the real reason flashed in his mind:

The war. The bloody damned war! If the boy is twenty-odd, he's liable to be called up for service. Young men are killed in wars. Even Argentineans. And we're not even in this war. Humberto Valdez Duarte's boy was killed—it was in La Nación—*at Stalingrad, of all places.*

The old man dotes on the boy. The mother is dead and the father a scoundrel. So the boy had been raised by the old man, and an aunt and uncle in Texas.

That's what this is all about. The old man doesn't want him killed in the war. So he's arranged to send him out of the country. He's a powerful man; he's arranged for him to be declared essential to Howell Petroleum. Sending him to Buenos Aires will keep him out of sight.

But who is the other fellow, Pelosi, coming with him?

We'll just have to wait and see.

He walked back to his desk, picked up a pen, and scrawled a note to his secretary, asking her (a) to please make reservations for an American gentleman, Señor Pelosi, at either the Alvear

Palace or the Plaza, for at least a week, starting November twenty-first (a small suite, to be billed to the SMIPP account); (b) to please remind him to inform his wife that they would be entertaining the young grandson of Cletus Marcus Howell for an indefinite period beginning November twenty-first; and (c) to please contact Schneider to ask if their meeting tomorrow could be rescheduled for later in the day; two-thirty or three, if possible, but no earlier than one-thirty.

[FIVE]
Aboard "The Ciudad de Rio de Janeiro"
(Pan American Airlines Flight 171)
1815 21 November 1942

One of the stewards (Clete Frade had serious doubts about his masculinity) came through the cabin, knelt in the aisle by each quartet of seats, and announced they were preparing to land in Buenos Aires. They should be on the ground—or, titter, on the water—in about fifteen minutes.

In fact, Clete's aviator's seat-of-the-pants instincts had already told him they'd been letting down slowly for about fifteen minutes. He had noticed a slight change in the roar of the Martin 156's quadruple thousand-horsepower engines, and a just barely perceptible change in attitude. Without taking it out of Autopilot, the pilot had just touched the trim control, lowering the nose maybe half a degree.

Clete was slept out and bored, so he had been doing his own dead-reckoning navigation since they'd left Rio de Janeiro. He used his Marine Corps–issue Hamilton chronograph and several sheets of the notepaper engraved "In Flight—Pan American Airways." Pan American had provided the paper—along with a good deal else—for the comfort of its passengers. He could only guess at the winds aloft, of course, but putting them at zero for his calculations, it was time to arrive in Buenos Aires.

He'd thought quite a bit about the watch, starting with the amusing notion that a diligent Marine Corps supply officer was almost certainly at this very moment trying to run down First Lieutenant Frade, USMCR, to make him either turn it back in or sign the appropriate form so the cost thereof could be deducted from his pay.

He got a strange feeling sitting in the softly upholstered seat of the Martin (every time they landed—first at Caracas, Venezuela, and then at Belém and Rio de Janeiro in Brazil—the crisp linen head cloths of the seats were replaced, and the ashtrays emptied) computing time and distance with the same watch he'd used when he had to wonder if he had enough gas to bring his Grumman Wildcat back to Midway or Henderson. Same identical watch, except for the strap. He replaced the old, mold-soaked strap with a new leather band in New Orleans.

It occurred to him that in his new role as a spy/saboteur/secret agent, he probably should put the watch away and wear one more appropriate to an oil industry executive.

That man is obviously a secret agent. You can tell by his watch!

But he had a strange, strong emotional reluctance to take it off. In a sense, the Hamilton and the Half Wellington boots he was wearing were his last connection with VMF-229, with Henderson and Guadalcanal, with the Corps, with Francis Xavier Sullivan. It was a connection he didn't want to break.

From the beginning in the hotel room in Los Angeles, he'd had doubts about the whole OSS operation. These had not only not diminished, they had grown more defined. He found it difficult to believe that the United States of America—faced with the problem that German submarines were being replenished by "neutral" freighters in Argentina—could not come up with a better solution than sending a fighter pilot, an immigrant electrical engineer, and a none-too-bright Italian boy from Chicago who was allegedly a demolitions expert to deal with it.

If General Frade had been in charge, he would have dispatched several Boeing B-17 bombers to Brazil with orders to bomb any suspicious-looking ship; and if the Argentineans didn't like it, fuck 'em. What were they going to do, declare war on the United States and bomb Miami? If the OSS knew about the ship, they would certainly know where it was. And it shouldn't be too hard to pass that information on to the bomber people.

On the other hand, it was also very true that the B-17s, the only aircraft Clete knew of with range enough to bomb Buenos Aires from a base in Brazil, weren't the invincible flying fortresses the Army Air Corps was advertising. B-17s had bravely gone out day after day from Midway and Henderson and Espíritu Santo to bomb Japanese ships; and so far as Clete knew, they hadn't been able to hit one of them.

They'd lost a bunch of B-17s—either to Japanese fighters, pilot

(or navigator) error, or lousy maintenance. At least some of the
Seventeen pilots must have known they were pissing into the
wind, but they kept their mouths shut and tried to do what was
asked of them, because that was the way things are in a war.

And that's how he felt about blowing up "neutral" freighters
in Argentina. He would give it a shot—and for that matter, even
try to make friends with his father—because that was what he
had been ordered to do. Phony discharge and draft card and civilian clothing aside, he was still a serving Marine Officer. He'd
taken an oath to "faithfully execute the orders of those officers
appointed him"; and simply because orders like these weren't
what he expected to get didn't release him from that oath.

All he could do was hope that "faithfully executing" his orders
wasn't going to get himself—and Pelosi and Ettinger—killed in
the process. And considering that the sum total of his knowledge
about how to be a successful secret agent could be written inside
a matchbook with a crayon—despite the mind-numbing, day-and-
night, relentless efforts of the mentors in New Orleans—getting
killed did not seem an unlikely possibility.

Ettinger seemed both smart and tough. Even telling his mother
that he was going to Argentina now seemed less stupid than it
did when Clete first heard it and ate him out about it. He had to
tell her something, obviously, and in the absence of a furnished
cover story—the OSS left things out, forgot things . . . this was
obviously not a comforting thought—the one he came up with
was a pretty good one. And someone who had lost his family to
Hitler's goons didn't have to be reminded that the Germans were
the bad guys.

Pelosi worried him more. Sure he knew his stuff, incredibly.
. . . Lieutenant Greene, the Navy Salvage officer, gave Pelosi
practice setting charges on a ship by giving him a to-be-scrapped
World War One destroyer to blow up. Greene came back from
Mississippi damned near glowing with tales of his expertise. But
Pelosi was a Second Lieutenant, a kid, who thought war was like
they showed it in Alan Ladd and Errol Flynn movies. Based on
his own recent experience in the role, Clete considered himself
an expert about the stupidity of second lieutenants. And he was
thus afraid that Pelosi would try to do something heroic—an excellent way to get yourself and the people with you killed.

When the opportunity presented itself—the mentors saw to it
there was no time for that in New Orleans—he intended to have

a long talk with Pelosi on the theme that discretion is often the better part of valor.

The mentors also ruined his plans to correct what was now a near-terminal case of Lackanookie. Finding a cure for that was the one thing he could reasonably expect to find in Buenos Aires. Three of their mentors had been there. They swore to a man that the women were both lovely and (sometimes) willing.

He remembered clearly very few of the nine million facts about Buenos Aires that they threw at him. But one of those few concerned Four Hour Hotels. Four Hour Hotels were set up for the express purpose of catering to unmarried people who wished to spend four hours alone together in a horizontal position without their clothes. That seemed to be a little too good to be true, but he was going to do his best to find out for himself.

Another steward came down the aisle, carrying a tray of glasses and a bottle of champagne wrapped in a napkin.

Clete nudged Pelosi, who was dozing in the seat beside him, waking him, and noting with surprise how his face was astonishingly dark with whiskers. Pan American had provided razors, but they both chose not to use them. Since it was unlikely either of them was going to be kissed on board, shaves could wait until they got to Buenos Aires.

Pelosi had a questioning look. And a hint of annoyance, as well.

"Champagne," Clete said.

"What are we celebrating?"

"Our arrival."

"Champagne, gentlemen?" the steward asked as he reached them.

"Thank you ever so much, and you can leave the bottle," Clete said.

The Martin set down into choppy water with a series of crashes. Water sprayed over the windows, so the seaplane was nearly stopped before Clete could look past Pelosi and see outside. The water was dirty. Or at least brown.

The seaplane turned, and the pilot shut down its engines. Punctuated only by the clangs of cooling metal and the lapping of water against the hull, the quiet felt strange. Then a string of boats appeared: The first four were outsize motorboats, with brightly varnished woodwork. And after them, in line, came four work boats, to take off the luggage and cargo. Clete had seen them load mailbags aboard in Miami and in Rio de Janeiro.

He wondered idly if there was other cargo. *It must cost a fortune to ship something air express, if that's what it's called. The bill for our tickets was more than the Marine Corps is paying me by the year as a first lieutenant on flight status.*

There was a flurry in the cabin as the passengers—thirty-six of them, thirty-four of them male, he had counted—started getting ready to get off. Pelosi saw them too, and began to get up.

Clete waved him back into his seat, and pointed out the window. The first of the passenger boats was still far from the Martin. No one would be getting off in the next couple of minutes.

Finally, they opened the door, and there was the smell of fresh air. And it was warm. The temperature rose quickly. He was sweating by the time it was their turn to pass through the hatch and step down onto what looked like a stubby second wing, and from that down to one of the powerboats.

The ride to shore cooled them off.

It's no hotter here than it was in Miami, Clete decided. *Maybe a little more humid.*

Just inside the terminal building he spotted a tall, brown-haired man with a massive mustache. The other man spotted him at the same moment.

Enrico Mallín. I know him. I told the old man I didn't remember him, but now that I see him, I do.

I remember something else about you, too, you sonofabitch! You made a pass at—what the hell was her name? Beth Fogarty— when I took old stand-up nipples Beth by the old man's house. What was that, the legendary hot-blooded Latin? If it wears a skirt, have a go at it, even if it's half your age?

Mallín gently but unmistakably pushed a uniformed man— probably customs—aside and walked up to Clete.

"Cletus, my young friend, how good it is to see you again!" he said, shaking Clete's hand and wrapping his arm around his shoulders.

"It's good to see you too, Enrico."

Clete sensed a certain stiffness at that, and realized that Enrico the Horny expected to be called "Mister."

Fuck you, Enrico, Little Cletus has grown up.

"And your friend? Associate?" Mallín asked.

"A little of both, actually," Clete said. "Tony Pelosi, this is Mr. Enrico Mallín."

"Welcome to Argentina," Mallín said as he shook their hands. "I am very pleased to meet you both. Shall we go?"

"What about the luggage?" Clete asked.

"My chauffeur is here with the wagon," Mallín said. "He will take care of the luggage."

"A *wagon?*" Tony blurted.

"A Ford," Mallín said, smiling condescendingly. "By and large, we have very few horse-drawn wagons on the streets these days."

That was a cheap shot, Enrico. What was that for? To pay me back for not calling you "Mister"?

"We can just walk out of here?" Clete asked. "What about Immigration?"

"Right this way," Mallín said. "We'll need your passports."

He led them to an unmarked door, pushed it open without knocking, and waved them inside ahead of him.

A middle-aged man wearing a better-quality uniform than the man outside gave them a look of indignation—who the hell are you to barge into my office?—but then he noticed Mallín. He stood up, smiled, and offered his hand.

"These are my friends," Mallín said.

"Welcome to Argentina," the man said in heavily accented English, and shook hands with them in turn. "Please, your documents?"

He took a rubber stamp and an ink pad from his desk, very carefully stamped the passports, signed his name carefully, handed the passports back, and shook hands with each of them again.

"I so very much appreciate your courtesy, Inspector," Mallín said.

"I am happy to be of service, Señor Mallín," the inspector said, and bowed them through a door behind his desk. They found themselves in a short corridor, and then came to another door, this one leading to the street, where a dark-green Rolls-Royce convertible and a 1941 Ford Super Deluxe station wagon were parked at the curb.

A short, plump man in gray chauffeur's livery smiled and touched the brim of his cap.

"If you will be so kind as to give Ramón your baggage checks, he will see to the luggage," Mallín said.

The baggage checks were handed over, and then Mallín opened the passenger door of the Rolls.

"I am so sorry that my home is simply not large enough to receive you both as my guests," he said. "I have taken the liberty to arrange for Señor Pelosi accommodations in the Alvear Palace Hotel, which I hope, Señor Pelosi, you will find satisfactory until other arrangements can be made. Cletus will stay with us; he's nearly—how do they say it in Texas?—kin.''

"Cousin Enrico," Clete said, smiling.

Mallín looked at him, and after a moment, smiled.

VII

[ONE]
Buenos Aires, Argentina
2005 21 November 1942

It was a fifteen-minute drive to the hotel—on, so far as Clete was concerned, the wrong side of the road; like the Australians the Argentines drove on the left (and would continue to do so until 1944). Mallín took them through a park, where people in proper equestrian clothing were riding fine-looking horses on bridle paths, and then down wide, tree-lined avenues. A statue of an ornately uniformed man on horseback seemed to stand at every major intersection.

Clete realized immediately that Buenos Aires was not the kind of place he'd expected. He had assumed that Argentina would be something like Mexico, and Buenos Aires something like Mexico City. It was not. It was unlike any city he had ever seen before.

They came to a park in which enormous banyan trees shaded neat walkways, and a moment later pulled off the street into the entrance of a hotel. A polished brass sign read: ALVEAR PALACE HOTEL.

A doorman in a top hat and a brass-buttoned linen coat which reached almost to his ankles walked quickly to the car and opened the passenger-side door.

Mallín stepped out of the car and held the seat back forward so that Pelosi could climb out of the backseat.

"I think you will find the Alvear comfortable, Mr. Pelosi," Mallín said, "and I would suppose that after your long flight, you greatly need a good night's sleep. I apologize again for not being able to take you into my home. . . ."

"This is really something," Pelosi said. "Like the Drake in Chicago."

It looks like the Adolphus, Clete thought, recalling the Dallas landmark. *Pre–World War I polished brass and marble elegance.*

"I will go in with you," Mallín said, "to make sure that everything is satisfactory."

A bellboy (a boy, Clete thought, he's not a day over twelve or thirteen) spun a revolving door for them, and they entered the lobby.

"This is Argentina," Mallín said. "It is unfortunately required to give your passport to the management. I thought perhaps you'd like a coffee, or something stronger . . ."

"Coffee would be fine," Clete said. "Or maybe a beer."

Mallín gave him another strained smile, and went on, ". . . while I take care of that for you. You'll find a bar by the elevators."

Mallín gestured for them to precede him, and they entered the bar. The headwaiter greeted Mallín by name and escorted them to a table.

"My American friends," Mallín announced, "will have something to drink while I take care of Mr. Pelosi's registration." He nodded in the general direction of Tony Pelosi.

"You will have to excuse, gentlemen, my English is not so fine," the headwaiter said.

"I'll have a beer, please," Clete said in Spanish, "but my first priority is finding the men's room."

"Ah, you speak Spanish," the headwaiter said in Spanish. "If you will cross to the door beside the elevator, the gentlemen's facility is one floor down."

"And perfectly," Mallín said. "I'd forgotten you spoke Spanish."

"But I don't know the word for that," Clete said in English, inclining his head in the direction of the bar, where a stunningly beautiful woman in a revealing linen dress was beaming at a man at least twice her age.

"The word for that is Miña," Mallín said. "They are one of the many treasures of Buenos Aires."

"Very nice!" Tony Pelosi said, with admiration.

"Expensive, no doubt?" Clete said.

"Yes, but not in the way . . . They are not . . . how does one say? 'Ladies of the evening.'"

"I think, Mr. Pelosi," Clete said, "that in time I could come to like Buenos Aires."

"I like it already," Pelosi said, looking at the Miña.

"I will see about your registration," Mallín said, and walked back through the lobby toward the reception desk.

Following the maître d'hôtel's directions, Clete crossed the lobby and started down a wide, curving, marble staircase. Halfway down, he encountered another young woman, just as stunning as the one in the bar. He smiled at her. She averted her eyes, ladylike, but he thought he saw a small smile curve her full lips.

To hell with the OSS! My priorities have just changed. First I will get laid, and then I will play Alan Ladd and lead my brave band of men to blow up the Nazi ship.

[TWO]
23 Calle Arcos
Belgrano, Buenos Aires
2105 21 November 1942

"I hope your friend will be able to fend for himself tonight," Enrico Mallín said as they sat with the Rolls's nose against his garage door, waiting for it to open.

"He's a big boy," Clete replied, and then chuckled. "He'll most likely have a quick shower and then spend the rest of the evening in the hotel bar, hoping another Mina will come in."

"Interesting young man," Mallín said. "He's from Chicago, you said?"

"That's right."

"That seems a long way from Howell Petroleum in Louisiana."

"It is. But if you're asking how he came to work for Howell, I'm just one of the hired hands, and I don't know."

One of the double doors to the garage opened inward, and then the other. An old man in a blue denim jacket smiled at them as they drove past. Two other cars were in the garage; after a moment Clete identified one of them. He remembered it because the name amused him—a Jaguar saloon. There was also a small van with LEYLAND on its grille. He had never seen a van like that, or heard of a Leyland. He did the arithmetic. Counting the station wagon, that made four cars.

The old man told me—in case Mallín became difficult—not to forget that he, and his father before him, have made a good deal of money out of Howell Petroleum, and to deal with him accordingly.

"I hope you don't mind coming into the house via the garage," Enrico Mallín said. "I hate to leave the car in front. I don't trust the old man to park it for me."

"Don't be silly," Clete said. "I'm flattered that you're having me in the house at all. I'm afraid I'm imposing."

A narrow, steep, and dark staircase led from the garage to a butler's pantry. A woman was waiting there for them.

"Welcome to our home, Mr. Frade," Pamela Mallín said. She was a tall, slim woman in a linen dress with a single strand of pearls and a simple gold wedding ring. "And forgive my husband for bringing you through the basement. I'm Señora de Mallín, but I do hope you'll call me Pamela."

Clete had always found English women attractive, and he decided that this one was ten degrees above the average: She wore her pale-blond hair parted in the middle and had startlingly blue eyes and a marvelous complexion.

"I'll call you Pamela if you call me Clete. And thank you for having me in your home. It's unexpected."

"It gives us much pleasure," Mallín said, and went on: "I suggest we give Clete a chance to freshen up—he's been on the airplane for thirty-six hours, at least—and then we can have a little chat over a cocktail before dinner."

"Ramón called," Pamela replied, with a look of disappointment on her face. "There was some trouble with the luggage. The officials, not only the customs people, were going through everybody's luggage dirty sock by dirty sock. He said they were obviously looking for something."

"He should have known enough to see Inspector Nore," Mallín said, annoyed. "When did he call?"

"About ten minutes ago. He wanted to know whether you wanted him to go to the Alvear first, or here."

"And you told him the Alvear, right?" Mallín asked, not pleasantly.

"In the absence of instructions to the contrary," Pamela replied, with a strained smile, "I thought that was the thing to do."

Mallín flashed a smile.

"Well, then," he said, "we can have a little chat now, and wait for your luggage, Clete. Sorry about this."

"Don't be silly," Clete said.

They followed her out of the butler's pantry through a dining room, where an enormous table was already set with five places, and then across a foyer to double doors, behind which was a sitting room. One wall was filled with books.

Pamela arranged herself gracefully on a dark-brown leather couch, then reached to a side table and pressed a button.

"Perhaps it would be easier if you told me what'd you'd like," she said. "Alberto's English is not as good as it could be. I *am* permitted to offer you a drink? Henry—perhaps I shouldn't say this—used the word 'boy.' "

In Spanish, Clete said, "A weak one. I had champagne on the plane, and a beer at the hotel. And a glass of water first, please? The airplane dehydrated me."

"He also didn't tell me that you spoke Spanish," Pamela said. "I'm disappointed; I looked forward to having someone in the house who speaks English."

Clete switched to English: "I don't speak English, but if you're able to put up with my American . . ."

"Beggars can't be choosers, can they?" she asked with a laugh.

A middle-aged male servant in a linen jacket appeared at the double doors, then walked into the room.

"Alberto, this is Mr. Frade, who will be staying with us. He speaks Spanish, but you are to speak Spanish with him only in an emergency. You understand? I am determined that you improve your English."

"Sí, Señora," he said.

"Mr. Frade will have first an agua con gas and then a scotch with a little water and ice; Mr. Mallín will have . . . what, Henry?"

"Scotch is fine."

". . . and if you have opened the dinner wine, I will have a Malbec. We *are* going to have a Malbec?"

"Sí, Señora," he said, and half backed out of the room.

Pamela turned to Clete.

"I believe polite custom requires me to ask, 'How was your flight?' "

"Very long," Clete said.

She laughed dutifully. "And now you can't get the authorities to release your luggage. I wonder what that was all about."

So do I. Am I already a paranoid secret agent, wondering why they were searching our luggage?

"What I'm wondering," Mallín said, "is what brings you to Argentina. Would it be rude of me to ask?"

"No, of course not. Actually, it's pretty silly. There are apparently paranoid people in our government who suspect that both crude from Venezuela and refined product from the States is being diverted to the Germans or the Italians."

"That's absurd!" Mallín flared.

"So my grandfather said," Clete replied. "But after extensive negotiations with the government, a solution was reached. If representatives of Howell, American representatives, were actually present in Argentina to more or less swear that our product is in fact staying in Argentina, the government would be satisfied. And I was chosen to come for several reasons—for one, my middle name is Howell; for another, I was recently discharged from the service and needed a job."

"Oh, you were in the service?" Pamela asked. "Which one?"

"I would like to know where the idea started that SMIPP could be involved with something like that," Mallín said indignantly.

"The Marine Corps, briefly," Clete said.

"And you were released?" Pamela asked. "Or shouldn't I have asked?"

"I was to be trained as a pilot," Clete said. "At the final physical, they found out that I have a heart murmur. Pilots—for that matter, Marines—cannot have heart murmurs."

That story came from Washington, with Adams the mentor. At one point Clete asked Adams why he had to deny that he was a pilot who had seen active service (at one point, Adams had told him that the best cover story was one which comes close to the truth, and which only alters or invents those facts that have a bearing on the deception). Adams replied that if Clete had a physical defect, his release from the service would be more credible than if he had actually become a Marine aviator. Clete didn't see the reasoning then or now, but Adams was supposed to be the expert in that sort of thing.

He was surprised at how easily he was able to tell both fabrications. He had previously thought of himself as a more-than-honest man who would have difficulty lying. That obviously wasn't the case.

Am I a natural-born liar, or can I do it now because this whole business is so unreal, like a game? Will I be able to lie as easily when it is important?

Or am I missing the point here and forgetting that these lies are important?

Alberto returned, bearing a silver tray on which were a crystal bottle with a silver "Scotch" tag hanging from its neck; a wine bottle; a silver bowl full of ice; a crystal water pitcher; a wineglass; and two large, squat crystal glasses. He made quite a ceremony of preparing the drinks, first pouring a sip of wine in the wineglass, then offering it—plus the cork, held in his palm—to Pamela for her approval.

She sniffed the cork, smiled, looked at Clete, said, "I think you will like our wines," and then sipped her wine. "That's fine, Alberto."

He filled her glass; then, with tongs, he added an ice cube to a crystal glass, and asked Clete, "Is sufficient, Sir?"

They were not large cubes.

"Two more, please," Clete said.

Then Alberto took what looked like a silver shot glass with a handle, held it carefully over the glass, filled it with scotch to the brim—and perilously over the brim—and only then dumped it. Then he picked up the water pitcher and, looking at Clete for orders to stop, added water. When Clete held up his hand, he stopped pouring and stirred the drink with a silver mixing stick.

If I drink all of that, I'll be on my knees.

"Gracias, Alberto."

Alberto repeated the ritual for Enrico Mallín. After Alberto placed the tray on a table and left the room, Mallín raised his glass.

"Welcome to our home, Clete," he said. "And to Argentina. May your visit be long and pleasant."

"Hear, hear," Pamela said.

"Thank you," Clete said, and took a sip. The drink was even stronger than he expected.

You will limit yourself to half of this, Clete, my boy. You had champagne on the airplane, a beer in the hotel, now this; and there is going to be wine for dinner, and you don't want to make an ass of yourself in front of these nice people.

The door opened again.

What now? Hors d'oeuvres?

He turned to see.

"Sorry, Mommy," the Virgin Princess said, "I didn't know you had a guest."

She looked to be about nineteen, as old as his "sister" Beth, and she was standing just inside the doorway. She spoke with Pamela Mallín's delightful British accent. She was wearing tennis clothes: a very brief skirt which showed most of her magnificent legs, a thin white blouse that pleasingly contained her absolutely perfect bosom, white socks, and tennis shoes. She carried two tennis racquets in covers under one arm, and held a red leather bag with the other hand. Her hair was long and light brown (probably shoulder length, Clete decided), swept up loosely and quite attractively at the back of her head. She had a wonderful innocence in her look and manner (innocent . . . but by no means childlike), yet she was confident too. Virgin and Princess.

"Come in, darling," Pamela said, "and say hello to Mr. Frade. He's an old friend of Daddy's; he will be staying with us."

The Virgin Princess crossed the room to her mother, kissed her, crossed to her father, kissed him, and then turned to face Clete. She put out her hand.

"Hello, Mr. Frade. I'm Dorotea," she said, offering him a glowing smile; her complexion was even more lovely than her mother's.

Her hand was warm and soft.

"Clete Frade," he said. His voice sounded strange to him. And his heart was beating strangely, too.

She's just a kid; she is the daughter of your hosts. Control yourself! What's wrong with you, pal, is that you haven't been laid since Christ was a corporal, and you are full of booze. Watch yourself!

"How was the game, querida?" Mallín asked fondly.

"My God, Daddy, it was hot out there! Even at this hour."

"Do you play tennis, Clete?" Pamela asked.

"Yes, Ma'am."

"Good, then we'll have a game. Henry plays well, but dragging him onto the courts is like dragging him to the dentist."

"I'd like that."

Ramón, the chauffeur, appeared in the doorway, holding his cap in his hand.

"I have had the gentleman's luggage sent to his room, Señor," he reported.

"What happened at customs?" Mallín demanded. "When there was a delay, why didn't you speak with Inspector Nore?"

"I did, Señor. He said it was out of his hands; it was an Internal Security matter."

Maybe I'm not so paranoid after all, Clete thought. *It is entirely possible that that charming Argentinean Consul in New Orleans warned them we were coming. Well, they found nothing. The last thing Adams did before we got on the train to Miami was go through our luggage to make sure there was nothing that could raise questions about us.*

Mallín grunted. "And the luggage of the other gentleman?"

"It is at the Alvear Palace, Señor."

"Thank you, Ramón. Would you ask Alberto to come in, please?" Mallín said, and turned to Clete. "Well, better late than not at all."

"Thank you, Ramón," Clete said. "And now, if I may be excused?"

"Alberto will show you to your room," Pamela said. "If you need anything, just ring. Should I order dinner for . . . say, in forty-five minutes?"

"That would be fine with me."

"I'll see you at dinner, Mr. Frade," the Virgin Princess said.

Clete nodded at her but did not trust himself to speak.

Alberto led him to a large, high-ceilinged bedroom. After he left, Clete found proof that the search of his luggage at the terminal had been thorough. While Clete was still in the house on St. Charles Avenue in New Orleans, Antoinette did his laundry. Specifically, she washed his socks and rolled them in her peculiar manner. He remembered thinking about that when he packed: Antoinette's rolled socks would pass the inspection of even the most critical, nasty-tempered drill instructor at Parris Island. The socks neatly laid out in a drawer in a chest of drawers here were neat, but not Antoinette neat. When they—*what did Mallín's chauffeur say? "Internal Security"*—examined his luggage they went so far as to unroll his socks.

Graham had told him that Argentine Internal Security was very good.

Did finding nothing satisfy them? Or just increase their curiosity?

Forty minutes later, after a long hot shower to remove the grime of the flight, and an even longer cold shower to force his libido under control, Clete dressed in a seersucker suit, went down the wide stairs to the foyer, and looked in the sitting room.

Mallín waved him in.

"Feel a little better?" he asked.

"Much better, thank you."

"Another little belt before dinner?" Mallín asked.

"Thank you, no."

"One is usually enough for me, too," Mallín said.

Christ, it should be. There must have been four ounces of scotch in the drink you gave me.

". . . and then I usually have a glass of wine for the appetite. May I interest you . . . ?''

"Thank you," Clete said.

Mallín poured him a glass of a red wine. Clete sipped it. It was very good. He said so.

"They call it Malbec. It . . . the vines, the cuttings, originally came from France. Bordeaux. This comes from a vineyard in Mendoza Province, near the Andes, in which I have a small interest."

"It's very nice," Clete said.

"There are those—your grandfather among them, by the way—who have been kind enough to suggest that Malbec is better than some French Bordeaux. I sent a few cases to him after my visit to your home in New Orleans."

"It's very nice," Clete repeated. "A little cleaner than most French Bordeaux, now that you mention it."

"If you like it, I am pleased," Mallín said.

"Papa?" a young male voice called from the door. Clete turned to see a boy of fourteen, fifteen, blond and fair-skinned, standing in the door. He was wearing short pants, knee-high socks, and a blazer with an embroidered insignia on the pocket.

That's obviously a school uniform, Clete thought. *He looks as if he's in the Third Form at St. Mark's, or one of the other St. Grottlesex schools patterned after English public schools. For that matter, he looks as if he's in his second year at Harrow.*

"Enrico, come in and greet our guest," Mallín said. "And since this is a special occasion, you may join us in a glass of wine."

The boy walked to Clete, looking at him with frank curiosity, and put out his hand.

"Enrico, this is Mr. Frade," Mallín said.

"How do you do, Sir?" the boy said.

"How are you, Enrico?"

"You are the gentleman from Texas?" Little Enrico asked, dubiously.

"Yes, I am. I left my horse and six-shooter in the garage."

"But you are wearing boots."

"Enrico!" Mallín protested. "Your manners!"

"I thought you had gauchos down here. Don't they wear boots?"

"We don't have gauchos in the house," Little Enrico said, shocked at the notion.

"Oh, I'm sorry to hear that," Clete said.

"Enrico, you owe Mr. Frade an apology. I can't believe you said that."

"He owes me no apology," Clete said. "We have a saying in Texas, Enrico, that you never have to apologize for the truth."

"Really?" Little Enrico asked delightedly.

"Unless that truth is that your friend's girlfriend is fat and ugly," Clete added.

Little Enrico laughed delightedly.

"Whose girlfriend is fat and ugly?" Pamela asked as she and the Virgin Princess walked into the sitting room. The Virgin Princess now had her hair swept neatly upward. She was wearing a yellow linen dress and a strand of pearls which rested in the valley of her breasts. She was wearing high heels, which made her calves even more perfect than when Clete first saw her.

"Enrico's," Clete said. "But he says he doesn't mind, he loves her anyway."

"I said nothing of the kind!" Little Enrico protested, but he giggled.

The Virgin Princess smiled at her brother; her mouth now wore an entirely delightful if faint coat of lipstick. Then she looked at Clete, and their eyes met for just a second, until, his heart jumping, he quickly looked away.

"Will you have some wine, darling?" Mallín asked.

"Yes, please."

"Dorotea?"

"Please, Daddy," the Virgin Princess said.

Mallín was still pouring the wine when Alberto appeared in the door and announced that dinner was served.

"No problem," Pamela said. "We'll just carry our glasses in with us."

That was done formally too. Pamela took her husband's arm. The Virgin Princess took Clete's, and they marched into the dining room with Little Enrico trailing along behind.

Clete did what he could to keep his eyes off the Virgin Princess during dinner. And he was torn between deep regret and enormous relief when Pamela announced afterward, "We'll say good night now, Clete. I know Henry and you have a good deal to talk about."

And the first thing we're going to talk about is finding an apartment for me tomorrow. If I don't get out of this house quickly, I won't be shot by "Internal Security." An outraged daddy will do it for making improper advances to his daughter.

"Thank you for a lovely dinner," Clete said.

"Good night, Mr. Frade," both Mallín children said politely, and both politely offered him their hands. For a moment, Clete's eyes again met those of the Virgin Princess.

Jesus Christ, I didn't know they came that beautiful!

[THREE]
Bureau of Internal Security
Ministry of Defense
Edificio Libertador
Avenida Paseo Colón
Buenos Aires
0915 22 November 1942

Comandante—Major—Carlos Habanzo, a stocky, dark-skinned thirty-one-year-old, stood at el Teniente Coronel Bernardo Martín's office door holding a large envelope and wearing a somewhat nervous smile. Habanzo was wearing a brown suit that was too tight around both the shoulders and the crotch, Martín noticed.

Martín waved him in.

"Buenos días, Habanzo," Martín said. "What do you have for me?" He was a tall, fair-haired, light-skinned man of thirty-five in a well-cut glen plaid suit and a regimentally striped tie.

"Buenos días, mi Coronel," Habanzo replied, then walked up to Martín's desk, laid the envelope before him, and stepped back from the desk.

Martín opened the envelope.

These are grainy, but very good, Martín decided. *There is only so much that can be done with a high-speed 35-mm negative, even one made by a Leica.*

As a gesture of friendship, el Coronel Grüner, the German military attaché—and the Abwehr's man in Buenos Aires; it was not much of a secret—had arranged for the Defense Ministry to buy a half-dozen Leica I-C 35-mm cameras, at giveaway prices. They were the best tool around for surreptitious photography, and for photographing documents.

"These were taken yesterday, mi Coronel," Habanzo offered. "When the Pan American Clipper landed, and at the Alvear Palace . . ."

"Which one is young Frade?" Martín interrupted.

"The tall one, mi Coronel."

"And he is staying at the Alvear Palace?"

"No, mi Coronel. He was taken to Señor Mallín's home by Señor Mallín. There are photos . . ."

"You recognized Señor Mallín, did you, Habanzo?" Martín interrupted again.

"Of course, mi Coronel."

Martín found the entry of Enrico Mallín into the puzzle fascinating.

"Thank you, Habanzo," Martín said. "Please give my compliments to whoever took these. They will doubtless prove very useful."

Habanzo beamed at the compliment.

"That will be all, Habanzo. Thank you," Martín said.

"Con permiso, mi Coronel," Habanzo said, came to attention, did an about-face, and marched out of the room.

Martín examined the photographs again. If one looked for it, one could see a strong family resemblance on young Frade's face. Martín had looked at enough photographs of el Coronel Frade to know his almost as well as his own.

Well, he's here, and he's his father's son. Now I'll have to bring The Admiral in on this, especially with the introduction of Mallín into the puzzle.

The Admiral was el Almirante Francisco de Montoya, the Chief of the Bureau of Internal Security of the Ministry of National Defense, to whom el Teniente Coronel Martín reported directly. Martín's most important responsibility (as Chief of the innocuously named Ethical Standards Office) was to keep an eye on the Grupo de Oficiales Unidos, which was strongly suspected of planning a coup d'état against the president.

The commonly accepted motive for a coup d'état was El Almirante's strong suspicion—shared by Martín—that President Ramón S. Castilló, who had pronounced pro-Axis sympathies, intended to remain in office no matter what was the result of the next election, and that the Grupo de Oficiales Unidos was determined to see that this did not happen.

Keeping an eye on the Grupo de Oficiales Unidos meant keeping an eye on el Coronel Jorge Guillermo Frade, who was both the brains and the money behind them.

The imminent arrival of young Frade had first been brought to Martín's attention a week earlier by a captain who worked with

Immigration. He set up an appointment, explaining to Martín's sergeant that he had information, unspecified, that el Coronel Martín would be interested in. He showed up, in uniform, at the appointed time, and then spent the better part of an hour telling, in great detail, what he knew.

Martín was by nature an impatient man, but he learned long ago to listen. More often than not, a careful listener could pick out a valuable gem of information hidden somewhere in a haystack of verbosity and minutiae. He heard the captain out:

A cable had been received from the Argentinean Embassy in Washington, D.C., stating that extended residence visas had been granted by the Consulate in New Orleans to two Americans, one of whom, Cletus Howell Frade, was born in Argentina. The cable had suggested that it might be of interest to look into Frade's relations in Argentina. Clearly, the Consul in Buenos Aires had smelled something not quite in order about the two Americans.

A routine investigation into Cletus Howell Frade was discreetly initiated. Since Frade was not an uncommon name in Argentina, there was no reason whatever for the Immigration Section to suspect that the best-known Frade of all had an American citizen for a son.

The investigation quickly determined that Cletus Howell Frade was born in the hospital of the University of Buenos Aires to one Elizabeth-Ann Howell de Frade, Citizen of the U.S. of America, and her husband, one Jorge Guillermo Frade, Citizen of Argentina, resident in Pila, Province of Buenos Aires. Jorge—George— and Guillermo—William—were even more common Christian names in Argentina than the surname Frade.

Beyond that, there was very little information in government files concerning Cletus Howell Frade. There was no record bearing his name in the files of the Ministries of Defense, Education, or Immigration. The files were linked. The Ministry of Education provided the Ministry of Defense annually with a list of physically fit sixteen-year-old males. This gave the Ministry of Defense a list to compare against the list of nineteen-year-old physically fit males who had registered for National Service under the Organic Military Statute of 1901 (according to which, without exception, one year's active military service was required of all physically fit males turning twenty years, followed by reserve service until age forty-five). If a boy's name was on the sixteen-year-old list and not on the nineteen-year-old list, why not? Where was he? One possibility was that he left the country. This could be ascertained by checking the list of sixteen-to-twenty-year-old males who had either left or reentered the country. The Ministry of Immigration furnished this list on a monthly basis.

Cletus Howell Frade's name was not on any of the lists, which suggested that he left the country before his sixteenth birthday and did not return. It was impossible to determine exactly when he left, because records more than five years old were routinely destroyed.

Thorough to a fault, the Immigration Section of BIS's investigators had searched the appropriate files for information on the parents. They could find nothing whatever about Elizabeth-Ann Howell de Frade, the mother. Which meant that she was not resident in Argentina, and, by inference, had last left the country more than five years before, since there was no record of her departure in that period. The records of the boy's father were, however, found in the files of Buenos Aires Province.

They indicated that he was still in Argentina, and still a legal resident of Pila, a small town about 150 kilometers from the City of Buenos Aires in the Province of Buenos Aires.

Further investigation revealed that he had good reason to live in Pila. The town was almost entirely surrounded by Estancia San Pedro y San Pablo, whose 84,205—more or less—hectares (one hectare equals about two acres) had been in the Frade family for more than a century and a half. On the death of their father, the estancia had passed to Jorge Guillermo Frade and his sister (now Beatrice Frade de Duarte, whose husband was Humberto Valdez Duarte, Managing Director of the Anglo-Argentinian Bank). Records of the Province of Buenos Aires revealed that shortly after her marriage, Señora de Duarte had sold her interest in Estancia San Pedro y San Pablo to her brother for an undisclosed sum.

At that point, the investigators realized they might be dealing not with *a* Jorge Guillermo Frade, but with *the* Jorge Guillermo Frade. Confirmation came from the records of the Ministry of Defense, which showed that el Coronel Jorge Guillermo Frade, formerly Colonel Commanding the Husares de Pueyrredón Cavalry Regiment,* one of Argentina's most prestigious units, had

---

*The Husares de Pueyrredón trace their heritage to the Pampas horsemen, turned cavalrymen, who rode with General J. M. Pueyrredón, one of the three officers (the others being Manuel Belgrano and José de San Martín) who led the war (1810–1816) for independence from Spain. In 1942, and today, the regimental dress uniform features a bearskin hat and a many-buttoned tunic bedecked with ornate imagery clearly patterned after the Royal and Imperial Hungarian Hussars of the Austro-Hungarian Empire.

upon his retirement eighteen months before listed his official address as Estancia San Pedro y San Pablo, Pila, Province of Buenos Aires.

And that changed the entire complexion of the investigation. The investigator in charge brought the matter to his captain's attention; and the captain immediately sought an audience with el Teniente Colonel Martín. He brought with him all the information the investigation had developed.

"Thank you, Capitán," el Teniente Coronel Martín said politely. "I will send a memo to el Coronel de Darre expressing my appreciation for your diligence and professionalism in this matter. And, of course, I'll take over this investigation from this point."

From that moment, Martín knew that at some point he would have to bring the problem to the attention of el Almirante. He had put off doing so, however, because of his sure and certain knowledge that once he was apprised of the problem, the Chief of the Bureau of Internal Security of the Ministry of National Defense would rise from his desk, lock his hands behind his back, stare for a moment out his window at the Río de la Plata, and then turn around and order him to do what he thought should be done under the circumstances.

In other words, nothing; he didn't think he would get any guidance, much less specific orders. El Almirante had no better idea than Martín if the likely coup d'état would be successful. If it was, it would obviously be better to have aligned oneself with the dissidents before the attempt. If it failed, it would obviously be better to have manifested some sign of loyalty to the preexisting regime.

Until the situation developed to a point where the success or failure of the coup could be reasonably predicted, the wise path for anyone in their business was absolute neutrality. Martín knew el Almirante devoutly believed—as he himself did—that the best way to preserve one's absolutely neutral status was to avoid any contact that was not absolutely essential with any member of either side.

And "contact" here meant bringing to the attention of el Coronel Jorge Guillermo Frade that Internal Security was prying into the subject of his son. And into the relationship between the Grupo de Oficiales Unidos and Señor Enrico Mallín, whose name had never come up before in that connection. And this meant that el Coronel Frade would become aware that Internal Security had added still more facets of his life to their investigations.

The previous incumbent of Martín's position was abruptly transferred back to the Artillery. When el Almirante was turning the job over to Martín, he told him matter-of-factly that the previous incumbent's transfer was engineered by el Coronel Edmundo Wattersly, who believed that Internal Security was adding information to his dossier he didn't want there. Wattersly was the third, perhaps fourth or fifth, most influential member of the Grupo de Oficiales Unidos. Frade was the most influential. Frade very possibly had the power to have el Almirante transferred back to the Armada—the Navy—and el Almirante knew it.

Adding to his dilemma, although he'd given the question a great deal of thought, Martín wasn't sure where el Almirante's loyalties lay—with the President? With the Grupo de Oficiales Unidos? Or was he still sitting on the fence?

But no matter where el Almirante sat, he would have to be made aware of this latest development. No matter what happened, Martín could not afford to have his loyalty to his superior questioned.

Martín reached for his telephone and dialed el Almirante's private, supposed-to-be-secure number.

"Martín, mi Almirante. I have something I'd like to discuss with you as soon as possible."

[FOUR]

Surprising Martín not at all, once the Chief of the Bureau of Internal Security of the Ministry of National Defense was apprised of the problem, he rose from his desk, locked his hands behind his back, stared for three minutes out his window at the Río de la Plata—it seemed longer than that—and then turned around to face Martín.

I will now be ordered to do what I think best under the circumstances, thus putting my neck and not his on the chopping block. But telling him is still the right thing.

"How, Coronel, do we know that the fellow who arrived from the United States yesterday is in fact el Coronel Frade's son?" el Almirante asked.

The question came as a surprise.

"Mi Almirante," Martín began, aware that he sounded as if he didn't really know what he was talking about, which was exactly how he felt, "he has a passport in that name."

El Almirante dismissed the passport with a wave of his hand.

"There are two possibilities," el Almirante said. "He is, or he isn't. As I would hope you have learned by now, Coronel, I am one of those who believe in assigning tasks to people in whom I have confidence and then letting them get on with it. But in this matter, I think a suggestion is in order."

"¿Sí, mi Almirante?"

"I would suggest that your next step would be to ascertain that Cletus Marcus Howell is, or is not, the son of el Coronel Frade..."

And how will I do that? Martín's mind raced. *Fingerprints? Even if I can get this fellow's fingerprints, what would I compare them to?*

"... and the way I suggest you do that is ask el Coronel Frade. In either possibility, I daresay that el Coronel could not help but be *interested* that a man representing himself to be his son has arrived in the country."

"Sí, Señor," Martín said, less as an acknowledgment of receiving an order than as an agreement that this was the way to deal with the situation.

"Let me know what you find out, Martín," el Almirante said, dismissing him.

[FIVE]
Estancia San Pedro y San Pablo
Near Pila, Buenos Aires Province
1225 23 November 1942

After his session with el Almirante, el Teniente Coronel Martín considered the possibilities:

The best would be that the young man was not the son of el Coronel Frade, but some sort of American agent. Then el Coronel Frade could not help but be impressed with the BIS's ability to find him out.

This was a credible scenario: It was a standard practice of intelligence agencies worldwide to issue spurious credentials in the name of a real person, often a dead one. There was no reason to think the Americans were less skilled than anybody else at that sort of thing. If, for example, an American intelligence functionary charged with reading newspaper obituaries had come across the name of a young man, or a child—or even an infant—stating that he had been born in Argentina, the name and statistics would have been filed away for possible future use.

There were several possibilities that were not as pleasant to consider. For instance, the young man could well be who he said he was. And from his looks, that was quite likely.

That's going to place me on dangerous ground with el Coronel Frade. I can't imagine a better way to antagonize a proud and powerful officer than showing him a photograph of his son and telling him that BIS thinks he might be an intelligence agent who is possibly operating against the best interests of Argentina.

And if he is el Coronel's son, that raises other embarrassing questions: What is the relationship between el Coronel and his son? Why has the boy never even been to Argentina before? That suggests that the boy is a skeleton in el Coronel's closet, whose door he felt sure was firmly closed . . . until BIS stuck its nose once again in his business.

And if the young man is both el Coronel's son and *an American intelligence agent—which is unlikely, but possible—is el Coronel aware of this? Is the son here because the Grupo de Oficiales Unidos has turned to the Americans for help? Or is the young man here to offer that help? And is the American government, which would dearly like to see President Castilló out of office, aware of the relationship between el Coronel Frade and the Grupo de Oficiales Unidos, and playing the father-son card?*

Perhaps it would have been better to snoop around a little more, perhaps even ask the Embassy in Washington or the Consulate in New Orleans to see what they could find out about "Cletus Howell Frade." But, following the session with el Almirante de Montoya, that was no longer an option.

Though Martín normally worked in civilian clothing and drove an unmarked Bureau of Internal Security Chevrolet, for his visit to el Coronel Frade he decided to wear his uniform (his basic branch was Cavalry) and arrange for an Army sedan with a soldier driver. Perhaps, if he was lucky, el Coronel Frade would be reminded that he was an officer, a Cavalry officer, simply doing his duty. He also decided not to call ahead and ask for an appointment; Frade was likely to be "unavailable" if he did that. But he would make sure that Frade was at home.

When he called Frade's Buenos Aires home, a large mansion at Number 1728 Avenida Coronel Díaz, he was told that Frade was at the estancia, and was not expected to return to the city for several days.

Which is understandable, Martín thought. *If I didn't have to be in the city in the middle of the summer, I wouldn't be here either.*

This required only a minor change in his plans. At 10:15 he left Buenos Aires in the backseat of an Army Mercedes open sedan, drove down Route Two to the turnoff to LaPlata, had a nice luncheon in the Hotel Savoy, then returned to Route Two and drove down it past Lake Chascomús to the Pila turnoff, and then down to Pila.

According to the map, the government road ended at Pila. But there was no visible evidence of this. A sign, of brick and wrought iron, at the side of the road read "San Pedro y San Pablo," but he saw no other indication he was now traveling on a private road.

Fifteen kilometers past the sign, he could see glimpses of the sprawling, white painted stone main building, sitting with its out-buildings in a two- or three-hectare manicured garden, all set within a windbreak of a triple row of tall cedars.

Those cedars were planted a long time ago, Martín thought. And then, *There are parks in Buenos Aires smaller than el Coronel Frade's garden.*

As he came closer, he saw a landing strip in a field outside the windbreak. Four airplanes were parked on it: a stagger-wing Beechcraft, a luxurious, six-place machine he had seen and admired at El Palomar, the civilian airport on the outskirts of Buenos Aires (this was almost certainly Frade's aircraft; he owned such an airplane); a two-place Piper Cub; and two Fieseler Störches. The Piper had civilian markings, while the Fieselers had Argentine Army markings. Fieselers were provided to the Army as another gesture of friendship and respect by the Germans.

The Fieselers and the Piper might well have just dropped into the Estancia San Pedro y San Pablo for a cup of coffee and a friendly chat with our old comrade-in-arms Jorge Guillermo Frade. But it's more likely that I've come upon a meeting of the Grupo de Oficiales Unidos.

So what to do now? Turn around and go back to Buenos Aires, hoping that no one has noticed an official Army car turn around close to the house? There are gauchos in the fields. It's entirely possible that they are posted as guards or lookouts, and that they sent one of their number galloping across the pampa to the house to report an Army car on the road. Cutting across the pampa, they can get to the house long before I do.

Innocence, I think, is the best face to put on this. If I were placing the Grupo de Oficiales Unidos under surveillance, I would hardly show up in uniform in an Army Mercedes.

A burly man in a brown suit stepped off the shaded verandah as Martín's driver was opening the door for him. There was something about him—his bearing, his immaculate shave—that made Martín suspect he had spent a large portion of his life in the Army, and probably in the Cavalry.

That has to be el Coronel's chauffeur and bodyguard, Martín decided. *Suboficial Mayor—Sergeant Major—Rodríguez retired with el Coronel Frade from the Husares de Pueyrredón.*

"Buenas tardes, mi Coronel," the man said.

"I would like to see el Coronel Frade," Martín announced.

"Does el Coronel expect you, mi Coronel?"

No question about it. The gauchos alerted them to my arrival, and this fellow is Suboficial Major Rodríguez, Retired.

"No, he does not."

"If you will be so kind to wait, mi Coronel, I will see if el Coronel is at home."

"Gracias."

Two minutes later, the retired soldier was back.

"If you will be so kind as to come with me, mi Coronel."

El Coronel Jorge Guillermo Frade, wearing riding breeches, boots, and an open-collared shirt, was waiting for him inside the house, in a large room with an enormous fireplace framed with carved and gilded wooden columns that looked as if they belonged in a museum. The floor was nearly covered with Persian carpeting, beneath which a red-tiled floor could be seen.

"I am Coronel Frade," he said, offering his hand. "Welcome to Estancia San Pedro y San Pablo. May I offer you a cup of coffee? Something stronger?"

Martín saluted before taking the hand.

"I am Martín. At your service, mi Coronel. No, thank you, Señor."

"How may I help you, Coronel Martín?"

Martín took his credentials from his pocket and extended them to Frade.

"How did an honest cavalryman become connected with the BIS?" Frade asked.

"It is a long and painful story, mi Coronel," Martín said, smiling.

"I am at your service, and that of Internal Security, Coronel."

"This is a delicate matter, mi Coronel," Martín said. "Absent more pressing duties, el Almirante de Montoya would have handled this himself."

"Why don't we get to the point, Coronel?" Frade said, more than a hint of impatience in his voice.

"I have some photographs, mi Coronel," Martín said, reaching into his briefcase for the envelope containing a dozen from the more than fifty photographs Habanzo had laid on his desk the day before. "May I show them to you?"

Frade went through them one by one. The first several showed three people getting into the ostentatious Rolls-Royce convertible Enrico Mallín insisted on driving.

There is something vaguely American about the other two men, he thought. *Where was this taken?*

The next several photographs showed everybody leaving the Rolls. He recognized the site. Avenue Alvear.

They're getting out of the Rolls at the Alvear Palace Hotel.
Who the hell are these people?
What's the interest of Internal Security in Enrico Mallín?
There is something very American about the tall one.
Holy Mary, Mother of Christ!

The balance of the photographs were views of the men in the lobby and lobby bar of the hotel.

One of them showed . . . *Christ, my son, my son!* . . . looking with obvious appreciation at a rather spectacular Miña fawning over an old fool standing at the bar.

There was another one of that. Cletus . . . *my son, my son* . . . sprawled in a chair, legs outstretched and ankles crossed, wearing boots . . . *what do you expect, he was raised in Texas, in Texas they stretch their legs and wear boots* . . . a glass of beer in his hand, and looking with healthy admiration at the Miña.

What in the name of the Blessed Virgin and all the saints is he doing in Argentina?

The last two pictures showed Cletus entering Mallín's car and driving off down the Avenue Alvear.

He handed the photographs back to Martín.

"Well? What was I supposed to see in those?"

"Mi Coronel, with respect, did you recognize anyone in those photographs?"

"Yes, of course. Enrico Mallín. The man with the mustache."

"Mi Coronel, with respect, no one else?"

"I have no idea who the short one is. The taller one is my son." He met Martín's eyes. "I didn't think you were asking if I recognized my son."

"Excuse me, mi Coronel. No offense was intended."

"No offense was taken. But I am, naturally, interested to know why BIS is interested in my son."

"There was some question, mi Coronel, whether or not he was in fact your son."

"A question in whose mind?"

"Mine, I am sorry to say, mi Coronel. I am paid to be suspicious of the innocent."

"Yes, I know," Frade said dryly.

"I will not trouble you further, mi Coronel," Martín said. "Thank you for receiving me without notice."

"I'm always pleased to be able to put the mind of the BIS to rest," Frade said.

"Mi Coronel. One final question. To close this matter, so to speak. So far as we know, this is the first time Señor Frade has visited Argentina. Could you comment on that?"

"I would presume it would have something to do with Howell Petroleum. It is a large norteamericano oil company owned by his grandfather. They do much business here. With Señor Mallín. Are you telling me you didn't know that?"

"Excuse me, mi Coronel. Do I understand you to say that you have no knowledge why your son has come to Argentina?"

"My son and I have been estranged since he was a small child," Frade said. "I haven't seen him in nearly twenty years. He is an American citizen. And I am surprised that Internal Security didn't know that, either."

"You didn't know he was here, Sir?"

"Not until you showed me those photographs. Is that all, Coronel? I have guests."

"I thank you very much for receiving me, mi Coronel."

"Not at all," Frade said, and put out his hand.

El Teniente Coronel Martín knew that he had been dismissed. He had a number of other questions he would have liked to ask, but he knew he would ask them in vain.

He shook Frade's hand, saluted, then marched out of the house and stepped into his car.

[SIX]

Frade watched Martín from the doorway as he got back in the
Mercedes and drove off. Then he went to a small room inside the
house furnished like a library, and took from a shelf a thin volume
bound in artificial leather. He thumbed through it until he found
the page he had often turned to before. On it were a number of
photographs of members of the Tulane University Class of 1940.
Below one of these was the caption:

> Cletus H. Frade
> "Clete" "Tex"
> BA
> Clete came to Tulane from Texas A&M
> and never quite got the sagebrush out of his hair.
> Tennis, Golf, the Aviation Club
> Going to Be a Marine Pilot

*He looks much younger in this picture than he did in the ones
Martín showed me, but there's no question that's him.*
*I wish I could somehow have kept some of those photographs.
What in the name of Sweet Jesus is he doing here?*
Doing here that has attracted the interest of Internal Security?
He closed the book and put it back on the shelf, then left the
library and walked across the entrance foyer to the sitting room.

"We were getting worried about you," el Coronel Guillermo
Kleber said.

"No cause for that."

"What did that man want?" el Coronel Edmundo Wattersly
asked, and went on without waiting for a reply. "You know who
he is, of course, Jorge?"

"His name is Martín and he's with Internal Security. It was a
personal matter."

"A personal matter?" Kleber asked incredulously.

"A personal matter, Willy," Frade said coldly. "It had nothing
to do with Grupo de Oficiales Unidos."

"I devoutly hope you're right," Kleber said.

"Can we move on to the business that brought you here?"
Frade said impatiently. "You make a very odd-looking nervous
old maid, Willy."

"He saw my airplane, I'm sure," Kleber said. "That makes me nervous."

"I'm quite sure BIS has all our names on a list," Frade said. "And I wouldn't be at all surprised if they have a much longer list of the times we have been together. But until they know what we're talking about, I don't think that's a cause for alarm. You were saying you believe the way to López's heart is through his pocketbook?"

Coronel Ricardo López commanded the 2nd Regiment of Infantry, stationed near Buenos Aires.

For a moment, it looked as if el Coronel Kleber was unwilling to drop the subject of the visit of el Teniente Coronel Martín to the estancia.

"Jorge, López has no independent means," Kleber said finally. "He is approaching retirement. For him the difference between a comfortable and a pinchpenny retirement is a promotion to general officer."

"You're not telling me he's asked for money? Or a guarantee of promotion when—if—we decide we must take action?"

"Of course he hasn't asked for money," Kleber said, almost angrily. "He's an honorable man."

"I'm glad to hear that," Frade said. "I have very strong feelings about buying people. Philosophical and practical. The people who back us must be concerned with the good of Argentina, not their own pocketbooks."

"It's easy for you to say that, Jorge, if you will forgive me."

"I will forgive you, Willy," Frade said. "If you will permit me to remind you that the practical reason why I am loath to turn an honorable Army officer into a mercenary—and that's the word to describe someone who fights for money and not for principle, mercenary—is that their allegiance switches to those who are willing to pay the most."

"All he's concerned about is his future, Jorge," Wattersly interjected.

"I'm concerned with the future of Argentina, Edmundo," Frade said. "With that in mind, I suggest you two visit el Coronel López and tell him to search his conscience. If he wants to join us, fine. If he does not, fine. And when the time comes, if López supports us, or does not betray us to Castilló's people, we will see that he is promoted to general. An honorable man deserves promotion. Of course, you won't tell him that."

"And if he receives his promotion, we could count on his continued loyalty afterward, right?'' Wattersly said.

"That thought has run through my mind," Frade admitted.

"Willy?" Wattersly asked.

"All right," el Coronel Kleber agreed. "Jorge's probably right."

Kleber always gives in at the end, Frade thought. *Is that because I am always right? Or because Willy is a weak man?*

"We've been at this long enough," Frade said. "I think we should at least break for a coffee."

VIII

[ONE]
23 Calle Arcos
Belgrano, Buenos Aires
1025 25 November 1942

Clete Frade was at the moment very much aware that his case of runaway carnal appetite was not a temporary anomaly brought about by a long period of enforced celibacy, a very long airplane ride, a good deal of alcohol, and the to-be-expected nervous excitement that went along with arriving in a foreign country as a secret agent charged with blowing up a ship.

If anything, his fascination with and hunger for the Virgin Princess had grown even more intense since he first met her four days before. He even dreamed about her, the dreams twice culminating in nocturnal emissions after he had worked his wicked imaginary way with her.

An hour earlier (he recalled in painfully exquisite detail as he watched her marvelous derriere, barely concealed by her tennis dress, ascend the stairs to the second floor) when the Virgin Princess bent over to retrieve a tennis ball and innocently offered him a glance down the opening of her blouse, his talleywacker popped to attention so quickly and with such intensity that he almost cried out in pain.

"How did the tennis go?" Pamela de Mallín asked, walking into the foyer.

"She's really quite good. She has an unusually strong forehand."

"From her father. My forehand stroke is my weak point. I'm sorry I couldn't go with you."

"We missed you."

"Dorotea enjoys playing with you. She says that you're so much better than she is that she's learning a great deal. It's nice of you to play with her."

"My pleasure. She's a really nice kid."

"And, of course, she's able to show off her older gentleman

friend to all her girlfriends," Pamela said with just a hint of a smile.

I wonder why I don't react to her other friends the way I do to her. Many of them are as good-looking as she is.

"You won't be having lunch, will you?" Pamela asked.

"No, thank you, I won't. I'm to meet Mr. Nestor for lunch. Will finding a cab be any trouble? And how far is it from here to the bank?"

"Oh, I'll have Ramón take you. And keep the car, Clete, I won't be going anywhere."

"That's kind, but unnecessary. I can take a taxi."

"Well, then, a compromise. Ramón will take you, and you can find your way back here on your own. What time are you to meet him?"

"I'd like to get there a few minutes before twelve."

"Then you'd better leave here," she looked at her watch, "at quarter past eleven. It's now almost ten-thirty."

"Then I'd better have my shower."

"I'll tell Ramón to bring the car outside at quarter past. And if I don't see you before you go, have a nice lunch."

"Thank you."

Clete smiled at her and went up the stairs. His room was to the right, as was the Virgin Princess's. And as he walked down the corridor to his room, he saw that the door to hers was slightly ajar. Ajar enough for him to glimpse her bed, on which her tennis clothes and undergarments lay after she had removed them prior to taking her shower. A moment later a delightful, if painful, image thrust its way into his mind—of the Virgin Princess standing under the shower with the water running down between her breasts to the junction of her legs.

Jesus Christ, Frade! You're really a dirty young man!

He took a long cold shower and then dressed. He decided on a cord jacket and trousers. As he examined himself in the mirror, he remembered where he bought the jacket—in Neiman-Marcus, in Dallas. And when—in the spring of 1940, just before he graduated from Tulane.

The Virgin Princess was how old then? Seventeen?

At the time, he didn't really want it. He suspected, correctly as it turned out, that he would not be permitted to wear civilian clothing when he went into the Corps; he went into the Corps three days after he graduated. But when he met Martha for lunch in the Neiman-Marcus restaurant before she flew out to Midland, she told him he looked like a ragpicker, that she was ashamed to be seen with him in public, and marched him into the men's store and bought the jacket for him.

And now I'm Cletus Frade, Secret Agent, about to wear it in Argentina, for my first meeting with the mysterious Jasper C. Nestor, Spymaster.

It's not happening the way it does in the movies. If Alan Ladd was sent down here to deal with the Dirty Huns, he would have met the spymaster in the middle of the night in some dark alley, and he'd have been wearing a trench coat.

"Why don't you come here, Frade?" Nestor had said on the telephone. He had a Boston accent. More precisely a Harvard Boston banker accent. "I'll introduce you to the people who will be handling your account. And then we'll have lunch. Have you eaten in the Plaza?"

"No, I haven't."

"El Grill, on the ground floor, is the oldest restaurant in Buenos Aires. Everybody who visits Buenos Aires should eat there at least once."

Is that what I'm doing, "visiting Buenos Aires"?

"Sounds fine."

"Come by the office—I'm on the third floor—say about noon?"

"Right."

"I'll look forward to it."

Aware that he was doing it because he was thinking about Martha, Clete pulled on a pair of boots Martha had had made to his measure by a bootmaker in Matamoros. They had walking rather than riding heels, and calfskin uppers which took a high shine. Dress-up boots, Martha had called them. So he wouldn't look like a saddle-bum when she made him take her to church.

Ramón drove him from Belgrano to the Banco de Boston Building in Florida in the Jaguar Saloon; and it turned out to be a disappointing car. It had a marvelous name, of course—it was hard to think of a Ford Saloon, or even a Lincoln Saloon, without smiling—and the body was beautiful, inside and out. But it didn't have any power. Ramón had to row it along with the gearshift.

I'll be glad when the Buick gets here.

The Banco de Boston Building, and the area around it, reminded Clete of Wall Street in New York City—1890s elegant, heavy, the facade elaborately decorated. The bronze doors of the main entrance, on a corner, were enormous; the entrance itself was floored and flanked with marble. He noticed, too, a brass plate mounted on the wall reading "Embajada de los Estados Unidos de America," with an arrow pointing to a doorway. Clete gave in to the impulse, took several steps backward on the sidewalk, and looked up. There it was, several floors above him, the American flag hanging limply from a pole.

He entered the bank and asked directions to Nestor's office.

Nestor looked the way he sounded on the telephone. He was a slim man, about forty, wearing a nearly black gray suit, a button-down collar shirt, and a maroon Harvard tie.

"Well, Mr. Frade," he said, flashing not much of a smile and offering a somewhat clammy hand. But, surprising Clete, he did his best to give him a painfully hard handshake. "I'm very happy to meet you. Had any trouble finding the place?"

"None at all, thank you."

"Can I offer you a cup of coffee? Or would you rather we tend to our business and then feed the hungry man?"

"No coffee, thank you," Clete said.

Nestor took a small leather card case from his jacket pocket, and peeled one off.

"My card. Feel free to call me at any time," he said.

"Thank you," Clete said.

Nestor took his arm and led him out of the office and back down to the main floor, where he introduced him to two Argentineans and two Americans, too low in the bank hierarchy to rate more than a desk and a chair for visitors in a long row of identical desk sets.

Each time he introduced Clete the same way:

"This is Mr. Frade, Mr. Cletus *Howell* Frade, of Howell Petroleum."

One of the Americans was David Ettinger, who gave no sign he had ever seen Clete before.

"Mr. Ettinger has just come down here himself," Nestor said. "He was in our New York office."

At the desk of one of the Argentineans, Clete was given a signature card to sign. He was then informed it would be a week or two before checks with his name printed thereon would be available; in the meantime, he should feel free to use counter checks; "the tellers will be alerted to the situation." He was handed a pad of a dozen counter checks, which were twice the size of an American check.

As they started out of the bank, Nestor touched his arm, and whispering as if he were about to impart a deep secret, asked, "I presume you're all right for ready cash? Or should I arrange something before we leave?"

"I'm fine, thank you," Clete said.

Nestor had a 1939 Buick Special Coupe parked in a garage near the Banco de Boston Building. The right fender and door bore red splotches. A body job was obviously in progress.

Apparently my new boss has not been able to adjust to driving on the left. Either that, or these people are as crazy behind the wheel as they seem. Or both.

Halfway to the Plaza Hotel, Clete concluded that it was both. Nestor was an inept, nervous driver, and a substantial percentage of the other drivers seemed to be insane.

"Well," Nestor finally asked, "how are things going?"

"Either today or tomorrow Pelosi is moving into an apartment on Avenida Corrientes. Mallín tells me the 'negotiations' for my apartment should be completed either today or tomorrow and that I should be able to move in as soon as they are."

"Where did you say that was?"

"Posadas 1354, Piso sexto"—sixth floor.

Clete had the strange feeling that a mechanical recorder had just started running in Nestor's brain: Once hearing that address, he would never forget it, and he would spew it back with perfect accuracy whenever called upon.

"And the telephone number?"

"I don't have that. One of the reasons the 'negotiations' are going so slowly was a disagreement over the price of the telephone."

"Yes," Nestor said.

"Where is Ettinger staying?"

"At the bank's guest house. An apartment near Recoleta. I'm working on an apartment for him. When I have an address and a phone, I'll pass it to you."

"Am I permitted to ask questions?"

"Yes, of course."

"What do you do if one of your agents doesn't have an independent income?"

"You mean for money?"

"Yeah. Mallín told me the man who owns the apartment wanted two hundred fifty dollars for the phone, and he was trying to get it down to two hundred."

"They've gone for as much as five," Nestor said. "And then there will be a bribe to the telephone company, probably for at least that much, to activate the line. You're lucky to have Mr. Mallín handling it for you." He paused and then turned and smiled at Clete. "We try very hard to recruit young men of independent means."

"Pelosi and Ettinger don't have independent incomes."

"Their expenses, within reason, for their telephone or to purchase automobiles, for example, will be reimbursed. I have funds for that. It's important, you see, Frade, that no questions are raised about whence the money, beyond a reasonable salary, cometh. In your case, of course, that's not a problem. Your middle name is Howell, as in Howell Petroleum. You can buy any kind of a car you want, and I suggest you do so as quickly as possible."

"I've shipped my car from New Orleans," Clete said. "You didn't know?"

"No, I didn't. Something ostentatious, I hope?"

"You tell me. It's a '41 Buick."

"Splendid. A convertible coupe would be even better."

"It's a convertible," Clete said.

I don't believe this conversation.

"May I call you 'Cletus'?" Nestor asked.

"I'd rather you called me 'Clete.' "

"The thing is, Clete, the way to avoid suspicion is not to act suspiciously. The word will gradually get around who you are, which is to say the heir apparent to Howell Petroleum . . ."

"That's really not so," Clete interrupted, with a smile. "I'm one of three grandchildren."

". . . and the son of Jorge Guillermo Frade."

"Mr. Nestor, do you know that I've never met my father?"

"Why don't you call me 'Jasper'?"

"Thank you."

"People won't believe, Clete, that you don't know your father." He smiled. "Everybody knows their father. They may not get along with him, but they know him."

"I thought I'd better mention it," Clete said.

"Yes. Of course," Nestor said. "As I was saying, Clete, the word will get around that you're a bachelor of means. That suits our purposes neatly. And, in one of the world's most sophisticated cities, with—in case you haven't already noticed—some of the world's most beautiful women."

Oh, I've noticed. The trouble is she just graduated from high school.

"It would attract notice if such a man did not take advantage of the repast fate has laid before him."

"I understand. Another question?"

"Certainly."

"When will I be able to get together with the other team leader?"

"I'm afraid that won't be possible," Nestor said.

"Sir," Clete protested politely. "If we are to be the backup team, shouldn't I know as much as possible about what they've got lined up?"

"Obviously, that would be the thing for you to do," Nestor said. "But, unfortunately, the team has disappeared."

With a sinking feeling in his stomach, Clete turned to look at Nestor.

"What do you mean, 'disappeared'?"

"Disappeared," Nestor repeated.

"You don't know what happened to them?"

"It's possible, but unlikely, that they are being held by the Argentines for interrogation, and that in a day, or a week, our ambassador will be summoned to the Foreign Ministry and handed a message condemning, in the strongest possible terms, this outrageous intrusion into Argentine internal affairs. But I don't think that will happen. Everybody knows the rules of the game."

"What are you saying? That they were caught and executed?"

"That seems the most likely scenario."

"Jesus Christ!"

"These things happen. They have to be expected. That's why your team was sent down here. To be available in case something went wrong."

"I suppose," Clete said.

I'm not terrified, Clete thought. *I've been terrified often enough to know that's not my reaction now. How about "scared shitless"? That fits in between "terrified" and "deeply concerned."*

"The United States has two important concerns here, Clete," Nestor said. "First, as a tactical objective with diplomatic overtones, the replenishment vessel has to be rendered hors de combat. And we have to accomplish that before the Brazilians decide to deal with it themselves. It is not in the interests of the United States that they go to war against Argentina at this time."

"The mentors from the Country Club discussed that in New Orleans," Clete said.

"Secondly, equally important, we have to teach the Argentines a lesson."

They just taught us one, didn't they? Don't mess with our neutrality.

"Yes, Sir?"

"I really wish you would call me 'Jasper,' " Nestor said. "I understand, force of habit, but someone hearing you might ask . . ."

"Sorry, Jasper. I'll work on it."

"The Argentines have to be taught that they can't stop us from making sure they stay neutral; that they can't close their eyes to the fact that the Germans are reprovisioning their submarines and surface raiders in the River Plate. More important, that even if they have eliminated one of our teams, we are capable of, and will in fact, send in another team. And another. And another. As many as it takes."

"I understand. Will there be another team sent down here now?"

"I'm sure there will be. No telling, of course, how long it will take to find the men, and then run them through the training school, et cetera, et cetera. For the time being, Clete, you're the varsity team."

"Varsity team"? Jesus Christ! We're here to blow up a ship, not play football!

"It will be important for you to keep in mind that we don't want to anger the Argentineans. Ideally, you would render the replenishment ship inoperable, rather than sink it, and do so without its coming out publicly that it was done by Americans."

"Who else would do it?"

"The British, for one. The Brazilians, for another. The point is that if it became public—as opposed to private—knowledge that the vessel was rendered inoperable by Americans, there would be an inevitable public outcry—fueled by the Germans—against American violation of Argentine neutrality."

"OK. I get the picture."

"Blowing the ship up would attract attention—especially if the ship was flying the flag of a neutral country."

"Is that what happened to the team that was eliminated?" Clete's mouth ran away with him. "They 'attracted attention'?"

If Nestor was offended by his sarcasm, or even noticed it, there was no sign.

"I don't actually know. Scenario One is that they were detected and eliminated while actually conducting the operation. Scenario Two is that they came to the attention of members of the Argentinean Navy who, with permission from the highest quarters, removed the perceived threat to Argentinean neutrality in such a manner that no questions could be asked. Scenario Three is that the threat to the Motor Vessel *Sundsvall* came to the attention of the Germans. They have a very good Sicherheitsdienst operation..."

"A what?"

"Sicherheitsdienst—Secret Service, literally. Actually a sort of a combination of our FBI and OSS."

"The Sicher... What is it?"

"*Sicherheitsdienst.* Yes. They're quite good. Scenario Three is that the team's intentions came to the attention of the Sicherheitsdienst, and the Sicherheitsdienst, regarding them as a simple military threat, eliminated them themselves. Or arranged for their elimination by Argentinean friends. As I am sure you know, there are many Argentineans, not only those of German extraction, who feel that God and reason are on the side of the Germans."

"And if the Sicherheydinn..."

"Sicher-heits-dienst," Nestor corrected his pronunciation.

"... finds out about us, are they going to try to eliminate us?"

"Possibly. The threat increases as the threat you pose to the replenishment operation increases. I'm leaving you at the Plaza after we have our lunch. When I do, I will leave my briefcase with you. In it you will find two Argentinean-manufactured copies of the Colt Model 1911A1 .45 automatic. Presumably they were stolen from the Argentinean Army. They were acquired illegally. It is against Argentinean law for any foreigner to own a pistol. A foreigner may obtain a permit to purchase a smooth-bore sporting firearm... a shotgun. Mallín, or your father, if you can strike up an acquaintance with him, can probably arrange a permit for you and Pelosi, without difficulty."

If there wasn't a bona fide threat from the Germans, he would not have come with the pistols.

"Turning to your father," Nestor went on. "I suggest you leave the initiative to him, for the next couple of weeks anyway. I don't think it will take long for him to find out that you're here. If he does not contact you during that time, you will have to take the initiative. Anyway, acquire permits and buy shotguns. The bird shooting here is magnificent, by the way. As soon as you have the shotguns, return the pistols to me."

"In other words, there *is* an immediate threat from the Sicherheitsdienst?"

"You pronounced it right that time," Nestor said. "I don't know. But it seems prudent to act on the presumption there might be. It took a good deal of effort and money to bring you down here. It would be a shame if the Sicherheitsdienst eliminated you before you accomplished your mission. Or if you eliminated yourselves by being found in possession of illegal firearms. Make sure Pelosi understands that."

"Does Ettinger have a pistol?"

"Yes. And I have had a word with him about the importance of discretion. Now, I don't want you, Clete, to think that any immediate action is required. Fortunately, we have some time."

"Sir . . . Sorry. I don't think I follow you."

"The replenishment vessel that was in the River Plate has left, presumably because it was out of supplies. Its replacement is almost certainly on the high seas, inbound from Europe, but won't be here for three weeks or so. We don't have a name. One possible candidate, of French registry, was sunk by a submarine off the coast of Morocco. The French blame the British; the British deny any knowledge and blame the Germans. The United States government has also denied any knowledge of the incident. That leaves three ships of interest now on the high seas; all of them are capable of the replenishment mission. As soon as I hear anything specific, *if* I hear of anything, I will, of course, let you know. You'll find the names in the briefcase."

Well, his intelligence is apparently good, if he has the names of three ships. But what good are the names if we don't know which ship it is? Or are we expected to take out all three of them?

"I have high hopes that David Ettinger will be helpful in finding out which of the ships is the one we're after," Nestor said, as if he knew what Clete was thinking.

"I don't follow that," Clete said.

"There are a number of Jews in the ship chandlery business here. One of the things the replenishment vessel cannot bring from Europe—it's at least a three-week voyage, more often a month—is fresh produce, meat, milk, and other nonfreezable perishables. Additionally, the more canned goods the replenishment vessel can buy here in Buenos Aires, the better for them; the longer they can remain on station. The only reason the *Sundsvall* left Argentinean waters was that her supply of torpedoes and diesel fuel was exhausted. So one of the things David will be looking for is a vessel which purchases more than the usual quantities of perishable goods or of canned and/or frozen supplies."

"You think people will tell him?"

"I hope so. He was trained as an investigator, for one thing, and more important, we were able to provide him with a list of names of Jews from Berlin now resident in Buenos Aires. It's likely that he will know some of them, or have mutual friends. He should be able, through them, to make contact with the people in a position to help."

"Here we are," Nestor announced, pulling into an off-the-street hotel entrance not unlike that of the Alvear Palace Hotel's. "We'll have a drink in the bar, and then have our luncheon. Did I tell you El Grill is the oldest restaurant in Buenos Aires?"

"I'll pass on the drink, thank you," Clete said.

"Oh, I think we really should have a drink," Nestor said, and there was a tone of command in his voice. "Taking an important client for a drink in the Plaza bar before lunch is the sort of thing a vice president of the Bank of Boston would be expected to do."

A uniformed doorman and a bellman walked to the car and opened the doors. The doorman greeted Nestor by name. Nestor took his briefcase and motioned for Clete to precede him into the hotel, then led him to a staircase and down it to the bar.

The room was paneled with dark wood. There was a bar, with stools, three quarters of them occupied, and a dozen tables, each with three or four leather upholstered chairs, half of them occupied.

Most of the customers were men, but there were some women. All but one of the women were striking; she was silver-haired, plump, and wearing a small fortune in diamonds on her fingers. She and the man with her, obviously her husband, were almost certainly Jewish.

And there were three Miñas, one at the bar, two at tables, one with a man old enough to be her father, the other with a young man in a beautifully tailored suit. When he saw Clete looking at the girl, his right eyebrow rose in indignant question. Clete smiled at him, and he smiled back.

Nestor led him on a tour of the bar, introducing him to three of the men there as "Cletus *Howell* Frade," just as he'd done in the bank. One of the men had a Miña with him. She was introduced only by her Christian name, Estrellita. Estrellita smiled shyly at him.

Then they took a table, and a waiter immediately appeared. Nestor ordered Ambassador-Twelve scotch. Clete had the waiter recite the short list of available bourbon, heard nothing he liked, and told the waiter he would have what Nestor was drinking.

The whiskey was served with a plate of hors d'oeuvres and with the same little ceremony that Alberto, the Mallíns' butler, had used.

It's classy, Clete decided. *They know how to do things down here.*

He glanced around the room. There were mirrors. He found himself looking at the reflection of the good-looking Miña with the young man in the beautifully tailored suit. And she was looking at him. He winked. A faint but unmistakable smile touched her lips.

"That's a nice touch," Nestor said. "I understand they're really quite comfortable."

What the hell is Spymaster talking about? What's "really quite comfortable"? The Miña? Come to think of it, I'll bet she is.

"Pardon me?"

"I just noticed your cowboy boots," Nestor said.

"These are *boots,*" Clete explained. *"Cowboy* boots are usually old, cracked, and covered with horseshit."

He glanced down at his boots, and flicked a dried spot of mud off the glistening left toe.

When he looked up, he sensed eyes on him and glanced around the room. The good-looking Miña was smiling at him.

If I can escape the Mallíns' hospitality, maybe I could come back here and see what develops.

[TWO]
23 Calle Arcos
Belgrano, Buenos Aires
1605 25 November 1942

The key to the lock on Clete's bedroom door was a massive device as long as his hand; and when he turned it, the bolt fell with an audible metallic clunk. It could probably be heard the length of the corridor; if so, it would probably make people wonder why he was locking the door.

But it couldn't be helped. He didn't want one of the servants barging in while he was going through the briefcase.

The afternoon was not going well. There was something about Jasper Nestor he didn't like, even if he couldn't put his finger on it. The three-ounce drink Nestor forced on him made him feel thick-tongued and stupid at lunch. And after he left the air-conditioned hotel into the summer heat, it made him dizzy and gave him a headache.

He decided in the taxi on the way to Pelosi's new apartment on Avenida Corrientes that it was probably a delayed reaction to coming from Guadalcanal, a to-be-expected resentment toward any military-age male who hadn't been there, who had been sitting around in a neutral country drinking whiskey with ice in it in an air-conditioned saloon, while he and the others were in the heat and mud and humidity of Guadalcanal eating captured Japanese food and wondering if today was the day the odds would catch up with you and your next takeoff in a battered and worn-out Wildcat was going to be your last.

And then he wasn't able to find Pelosi. Carrying the pistols in a briefcase like a Chicago gangster, he went to the apartment on Avenida Corrientes. But Pelosi wasn't there—the building manager said he would return tomorrow and finish moving in. So Clete tried the Alvear Palace Hotel.

When Pelosi wasn't there, either, Clete decided he was following his orders to familiarize himself with Buenos Aires. Clete had told him to get on a bus, any bus, and ride it as far as it went.

The bus-riding was one of the really helpful, practical suggestions they'd gotten from the mentors in New Orleans. That Pelosi was following his orders reminded Clete that he himself was violating the military equivalent of the Golden Rule: that a commanding officer should never order his men to do anything he wasn't willing to do himself. He had yet to ride on a bus. His rationale, which he knew was empty, was that he'd been too busy, and when the Buick arrived, he would make up for his failure by driving around the city.

He left a note for Pelosi in an envelope at the concierge's desk in the Alvear Palace, telling him he would meet him there at ten in the morning.

He sat down on the bed and opened Nestor's briefcase. Two envelopes were inside, unsealed. In one was a single sheet of paper on which was typed:

```
Sud Atlantico Mercader—Cádiz—19 Nov
Reine de la Mer—Lisbon—23 Nov
Águila del Mare—Barcelona—16 Nov
```

Those are the names of the three possible ships—where the hell is Cádiz? I should have paid attention in geography class. And when they sailed. Nestor probably gave them to me in case I hear something on my own about them. He said the voyage was at least twenty-three days. Twenty-three days minimum from where? Anyway, that means the first of them will be here in the next couple weeks.

He found a sheet of paper in the writing desk and copied the names down for Pelosi.

I don't think Pelosi stands any better chance of learning anything about these ships than I do, but if Nestor thinks there's a chance—and he's the expert—no harm can be done. And even if we don't learn anything on our own, Pelosi will at least know what we're looking for.

The second envelope contained a thick stack of money, American twenty- and fifty-dollar bills. And a sheet of paper, on which was typewritten:

> Receipt of Two Thousand Five Hundred
> Dollars ($2500.00) in reimbursement of
> expenses incurred in the Service of The
> United States is acknowledged.
>
> _____
>
> Cletus H. Frade
>
>   25 November 1942

Well, that's interesting. Nestor forgot to have me sign for what is obviously our expense money. He didn't even mention the money. Maybe his mind was on other things, once he met me. Such as "What is the OSS thinking of to send an absolutely unqualified airplane driver down here to do something important?"

What do I do about it? Drop the signed receipt off at the bank in an envelope? Or let him ask for it? "What twenty-five hundred?"

He'll ask for it. Probably telephone. And if he does, I can ask him how I can get together with Ettinger. I'm pretty forgetful myself, especially when I have three ounces of scotch in me before lunch.

He took the pistols from the briefcase and laid them on the chest of drawers. They were each in holsters, separately wrapped in small towels. The holsters were different from U.S. military issue. They were stiff—molded—and had a hard molded cover, fixed in place with a rather ornate catch instead of the flap used by American armed forces. And they had a pocket holding an extra magazine sewn to the long side.

The two magazines provided for each pistol were loaded. When he thumbed the cartridges out, he saw that while they were identical to the .45 cartridges he was familiar with, their head stamps (which he didn't understand) were foreign.

I guess they make their own down here. Why not?

While the pistols themselves functioned identically to the Colt he'd carried in the Pacific, they were not exact copies. He couldn't put his finger on the difference, but there was a difference.

The grip safety? The horn, or whatever it's called, looks longer. And the safety on the side of the receiver. That's shaped differently, too, I think.

What does it matter, so long as it goes off when you pull the trigger?

He stripped and then reassembled both pistols. Both were dirty and required cleaning and lubrication. And there were pits in both barrels. He used a handkerchief and a toothbrush to clean them. And for lubrication he used what was left of the jar of gray U.S. Navy Medical Corps paste he was sure was Vaseline.

He had just about finished with the pistols when there was a knock at the door.

"Sí?"

"Teléfono, Señor."

That must be Nestor, who's remembered I didn't sign the expense money receipt.

"Gracias," he called. He stuffed everything back into Nestor's briefcase and then locked the briefcase in the enormous wardrobe that covered just about all of one wall. He then unlocked the door with a loud clank and went quickly downstairs to the sitting room, to the nearest telephone.

The Mallíns were there, Mommy, Daddy, and the Virgin Princess.

"It's a woman," Mallín said, somewhat indignantly. "She wouldn't give her name."

A woman? Ah. Nestor's secretary. I was right.

He sensed the eyes of the Virgin Princess on him. She looked either angry or hurt or both.

What's that? She doesn't like the idea of a woman calling me? You want to keep your Older Gentleman Friend to yourself, do you, Princess, and not share him with the other virgins at the Belgrano Athletic Club?

He went to the telephone and picked it up.

"Hola?"

"Señor Frade?" a woman's voice asked.

"Sí."

"Un momento, por favor," the woman said.

A man came on the line and asked, "Cletus? Cletus Frade?"

"Who is this?"

"This is your father."

Jesus Christ! What do I do? What do I call him? "Dad"? "Father"?

Nestor was right. He did find out that I'm here, and quickly.

"I don't know what to say," Clete said.

There was a chuckle, a deep one.

"Now that I have you on the line, neither do I. What about 'Hola, Padre'?"—Hello, Father.

"Hola, Padre," Clete said.

"Hola, Cletus. I only learned that you were in Argentina three days ago. It was impossible for me to come to Buenos Aires until today."

Clete said nothing.

"Is it an embarrassment for you if I call there?" Jorge Guillermo Frade asked.

"No, Sir. Not at all. You just caught me a little off base."

" 'Off base'? Of course, the baseball."

"Yes, Sir."

"I would like to see you, Cletus."

"Yes, Sir."

"Would tomorrow be convenient? Luncheon, perhaps, here at my home. I could send a car for you . . ."

"No," Clete said. *Why did I say "no"?* "I have business downtown tomorrow morning. At the Alvear Palace Hotel. Could we meet there?"

"Certainly. Give me a time."

"Noon. I'll meet you in the lobby at noon."

"I will be there."

"How are you going to recognize me?"

"That will be no problem," his father said. "I will look forward to seeing you at noon. Thank you, Cletus."

The phone went dead.

I have just talked to my father. He found out I'm here and called me up. He invited me to lunch. A belated sense of being a father? Simple courtesy? Or simple curiosity. If I had a son, I'd at least want to see what he looks like.

"I'll be goddamned!" Clete heard himself say.

Nice, in front of the Mallíns.

He exhaled audibly as he replaced the telephone in its cradle, then turned to face Mommy, Daddy, and the Virgin Princess. They were all looking at him with understandable curiosity.

"That was my father," Clete announced.

The looks on the faces of Mommy and Daddy changed from curiosity to surprise, or confusion. The look on the face of the Virgin Princess changed to disbelief.

"Your *father?*" Enrico Mallín asked, visibly baffled by the announcement. "He's here? In *Buenos Aires?*"

Clete was surprised at Mallín's reaction. Considering that Enrico Mallín had been doing business with Howell Petroleum for years, and had actually stayed with the old man on St. Charles Avenue, he had naturally presumed that Mallín had been treated, at least once, to the old man's standard "Oh, let me tell you about that three-star sonofabitch Hor-gay Goool-yermo Frah-day" diatribe, and that good manners, not ignorance, were the reason why the subject of his father had not come up.

Is that yet another example of the old man's "The Bottom Line Is All That Matters" philosophy? He didn't want to lose Mallín as a source of revenue. And that might have happened if Mallín— or Mallín's father—had known about the bad blood between the old man and my father.

"He lives here," Clete said. "I was born here. Until just now, I thought you knew."

"No, I didn't," Mallín said. "He lives here? He's an Argentine?"

"A retired Army officer," he said.

"But you're an American," Pamela blurted.

"My mother died when I was very young," Clete said. "I was raised by my grandfather and my aunt and uncle in the States."

"I see," Mallín said.

"If you were born here," the Virgin Princess announced, "and if your father is an Argentinean, then you're an Argentinean." She seemed pleased.

"No. I'm an American citizen."

"No, you're not," the Virgin Princess insisted.

"I can't imagine . . ." Mallín said. "How is it . . . ?"

"I've never met my father," Clete said.

"Henry, this is really none of our business," Pamela said.

"Who is your father?" Mallín asked, ignoring her. "You say he's a retired Army officer? What's his name?"

"Jorge Guillermo Frade," Clete said, hearing his grandfather's acidic pronunciation as he spoke. "El Coronel Jorge Guillermo Frade."

"My God, he's a friend of mine!" Mallín exclaimed. "And, Cletus, if you don't know this, he is not just 'a retired Army officer.' He's one of the most prominent men in the country."

"So I've been told," Clete said.

"You've never met him?" Pamela asked.

"There is bad blood between my grandfather and my father."

"How sad," Pamela said. "But—I couldn't help but over-hearing—you're going to meet him tomorrow?"

"Yes, I am."

"He's Alicia Valdez's uncle," the Virgin Princess said. "She introduced me to him on Independence Day. At the reception at the officers' club."

"Who?" Pamela asked.

"Alicia," the Virgin Princess said.

"I really wish I had known all this," Mallín said. "I can't imagine what your father is thinking. You here, in my home, and . . ."

"If I have in any way embarrassed you, I'm sorry," Clete said. "But I . . . I simply presumed you knew."

"You haven't embarrassed us," the Virgin Princess said, walking across the room to him and touching his arm. "Has he, Mother?"

"Of course he hasn't," Pamela said. "It was a simple misun-derstanding."

"When I see my father tomorrow, I will make sure he under-stands that you didn't know my relationship to him," Clete said.

"Funny," the Virgin Princess said, rubbing his arm and looking up into his eyes, "you don't look like an Argentinean."

Clete averted his eyes, which meant that they fell on the V of her dress, and into the valley between her breasts.

She's no older than Beth. And her feelings for you are as innocent as Beth's. Remember that.

"But you are, you know," the Virgin Princess went on, her fingers still on his arm. "An Argentinean. It was a question in a political science examination."

"No, I'm not, Princess," Clete said firmly.

Pamela laughed.

"Princess? Why do you call her 'Princess'?" Pamela asked, smiling.

"Yes, why do you?" the Virgin Princess asked.

"Princesses are beautiful young girls, adored by their parents, who live in a castle like this one, waiting for their knight in shining armor to ride up on his horse," Clete said.

"I don't think I like the 'young girl' part. And why should my knight have to wear shining armor? Why not cowboy boots?"

"Dorotea, you're embarrassing Clete," Pamela protested.

"Am I embarrassing you, Clete?"

"Yes, you are."

"You can go to hell," the Virgin Princess said.

"Ignore her, Clete," Pamela said, one adult to another. "All of her friends think it's chic, and makes them seem mature, to swear like sailors."

[THREE]
Office of the Managing Director
Sociedad Mercantil de Importación de Productos
Petrolíferos
21st Floor, Edificio Kavanagh
Calle Florida 1065
Buenos Aires, Argentina
1030 27 November 1942

"Excuse me, Señor Mallín," his secretary said, walking to his desk and extending a visiting card to him. "This gentleman says it is quite important that he see you."

Mallín took the card and looked at it.

Alejandro Bernardo Martín

Teniente Coronel
Ministerio de Defense

Goddamn it! I knew something like this was going to happen!
"Ask him to come in, please," he said.

Martín, in a tweed jacket and gray flannel trousers, came into the office smiling and held his hand out.

"I very much appreciate your time, Señor Mallín," he said. "I know that you're a very busy man."

"I always have time for the Ministry of Defense, mi Coronel," Mallín said, shaking his hand. "May I offer you a coffee?"

"If it would not be an imposition?"

"Not at all."

Martín walked to the window.

"What a splendid view."

"It may not be modest of me to say so, mi Coronel—but I say this as a tenant, not as the owner—I think it is the best view in all Buenos Aires."

Martín waited until the coffee had been served and Mallín's secretary had left them alone. Then he reached in his pocket, took the leather folder which held his Internal Security credentials, and extended it to Mallín.

Internal Security. Goddamn it, now what?

"I see," Mallín said. "And how may I assist Internal Security?"

Martín noted the signs of nervousness in Mallín's eyes and body language.

I wonder why? There's nothing in the files to suggest that he's anything but what he purports to be, a well-educated, wealthy, successful importer of petroleum.

Martín had taken another look at Mallín's dossier just before driving to the Kavanagh Building: He had done his active military service honorably, but without distinction, and had no more to do with the military afterward than the law required. He was friendly, but not intimate, with members of the major political factions—a skillful tightrope walker. His only recorded violation of the laws of God and/or the Republic of Argentina—aside from an extraordinary number of citations for illegal parking—was to maintain one Maria-Teresa Alberghoni, twenty-one, in Apartment 4D at 2910 Avenue Canning in Palermo. And Martín would have been surprised if Mallín did not maintain a Mina.

"Let me begin by saying that the BIS does not really eat babies for breakfast, Señor Mallín, and there is no Tower of London here in Buenos Aires where we chop heads off."

"Well, I'm glad to hear that."

"But we do try to keep an eye on things, find answers to questions which interest us."

"Of course."

"We are interested, frankly, in your houseguest, Señor—or should I say 'Mister'?—Cletus Howell Frade. Could you tell me what he's doing here?"

Be very careful, Enrico. This could be a very dangerous conversation.

"You are aware, mi Coronel, that SMIPP, in addition to other associations, of course, represents the interests of Howell Petroleum (Venezuela) in Argentina?"

Martín nodded.

"Howell Petroleum (Venezuela) is a subsidiary of Howell Petroleum, which has its offices in New Orleans, Louisiana. Señor Howell, my houseguest, is the grandson of Cletus Howell, the owner. When I was in the United States, I was a guest in his house . . ."

He left the rest of the sentence unspoken. Martín would certainly understand reciprocal hospitality. A nod of Martín's head suggested that he did.

"As to what he's doing here: The United States government has somehow concluded that certain petroleum products—Howell Petroleum Products—are being illegally diverted. To the Germans or the Italians, presumably. They are of course sold to us with the understanding that they will be consumed in Argentina and not transshipped anywhere."

"And is that happening? Are there products being transshipped?"

"Not to my knowledge. For one thing, it would be quite difficult. The Americans know what we consumed before the war, and they have been unwilling to raise the amount of product shipped to us, although our demand has risen. If I wanted to, I would not be able to divert any product. In fact, my clients are increasingly unhappy that they can't get what they need. Cutting that amount would be simply impossible, since the government knows to the last liter how much product I receive."

"Nevertheless, the American government has the idea that— what was the term you used? 'product'?—is being diverted, and Mr. Frade's presence in Argentina has something to do with that?"

"As he explained it to me, he will verify to the U.S. Embassy that Howell product is in fact entering our supply channels and is not being diverted."

"Well, that explains his presence here, doesn't it?" Martín said. "Meanwhile, I have a couple of other questions in my mind that probably fall into the category of personal curiosity, rather than official queries."

"I don't quite understand."

"I was wondering how a young man, a man his age, in apparently good health, could avoid military service in the United States. In wartime, that's seems a little odd."

"As I understand it, mi Coronel, he was called up for training as a pilot, and then was physically disqualified and discharged."

"That happened to a cousin of mine when my class was called," Martín said. "He served three weeks."

"I think he finds it rather embarrassing," Mallín said. "That it somehow makes him less a man."

"It will also keep him from getting killed. In time, he will probably decide he was lucky."

"When my class was called up," Mallín said, "I didn't want to go. I was in love. But on the other hand, I was afraid that I would not pass the physical examination."

"Precisely," Martín said, smiling. "And my last question, which obviously has nothing to do with internal security, is why Mister Frade is staying with you, and not with his father."

I knew he'd come to that. Of course that would interest BIS. Anything to do with Frade interests them, and now a son that nobody's ever heard of suddenly shows up, and instead of staying with his father or another member of the family, he stays with me. As if he doesn't want it known, or el Coronel Frade doesn't

want it known, that there is a son, or that he's here. I would be
suspicious of that myself.

"Well, for one thing, el Coronel Frade wasn't in town when young Frade arrived," Mallín said, hoping he sounded more at ease than he felt. "He was at his estancia, I believe. And for another, I welcomed the opportunity to repay the hospitality of Mr. Howell."

"I have heard—what, 'gossip'?—that there is some problem between father and son. Would you feel awkward talking about that?"

"I don't know anything about that," Mallín said. "I would suspect that it is, as you suggested, simply gossip. I do know that young Frade and his father are having lunch today."

"Oh, really?"

"At the Alvear Palace, if that's of interest to you."

"Only in that it puts the gossip to rest," Martín said. He stood up. "I won't take any more of your time, Señor Mallín. Thank you very much for seeing me."

"It was my pleasure, mi Coronel," Mallín said, walking with Martín to the door.

"May I make a suggestion, Señor Mallín?"

"Of course."

"I would suggest that you not mention to Mr. Frade, or his father, that we had this little chat. Internal Security has an unfortunate—and as far as I am concerned, unjustified—reputation. You have more than satisfactorily answered both my official queries and my personal curiosity. I can see no point in causing either of the gentlemen in question undue concern. Can you?"

"I take your point, mi Coronel."

"Thank you again," Martín said, smiled, shook Mallín's hand, and walked out of the office.

Enrico Mallín walked to the window overlooking the Río de la Plata and rested his forehead on the cool glass.

He went over the entire conversation in his mind. He could think of nothing he said that was either untrue or could cause difficulty. But that did not alter the underlying unpleasant truth, which was that Internal Security was interested in his houseguest, and by association, in him.

Everybody knows that el Coronel Jorge Guillermo Frade is deeply involved with the Grupo de Oficiales Unidos. Will Internal Security now suspect that because I am close enough to Frade to entertain his son in my home, I am also closely connected with Grupo de Oficiales Unidos?

God, if I had known who his father was, I wouldn't have had him at the house for so much as a cocktail!

Goddamn the old man for not telling me who his grandson is!

That could have been innocent, of course. A natural reluctance to keep intimate family business private. But Clete should have said something; after all, he was a guest in my house! He should have known—of course he knew—that we would be interested to know who his father is. He didn't tell us until he had to! Why?

And I don't like the way he looks at Dorotea, either. Or the way she looks at him. How dare he call her "Princess"?

Well, he'll be gone tomorrow, or the day after, and after that, I will simply, tactfully, increase the distance between us.

IX

[ONE]
Edificio Kavanagh
Calle Florida 1065
Buenos Aires, Argentina
1105 27 November 1942

El Teniente Coronel Martín found a pay telephone in a cigar-and-candy kiosk around the corner from the Edificio Kavanagh and called his office.

El Comandante Carlos Habanzo answered. It was not a Comandante's function to answer the phone; there were enlisted men and junior officers to do that. But in this case Martín decided to say nothing. For one thing, he was aware that he had been finding fault with just about everything Habanzo was doing; and for another, he wanted to speak to him.

"Habanzo, I need two good men—well-dressed, who won't look like whores in church—to be in the lobby of the Alvear Palace, with cameras, from eleven-thirty. They are to surveil a meeting between el Coronel Jorge Guillermo . . ."

"Mi Coronel, I regret that we have no one available at the moment."

"What do you mean, no one's available?"

"Mi Coronel, you reviewed and approved the assignment list this morning. I can, of course, call two men back from the pistol range, but there is no way they can reach the Alvear Palace by eleven-thirty."

"Comandante Habanzo, are you wearing a clean shirt?"

"Sí, mi Coronel."

"The lobby of the Alvear Palace Hotel from eleven-thirty, Habanzo. Do not say hello to me. We'll dispense with photography."

"Sí, mi Coronel. Mi Coronel, I could bring a camera."

"That won't be necessary. Just be there. You will be able to recognize young Frade?"

"Of course, mi Coronel."

[TWO]
1728 Avenida Coronel Díaz
Palermo, Buenos Aires
0945 27 November 1942

El Coronel Jorge Guillermo Frade was already awake and out of
bed, bathed, shaved, and sitting, dressed in a summer-weight red
silk dressing robe, in an armchair reading yesterday's *La Nación**
when Antonio, his butler, wheeled in the breakfast cart.

"Buenos días, mi Coronel."

"I was wondering what happened to you," Frade said. He
dropped the newspaper on the floor, walked to the cart, and lifted
silver covers from several dishes on it.

"It is quarter to ten, mi Coronel," Antonio said, which was
both an announcement of the time and a statement that breakfast
was being served at the time it was supposed to be served.

Frade looked at his watch.

"So it is," he said. "I think melon and ham, Antonio, and a
couple of eggs. Presuming they are neither raw nor hard-boiled."

"Four minutes exactly, mi Coronel," Antonio said. "I boiled
them myself."

"That's what I was afraid of," Frade said.

Antonio began moving items from the breakfast cart to a table,
as Frade picked up a chair and carried it to the table. He sat down
and watched as Antonio poured orange juice and then coffee, and
then began to cut the meat from a cantaloupe.

Frade picked up the orange juice.

"And what are we going to wear today, mi Coronel?"

"A suit. I have an important lunch."

"The double-breasted gray?"

"That should do," Frade said. "With one of the new shirts."

"Sí, mi Coronel."

"And for a tie?"

"Lay several out," Frade said.

"Sí, mi Coronel. And the black wing tips?"

Frade nodded.

"The Señora asks that you call when you have time," Antonio
said. "At her home."

"Here? She's in town?"

---

*The most conservative of Buenos Aires' daily newspapers.

"Sí, mi Coronel."

"The Señora will have to wait. If she calls again, please tell her I will try to call her this afternoon. And while you're on the phone, call the Centro Naval* and tell them I may require my table for luncheon."

"For how many guests, mi Coronel?"

"One."

"Sí, mi Coronel," Antonio said as he picked up a silver coffeepot and refilled el Coronel's cup. "You will require the car when, mi Coronel?"

"My appointment is for twelve, at the Alvear Palace."

"Eleven-thirty, mi Coronel?"

"A little earlier, I think. I don't want to be late."

"Sí, mi Coronel."

At ten forty-five, when el Coronel descended the wide marble staircase to the entrance foyer and looked out the window, his car was not standing before the door.

He turned and went down a corridor into the kitchen. Antonio was sitting at the kitchen table with the housekeeper and one of the maids, drinking coffee.

"Mi Coronel, you said eleven-thirty," he said with reproof in his voice, as he stood up.

"It is not a problem," Frade said, walked past him, and passed through a door leading to the basement garage.

Enrico was there, his suit jacket off, his shirt sleeves rolled up, polishing the hood of the Buick station wagon. He was carrying a .45 automatic in a shoulder holster.

"Antonio said eleven-thirty, mi Coronel," he said.

"Better to be early than late," Frade said.

"Where are we going, mi Coronel?"

"We are not going anywhere. I will not need you this morning, Enrico."

"¿Mi Coronel?"

"I am going to the Alvear Plaza, and then to the Centro Naval. And I wish to be alone."

Enrico was visibly unhappy with this announcement.

"Mi Coronel . . ."

"Are the keys in the Horche?"

"Sí, mi Coronel. Mi Coronel, I can wait in the car."

---

*Literally, Navy Center. An officer's club serving both services on Calle Florida.

"Open the doors like a good fellow, Enrico," Frade said, and then added, "Enrico, I will be all right."

Enrico expressed his displeasure with Frade by showing him a stony face as he opened the door to the Horche, then went to open the garage doors. Frade started the engine, let it warm a moment, and then drove out of the garage and headed downtown.

He decided to leave the Horche at his sister's house on Avenue Alvear. It was only two squares from the hotel, the walk would do him good, and inside her tall fence *(there is no good reason I can't close the gates myself)* it would be safe from both the idiot drivers on the street and the greasy hands of the curious. And with just a little bit of luck, she wouldn't even know it was there.

The Horche was important to him. He truly believed that he indulged himself in few personal luxuries; and if he was extraordinarily sensitive about his 1940 Horche droptop touring sedan, so be it. In his judgment, the Horche was the finest automobile in the world. Certainly better than the Cadillac or the Mercedes-Benz or the Rolls-Royce or the Packard, and far superior to every lesser car he had ever driven. His was one of the very last Horches to leave the factory, before the factory started to make trucks or cannon or whatever for Hitler's military.

It was built like a battleship would be built if Swiss watchmakers built warships. It not only handled beautifully and was powered by a smooth, very strong engine, but was beautifully furnished inside, with fine leather seats and gnarled walnut on both the dashboard and in the passenger compartment. With reasonable care, it would last not only through the war—however long that lasted—but indefinitely thereafter. He personally supervised its care, and often did the work himself.

The problem was little things. If there was a fender-bender, he had absolutely no way to replace a bumper, a headlight ring, or one of the clever little lights that sat on the fenders and indicated (controlled by a switch on the dash) which way the driver intended to turn. There were simply no parts available in Buenos Aires.

Therefore, it seemed entirely understandable to him that he never permitted anyone to drive it but himself, and on rare, absolutely unavoidable occasions, Enrico. First of all, he was as good a driver as he knew—fast but skillful, and thus safe. Secondly, no one else could be expected to share his full appreciation of the mechanical and aesthetic superiority of the Horche, and therefore no one else could be expected to handle the car with the respect it deserved. He had no intention of entrusting the Horche to one of the Alvear Palace Hotel's bellmen to park.

Leaving it at his sister's house seemed a perfectly satisfactory solution to the problem of driving the Horche downtown to meet Cletus.

Luck was not with him. Two of Beatrice's servants were adjusting cobblestones in the drive, and it wasn't until too late that he saw Beatrice herself, in a mourning-black dress, standing there watching. Or believing she was supervising.

Her face lit up when she saw him; her eyes were at once bright and vacant.

Mother of Christ, she's still taking those pills! What the hell is the matter with her husband?

"Jorge, how nice!" she said as he stepped out of the Horche.

He walked to her and she raised her cheek to be kissed.

"I didn't expect to see you," he said. "All I wanted to do was use your drive to park the car."

"The cobblestones are washing loose," Beatrice said, pointing. "Ricardo thinks that water is coming under the drive out of the drainpipes from the roof."

One of the workmen, hearing his name, looked up and smiled at Frade.

"Buenos días, mi Coronel."

"Buenos días," Frade said. "Beatrice, you'll have to excuse me. I have a business appointment at noon." She looked at him with empty eyes and a smile. "At the Alvear," he added, nodding down Avenue Alvear.

Beatrice put a hand to her bosom and lifted a lapel watch.

Damn, she has a watch. I'm surprised she knows what day of the week it is, but she has a watch.

"It's eleven-fifteen," Beatrice announced. "You have forty-five minutes. It will take you two minutes to walk to the Alvear. We have time for a coffee."

"It's an important meeting. I don't want to be late."

"You have time. And I have so much to tell you about the arrangements."

She took his arm and led him into the house, to the sitting room.

"Ambassador von Lutzenberger has been to see Humberto—"

"I know," Frade interrupted her. "He called me first, and I suggested he call Humberto."

Alberto came into the library.

"We will have two coffees, please, Alberto. And if there are any candied orange slices . . . el Coronel likes candied orange slices; he has since we were children."

"Sí, Señora," Alberto said, and left.

I don't like candied orange slices. I haven't liked them since I was fourteen or fifteen. Good God!

"Ambassador von Lutzenberger told Humberto that Jorge is to be decorated, posthumously, by the German government," Beatrice said.

"He mentioned that to me."

"And—I thought it would be nice, I'm trying to work it out with Monsignor Kelly—do you know him?"

Frade shook his head no.

"Very nice man. He handles important ceremonies for the Archbishop."

"I haven't had the pleasure."

"Well, I thought it would be nice to have that ceremony—they pin the decoration to the flag, which will be covering the casket—outside Our Lady of Pilar. On the plaza, *before* the Archbishop celebrates the high requiem mass. Or do you think it would be better to do it after the mass, and before we take the casket to Recoleta?"

Has it occurred to you, my poor darling, that you are talking about a decoration to be awarded in the name of a mass murderer? For political reasons, not because poor Jorge did anything valorous?

"If you want my opinion, Beatrice, I would say that sort of decision would best be left to the Monsignor. You said his name was Kelly?"

"Yes. Monsignor Kelly. A fine and holy man."

"Why don't you tell him to do what he thinks is best?"

"You're right, of course," she said. "Have I told you about the reception?"

"No. You haven't."

"I was wondering . . . We'll have it here, of course. It was Jorge's home. Getting people in and out of their cars will be a problem. Especially if it rains. Otherwise, I suppose they could park their cars by Our Lady of Pilar and walk here from Recoleta. But if it rains, that would pose a problem, of course."

"What were you wondering, Beatrice?"

"Mommy's punch bowl. Do you have it here in the city? Or is it at the estancia?"

Mother's punch bowl?

It was enormous. He suddenly remembered that he and Beatrice were whipped as children after filling it with a litter of nearly grown Llewellyn setters.

"I was thinking it would look so nice," Beatrice explained, "filled with flowers, if we put it in the center of the foyer. We could move in one of the tables from the library and put it on that."

"I think it's here," Frade said. "If it's not . . . if it's at San Pedro y San Pablo, I'll have it brought to you."

"Just the punch bowl. Not the cups."

"Just the punch bowl."

"You are always so kind to me, Jorge. I don't know what I'd do without you."

"Don't be silly, Beatrice."

Alberto appeared with the coffee on a silver tray, a *cortado* for his mistress, and a *café doble* for Frade.

"Everything for the invitations is ready, except the date. We won't know the date, of course, until the *General Belgrano* arrives. Humberto spoke with someone at the shipping company . . ."

"L.M.A.E.," Frade said without thinking—Líneas Marítimas de Argentina y Europa.

"Yes," Beatrice said, ever so genteelly letting him know she didn't like the interruption. "L.M.A.E. The *General Belgrano* sailed November eighth, so it's due here around the first of the month. In a week or so. The casket is to be brought here. Humberto wanted to put it in the library, but I said there will be so many people that we'll have to put it in the foyer, to keep the traffic moving, so to speak. Don't you agree?"

If I don't escape from here in the next thirty seconds, I am going insane!

"Yes, Beatrice, I agree."

He looked at his watch.

"Beatrice, I must go."

"You haven't finished your coffee."

"I drink too much coffee. It's bad for my nerves. I can't sleep."

"Those Brazilian cigars of yours are what keeps you awake,"

Beatrice proclaimed. "I read an article . . ."

"Beatrice, I'll have the punch bowl sent over to you as soon as I can; within the next several days."

"And there's one more thing," Beatrice said.

"Yes?"

"There's nobody in your house but you, so I wondered if it would be a terrible inconvenience for you to put up Captain von Wachtstein for a while, at least until the funeral is over."

"Captain who?"

"Captain Hans-Peter von Wachtstein. He is the officer bringing Jorge home. Ambassador von Lutzenberger said that he comes from a fine Pomeranian family; and that his father is a Major General. I don't think he would be comfortable here, Jorge, and we certainly can't put him into a hotel."

In that case, let the goddamned German ambassador take care of him!

"Certainly, Beatrice. I'll tell Señora Pellano to set up an apartment for him in Uncle Guillermo's."

"The Guest House?" she asked, surprise and hurt in her voice. "Not in your house?"

Beatrice, for the love of God!

"I think he would be more comfortable in the Guest House. My house will probably be full of senior officers."

"Yes, of course it will," she replied, after considering that. "The Guest House will be better, won't it, for the Captain?"

"I think so. I will arrange for an officer of suitable rank to be with him."

"Muy bueno," Beatrice said, then changed the subject: "I have the proofs, or whatever they're called, of the invitations. Would you like to see them?"

"I'd love to, Beatrice, but I have to go."

He kissed her and fled. She called his name as he was passing through the front door, but he pretended he didn't hear. He walked quickly down the Avenue Alvear toward the Alvear Palace Hotel.

El Coronel Jorge Guillermo Frade did not believe in drinking during the day. A glass or two of wine with lunch was not drinking, of course, and a glass or two of beer in the afternoon never hurt anyone; but he often said that he learned as a young officer that drinking spirits during the day caused nothing but trouble.

Right now, after that pathetic scene with Beatrice, he wanted a drink, a good stiff drink, very badly. He told himself that he would nobly resist that temptation, of course. He didn't want his son to smell alcohol on his breath at their first meeting and get the wrong idea.

As he waited for two women to negotiate the revolving door to the lobby of the Alvear Palace, he glanced at his watch. It was eleven forty-five—specifically, 11:46:40.

He looked around the lobby, in case Cletus might have arrived early.

No. He will arrive late. Stylishly late. Five or ten minutes late. I have plenty of time for a drink. There is no reason at all why I should not have a quick one.

I would not be at all surprised if Beatrice's emotional difficulties are contagious. I pity poor Humberto.

He walked up to the bar. It was crowded.

I wonder what work these people do that allows them to come in here at noon and drink whiskey.

He found an empty stool near the end of the bar and slipped onto it. One of the bartenders came to him immediately.

"¿Mi Coronel?"

The man sitting to his right, on the last stool of the bar, had a bottle of Jack Daniel's American whiskey sitting in front of him.

If you must take a drink for medicinal reasons in the middle of the day, you might as well do it right. Bourbon whiskey was not at all subtle. When you drink American bourbon whiskey, you know instantly you are drinking.

El Coronel Jorge Guillermo Frade pointed at the bottle of American bourbon whiskey, then held up two fingers, meaning a double. He pointed at the ice bucket sitting in front of the man next to him and shook his index finger. No ice. He pointed to the water pitcher, then to a small glass, signaling he wanted water on the side.

"Sí, mi Coronel," the bartender said, smiling, and made the drink.

He picked up the glass of bourbon and took a healthy swallow. He felt a burning sensation in his mouth and then in his throat. Warmth began to spread in his stomach.

Precisely what I needed. Good decision, the American bourbon.

He set the glass down and almost immediately picked it up and took another swallow.

It gave him the same reaction, except the burning sensation didn't seem as harsh or as enduring.

I will ask the barman for a slice of lemon, and eat it, pulp and rind, just before I go upstairs. I don't want Cletus imagining the reek of his father's alcohol fumes when he recalls the first time in his adult life he ever met him.

He sensed the attention of the gentleman sitting beside him, and turned to glower at him. It was no one's business but his own if he wanted to take a couple of quick swallows of American bourbon whiskey.

"Excuse me, Sir," the man asked in Spanish. "But are you Colonel Frade?"

"Sí, Señor. Yo soy el Coronel Frade," Frade said, the words coming out before he could stop them.

"My name is Frade too," Clete said.

"I know full well what your name is," Frade snapped. He was horrified at the sound of his own words, but they just kept coming. "You were supposed to meet me in the lobby at noon."

Frade saw anger form in Clete's eyes, in the tightening of his lips, in a faint reddening of his cheeks.

God, what have I done?

Then Clete's lips loosened, and turned into a smile.

"I see that I'm not the only one who needed a little liquid courage for the great confrontation."

"Is that how you view it, as a 'great confrontation'?"

"Isn't that what it is?"

The barman appeared, asking with the inclination of his head whether Clete wanted another drink. Clete pushed his empty glass across the bar to him.

"Do you customarily drink whiskey at the noon hour?" Frade asked, and was again horrified at the sound of his words.

What in God's name is wrong with me?

"Only when about to confront a great confrontation," Clete said. "What about you?"

God, he's insolent! No one talks to me like that! Now watch what you say!

"Actually," Frade said, "it's not you. I just had an unpleasant *confrontation* with my sister. Your aunt Beatrice."

"I didn't know I had an Aunt Beatrice," Clete said quietly, and then asked flippantly, "And Aunt Beatrice drove you to drink whiskey at the noon hour?"

I'd like to slap his face! I'd like to punch him square in the nose! How dare he talk in that manner about Beatrice?

And again the words came out of control.

"She's ill, Cletus. Emotionally disturbed," Frade heard himself say. "She's on something, God only knows what, that her psychiatrist prescribed."

"I'm sorry," Clete said. "I didn't know . . ."

"You had no way of knowing. You didn't even know she exists," Frade said.

"No, Sir, I didn't."

"Beatrice lost her son, her only son, your cousin Jorge," Frade heard himself saying.

"I'm sorry," Clete said.

"He was killed at Stalingrad. Beatrice has . . . been disturbed since."

I had a cousin in the German Army? Clete thought. *Jesus H. Christ! The Old Man was right. They're all Nazis down here!*

"Stalingrad? What was he doing at Stalingrad?"

"He was assigned as an observer," Frade said. "He was not supposed to be at Stalingrad, much less involved in anything that would place him in danger. He gave me his word to that effect before I agreed to his assignment."

Well, there were for sure no Argentine "observers" on Guadalcanal. What did he say? "Before I agreed to his assignment"?

"Before you agreed to his assignment?"

Frade met his son's eyes.

"I have a certain influence within the Argentinean Army," he said. "Jorge would not have been given that assignment without my approval."

"And now you're blaming yourself because he was killed?"

"Obviously, to a certain degree, I feel responsible."

"What was he? What rank?"

"A captain."

"People get killed in wars. If he didn't know that, he shouldn't have been a captain."

Frade looked at Clete, thinking: *That's damned cold-blooded. When I told myself the same thing, I was ashamed of myself.*

"How was he killed?"

"As I understand it, he was flying a Storch on a reconnaissance mission, and was shot down."

He was a pilot? Clete thought.

"He was flying a what?"

"A Fieseler Storch. A small, high-wing, two-place observation airplane," Frade explained. "Something like the Piper Cub, except larger and more powerful."

Clete shook his head, signifying he had never heard of the Storch.

"What ever happened to your plans, Cletus, to become a pilot? A Marine pilot?"

How the hell did he hear about that?

Clete looked at his father. For the first time, their eyes met.

I don't want to lie to this man.

"I was discharged about three weeks ago," Clete said. "They found a heart murmur. You can't be a Marine Aviator with a heart murmur."

"They discovered it when you were in training?"

Clete met his father's eyes and saw genuine concern in them. And realized that he could not lie to him.

"No."

"You saw active service, then?" his father asked.

"They discovered the heart condition when I came back from the Pacific. From Guadalcanal."

"You flew at Guadalcanal?"

"Yes. And I was at Midway, too."

"I didn't know that," Frade said. "We read about Midway and Guadalcanal in the newspapers, of course. And there have been newsreels in the cinema."

The father saw the newsreels again in his mind's eye. American fighter planes, and their young pilots, rising into the sky from a jungle airstrip.

Did I see Cletus? Was he one of those tired-looking young men?

He was one of them, whether or not I saw him. And that explains why he can be so cold-blooded about Jorge. He is a soldier. He has the right to think that way, and say what he thinks.

"What about your heart? A murmur, you said?"

"Nothing serious," Clete said. "It just disqualified me from flying for the Marines. Thank you for your service, and don't let the doorknob hit you in the ass on your way out."

He's bitter. That's understandable.

"Otherwise you weren't injured?"

"I got dinged a couple of times. Nothing serious."

Spoken like an officer. And why not? The blood of Pueyrredón runs in his veins.

"Would it be impolite of me to ask what you are doing in Argentina?"

Clete met his father's eyes. "No. Why should it be? I'm working for my grandfather . . ."

"And how is Mr. Howell? Well, I hope?"

"Yes, he is, thank you," Clete said. *The Old Man would shit a brick if he knew the two of us are sitting here like this.*

"And your uncle James and your aunt Martha? They are well, I trust?"

"Uncle Jim died when I was in the Pacific. A heart attack."

"I am so sorry," Frade said.

He sounds as if he means that.

"And my aunt Martha is well, thank you."

Frade nodded. "You say you are working for your grandfather?"

"The U.S. government seems to think that somebody down here is diverting Howell petroleum products to the Germans. I was sent down to make sure they aren't."

"I can't believe Enrico Mallín would be involved in that kind of thing," Frade said. "Not only is he an honorable man, but I'm sure his sympathies lie with the English and the Americans in this war."

Well, I guess I am a pretty good liar, after all. He swallowed that hook, line, and sinker. And where do your sympathies lie, Dad?

"I don't think he is either," Clete said. "But the deal the Old Man worked out with the government meant sending me down here to make sure he isn't."

"I am glad you are here," Frade said. "To finally meet you."

"Yeah, me too," Clete said.

"Perhaps there will be an opportunity for us to know one another," Frade said.

"Yeah," Clete said. "Maybe there will be."

"But the immediate problem before us is lunch," Frade said. He pushed his glass of bourbon away from him. "I have had enough whiskey."

He beckoned, rather imperiously, for the bartender to bring the bill. When it came, he scrawled his name across it.

"Gracias, mi Colonel," the barman said.

"The Centro Naval—the Navy Officers' Club—is not very far from here. They usually serve a very nice lunch," Frade said. "How does that sound, Cletus?"

"That sounds fine."

"Well, then, I suggest we go," Frade said.

Clete slid off the barstool and followed his father up the circular staircase to the lobby. They were halfway across the lobby when his father suddenly veered to the right, toward the concierge's desk.

It looks like he's chasing that guy.

Frade caught up with a man who pretended, not too successfully, to be both delighted and surprised to see him. They shook hands, and then Frade propelled him across the lobby to where Clete stood.

"Coronel, I want you to meet my son. Cletus, this is Teniente Coronel Martín, of the Internal Security Service."

Teniente Coronel Martín could not conceal his discomfort.

"How do you do?" he said in English.

"A sus órdenes, mi Coronel," Clete replied.

"Welcome to Argentina," Martín said, still in English.

"Thank you," Clete said, switching to English.

There was a long, awkward silence.

"Well, it was very nice to make your acquaintance, Mr. Frade," Martín said. "And to see you, mi Coronel."

Frade nodded coldly but didn't speak.

Martín walked out of the lobby into the driveway.

"Who was that?" Clete asked.

"An officer of our intelligence service," Frade said. "The Bureau of Internal Security. It was from him that I learned you were here."

"Oh?"

"He was naturally curious why you were staying with Señor Mallín and not me."

"I'm surprised he knew about me at all," Clete said.

"I thought it a bit odd myself," Frade said. "Unless, of course, you're not here for the reason you gave me."

"I don't know what you mean," Clete said. "I'm here because my grandfather needed someone down here, and I speak Spanish and needed a job."

He knows I'm lying. Whether because I'm not a very good liar, or because he's put two and two together. Whatever else he is, this man, my father, is no fool.

The question is, where does that leave us?

"You speak Spanish very well," his father said, dropping the subject. "Shall we go?"

Frade led Clete through the revolving door to the entrance driveway before he remembered where the Horche was. Taking

Cletus there would be unwise. Beatrice would almost certainly see him.

"I have the car parked a block or so away," Frade said.

"All right."

"Why don't you just wait in front for me."

"I don't mind walking."

"Please wait for me in front," Frade said. It was unquestionably an order.

"All right," Clete said.

Clete watched his father march down Avenue Alvear. Then nature called. He went back into the hotel and down the stairs again to the men's room. An attendant patiently waited for him to relieve his bladder, then stood by with soap, a towel, a comb, cologne, and an open hand.

When Clete reached the entranceway again, his father was already there, standing impatiently by the open door of a magnificent, gleaming, four-door convertible. A Horche, according to the grille.

What the hell is a Horche?

"I wondered what happened to you," Frade said.

"That's one hell of a car," Clete said.

"I rather like it myself," Frade said. And then he heard himself say, as he extended the keys to his son, "Would you like to drive?"

[THREE]
Centro Naval
Avenida Florida y Avenida Córdoba
Buenos Aires
1325 27 November 1942

"I don't usually take spirits at lunch," el Coronel Jorge Guillermo Frade announced solemnly as he waved Clete into a leather-upholstered chair in the dark paneled bar of the Officers' Club, "but this is an occasion, no? Our 'great confrontation'?"

He turned to the white-jacketed waiter who had trailed them from the door. "Dos Jack Daniel's, dobles, por favor, Luis."

Clete looked around the room. He saw no women. Most of the men were in civilian clothing, but something about them suggested they were officers. *Not officers,* he corrected himself,

brass. Hardly anybody in here is my age. Lieutenants and cap-
tains not welcome, and please keep off the grass on your way
out.

He looked at his father. His father was making a visual sweep
of the room. He gave a curt nod of recognition to a few men,
smiled faintly at others, but at two in particular he smiled widely
and nodded his head as if in approval.

As soon as the whiskey was delivered, while the waiter was
carrying out the little routine of overflowing the silver shot glass
on a handle, a procession of brass making their manners came to
the table.

The introductions followed the same pattern:

"Coronel, I have the honor to present my son, Cletus, late
Teniente of the air service of the U.S. Marine Corps, who has
been medically retired after service in the Pacific at Guadalcanal.
He is here on business, which I hope will take a long time to
complete."

Like blowing up a neutral ship in your river.

Once, his father rose to his feet, and Clete followed him.

"Mi General," his father said, "I have the honor to present
my son, Cletus, late Teniente of the air service of the U.S. Marine
Corps, who has been medically retired after service in the Pacific
at Guadalcanal. He is here on a visit. Cletus, I had the honor to
succeed el General Sussman as Colonel Commanding the Hus-
sares de Pueyrredón."

"A sus órdenes, mi General," Clete said.

The introduction seemed to both please and surprise the General.

"You served at Guadalcanal, Teniente?"

"Sí, mi General."

General Sussman examined him closely, and nodded approvingly.

"I am very happy to make your acquaintance," he said in
somewhat awkward English. "Welcome to Argentina."

I don't think you would say that if you knew why I am here,
General.

"Gracias, mi General."

Frade waited until the General was out of earshot, then announced, "Coronel Sahovaler—the fat, bald one—succeeded me
at the regiment. I should have introduced him that way."

Dear old Dad, Clete realized, *is half in the bag. And if he is,*
you almost certainly are. So watch yourself.

That triggered another thought, a somewhat alarming one: *His only reaction when he realized I was lying to him was to change the subject, and then let me drive that car of his. Is it possible that he intends to get me drunk to see what he can worm out of me? Of course it's possible. It's even likely.*

Without asking, the bartender delivered another Jack Daniel's *doble* long before either of their glasses was empty.

"I think we should carry these into the dining room and put something into our stomachs," Frade announced somewhat thickly after draining the first drink and picking up the second. "As you may have noticed, the Porteños are very dangerous drivers. One must be in full control of one's faculties to survive."

The booze flows like water—if that's really whiskey he's drinking—and he wants me to think he's drunk. Of course, he's trying to get me drunk enough to confide in him, father-to-son. Well, why are you surprised? The Old Man told you often enough he's a three-star sonofabitch. Well, screw you, Dad. I may be an amateur at this business, but I am not stupid.

"Excuse me?" Clete asked politely, smiling, as he rose to his feet. "The what? Porteños?"

"Natives of Buenos Aires," his father explained. "As opposed to those who come from the country. They drive like madmen. They seem to believe that an automobile has two speeds, on and off."

Clete chuckled.

The headwaiter of the dining room followed them to their table.

"Edmundo," el Coronel ordered, "see if they can find something nice, a Beaujolais perhaps, in my stock."

"Sí, mi Coronel."

And now wine, on top of the whiskey, Clete thought.

"This is an occasion. I have the honor to introduce my son, Cletus, late Teniente of the air service of the Marine Corps of the USA."

And fatherly pride and charm on top of the wine. Mi Coronel, mi Papá, you are a clever sonofabitch, aren't you? What I would like to do is just walk out of here. But I have a feeling I should stick around. Maybe I can learn something from you.

"A great privilege and honor, mi Teniente," the headwaiter said. "El Coronel would prefer some of the French?"

"French or Argentine, Cletus?"

"Argentine, please," Clete said.

"I personally believe our wines are superior—the stock I keep here at the club is from a small vineyard the family has an interest in—but I am of course prejudiced.''

"The Argentine wine I've had so far has been great," Clete said.

"And we are known for our beef, too," Frade said. "Might I suggest a lomo? With papas fritas?''—a filet mignon and french-fried potatoes. "And a tomato and onion salad?''

"Sounds fine, thank you.''

"One should not eat heavily in the middle of the day," Frade declared. "It slows the blood, and thus one's ability to think clearly.''

"Yes, Sir, I agree.''

When a waiter delivered the bourbon, Frade ordered their meal.

"One day," he said, "I hope you will find the time to tell me about Guadalcanal. As a soldier, I am of course interested.''

I guess that's Question Number One.

"Yes, Sir. I'd be happy to.''

"Will there be time? When will you return to the United States?''

And that's Question Number Two.

"I don't know. I'll be here indefinitely.''

"I did not know that," Frade said. "Cletus, certainly you cannot take advantage of Señor Mallín's hospitality indefinitely.''

"No, Sir. I don't intend to. Señor Mallín has found an apartment for me. I'm to move in tomorrow.''

"Where?''

"Posadas 1354 Piso sexto.''

"That's absurd," Frade declared, and belched. "I beg your pardon.''

What the hell does that mean?

"The Guest House is yours," Frade declared with a grand wave of his hand. "For as long as you're here.''

"Excuse me?''

"It will be perfect for you," Frade said. "All it does most of the time is sit there and eat up my money anyway. It's settled.'' He then had a second thought. "Unless, of course, it is not to your liking.''

"Sir, I don't understand what you're talking about.''

"I would ask you to share my home," Frade said, "but I was once your age, and I know how it is with young men. From my own experience.'' El Coronel Frade winked, man-to-man, at his son. "Before I met your mother, of course.''

That's the first mention of my mother.

"It is on the Avenida Libertador, across from the Hipódromo de Argentina, our major horse track," Frade went on. "It was built by my uncle Guillermo. He would be your granduncle Guillermo. He was a horseman. Unfortunately—within the family—we concede that is about all he was, a horseman. Charming fellow. Played six-goal polo in his sixties. When he was younger, he raced thoroughbreds. If he just raced them, which is quite expensive enough, he would have been all right, but he insisted on gambling on them as well, and he was not at all good at that."

A waiter delivered a bottle of wine, and he and Frade went through a ritual of cork-sniffing and sipping.

"That will do," Frade announced. "Well, as they say in America," he went on, picking up his Jack Daniel's *doble* and draining it, "waste not, want not."

He looked at Clete, who took a very small sip of his drink and set the glass down.

I wish I could think of some way to get rid of the rest of this. Except that if I poured it out someplace, there would be another instant refill. Better to just pretend to sip on it.

"When your granduncle Guillermo—who never married, by the way—built the Avenida Libertador house, he put the master suite on the fourth floor. This was so that he could watch the races without having to mingle with the crowds, *he* said. My father, your grandfather, said it was because he could entertain ladies in his bedroom between races. Guillermo was my father's older brother. They were very close."

Now he's giving me this rundown on the family—my granduncle who played the ponies and chased women—to make me feel close and part of things. If you can't trust your own family, who can you trust?

"Shortly after the house was built, your granduncle Guillermo bet more money than he could afford on a horse he owned. It lost, and he found himself in trouble and had to turn to his father for help. He would be, of course, my grandfather and your great-grandfather. Your great-grandfather married María Elena, the second daughter of Edwardo Pueyrredón, which is where you and I, Cletus, get our Pueyrredón blood."

That's nice. What the hell is Pueyrredón blood?

"As my father related the story to me, Grandfather helped Uncle Guillermo out of his financial difficulties. Of course, Uncle Guillermo knew he would, for the honor of the family. He had done so before, and he would do so again. But this time Grandfather extracted a price. He bought Uncle Guillermo's house. Uncle Guillermo used the money to pay his debt of honor. And then Grandfather told him he intended to put it on the market, since he didn't need it, and Guillermo could not afford to buy it back. Thus, it would be necessary for Uncle Guillermo to move out, and to live and work at San Pedro y San Pablo until such time . . .''

"Saints Peter and Paul?" Clete asked, confused.

"Our estancia," Frade explained. "Since you are going to be here for some time, you will of course visit there. It will, of course, be yours one day. Someday, I hope, in the far distant future."

Did I hear that correctly? I have suddenly become heir apparent? Good thought, Pop. The heir apparent will certainly tell you anything about himself you care to know.

"Uncle Guillermo, of course, thought this would be a temporary arrangement, that he would spend a couple of months at San Pedro y San Pablo until things calmed down with Grandpapa. But Grandpapa was annoyed with him (though Grandpapa was not serious about putting the house on the market). When Daddy—your grandfather—married, his father—your great-grandfather—gave the house on Libertador to him as a wedding present. I was born there. When your grandfather died, he passed his home to my father. I live there now—a money sewer on Avenida Coronel Díaz in Palermo. My father did not wish to sell the Libertador house, for even then they were talking of building apartment buildings along Libertador, and the land value was rising, so he turned it into a guest house. I have always felt that Daddy would give the house to me on my marriage, but God called him home before that could happen."

El Coronel Jorge Guillermo Frade stopped, quickly pulled the crisp white handkerchief from his breast pocket, grimaced, and loudly blew his nose. "Disculpeme"—excuse me—he said.

My God, he's crying! Am I supposed to believe that's for real?

"Disculpame," he repeated, dabbing at his eyes with the handkerchief. "Something was stuck in my throat. As I was saying, when your mother came here as my bride, we lived in the Libertador house when we were in the city. To her, living in the house on Avenida Coronel Díaz was like living in a museum. You were not born there, Cletus, but it was from the Libertador house, when your mother's time came, that I took her to the hospital where you were born.''

He blew his nose loudly again, and picked up his wineglass and drained it.

He's really shameless. And good. If I hadn't figured the son-ofabitch out, I'd really start to think he was shedding tears at the memory of my mother.

"After we have our lunch, if they ever get around to serving it," he said, "we will drive over there and you will decide if you would be comfortable there."

[FOUR]

Clete was to remember the drive from the Officers' Club to the house on Libertador for a long time. His father drove. He left the Officers' Club with a squeal of tires on the cobblestones, then raced through town practically flat out, blowing the very loud horn at whoever had the effrontery to place a car in his path, weaving in and out of the traffic—which was six lanes in each direction along Avenida Libertador. Just as Clete noticed the entrance to the racetrack, he made a sudden U-turn, tires squealing again, the huge Horche leaning dangerously, and pulled up before a stone building with an elaborate facade, where he slammed on the brakes.

His father stared at him triumphantly.

"It will be necessary to place the fate of the Horche in the merciful hands of God," he announced. "It takes them forever to open the damned gates, and I have urgent need of the baño''— a toilet.

He left the car and walked quickly to the door of the house, where he lifted a huge brass knocker and banged it half a dozen times. The door was opened by an attractive young woman in a maid's uniform. Frade walked past her, called over his shoulder, "You will please excuse me a moment," and disappeared through a door.

The power of suggestion, Clete thought. *My back teeth are now floating.*

He was alone for perhaps two minutes, looking around the sparsely furnished room—heavy, wooden, leather-upholstered chairs and couches, and a round table with a silver bowl of flowers in the center—and then a short, plump, gray-haired woman in a gray dress appeared. She smiled.

"May I offer you something, Señor? A cup of coffee perhaps?"

"Yo soy Cletus Frade," Clete said. "I am waiting for my father."

"Pardon?"

"I am Cletus Frade, el Coronel Frade's son. I am waiting for him."

The woman clapped her hands in front of her, fingers extended. She did it again and again.

"Madre de Dios," she said; tears ran down her face and she began to sob.

"It would be a kindness, Cletus," his father's voice came softly, from behind him, "if you permitted Señora Pellano to embrace you. She cared for you as an infant."

Cletus looked back at the woman and then, somewhat embarrassed, held his arms open. She wrapped her arms around him, put her face on his chest, and sobbed unashamedly.

"A bit overemotional, perhaps," Frade said. "But she means well."

Clete, very uncomfortable, nevertheless gave the woman all the time she wanted, until she finally pushed herself away.

"Pardon, Señor," she said.

"I am very pleased to meet you, Señora," Clete said. It was the only thing he could think of to say.

"You can see his mother in his eyes, God grant that she rests with the angels and in peace," Señora Pellano said.

"Yes, I saw that," el Coronel Jorge Guillermo Frade said with emotion, and then found it necessary to blow his nose again. Then he cleared his throat. "Señora Pellano, I am going to show Cletus the house. If he finds it to his liking, he will be staying here. Perhaps you would be good enough to bring some coffee to the master suite?"

"Sí, mi Coronel," Señora Pellano said.

I'm surprised he didn't order more booze. Why? Probably because he figures now that I've been convinced that we're all one big loving family, he wants to make sure I'm not too drunk to answer his questions when the questioning session begins.

The tour ended when Frade ushered his son up a narrow flight of steps in the back of the house into a large suite on the top floor.

"There's an elevator," el Coronel said, pointing. Clete turned and saw a sliding door. "The stairs are for the servants, or, it was said, for ladies whom Uncle Guillermo brought in by the rear door.

"You normally keep shutters closed against the afternoon sun in the summer," Frade went on as he walked to the front of the room from the elevator, "but I will raise them to show you the vista."

He pulled hard, grunting, on a strip of canvas next to one of the windows, and a vertical shutter covering a French door leading to a balcony creaked upward.

"There, of course, is the Hipódromo," he said, pointing. "And the English Tennis Club. Beyond it is the River Plate. One day there will be an aeropuerto between here and the river; and there is talk of building a course for el Golf over there to the left. Do you play golf, Cletus?"

"Yes, Sir."

"Of course, and tennis, too. I will arrange for guest memberships at the English Tennis Club and at my golf club."

How the hell did he know I play tennis?

"In the afternoon, and at night, when the sun is down, you catch the wind from the river," Frade said.

Clete heard the elevator and turned in time to see the door slide open. Señora Pellano and the young maid who had opened the door were inside a beautifully paneled small elevator. Señora Pellano was carrying a coffee service, and the maid was carrying a tray with whiskey.

"So what do you think, Cletus? Would you be comfortable here?" Frade asked as he collapsed into a leather armchair.

"The house is beautiful," Clete said.

It was not as large as it looked. Most of the rooms were small. In square feet, it was probably not as big as the house on St. Charles Avenue. And for that matter, there were probably more square feet in the houses in Midland and on the ranch. But it was inarguably more elegant than any of them, with crystal chandeliers in most of the rooms and corridors, and ornate bronze banisters on the stairway. And the luxuriously furnished suite which occupied all of the top floor certainly proved that Granduncle Guillermo knew how to take care of himself.

"Señora Pellano," Frade said as she poured him a scotch, "if Señor Cletus were to move in here, have I your promise you will care for him well?"

"With joy, mi Coronel."

"Then it's settled. Telephone to Señor Mallín's Alberto, por favor. Tell him to pack Señor Cletus's things, and that Enrico will be there immediately to pick them up. And then telephone Enrico at the Big House and tell him to go there and bring Señor Cletus's things here."

"Sí, mi Coronel," Señora Pellano said, and smiled warmly at Clete.

"Sir," Clete began—and wondered again why he could not bring himself to say "Father"—"wouldn't it be better if I went over there and got my things, and said good-bye and thank you?"

"I do not think I quite understand . . ."

"Sir, this strikes me as perhaps a little rude, just sending someone there to get my clothing."

"No, not at all. So far as good manners are concerned, I will have flowers sent in your name to Señora de Mallín, and some small gifts to the children, and a case of whiskey to Mallín himself. I will send him something else as well—perhaps a set of silver cups engraved with the crest of the regiment and my name. I think he would like that, as a token of my appreciation for his hospitality to you. That should take care of things."

"Well, if you say so."

"And then, of course, I suspect Mallín will be rather glad to have you out of his house."

"I beg your pardon?"

"You remember Teniente Coronel Martín—the fellow we 'bumped into' in the hotel? . . . I still haven't worked that out; he's too important in the BIS to conduct surveillances himself. . . . Martín came to see me, asking about you and your friend. If he did that, it follows that he has also been to see Mallín, or else will shortly do so. I suspect Mallín will be pleased that you will no longer be a guest in his house."

"You make the BIS sound like the Gestapo."

"I don't think they're quite that ruthless. But they are good. Don't worry about them. Since you're here simply to ensure that Venezuelan petroleum is not diverted to the Germans, once they convince themselves of that, they will have no further interest in you."

What's that? My invitation to tell you what I'm really doing here? No way, Daddy.

Clete forced himself to look at his father. His father was reaching over the side of his chair to pick up his drink. Clete walked to the window and looked out.

There was activity at the racetrack. Exercise boys were walking horses back to stables after a race. Clete watched as a rambunctious horse got away from its handler and trotted insolently down the track, obviously enjoying itself.

He turned to face his father, to play it by ear.

That's all I can do, play it by ear.

His father was slumped in the armchair, his hand holding the whiskey glass on the armrest. But his head was bent forward, his mouth was open, and his eyes were closed; he was asleep, and snoring.

I'll be damned, he's passed out, or the next thing to it. He really was putting all the booze away.

Clete felt nature's call and found the bathroom. In it he found proof that Granduncle Guillermo expected female guests in his room. The bathroom was equipped with a plumbing fixture Clete had first seen on the island of Espíritu Santo, in the house of a French plantation owner taken over as a transient quarters. Sullivan had used it, with some success, to cool bottles of Australian beer.

Clete examined the fixture with interest, wondering exactly how it worked. When he completed his primary purpose in the bathroom, he bent over the fixture and tried the faucets, one at a time. The prize for his curiosity was a sudden burst of water at his face from what he thought was a drain.

He dried himself, torn between amusement and humiliation, and returned to the apartment.

Señora Pellano was there, along with a burly man in a brown suit. They were both looking down at the soundly sleeping Coronel.

"Who are you?" Clete demanded.

"I am Enrico, mi Teniente," the man said. "I have come to take care of el Coronel."

"I see," Clete asked, and then blurted, "Does he do this sort of thing often?"

"No, mi Teniente," Enrico said, and then, "Permission to speak, mi Teniente?"

"Certainly."

This guy is—or was—a soldier. He looks like a Marine gunnery sergeant with six hash marks; that "permission to speak" business is the mark of an old-timer enlisted man.

"El Coronel would be very embarrassed to remember himself

as he is now, mi Teniente. It would be a kindness if he were not reminded of it."

"OK."

"Gracias, mi Teniente."

"What was the occasion today?"

"You were, mi Teniente," Enrico said. "Con permiso, mi Teniente?"

Clete nodded.

Enrico bent over the inert body of el Coronel, wrapped his arms around him, and with a heave and a grunt hoisted him to his feet. Then, with an ease that showed he had done this sort of thing before, he stooped and allowed Frade's body to fall over his shoulder. Then, grunting again, he stood erect. He was now carrying Clete's father in the "Fireman's Carry."

He carried him to the elevator. Señora Pellano entered with him, and the door slid closed.

Powerful man, Clete thought. *My father is a large man, and he was really out. Took a lot of muscle to carry him that way.*

And since he was really out, what does that mean?

Enrico said, and I don't think he was lying, that he doesn't often pass out drunk.

So what does that do to your theory that he was pretending to drink so that you would get drunk and start running off at the mouth?

Christ, I don't know what to think!

X

[ONE]
Calle Agüero
Barrio Norte
Buenos Aires, Argentina
1515 28 November 1942

David G. Ettinger was sure he had the right number, but he checked again, taking from the breast pocket of his seersucker suit the slip of paper with "Ernst Klausner, calle Agüero 1585" written on it. He crossed the cobblestones of calle Agüero and stopped before Number 1585. The house number looked European—blue numbers on a white background, a porcelain medallion mounted to a brass plate.

The houses along both sides of the street were built up to the wide concrete sidewalks. Every twenty yards or so the thick trunks of elm trees pierced the sidewalk, their branches almost touching, shading the street and the sidewalks. The exterior walls of Number 1585 were of exposed aggregate concrete, and the windows had roll-down shutters in place, possibly because of the afternoon sun, or maybe because no one was at home.

The whole neighborhood looks European. Buenos Aires looks European. This could be a street in Madrid; for that matter in Berlin—say Tegel, or Wilhelmsdorf. In Berlin, the walls would be of concrete, carefully smoothed and marked to suggest stone blocks, but that's the only real difference.

Except in Germany, a Jew would live in a Jewish neighborhood.

This neighborhood had no national flavor. He'd ridden several times on his bus rides through a section of town that could have been a suburb of London, and was in fact where many British lived. Pelosi had told him he had found an Italian section. Presumably there would be other neighborhoods with some kind of national identity, but this wasn't one of them. This section of town looked—Argentinean.

First without realizing he was doing so, and then quite intentionally, he had looked for some outward sign—a kosher butcher shop, something like that—which would announce, "Here Live the Jews." He'd seen signs for kosher meats two or three times, but not today, and not in this neighborhood.

And realized, *The six pointed Jewish stars on the butcher shops here, as in the United States, are printed in gold, to attract the business of those who keep a kosher kitchen. This isn't like Germany, where they are painted crudely in white on the plate glass, in compliance with provisions of the Racial Purity Act of 1933, to warn innocent Aryans they are about to risk contamination by entering the business premises of a Gottverdammte Jude.*

Ettinger realized that he was feeling very powerful emotions now. There were probably several thousand people named Ernst Klausner in Germany . . . or there once were. But he had a strange feeling that this was the Ernst Klausner he knew. Ernst Klausner, of Heinrich Klausner und Sohn, G.m.b.H. The firm had been wholesale paper merchants, with their headquarters in Berlin, and branches all over Germany. They had lived in a villa in Berlin-Lichterfelde.

Ettinger walked up three shallow steps to the door of Agüero 1585, found the doorbell, and pressed it. He could not hear a sound from inside, and had just about decided that no one was home, when the door opened. A girl of about twelve or thirteen, her blond hair—*Inge Klausner had been blond!*—done up in rolled braids. She smiled a bit nervously and asked, "¿Señor?"

"Guten Tag, Fräulein," Ettinger began, and saw relief in the girl's eyes that she did not have to cope with Spanish. "My name is Ettinger. Is your mother or father at home?"

"No, I'm afraid not."

"I'm looking for Herr Ernst Klausner, formerly of Berlin. Have I the right home?"

Concern came back in her eyes.

"My father will be here at six," the girl said. "Perhaps it would be better, mein Herr, if you came back then."

"The Frau Klausner I am looking for is named Inge," Ettinger said.

From her eyes, Ettinger could see that he had hit home, but the concern in her eyes did not go away, and she didn't respond directly.

"It would be better, mein Herr, if you came back when my father is here. At six, or a little after."

"And if this is the home of Ernst and Inge Klausner, then you would be Sarah," Ettinger said. "Who I last saw as a small child."

She looked intently into his eyes. They were frightened, and he was sorry he had said what he had.

"Please," the girl said. "Come in. I will telephone to my father."

"¿Hola?"

"Ernst?"

"Who is this?"

"An old friend from Berlin, Ernst. David Ettinger."

"Ach du lieber Gott!"

"Wie geht's, Ernst?"

"You got out!"

"Obviously."

"And your father and mother?"

"Mother is in New York. The others . . ."

There was a long silence.

"How did you find me?"

"Your daughter was kind enough to call you for me."

"You are at my home?"

"Yes."

There was another perceptible pause.

He doesn't like me being here.

"I can't leave here now, David. Could you come back to the house tonight? After six?"

"I have nothing else to do. I could wait for you."

"Of course," Ernst said. "Have you money, David? There is some in the house. I will tell Sarah to get you something to eat . . ."

"I have money, thank you. And I had an enormous Argentinean lunch before I came here."

He thinks I am a refugee. I am, but not the way he thinks.

"I can't leave here now. I will come, we will come, as soon as we can. Would you put Sarah on the telephone?"

Inge sobbed and dabbed at her eyes when she embraced him, but quickly recovered and announced, "We will have a coffee, David. Like old times."

She motioned with her head for Sarah to come with her, and went into the kitchen, leaving Klausner and Ettinger alone.

"So, David," Klausner said. "You are really all right? You need nothing?"

"Nothing, but I thank you for the thought."

Klausner smiled. "You look prosperous. Can I ask? Did you bring anything out?"

"My Spanish cousins have been more than generous; and so far, I understand, they have kept the business from being sold to some deserving National Socialist." He paused, then decided he could, should, tell Klausner everything. "I sold my interest in the German businesses to them. Technically, they are now owned by Spaniards. Germany has yet to expropriate Spanish-held property."

"And you're now living in Spain?"

"No. In the United States. Ernst, not for Inge's ears, I am in the American Army." He paused and chuckled. "I am a staff sergeant in the United States Army."

Ettinger expected surprise at that announcement, but not the look of total bafflement that came to Klausner's face.

"I was working in New York City," Ettinger went on. "When I went to America, I took the examination for radio engineer, and I was working for RCA, the Radio Corporation of America . . . you know the name Sarnoff, Ernst, David Sarnoff? A Russian, a Jew, one of the great geniuses of radio . . . ?"

"Why did you leave Spain?" Klausner interrupted.

The question surprised Ettinger.

"I didn't, I don't, trust Franco," he said. "It is only a matter of time before he joins the Axis. I'm surprised it hasn't happened already. What happened in Germany will happen in Spain."

Klausner closed his eyes and shook his head, as if shocked and saddened by Ettinger's stupidity.

"Franco is not as bad as you think, David," he said.

What the hell is that all about? Franco is El Caudillo *only because of the Germans, their Condor Legion, and all their other military support. He is as much a fascist as Mussolini and Hitler. But this is not the time to debate that.*

"I was working for RCA, and I registered for the draft . . ."

"The what?"

"Military service, conscription," Ettinger explained. "And Mr. Sarnoff—Ernst, you must know who he is. He worked with Marconi . . ."

Klausner was obviously wholly uninterested in a Russian Jew named Sarnoff, radio pioneer and genius or not. And Ettinger realized his attitude annoyed him.

"Mr. Sarnoff called me to his office. He said my work was essential to the war effort, and I did not have to go into the Army; all I had to say was that I did not wish to go, and he would arrange it."

"So why are you in the American Army?" Klausner asked.

"I told Mr. Sarnoff that I wished to be an American citizen, and that I felt it my duty to serve."

There he goes, shaking his head again. Or has his head ever stopped shaking, as if he is dealing with a pitiful idiot?

"And Mr. Sarnoff said to me, I know how you feel. I myself am going in the Army. And he told me when the war is over, I will not only have my job back, but that while I am in the Army, RCA will pay the difference between my Army pay and what I was making at RCA."

"If the Americans win the war," Klausner said.

"There is no 'if,' Ernst," Ettinger said. "The Americans will win."

Klausner shrugged.

Why am I growing so angry?

"When I was in an Army school in Baltimore," Ettinger said, "I was taken, Ernst, to a shipyard in Kearny, New Jersey, which is right across the river from New York City. They are building one ship a day in that shipyard, Ernst. It takes them three weeks to build a ship. Every day, seven days a week, they launch a ship. And they told us they were not up to speed."

"What?"

"Up to speed. It means that soon they will be making two ships a day, or three, or even four. And that is not their only shipyard. They have—I don't know, ten, twenty shipyards, maybe more. Germany cannot make enough torpedoes to sink that many ships."

Klausner shrugged again.

"On the way to Kearny, we passed the airport in Newark. It is bigger—three or four times the size of Tempelhof—and as far as I could see, enormous bombers were about to be flown to England. Not shipped, Ernst, flown."

Klausner held up his hand to silence him. Ettinger followed his eyes. Inge was coming into the room with a tray.

"They are worse than the Viennese here," she said, putting the tray down in front of him. It held an assortment of pastries. "They take a Viennese recipe. If it says 'six eggs,' they use twelve. If it says 'one cup of sugar,' they use two. And the meat!''

"The meat is incredible," Klausner agreed. "Cheap. Marvelous."

Sarah put a coffee service on a low table. Inge poured coffee, handed cups to Ettinger and her husband, then started to pour a cup for herself.

"Liebchen," Klausner said. "Why don't you take Sarah for a little walk?"

It was said softly, but it was an order. She put the pot down and smiled.

"We will talk later, David," she said. "You'll stay for supper, of course."

"We will talk," Ettinger agreed.

"I am so happy that you are here," Inge said.

"I am so happy to see you all," Ettinger said.

Klausner waited until his wife and daughter had left the house.

"If you are in the American Army," he challenged, "what are you doing in Buenos Aires, not in a uniform?"

"That, Ernst, I cannot talk about."

"You are a spy."

Ettinger laughed. "No. A spy? No."

"I don't believe you," Klausner said. "I understand why you feel you must lie to me, David, but I don't believe you."

"I am sure we—we Americans—have spies here, but I am not one of them."

"What are you doing here?"

"I cannot tell you."

"A spy by another name. You are playing word games."

"I am here to harm the Germans, Ernst."

"Yes, of course you are. Thank you for your honesty."

"Not the Germans. The Nazis."

"Word games again. There is no difference between them. You should know that. You do know that."

This time Ettinger shrugged.

"Let me tell you about the Argentineans, David. We Argentineans. I am not a German anymore. I speak the language. I read Goethe and Schiller, I eat apfelstrudel. But I am no longer a German. I am an Argentinean."

"You are also a Jew."

"I am an Argentinean who happens to be a Jew."

"You are a German Jew who has lost his life and his family to the Nazis."

"I am an Argentinean whose family, Inge and Sarah, has been saved by the Argentineans. I am an Argentinean. I became an Argentinean. I swore to defend this country, David, to obey its laws. Argentina is neutral. I want nothing to do with a spy from the United States of America or anywhere else."

"They killed our people. They are killing our people."

"I think it would be best if you left, David, before Inge and Sarah come home," Klausner said.

Ettinger stood up, then looked down at Klausner.

"Because we were friends together in Germany," Klausner said, "I will not report you to Internal Security. But please, please, do not come back, and do not tell anyone that you knew me in Berlin."

"As you wish, Ernst," Ettinger said.

"Auf Wiedersehen, mein alt Freund. May God be with you," Ernst said.

[TWO]
4730 Avenida Libertador
Buenos Aires
0900 29 November 1942

Clete was wakened by Señora Pellano, who set a tray-on-legs with orange juice and coffee on his bed.

"Buenos días, Señor Cletus."

" 'Días, muchas gracias," he said, smiling at her, carefully trying to sit up without upsetting the tray.

"Would you like me to bring you something to eat?"

"Let me come downstairs," he said, smiling at her. "Give me thirty minutes to shower and shave."

"I would be happy to serve it here."

"Downstairs, please."

"Sí, Señor Cletus," she said, and went to the wardrobe and took out a dressing gown and laid it on the bed before leaving.

Even in the house on St. Charles Avenue, he thought, *I was never treated this well, like an English nobleman in the movies.*

There were two maids, so that no matter what hour of the day, his needs would not go unattended. There was also a cook and a houseman, a dignified old man named Ernesto. The staff was run with an iron hand by Señora Pellano, who, his father had told

him, came from a fine family who had been in service to the
Frades for three generations. One of the maids was a *Porteño*, the
other from a family who lived on Estancia San Pedro y San Pablo.
Both were young and attractive, which made him somewhat uncomfortable. He would have preferred maids twice their age.

Despite the physical comforts, he had spent an uncomfortable
night at the house on Libertador—his second night there—primarily because he was bored. Exploring Granduncle Guillermo's
playroom, which is what he finally did after everything else failed,
didn't really help to cure his boredom.

At ten of the morning after their meeting, his father called to
ask if he was comfortable, and to apologize: He had to leave town
and would be in touch in a couple of days, after he returned; if
Clete needed anything in the meantime, Señora Pellano would
provide it. He did not mention how they parted the day before.

When Clete tried to call Mr. Nestor at the Bank of Boston to
tell him where he was living, he was told that Nestor, too, was
out of town.

"And is there a message, Señor?"

"No, thank you. I'll call again."

And Pelosi was unavailable. Mallín had arranged a tour of the
tank farm for him, and he would be gone all day.

Clete took a stroll around the neighborhood, including a walk
through the stables of the Hipódromo. The horses were magnificent, and he liked their smell. It was comforting.

But with that out of the way, he couldn't find much else to do.
Except explore Granduncle Guillermo's playroom. It was still relatively early in the evening when he searched through an absolutely gorgeous, heavily carved desk, made from some kind of
wood he didn't recognize, and came across a locked compartment
at the rear of one of the large drawers.

Feeling childishly mischievous, he looked for keys. None of
the two dozen he could find fit the simple lock. So, telling himself
that he knew better than what he was doing—but his father *did*
tell him the place was his—he went downstairs and asked Señora
Pellano were he could find tools.

"If anything needs fixing," she told him patiently but firmly,
"I will fix it myself; or else the houseman will do it."

"All I need is a screwdriver," he said. "A small one. And
maybe a small knife. I'll take care of it myself."

She led him to a toolbox in the basement. The box held both
a penknife and a screwdriver.

The locked drawer quickly yielded to the removal of the brass screws of the lock.

It contained more evidence of Granduncle Guillermo's preoccupation with the distinguishing characteristics of the opposite gender. The drawer contained two leather-covered boxes, each containing fifty or sixty lewd and obscene photographs.

Clete had never seen anything like them (even at stag movies at his fraternity house at Tulane). They were glass transparencies, about four by five inches. Not negatives, positives. He suspected that there was probably some kind of a projector, to project them on a screen.

To judge by the appearance of the women, they had been taken a long time ago, certainly before the First World War, possibly even before the turn of the century. The women were far plumper—plusher—than currently fashionable, and wore their hair either swept up or braided, while all the men had mustaches and were pretty skinny.

Holding them up to the light, he examined every last one of them, concluding that they knew the same positions then that he was used to. The women far outnumbered the men, and it was possible to suspect that the women were more interested in other women than in the scrawny men in their drooping mustaches.

After carefully replacing the glass plates in their boxes and relocking the drawer, Clete realized that he was going to have to commit the sin of Onan. Somewhat humiliated by the process, he did so.

At least I won't stain the sheets tonight, he thought afterward.

Unfortunately, things didn't work out that way. He woke up from a painfully realistic dream—Princess Dorothea the Virgin was exposing her breasts to him—to find that he had soiled the sheets after all.

He took a shower, hoping that by morning the sheets would be dry and the maid would not notice, and tittering, report her finding to Señora Pellano.

Clete drank the orange juice and half the coffee, took another shower, put on a short-sleeve shirt and a pair of khaki pants, and rode the elevator down to the main floor. The twelve-seat dining-room table had been set for one and laid out with enough food to feed six hungry people.

Halfway through his scrambled eggs, he heard the telephone ring, and a minute later, Señora Pellano set a telephone beside him. It looked as if it had been built by Alexander Graham Bell himself.

"It is a Señor Nestor. Are you at home, Señor Clete?"

He picked up the telephone.

"Good morning, Sir."

Shit, I'm not supposed to call him "Sir."

"Good morning, Clete," Nestor said. "Jasper Nestor of the Bank of Boston here."

"I tried to call you yesterday to tell . . ."

"I called the Mallín place, and they told me where to find you."

"My father offered me this pla—"

"The reason I'm calling, Clete," Nestor interrupted, "and I know this is damned short notice. The thing is, there's a small party at the Belgrano Athletic Club this evening. We sponsor, the bank, one of the cricket teams. Nothing very elaborate—no black tie, in other words. Just drinks and dinner. There's a chap I want you to meet. I introduced you at the bank, if you'll remember. Mr. Ettinger?"

"Yes, I remember meeting Mr. Ettinger."

"Well, you have things in common—being newcomers and bachelors. Why don't we put you two together and see what happens? Or do you have other plans?"

"No. Thank you very much."

"Perhaps we'll have a few minutes for a little chat ourselves. Right about seven? Would that be convenient? Do you know where it is, can you find it all right?"

"Yes. I have a guest card. I've played tennis there."

"Good. Look forward to seeing you about seven."

[THREE]
The Belgrano Athletic Club
Buenos Aires
1925 29 November 1942

I wonder what the rules of that game are, Clete thought as he looked out the window of the bar at a cricket game being played under field lights.

He held a scotch and water—he had told the barman to give him a very light one—and was munching on potato chips, waiting for Nestor to show up.

The Belgrano Athletic Club looked as if it had been miracu-
lously transported intact from England. In the bar, a paneled room
with photographs on its walls of the Stately Homes of England,
the conversation was in English—English English—and even the
bartender spoke as if London was his home.

The bar was for men only, but there were a good number of
women outside in the stands watching the game, and parading
past the windows of the bar. Good-looking, long-legged, nice-
breasted blond women, in lightweight summer dresses.

*Just what I don't need after Granduncle Guillermo's dirty pic-
tures.*

I wonder what the boys on Guadalcanal are doing right now.

"Ah, there you are, Clete!" Nestor said behind him. "Admiring the view, are you?"

Clete turned to face him. Ettinger was with him.

"Good evening."

"You remember David, of course. You met him at the bank?"

"Yes, of course. How are you, Mr. Ettinger?"

"We're quite informal here," Nestor said. "It really should be
'David' and 'Clete.' "

"Nice to see you again, David," Clete said.

They shook hands.

"Let me find us something to drink. You all right, Clete, or
will you have another?"

"I'm fine, thank you just the same."

As soon as he was out of sight, David asked, "No Tony? I
thought maybe I'd be introduced to him too."

"He wasn't invited. He's not even supposed to know who Nestor is."

"I meant I thought Nestor the banker might invite him as a
courtesy to an employee of Howell Petroleum. One of the things
I've learned is how much Howell money flows through the Bank
of Boston."

Clete shrugged.

"Maybe later. Nestor strikes me as a very cautious man." He
smiled at Ettinger. "All things considered, you like being a
banker?"

Ettinger looked at Clete a moment as if wondering if he should
say what he wanted to. He glanced around to make sure no one
was within eavesdropping range, and then said, "I had a very
strange, disturbing thing happen to me yesterday."

"What was that?"

"I went to see some people I used to know . . ."

"Used to know"? Oh. In Germany. One of the Jewish families on Nestor's list.

"People named Klausner. A man named Ernst Klausner. We were rather close at one time. Until he found out what I was doing here—"

"You told him?" Clete interrupted, shocked and then angry.

Jesus Christ, here he goes again. First he tells his mother he's going to Argentina, and then he tells somebody he used to know—

"I told him I was in the Army, nothing else. At that point, he pulled the welcome mat out from under my feet. He told me he was now an Argentinean, not a German, and that as an Argentinean, he should report me to the authorities. For auld lang syne, he wouldn't, but don't come back."

"Jesus! Was this before or after you asked him about the ships?"

"I didn't get as far as asking him anything. And he didn't seem at all concerned what the Germans are doing to Jews in Germany. He's out, and that's all he cares about it."

"Did you tell Nestor?"

"Of course."

Well, Nestor is the Station Chief. If he's not upset that David ran off at the mouth, why should I be?

Because if we get caught, we go to jail, or worse, not Nestor.

"And what was his reaction?"

"He said there were a lot of other names on the list."

Two other men came to the window, effectively shutting off further conversation. A moment later, Nestor rejoined them.

"We owe you an apology for keeping you waiting, Clete," he said, handing Ettinger a drink.

"Not at all."

"We were out buying David a car."

"Really?"

"A '39 Ford, with the steering wheel on the wrong side," Ettinger said.

"You'll have to take me for a ride in it," Clete said.

"As soon as I actually get it, I'd be delighted to."

"This is Argentina, Clete," Nestor explained. "You don't buy a car and drive off the lot with it the same day. With a little bit of luck, David may lay his hands on it in a week or ten days."

"I love the view from here," Ettinger said. "Look at that blonde!"

Clete had noticed her too. A stunning female, wearing a wide-brimmed straw hat and a pale-yellow dress.

"Her husband is probably standing at the bar," Clete said, laughing.

"He's not," Nestor said. "He's one of ours at the bank. And he's out of town. But if he was here, he would take it as a compliment."

"It was intended as one."

"I think maybe we better wander in," Nestor said.

"Wander in where?" Clete asked.

"To the lounge."

"I hate to walk away from the parade," Clete said.

"They'll be in the lounge," Nestor said. "They're not allowed in here, which I think is a rather good idea. But they will be in the lounge, and they will, of course, be at dinner."

Clete's companion at dinner turned out to be the blonde who had caught David's attention.

Her name, she told him in a delightful British accent, was Monica Javez de Frade. But they were not related.

"We're not even a poor branch of your family. No relation at all."

Which means that Nestor told you who I am. Or that word had spread around the bank who I am—who my father is—after Nestor introduced me around his office.

The proof of that theory seemed to come when she told him that Pablo, her husband, was in "real estate" at the bank, and worked closely with Nestor.

"Agricultural real estate, unfortunately," Monica added, "which means that poor Pablo spends most of his time in the country, leaving poor Monica to spend most of her time alone in the city."

Clete smiled politely, telling himself that her remark had the meaning he was giving it only because his near-terminal chastity—and Granduncle Guillermo's dirty pictures—had inflamed his imagination.

But during supper, and during the award afterward of small silver cups to the triumphant members of the Banco de Boston cricket team, Monica's knee kept brushing against his. At each encounter, Clete quickly moved his knee away . . . until he decided to leave his knee there. Then the pressure of her knee against his increased. He withdrew it then, telling himself that the cure for his near-terminal chastity should not involve a married woman, and especially one whose husband worked closely with Jasper Nestor.

Laying her hand on his arm to distract his attention from one of the cricket players' lengthy tribute to his teammates—*and for no other purpose, Clete, get your imagination under control*—Monica asked if he had found an apartment, or whether he was staying with his father.

"My father has a guest house. I'm staying there."

"On Avenida Libertador?"

"Yes. You know the house?"

"I know about it," she said. "The place one of the legendary Frades built with the master apartment on the top floor so he could watch the races at the Hipódromo without crossing the street?"

And for other purposes.

"That's the place."

"I've always wanted to see it."

"Anytime. It would be my pleasure."

The cricket player finally finished his speech, there was unenthusiastic applause, and a short man with a bushy mustache stepped to the lectern to announce the conclusion of the evening's events. He told everyone he wished to thank them for coming, and especially the Banco de Boston for their generous support.

People started rising to their feet, including Monica, who managed to brush her breasts against Clete's arm in the process.

Nestor appeared.

"About ready, Clete? I'd love to stay for the dancing, but I have an early-morning appointment."

"Thank you, Señora de Frade."

"Oh, Monica, please."

"Thank you, Monica, for the pleasure of your company."

"Perhaps we'll see each other again," she said, giving him her hand.

"When is Pablo due back, Monica?" Nestor asked.

"The day after tomorrow."

"It's always a pleasure to see you," Nestor said. "Clete?"

Clete followed him to the door, where Ettinger was waiting.

"Well, now that you and David have been introduced," Nestor said as he drove down Avenida Libertador, "it will seem perfectly

natural that you meet for lunch or dinner. Two bachelors, so to
speak, out on the town.''

"Yes," Clete agreed.

"You seem to have made quite an impression on the de Frade
woman, Clete," Nestor added. "Which might not be a bad
thing."

"I don't think I understand."

"With her husband out of town as much as he is, hostesses are
always looking for a suitable bachelor to be her escort at dinner.
You really should be socially active."

No way, thank you very much.

"I volunteer," David said from the backseat.

"She didn't seem nearly as interested in you, I'm afraid, David." Nestor laughed. "And they always ask the husband-less
woman if the proposed dinner partner is satisfactory to her before
they invite him."

Señora Pellano was waiting up for him in the foyer of the Guest
House.

"I thought perhaps you might like a little something to eat,
Señor Cletus."

"No. Thank you very much. And you don't have to wait up
for me like this, Señora Pellano."

"It is my pleasure, Señor Cletus."

"I'm going to turn in, Señora Pellano. Good night."

"Buenas noches, Señor Cletus."

He started toward the elevator. The telephone rang.

"A gentleman called before," she said. "Not an Argentine.
His Spanish was not very good. He said he would call again.
Perhaps that is him."

Pelosi. I wonder what he wants.

Clete waited for her to answer the telephone.

"It is a lady, Señor Cletus," she said, and handed him the
telephone.

"¿Hola?"

"Cletus, Monica. I wondered if you would really go home."

"I really went home."

"I'm still at the club. I stayed for the dancing. I'm bored."

"I'm sorry."

"Cletus, did you mean it when you said you would show me
the Guest House?"

"Of course."

"You also said 'anytime.' I could be there in fifteen minutes."

"Why don't you come over, Monica? I'll show you my etchings."

"Oh, that sounds delightfully wicked. I'll be right there."

Or maybe Granduncle Guillermo's dirty pictures.

"I'm driving myself," Monica said. "And I'd really rather not drive home to drop the car off and look for a cab. Is there room in your garage?"

There was only one car in the basement garage, which was large enough for four cars, a Fiat sedan used by Señora Pellano.

"Yes, there is."

"Then be a dear and have it open when I get there, will you? We don't want people talking, do we? Or would you prefer that I take a taxi?"

"I'll have the gates and the garage open."

"Fifteen minutes," she said, and hung up.

He hung up the telephone and turned to find Señora Pellano looking at him.

"I'm to have a guest," he began. "She wants to park her car in the garage."

"I'll have Ernesto open it."

"I can do that."

"And I'll set out some agua mineral con gas and some ice in the reception room," she said. "Unless you would prefer it in the apartment? Señor Cletus?"

"The reception room will be fine, thank you."

"And then I will say good night, Señor Cletus."

"Thank you, Señora Pellano."

"I hope you have a good alarm clock," Monica said, looking at him over the rim of the scotch and water he had made her. "I absolutely have to be home by seven. If I'm not, the children are liable to wake up and ask where Mommy is."

Children? Of course, children. She's a married woman. Married women have children.

This is not the smartest thing you have ever done, Clete. It may turn out to be the dumbest. But there doesn't seem to be any question that you are about to return to the ranks of the sexually active.

Maybe that will put the Virgin Princess out of your mind.

"I think there's one in the apartment. Shall we go have a look?"

"Splendid idea," Monica said. "And why don't I carry this tray along with us, so you won't have to wake the servants?"

She picked up the tray with the ice and soda water on it, smiled at him, and waited for him to show her the way to the bedroom.

[FOUR]
4730 Avenida Libertador
Buenos Aires
1745 30 November 1942

Cletus Howell Frade, First Lieutenant, USMCR, and Laird of the Manor, in T-shirt and khaki trousers, was sitting on a heavy wooden chair—so heavy it absolutely could not be tipped back on its rear legs, and he had really tried—on the balcony outside his bedroom. A liter bottle of Quilmes Cerveza (beer) rested on his abdomen. His feet, in battered boots he'd owned since before he went to College Station to join the corps of cadets at Texas A&M, rested on the masonry railing. And he was watching an exercise boy let a magnificent Arabian run at a full gallop at the racetrack across the street.

"I wish I was up there with you, you lucky sonofabitch, who-ever you are," he announced to the world in general.

And immediately regretted it. Every time he opened his mouth and a sound came out, even a cough, either Señora Pellano or one of the maids appeared with a warm smile on her face and inquired, "¿Sí, Señor?"

He glanced over his shoulder to see if one of them was headed his way. No one was coming through the bedroom—or Grand-uncle Guillermo's playroom, as he had come to think of it.

He looked back toward the river and the racetrack. Thirty or forty sailboats were on the river, and there was activity at the racetrack, as if they were preparing for a race. He took another pull at the neck of the bottle of cerveza.

Damned good beer. They really know how to eat and drink down here.

He was not looking forward to the evening. He was going to dinner, where he would meet his aunt Beatrice and his uncle Humberto for the first time. Until three days before, he had been blissfully unaware that he had an Uncle Humberto or an Aunt Beatrice or a Cousin Jorge who got himself killed at Stalingrad.

And whose death, his father said, left Aunt Beatrice shattered enough to need a psychiatrist's attention.

There was of course no way to get out of going.

"Beatrice will inevitably find out that you are in Buenos Aires," his father told him on the telephone, "and would be deeply hurt if you do not pay your respects."

"I understand."

"Beatrice and your mother were close, Cletus. They were brides together, and young first mothers. She held you as a baby."

And now she'll want to know how come her baby is dead, and I'm alive.

Shit.

"I will try to make it an early evening. May I send a car for you at nine forty-five? They usually sit down to dinner at ten-thirty or eleven."

An early dinner?

"Thank you."

He was also having troubling feelings about the events of the previous evening.

After their first coupling—which took place no more than ninety seconds after they stepped off the elevator and walked into the playroom, and lasted about half that long—Monica confided to him that a combination of Pablo's diminishing sexual drive and the attention he was spending on his Mina had combined to almost entirely deny her the satisfactions of the connubial couch.

Their initial coupling was followed by three others. The last two shattered the hope that his near-terminal chastity was solely responsible for his carnal thoughts about the Virgin Princess, and that once that condition was cured, his shameful thoughts about her would disappear.

That didn't happen. He managed to perform—although he wasn't too sure he could the last time Monica reached for it—in a manner that did not bring shame on the reputation of the commissioned officer corps of the United States Marines. But clear images of the pert, yet ample virgin breasts of Señorita Dorotea Mallín kept flashing into his mind, even as he was somewhat feverishly attending to the business at hand.

Which is what you get, you pre-vert, for looking down the front of her dress whenever you have the chance.

At least I got out of her house before I made an ass of myself. I think Mallín was looking at me funny toward the end, which means that he caught me looking at her.

On the other hand, there's no denying that I miss her something awful. Just seeing her, hearing her talk and laugh. Just having her look at me. The funny thing is that when I think about her— except when I'm banging a thirty-two-year-old mother of three— it's not her breasts, or even that absolutely perfect ass, but her eyes. Christ, she has beautiful eyes!

Thank God, I got out of there before I made any kind of a pass at her.

Or am I going to be a fool and call her up when the Buick comes and ask her if she'd like to go for a ride?

In his mind he heard her voice: *"I have never been in a Buick droptop, Cletus. Will you take me for a ride when it arrives?"*

"Convertible, Princess. Convertible. Sure. Be happy to."

"Señor Cletus, Señor Nestor wishes to see you," Señora Pellano announced, startling him—he hadn't heard her come up.

"He's here?"

"Sí, Señor. In the reception."

What the hell does he want?

"Ask him to come up, please, Señora Pellano," Clete said.

When, a minute or so later, he heard the sound of the elevator door opening, he took his booted feet off the railing and stood up and smiled at Jasper C. Nestor. The Spymaster was wearing a seersucker suit, and he was carrying a soft-brimmed straw hat in one hand and a package in the other.

"I'm glad I caught you at home, Clete," Nestor said, thrusting the package at him. "A little housewarming gift."

The package gurgled. It was booze of some kind.

"Thank you," Clete said. "I'm a little disappointed, though, frankly."

"How's that?"

"From Humphrey Bogart movies, I had the idea that spies met in an alley in the tough part of town at midnight, not at someplace like the Belgrano Athletic Club. And I certainly didn't expect the Spymaster to show up bearing a housewarming gift."

He'd intended to be witty. From the strained smile on Nestor's face, Clete saw he hadn't been taken that way.

I will henceforth go easy on the humor.

"We're not spies, Clete," Nestor said after a moment. "We're gentlemen. The FBI are the spies."

"And not gentlemen?"

"Rarely, Clete, rarely. There is always an exception."

Clete shook the package.

"Would you like a little of whatever this is? Or something else?"

"I would prefer one of those," Nestor replied, indicating Clete's beer. "If that would . . ."

Clete pushed the call button. They were all over the house. Granduncle Guillermo knew how to live.

Señora Pellano appeared immediately.

"Would you bring the Señor a beer, please? And a glass. Señor is a gentleman."

"Actually, on a hot day, I rather like to drink from the bottle," Nestor said, smiling, and then turned and gestured off the balcony. "Beautiful view from here."

"It's a beautiful house," Clete said.

"And how kind of your father to make it available to you."

"I thought so."

"There are other advantages as well."

"Such as?"

"It establishes you as the beloved son of el Coronel Jorge Guillermo Frade," Nestor said. "That could prove very valuable."

Clete nodded.

"Have you thought about calling Señora Frade? You seemed to be getting along splendidly with her last night. A—I almost said 'affair'—*relationship* with her might be valuable to us."

"She called me," Clete said. "The phone rang the minute I walked in the door last night."

"And will you see her?" Nestor asked, then caught the look on Clete's face. "Really? Good boy."

"Is that why I was at the dinner? You wanted me to meet her?"

"I wanted you to meet David in a credible situation," Nestor said. "Señora Frade, so to speak, was an unexpected bonus. Letting it travel around town that she has added you to her list of admirers—her long list of admirers—will paint the sort of picture about you we want."

Her long *list of admirers? Incredible!*

"Inasmuch as you elected to ignore your instructions vis-à-vis your cover," Nestor went on, "that may prove quite valuable. More gossip-worthy, so to speak."

"Sir, I'm afraid I don't know what you're talking about."

"Your father proudly introduced you to a number of important officers as 'my son, late Teniente of the air service of the U.S.

Marine Corps, who served at Guadalcanal.' ''

"How did you hear about that?" Clete asked, surprised.

"I have a number of friends in the Argentine military. I presume you had reason to ignore your instructions about your cover?"

"I suppose I could tell you that it just slipped out. But the truth of the matter is, I was a little drunk at the time, and didn't want my father to think I was shirking my duty to God and country."

"From what I hear, the both of you were three sheets to the wind. I'm sure meeting him was emotional for the both of you, but you might consider the ill-wisdom of excessive alcohol."

"Yes, Sir."

Señora Pellano came onto the balcony with a bottle of cerveza and a glass on a tray.

Nestor stopped her when she started to pour, took the bottle from her, and put it to his lips.

Is he doing that because he really likes to, or to play "I'm just one of the boys" with me?

"I hope I haven't disturbed anything?" Nestor asked.

"No. Not a thing. I was sitting here catching the breeze and feeling sorry for myself."

"Why sorry? Don't tell me Señora Frade didn't turn out to be as advertised."

"I miss flying. I even miss the goddamned Marine Corps. I'm a much better Naval Aviator than I am a saboteur."

"Perhaps your father will let you fly his airplane. Or one of them."

"I didn't know he had an airplane."

"He has a Beechcraft biplane, and at least one Piper Cub."

"You mean a stagger-wing Beechcraft?"

"Your father's has the top wing behind the lower . . . yes, I suppose it would be a 'stagger-wing.' And as I say, at least one Piper Cub. The use—on the larger estancias—of small aircraft is quite common."

"They were getting into that in Texas and Oklahoma, too," Clete said.

If my father has a Beech stagger-wing, he'll probably let me fly it.

"We considered, of course, that you might not find your father to be the ogre Mr. Howell paints him to be. And in time, that you might manage to get close to him. We didn't think it would happen so quickly.

"Do you think he'll turn out to be useful to us?"

"How do you mean, useful?"

"Tilt this country toward us, and away from Mr. Hitler and Company."

"My initial impression of my father is that he's a strong, intelligent man, who will tilt the way he decides to tilt, completely unaffected by his son's nationality, or by what his son thinks or asks him to do. Incidentally, I'm quite sure he's figured out that I'm not down here to make sure Mallín isn't diverting crude to the Germans."

"What makes you think so?"

"He as much as told me. It was by shading, innuendo, not in so many words."

"What were the circumstances?"

"There was an Internal Security officer. A lieutenant colonel named Martín . . ."

"Not just 'an Internal Security officer,' Clete," Nestor interrupted him. "Colonel Martín is Chief of the Ethical Standards Office of the Bureau of Internal Security. He reports only to the Chief of Internal Security, an admiral named de Montoya. A very competent, and thus dangerous, man."

"My father said he'd been to see him, asking about me. As a matter of fact, he said that's how he learned I was in Argentina."

"That was quick work on Martín's part," Nestor said admiringly. "They apparently made the connection between you and your father more quickly than we thought they would. Go on."

"Anyway, this Colonel Martín was in the Alvear Palace when I met my father."

"Possibly surveilling your father. But that's unlikely. He's too important for something like that."

"My father introduced us," Clete went on, aware he was growing annoyed at Nestor's frequent interruptions. "Later he told me who Martín was. And this is the innuendo I meant: He told me that I have nothing to worry about since I'm down here only for Howell Petroleum—to make sure Mallín is not diverting petroleum products."

Nestor grunted.

"And does Mallín have any idea that you're not down here to do that?"

"No. Or at least he didn't. My father said Martín would probably go to see him. And that would arouse his suspicions."

"Worst possible scenario: You will be expelled from Argentina despite your father, or possibly because your father will arrange it. You would probably have time to go underground, but that would be sticky."

I can think of a worse scenario: The same thing will happen to me, to all three of us, that happened to the last OSS team.

"Alternative scenario," Nestor went on. "Even if Martín has questions about your cover, he won't connect you with the re-plenishment-ship problem yet, and you will *not* be expelled from Argentina." He paused a moment, then finished that thought. "Both Martín and Admiral de Montoya are obviously reluctant to anger your father. But he will keep you under surveillance."

"I understand."

"You will have to be extra careful when you go to Uruguay. Which brings us to that."

"Uruguay?"

"How soon do you think you can tear yourself away to go to Uruguay?"

"What will I do in Uruguay?"

"You and Pelosi are going to Montevideo, where you will hire a car and drive to Punta del Este. It is a rather charming little town on the Atlantic coast, quite popular with Argentineans escaping the heat of Buenos Aires. After you take the sun on the beach at Punta for a day or two, you will drive north—I'll furnish a map—to near the Brazilian border. A quantity of explosives and detonators will be air-dropped to you there."

"Air-dropped from where?"

"From Brazil, onto a rice field we have used before."

"How do I get the explosives past Argentine customs when we come back? Or past Uruguayan customs leaving Uruguay?"

"The explosives themselves should pose no problem. They have been molded into a substance that looks exactly like wood, and precut to form the parts of a wooden crate. You will assemble the crates—there will be two of them, with a total weight of just over twenty-two pounds—and fill them with souvenirs of your holiday . . . not too heavy souvenirs; the explosives only look like wood and don't have wood's strength. They make some rather attractive doodads of straw, in the shape of chickens, horses, cows, et cetera. These would be ideal. You will quite openly carry the crates onto and off the ferry and through Argentine customs."

Now this is more like Errol Flynn battling the Dirty Nazis. The problem is, although I know Nestor is dead serious, I'm having trouble believing that I am about to go to some field near the

Brazilian border and have explosives air-dropped to me.

"The detonators will pose a problem. There will be a dozen of them. They're quite sensitive. Probably the best way is for one of you to tape them to your body. Argentine Customs is very unlikely to submit you to a body search." He paused and smiled. "Or perhaps you could wear your cowboy boots. I'm sure you could conceal them in your boots."

And blow my goddamned leg off!

"Is there any way I could take Ettinger instead of Pelosi?" Clete asked. "Pelosi is young. Excitable. And doesn't speak Spanish well."

"But knows about explosives and airdrops," Nestor said, shaking his head no. "Besides, I want Ettinger to continue what he's doing with the Hebrew community here."

"We've discussed that. He knew only one family on that list of names, and they told him to bug off."

"He's going to have to go back to Klausner and try again."

"He's convinced me that would be a waste of time, and that Klausner would very possibly turn him in. Or at least report to Internal Security that Ettinger has contacted him."

"He'll have to go back."

"You tell him."

"I have information that may change Klausner's attitude," Nestor answered, ignoring Clete's last remark.

He took what looked like several sheets of folded yellow paper from the inside pocket of his seersucker jacket and handed them to Clete. When Clete started to unfold them, he saw it was really one long sheet of paper, and recognized the carbon copy from a radio-teletype machine.

"This will be released to the Argentinean press in the morning. Even if they run it, Herr Klausner might not see it," Nestor said as Clete started to read it.

FROM SECSTATE WASHINGTON 0645 28 NOVEMBER 1942
VIA PANAMA TO ALL AMEMBASSIES SOUTHAMERICA FOR IMMEDIATE PERSONAL ATTENTION AMBASSA-DORS

(1) SECSTATE DESIRES IMMEDIATE TRANSMITTAL AT AMBASSADORIAL LEVEL TO HIGHEST POSSIBLE

LEVEL HOST GOVERNMENT OFFICIAL, FOLLOWED BY
WIDEST POSSIBLE DISSEMINATION TO ALL CHAN-
NELS OF PUBLIC INFORMATION.

DECLARATION BEGINS:
THE UNITED STATES OF AMERICA
THE DEPARTMENT OF STATE
WASHINGTON, DC
28 NOVEMBER 1942

FRANKLIN DELANO ROOSEVELT, THE PRESIDENT OF
THE UNITED STATES OF AMERICA; HIS MAJESTY
GEORGE VI, KING OF ENGLAND AND EMPEROR OF THE
BRITISH EMPIRE; JOSEF STALIN, CHAIRMAN OF
THE SUPREME SOVIET OF THE UNION OF SOVIET SO-
CIALIST REPUBLICS; AND GENERAL CHARLES DE
GAULLE, CHAIRMAN OF THE FRENCH NATIONAL COM-
MITTEE, ON BEHALF OF THEIR GOVERNMENTS, AND
IN THE NAME OF THEIR PEOPLE, HEREWITH DE-
CLARE:

THE GERMAN GOVERNMENT, NOT CONTENT WITH DE-
NYING TO PERSONS OF JEWISH RACE IN ALL THE
TERRITORIES OVER WHICH THEIR BARBAROUS RULE
HAS BEEN EXTENDED THE MOST ELEMENTARY HUMAN
RIGHTS, ARE NOW CARRYING INTO EFFECT HI-
TLER'S OFT-REPEATED INTENTION TO EXTERMI-
NATE THE JEWISH PEOPLE IN EUROPE.

FROM ALL THE OCCUPIED COUNTRIES, JEWS ARE BE-
ING TRANSPORTED, IN CONDITIONS OF APPALLING
HORROR AND BRUTALITY, TO EASTERN EUROPE. IN
POLAND, WHICH HAS BEEN MADE THE PRINCIPAL
NAZI SLAUGHTERHOUSE, THE GHETTOS ESTAB-
LISHED BY THE GERMAN INVADERS ARE BEING SYS-
TEMATICALLY EMPTIED OF ALL JEWS EXCEPT A FEW
HIGHLY SKILLED WORKERS REQUIRED FOR WAR IN-
DUSTRIES.

NONE OF THOSE TAKEN ARE EVER HEARD OF AGAIN.
THE ABLE-BODIED ARE SLOWLY WORKED TO DEATH IN
LABOR CAMPS. THE INFIRM ARE LEFT TO DIE OF

EXPOSURE AND STARVATION, OR ARE DELIBERATELY
MASSACRED IN MASS EXECUTIONS.

THE NUMBER OF VICTIMS OF THESE BLOODY CRUEL-
TIES IS RECKONED IN MANY HUNDREDS OF
THOUSANDS OF ENTIRELY INNOCENT MEN, WOMEN
AND CHILDREN.

THE GOVERNMENTS OF THE UNITED STATES OF AMER-
ICA; THE KINGDOM OF ENGLAND AND THE BRITISH
EMPIRE; THE UNION OF SOVIET SOCIALIST
REPUBLICS; AND THE FRENCH NATIONAL COMMITTEE
CONDEMN IN THE STRONGEST POSSIBLE TERMS THIS
BESTIAL POLICY OF COLD-BLOODED EXTERMINA-
TION.

DECLARATION ENDS.

(2) SECSTATE DESIRES NOTIFICATION BY MOST
EXPEDITIOUS MEANS OF COMPLIANCE, TO INCLUDE
NAME AND TITLE OF FOREIGN OFFICIAL TO WHOM
DECLARATION DELIVERED, AND DATE AND TIME.

CORDELL HULL
SECRETARY OF STATE

"Jesus H. Christ!" Clete said.

"Rather nauseating, isn't it?" Nestor said.

"Hundreds of thousands of people murdered?" Clete asked
incredulously.

"The ambassador said he's been led to believe it's many more
than that," Nestor said evenly. "He thinks there was probably
quite a discussion in Foggy Bottom..."

"What?"

" ... at the Department of State," Nestor explained somewhat
condescendingly. "They call it 'Foggy Bottom' in Washington.
The ambassador thinks there was probably quite a discussion—
with the decision made at the highest levels, perhaps by the Secretary himself—before they came up with the 'hundreds of
thousands' language. Even that boggles credulity. One's mind can

accept the death of one person, a hundred persons, even a thousand. Credulity is strained at tens of thousands, hundreds of thousands. The death, much less the murder, of millions is simply—beyond human comprehension.''

"In other words, you believe this?"

"We know it to be a fact; our people have seen the death camps."

"Jesus!"

"Give me a call when you return from Punta del Este. Have a good time. I've been there. The women on the beach are stunning; made me wish I was a bachelor."

He put his beer bottle down on the banister.

"I can find my way out," he said.

XI

Second Lieutenant Anthony J. Pelosi, Corps of Engineers, Army of the United States, wearing a short-sleeved white shirt and dark-blue cotton trousers, was wet with sweat when the bus finally arrived in La Boca. The bus was old, battered, noisy, and as crowded as the El at the Loop during rush hour—*more crowded; I feel like a goddamned sardine.*

Lieutenant Frade had ordered him to spend as much time as possible riding the buses, "to get an idea of the terrain." The mentors in New Orleans had suggested the idea, and it was a good one, but Pelosi couldn't help but notice that Frade wasn't riding around in fucking buses himself; he was either getting chauffeured in one of Mallín's cars or catching cabs.

Pelosi stepped off the bus, took half a dozen steps, and then pulled the sweat-soaked shirt away from his chest and back.

Lieutenant Frade had also ordered him to start "laying in whatever you think you're going to need to blow a hole in a ship. No explosives, no detonators, they'll be provided. Everything else."

What the fuck is everything else? You need five things to blow something: explosives, detonators, wire, damping material—sandbags are usually best—and a source of juice to blow the detonators. A proper magneto controller is best. You hook up the wires, give it a crank, and boom!

I'm not as dumb as Lieutenant Frade—and for that matter, Ettinger—think I am. Laying in everything else does not mean I should find some engineer supply store and walk in and announce, "Hola! I'm interested in a good high-explosives controller. A Matson and Hardy Model Seven would be nice. What am I going to do with it? Why, I'm going to blow the bottom out of a ship in your harbor, that's what I'm going to do."

I don't really need a controller. I can get by with a couple of six-volt dry-cell batteries; Christ knows I've done that often enough. So what I'm doing here is looking for wire and a half-dozen dry-cell batteries. Big fucking deal.

What I really need is a magnet, a great big fucking magnet, so I can make something like the thing Lieutenant Greene, Chief Norton, and Bo'sun Leech showed me at the shipyard in Mississippi.

That device really impressed Tony. It was designed to pierce armored steel, like on a tank; and it was improvised from a limpet mine the Navy had gotten from the English, Chief Norton told him. It was constructed of magnetized steel. Its bottom was flat and was attached to the steel of a ship's hull. The top was of much thicker steel, and dome-shaped. The explosive went inside the dome; but the dome also served as a damper, directing the explosive force inward. Even better, the charge itself was molded—Chief Norton called it a "shaped charge"—so that it *really* directed all the force inward.

Tony could think of a lot of uses for shaped charges in the business. Blowing concrete-sheathed structural steel, for example. And if you put a bunch of small shaped charges around the base of a smokestack, you could really drop the sonofabitch in on itself.

The only thing Tony found wrong with the limpets was that you could hardly put a couple of them in your luggage and board the airplane in Miami.

He didn't think now that he would be able to lay his hands on a dome-shaped piece of steel, even make one himself. But he could probably weld together a box—thin steel on the bottom, heavier on the sides and top—which would be maybe nearly as good as a dome. He would have to figure out some way to magnetize it. And he would try to mold some explosive himself into a shaped charge. If he could do that—he thought he could, with a big pot of boiling water—then he would have something just about as good as what the Navy showed him.

The one thing Tony could absolutely not figure out—with people around like Lieutenant Greene, Chief Norton, and Bo'sun Leech, who knew all about explosives and ships—was why *they* weren't down here, instead of a Gyrene fly-boy, Ettinger, and him. When Ettinger came to his apartment, he talked to him about that. Ettinger thought it was probably because Frade had connections in Argentina, and he and Ettinger spoke Spanish.

That was true, maybe. But Ettinger was supposed to be the

communications sergeant of the team, and so far they didn't even have a telephone, much less a radio.

This is really one fucked-up operation!

He walked to the edge of the water and bought an ice cream and a Coke from a street vendor. The ice cream was all right, but the Coke was room temperature. And the bottle was in shitty shape. When Tony was in the eighth grade at St. Teresa's, they took them on a tour of the Coke place. Half a dozen women there did nothing all day but sit at a conveyor belt and push off bottles that had chipped tops, or just looked bad. He wondered then what they did with all the bad bottles.

Now I know. They load them on ships and bring them down here.

He found an old-timey ship—it had both masts for sails and a smokestack—tied up at the stone wharf. Tony could read enough of the sign on the wharf to find out that the ship had sailed to Antarctica. He gave in to the impulse and bought a ticket and went on board.

A guy in what looked like some kind of Navy uniform guided him around. Tony scarcely understood what he was saying; but the map he pointed out showed that the boat had gone to the Antarctic not once, but half a dozen times.

Whoever sailed down there on this little thing really had balls. But what the hell, so did Columbus.

The guy kept talking too fast for Tony to understand much of what he said; but Tony nodded and shook his head and said "sí" a lot, and he had the idea when the tour was finished that the guy really didn't suspect that he was an American.

He gave him some money, and from the way the guy beamed, suspected he had given him way too much.

Well, fuck it! Lieutenant Frade gave me two hundred bucks for miscellaneous expenses. This is a miscellaneous expense. I'm looking at ships.

When he went back on the wharf, he was tempted to have another ice cream, but remembering the room-temperature Coke, decided that wasn't such a hot idea.

Maybe I can find a restaurant with some Italian food, and something cold to drink. Then I will go buy some fucking wire. If they ask me what I want it for, I'll tell them I'm putting in a telephone extension.

He found what he was looking for: Ristorante Napoli. It was

three blocks down a narrow cobblestone street, on the ground floor of a run-down building with light-blue shutters. The shutters were painted with what looked like watercolor paint that didn't cover the wood underneath all the way.

Every other Italian restaurant in Chicago is called Ristorante Napoli.

Inside, it was a dump. A small room and eight rickety tables covered with oilcloth. He walked in and looked down at one of the tables, not pleased with the cheap tableware and the battered glass, into which was rolled a thin paper napkin. But then the smell of basil, garlic, and fennel came to his nostrils, and he sat down.

A waiter, or maybe the owner, a none-too-clean white apron around his waist, walked into the room.

"Buenas tardes, Señor."

"Parli Italiano?"

"Of course. You are Italian?"

"Yes."

"From the North," the man said, and then tapped his ear. "I myself am from Napoli, but I can hear the North."

Actually, I'm from Cicero, Illinois. I don't think I should tell you that, so·if you think I am from the North of Italy, fine.

"Where?"

Shit! I know as much about Italy as I do about Argentina. Zero. Zilch.

"Far north. Up by the border."

"Perhaps near Santa del Moreno?"

"Not far," Tony said. He tapped his ear. "You have a fine ear, Señor."

"It is something like a hobby for me," the man said. "I am told that I am very good at it."

"You're amazing."

"And how may I help you, Señor?"

"I would like something cold to drink, and then I would like to eat."

"We have the Coca-Cola, and agua con gas."

"Coca-Cola."

"And have you considered what you would like to eat?"

Tony heard his father's voice in his ear:

"This only works in a little restaurant," he said. *"But if the guy running it is pushing something, take it. It's one of two things: He personally made it and he's proud of it. Or they made it*

yesterday and he's trying to get rid of it. You can always send it back.''

"You surprise me," Tony said.

"I will try to please. And a wine."

"You surprise me."

The first thing that appeared was the Coke and the wine. The Coke was cold, and Tony drained it and burped.

"Excuse me."

"It is nothing."

There was a whole bottle of wine.

All I wanted was a glass, but what the hell.

The man went through the wine-tasting ritual.

In a joint like this? But what the hell, he's trying.

"Very nice," Tony said. The man beamed and filled Tony's glass.

"What do you call it?"

"Vino tinto Rincón Famoso. It is Argentine. I would not want my mother to hear me say this, but I prefer it to the Italian."

"Very nice," Tony said, meaning it, even if it wasn't the Chianti he had hoped for.

Next came prosciutto—*damned good prosciutto*—on a plate with french fries.

"What do you call this in Spanish?"

"Jamón cocido con papas fritas."

"Jamón cocido con papas fritas," Tony repeated. "Jamón cocido con papas fritas."

"Fine," the man said. "In no time you will learn Spanish. It is not that different from Italian."

"I hope," Tony said.

Yeah, it won't be long. I'll speak Spanish in a couple of months. If I'm still alive in a couple of months.

Next came a small plate of vermicelli with a tomato-and-pepper sauce. Washed down with a couple of glasses of vino tinto, it wasn't at all bad; but Tony was disappointed. He could have eaten two, three times as much.

The small portion was explained with the delivery of some kind of chicken.

"What's this?"

"Suprema à la Maryland."

"Maryland?"

The man shrugged. "It is something my mother taught me. The

sauce is from bananas and corn. Perhaps it is Argentinean, not Italian.''

You bet your ass it's not Italian. Grandma told me the first banana she ever saw was in Chicago, and that she tried to eat the peel, it looked so good.

Washed down with the rest of the bottle of vino tinto, the Suprema à la Maryland wasn't half as bad as he thought it would be.

Tony declined another bottle of wine—*the last thing I can afford to do is get shitfaced*—and dessert. He was full up.

"Magnifico," he declared, and asked for the bill. It was a hell of a lot cheaper than the last meal he'd had downtown.

"Do you know someplace I can buy some telephone wire?"

"Right around the corner," the man told him.

Tony consulted his pocket-sized Spanish-English/English-Spanish dictionary before entering the hardware store.

"Cable para el teléfono, por favor?"

What looked like a hundred-foot roll of multistrand 16-gauge steel wire was produced. He would have preferred copper, but this would do.

And, hey, look at me, I'm speaking Spanish!

"How much?"

"How many meters will Señor require?"

"All of it."

"This is all I have."

So what?

"I will require all of it. Where I wish to place the telephone is a long way from the wall."

The man shrugged, announced a price, and Tony paid him. The wire was neatly wrapped in an old newspaper and tied with string.

Tony returned to the street and headed back toward the waterfront. As he neared Ristorante Napoli, he saw a fine-looking female coming the other way. She looked out of place here—too well-dressed, like one of the Miñas in the hotel. He wondered what she was doing in this neighborhood.

They met near the door to Ristorante Napoli. Tony smiled at her. She didn't respond, although he was sure she saw him smiling at her.

She looked right through me. Well, what the hell, the way I'm dressed, she probably decided I don't have any money. Or maybe she's not a Miña after all. She looks like a nice girl. Nice girls, nice Italian girls, always play hard to get.

And then she pushed open the door to the Ristorante Napoli and went in.

I'll be damned. That gives me two reasons to come back here.

He reached the waterfront and started toward the bus stop.

He saw a taxi.

Fuck the bus. Lieutenant Pelosi has made all the sacrifices in the service of his country he intends to today.

He flagged the taxi down and told the driver to take him to the Alvear Palace Hotel.

Jesus, that was a good-looking woman!

[TWO]
Aboard MV Colonia
Río de la Plata
0115 8 December 1942

"What do you say we go on deck and take the evening breeze?" First Lieutenant Cletus Howell Frade, USMCR, said to Second Lieutenant Anthony J. Pelosi, CE, USAR, as the waiter cleared their table.

"All right," Tony replied.

Clete stood up, peeled a couple of bills from a thick wad and tossed them casually on the table, then walked out of the dining room onto the deck.

The dining room, like their cabin, was on the bridge deck. There were benches along the bulkheads, and a dozen or so deck chairs. All the deck chairs were occupied, and people were scattered along the benches.

Clete looked aft. There was a glow on the horizon, obviously the lights of Buenos Aires. He estimated they were twenty-five, maybe thirty miles into the river. It was about a hundred twenty-five miles from Buenos Aires to Montevideo. The *Colonia* looked like a miniature ocean liner, and carried probably two hundred people. It sailed from Buenos Aires just after midnight, and would arrive in Montevideo at about nine in the morning. There were cabins, a dining room, a lounge, and a bar. You came aboard, had a drink and dinner, and then went to bed. When you woke up, you were in Uruguay. A couple of times Clete took the overnight boat from New York to Boston with his grandfather, when the Old Man had business with the Bank of Boston that had to be handled in person. The *Colonia* reminded him of that.

He led Pelosi forward, then down a ladder, then forward again, and down another ladder to the main deck. They stepped over a chain, with a sign in Spanish, "No Entry—Crew Only," hanging from it, and walked forward to the bow.

"That sign meant 'off limits,' didn't it?" Tony asked.

"Well, if somebody comes, we're just a couple of dumb Norteamericanos who don't speak Spanish. Besides, what they're worried about is a bunch of people out here lighting cigarettes, which will keep the helmsman and the officers on the bridge from seeing. No lights forward, in other words."

"No shit?"

"Would you like one of these?" extending to him a leather cigar case.

Tony considered the offer for a moment... *He gives me a speech about no cigarettes up here, and then pulls out cigars...* and then took a long, thin, black cigar.

"Thank you," he said.

"A fine conclusion to a splendid meal," Clete said.

"If you like eating at midnight."

"I wonder what they were serving at the O Club at Fort Bragg tonight? Three'll get you five it wasn't what we had."

"Jesus, their food is good, isn't it?" Tony said. "First-class steak!"

Clete handed him a gold cigarette lighter.

"You have to flip the top up first, and then spin the wheel," Clete explained. "I have the feeling that was made sometime around World War One."

Pelosi lit his cigar, then, hefting it, handed the lighter back.

"Heavy. Gold?"

"I'm sure it is. Nothing was too good for my uncle Bill."

"Excuse me?"

"My granduncle Guillermo. That was probably his. I found it and the cigar case in a drawer in his—now my—bedroom. I decided that if he had known what a splendid fellow I am, he would have left me both in his will, so I took possession."

Tony had to smile. He was glad it was too dark out here for the Pride of the Marine Corps to see his face.

"And the house, too?"

"The house belongs to my father. Uncle Bill lost it betting on the horses."

"No shit?"

"Uncle Bill was a man after my own heart. According to my father, he spent his life drinking good whiskey, laying all the women in Buenos Aires, gambling on horse races, and playing polo. I have decided I want to be just like him."

"You know how to play polo?"

"We used to play it at A and M. We called it polo, and I guess it was. But we did it on cow ponies, using brooms and a basketball."

"What's A and M? For that matter, what's a cow pony?"

"A and M, you ignorant city slicker, is the Texas Agricultural and Mechanical Institute. You really never heard of A and M?"

"Yeah. Now I know what it is. You went there?"

"For two years. I finished up at Tulane in New Orleans."

"So what's a cow pony?"

"A horse, most often what they call a quarterhorse, a small one, trained to work cattle. When we played 'polo,' the cow ponies made it clear they thought we were insane. We had them running up and down a field, and we were yelling and making a lot of noise, and there wasn't a cow in sight."

Pelosi chuckled.

"But you never played real polo?"

"No. I've been wondering if I could. Maybe. Christ knows, I grew up on a horse."

"Really?"

"On a ranch in West Texas. I was raised by my aunt and uncle."

"So those cowboy boots are for real? I thought maybe you thought they just looked good."

"They feel good. When I went in the Corps and had to wear what they call 'low quarter' shoes—do they call them that in the Army?—I felt like I was running around barefooted."

"Yeah, they do. When I went in the Army, the goddamned boots killed me. I was blisters all over. Then I got used to them, and then I got to wear jump boots, and they're really comfortable, and I felt the same way, barefoot, when I had to start wearing civilian shoes again."

"Well, keep your fingers crossed, and maybe pretty soon you can put your jump boots on again and get back to jumping out of perfectly functioning airplanes."

"Don't knock it 'til you've tried it," Tony said. "I like parachuting."

"I don't," Clete said. "I tried it once and hated it."

"How come you tried it?"

"There was a Japanese pilot who was much better than me," Clete said.

"No shit? You were shot down?"

"They warned us that the Japanese liked to shoot at people in parachutes, and that the thing to do was not pull the handle . . ." He made a pulling gesture across his chest.

"The 'D Ring,' " Tony furnished.

". . . until you were close to the ground. Or in my case, the water. So there I was," he gestured with his hands, "doing somersaults in the air, and every time I turned around—which seemed like twice a second—I looked at the water and tried to decide how close I was. Finally, I figured fuck it, and pulled the handle . . ."

Tony, chuckling, corrected him again: "The D Ring."

". . . and all of a sudden, it goes 'bloop,' jars the living shit out of me—I was sore between the legs for weeks—and then there's the water. Water is not always soft. And have you ever tried to swim wrapped in three square miles of parachute silk?"

"You didn't have your harness tight," Tony said. "That's one of the first things you learn, to make the harness tight."

"As I said, I tried it once and didn't like it. But you have fun, Tony. Each to his own."

Jesus, Mary and Joseph, Tony thought. *That's a true story. He was out fighting the Japs and got shot down, and jumped, and fucking near killed himself not opening his 'chute in time. He may be a little stuck up, but he's no candy-ass.*

"But you came out all right."

"They had PT boats patrolling between Guadalcanal and Tulagi. One of them saw me coming down, and they started firing at the Zero who was strafing me, chased him off, and then fished me out of the water. There was a guy—he commanded one of the other fighter squadrons, VMF-229—who went in the drink and spent twenty-four hours out there, floating around all by himself, before he was spotted and fished out. I don't think I could have taken that."

"Huh?"

"Waiting for the sharks. I think I would have gone nuts."

Tony could imagine that. He felt a chill.

"You ever shoot down any Japs?"

There was a moment before Clete replied, "I got lucky a couple of times."

"You going to tell me how many times?"

"Seven."

"You're an ace, then."

"Before I was dumb enough to volunteer for this, the Marine Corps was about to put me and a dozen other aces on display on the West Coast to sucker other innocent young men into volunteering for the crotch."

"The crotch"? What the hell is "the crotch"? Oh! He means the Marine Corps. If I called it "the crotch" he'd shit a brick.

"Was it as bad as they say on Guadalcanal?"

"It was unpleasant, Tony. Hot, humid, filthy, lousy food—much of it captured from the Japs—all kinds of bugs. And flying beat-up, shot-up, worn-out airplanes against Zeroes . . . a much better airplane, flown by pilots who were better than we were."

They weren't all better than you. Not if you shot down seven of them.

"You never talked about it before."

Clete shrugged. "Most people, civilians especially, don't understand."

"Can I ask you a question?"

"Sure."

"What are we doing here?"

"Hell, I thought you knew, Lieutenant Pelosi. Our contribution to the war effort is going to be to blow up a ship. That is, if people we must presume are far wiser than we are can make up their minds which ship, and tell us where it is, and how the hell we are supposed to blow it up."

Tony chuckled.

"I meant, where we're going?"

"Tomorrow morning, when we dock in Montevideo, we are going to a crude-oil terminal and make believe we know what we're doing as we examine the pipes and tanks and look at the books. Then we are going to a gambling casino for the night."

"A gambling casino?"

"You ever hear that line, 'theirs not to reason why, theirs but to ride into the valley of death'? In our case, it's walk into a gambling casino."

"And then what?"

"The next morning, we drive a rented car to a place called Punta del Este, where we take a swim. If Nes—the man who gave me our orders wasn't pulling my leg, the beaches of Punta del Este are crowded with good-looking women. Then, at night, we drive up to the Brazilian border, where they will air-drop your explosives to you.''

"How are they going to do that?"

"I would presume from an airplane."

Tony chuckled.

"I meant how are we going to communicate with the drop aircraft?"

"I was told you were the air-drop expert."

"You need a radio to talk to the drop aircraft."

"I wondered about that. I do know that at specified times we are to turn the headlights on and off for sixty-second intervals. Maybe that'll be enough to let the guy flying drop the stuff to us."

"Who gives us our orders?"

"I can't tell you his name, Tony, sorry. But I think he knows what he's doing," Clete said seriously. "And I'm sure he's right about the way they do things. If you don't know his name, you can't tell anybody . . . if, for example, we get caught and they start roasting you over a slow fire, or pulling your fingernails out.''

"Can that happen?"

"I hope not."

"If everything goes all right, if everything works, and we blow up this fucking ship, then what? What happens to us?"

"I don't know. Maybe they'll want us out of Argentina, and maybe they'll want us to stick around doing something else until we do get caught, or until we win the war, whichever comes first."

"I wish to Christ I was back in the 82nd Airborne."

"And I almost wish I was back on Guadalcanal," Clete said. *No, I don't,* he thought. *There is no Virgin Princess on Guadalcanal.* "For what the hell it's worth, Tony. We had Marine paratroops on Tulagi, a battalion of them. They landed by ship, not by jumping. They got shit kicked out of them. More than ten percent killed. I think our odds are a little better than that; and in the meantime, it's clean sheets, steaks, and with a little bit of luck, a piece of ass in Punta del Este.''

"I could use a little," Tony said. "I saw the most beautiful girl I ever saw in my life in Buenos Aires. I get a hard-on just thinking about her."

"Much the same thing, oddly enough, happened to me," Clete said.

He flicked his cigar over the rail.

"What do you say we hit the sack?"

"I never slept on a boat before," Tony confessed. "Do you get seasick in your sleep?"

"A ship," Clete corrected him. "A *boat* is a vessel you can carry aboard a ship. And no, if you were going to get seasick, you would be seasick by now."

[THREE]
El Casino de Carrasco
Montevideo, Uruguay
2000 8 December 1942

"Very nice," Lieutenant Pelosi observed to Lieutenant Frade as he inspected their suite—two bedrooms, plus sitting room and foyer.

"Try to remember you're an officer and a gentleman," Clete said, "and don't piss in the bidet."

"Screw you, Clete!"

Pelosi went to a window and hauled on the canvas tape that raised the heavy blinds over the French doors.

"Hey, the ocean's right out here!" Pelosi said, and then began to raise the other blinds.

"Jesus Christ, it really gets around, doesn't it? The last time I looked, it was in Miami."

"I mean we're facing the ocean, wise guy," Tony said, and opened one of the French doors. "And there's a balcony."

Clete followed him outside.

They were on the top floor of the ornate, stone, turn-of-the-century building. The balcony indeed faced an open body of water.

"The water's dirty," Tony observed.

"I think this is still the River Plate," Clete said. "You don't get to the Atlantic until you're in Punta del Este. That's up that-a-way, about a hundred miles." He pointed.

"That breeze feels good. Jesus, I hate this hot weather. You realize it's only a couple of weeks 'til Christmas? Sweating on Christmas!"

"Why don't we open all the blinds—in the bedrooms, especially—and the doors, to let the breeze in. And then go down and have dinner and see what happens? Play a little roulette, maybe?"

"Jesus, I'm still recovering from lunch, and we didn't eat that until three," Tony replied. "I think I'll just sit out here and watch the water go up and down."

"I don't think Ne—we were sent here to try our luck," Clete said. "And if someone were trying to contact us, they'd prefer to do it in a crowd, rather than up here in the room."

Tony considered that a moment, then said, "Let me take a leak. I'll be right with you."

When he came out of his bathroom, Clete handed him five fifty-dollar bills.

"What's this for?"

"To gamble. It's your Christmas present from the taxpayers of the United States."

"And what if I win?"

"You will be expected, of course, to turn all your winnings over to the government."

"In a pig's ass I will."

"Shame on you, Lieutenant Pelosi!"

They had a very good dinner in the dining room. It was in the center of the building, a large, somewhat dark space from whose three-story-high ceiling hung four enormous crystal chandeliers. A grand piano was at one end of the room, beside the bar, and a pianist played light classical music for most of their meal. Later it was replaced with a string quartet.

The room was full of prosperous-looking people, Clete thought; but nobody there was an aristocrat. Successful businessmen, he decided. Or ranchers in from the country for a night on the town. Moneyed, but not rich-rich like the sixteen or so people at Aunt Beatrice's and Uncle Humberto's dinner table.

Uncle Humberto's guests were rich-rich; they smelled of money and privilege. And they were simply fascinated with Dear Jorge's long-lost son. Half a dozen of them simply refused to speak Spanish with him, insisting on proving their worldliness by showing they spoke a second language as well as their native tongue.

He'd heard somewhere that in the Russian Court—before they booted the Czar out and murdered him and his family and threw their bodies down a well—the official language was French.

Clete thought of that after noticing that just about everybody had a pronounced loathing for the Russians, with a lesser but concomitant sympathy for the Germans.

Dear Beatrice's Poor Jorge had been murdered by the filthy communists, not killed in battle in Russia while accompanying an invading army. The Germans did not shoot their aristocracy, and they were engaged in fighting the filthy, godless communists. Thus, they could not be all bad.

This talk bothered him; but he managed to resist a growing temptation to mention the Germans' murder of several hundred thousand Jews—he was not sure if he believed Nestor's several millions figure; he didn't want to. But he didn't want to get in an argument with anybody either, not when Aunt Beatrice was liable to pop up at his side at any moment, and tell him again how much he looked like his mother and Poor Dear Jorge, both of them now together and with God and all the blessed angels . . . and how they took baths together and splashed and laughed and were so happy when they were infants.

Aunt Beatrice was out of her mind; there was no question about that. But Uncle Humberto was worse. He was not floating around on a drug-induced cloud. He was in the here and now and knew what was going on. Humberto kept looking at Clete out of big, dark, immensely sad eyes—*How is it that you are alive, and my Jorge is dead?*—until he saw Clete looking back. Then he put on a wide, toothy, absolutely phony smile and gave him a thumbs-up sign.

The Mallíns were there, of course. Not only were they part of that social circle, but it would be unthinkable not to invite them after they were so kind to Dear Cletus when he arrived.

The Mallíns, less the Virgin Princess. Aunt Beatrice's dinner to meet Dear Jorge's son had been a grown-ups' party; children not welcome. Clete wasn't sure at first if he was relieved or disappointed, but soon admitted he was goddamned disappointed.

At least I could have looked at her every once in a while.

All things considered, it was a lousy evening at Aunt Beatrice's and Uncle Humberto's.

No one tried to speak to Clete or Tony at dinner, and there wasn't even any eye contact from the other diners.

Nor was there anyone who paid the slightest bit of attention to them in the casino, except when Tony delivered a loud Cicero,

Illinois, "Oh, shit!" when he drew a king to a pair of fives and a two at the Vingt-et-Une table and dropped almost a thousand dollars.

By then it was midnight, and Clete decided he had been wrong about a possible contact in the casino. Nestor told him to spend the night here, he decided, because that's what an American in Uruguay on business would be expected to do.

"Let's go to bed," he said to a sad Tony Pelosi as he counted what was left of his money.

Tony was sad, but without good reason.

"I'm up six hundred over the two fifty you gave me," he announced in the elevator. "And if I hadn't gotten that fucking king!"

"Don't be greedy. Greedy gamblers always lose."

"My father says that all the time," Tony agreed. "You say that too?"

"I thought I made it up," Clete said, straight-faced.

Pelosi was in his room less than two minutes when Clete heard him call, excitedly, "Hey, Frade! Come in here."

Clete walked across the sitting room. Tony was in his underwear, and he was holding what looked like an oversized telephone to his ear.

"What the hell is that?"

"It's a walkie-talkie."

"A what?"

"A radio. A two-way radio!"

"That little thing?"

"I seen them demonstrated at Bragg. They're new. Not yet issued."

Pelosi pointed to a small leather bag on the bed, not much larger than a woman's purse.

"That was on the rack at the foot of the bed when I came in," Pelosi said. "With this inside."

He handed Clete a three-by-five-inch filing card—obviously American—on which was typewritten:

```
(1) Speak English

(2) Your call sign is ''Hunter.''

(3) You will contact ''Mallard.''
```

(4) You have 45 mins possible, 1 hr stretching it, battery power. (90 mins, 2 hrs, using spare set)

(5) Leave walkie-talkies in Wardrobe Punta de E. on departure.

Clete took the radio from Tony and examined it dubiously.

There was a nameplate on it: AN/PRC-6 MOTOROLA CORP. CHICAGO, ILL.

"These things really work?"

"Yeah. Well, now we know how we talk to the drop plane."

Clete put the walkie-talkie to his ear and heard a hiss.

"There's two of them?" he asked.

"Yeah. Take that one into your room, and we'll see if they work."

Clete went back to his room, examined the walkie-talkie again, pulled out an antenna that looked as if it should be mounted on a car fender, put the radio to his ear, and depressed a two-inch-long lever marked PRESS TO TALK.

"Dr. Watson, can you hear me?"

"Yeah. You're coming in five by five."

"I will be damned. Dr. Watson, over and out."

He walked back to Tony's room.

"What's the range of these things?" he asked.

"I don't know," Tony replied, thinking about it. "Maybe a mile. Maybe longer if we're talking to an airplane."

"Start thinking about how we can get these into Argentina," Clete said.

"We're supposed to leave them in the hotel in . . . Where we going? Punta someplace?"

"Punta del Este. Fuck 'em. The first thing a Marine learns, Tony, is that when he puts his hands on a piece of equipment that works, he keeps it."

[FOUR]
La Posta de la Congrejo Hotel
Punta del Este, Uruguay
0005 10 December 1942

"You want to put the top down?" Lieutenant Frade inquired of Lieutenant Pelosi as they prepared to get in their rental car.

"Why not? We could see better."

The car was a 1937 Ford convertible sedan. They had a good deal of difficulty pulling the top down.

"The President probably has people who do this for him," Clete observed.

"What?"

"I said, Roosevelt probably has people who do this for him."

"What the hell are you talking about?"

"President Roosevelt has a car just like this. I don't think he could put the top down himself; he probably has an official top-putter-upper-and-downer."

"He's crippled. Polio. How the hell can he drive a car?"

"It has levers on the steering wheel. You never saw it in the newsreels?"

"Yeah, now that you mention it."

"How far is this place?"

"A hundred and twenty-five miles," Clete said. "According to the map, the road's a highway. I figure we can make forty miles an hour; that's three hours to get there. We have an hour, an hour and a half's, cushion."

"You figuring this in miles or kilometers?"

"Miles. You know how to convert?"

"Sure," Tony said.

Bullshit. You don't know, but don't want to admit it.

"To get miles from kilometers, you divide the kilometers by eight, then multiply by five. Two hundred kilometers divided by eight is twenty-five. Times five is one twenty-five."

"Yeah, right. You want me to drive?"

"I'll drive. You work the map. I wish to hell we had a flash-light. Flashlights, plural."

"I got one," Tony said. "In the bag with the walkie-talkies."

"Good for you! You bring it with you?"

"No. But when I figured we would need one, I went to that little store on the main drag and said, 'Señora, una linterna, por favor,' and she sold me one."

"You should have bought two."

"I did, Lieutenant, Sir. I knew I had to take care of you."

"Insolence does not become you, Lieutenant."

The first fifty miles were on a macadam road on which they met few cars but a large number of open-bodied trucks of all sizes. In the direction of Montevideo, most of these were heavily laden with everything from firewood to cattle; but they were mostly empty headed north. Clete was not surprised when they reached the city of Rocha to find an all-night truck stop. He pulled in, gassed the car, and then he and Tony ate brochettes of beef, peppers, and onions cooked on an open fire. The beef was so tender, it had to be filet mignon.

A few miles out of Rocha, the pavement stopped abruptly, and they found themselves on a gravel road.

Christ, I should have thought about that! Clete realized, angry with himself. *This is Uruguay, not Louisiana.*

His concern proved unnecessary. The gravel road was wide and smooth and well cared for. Twice, the headlights picked up Caterpillar Road Graders and tractors with grading blades parked by the side of the road, which explained it.

Forty miles farther along, they came to a small town called Castillos, dark except for the bright lights of another all-night truck stop. Thirty-five miles past that they came to a still-smaller town, La Corinilla. They were almost at their destination. Finding it proved far easier than Clete thought it would be. Nestor's map was right on the money.

Three point seven miles past La Corinilla's Abierto Las 24 Horas truck stop, they turned right, drove 2.1 miles down a slightly more narrow, but equally well cared for gravel road, and then .6 miles down that, turned right again onto another fairly narrow road, drove .3 miles, and stopped.

In front of the car, as far as the headlights permitted him to see, the road was straight and level. On either side of the road there appeared to be swamp, but Clete finally realized these were rice fields.

He made a note of the odometer reading so he could return to this spot. And then they drove down the road. He went exactly a mile and stopped. The road and the rice fields stretched on, apparently to infinity. He looked at his watch, the Hamilton chronograph. It was two forty-five—0245. Even stopping for the brochettes and gas, they'd made much better time than he thought they would. And they weren't supposed to start flashing the headlights until 0400. They had an hour and fifteen minutes.

He turned the Ford around and headed back toward La Corinilla.

"Where are we going?" Tony asked.

"We have more than an hour. I don't think it's a good idea to just sit here. It might make somebody curious."

Do I mean that, or do I want a beer at that all-night truck stop?

"Shit, there's nobody out here. We haven't seen a car—or a light, for that matter—since we left that village."

"OK. You wait here, and I'll go back to the truck stop for a beer."

"The hell I will."

"I've been thinking about those whores," Tony announced as a plump woman in a dirty apron poured from their second liter bottle of cerveza.

Three minutes after they had put the walkie-talkies away, there was a knock at their door in the casino. Two very attractive, well-dressed women stood outside, in the corridor. The taller of the two—she had luxuriant reddish-brown hair—wondered if they might be interested in some companionship, if they hadn't lost all their money in the casino. Clete replied that would be a delightful experience, but unfortunately, he was waiting for his wife.

"First of all, they weren't whores, they were prostitutes; there's a difference. And secondly, shame on you."

"You weren't interested?" Tony asked. "Christ, they were really good-looking!"

"Well, I have this problem, Tony. I have the honor of the Marine Corps to think of. Marine officers don't pay women; it's the other way around."

"Oh, shit," Tony groaned.

"There wasn't time, and I didn't think it was such a good idea," Clete explained.

Not for the sake of the efficient execution of my assigned mission, he thought, *but because the dark and innocent eyes of the Virgin Princess seemed to be looking at me.*

"Well, I don't mind telling you I was tempted. I haven't had any in a long time. You bastards didn't give me any time in New Orleans . . ."

"We bastards?"

". . . and when I was on leave at home, my brothers insisted on showing me a good time; they never left me alone."

"Your brothers don't like women?"

"One of them is a priest."

"Oh. Tough luck. Well, you shouldn't have any trouble getting the wick dipped in B.A., Tony. There's women all over."

"I'm working on a little something," Tony said. He was thinking of the girl he had seen go in the Ristorante Napoli in La Boca.

I'm going back there and just hang around and look for her, he thought. *That is, if we get back, and don't get stood against some wall and shot for trying to smuggle twenty pounds of molded Composition C4 and walkie-talkies into Argentina.*

He picked up his beer glass.

"Isn't it about time we started back?"

"Jesus Christ, it's dark out here," Tony said. "There's not a goddamned light anywhere!"

"Shut up!" Clete ordered abruptly.

He thought he had heard the sound of an aircraft engine, a little one, probably a Lycoming. And then he was sure.

"Get on the horn," he ordered as he reached for the headlight switch.

"It's not 0400," Tony protested.

"Goddamn it, do what you're told."

"Mallard, Mallard," Tony complied. "This is Hunter, Hunter. Over."

There was an immediate reply.

"Hunter, Mallard," an American voice said. "How do you read? Over."

"Five by five. Over."

"Hunter, leave your lights on."

"Mallard, roger your lights on," Tony said, and then repeated the order to Clete.

"Roger, I have you in sight. Is the road clear? How do you estimate the wind?"

"He wants to know if the road is clear and about the wind," Tony relayed.

Clete stuck his index finger in his mouth and then extended his arm over his head. Then he took the walkie-talkie from Tony and pressed the PRESS-TO-TALK switch.

I think that crazy sonofabitch is about to try to put it down! Why else would he ask about the road being clear?

"Mallard, winds from the north negligible, I say again, negligible. The road is paved with gravel and clear. I say again, paved with gravel and clear."

"OK, Hunter, here we go."

Without realizing they had done so, both Tony and Clete had gotten to their feet, and they were now standing on the seat of the Ford, their waists about at the level of the top of the wind-

shield. They could hear the sound of the aircraft engine, but all
they could see of it was the orange glow of the engine exhaust,
and there was no way to judge from that where the aircraft was.
And then the exhaust glow disappeared.

Suddenly, blinding them, a landing light came on, and the
sound of the engine changed as the pilot retarded the throttle. The
landing light lined up with the road, and dropped lower and lower.
It was impossible to see the airplane against the brilliance of its
landing light, but Clete heard a chirp of wheels and then a rumble
as it touched down. The landing light died into an orange glow,
but it took their eyes some time to readjust.

And then there was an orange Piper Cub taxiing up to the grille
of the Ford.

"I will be a sonofabitch!" Tony said as he jumped over the
side of the Ford. Clete went over the other door and followed
Tony to the airplane as the pilot, in a summer-weight flying suit,
got out.

"God bless the Army Air Corps," Clete said to the pilot as he
put out his hand.

"Actually, I'm an Engineer officer," the pilot said. "I'm an
Army Liaison Pilot, teaching the Brazilians to direct artillery
fire."

"Corps of Engineers?" Tony said delightedly. "Me too."

"I thought you guys were in the OSS," the pilot said.

"Never believe what anybody over the grade of captain tells
you," Clete said, "as we say in the Marine Corps."

"Marine Aviator? You sounded like a pilot, on the horn."

"Fighter pilot, way out of his element," Clete said. "I thought
you were supposed to air-drop this stuff."

"The Air Corps wanted to. They were going to make a big
deal of this, come in with a C-47, drop some pathfinder in first,
then drop this stuff with a great big fucking cargo parachute, you
know how they are. I figured, shit, this stuff doesn't weigh fifty
pounds altogether, I can put it in the backseat. So I came over—
lost, of course—here yesterday, and took a look, and here I am.
What is that stuff, anyway? It looks like boards."

"It's supposed to," Tony said. "It's Composition C4. They
molded it to look like wood boards."

"Then that explains what your guy meant when he said 'be
damned careful with these.' Detonators, right?"

Tony took the small package the pilot extended to him and
opened it.

"Right," he said. "I hope you didn't have this near the explosives."

"I had it on my lap."

"Jesus!" Tony said.

"Let's get me unloaded and out of here," the pilot said. "I'd love to stay and chat, but I really don't want to know what you guys are going to do with that stuff, and I don't want to spend the war in a Uruguayan jail."

Three minutes later, he was gone.

When Clete got behind the wheel of the Ford and pressed the starter, the battery was dead. Tony, sweating and swearing, had to push the car to get it started. But in another three minutes, they too were gone.

XII

[ONE]
Aboard the *General Belgrano*
Río de la Plata
0945 13 December 1942

Shortly after they sailed from Lisbon, Captain Manuelo Schirmer, master of the *General Belgrano,* began to extend to Hauptmann Freiherr von Wachtstein of the Luftwaffe certain privileges. First, that of his table. At the start of the voyage, Peter was assigned to an eight-place table in the dining room. When he arrived for lunch, six other people were there, a middle-aged Argentinean couple and a somewhat younger German couple and their two children. When he politely asked about their home, they replied they were from Heidelberg, then made it quite clear they were not interested in conversation.

When he went in for dinner, the steward intercepted him and led him to the captain's table. This was placed lengthwise across the back of the room and was set with ten places, all on one side.

"Mi Capitán," the steward said, addressing a stocky, blond-haired man in his forties, who was wearing a uniform blouse with four gold stripes on each sleeve over a navy-blue turtleneck sweater. "El Capitán von Wachtstein."

"I am Kapitän Schirmer, Herr Hauptmann," Schirmer said in German, examining him carefully and unabashedly, "I thought you might be more comfortable taking your meals here."

"That's very kind of you, mi Capitán," Peter replied in Spanish. "Thank you."

"Ah, you speak Spanish. Good."

Schirmer then introduced him to the other officers at the table. Not all the ship's officers came to the first dinner, but eventually Peter understood that these included Schirmer, his first, second, and third mates; the chief engineer, his first, second, and third assistant engineers; and the ship's doctor. There were no other passengers at the table; obviously he was being given a special privilege.

The next morning, at breakfast, Schirmer invited him to visit the bridge. And when Peter went up later that morning, waiting for permission to enter, Schirmer loudly and formally announced, "Hauptmann von Wachtstein has the privilege of the bridge."

Peter knew virtually nothing about the customs and protocol of the sea. But he was a soldier, and understood that an order had been issued, and that he was being granted the privilege of permanent access to the bridge—this was not a good-for-only-one-visit invitation. Schirmer showed him around the bridge and the chart room, introduced him to his second mate (who had not been at dinner the night before), and then announced that Peter would be more comfortable in the supercargo cabin on the bridge deck, not presently in use, and that if he had no objection, he would have the steward move his things from his cabin on the passenger deck.

"Mi Capitán," Peter replied, "I don't know what 'supercargo' is. It sounds like either gold bullion, or diamonds, or something stowed outside on the deck under a tarpaulin, rather than downstairs in the hold."

Schirmer laughed.

"*Below decks,* Herr Hauptmann, not downstairs," he said, and then went on to explain that there was a cabin reserved for the senior hierarchy of L.M.A.E.—a company executive, for example, or an L.M.A.E. master or chief engineer traveling as a passenger.

"In that case, mi Capitán, I accept," Peter replied. "Thank you very much."

Peter had a strong temptation to suspect that he was being given all of these privileges because he was such a naturally charming fellow, but he resisted it. More likely, Schirmer, whose name was obviously German in origin, was extending a sort of Germanic privilege. Or else Capitán Schirmer was possibly treating Hauptmann von Wachtstein like a fellow officer.

By the third day out of Lisbon, they were on a partial first-name basis: Schirmer started to call him "Peter." Peter, however, decided that good manners and protocol required that he continue to call Schirmer "Capitán," and did so.

On the fifth day out, very late at night, as they were playing chess in Capitán Schirmer's cabin, Schirmer told him the real reason he granted Peter the privilege of the captain's table and the supercargo cabin. Of the one hundred and five passengers aboard the *General Belgrano,* thirty-nine, including the couple from Heidelberg and their children, were Jewish.

"I didn't know, Peter, whether or not you were a Jew-hating Nazi," Schirmer said, meeting his eyes, "but it was clear to me that you were making the Steins uncomfortable. And making things worse, the Argentineans at the table are rooting for the English in this war. He was educated in England and works for our railroad, which was designed and built by the English."

"I am not, mi Capitán, either a Nazi or a Jew-hater."

"I didn't think you would be, just to look at you, but I had no way of knowing."

"I wonder how they got out of Germany," Peter blurted, thinking aloud.

"I have no idea," Schirmer replied. "The L.M.A.E. office in Lisbon makes sure they have an entrance visa to Argentina and a paid-for ticket, and that's all we care about."

"There are a number of Germans, mi Capitán, myself and my father and many of our friends included, who loathe the Nazis and are ashamed at their treatment of Jews."

"As far as I am concerned, the subject is closed. All *is* well that ends well, Peter. I find you a delightful dinner companion and an even more delightful opponent at chess. You are not quite as good as I am, but you're good enough to give me a very good game."

"Our final breakfast, Peter," el Capitán Schirmer said on the morning of December 13, as they lingered over their coffee. "I shall miss your smiling face, an island of joy in this sea of sourpusses."

The Chief Engineer snorted. "There is something wrong with a man who leaps out of bed when he doesn't have to," he said.

"You Spaniards feel that way," Schirmer said. "We of German stock regard each day as a glorious opportunity to do something constructive."

"Carajo!"—roughly, Oh shit!

"Pay no attention to him, Peter. He has been bitter since the day he discovered he is known as 'Tiny Prick' among the girls under the El Puente Pueyrredón"—a railroad bridge in La Boca.

The Chief Engineer stood up and held out his hand to Peter.

"If I don't see you again, it's been a pleasure, Peter. I'm in the telephone book. If you have a free moment, give me a call, and I will take you to El Puente Pueyrredón and ask the girls themselves to tell you what they call el Capitán."

Peter stood up.

"Thank you, Sir, for the privilege of your company."

As they shook hands, there was a subtle change in the ambient vibrations of the ship. The Chief Engineer cocked his head.

"Stop engines," he said. At the same instant, Peter reached the conclusion that the vibration was gone, and that meant the engines had stopped.

Schirmer nodded, and turned to Peter.

"They were on the radio this morning," he said. "They are sending people to meet you aboard the pilot boat. Maybe you should get dressed."

For the last ten days of the voyage Peter had been dressing just as the ship's officers dressed—in white shirt and shorts loaned to him by Capitán Schirmer.

"Yes, Sir. I suppose I'd better. Con su permiso?"—With your permission? (May I leave you?)

The officer's steward had his perfectly pressed and starched summer khaki uniform hanging on the door of his cabin.

I wonder how much I should tip him. He's really taken good care of me. I should have asked Schirmer. I will miss him. I will miss the whole damned thing, the steward, the good food, the officers at the table, but especially Schirmer.

When he left his cabin, he saw Schirmer standing on the flying bridge, looking down at the sea. He went to him and asked about the tip. Schirmer told him, then pointed down.

Peter turned. A good-looking launch, with a good deal of varnished wood and gleaming brass, was alongside. A ladder had been put over the side, and a tall stocky man in an ornate uniform was very carefully climbing up it. Waiting to follow him was a much thinner man in a Wehrmacht colonel's uniform. He removed his cap and dabbed at his forehead and shaved head with a handkerchief.

Those are winter uniforms. Why the hell are they wearing winter uniforms in this heat?

The *Belgrano*'s second mate was on deck with a couple of sailors.

Probably waiting for the clown in the ornate uniform—what the hell is that, anyway?—to fall off the ladder.

"I suppose I'd better go down there," Peter said.

Schirmer nodded and grunted.

Peter went down the two ladders to the main deck. He reached the railing as the second mate helped the clown in the fancy uniform onto the deck.

Peter noticed for the first time that there was a brassard with a red swastika on the clown's left sleeve.

That makes him a Nazi.

The clown looked at Peter sternly.

The sonofabitch expects me to salute him. Fuck him. That's not a military uniform. Maybe Nazi party, probably diplomatic corps. I am a soldier; I exchange salutes with soldiers.

"Guten Morgen," Peter said politely.

The Wehrmacht Colonel came on deck a moment later.

Peter saluted, a military salute.

"Guten Morgen, Herr Oberst."

"Herr Hauptmann," the Colonel replied as he returned the salute.

The clown in the fancy uniform held out his right arm stiffly in the Nazi salute. Peter glanced up at the flying bridge. Schirmer was still leaning on the rail, watching the little ceremony. He was smiling, as if amused.

"I am Anton von Gradny-Sawz, First Secretary of the Embassy of the German Reich to the Republic of Argentina," the clown announced, "and this is Oberst Karl-Heinz Grüner, the Military Attaché."

"Hauptmann von Wachtstein," Peter said, "and this is Claudio Saverno, Second Officer of the *Belgrano.*"

"Welcome aboard the *Belgrano,*" Saverno said in Spanish.

A third man, in mussed civilian clothing, stepped off the ladder onto the deck.

"Mi Capitán," Saverno said. "El Capitán Schirmer is on the bridge. Would you care to join him?"

"Hola, Bernardo!" Schirmer called down loudly. "Come on up!"

"Is there somewhere we can talk?" Gradny-Sawz asked.

"Claudio, may I use the mess?" Peter asked.

"Of course, Peter. I'll send the steward with coffee and whatever."

"Gracias, amigo."

Peter gestured to show the way.

"Will you follow me, please, gentlemen?"

He led them to the mess.

"I was led to believe, Herr Hauptmann," Gradny-Sawz opened the conversation, "that you have been invested with the Knight's

Cross of the Iron Cross. May I ask why you are not wearing it?"

"I wasn't aware this was a formal occasion."

"It is a very formal occasion, Herr Hauptmann," Oberst Grü-ner said dryly.

"And can you get into a proper uniform?" Gradny-Sawz asked.

"By proper, mein Herr, I gather you mean winter?"

"The Colonel commanding the Husares de Pueyrredón," Colonel Grüner said, "was kind enough to advise me the uniform of the day for the ceremony on the dock will be the winter dress uniform."

"Jawohl, Herr Oberst."

"A squadron of the Husares, plus a military band, and a delegation of Argentine officials, military and civilian, will be on the dock," Grüner went on, "to accept the remains of Hauptmann Duarte from your custody. We will accompany them from the dock to the late Hauptmann Duarte's home. Here is the schedule we have been given. Do you speak Spanish?"

He handed Peter two sheets of paper stapled together.

"Jawohl, Herr Oberst," Peter repeated.

There was a vibration as the engines engaged.

"Following which," Gradny-Sawz said, "you will be taken to the Frade Guest House. Until the ceremonies are completed, you will reside there as the guest of Colonel Jorge Guillermo Frade, uncle of the late Hauptmann Frade, and former colonel commanding the Husares de Pueyrredón. I wish to speak to you about that."

"Oh?"

"It is a singular courtesy on the part of the Frade family to you. Your conduct during that period is of great importance, if you take my meaning."

In other words, I am not to get drunk and piss all over the carpet, right?

"I understand."

"Though it is his custom to have newly assigned members of the embassy staff as guests in his home, under these circumstances, Ambassador Graf von Lutzenberger will not be able to share his home with you. He has asked me to express his regret."

"That is very gracious of the Ambassador," Peter said.

"In other words, you will be at the service of the Frade family tonight and tomorrow," Oberst Grüner said. "We don't know what plans, if any, they have for you. But if they have made plans, and you were not available, there is a question of bad manners."

"I understand, Herr Oberst."

"And what plans have you made for the removal of the late Hauptmann Duarte's remains from this ship?" Gradny-Sawz asked.

"I believe el Capitán Schirmer will remove them from the hold with a crane and lower them onto the dock," Peter said, with a straight face.

He thought he saw a glimmer of amusement in Colonel Grüner's eyes.

"I don't know how long it will take us to reach the dock," Gradny-Sawz said, Peter's subtle sarcasm having escaped him, "but may I suggest that you change into a proper uniform, including the Knight's Cross, Herr Hauptmann?"

The Husares de Pueyrredón were mounted on absolutely beautiful horses and looked as if they were about to charge into Bosnia-Herzegovina and lop off rebellious heads with their sabers, or impale rebellious bodies on their lances, thus keeping peace in Emperor Franz-Josef's domain.

The Army band, not nearly so ornately uniformed as the Husares, played "Oid, mortales" ("Hear, O Mortals"—the Argentinean national anthem) as the casket was lowered off the *Belgrano* onto a horse-drawn artillery caisson. Salutes were exchanged between German and Argentinean officers, and then the official party formed up behind the caisson.

With the drums of the band beating out the Argentinean equivalent of "slow march," the procession marched off the dock and into the streets of Buenos Aires, with the cavalry bringing up the rear. Policemen halted traffic. Pedestrians stopped and faced the street as the procession marched by—some of them respectfully removing their hats, and most of them crossing themselves.

It was a long walk to the Avenida Alvear, and it was almost brutally hot. First Secretary Gradny-Sawz, Peter noticed with some pleasure, was not only sweat-soaked, but had not managed to avoid stepping into the horse dung left by the six animals drawing the caisson.

They had some trouble passing the caisson through the gate at the Duarte mansion—the lead horse tried several times to rear. But finally the caisson was in place, and eight Husares—almost certainly officers, Peter decided, although he could not read Argentinean insignia—unstrapped the casket, and struggling under its weight, carried it into the foyer of the mansion.

The official delegation followed. A man and a woman stood just inside the door, with a rank of servants behind them. The woman was in mourning black, broken only with a strand of very large pearls, her face concealed behind a veil.

A short fat officer who looked almost ludicrous in his Husares uniform was ahead of Peter in the line. When he reached the couple, he said, "Señor Duarte, Señora de Duarte, I have the honor to present Capitán Freiherr von Wachtstein of the German Air Force, who had the sad duty of bringing Capitán Duarte from Germany."

Duarte's father shook his hand limply and said, "How do you do?"

"May I extend the condolences of the Luftwaffe and the German people on your loss?" Peter said.

"Thank you," the father said.

"My son is now home, thanks to you, Captain," the mother said. "And with the Blessed Jesus and all the angels in his heavenly home."

Peter felt like crying.

You dumb shit, he thought angrily, *you left* this *to go fly a Storch and be a hero at Stalingrad? It wasn't even your goddamned war!*

The short fat man tugged at his arm and led him away.

"I am Coronel Alejandro Sahovaler," he said. "I have the honor of commanding the Husares de Pueyrredón."

"A sus órdenes, mi Coronel."

"El Coronel Jorge Guillermo Frade, uncle to the late Capitán Duarte, has arranged for you to be put up at the Frade family guest house. Unfortunately he had pressing business at his estancia, and could not be here today. Señora de Duarte telephoned me this morning to ask me to take you to the guest house. I was of course honored to be of service. May I do that now?"

"You're very gracious, mi Coronel," Peter said, and then spoke what came into his mind: "My luggage? It's still aboard the ship."

"It has been taken to the Avenida Libertador house," Sahovaler said. "It is no problem."

Well, in that case, I suppose that nobody closely examined my luggage and found the money.

"May I have a minute to speak with el Coronel Grüner, mi Coronel?"

"Of course."

Grüner was standing with Gradny-Sawz. Grüner and Sahovaler knew each other, while Gradny-Sawz had to be introduced. Peter explained that Sahovaler had offered to drive him to the guest house. The announcement visibly pleased Gradny-Sawz.

"I will be in touch, Hauptmann von Wachtstein," Gradny-Sawz said. "If not sooner, within a day or two."

"Thank you," Peter replied.

Sahovaler had an open Mercedes sedan—an Army car—waiting outside. The driver was wearing a Husares uniform, complete to bearskin hat. They rode regally from Avenida Alvear to Avenida Libertador. On the way, Coronel Sahovaler told Hauptmann von Wachtstein that he was sure el Coronel Frade would be in touch with him very shortly to make sure he was not left alone in the Guest House.

[TWO]

Coronel Sahovaler was wrong. Since el Coronel Jorge Guillermo Frade had no intention whatever of participating in the nonsense on the pier, or to put on a hot dress uniform to march through horse droppings on the streets of Buenos Aires in the heat of summer, and since Cletus had "business" in Punta del Este— Frade hoped this was nothing more dangerous than meeting young women in brief bathing costumes—he had indeed found pressing business at Estancia San Pedro y San Pablo.

It happened to be legitimate. He was entertaining overnight el Coronel Ricardo López, commander of the 2nd Regiment of Infantry. Wattersly had informed Frade that when he and Kleber talked with him, they were unable to move him off the fence. Wattersly suggested that Frade talk to him himself. Under the circumstances, he had had no choice but to go along.

He would entertain López royally. And if there seemed to be an opportunity, he would reason with him himself. If that failed, the 2nd Regiment of Infantry would have to be placed in the Against column. There were only two columns, For and Against. If the 2nd Infantry went in the Against column, it would have to be neutralized.

He also completely forgot that he had promised his sister to arrange to put up the German officer at the Guest House. Knowing her brother's tendency to let promises slip his mind, Señora

Beatrice de Duarte had called the Guest House and checked. When it turned out he had indeed forgotten, she asked Señora Pellano to take very good care of the young German officer who brought Dear Jorge back to Argentina. Then she called el Coronel Sahovaler to make sure he had a ride.

[THREE]
Customs Shed
Buenos Aires, Argentina
2135 13 December 1942

The plan to smuggle the walkie-talkies past customs was Tony's. It was novel, simple, and it worked:

"If you never saw one of these before," Tony said, "the odds are that nobody here has."

"So?"

"We'll tell them they are portable radios that don't work."

"You've lost me."

"We don't try to hide them. We make believe we took them over there to listen to music on the beach."

Clete could think of no better way to bring the radios into Argentina. Besides, even if the ruse didn't work and they confiscated the radios, it would divert attention from the "wooden" boxes loaded with straw chickens, ducks, and fish.

They pried the AN/PRC-6 MOTOROLA CORP. CHICAGO, ILL. labels from the walkie-talkies; then they each put one of them on clear display in their luggage.

The customs officer was fascinated with the radios, and very sympathetic. After he put a radio to his ear and heard only a hiss, he offered the professional opinion that they probably dropped them, or else got them wet on the beach.

He pawed perfunctorily through the chickens, ducks, and fishes in the "wooden" boxes, smiled, and waved them through.

"Buenas noches, Señores."

"Buenas noches," Clete replied, and motioned for a porter to carry their luggage toward the taxi line. He carried one of the "wooden" boxes and Tony carried the other.

As they walked toward the line, he asked Tony if he wanted to have dinner at the guest house, or else go out somewhere.

"Thanks, no, Clete," Tony replied. "What are we going to do

with this stuff, now that we've got it?''

"I'll keep it," Clete said. "That would probably be the safest thing."

"I was thinking that maybe you could give the radios to Ettinger. Maybe he can figure out what to do when the batteries go dead."

"Right."

"And I'd like to take the detonators. I want to take a good look at them, to make sure how much dry-cell juice I'm going to need."

"Good thinking. But we can drop the radios off at Ettinger's apartment on the way to yours. And then we'll drop the detonators at yours, and get some dinner."

"I think I'll pass, Clete," Tony said. "Unless you really want some company."

"Just an idea. I'll bring the radios to David tomorrow."

"What I'm going to do, Clete," Tony said, as if worried that he'd hurt Frade's feelings, "is go find a church. Light a candle. Say 'thank you.' You want to come along?''

"I think I'll pass on that, Tony," Clete said. "If I went to church, the steeple would fall off. But say 'thank you' for me, too, will you?''

"I will," Tony said, wondering if it was a sin for him to be glad Clete didn't want to go to church with him. The church he had in mind was near the Ristorante Napoli. Afterward, he would drop in to the Ristorante Napoli for his dinner. She just might be there.

Hell, she might even be in the church. Odds are that she's Catholic, and nice Catholic girls go to church.

They took their turn in the taxi line, and finally climbed into one. Clete told the driver to take them to Tony's apartment on Avenida Corrientes.

It was quarter past ten when the driver pulled up before the gate at 4730 Avenida Libertador. There were lights on over the drive and above the door, but the gates were closed, and the smaller pedestrian gate beside the vehicular gate was locked; he could see no light coming from the servants' quarters. Since Señora Pellano had not known when to expect him, he presumed she had simply gone to bed.

Finding the keys he needed, then wrestling with the ancient lock on the gate, and then carrying his luggage and—carefully—

both "wooden" boxes from the cab to the front door took another five minutes.

He paid the cabdriver, then moved everything inside the house.

I'll bring these boxes upstairs—duty first. I'll take them apart, put the pieces on a shelf in one of my closets, and then I'll come down here and have a very stiff drink. I was more afraid smuggling this stuff past customs than I let on.

He was almost to the elevator when he heard, faintly, Beethoven's Third Symphony on the radio or the phonograph. Then he saw a crack of light under the double doors to the library.

Who the hell can that be? My father?

He walked to it and pushed it open with his foot.

A young man in a quilted, dark-red dressing gown was slumped in one of the armchairs, a cognac snifter resting on his chest. A cigar lay in the ashtray on the table beside him.

Who the hell is this?

"Buenas noches, Señor."

The young man was startled. He quickly put the cognac snifter on the table, rose, and smiled.

"Buenas noches," he said.

"Yo soy Cletus Frade."

"El Coronel Frade?" the young man asked incredulously.

"No," Clete chuckled, "el Teniente Frade. El Coronel is my father."

The young man bowed and clicked his heels.

"Mucho gusto, Teniente. Yo soy el Capitán Hans-Peter Freiherr von Wachtstein, de la Luftwaffe."

Holy shit! This must be the guy who brought the body from Germany. And you told him you were a lieutenant. Brilliant, Frade, fucking brilliant! He speaks Spanish perfectly.

"Señor, please, Capitán. I am no longer a lieutenant. Better yet, please call me Clete."

"I'm called Peter," von Wachtstein said, offering his hand. "Am I in your chair?"

"Sit down," Clete said.

"The lady who runs this place told me to make myself at home. So she asked if it would be all right if she went to evening mass," Peter said. "I took the liberty of coming down here and playing the phonograph, and helping myself to the cognac. Was that all right?"

"The cognac is a fine idea. Give me a minute to take my things to my room, and I'll join you."

"Let me help you."

"Not necessary."

"I would like to."

"Thank you."

Peter followed Clete back into the reception foyer and picked up the second "wooden" box.

"Delightful," he said, admiring the straw chickens, ducks, and fishes. "For your children?"

"I have no children that I know of," Clete said as they stepped into the elevator.

"I have none that I acknowledge," Peter replied.

They smiled at each other.

"I was drinking when I bought these," Clete said. "At the time it seemed like a splendid idea."

Peter chuckled.

"Señora Pellano has a herd of grandchildren," Clete said. "They will not go to waste."

"How nice for the grandchildren."

They put the "wooden" boxes inside the door to Clete's apartment, then made a second trip with his luggage, and finally returned to the library.

"It's a beautiful and unusual, house," Peter observed as Clete helped himself to the cognac.

"To your health, Peter," Clete said, raising his glass.

"And yours, Clete," Peter replied in English.

"The house was built by my granduncle Guillermo," Clete said, and went on to relate the history of Uncle Bill and the house.

It'll give me a chance to decide how to handle this, he thought. *I am obviously in the presence of mine enemy.*

Capitán von Wachtstein was properly appreciative of the story of Granduncle Guillermo, chuckled a final time, and then met Clete's eyes.

"You said you were formerly a lieutenant," he asked amiably. "In the Argentine Army?"

"No," Clete said.

"I could not help but observe your watch," von Wachtstein said in a polite challenge. "I have seen such watches before."

"Have you?"

"On the wrists of American aviators shot down over France and Germany. They are very good watches."

"You are a very perceptive man, mi Capitán."

"Possibly. And you have a very interesting Spanish accent.

Why do I think that my being here may be very awkward for both of us?''

''I am not a professional officer, mi Capitán,'' Clete said. ''I have no idea what conduct is expected of an officer, even a former officer, when he meets an enemy officer in a neutral country.''

''And in his father's house,'' Peter replied. ''I, on the other hand, am a professional officer, and I haven't the faintest idea either. My father, however—my father is a Generalmajor, and presumably should know about these things—served in France in the First World War and often told me about the armistice, the unofficial armistice, declared between the English and the Germans on Christmas Eve. Do you suppose, as officers and gentlemen, that we might pretend it's Christmas Eve? We'd only be off by a couple of weeks. Less.''

''I think that would be a splendid solution,'' Clete said. ''Merry Christmas, Captain. *Peter.*''

They shook hands.

''Fröhliche Weihnachten, Clete,'' Peter said. ''You were a pilot, right?''

Clete nodded.

''I could tell,'' Peter said. ''Not only by the watch. Pilots are better-looking, more charming, and far more intelligent than other officers.''

''More modest, too,'' Clete said.

''Absolutely. What did you fly?''

''Wildcats, Grumman Wildcats.''

''You're a fighter pilot. So am I. Most recently Focke-Wulf 190s. I had a Jaeger squadron near Berlin.''

''I was in the Pacific. Midway and Guadalcanal.''

Their eyes met and locked for a moment.

''We heard about Guadalcanal,'' Peter said. ''My father told me that the Japanese military attaché assured him that the Americans would be forced into the sea within weeks. My father said he did not think so.''

''We were hanging on by our teeth for a while,'' Clete said. ''But we're there for good now, I think.''

''Are the Japanese pilots competent? And their aircraft?''

''The Zero is a first-class fighter,'' Clete said. ''And some of the Japanese pilots, two in particular, were very good.''

Peter chuckled in understanding.

''You were shot down twice?''

"Shot down twice, disabled once. I was able to bring it in dead-stick."

"Over Russia, especially in the Steppes, losing an engine is not much of a problem. You can sit down almost anywhere. Over Western Europe, it is a problem. The farms are smaller, and in France, in Normandy in particular, the edges of the fields are fenced with rock."

"I guess you know from experience?"

"Yes. Your Flying Fortress—B-17?"

Clete nodded.

". . . is formidable."

"We have a saying—about pilots and watches—that you can always tell a B-17 pilot in the shower. He's the one with the big watch and the small prick."

He had to explain "prick" to Peter, the Mexican-Spanish vulgarism not being the same as the Spanish-Spanish; but eventually Peter laughed appreciatively.

I'm running off at the mouth, Clete thought, somewhat alarmed, *which means I'm getting drunk. Why? I've only had three of these. What I should do, obviously, is politely tell mine enemy "good night," go to bed, and sort this all out in the morning. To hell with it. We have a gentleman's agreement that it's Christmas Eve, and I like this guy.*

He picked up the cognac bottle, poured some in Peter's glass, and then refilled his own.

"I will not ask what an American Air Force officer is doing in Argentina," Peter said.

"Thank you," Clete said quickly. "An *ex*-officer. And I was a Marine, not in the Air Corps."

"A Marine? What is a Marine?"

"Soldiers of the sea," Clete said.

"Ah, yes. I have heard of the Marines. An elite force. They are like our SS."

"An elite force," Clete said coldly. "But not at goddamn all like your SS."

Their eyes locked again.

"There is propaganda on both sides in a war," Peter said. "Some of the SS—perhaps most—are fine soldiers."

"I think we better change the subject, Peter."

"And some are despicable scum," Peter went on.

"I know why you're here," Clete said. "You escorted Jorge Duarte's body, right?"

Peter nodded, then said, "My father arranged it. He wanted me out of the war, out of Germany."

Gott, I must be drunk! Peter thought. *Why did I tell him that?*

"I don't understand."

"I lost my two brothers, and my mother, in this war," Peter said. "My father wanted to preserve the family."

"I'm sorry," Clete said.

That was sincere, Peter thought. *He meant that.*

"Just before you came in here, I was wondering, with the assistance of Herr Martel"—he held up his brandy snifter—"if I have done the honorable thing."

"You said your father arranged it. Could you have stopped him?"

"I was wondering about that too. I didn't try."

"I was glad to get off of Guadalcanal," Clete said. "I figured I was running out of percentages."

"Excuse me?"

"You can only go up and come down in one piece so many times," Clete said. "Eventually, you don't come back. We call it the percentage."

"Yes," Peter agreed. "But you felt no . . . obligation of honor . . . to remain?"

"I did not ask to be relieved, but I was glad when I was."

"I got drunk when I was relieved," Peter said. "I told myself I did it because I did not wish to be relieved. Now I am wondering if I really wasn't . . . glad."

"I thought maybe you were with Duarte when he was killed," Clete said.

"Never met him. I was told he was killed at Stalingrad flying a Storch, a little high-wing monoplane used for artillery spotting, carrying people around, that sort of thing."

"That he wasn't supposed to be flying in the first place. My father told me that if he had any idea he was putting him in the line of fire, he never would have let him go over there."

"What sort of a fellow was he?"

"I never met him," Clete said.

"Really? I thought he was your cousin."

"He was. But I never met him. Or his parents. Or, for that matter, my father, until a couple of days ago."

"I met them this afternoon. That was very difficult. I had the feeling they were asking, 'What are you doing alive when our son is dead?' "

"I had exactly the same feeling when I met them," Clete said.

"How is it you never met them?"

Clete told the story, including the cover story of his heart murmur and his job down here making sure the Argentines weren't diverting American oil products to the Germans. The lies made him uncomfortable, especially after "mine enemy" had been so openly sincere.

"Does that mean you can't fly anymore?"

"No. It just means I can't fly for the Marines."

"I miss flying," Peter said. "And I don't think I'll be doing much, if any, flying here."

"My father has a light airplane. If I can persuade him to let me use it, I'll take you for a ride."

"I would like that," Peter said seriously. "Thank you very much."

Señora Pellano came into the library a few minutes after one to find Señor Cletus and the young German officer standing by the fireplace making strange movements with their hands, like little boys pretending their hands were aeroplanes.

They seemed embarrassed that they had been drinking. There was no reason for that.

She told them she had gone to midnight mass at the Basilica de Nuestra Señora del Pilar, which was why she was so late, and asked them if they would like anything to eat.

But they thanked her and said they were about to go to bed.

For about half an hour she sat on a little stool behind the door of the corridor that led from the foyer to the kitchen, until she heard them—sounding very happy if perhaps a little drunk—tell each other goodnight.

[FOUR]
Calle Olavarría
La Boca, Buenos Aires
1135 13 December 1942

As he prepared to enter the Church of San Juan Evangelista, Tony was telling himself for the tenth or twelfth time that he was making a fool of himself, a church seemed to be on every other corner, and the odds of her showing up at this one were one in nine zillion. That was when he saw her coming around the corner from the direction of Ristorante Napoli.

She wasn't as well-dressed as the last time he saw her. She was wearing a simple cotton dress and sandals, with a shawl around her shoulders and over her head. But she was even more beautiful than he remembered, like one of the statues of the Virgin Mary in St. Rose of Lima's, back in Cicero.

Seeing him standing by the church door seemed to surprise her, even to frighten her, as if he might do something bad to her, and she quickly averted her eyes.

Tony had gathered his courage. "Buenas noches, Señorita," he said, smiling. It wasn't all that much different from Italian.

She looked at him and just perceptibly smiled, but did not speak.

He waited a good three minutes before following her inside the church, among other things debating the Christian morality of trying to pick up a girl there. He finally decided it was all right, he wasn't trying to fuck her or anything.

He had a little trouble finding her in the church; it was dark inside. And when he did find her, he had trouble finding a seat that would give him a view of something besides the back of her head.

But even that wasn't so bad. He stepped on some old lady's foot and she yelped, and he said without thinking, "Scusi," in Italian, and the old lady answered him in Italian. She said he was a clumsy jackass, but she said it in Italian, and that made him think that maybe the girl also spoke Italian—why not? She had gone into the Ristorante Napoli, and this was an Italian neighborhood. Maybe if he had a chance to say hello to her again, he could try it in Italian and wouldn't sound like the neighborhood idiot trying to talk to her in Spanish.

He said a prayer for his family, and thanked God for not getting caught in Uruguay. And he asked God's protection when they tried to blow a hole in the ship. And then he asked God, "Please let me meet her." And for a moment he wondered if he should have done that, but decided there was nothing wrong with it, he had no carnal lusts for her or anything like that.

Once she turned around and saw him. And even in the dim light—he didn't think there was a bulb bigger than forty watts in all of Argentina, and the ones in here looked like refrigerator bulbs—he thought he saw her blush.

When she stood up and left, walking past him out of the church, she didn't look at him, although he knew damned well she had seen him. He hurried after her, and saw her heading toward the Ristorante Napoli. He waited until she disappeared around the corner and then walked quickly after her.

What the hell, it was three blocks to the ristorante, maybe I can catch up with her.

She turned another corner, a block away from the Ristorante Napoli, and he walked faster so he wouldn't lose her. And in case she went in some house or something, he would know where she lived.

When he turned the corner, she was waiting for him.

"If my father sees you following me, he will cut out your heart with a knife," she said. In Italian!

His mouth went on automatic. He was startled to hear himself say, "Oh, please don't tell your father. I am just a poor Italian boy far from home and all alone."

Boy, did I put my foot in my mouth with that stupid line.

But she smiled.

"You're telling the truth?"

Tony held up his right hand.

"I swear to God!" he declared passionately.

"Where are you from? The North?"

"Cicero."

"Where?"

"Cicero, Illinois. Outside Chicago. In the United States of America."

"You're telling the truth?"

"I swear to God, on my mother's honor."

"I have never heard of Cicero, Illinois," she said.

"It's a nice place. You would like it. You ought to visit there sometime."

There you go again, asshole! Think before you open your god-damned mouth!

"You are an American?" she asked in disbelief.

"I am an American."

"If you are an American, you must speak English."

"I do."

"Say something in English."

"What do you want me to say?" Tony asked in English.

"Say you are a poor Italian boy far from home and all alone."

"I really am," Tony said in English.

"You can't speak English!"

"I am a poor Italian boy far from home and all alone," Tony quickly said in English.

Her eyes widened.

"I think I maybe believe you," the girl said.

"I swear to God."

She smiled and took his arm.

"It is not right to be alone and far from home," she said. "Come, I will take you home with me and we will have a glass of wine for you, and a cake."

I don't believe this! Thank you, God!

She took him to the Ristorante Napoli, which was closed, and through a door that opened on a stairway that led to a little apartment over the restaurant.

Her father—Tony recognized him as the guy who gave him the good meal the first time he went to the restaurant—and her mother and some younger brothers and sisters were there.

Her father didn't recognize him.

Thank God, after that bullshit story I handed him about being from some village near the Austrian border!

The girl told her family they had met in the church and that he had told her he was alone, and she had brought him home for a glass of wine and a cake. Her mother raised her eyebrows the way Tony's grandmother used to raise hers; but her father gave him a glass of wine, and then another, and some kind of pastry her mother said she made special for the family and not for the restaurant. And then everybody just sat there sort of uncomfortable, so Tony took the hint and decided he better get the hell out of there before he made a pest of himself, and started to go.

He shook hands with everybody and then the girl went down the stairs with him to the street, and he gathered his courage and blurted, "I'd really like to see you again."

"Impossible."

"Why is it impossible? We could have a cup of coffee or something. Dinner."

"It's impossible."

"Why is it impossible?"

"I have a job. I work all week."

"You have to have some time off."

"Very little."

"You have to have some," Tony argued. "You're off now, for example. Are you working tomorrow? Tomorrow's Sunday!"

She hesitated before replying, "No. But my family will be visiting relatives."

"All day?"

"From five."

"What about between now and five?"

"It's not a very good idea."

"Please!"

"It's crazy."

"Let me at least buy you a cup of coffee."

"I should not do this, but . . ."

"But what?"

"You come here at nine-thirty tomorrow. We take the train to El Tigre. We have a cup of coffee, maybe a little sandwich, and then we come back. OK."

What the hell is El Tigre? Tony wondered. *"The Tiger"? What the hell does that mean? Who the hell cares?*

"Nine-thirty," he said. "I'll be here."

"It's crazy," she said one last time, and then turned and went up the stairs.

[FIVE]
4730 Avenida Libertador
Buenos Aires
0925 14 December 1942

First Lieutenant Cletus Howell Frade, USMCR, opened his eyes and found himself staring at Hauptmann Freiherr Hans-Peter von Wachtstein of the Luftwaffe, who was in a khaki uniform. Clete noticed the swastika on his pilot's wings. It made him uncomfortable.

"What the hell do you want?" he inquired, somewhat less than graciously.

"It is almost half past nine," von Wachtstein said.

"What the hell are you, a talking clock? Get the hell out of here!"

"There is an officer here to move me to a hotel," Peter said.

Clete sat up. His brain banged against the interior of his cranium. His dry tongue scraped against the cobblestones on his teeth. His stomach groaned. His eyes hurt.

"What did you say?" he asked.

Behind Peter, he saw Señora Pellano carrying a tray on which was a coffeepot, a large glass of orange juice, and a rose in a small crystal vase. She was smiling at him maternally.

"Buenos días, Señor Cletus," she said.

Christ, that's all I need. A smiling face and a goddamned rose!

"Buenos días, Señora Pellano," he said, and smiled. It hurt to smile.

"There is an officer here, a Coronel Kleber. He is to move me to a hotel," Peter said. "He claims it is to make me more convenient to your uncle's house. But I think someone finally remembered that you are living here."

"Oh, Christ," Clete said.

"Our armistice is over, I am afraid," Peter said.

"Looks that way."

"I would suggest, Clete, that our armistice be a secret between us; that we both say we were unaware the other was in the house. There are those, I am afraid, who would not understand how it was between us."

"Oh, shit!" Clete said.

"You agree?"

"Oh, hell. Yeah, sure. You're right."

"I thank you for your hospitality, Clete," Peter said, and put out his hand. Clete shook it.

Peter took his hand back, came to attention with a click of his heels, and saluted.

With a vague movement of his arm, Clete touched his hand to his right eyebrow, returning the salute.

Von Wachtstein did an about-face and marched out of the room.

I shouldn't have been so fucking casual with that salute. He meant his. I'll be damned if that bullshit they gave us at Quantico isn't true—that a salute is a gesture of greeting that is the privilege of warriors. The least I could have done was return it, not wave at him. Nice guy. Damned nice guy.

"Señora, I very much appreciate the breakfast, but could you come back in a couple of hours?"

"Señor Clete," Señora Pellano said, setting the tray on the bed and fluffing his pillows, "it would be better if you had the coffee. Señor Nestor will be here in twenty minutes."

"Señor Nestor?"

"I told him you were not feeling well, and he said it was very important."

"Thank you, Señora," Clete said, and reached for the orange juice. "I will receive him."

"Sí," she said, and then, "And you may have your car at any hour between twelve and three."

"What car?"

"There was a call from Señor Mallín's secretary yesterday. Your car has arrived. The necessary papers have been accomplished, and you may go to the customs at any hour between twelve and three to take it from them."

"On Sunday?"

"It is a courtesy to Señor Mallín," Señora Pellano said. "Or perhaps to your father."

"Won't it wait until tomorrow?"

"The officials will be there waiting for you, Señor," she said.

In other words, you ungrateful bastard, go pick up the god-damn car.

"Thank you," Clete said. "Señora, would a little present for the man who has my car be in order?"

"A small gift of money would be nice. Or perhaps a few bottles of wine."

"Is there any here?"

"But of course. I will pack something appropriate for a small gift."

Sixty seconds after he stepped under the shower, there was a telephone call for him, surprising him not at all.

"Have them call back!" he ordered.

"It is your father, Señor Cletus."

"Good morning, Cletus. It is your father calling."

"Good morning."

"I only a few hours ago learned—I am at Estancia San Pedro y San Pablo—that you have returned from Uruguay."

"I got in late last night."

"And was an angry man with a pistol chasing you?"

"I beg your pardon?"

"I thought perhaps that a jealous husband had cut short your stay."

"No. Nothing like that. I just had enough."

"When I was your age, I never had enough. Did you meet the other guest at the house?"

Clete hesitated just perceptibly before replying.

"Just to say hello, to wish him a Merry Christmas. Señora

Pellano tells me that he has left.''

"It is of no importance. The people who arranged for him to stay there were not aware that it is now your residence,'' Frade said. "Tell me, have you plans for the day?''

"No, Sir.''

"May I make a suggestion?''

"Certainly.''

"I will send Enrico in the station wagon to you. He will bring you to the estancia, and you and I will have an American dinner. A rib of beef, with Worcestershire pudding. And perhaps a ride afterward. How does that sound to you?''

He means Yorkshire, Clete thought, smiling, and then: *Is he alone out there? Lonely?*

"I have someone coming to see me now; and, between twelve and three, I have to pick up my car at the port.''

"Excuse me?''

"My car has arrived from New Orleans. Señor Mallín has arranged for me to pick it up today between twelve and three.''

"Then you do not wish to come?'' His disappointment was evident.

"No, Sir. I'm just telling you what I have to do before I can come.''

"I will call a friend in the Ministry of Customs,'' Frade said. "When you arrive at the port, there will be no problems.''

"I think Señor Mallín has already arranged that.''

"I will call my friend. There will be no problems with Customs. And then Enrico, in the station wagon, will come from here to there and lead you back to the estancia.''

"I can read a map. Is there someplace I can get a map?''

"Yes, of course you can read a map. Ask Señora Pellano to prepare one for you.''

"Well, then, I'll be there as soon as I can.''

"I will be waiting with great expectations,'' el Coronel Jorge Guillermo Frade said, and the phone went dead.

Señora Pellano was standing there during the conversation, making Clete a little uncomfortable—he was wearing only a towel around his waist.

"Señora, could you make a map showing me how to drive to my father's estancia? I am going to have dinner with him.''

"Marvelous,'' she said. "He will be pleased. I will draw you a map.''

"I have a better idea,'' Clete said impulsively. "Why don't

you ride down there with me? And show me the way?''

"I am not sure el Coronel would be pleased."

"You don't work for him, you work for me," Clete argued.

She considered that a moment.

"Yes, that is true," she said. "And I could see my family, my sisters, my brother, my aunts."

"Then you're coming," Clete said.

"If you wish, Señor Cletus," she said.

XIII

"It's a little early for that, isn't it?" Jasper C. Nestor asked with disapproval, indicating Clete's beer. But he softened the criticism by smiling and adding, "Is beer drinking at this hour another of those barbarous Texas customs we hear so much about?"

"It's medicinal," Clete said. "My uncle Jim taught me that. When you are all bent out of shape the morning after, a beer is far superior to coffee, prairie oysters, et cetera, et cetera. Can I offer you a cup of coffee? Tea?"

"I'll have coffee, thank you, if that would be convenient," Nestor said. "I presume you were celebrating your successful trip to Punta del Este."

"Our successful passage through Argentine customs with our souvenirs," Clete said. "I was really worried about that."

"Speaking of souvenirs, Clete: They didn't find the walkie-talkies in your room."

"I regret to inform you, Sir, that you'll have to fill out the appropriate form certifying that the walkie-talkies were lost in combat."

"If you need radios, Clete, ask me for them."

"All right."

"Where are they?"

"The explosives are here," Clete said, pointing at a large wardrobe. "Pelosi has the detonators."

"And the radios?"

"You mean the radios that were expended in the service of the United States? Those radios?"

"They're really upset about those radios. Apparently they are in very short supply."

"I thought they might be. Pelosi tells me they're brand-new."

Nestor's face tightened, but he didn't respond. He changed the subject: "The ship we're talking about has been positively identified. It's the *Reine de la Mer*. She sailed from Lisbon November thirteenth, so she should be arriving here in the next day or two. She may call at Montevideo first.''

"OK.''

"The next step will be locating her when she arrives in Argentinean waters. We're working on that,'' Nestor said, and then changed the subject. "Did Ettinger have any luck with Klausner when he went back to see him?''

"I haven't seen him since we got back. I thought I would drop by his place this morning. But since we know what ship it is, isn't that moot?''

"It is entirely possible that one of the other ships is also a replenishment vessel. This business is important to the Germans, and they have a reputation for being thorough.''

"I don't know if he went back to see Klausner or not,'' Clete said. "But if he did . . . I can't believe that declaration won't affect Klausner. Even if Ettinger doesn't tell him the figure is millions of people murdered, not thousands.''

"You say you plan to see David today?''

Clete nodded. "This morning.''

"Ask him to call me at home, please,'' Nestor said. "Better yet, ask him to come for drinks and dinner—say, at seven.''

"Yes, Sir.''

"I suppose that habit is hard to break, isn't it? The Southern custom of addressing one's elders as ''Sir.' Military courtesy only buttresses it.''

"Sorry,'' Clete said. "I'll try . . .''

"Why don't you come for drinks and dinner too?''

"Thank you, but I have a previous engagement. As soon as I pick up my car at the port, I'm driving to my father's estancia. Unless you . . .''

"That is more important. How long will you be there?''

"I don't know. I hadn't thought about that.''

"I'm sure you'll return in time for the Duarte boy's funeral.''

"He wasn't a boy,'' Clete said. "He was a captain. Maybe a foolish one, but a captain.''

"Figure of speech. No slight intended.''

"I had an interesting conversation about el Capitán Duarte last night,'' Clete said. "With Captain von Wachtstein of the Luftwaffe.''

"With whom?'' Nestor asked. His surprise was evident.

"The German officer who escorted my cousin's body home,''

Clete said. "Somebody's signals crossed—the arrangements were probably made long before I showed up down here—and they put him up here in the Guest House. He was in the library when I came in last night."

"And?"

"It was really very civilized. We wound up talking about flying. Somebody, some German officer, came and fetched him this morning. I rather liked him, as a matter of fact."

"He's an enemy officer, for God's sake! And you were drinking!"

"What should I have done?" Clete asked.

"You told him you were a Marine officer?"

"An ex–Marine officer, with a medical discharge for a heart murmur. He's a clever fellow. He saw my watch." Clete raised the Hamilton chronograph. "And recognized it as a military pilot's watch."

"If you weren't wearing that watch . . ."

"I thought about that, Mr. Nestor, before I came down here: If my cover story were true, and I had acquired a watch like this, would I wear it? The answer was yes, I would. They're very good watches."

"By now, you must realize that Colonel Grüner, the German military attaché—and the representative of the Sicherheitsdienst—knows that you are a Marine officer."

Clete felt anger welling up in him. Nestor was making it clear he thought Clete was a fool.

I may be an amateur down here, but I'm not a fool.

"Perhaps not," he said. "Von Wachtstein might have elected to tell Colonel Whatsisname—the attaché—nothing more than that he met me. And isn't it likely that Colonel Whatsisname has friends in the Centro Naval? Wouldn't they already have reported to him that my father introduced me there as a former Marine?"

For a moment, Clete thought Nestor was about to chew him out. His face showed that he didn't like being argued with. But finally, he smiled.

"Well, then," he said. "With the exception of this unfortunate encounter with the German captain, things seem to be going well, don't they? Falling into place, so to speak."

"They seem to be."

"Except, of course, for those walkie-talkies. I wish you would reconsider that, Clete."

"You mean the walkie-talkies that fell in the rice paddy and were lost? Those walkie-talkies?"

Nestor met his eyes and then put out his hand.

"Well, Clete. Have a good time at your father's estancia. Call me when you come back and tell me about it."

"Yes, S—Jasper."

"Better," Nestor said, then smiled and walked toward the elevator.

[TWO]
Calle Monroe 214
Belgrano, Buenos Aires
1100 14 December 1942

"Got a present for you, David," Clete said when Ettinger let him into his apartment. "I know you've always wanted your very own handmade straw chicken."

Ettinger looked at him strangely.

There was indeed the head of a straw chicken sticking out the top of the shopping bag Clete had borrowed from Señora Pellano.

"I'm glad to see you back, Clete. Everything apparently went well?"

Clete removed the chicken from the bag, then the two walkie-talkies.

"These are portable radios," Clete said. "They work well. I didn't return them to the people who left them in our room in Montevideo. They—and Nestor—are very upset about that. But I thought we might be able to use them. If Nestor asks, you don't know anything about them."

"He's the Station Chief, Clete."

"I've been thinking about that," Clete said. "I've concluded that from time to time, as the commanding officer of this team, I'm going to have to do things the way I call them. Such as 'losing' these radios. If you can't live with that, tell me now."

"I've been thinking about that too," Ettinger said after a moment. "It says in the Bible that a man cannot have two masters. So far as I'm concerned, you're calling the shots, Lieutenant Frade."

"Thank you," Clete said. "Now tell me, are these radios going to be useful?"

Ettinger picked up a walkie-talkie and looked at it.

"I've seen schematics for these," he said. "This is the first one I've ever actually looked at. If this works the same as the one in the schematics, the frequency is crystal controlled. Unless I can get my hands on some crystals, we can only talk to each other . . . or to somebody on the same frequency. I think I can up the power, though, to maybe five, six watts. And maybe if I can rig a wire antenna, instead of this telescoping one, I can get us some additional range." He paused thoughtfully, then said, "To answer your question, Lieutenant, yes, I think they'll be very useful."

"Any chance you could find crystals here?"

"Not from the Argentines," Ettinger said. "But maybe from the Navy."

"The Argentine Navy?"

"*Our* Navy," Ettinger said, and smiled when he saw Clete's confusion. "I've been having long lunches in the dock area, trying to pick up anything I could overhear. Yesterday a Teniente of the Armada Argentina let a salesman from S.A.P. know that he—"

"What's S.A.P.?"

"It stands for Servicios de Proveedores Asociados, literal translation, Associated Service Providers. They are actually ship victualers. Anyway, this Teniente was looking for a little gift in exchange for steering a little business toward the S.A.P. guy . . . specifically, providing fresh meat, fruits, and vegetables to a United States Navy destroyer, which will call at Buenos Aires over Christmas. The *Alfred Thomas,* DD-107."

"You even know the name?" Clete said. "I'm impressed."

"Her arrival here is probably classified SECRET," Ettinger said. "It's really true, Clete, that loose lips sink ships."

"What's she doing here?"

"I think we're just showing the flag. To let the Argentines know that we control the seas down here, and all the Germans can do is sneak the odd submarine in and out of the Bay. Or maybe they just wanted to give the sailors aboard shore leave on Christmas. Or they have been running all over the Atlantic looking for German submarines and are out of food. Who knows?"

"A destroyer would have aboard the crystals you're talking about?"

"Probably. If they did, could we get them?"

"I don't know. If I ask Nestor, that'd be admitting I have the walkie-talkies; and he'd want them back. Let me think about it.

In the meantime, you don't let Nestor know that you have them."

Ettinger smiled at him. "What radios?"

"We better not count on help from the Navy."

"OK. Just a thought. Rigging a power supply for it will be no problem. All I'll need is regular flashlight batteries, and some tape to hold them together."

"You are a very clever fellow, aren't you, Dave?"

"Flattery will get you everywhere, mi Teniente."

"I've got to go," Clete said. "I'm on my way to pick up my car, and I have my father's housekeeper waiting in the taxi. Christ, I almost forgot: You're invited for dinner at Nestor's. Drinks and dinner. Seven o'clock. He wants to know if you showed Klausner that declaration."

"I did, and he doesn't believe it. Damn him!"

"On the face of it, it's incredible."

"It shouldn't be to Klausner," Ettinger said bitterly. "Well, I'll see you later, then?"

"No. I'm not going to be at Nestor's. I'm going to my father's ranch."

"Really? What do you think of him now that you've met him? Or shouldn't I ask?"

"I really haven't made my mind up," Clete said. "His fangs and horns aren't nearly as long as I have been led to expect."

Ettinger chuckled.

"Thank you, David."

Ettinger put out his hand.

"A sus órdenes, mi Teniente," he said.

Clete left the apartment and went downstairs to Señora Pellano and the waiting taxi.

[THREE]
Suite 701
The Alvear Palace Hotel
Buenos Aires
1115 14 December 1942

The medical treatment considered most efficacious by Hauptmann Freiherr Hans-Peter von Wachtstein of the Luftwaffe for overindulgence in spirits was, perhaps not surprisingly, exactly that considered most efficacious by First Lieutenant Cletus Howell Frade,

USMCR. Almost immediately after he was taken to his new living quarters, Peter called Room Service and had them send up a bottle of beer.

When the treatment seemed to work, he called Room Service again and repeated the order.

When it was delivered, he carefully locked the door, then dragged a large steamer trunk from the corner where the bellman left it and opened it. And then, with the blade of a pocketknife issued to all Luftwaffe personnel on flying status, he began to pry loose the cardboard covering the trunk's bottom.

The removal of the cardboard revealed a half-inch-thick layer of currency, neat stacks of Swiss francs, English pounds, United States dollars, and Swedish kronor. According to his father, he now had the equivalent of just over five hundred thousand dollars in American money. His father would additionally apply for permission to transfer to Peter the equivalent of five thousand dollars American to defray the costs of establishing himself in Buenos Aires in a manner befitting an official representative of the German Reich, with monthly payments of one thousand dollars to follow.

"Some Foreign Ministry bureaucrat will almost certainly lower those numbers, just to feel he's doing his duty to the Austrian Corporal," Generalmajor Graf Karl-Friedrich von Wachtstein had said, "but I'm sure they will not deny the request entirely. Just try not to spend it all on the same Señorita."

When the memory brought tears to his eyes, Peter told himself that the cognac of the previous evening was working on him, as well as the beer now, not foolish and maudlin sentimentality.

He thumbed through a stack of United States twenty-dollar bills, then pulled one out in curiosity and examined it. On one side was a picture of a long-nosed man with flowing silver hair. His name was Jackson. He seemed to recall the Americans had a President named Jackson.

And a general named Jackson. Stonewall Jackson. Defeated the British at New Orleans in 1812. 1812? Same man? Did the Americans put pictures of general officers on their currency? Did American generals become Presidents?

On the other side of the bill was a picture of the White House.

A very attractive, if not very imposing, edifice. Didn't the British burn this building to the ground in 1812? Or was it . . . the what? The Rebels—the Confederates—*in the* Civil War *who burned it? There was a Confederate cavalry officer by the name of J.E.B. Stuart . . . a magnificent warrior. Graf Wilhelm Karl von Wachtstein, then an Oberstleutnant, rode with him as an observer. Because J.E.B. Stuart was not a professional officer, he did not know it was impossible to haul artillery around the battlefield with cavalry horses. The proper method of employing artillery required building emplacements, and then spending a good deal of time and effort "laying in" the cannon, so that the field of fire was known. Ignorant of all this, Stuart hauled his cannon about the battlefield at a gallop, and fired his cannon at the enemy with no preparation whatever, except loading the piece.*

With great effectiveness.

Great-grandfather came home to Germany and wrote a book about his experiences, devoting a substantial portion of it to the proven merits of attaching artillery to cavalry, for great mobility and firepower on the battlefield. Peter's father told him they used the book as a reference at the War College, and that he knew for a fact that it greatly affected the thinking of General Hasso von Manteuffel when he was a student. And consequently it had a great effect on the evolution of the *Blitzkrieg* philosophy that proved so effective against France and, at least initially, against Russia.

There was a knock at the door.

Who the hell is that?

"I am asleep, come back in two hours!"

"Please, Hauptmann von Wachtstein, open the door," someone replied in German.

Peter quickly closed the steamer trunk and went to the door and opened it. A small, skinny, middle-aged man in a business suit stood there, holding a gray homburg in his hand.

"May I please come in, Herr Hauptmann? I am Ambassador von Lutzenberger."

"I beg your pardon, Your Excellency, I had no idea," Peter said. He opened the door wide, and then with a curt bow and a click of his heels, he stepped aside.

"I've been told you often open your mouth before you think," von Lutzenberger said.

He walked around the suite, opening doors, even looking into the bathroom, and then returned to Peter.

"It is important that we have this conversation," he said. "And more important that no one else is privy to it."

"Jawohl, Exzellenz."

"I was given a rather interesting appraisal of your character by

Generalmajor Dieter von Haas," von Lutzenberger said. "It came to me out of the normal channels. By hand specifically, from the Ambassador of Portugal. Do I make my point, Herr Hauptmann?"

"Yes, Sir."

"Dieter von Haas wrote that you are a fine young officer . . . but with a lamentable tendency to drink and talk too much for your own good—and the good of people around you."

"I regret that Generalmajor von Haas has such a low opinion of me, Your Excellency."

Von Lutzenberger ignored the reply.

"I presume the money came through safely, and without official notice?" he asked.

"I was checking when you knocked," Peter said, nodding at the steamer trunk.

"In a week or so, I will be in a position to make suggestions about its disposition," von Lutzenberger said. "Von Haas's letter reached me only a few days ago, and I have not had the time to make the necessary inquiries. I think it will be safe enough with you for the time being."

"Yes, Sir."

"There are several questions of immediate importance. First, when you were at the Frade house, did you happen to meet the son?"

"Yes, Sir."

"And?"

"We had a drink."

"That's all?"

"He told me he served in the American Corps of Marines. He was a pilot."

"Do you think he is a former officer? Or is he still serving?"

"I have no way of knowing, Your Excellency."

"His father is a very important man in Argentina." He met Peter's eyes for a moment, then continued. "I do not have all the details as yet about the son's actual business here. We may safely assume, however, that he is a serving officer and that he is not here on holiday. But his father may be of great use to us, presuming I can somehow convince the Abwehr and Sicherheitsdienst to do nothing foolish. Which brings us to the Abwehr and Sicherheitsdienst in the Embassy, where they are embodied in one man, Oberst Karl-Heinz Grüner. You will explain to Grüner— and you'll tell my first secretary, Herr Gradny-Sawz, the same— that while you encountered the Frade boy, there was nothing more than an exchange of brief courtesies. You will pretend to be greatly surprised if they inform you he is an American officer.''

"Jawohl, Excellenz."

"My residence, my office, and my telephone lines are regularly inspected to detect listening devices. I am regularly assured there are none—by Oberst Grüner. Consequently, I am very careful of what I say in my office, in my home, and on the telephone. Do you take my point, Herr Hauptmann?''

"Yes, Sir."

"After you are presented to me tomorrow by Grüner, I will, as a courtesy to your father, whom I know socially, have you as a guest in my home. You will remain there until you have completed your duties vis-à-vis Hauptmann Duarte and my staff can find you a suitable apartment. I regret that our relationship thereafter will be formal and distant. This is doubly unfortunate, inasmuch as Frau von Lutzenberger and your mother were close, and I myself hold your father in the highest regard,'' he met Peter's eyes again, "in these difficult times."

"I understand, Your Excellency."

"This conversation never took place."

"Yes, Sir."

"Watch your drinking and your mouth, von Wachtstein."

"Yes, Sir."

Ambassador von Lutzenberger nodded, turned, and walked out of the room.

[FOUR]
The Port of Buenos Aires
1200 14 December 1942

When Clete and Señora Pellano left the taxi, the Buick was waiting for him, along with half a dozen customs officials. The Buick looked like hell, despite an obviously fresh, if none-too-skillful, wash job.

The paperwork was taken care of. All he had to do was sign an acknowledgment of receipt of the vehicle in an undamaged condition.

A customs officer—*obviously the senior man,* Clete decided, *in deference to my father or Señor Mallín or both*—walked to the car with him and watched somewhat nervously as Clete threw his and Señora Pellano's bags on the backseat, then got behind the wheel.

The engine fired as soon as he stepped on the starter; and it quickly settled down to produce its entirely satisfying Buick Straight Eight exhaust rumble. The smoothness, so quickly, surprised Clete, and he looked at the water-temperature gauge. The engine was warm; it had obviously been running recently. He remembered now that the customs officer standing by the side of the car exhaled audibly in relief when the engine started.

Having friends—or a parent—in high places is very nice.

"Excuse me, Señor," the customs officer said. "Be so kind. Inform me how you did that?"

"Did what?" Clete said, and then understood.

"On this model the starter is mounted with the accelerator pedal. To start the engine, it is necessary only to press the accelerator."

"Magnífico! We looked—I myself looked—for the starter button, and could find none. It was necessary to call a mechanic to ... how you say, jump-start?"

"Short the starter leads," Clete furnished.

"Precisely," the customs officer said. "A marvelous invention!"

"Thank you, and thank you for your many courtesies."

"De nada," the customs officer said, offering his hand. After Clete shook his hand, he stepped back and saluted.

Clete put the Buick in gear and drove off, feeling fine, wondering if the Virgin Princess would be as fascinated with the step-on-the-gas-pedal starting technology as the customs guy was.

If I am goddamn fool enough to actually call her up and ask her if she still wants to take the ride she asked for.

Jesus Christ, why does she have to be only nineteen goddamned years old? And an innocent, virginal nineteen-year-old at that?

The good feeling about the Buick lasted until he reached the port gate and its guard shack. The heavy steel gate was open, and the guard on duty smilingly waved him through. Just outside the gate, there was a small, permanent watercourse, about six inches deep and perhaps a foot wide.

When he crossed it, there was an awful thump, as if the whole goddamned rear end were about to fall off.

He drove, very slowly, for a block or two, listening for the sounds of a fatal defect—the clutch tearing itself to pieces, for example—and then pulled into a side street, stopped, and got out.

He tried to slam the door. It wouldn't close. He tried it again, then took a closer look to see what the hell was wrong with it.

The door panel was falling off.

Jesus Christ! How did that happen?

He tried to push the little clips back in place with his thumb. That didn't work. They needed the jolt from a hammer. There was—at least the last time he looked—a tool kit in the trunk. He reached through the window and pulled the key from the ignition.

"There is trouble, Señor Clete?" Señora Pellano asked.

"I don't think so. Just checking."

When he opened the trunk, the mysterious thump was explained. The spare tire was not mounted where it should have been: flat on the trunk floor against the right fender well and held in place with a bolt passing through the floor plate. When he passed over the bump, the tire flew up and down.

How the hell did that come loose?

I'll be a sonofabitch; they searched the car. They took the spare out to see what I might have hidden in there, and they didn't know how to put it back the way they found it. That also explains the loose door panel.

He pressed hard on the sidewall of the spare. It had been deflated, obviously to dismount it. And he found scratches on the paint of the wheel. And then they forgot to reinflate it—or else they didn't have time to do that.

He bolted the spare wheel in place, found the hammer, and tapped the door-panel clips on both doors back in place. They had managed to properly reinstall the rear seat panels, however, which fastened with screws.

He finally slipped behind the wheel and started the engine again.

"All fixed, Señora Pellano," he said. "Among my many other accomplishments, I am a master mechanic."

"I am not surprised," she replied seriously.

Sorry, Princess. No ride in the Buick. If Internal Security is watching me this close, you don't want to be anywhere near me. What the hell was I thinking about?

[FIVE]
Estancia San Pedro y San Pablo
Near Pila, Buenos Aires Province
1715 14 December 1942

A dark-maroon Beechcraft stagger-wing and a Piper Cub were
parked beside a wind sock about a thousand yards from the grove
of trees surrounding the ranch house—the trees looked to Clete
like several acres of long-established, at least a century old, hard-
wood. He wondered if his father flew the Beechcraft, then decided
that was unlikely. Since there was probably a pilot, that would
probably complicate his laying his hands on the stagger-wing.

And then there is that other problem, Cletus, my boy, you've
never flown a stagger-wing. Well, so what? You never flew a
Wildcat either before the first day you flew one. If you can fly a
Wildcat, it would seem logical that you can fly a stagger-wing.

When Clete pulled up, el Coronel Jorge Guillermo Frade was
sitting in an armchair on the wide verandah of the ranch house.
He held a large, very black cigar in one hand; and in the other
was a large, squat glass, dark with whiskey. He was wearing a
white polo shirt, riding breeches, and glistening boots.

"Welcome to San Pedro y San Pablo," Frade said, moving
down the shallow stairs toward the car.

The cigar, Clete saw, was freshly lit. The drink was fresh. So
was the shave: A dot of shaving cream was by his father's ear.

He got all dressed up to meet me. Jesus, that's nice.

"I brought Señora Pellano along with me to show me the
way," Clete said as he shook his father's hand.

"I hope that is all right?" Señora Pellano asked.

"Of course it is, Marianna," Frade said. "I should have
thought of it myself."

"Gracias, mi Coronel," she said.

"Nice-looking automobile," Frade said. "The latest model?"
He took a closer look and proclaimed indignantly, "It's filthy."

"It just came off the ship."

"They should have prepared it for you at the dock," Frade
said indignantly. "I was assured that everything would be taken
care of." But then he brightened. "No problem. Enrico will see
to it that it is washed and waxed."

"That's not necessary," Clete protested.

"Nonsense. Enrico will be pleased. He admires fine automo-

biles. Marianna, would you be good enough to have someone take
care of Señor Cletus's luggage, and have someone send for Enrico, and then ask if they can prepare a little snack for Señor
Cletus and myself?''

"Sí, mi Coronel."

"Come sit on the porch with me," Frade said. "I do not normally take spirits before seven, but your visit is a special occasion
for me. And perhaps you would like a little something . . . what
is it they say, 'to cut the dust of the trail'?''

"Yes," Clete said, restraining a smile. "Thank you, I would."

Señora Pellano walked into the house. Thirty seconds later, a
procession of three servants marched onto the porch, one of them
heading for the car, the other two pushing wheeled tables. On the
first of these was arrayed an enormous plate of hors d'oeuvres.
And on the second Clete saw enough whiskey of various sorts
for a party of eight.

*He had that set up, too. It took half an hour to make that tray
of food. How did he know exactly when I would arrive? Ah hah,
those guys galloping over the fields on those beautiful horses with
the funny-looking, hornless saddles. He had people out there waiting.*

"We will have a drink, or perhaps two, and then you will
decide when we should have our dinner. It will be simple, just
you and I. It will take no more than an hour to prepare."

"Thank you," Clete said.

"I did not know when you would arrive, of course, so I was
about to take a ride," Frade said.

Sure you were. Where's the horse, Dad?

"I saw some beautiful animals a couple of miles back," Clete
said.

"We take pride in our animals," Frade said. "I am sure that
your uncle James taught you to ride?"

"Yes, Sir."

"Perhaps we will have time to ride tomorrow."

"I'd like that," Clete said.

"I don't know about riding clothes . . ." Frade said, almost in
alarm.

"I'm wearing all I need," Clete said, hoisting his trousers to
reveal his boots. "Anyway, Uncle Jim always said that a man
who couldn't ride bareback really couldn't ride."

"Yes, I recall, James was a fine horseman. And your mother

rode extremely well for a woman. So it is in your blood from both sides.''

Enrico appeared. There was no look of recognition on his face.

''¿Mi Coronel?''

''Enrico, this is my son, Señor Cletus, former Teniente of the U.S. Marine Corps. Cletus, Enrico is former Suboficial Mayor''— Sergeant Major—''of the Husares de Pueyrredón. We were together there for many years, weren't we, Enrico?''

My father doesn't know how he got home from the Guest House the night he passed out. Or he knows, and we are pretending we don't.

''Sí, mi Coronel. A sus órdenes, mi Teniente.''

Enrico smiled at him warmly as Clete shook his hand.

Whaddayasay, Gunny? How they hanging? Still one below the other?

''Be so good, Enrico, to prepare Señor Cletus's automobile. Have it washed and waxed, and you—personally—check all the mechanicals.''

''Sí, mi Coronel.''

The drink prepared by the maid was at least a triple. Clete sipped a small swallow, put it down, and then stood up.

''I need the gentlemen's,'' he said.

''Emilia, show Señor Cletus to his apartment,'' Frade ordered the maid who was passing the hors d'oeuvres and mixing the drinks.

He was distracted by other things before he reached the apartment. When he entered the house, he found himself in an enormous foyer. Off of this opened three corridors. The maid led him down one of those, and then Señora Pellano intercepted them.

''I wish to show you something, Señor Cletus,'' she said, and opened the door of one of the rooms.

Whatever I'm about to be shown, the maid doesn't like it a goddamned bit, to judge by that horrified look on her face.

Señora Pellano entered the room ahead of Clete, snapped on the lights, then stood to one side.

It was something like a small library. There was a leather armchair, with a footstool and a chair side table on which sat a cigar humidor and a large ashtray. There was a library table, on which rested a stack of leather-bound albums. And hanging over the fireplace there was a large oil portrait of Elizabeth-Ann Howell de Frade with her infant son Cletus in her arms.

Cletus Marcus Howell smiled rather artificially in a photograph taken before the altar of the Cathedral of St. Louis on Jackson Square in New Orleans. The Old Man was in morning clothes, standing beside His Eminence, the Archbishop of New Orleans, Uncle Jim, and the bridal couple.

There was a wall covered with framed photographs: Clete Frade, aged nine, taking first place in the Midland FFA Sub-Junior Rodeo Calf-Roping Contest; Cadet Corporal Cletus Frade in the boots and breeches of the Corps of Cadets of the Texas Agricultural and Mechanical Institute; Clete Frade, looking as if he had already been at the post-tournament refreshments, with the rest of the Tulane Tennis Team . . .

"Marianna! How dare you bring him in here!" el Coronel Jorge Guillermo Frade said, almost shouted, from the door.

Señora Pellano was unrepentant.

"No, Señora Carzino-Cormano is right, and you are wrong, mi Coronel," she said. "It is wrong for you to let him think he was not in your mind and heart all these years."

It was a moment before the Colonel spoke. "If it meets with your approval, Cletus, we will dine in an hour," he said. Before Clete could reply, he turned and left the room, slamming the door behind him.

"I will leave you, Señor Cletus," Señora Pellano said, and left the room.

What did she say? "Señora Carzino-Cormano is right"? Who's she?

Clete walked to the wall of pictures and examined all of them.

It's a scrapbook on the wall. I wonder what's in the scrapbooks?

He went to them. They were full of photographs and newspaper clippings. In a town like Midland, with a thrice-weekly newspaper, one tends to find one's name in one's local newspaper far more frequently than, say, if one lives in New York City and subscribes to the *Times*.

Whoever did this clipping job worked hard at it. Every time Clete's name was mentioned in the *Midland Advertiser*—as a guest at some six-year-old's birthday party, for example—the item was clipped out and somehow sent down here.

He was deeply touched. His eyes teared, and his throat was tight.

Well, the Old Man is obviously wrong. My father did not simply put me out of his mind as if I never happened. A lot of effort went into collecting all this stuff. And he displays it, protects it, with

*. . . what? reverence? Maybe not reverence but something damned
close.*

Then why the hell did he never try to get in touch with me?

*The Old Man could have stopped him from doing that when I
was a kid—and he's certainly capable of that. But not when I
went to A&M or Tulane. And my father damned sure knew that
I was there, and when I was.*

Fascinated with the idea that his father had actually gone to
such trouble, as well as with the clippings themselves, Clete went
through each of the seven albums he found, one page at a time.

Finally, desperately wishing he'd brought the triple scotch with
him, he left the room.

And now where the hell is my bedroom?

Señora Pellano was in the corridor outside.

"Your father, Señor Cletus, spent many hours in there."

"Thank you, Señora Pellano, for showing it to me."

"I felt I should," she said. "I will show you to your room."

The room turned out to be a three-room suite; and he was not
surprised to find that his clothing had been unpacked and put
away. On the desk in the sitting room sat a package decorated
with a red ribbon and bow. Inside a small envelope was a card,
embossed with what must have been the Frade coat of arms. The
card read:

*This belonged to your grandfather, el Coronel Guillermo Ale-
jandro Frade, who carried it while commanding the Husares de
Pueyrredón. I thought it would be an appropriate gift from one
soldier to another. Your father, Jorge Guillermo Frade.*

Clete opened the package. In a felt-lined walnut box—with 20
rounds of ammunition and accessories, including a spare cylinder—was a Colt Army .44-40 revolver, the old Hog Leg. It was
in good shape, but it was obviously a working gun. The blue was
well worn, as were the grips, which were nonstandard—person-
alized. They were of some wood Clete did not recognize, inlaid
with silver wire. On one side was again probably the Frade coat
of arms; and on the other was probably the regimental crest of
the Husares de Pueyrredón, whatever the hell that was.

He removed the cylinder and peered down the barrel. No rust,
no pits, but evidence (the lands were worn smooth) that it had
been fired a good deal. He replaced the cylinder and was returning
the pistol to its box when he heard a knock at the door.

"Dinner will be at your pleasure, Señor," someone called.

"Be right there," Clete called.

*   *   *

El Coronel Jorge Guillermo Frade stood at one end of a table with enough side chairs to seat at least twenty people. It was set, at that end, for two. There was a large centerpiece, a sterling-silver sculpture of a horse at full gallop. There were two silver bowls filled with freshly cut flowers. There were four wineglasses for each of them, and a dazzling display of silverware. An enormous standing rib of beef rested on a large silver platter, and there were at least a dozen other serving dishes, each with a silver cover.

"You had time to freshen up?" Frade asked.

"Yes, Sir. Thank you for the pistol. I'm sorry, I didn't bring . . ."

"I didn't expect you to."

He snapped his fingers. A man in a gray cotton jacket appeared immediately and poured a splash of wine in one of the four wine-glasses in front of Clete's plate.

"This is a Pinot Noir, from a vineyard in which the family has an interest," he said. "I tend to feel it whets the appetite for beef. Is it all right?"

Clete sipped the wine.

"Very nice," he said, nodding at the man in the gray jacket, who then filled the glass before moving to the colonel's glass.

"That's a fascinating room," Clete said. "How did you get all those clippings down here?"

Frade did not reply. He stood up, and with an enormous knife cut the beef. He laid a two-inch-thick rib on a plate held by a maid, who carried it to Clete and then returned to Frade, who was now holding out a vegetable bowl to her.

Frade waved impatiently at her.

"I will ask her to serve the vegetables and the sauce and the pudding," Frade said. "It is less complicated."

"How did you get your hands on those clippings?"

Frade sat down, pursed his lips, and shrugged.

"Very well," he said. "When your mother came to me as my bride, her dowry was an interest—approximately one quarter . . ."

It wasn't approximately a quarter, it was twenty-four-point-five percent, precisely. Christ knows, I've heard that figure often enough!

" . . . of the outstanding stock of Howell Petroleum. It wasn't then worth what it is now, but even then it was of considerable value. When God called your mother to her heavenly home . . ."

Well, that's one way of putting it, I suppose.

" . . . it came to me. I considered it, of course, to be yours . . ."

Jesus Christ! That means that with the third of the twenty-four-point-five percent of Howell Stock Uncle Jim owned and left me, I will own thirty-two point something of Howell. And if the Old Man leaves me a third of his stock—a third of fifty-one percent is seventeen percent, seventeen and thirty-two-point-something is forty-nine-point-something—I will be majority stockholder in Howell Petroleum. And I think he'll leave me more than a third. Sarah's girls don't need the money, and the Old Man likes me best.

Jesus Christ, Cletus Frade, you are an avaricious sonofabitch, aren't you?

" . . . to which end I engaged an American attorney, who established a trust fund for you managed by the First National Bank of Midland. I asked him to keep an eye out for anything . . ."

"And he hired a clipping service."

"I presume."

"I've been told some unpleasant stories of my mother's death," Clete heard himself say.

"If you don't mind, I would prefer not to discuss the matter."

"I would prefer that you did."

"No one dares talk to me like that. Just who do you think you are?"

"I'm the only son you have."

"You are a guest in my house, and you are insufferably rude."

"I told you, the rules are different. I want your version of what happened. If you don't want to give it to me, I will have to presume that my grandfather's version is true. . . . It paints you as the unmitigated sonofabitch of the century. And if it is true, I don't think I want to be here."

"You dare to call your father a sonofabitch?"

"That's what it looks like from where I'm sitting."

Frade stared down at his plate, then suddenly, furiously, pushed it away from him. It slid a third of the way down the table and then crashed to the floor. The maid made a faint yelping noise and rushed to clean up the mess.

"Get out! Get out!" Frade ordered.

She scurried from the room.

"You take that from your mother," Frade said to his son. "I know when to stop. Your mother . . . your mother had a will of iron."

"Is there something wrong with that?"

"There is a time to bend. Nothing is black and white."

"For example?"

"It was necessary for your mother to join my church in order to marry me. For a long time she absolutely refused. I tried to explain to her that I personally didn't care if she lit candles to Satan himself, but that Argentina is by law a Catholic country. To be legally recognized, a marriage has to be performed in a Catholic church. Otherwise, there would be serious problems about our children. In the eyes of the law, they would be bastards, and there would be all sorts of difficulties about inheritance.

"So she said she would talk with a priest in New Orleans. An ordinary priest was not good enough for your grandfather. If his daughter talked to someone, she would deal with someone important, in this case, his golf-playing friend, the Archbishop. I met that sonofabitch when I was there. I blame a good deal of what happened on him."

On the Archbishop? That's stretching things a little, isn't it?

Clete's father made sudden angry stabbing motions with his leg. For a moment, Clete thought there was a rat or a mouse under the table. But when the maid reappeared, he understood that the call button was mounted on the floor under the table.

"Bring whiskey," Frade ordered. "Scotch."

"And for the young Señor?"

"Bring him whatever he wants, of course."

"Nothing for me, thank you."

"Then I received a letter from your mother. She wrote that she had been wrong, and that she now understood. She would now be confirmed in my Church and place her life in God's hands and mine. I didn't pay a lot of attention. I have never pretended to understand women and God. But the immediate problem, marriage in church, was over."

The whiskey was delivered. Frade watched impatiently for about thirty seconds as the maid fussed with a silver-handled shot glass, then he took the bottle from her and poured an inch and a half in his glass.

"And then get out," he concluded to her. He waited until the maid fled again before going on.

"So we were married. We went to Europe. It was a splendid time. And then she became pregnant with you. And fell ill. Her doctor informed me that further pregnancies were ill-advised. That was fine with me. We were to have a baby. Two or three babies might increase the chances of having a son, but if the choice was between a second baby and your mother . . ."

He took a healthy swallow of his drink.

"I told her, before you were born, that there is some sort of an operation performed during—what is the word—*delivery* that prevents future pregnancies. She flatly refused. She said her life was in God's hands; God would protect her. She had sworn a vow before God; she was honor bound.

"I thought I would talk her out of this nonsense at a later time. There are . . . certain measures . . . one can take to prevent pregnancy. After a while, after you were born, she told me she had discussed this question with her confessor, and the priest told her there was only one thing she could do to avoid children. You know what I mean."

No, I don't. Oh, yeah. Abstinence.

"What happened thereafter is clearly my responsibility," Frade said. "I knew the risk, and out of selfishness, I took it. And you know what happened. But I loved her so much, with such passion . . ."

"Why did you leave me in the States?"

"Your grandfather hated me, with obvious good cause. Your uncle James hated me."

"You could have told them."

"They would not have believed it. And I could not, in any event, try to blame your mother's religious fanaticism for what happened. God didn't make her pregnant, I did."

He looked at Clete.

"I asked you, why did you leave me in the States?" Clete said.

"I hoped not to get into this, Cletus."

"Get into it."

"When I went to Midland and drove to the ranch, I was arrested—by two Texas Rangers, by the way—and charged with trespassing. I was sentenced to ninety days in the county prison. When I was finally able to get a lawyer—I was employed on the county roads, clearing drainage ditches—he told me that an appeal of my jail sentence, much less an application to the courts to have you returned to me, would be a waste of effort."

The Old Man is certainly capable of arranging that.

"The lawyer did tell me that he could have the sentence vacated on my promise to leave Texas and never return. So I accepted that offer and sought other legal counsel. When I arrived at the courthouse seeking an injunction to have you returned to me, I was rearrested by the Texas Rangers for parole violation, and returned to Midland to complete my sentence."

"I never heard any of this."

"I'm not surprised," Frade said simply. "When I was released from jail, officials of the Immigration Service were waiting outside. My visa had been revoked on allegations that my morals were not up to the standards required of visitors to the United States. I was taken to El Paso, Texas, and escorted across the Mexican border."

"Incredible!"

"In Mexico City, a firm of lawyers—I was assured they were the best around—informed me that my case was virtually hopeless. In order to petition a Federal Court for your return to me, I had to be physically in the United States. Otherwise—I remember the phrase well—I 'had no legal status' before the court. And I could not, of course, obtain another visa to enter the United States. Your grandfather hates with a great depth, Cletus. In a way, it's admirable."

"My mother was his only daughter," Clete said softly.

"Yes, of course. In Buenos Aires, I consulted with our Foreign Ministry, who took the case to the Argentine Ambassador in Washington." He shrugged, holding out his arms helplessly. "Little pressure could be brought to bear . . . especially now that several United States senators had already brought the case to the attention of the State Department. The senators were furious that an American child might be expatriated into the care of a father whose morals were . . ."

"Jesus H. Christ."

"I considered having you taken—kidnapped. But I finally . . . Your aunt Martha loved you. I knew that. She would be a mother to you. I was alone. It would be better for you to be raised by Martha than by my sister, who has never been entirely sound mentally. Or by servants. So I quit, Cletus. Gave up."

"All I can do is repeat that I knew nothing."

"I was right about one thing. Jim and Martha raised you well." Very hesitantly, one of the maids entered.

"We do not wish to be disturbed," Frade said softly.

"The Señora is here, mi Coronel. She asks to be received."

"I will be a son of a bitch!" Frade exclaimed.

"The Señora?" Clete asked.

"She is the Carzino-Cormano widow," Frade explained. "She has an estancia nearby. Pushy woman. Comes here whenever she feels like it. Does not have the good manners to telephone to see if it would be convenient. I had hoped she would spare me today.'' He turned to the maid. ''Tell the Señora that we will join her shortly.''

The door opened again and a svelte woman in her fifties walked into the dining room. Her gray-flecked, luxuriant black hair was folded up under a hat with a veil; a double string of pearls hung from her neck; and a golden sunburst with diamond-chip decorations was pinned to the right breast of her black silk dress.

''I was planning to bring him by to meet you tomorrow,'' Frade said.

''So you said,'' she said. She looked around the room, and turned to the maid. ''Clean up the mess on the floor, remove the whiskey, and bring champagne. I told Ramona to chill half a dozen bottles this morning.''

The maid hurried to obey her orders.

''I have not finished my drink,'' Frade protested.

''Yes, you have,'' she said. She walked to Clete. He rose to his feet as she put out her hand. ''You are Cletus. I am Claudia de Carzino-Cormano. You may call me Claudia.''

''Yes, Ma'am.''

She turned to Frade. ''There is much of his mother in him, but also much of you. Which may not be entirely a good thing.''

Three maids entered the room, one stooping to clean up the mess on the floor, the others carrying a silver wine cooler and a tray of glasses.

''Can you open that?'' Claudia inquired. ''How much have you had to drink?''

''I have had this one drink.''

''And how many before? You were as nervous as a virgin on her bridal night when I talked to you this morning.''

This woman is not simply a pushy widow woman from the next spread, Clete thought.

Claudia took the champagne bottle from the cooler, expertly uncorked it, and poured.

She handed Clete a glass, then handed one to his father, and finally picked hers up.

''Welcome to Argentina,'' she said, and raised her glass. Clete followed suit.

Claudia held up her hand to stop the toast.

''No,'' she said. ''More importantly. Welcome home, Cletus. Your father has been waiting for you for a long time.''

"Thank you," Clete said, and his voice broke.

Claudia walked quickly to him and laid a hand on his cheek. Then, with a little hug, she kissed him. He could smell expensive perfume.

"It is all right to cry," she said. "Your father cries often."

She was right. When Clete looked at his father, tears were running down his cheeks.

[SIX]
Bureau of Internal Security
Ministry of Defense
Edificio Libertador
Avenida Paseo Colón
Buenos Aires
2045 14 December 1942

El Teniente Coronel Bernardo Martín, in a foul mood, parked his car directly in front of the main entrance of the building and stormed inside.

It is almost nine o'clock, after all, and unless Paraguay or Chile has invaded Argentina as an evening surprise, there will be no one superior in rank to me in the building, and I can park wherever the hell I choose.

The ornately uniformed guards standing by the door moved from parade rest to rifle salute as he passed (the formal guards at the Edifico Libertador wear the dress uniforms of the Patricios Regiment, circa 1809). Martín, who was wearing civilian clothing, forgot that he wasn't in uniform and returned the salute.

The door to the building was locked, and he pressed the bell button impatiently. A sargento appeared, immediately followed by a teniente, to tell him the building was closed. These men were in the field uniform, with German-style helmets and accoutrements, of the army unit charged with actually protecting—as opposed to decorating—the building.

He finally produced his Internal Security credentials. He disliked using them—and did not, unless he had to—because there was a lamentable and uncontrollable tendency on the part of people like this to remember him and point him out to their girlfriends: *See the funny man? He's Internal Security!*

With profound apologies, the teniente finally opened the door.

He would now almost certainly remember him; he could tell all his friends that Internal Security, ever vigilant, worked all night. Martín walked across the lobby and took the elevator to his seventh-floor offices.

The sargento on duty and Comandante Carlos Habanzo were waiting for him there. They rose to their feet as Martín walked through the door.

"Buenas noches, mi Coronel."

"I was playing bridge with the father-in-law when you called, Habanzo. I hope your reasons are important," Martín said, and waved at Habanzo to follow him as he walked to the door of his office and opened it.

"I took the liberty of putting the agent's reports on your desk, mi Coronel," Habanzo said.

Martín sat down at his desk and read the reports. They told him nothing that Habanzo had not told him—or hinted at—on the telephone.

"Why did this idiot not follow young Frade and the other one to Uruguay?"

"Mi Coronel, as you yourself have often said: Without specific, previous authorization, an agent's authority stops at the water's edge."

If I say now what I would like to say, I will regret it.

"Habanzo," he said a full thirty seconds later—which of course seemed much longer to Comandante Habanzo—"I will explain our policy to you one more time. I would appreciate it if you would not only remember it, but pass it on to our agents: The authority of an agent does indeed end at the water's edge. But this agent's instructions were to surveille young Frade, not arrest him. No authority is needed to follow someone across a border. Do you see the difference?"

"Sí, mi Coronel," Habanzo replied. "Mi Coronel, in this specific case, in addition to his misunderstanding of his authority, our agent did not have sufficient funds to take the boat to Montevideo for an unknown period of time. There would have been a hotel bill. Perhaps he would have been required to rent an automobile . . ."

Martín held up his hand to stop him.

"Be so good as to refresh my memory, Habanzo."

"I will try, mi Coronel."

"Do we have an officer on our staff who is charged with seeing that our agents are properly equipped to perform their duties?"

"Sí, mi Coronel," Habanzo said, somewhat unhappily, now sensing what was coming.

"Charged, in other words, with providing them with automobiles, appropriate documents, weapons where necessary . . . and of course sufficient funds to fulfill their duties?"

"Sí, mi Coronel."

"And who, precisely, is that officer on our staff, Habanzo? What is his name?"

"It is I, mi Coronel. I have obviously failed to carry out my duty."

"Unfortunately, that is the conclusion I myself have reached."

He let him sweat for a full minute before he went on.

"The damage is done, Habanzo. We will speak no more of it."

"It will never happen again, mi Coronel. Gracias, mi Coronel."

"We know from this," Martín said, tapping a document on his desk, "that young Frade and the other one . . ."

"Pelosi, mi Coronel. Anthony—it is the English for Antonio—Pelosi."

". . . returned from Uruguay at approximately nine-thirty last night."

"Whereupon, mi Coronel, surveillance of the subjects was resumed by our agents, who were stationed at customs in the expectation that they would return."

"Did it occur to them to speak with the customs officer who inspected their luggage?"

"No, mi Coronel, it did not," Habanzo replied, and hastily added, as he saw the clouds form on Martín's face: "I personally went to the individual concerned and questioned him myself."

Proving, I suppose, that you are only half stupid.

"And?"

"There was nothing suspicious in their belongings, mi Coronel. They had boxes of straw ducks, chickens . . . you know what I mean. And two beach radios that didn't work."

"One thing at a time. The straw ducks. Why would two bachelors have boxes full of children's toys?"

"I have no idea, mi Coronel," Habanzo confessed. "Perhaps for the children of their servants.".

"And perhaps they contained enough explosives to blow up the Edificio Libertador! Did that occur to you?"

Habanzo considered the question seriously.

"I do not think it was possible that the boxes contained that quantity of explosives, mi Coronel."

"I was speaking figuratively, Habanzo."

"Yes, of course, mi Coronel."

"Tell me about the beach radios."

"You know the type, mi Coronel. They are powered by batteries, and you can take them with you. To the park, for example, or the beach. Theirs did not work."

"They had two *portable* radios? And they did not work?"

"Sí, mi Coronel. They did not work. The customs man tried them, and all he heard was a hiss."

"You don't think it suspicious that *each* had a radio?"

Habanzo shrugged and held up his hands helplessly.

"Did he tell you what these portable radios looked like?"

"Like oversized telephones."

Habanzo, you are an idiot of unbelievable magnitude!

"Habanzo, two months ago, through the courtesy of el Coronel Grüner of the German Embassy, I was treated to a lecture of the latest German communications equipment. One of the items he was kind enough to show me was a portable communications radio. It had a range of several kilometers, weighed three kilograms, and looked like an oversized telephone, to which was attached an automobile antenna. Do you suppose that only Germans possess such electrical genius, or do you think it is possible that the norteamericanos might come up with something comparable?"

"You think they were communications radios, mi Coronel?"

"I think we must consider that possibility, don't you?"

They didn't go to Uruguay to pick up a couple of radios. Those would have been sent to them via the diplomatic pouches of the American Embassy. So what were they doing in Uruguay?

"I could send someone into the Frade guest house, mi Coronel, to examine the radios. If they are still there."

"If they are still there?"

"On his way to the port to pick up his car, Frade stopped at Calle Monroe 214, in Belgrano, at the apartment of Señor David Ettinger, an employee of the Banco de Boston. He carried a shopping bag containing a straw chicken. He did not have the straw chicken with him when he left."

"We must consider the possibility, mustn't we, that the straw chicken was a present from Señor Frade to Señor Ettinger?"

"The shopping bag was large enough, mi Coronel, to also contain the radios. Or something else."

"Permission denied," Martín said after a moment. "I don't

want any intrusion into the living quarters of any of these three without my specific approval. Understood?''

''Sí, mi Coronel.''

''Who inspected young Frade's automobile at the port?'' Martín asked, picking up a report from his desk.

''Two of our men, under my personal supervision, mi Coronel.''

In that case, he could have smuggled in two elephants.

''And?''

''Absolutely nothing, mi Coronel.''

Three elephants.

''And was the investigation conducted carefully? Will it go undetected?''

''Absolutely, mi Coronel. You have my personal assurance about that.''

Which means he will know we searched his car.

''And where is he now?''

''We have just had word from our man at Estancia San Pedro y San Pablo that he is with his father.''

''I don't want him lost again, Habanzo.''

''I understand, mi Coronel.''

''Provide whatever personnel are required. See that they have adequate funds to cover any contingency.''

''Sí, mi Coronel.''

''My function, Habanzo, is to know everything there is to know about el Coronel Frade and his associates. I think that his son could be considered an associate, don't you? His long-lost, recently returned son, who just happens to be—he says—a recently discharged American officer?''

''Yes, of course, mi Coronel.''

XIV

[ONE]
Estancia San Pedro y San Pablo
1115 15 December 1942

Two gauchos, sprawled on the wide steps to the verandah, were waiting for them when they returned from their ride. As they approached, Clete's horse, a magnificent sorrel, shied at something and, with a shrill whinny, reared. Despite the strange saddle, Clete managed to keep his seat and to control the animal, and more than a little smugly noticed both surprise and approval on the faces of the gauchos.

The Norteamericano did not get his ass thrown. Sorry about that, guys!

The gauchos took the reins of the horses and led them away. And Clete followed his father and Claudia Carzino-Cormano onto the verandah. The more he saw this woman, the more he liked her. If she and Aunt Martha met, they would form an instant mutual admiration society. Like Martha, Claudia was a first-class horsewoman; and like Martha, she said what was in her mind, rather than what she thought a lady should say. And, like Martha, she ran a ranch. An estancia almost, but not quite, as large as San Pedro y San Pablo.

He was touched and amused at his father's blustering attempts to paint her as just a platonic acquaintance who happened to drop by now and again. The servants obeyed her orders the way they'd obey the mistress of the place. And last night, when his father suggested, "Since it's late, Claudia, why don't you spend the night? I'll have one of the guest rooms set up for you," she winked at Clete and smiled.

"Thank you for your hospitality, Jorge," she said.

And when he got up the next morning and went looking for something to eat, Claudia was already up too, wearing a white blouse and baggy trousers, and soft, black, tight-over-the-calf leather boots, obviously a gentle lady's riding costume—which his father apparently expected him to believe just "happened" to be in the house.

"Your father is insufferable until he has had his second cup of coffee," she greeted him. "It is best to ignore him, or anything he says."

Clete had ridden hornless saddles before—at Texas A&M, the ROTC horses had Army-issue McClellan cavalry saddles—and after a few minutes, he became accustomed to the Argentine saddle. It was called a *recado,* Claudia told him. Although everyone else in the area had been using "English" saddles since the turn of the century, his father insisted on keeping them, because he was too cheap to throw anything away.

When Clete's father overheard her tell Clete that, he flared up at her: "I am not cheap, my dear. I am frugal, and I respect our traditions. Since they have been properly cared for, they have not worn out." She rode close to him then, murmured, "Precioso, I'm sorry," and leaned out of her *recado* to kiss him.

Acting as if the kiss—which calmed him down immediately—never happened, Clete's father then delivered a lecture on the history of their saddles. A brilliant saddler made them on the estancia during the tenure of Clete's great-grandfather. The shape of the seat, he went on to say, together with *estribando largo*—long stirrups—permit the rider to sit in an almost vertical position, the merits of which for herding cattle over long hours do not have to be explained. Except perhaps to a woman.

"Sí, mi jefe," Claudia replied, laughing.

When they came onto the verandah, Señora Pellano was supervising the arrangement of a little "after the morning canter" refreshment. There were two bottles of champagne in coolers, and an array of sweets and cold cuts.

"I would suggest, Cletus," Frade said, "that you pass up the champagne."

"Why?" Claudia demanded.

"I am reliably informed that it is not wise to fly an aircraft under the influence of alcohol."

"Is he going flying?"

"I thought—it is a lovely day—that we would return you to your home in the Beechcraft. I will arrange for your car to be delivered there."

"And Cletus will fly the airplane?"

"Certainly. Why not? He is an experienced military pilot. He probably knows more about flying than el Capitán Delgano."

"Cletus?" Claudia asked, a hint of doubt in her voice.

"After flying the Wildcat fighter, Claudia," his father persisted, "as he did in Guadalcanal, flying the Beechcraft will be like riding a tame old mare."

"I'm sure I can fly it," Clete said. "But I'd like to solo it an hour or so before I carry passengers."

"Solo it?"

"Fly it alone for an hour."

"Not only experienced, but cautious," Frade said. "It is settled. We will have our sandwiches, and he will have coffee. And afterwards he will *solo* for an hour, and then we will fly you home. I'm sure your daughters will like to meet him. Perhaps he can take them for a ride. You might wish to call to make sure they are at home."

"Precioso," Claudia said, laughing, "if it is your intention to marry him off to one of the girls, as I suspect it is, you are going about it in exactly the wrong way. Young people never like the young people their parents consider suitable for them."

"I have no idea what you're talking about," el Coronel Jorge Guillermo Frade said.

"El Teniente Frade is a fine pilot, mi Coronel," el Capitán Gonzalo Delgano, Air Service, Argentine Army, Retired, reported. The two of them had just taken the stagger-wing Beechcraft on a thirty-minute orientation flight, with half a dozen touch-and-go landings. "As fine a pilot as I know."

Don't let it go to your head, Cletus, my boy. Unless you had dumped that airplane, it was the only thing he could say about the boss's son's piloting skills.

He also doesn't like it a bit that I'm flying what he thought of as his personal airplane. But there's nothing he can do about that, either, except smile.

"Then we can go?" el Coronel asked. "I will send for Señora Carzino-Cormano."

"Not yet," Clete said. "I'd like to solo it first."

His father looked disappointed and a little annoyed, but finally said, "Whatever you think is best, Cletus."

"I won't be long," Clete said, and walked back to the airplane.

The pilot in him now took over. He had no doubt that he could fly the airplane, but that presumed nothing would go wrong. A lot of things could go wrong: The checkout had been really inadequate, and there was no civilian equivalent of a Navy BuAir Dash One, "Pilot's Instruction Manual," to study for the CAUTION notices, which warned pilots what they should not do.

But I have to fly it. And not just to take Señora Carzino-Cormano safely home.

While he was looking the plane over earlier, he noticed a low-level chart in a compartment on the door, an Argentine Army Air Service map of the area. He examined this with great interest. In addition to pointing out the few available navigation aids, a dozen or so civilian airstrips—one was at the Estancia Santa Catharina, Señora Carzino-Cormano's ranch—and a military air base ninety kilometers to the south, the chart showed the entire mouth of the Río de la Plata, including all of Samborombón Bay and a couple of miles of the coastline of Uruguay.

Within a day or two, he thought with sudden excitement—*presuming she's not already here—the* Reine de la Mer *will be anchored out there, waiting to replenish German submarines. I'm supposed to find her and blow her up. I didn't come here with the idea of finding her myself, but I can't pass up the opportunity to see if I can.*

He strapped himself in and looked out the window for el Capitán Delgano. When they first fired up the stagger-wing, Clete stood by the fire extinguisher for Delgano. And he expected Delgano to do the same for him; but Delgano was nowhere in sight. Clete pushed himself out of the leather-upholstered pilot's seat, went back through the cabin, and opened the door.

"Something is wrong?" his father asked.

"I need the fire extinguisher, Dad," Clete said. "I'm about to start it up. What happened to el Capitán Delgano?"

"That is the first time you have ever called me that," his father said.

Christ, he looks as if he's going to cry again!

He was touched by his father's emotion, and felt tightness in his throat. And his own eyes grew moist. *Jesus.*

As if the display of emotion embarrassed him, Frade looked around for Delgano.

"He probably had to relieve himself," he announced, and then indignantly, "He should have waited for you."

"No problem, Dad. All you have to do is stand there while I start the engine, and give it a shot if it catches fire."

It was immediately evident that el Coronel Jorge Guillermo Frade had no idea where he was to stand, or for that matter, how to operate the extinguisher.

Clete conducted a quick course in fire-extinguisher operation during aircraft engine start, then climbed back into the Beechcraft, strapped himself in, and slid the pilot's window open.

"Clear!"

"Clear!" his father responded, with obviously no idea what he was saying.

Clete turned on the MAIN switch, then pushed ENGINE PRIME, and finally ENGINE START.

The engine coughed to life on the first try, and he saw his father smile triumphantly at Claudia, who had come to the airstrip from the house to watch him. Clete looked at her and gave her a thumbs-up. She crossed herself but smiled, making it a joke.

As the needles came off the peg, he removed the brakes, checked the wind sock, and began to taxi to the gravel strip, then down it. By the time he had turned it around, everything was in the green.

"Engage brain before beginning takeoff roll," he said aloud, and shoved the throttle forward.

At just about the moment the airspeed indicator began operating, indicating forty, he felt life come into the wheel. The tail wheel lifted off. He held it on the ground, deciding it would take off at sixty or seventy. At sixty, it lifted into the air of its own accord. He eased back on the wheel and saw the ground drop away.

Claudia was waving cheerfully at him.

He put it into a shallow climb to the north, in the direction of Estancia Santa Catharina and Samborombón Bay. When he reached 4,000 feet, he played with it a little—more than he felt he could do with Delgano sitting beside him—to see how it flew. It wasn't a Wildcat, but it was a damned nice little airplane.

He found Claudia's estancia and landing strip without trouble. Giving in to the impulse, he made a low-level pass over it, rocking the wings as he did so. So far as he could tell, this dazzling display of airmanship went wholly unnoticed.

He looked at the elapsed time function on his Hamilton, and saw that it had taken him fifteen minutes to reach the estancia.

If I'm gone more than an hour, they will start shitting bricks. So I have to be back in forty-five minutes. Half of forty-five is twenty-two thirty. I can fly over the Bay for twenty-two thirty. If I can't find the Reine de la Mer *in twenty-two thirty, I'll have to quit.*

Eighteen minutes later, ten minutes after crossing the coastline, all alone on a vast expanse of bay, he spotted a ship dead in the water. He put the Beechcraft in a shallow descent from 5,000

feet, taking it right down to the waves. He retarded the throttle—
watch it, Clete, you don't want to stall it into the drink—and
approached her from the stern. Her sternboard had a legend,
which at first he couldn't see.

He flew closer.

Don't run into the sonofabitch!

A flag was on her stern pole. The wind was such that it was
flapping, fully extended. Surprising him, he recognized it as Portuguese from one of the briefings Adams had given them in New
Orleans.

And then the letters on her sternboard came into focus: *REINE
DE LA MER—LISBOA.*

There you are, you sonofabitch!

He banked sharply to pass her on her port side, and waved
cheerfully as he flew past.

Twenty crewmen waved cheerfully back, most of them standing beside canvas-draped objects that he strongly suspected were
searchlights and machine-gun mounts.

He put the Beechcraft into a shallow turning climb until he was
on a heading for Estancia San Pedro y San Pablo.

*No wonder those other guys got themselves killed. There is no
way to approach a ship like that, at anchor twenty miles off shore,
without being detected. Certainly not in the daytime. And even at
night if you rowed out there, so they wouldn't hear the sound of
your engines, if that captain knows shit from shinola, he's going
to use his searchlights every couple of minutes to see what else
is floating around out there.*

So how do we fix explosives to her hull?

*It can't be done, not the way we've planned. I'll have to come
up with something else.*

*What? Find some excuse to bring a boat alongside and have
Tony fix his charges while I go on board and . . .*

And what?

*The last team was probably eliminated trying something just
like that.*

By air?

*Not with this airplane, certainly. Not even with a Wildcat. You
can't take out something that large with .50-caliber machine
guns. I know that for a fact. And that ship has more antiaircraft
weaponry on it than any Jap freighter I ever strafed.*

What the hell do I do now?

[TWO]
Estancia Santa Catharina
Buenos Aires Province
1425 15 December 1942

"Take a good look, my darlings," Claudia said to the two very beautiful, black-haired, stylishly dressed young women who came out to the Beechcraft as Clete was tying it down, "this is Cletus. El Coronel has decided that Cletus will marry one of you. Which of you will have him?"

"I said nothing of the kind," el Coronel protested as the girls gave him their cheeks to be kissed.

The younger girl—she looked about twenty—blushed, giggled, and smiled. The other girl, who looked several years older, was obviously not amused.

"How do you do?" she said in English. "I have seen your pictures, of course. I am Isabela Carzino-Cormano. I am very pleased to make your acquaintance."

It sure doesn't sound like it.

"I am overwhelmed," Clete said. "How soon do you think we can schedule the wedding?"

"I see that you take after Uncle . . . your father," Alicia, the younger one, said with a giggle.

Isabela treated both of them to an icy smile.

They started to walk toward the ranch house.

"Somehow, I don't think she intended that as a compliment," Claudia said. "You may have to settle for Alicia."

"Can't I have both?"

"That's an idea," el Coronel said. "That is an American custom. The Mormons in Utah can have as many wives as they wish."

"Really?" Alicia asked. "That's terrible!"

"A man must be prepared to make many sacrifices in life," el Coronel said. "Two wives, four, six . . . whatever duty requires."

"Now, I am not amused," Claudia said. "Jorge, you always go too far!"

She said that because she's pissed that he hasn't proposed marriage to her. Why not? I have no idea.

The faces of Claudia's daughters showed that they had made the same interpretation.

"I saw you, Cletus," Alicia changed the subject quickly, "at the English Tennis Club, playing with Dorotea Mallín.''

"If you two play hard to get," el Coronel said, "I am sure that Dorotea would be happy to have him.''

"She's only a kid, Dad," Clete blurted.

"She's what, eighteen, nineteen years old," his father said. "That's old enough.''

"And she looked at him as if he gives milk," Alicia said. "Everybody at the English was talking.''

"That is quite enough!" Claudia Carzino-Cormano flared. "You're embarrassing Cletus. That includes you, Jorge!''

El Coronel did not seem at all repentant, but he moved to another subject.

"We have decided, your mother and I, about the travel arrangements for tomorrow," he announced to the girls, then stopped. "Why don't we go into the house? I don't suppose that you have any champagne chilled, Claudia?''

"You can have coffee. You have had quite enough champagne.''

"A few glasses . . .''

"Most of two bottles. You convinced yourself that Cletus wrecked the airplane, and that it was your fault. Coffee!''

"As you wish," Frade said, and marched across the verandah as if he owned it, to sit in a leather armchair. To judge by the cigar humidor and ashtray on a table beside it, he had used the chair before. He opened the humidor, extended it to Clete, who took one of the large black cigars inside.

"I was not at all concerned with Cletus's ability to fly the airplane. I thought perhaps he had mechanical difficulties, or ran out of fuel.''

"Or became lost, or the wings or the engine fell off. You have an active imagination, precioso, and it was running at full speed.''

"I was speaking of the travel arrangements for tomorrow," el Coronel said, changing the subject. Again he addressed Isabela and Alicia. "This afternoon, Enrico will come here in the station wagon for the luggage. He and Señora Pellano will carry it to my house, where she will arrange things for your stay. In the morning, your mother and I will drive to Buenos Aires in my Horche, and you will go with Cletus in his Buick. You will have to direct him to my house, as he does not know the way.''

"Is he going to the funeral?" Isabela asked, surprised. Unpleasantly surprised, it was immediately clear.

"Of course he is," Claudia Carzino-Cormano said quickly, and a little sharply. "Jorge was his cousin."

"If I have a choice in the matter, I would prefer to drive into Buenos Aires this afternoon with Enrico in the station wagon," Isabela said.

What did I ever do to you, honey? As far as I'm concerned, I don't want to go to the goddamned funeral in the first place, and so far as I'm concerned, you can walk to Buenos Aires.

"You will not go with Enrico and Señora Pellano in the station wagon," her mother said flatly. "It would be unseemly for Cletus and Alicia to travel alone."

"And it won't be unseemly for him to be at the funeral?"

"You are excused, Isabela," Claudia Carzino-Cormano said furiously.

Claudia waited until the sound of Isabela's high heels on the tile floor of the house had died.

"I'm am so sorry, Cletus," she said. "I apologize."

"Did I somehow give offense?"

"She was close to Jorge," Claudia said.

"Not really," Alicia added. "But now that he's dead, she's convinced herself she was in love with him."

Her mother looked angrily at her.

"That's a terrible thing to say!"

"It's true. She'd wear widow's black if she thought she could get away with it. It draws attention to her."

Claudia glowered at her, then shrugged her shoulders and let the remark go unchallenged.

"I always thought that Isabela and Jorge . . ." el Coronel said, leaving the rest unsaid. "But that certainly doesn't give her the right to treat Cletus as if . . . as if he's an enemy officer."

"Jorge, she wasn't doing that at all!" Claudia said.

"Why else would she feel it was unseemly for Cletus to be at Jorge's funeral?"

"Because she is a fool, Uncle Jorge," Alicia said.

"Alicia, that's the last word I want to hear from you," Claudia said angrily, and turned to el Coronel. "Honey," she said almost plaintively, "I'll speak to her. I'll make sure she understands that it was the anti-Christ communists who killed Jorge, not the Americans."

While he was flying an airplane for the Germans, who are murdering hundreds of thousands of women and children.

"Please·do," Frade said, not pleasantly. "I think an apology to Cletus is in order."

That was not a suggestion from a visitor. Obviously, my father has the same kind of authority in this house as Claudia does in his. I wonder why he never married her. He said she was a widow.

"No apology is necessary," Clete said. "Except from me. I'm sorry to be a source of unpleasantness, Claudia."

"Oh, honey, you're not," Claudia said, and kissed him. "You're a source of joy."

"Speak to her," el Coronel Frade said.

"You mean right now?" Claudia asked.

"Yes, I mean right now," el Coronel said. There was a tone of command in his voice, and Claudia reacted to it.

"Excuse me, please, Cletus," she said, and went in the house.

"Alicia," el Coronel Frade ordered, "would you have someone bring us some champagne?"

"Do I get any of it?"

"If you can drink it before your mother comes back," Frade said with a smile.

"Sounds fair enough," Alicia said, and went quickly into the house.

Now that was a father talking to his daughter, and vice versa. What the hell is their relationship?

"I'm sorry about this, Cletus," el Coronel said.

"No problem, Dad. I was raised with Uncle Jim's girls. They drove both of us crazy, too."

[THREE]
The Plaza Hotel Bar
Buenos Aires
1710 15 December 1942

Señor Enrico Mallín, with Señorita Maria-Teresa Alberghoni on his arm, entered the bar via the street entrance rather than through the lobby. They had just come from her apartment.

In her apartment earlier, watching her postcoital ablutions through the glass wall of her shower, and then watching her dress, he told himself she was not only an exquisitely lovely young woman, but a sweet and gentle one as well, worth every peso she cost him.

It was not impossible, he also told himself, that she was beginning to love him for himself—she certainly acted like it in bed. Perhaps she was not submitting to his attentions solely because of the allowance he gave her, and the apartment, and his guarantee of her father's loan at the Anglo-Argentinean Bank. He was flattered by such thoughts, of course, but he was at the same time aware that they were not without a certain risk . . . if she let her emotions get out of control, for example.

An arrangement was an arrangement. And its obligations and limitations had to be mutually understood between the parties. She would never become more than his Miña, and he would never be more than her good friend, her protector. She was expected to be absolutely faithful to her good friend—the very idea of another man touching Maria-Teresa, those exquisite breasts, those soft, splendid thighs, was distasteful. And he was expected to be faithful to her. Excepting of course, vis-à-vis his wife.

The relationship was an old—he hesitated to use the word "sacred"—Buenos Aires custom. His father had a Miña; his grandfather had a Miña; and most of the gentlemen of his professional and social acquaintance had Miñas. When he was a young man, his father explained to him the roots of the custom: It first developed in the olden days, when marriages were arranged with land and property, not love, as the deciding factor, and a man could not be expected to find sexual satisfaction with a woman who might have brought 50,000 hectares as her dowry but was as ugly as a horse.

In the olden days, a gentleman was expected to provide for the fruit of any such arrangement. And he was ostracized from polite society if he failed to do so. Some of the affluent Buenos Aires families (those who were perhaps a little vague about their lineage) could often trace their good fortune back to a greatgrandmother or a great-great-grandmother who had an arrangement with a gentleman of wealth and position.

Just before the turn of the century, when Queen Victoria was on the British throne, the custom was buttressed by Queen Victoria's notion—shamelessly aped by Argentine society, as were other things British in those days—that ladies could have no interest in the sexual act save reproduction. A man, a real man, needed more than a woman who offered him her body only infrequently and with absurd limitations on what he might do with it.

In exchange for certain considerations, a Miña well understood her sexual role.

In more recent times, the necessity for permanence in the relationship between a Miña and her good friend died out. This was because the efficacy of modern birth-control methods obviated the problem of children. On more than one occasion, however, Enrico Mallín considered giving Maria-Teresa a child. He loved his own children, of course, but they had inherited their mother's English paleness. He thought it might be nice to have a child or two with Maria-Teresa—a child who would have his olive skin and dark eyes, his Spanish blood.

Of course, on reflection, he realized the foolishness of this notion, and ascribed it to his fascination with her olive skin and dark eyes.

Because a Miña was not a whore or a prostitute, it would be ungentlemanly to conclude an arrangement with her in such fashion that she was forced into one of those professions afterward. Hence the allowance, at least a part of which the girl was expected to save for a dowry—which she could use after the arrangement came to an end. And hence the note at the Anglo-Argentinean Bank which Enrico had guaranteed for her father's business. When a Miña had enough money to wish to begin her married future, it was usually time for her good friend to wonder whether the grass might be greener elsewhere.

Maria-Teresa Alberghoni was Enrico Mallín's third Miña, and she had been with him for four years. While he couldn't imagine replacing her, in the back of his mind it seemed to him that their arrangement would doubtless come to an end in another two or three years . . . though in truth, he didn't really want to do without Maria-Teresa. The grass is rarely greener than where you are standing.

Although one of the best in Buenos Aires, the Plaza Hotel is, after all, nothing more than a hotel. A hotel accommodates travelers . . . or sometimes a man and a woman not married to each other who require a bed behind a locked door.

Appearances are important. Unless it is for some specific function—such as a ball, or a wedding reception that their husbands are unable to attend—ladies should not risk gossip by being seen in a hotel without their husbands. Specifically, a lady would not think of entering the bar at the Plaza Hotel without her husband; and gentlemen of Enrico Mallín's social and professional circle had an unspoken agreement never to take their wives to the bar at the Plaza under any circumstances.

This left the gentlemen free to take their Miñas there in the almost certain knowledge that they were safe from their wives.

The girls liked the system too. They could move from table to table chatting happily with their friends, while the gentlemen were afforded the opportunity to show off their Miñas to their peers, and to have private conversations about business, or whatever else needed to be discussed in confidence, in a place where the walls do not have ears.

As a matter of fact, in Enrico Mallín's judgment, the showing-off aspects of the custom had recently started to get a little out of hand. For one thing, certain gentlemen were beginning to bedeck their Miñas in jewelry and furs. There was nothing wrong, certainly, with giving your Miña a couple of small gold trinkets, or even a silver-fox cape, especially if she had done something to make you extraordinarily happy, or as a farewell gift, if the relationship was drawing to an end.

But these weren't trinkets, these were diamonds and other precious jewels, and heavy gold bracelets, and quite expensive fur coats. Once one or two gentlemen started this practice, all the Miñas would begin to expect it.

And worse than that, certain gentlemen started to appear in the Plaza bar with a Miña on each arm. And there was one old fool, Hector Forestiero—he was as bald as a cucumber and must be in his seventies—who was showing up with three. Enrico had no idea what exactly he thought he was proving by this—to suggest that he had enough money for three Miñas, or that he was still virile enough to handle a *ménage à quatre* in bed.

The Plaza bar was L-shaped. The bar itself, with its comfortable stools, occupied a corner of the room. On either side, there were leather-upholstered chairs and tables under large mirrors and mahogany paneling.

The place was full, but that was not unusual.

When the maître d'hôtel saw Mallín and Maria-Teresa, he came quickly to them and led them to a table at one end of the L. He snatched a brass "Reservado" sign from it and held Maria-Teresa's chair as she sat down.

Enrico looked around the room and nodded to several gentlemen of his acquaintance. A waiter appeared a few minutes later, automatically delivering a plate of hors d'oeuvres; a Johnnie Walker Black with two ice cubes and a little water for Mallín; and a gin fizz for Maria-Teresa.

The waiter barely had time to prepare Mallín's drink when Alejandro Kertiz appeared. Kertiz was a lawyer with a pencil-line mustache and a taste for flashy clothing. His Miña was cut from the same bolt of cloth. Her clothing was too tight, too revealing, and she apparently applied her lipstick with a shovel.

Enrico Mallín did not like Alejandro Kertiz. His grandmother—perhaps even his mother—was probably a Miña. You don't need a good family to be a successful lawyer, just a devious mind and a complete lack of morals. Mallín avoided Kertiz whenever possible. He certainly did not want to give the impression that he and Kertiz were anything more than casual acquaintances.

"My dear Enrico," Kertiz began. "Would there be room for us with you? The place is jammed."

"I would be honored," Mallín said.

The two sat down after Kertiz's Miña leaned across the table to kiss Maria-Teresa's cheek.

"I was hoping to run into you," Kertiz said, and started looking around for a waiter.

Even the waiters recognize you for what you are and try to ignore you.

By snapping his fingers so loudly and so often that everyone in the room was looking their way, Kertiz finally attracted the attention of a waiter, and grandly ordered "whatever Señor Mallín and the Señorita are having, plus a Dewar's White Label, *doble,* with soda, for the Señorita and myself."

Good manners require that I protest and tell the waiter to put that on my bill. To hell with him. Let him buy his own whiskey. On the other hand, if I permit him to buy me a whiskey, I am indebted to him.

"Put that on my bill, por favor," Mallín ordered.

Kertiz waited until the waiter delivered the drinks, then said, "Corazonita,"—Little Heart—"why don't you go powder your nose and take Señor Mallín's little friend with you? I wish to discuss something in confidence with him."

The young women left the table.

"She's so very attractive," Kertiz said, obviously referring to Maria-Teresa, and then added, "Pity."

"Yes, I think she is," Mallín said. "What do you mean, 'pity'?"

"None of them—sadly—seem able to deny themselves the attentions of a young man," Kertiz said. He reached into his pocket, produced a brownish envelope, and handed it to Mallín.

There was a photo inside. It showed Maria-Teresa standing by the railing of the canal across from the English Yacht Club at El Tigre. She was holding the hand of a dark-skinned young man.

His back was toward the camera; his face could not be seen, but Mallín could see his dark skin, and that he was touching Maria-Teresa's face with his hand.

Another goddamned Italian! Mallín thought furiously. *A stevedore from La Boca, or a vegetable salesman, all dressed up in his one suit of "good" clothes.*

"I took my family out to El Tigre yesterday," Kertiz said. "To the Yacht Club. You know that my wife's grandfather was one of the founding members?"

"I had heard something like that," Mallín said.

While your grandmother was a Miña.

"And I had the camera with me, a Leica I-C, with a shutter speed of one one-thousandth of a second. With the new American film and the Leica, one can take photographs with practically no light."

"Fascinating!"

How dare the ungrateful little bitch do this to me!

"I wasn't sure at first that it was actually your little friend, but I took the shot anyway, and I developed the film. . . . I have my own laboratory, I think you know, complete in every detail."

"How nice for you."

"And I examined the negatives, and then made an enlargement, so I could tell for sure."

"It is her cousin Angelo," Mallín said. "I know the boy well. He works in her father's restaurant."

"Oh, I am so happy to hear that," Kertiz said, making it quite clear that he thought that possibility was remote indeed. "I would hate to think that she does not find satisfaction with you, my friend."

"May I have this?" Mallín asked.

"Of course. I made it for you."

"Muchas gracias."

"De nada."

Soon after the girls returned to the table, without the manners to excuse himself, Kertiz jumped up and walked across the room to invite himself to sit with another gentleman and his Miña. A minute or so after that, he rather imperiously waved for his Corazonita to join him.

Of course, you sonofabitch. You accomplished at my table what you set out to do. Rub this disloyal bitch's philandering in my face.

"I didn't think to ask, Teresa," Mallín said when they were

alone. "Did you have a pleasant Sunday?"

"Yes, thank you."

"And what did you do?"

"Well, I went to an early mass at San Juan Evangelista, then we had a family dinner, and then visited with relatives."

You are a bad liar.

Did you really go to mass? Or were you in bed all morning with your vegetable salesman? Perhaps in bed with your young man in the apartment I provide for you? After you told your father you were going to mass, did you then take your vegetable sales- man into our bed?

"I was thinking that perhaps one day we should drive out to El Tigre," Mallín said.

Well, that caused a reaction, didn't it? Your eyes are fright- ened.

"El Tigre?"

"I thought we might go out there for lunch," he said. "Get out of the heat of the city."

"That would be very nice," Teresa said.

"It's been some time since I have been there," he said. "When was the last time you were there?"

Teresa shrugged.

"A long time ago. I don't remember."

Mallín stood up, so suddenly it frightened her.

"I am leaving you now, Maria-Teresa," he said.

"Excuse me?"

He threw Kertiz's photograph on the table.

"If you want to go out to El Tigre, have your vegetable sales- boy take you there."

"Enrico!"

"Get your things out of the apartment today," he went on. "And please tell your father that I am no longer able to guarantee his loan at the bank."

"Enrico, amado"—beloved.

"Don't 'amado' me, you treacherous little bitch!" Mallín said, louder than he intended. He glanced around the bar. People were looking at him. Kertiz had a smug look on his face.

He marched out of the bar with as much dignity as he could muster.

There wasn't a taxi in sight. There was never a taxi when you needed one.

He felt like crying.

Finally, a taxi appeared and he flagged it down and told the driver to take him to the Edificio Kavanagh. He would get the Rolls and drive around until he had his emotions under control, and then he would go home, where he would have several stiff drinks.

Pamela would be pleased to see him. She didn't expect him for several hours. Perhaps he would surprise everyone, Pamela, Dorotea, and Little Enrico, and take everybody out for dinner.

[FOUR]
4730 Avenida Libertador
Buenos Aires
1730 16 December 1942

Clete put the top up on the Buick convertible, marveling again that the General Motors automotive engineers had the ingenuity to come up with a device that would raise and lower the top at the push of a button (unlike the do-it-yourself bullshit he and Tony had had with the '37 Ford in Punta del Este). Then he carefully locked the car and walked into Uncle Guillermo's house.

A man was loitering at the corner of Calle Jorge Newberry, and Clete wondered whether the man was there to watch him.

He was in an unpleasant mood. *Who the hell was Jorge Newberry, anyway?* he thought as the man on the corner glanced his way, then averted his gaze.

The plan was to leave Estancia San Pedro y San Pablo for Estancia Santa Catharina sometime in the morning. To Clete's way of thinking, that meant sometime before ten-thirty. But it was twelve-thirty before the two-car, Horche-Buick convoy finally set out down the gravel road to Estancia Santa Catharina. During the forty-mile trip, he had to swallow the dust from his father's Horche.

And, of course, Claudia's daughters were not prepared to leave when they arrived. *Argentina, while very unlike Mexico, had* mañana *in common with the republic immediately south of the Rio Grande.*

"Since you have nothing to do in Buenos Aires," his father said cheerfully, "I'm sure you won't mind waiting for the girls to finish their packing while Claudia and I drive ahead. The girls will show you the way."

"Fine," Clete said.

The trouble was that he had something to do in Buenos Aires. He had to get in touch with Nestor and tell him he had found the *Reine de la Mer* and that he could forget taking her out by planting a charge against her hull. It couldn't be done that way. And since he could think of no way to do it himself, that would be up to Nestor to figure out.

On the flight back to the ranch, inspired by an Errol Flynn Battling the Dirty Nazis movie he vaguely remembered, he considered sneaking aboard the ship, overpowering the crew, placing scuttling charges, and then slipping away.

It worked for Errol Flynn. But, he finally remembered—shooting down the only idea he had been able to come up with—that ship in the movie was tied up at a wharf, not anchored twenty-odd miles offshore.

But of course he could not tell his father that, so he smiled and waited patiently for the girls to put their goddamned gear together. He occupied himself by putting the convertible top down, because he would no longer be swallowing his father's dust.

When she finally came out to the car, Isabela Carzino-Cormano insisted on riding in the backseat. Fine gentleman that he was, knowing that riding in the backseat of a convertible going as fast as he intended to drive was no fun, he put the roof up.

That situation lasted perhaps two miles, until Isabela tapped him imperiously on the shoulder and asked him if he would be good enough to please raise the windows. The wind was mussing her hair and she was getting dusty.

That was the last word Isabela spoke before they reached Buenos Aires. It was hotter than hell in the Buick with the roof up.

Alicia Carzino-Cormano tried to make conversation. "Now tell the truth, Cletus," she asked him, "aren't you really just a *poco* interested in Dorotea Mallín?" Watching them play tennis, she saw him looking at her in a *certain* way.

Actually, Alicia, you saw me looking down her dress and at her crotch, because I am a perverted dirty young man.

"Alicia, don't let your imagination run away with you. And since you're so curious, there is a young woman in America I'm involved with."

He was glad to get rid of both of them at his father's house on Avenida Coronel Díaz and drive quickly to the Guest House.

One of the maids greeted him at the door, then asked him if

he would like her to park the Buick.

Thank you, no. Sweetheart. You are probably a worse driver than my father.

"No, gracias. I'm going to leave it right where it is."

His answer brought him a lecture about petty crime on the streets of Buenos Aires. She assured him that if he left the car outside overnight, in the morning there would be nothing left but the windshield, and perhaps not even that.

Getting the car into the garage also posed a problem. They couldn't find the keys. Señora Pellano would of course know where the keys were, the maid told him, but Señora Pellano was unfortunately at the house on Avenida Coronel Díaz. They wound up telephoning Señora Pellano and asking where the keys were.

Finally, stopping off at the kitchen to load a silver champagne cooler with ice and two bottles of cerveza, Clete was able to take the elevator to Uncle Guillermo's playroom and get on the horn to Nestor. Predictably, Nestor was not thrilled to hear from him.

"I saw that boat you were talking about, the one you're thinking of buying? *Reine de la Mer,*" Clete said.

"I'd really rather hear it from you in person, Clete. Why don't you come here?"

"Certainly."

"You have your car?"

"Yeah."

"We can take a ride."

"I'm on my way," Clete said.

[FIVE]

Jasper C. Nestor came out of his house and got in the Buick. As soon as he was seated, Clete said, "There's a Fiat parked down the street that was parked across the street from the Guest House when I drove out of the garage."

"Well, they can't hear us as long as we're driving. You implied that you know where the *Reine de la Mer* is?"

"She's at anchor twenty miles or so offshore in the Bay of Samborombón."

"How do you know that?"

"I saw her there. I was flying my father's airplane."

"You're sure it's the *Reine de la Mer?* How can you be sure?"

"Because I flew close enough to read her sternboard. And as

a bonus, I got a good look at all the nice searchlights and machine-gun mounts on her superstructure.''

"You ... flew close enough to read her sternboard?"

"I buzzed her, all right? That was the only way I could get
close enough to read the sternboard.''

"I'm not sure that was wise.''

"Why?" Clete asked incredulously.

"We would have found her.''

"You didn't, did you?''

"And now they know you've found her.''

"Mr. Nestor, I don't think there's any way to get close enough
to her to blow her up. At least, I can't think of one.''

"Point one, Frade, is that you're not to blow her up, you are
to disable her. And as quickly as possible, certainly within the
next week or ten days. If she replenishes one German submarine,
that's one too many. Point two is that you seem to have forgotten
that it is not your function to question your orders, but to obey
them.''

"Did you hear what I said? There is no way to get close to
her where she lies. And even if we could, I don't believe that the
explosives we have would do much damage.''

"There's enough explosives—you have more than twenty
pounds. If judiciously placed, that's more than enough to disable
her. That's what we're after.''

"If we could get to her steering ... or to her engines, and had
an hour or so to do it, possibly. Pelosi is very good at what he
does, but ...''

"But what?''

"There's no way to get close to that ship, much less get aboard
her.''

"You have to try.''

"I'll have a shot at anything that looks like it has a chance of
succeeding, but I'm not going to commit suicide.''

"What did you say?''

"I said I'm not going to commit suicide. I respectfully suggest
you send a message to Colonel Graham ...''

"Colonel Graham is the Deputy Director of the OSS. I have
no intention of bothering him with something like this. What he
expects from me, and what I expect from you, is that we carry
out the mission assigned by the OSS.''

"I respectfully request, Sir, that you send a message to Colonel
Graham and tell him that I said there's no way to take the *Reine*

de la Mer out with the men and materiel I have.''

"It doesn't work that way, Frade," Nestor said. "We receive our orders and we carry them out to the best of our ability.''

What is this "we" crap? You'll be in your office in the Bank of Boston.

"Why didn't *we,* or the English, sink the *Reine de la Mer* off Lisbon, once she was identified? Or here, as she came into the Río de la Plata estuary? The Navy is operating in the South Atlantic. And there's even a destroyer, the *Alfred Thomas,* making a port call here the day before Christmas.''

"Where did you hear about the *Alfred Thomas?*" Nestor interrupted.

"Apparently it's common knowledge.''

"I asked you how you heard about it. Did Ettinger tell you?''

You don't like it that Ettinger told me about the destroyer and didn't tell you. And that I didn't tell you either. But screw that. I'm not going to let you get on Ettinger's back for that.

"No, I heard it from Enrico Mallín. Why can't this destroyer sink the *Reine de la Mer?*"

"It's not your business to question decisions like that, if I have to point that out to you. But the reasons seem self-evident. The *Reine de la Mer* is a Portuguese ship. Portugal is neutral. The United States does not torpedo neutral ships.''

"But it's all right for the three of us to sink it? What's the difference? Aside from the fact that a destroyer has the capability to take it out, and we don't?" Clete asked, and then went on without waiting for a reply: "I'd like to plead my case up the chain of command.''

"It doesn't work that way. You're in the OSS now. You take your orders from me, and you don't have the privilege of questioning them. What's the matter with you, Frade?''

Clete felt frustration and anger sweep through him.

"I know what orders are, Mr. Nestor, and I'll try to obey mine," he said. "All I'm asking you to do is pass the word up the chain of command. Tell them that I told you that I'll need more to take out the *Reine de la Mer* than good intentions and twenty pounds of explosives. A very fast powerboat, maybe. Certainly another two hundred pounds of high explosive. Or a TBF from Brazil. Something.''

"A what from Brazil?''

"A TBF," Clete repeated. And then, when he realized that

Nestor had no idea what a TBF was, he added, "A torpedo bomber."

"A *torpedo bomber?*" Nestor asked sarcastically.

"I'm a fighter pilot, but I can fly TBFs. I could go to Brazil, pick up the plane, fly it to that dirt strip we used for the airdrop in Uruguay, where Pelosi would be waiting with enough avgas to get me to the *Reine de la Mer* . . ."

Nestor looked at him with incredulous contempt.

". . . and put a torpedo in her."

Nestor shook his head sadly, as if he had failed to make a point to a backward child.

"Frade, that would be just as much an act of war as the *Alfred Thomas* attacking the *Reine de la Mer*."

"I could then fly over my father's estancia, put the plane on a course that would carry it out over the Atlantic, and bail out," Clete said.

"And that's what you want me to suggest to my superiors?"

"Yes, Sir."

"You simply refuse to understand the situation. Sinking the *Reine de la Mer* with a torpedo bomber was, I am quite sure, one of the options considered. It was obviously discarded. It's out of the question. Quite impossible."

"So is doing the *Reine de la Mer* any harm with twenty pounds of explosive. And I will not order my men to do something that has no chance of success, and that will get them killed," Clete said. "I respectfully request that you pass that up the chain of command."

"I don't think there is any point in continuing this conversation, Lieutenant Frade," Nestor said. "You leave me no choice but to report your insubordination—if that's all it is—up, as you put it, 'the chain of command.' "

"What do you mean, 'if that's all it is'?" Clete demanded, coldly angry.

"What would you call it when an officer refuses to obey an order because there is an element of personal risk involved?"

Clete pulled to the curb and slammed on the brakes.

"Get out," he ordered. "Before I punch you into next week."

Nestor looked at him in surprise, then opened the door and stepped out.

[SIX]
Avenida Alvear
Buenos Aires
1815 17 December 1942

"And here we are at the Alvear Palace Hotel," Oberst Karl-Heinz
Grüner, military attaché of the Embassy of the German Reich to
the Republic of Argentina, said quite unnecessarily to Hauptmann
Freiherr Hans-Peter von Wachtstein, who was residing there.
"Just a few minutes' walk from the Duarte mansion."

They were both in civilian clothing, and had just come from
Peter's formal introduction to Ambassador von Lutzenberger at
the embassy.

"I estimate a three-minute walk, Herr Oberst," Peter said
straight-faced.

"No more, I am sure."

*The military mind at work. Or an oberst-and-higher's mind at
work. My father can't park a car without a detailed operational
plan. Why should this man be any different?*

"It was the original intention of the Argentines to line with
cavalry from the Husares de Pueyrredón both sides of Avenida
Alvear from the Frade mansion to the Basilica of Saint Pilar,
which is approximately a kilometer in that direction," he pointed.
"I talked them out of that."

"Yes, Sir?"

"The avenue will be lined from a point approximately twenty-
five meters from the Duarte mansion with troops of a regular
regiment—the Second Regiment of Infantry. There *will* be a
representative honor guard of the Husares de Pueyrredón at the
mansion itself. On my side, I thought it would be best. for public
relations purposes, to have regular troops in field gear—they wear
our helmets, you know, and are armed with Mausers, and look
very much like German troops. And on their side, I suspect they
were pleased at the suggestion. With that many men in those
heavy winter-dress uniforms, in this heat, it was statistically certain that a number of Husares would faint and fall off their
mounts."

He looked at Peter with what could have been the suggestion
of a smile.

"It is always embarrassing, Herr Oberst, when men faint while
on parade."

"Precisely," Grüner said. "I had a tactical officer at the infantry school who used to quite unnecessarily threaten us that anyone who fainted on parade would regret it."

Peter now felt quite safe in smiling at Grüner, and did so. Grüner smiled back.

"The Husares de Pueyrredón, the mounted troopers," he went on, "will line the path of the procession from the point where Avenida Alvear ends at the Recoleta Park, at the foot of this small hill." He pointed again, and resumed walking.

When they reached the foot of the small incline, he stopped and pointed again.

"There is the Basilica of St. Pilar," he said. "Did you have the opportunity to visit churches when you were in Spain?"

"On one or two occasions, Herr Oberst. I am Evangelisch" — Protestant.

"Yes, I know. So am I," Grüner said. "And there are not very many of us in Bavaria. The Recoleta Cemetery, where Hauptmann Duarte's remains will be interred, is immediately behind the Basilica. What I started to say was that if you visited a Catholic church in Spain, you will feel quite at home in this one. It is jammed with larger-than-life-sized statues of various saints—I have often wondered if the admonition against making even graven images is in the Catholic version of the Ten Commandments . . ."

Peter chuckled, and Grüner smiled.

". . . including one of St. Pilar," Grüner continued, "the source of whose prestige in the Catholic faith remains a mystery to me, plus the to-be-expected Spanish Baroque ornamentation covering every inch of the place."

Peter chuckled again as Grüner started across the street, and they started walking up a fairly steep hill toward the Basilica.

"How the Husares will keep their mounts' footing on this incline," Grüner observed, "is fortunately not my problem."

They reached the church and stopped in a small exterior courtyard.

Grüner pointed again.

"Following the high requiem mass, the casket will be brought to this point. By that time, the dignitaries—including you and me, of course—will be standing there, against that wall. The Ambassador will step forward, and you and I will also step forward, stopping one pace behind him. The Ambassador will then briefly express the condolences of the Führer and the German people to the Duarte family and the government of Argentina. He will then take one step backward, and I will take one step forward.''

"Yes, Sir.''

"You will be holding a small pillow on which will rest the Knight's Cross of the Iron Cross.''

"Yes, Sir.''

"I will then read the order of the Oberkommando of the Wehrmacht posthumously awarding, in the name of the Führer, the Knight's Cross of the Iron Cross to Hauptmann Duarte. I will then take three steps forward to the casket. You will follow me, do a left face to me, and extend the pillow to me. I will take the decoration from the pillow and pin it to the Argentine colors that will be covering the casket.''

"Yes, Sir.''

"How do you feel about that, Herr Hauptmann?''

"Sir?''

"I personally felt the Knight's Cross was a bit much,'' Grüner said. "It is a decoration that should be won because of outstanding valor. A simple Iron Cross would be sufficient, I think.''

"Herr Oberst, it is not my place to question the award of a decoration by the Oberkommando of the Wehrmacht.''

"Nor mine,'' Grüner said. "But between soldiers . . .''

Peter did not reply.

"We will then, at my command, do the appropriate facing movement, so that we are facing the casket. On my command, we will take two steps backward and then render the German salute. The Navy somehow gets away with the hand-to-the-temple salute, but those of us in the Wehrmacht and the Luftwaffe must obey the Führer's order to render the German salute. Don't forget!''

"No, Sir.''

"On my command again, we will conclude the salute, do an about-face, and march back to our positions behind Ambassador von Lutzenberger.''

"Yes, Sir.''

"The casket will then be carried out of this courtyard, to the right and through the main entrance to the cemetery. You will remain behind, and when the last of the dignitaries has left the courtyard, you will enter the cemetery through that gate.''

He pointed, then walked to a small iron gate in the wall, which turned out to be locked.

"I will see that it is unlocked,'' Grüner said. "For now, we will enter the cemetery by the main gate.''

"Yes, Sir."

"You will pass through that gate and—you will probably have to move quickly—proceed to the Duarte tomb, where you will remain until the casket has been placed inside. After the family has departed, you will remove the Knight's Cross from the casket, return it to its box, and proceed to the Duarte mansion, where, exercising great tact, you will present the decoration to Señor Duarte."

"Yes, Sir."

"I say 'exercising great tact' because of the mother. She is, poor lady, not in the best of health, mentally speaking."

Oberst Karl-Heinz Grüner made a circling motion with his index finger at his temple.

"I understand, Herr Oberst."

"We will now locate the Duarte tomb for you, and the path from the small gate in the courtyard."

"Yes, Sir."

That took about five minutes. Peter found the cemetery fascinating. It was almost literally a city of the dead, with every inch except the walkways covered with elaborate tombs, some small and some as large as small houses. In fact, they all looked like houses. Almost all of them had a glass-covered wrought-iron door, through which small altars could be seen. The altars were usually complete to either a large brass cross or a statue of Christ on His cross, or both. And in each tomb/chapel a casket could be seen, either on the altar itself or in front of it. Several of the caskets were small and white, children's caskets, which made Peter uncomfortable.

When Oberst Grüner saw him looking into the tombs, he explained:

"The most recently deceased has his casket left on or in front of the altar until the next death in the family, whereupon it is placed in what for a better word I think of as the basement of the tomb. There are three, four, as many as six subterranean levels, I'm told."

"Fascinating."

"Bizarre, is more like it. Catholic bizarre, plus Spanish bizarre. Incredible!"

Something else raised Peter's curiosity as they walked through the cemetery, a tomb with no Catholic symbols or pious words— the burial place of an atheist and his family? He asked Grüner about it: "I thought only Catholics could be buried in a Catholic cemetery."

"So did I, until I came here." He paused and shook his head at the failure of Argentines to be logical. "Consecrated ground, they call it. No heathens or Evangelische need apply. The last time I was here—it's over there someplace—I even came across a tomb reserved for Freemasons. I thought the Catholics hated Freemasons about as much as the Führer." He smiled. "There is no explanation, except that this is Argentina, and Argentina is like nowhere else in the world."

Finally, they were through, just outside the cemetery's main gate. Grüner made Peter recite, in detail, his role in the funeral of Hauptmann Duarte.

I expected this. Sound military practice. You tell someone what you're going to teach him. You teach him what you want him to know. And then you make him tell you what he has just been taught.

"So, this is done," Grüner said. "And what do you suppose we should do now?"

"I have no idea, Herr Oberst," Peter replied.

"What do all soldiers, from private soldiers to Feldmarschalls, do when they have finished their assigned duties and there is no superior officer around?"

"Look for a woman?" Peter blurted.

Grüner chuckled. "Close, but I was thinking of finding a beer," he said. "Fortunately, we are close to a place where we can do just that. And who knows, there just might be someone there who catches your eye."

XV

[ONE]
Restaurant Bavaria
Recoleta Plaza
Buenos Aires
1905 17 December 1942

With Peter moving in step beside him, Oberst Karl-Heinz Grüner marched across Recoleta Plaza to a restaurant. A brass sign mounted on the wall identified it as Restaurant Bavaria. Peter stepped ahead of Grüner and opened the plate-glass door.

A heavyset, barrel-bellied man in his fifties approached them the moment they were inside. He was wearing a stiffly starched shirt and a suit that looked too tight, and he was immaculately shaved, except for a Hitler-style mustache on his lip.

"Guten Tag, Herr Oberst," he said, with a snap-of-his-neck bow. "What a great pleasure it is to see you."

Grüner nodded somewhat imperiously.

"Herr Krantz," he said, "I have told this young gentleman that the imitation schnapps in this pathetic copy of a gasthaus is sometimes drinkable."

"I like to think it is decent."

"This young gentleman is my new assistant, Hauptmann Freiherr von Wachtstein, of the Luftwaffe," Grüner said, waited until Krantz had made his little bow, and then added, "holder of the Knight's Cross of the Iron Cross."

Krantz snapped his head again.

"A great honor, Sir," he said.

It is apparently true, Peter thought. *The Knight's Cross and a Reichsmark* will *sometimes get you a glass of schnapps.*

"Herr Krantz," he said.

Peter looked around the restaurant. It not only had solid, Germanic-appearing furniture, but the walls were decorated with the crests of the German states and some of the larger cities, and with horned rehbock skulls and mounted boar heads. It looked truly

358   W.E.B. GRIFFIN

German; it could have been in Munich or Frankfurt am Main or Berlin.

"Would the Herr Oberst and the Herr Freiherr prefer a table by the window, or . . ."

"One of the rooms upstairs, Krantz, overlooking the Recoleta, would be preferable," Grüner said. "I have told the Freiherr that some of the prettiest women in Buenos Aires march past your windows at this hour. And we are going to have a little private chat."

Krantz led them to the rear of the restaurant and up a flight of stairs, then down a corridor and into a small room with windows overlooking the Recoleta.

"Would this be satisfactory to the Herr Oberst?"

"Thank you, Krantz," Grüner said. "This will do."

"Perhaps I might interest the Herr Oberst in something besides a schnapps?"

"With the outrageous prices you charge, schnapps—imitation schnapps is all . . ."

"The Herr Oberst forgets that I have told him time and time again that his money is not acceptable here," Krantz said.

"How kind of you, Krantz," Grüner said, and added to Peter: "Herr Krantz is a good German, Herr Hauptmann. A leader of the German colony here."

Krantz beamed.

"Permit me, Herr Oberst, to send you something of my choice."

"How kind of you, Krantz," Grüner said.

Grüner disappeared.

"He has been very valuable, helping us get officers from the *Graf Spee** out of the country," Grüner said. "You'll become involved in that, of course."

*The German pocket battleship *Graf Spee*, under the command of Captain Hans Langsdorff, was engaged in destroying British shipping in the South Atlantic when located and damaged by three British cruisers She sought refuge in the neutral port of Montevideo, Uruguay. Two British cruisers followed her, and patrolled outside the harbor. A British aircraft carrier and a British battleship were en route to Montevideo when, on 17 December 1940, under British diplomatic pressure, the Uruguayan government insisted on compliance with International Law and that she leave Uruguayan waters after seventy-two hours or be interned Langsdorff then took her to sea, but rather than risk her capture by the British, blew her up just outside Montevideo. A flotilla of tugs and other small craft hastily organized by the German colony in Buenos Aires carried Captain Langsdorff and his thousand-plus-man crew to Buenos Aires There, after learning his crew would be interned and that he could do nothing else for them, and to prove that it was fear of

"How many of the *Graf Spee*'s men are here?" Peter asked. He remembered the loss of the *Graf Spee* and the suicide of her captain, but it never entered his mind to wonder what happened to her crew.

"Eight hundred and something other ranks, and about forty-nine officers," Grüner said. "Getting the officers out is a high priority for me, largely because Admiral Canaris has an understandable personal interest."

Admiral Wilhelm Canaris was Chief of German Intelligence (Abwehr).

"Excuse me?"

"Canaris was himself interned here during the First World War, and escaped."

"I didn't know that," Peter confessed.

Strange that I didn't. Admiral Canaris and my father are close. I wonder if Grüner knows that. I wonder how much he knows about my father, or for that matter about me. Did they send a copy of my service records over here? Or my Abwehr dossier? More than likely.

Krantz came back, bearing a bottle in his right hand and holding the stems of three glasses between the fingers of his left.

"I know the Herr Oberst likes a little Slivovitz to whet his appetite, and I thought the Herr Freiherr might like a taste."

"Good of you, Krantz," Grüner said as Krantz poured the liquor.

"I am chilling some champagne, Argentinean. The German is gone, and I didn't think French appropriate to properly welcome the Herr Freiherr to Argentina. And then with the Herr Oberst's approval, I thought perhaps a nice Schnitzel, *mit Kartoffeln und Apfelbrei*—breaded veal cutlet, potatoes, and applesauce.

"We place ourselves in your capable hands, Krantz," Grüner said.

Krantz picked up his glass and raised it.

"Herr Oberst," he said, "Herr Freiherr, unser Führer!"

Grüner and Peter stood and made the toast.

"To victory!" Grüner said.

"Death to our enemies!" Krantz said passionately.

Cletus Frade is by definition my enemy. But I don't wish to see

---

British capture of his warship, and not fear of death at the hands of the enemy, that made him scuttle his command, Langsdorff arranged himself so his body would fall on the *Graf Spee*'s battle ensign and shot himself in the temple.

him dead. I just don't want him to kill me. Why do people who have never worn a uniform—who have never had to kill anyone— seem to be in love with death and killing?

The Slivovitz burned his throat. But he remembered that his mother liked it. There was a dinner at the Drei Husaren Restaurant in Vienna, near St. Stephen's Cathedral . . .

"How long have you been in Argentina, Herr Krantz?" he asked.

"I was born here," Krantz replied. "My father was brought here as a small child."

That explains your bellicosity, doesn't it? You've never heard a bomb fall, or the screams of the dying, or seen the body of the enemy burned to a crisp.

"But you have visited Germany?"

"Only once, as a child. I intend to go after the war."

This man is an amiable idiot. Still, Grüner says he's useful. What's the matter with you, anyway? All this man is doing is being polite and patriotic. No. Polite and treasonous. If he was born here, doesn't that make him an Argentinean, not a German? He owes his allegiance to Argentina, not Der Führer.

"One more," Krantz said, refilling his and their glasses. "What is it they say? A bird who flies with only wing does so badly?"

Grüner and Krantz drank theirs at a gulp. Peter returned his glass to the table barely touched. He didn't like Slivovitz, and he was concerned about alcohol loosening his tongue—Krantz was sending champagne, and there would probably be more than one bottle. It was entirely likely that the purpose of Grüner's friendliness was to feel him out. Ambassador von Lutzenberger warned him to be careful around him.

Krantz finally left.

"No more of this for you?" Grüner asked as he picked up the Slivovitz bottle.

"Thank you, no, Herr Oberst."

"You don't like it, or you're a little afraid of drinking with your new commanding officer?"

"A little of both, Herr Oberst."

"Good for you. In my line of work, alcohol is a dangerous thing. And I suppose the same is true with flying."

"We have a saying in the Luftwaffe, Herr Oberst, that there are old cautious pilots, somewhat fewer old bold pilots, and no old drunken pilots at all."

Grüner smiled his appreciation of that.

"In my line of work—it will now to some degree be your line of work as well—a tongue loosened by alcohol is a dangerous thing. One is often possessed of knowledge that should not be shared with others."

"I'm sure that's true, Herr Oberst."

"I have, for example, two pieces of information about you that I elected not to share with Ambassador von Lutzenberger."

"Whatever the accusations, Herr Oberst, I plead guilty and throw myself on the mercy of the court."

Grüner laughed.

"The first makes Krantz's free champagne especially appropriate," Grüner said. "The Ambassador will soon be notified, and he will in his own diplomat's good time notify me, that you have been promoted major."

"Really? You're sure, Herr Oberst?"

"The reason I am sure is that my source is impeccable," Grüner said, obviously pleased with himself. "A source about whose credibility I have absolutely no doubt."

"The Führer told you I was being promoted?"

"No." Grüner chuckled, then reached into his pocket and tossed a photograph on the table.

Peter picked it up. It showed two pilots standing under the engine nacelle of a Messerschmitt ME-109, holding between them the bull's-eye fuselage insignia torn from a shot-down Spitfire. Both wore black leather flying jackets, each of which was adorned with brand-new second lieutenant's insignia and brand-new Iron Crosses. One was Second Lieutenant Freiherr Hans-Peter von Wachtstein and the other was Second Lieutenant Wilhelm Johannes Grüner.

Did I shoot that Spit down? Or Willi? Or was that piece of fuselage fabric just one of the half-dozen around the officers' mess, and we picked it up to have the photo taken?

"Willi," Peter said. "France. Calais, I think. Or maybe Cherbourg. 1940."

Why the hell didn't I make the connection? I knew Willi's father was an officer, an Oberstleutnant. Because I don't like to think of Willi Grüner? Because the last time I saw Willi was outside London. His aircraft was in flames, and he was on his way down by parachute.

"Willi," Grüner repeated.

"Have you heard from him?" Peter asked, remembering only now that there had been word from the International Red Cross.

Willi was a POW, alive but injured.

"You weren't paying attention," Grüner said. "I learned about your promotion from Willi."

"I don't understand."

"He had himself named escort officer for a group of seriously wounded prisoners exchanged via Sweden. He's now in Berlin. *Hauptmann* Willi."

"I was with him the day he was shot down," Peter said.

"Yes, he told me. He also told me that you followed him to the ground to make sure the English didn't use him for target practice."

"He would have done the same for me," Peter said.

"In any event, Willi was in Berlin, and looking for you. At the Oberkommando of the Luftwaffe, he found that you've been sent here, but promoted major as well."

"I'm surprised the word got here so quickly," Peter thought aloud. "It almost got here before I did."

"Well, there is Condor service, of course. Willi's letter was on last week's flight." German four-engine transports, called "Condors," were engaged in transatlantic service via Spain and Africa. "It used to be twice a week, but it's down to once a week, sometimes once every other week. The aircraft have been temporarily diverted to supply von Paulus at Stalingrad."

Well, scratch the Condors from the property books. Stalingrad is lost, and so will be the aircraft trying to supply von Paulus.

"If you have his address, I'd like to write him," Peter said.

"Of course. I'll see that it goes in the diplomatic pouch."

Krantz returned, leading a two-waiter procession bearing champagne bottles in coolers.

"I think you will find this satisfactory, Herr Freiherr," Krantz said as he popped the cork and began to pour. "It is not quite as good as German, of course, but it is drinkable."

Peter took a sip and pronounced it very nice.

The bottle was empty by the time they finished their meal, and then Krantz produced a bottle of French cognac.

During the meal, Peter couldn't fail to notice that there *were* indeed an extraordinary number of good-looking, long-legged, nicely bosomed young females parading down the sidewalk outside.

"The French," Herr Krantz proclaimed as he poured the cognac, "may well be a decadent people, but they do know how to make brandy." Krantz's face was flushed, doubtless from sampling the brandy himself.

And he took a long time to leave.

"He attaches himself like a leech," Oberst Grüner observed. "But his food is not only first-class, but free. And you can bet he will invite you to return as often as your duties permit."

"That would be very nice."

"Tell me, Peter," Grüner said, for the first time addressing Peter by his Christian name, "how much of Frade's son did you see when you were in Oberst Frade's guest house?"

Now it comes. Even though Willi and I are close. He is after all, as von Lutzenberger put it, the "embodiment" of the Sicherheitsdienst and the Abwehr in the embassy.

"Not much. I was there when he walked in. He said hello, had a glass of cognac with me, and went to bed."

"He is a serving officer of the American Marine Corps. Did you know that?"

"No, Sir. Really?"

You have just violated the Officer's Code of Honor, Hauptmann von Wachtstein. An officer has asked you a question in the execution of his office, and you consciously and deliberately lied to him. That von Lutzenberger told you to is not justification, and you know it. So why did you do it? Who are you to criticize Herr Krantz for not knowing his allegiance?

"You're familiar with the American Marine Corps, of course?"

"No, Sir."

"An elite force, like the Waffen-SS," Grüner said.

"Really?"

Cletus was furious when I made that comparison.

"Like yourself, he is an aviator. His father introduced him at the Centro Naval—that's the downtown officers' club, used by both services, I will get you a guest membership—as a veteran of the Pacific, specifically Guadalcanal."

"Interesting. What is he doing in Argentina, if I may ask? For that matter, how did he wind up in the American Army—"

"Marine Corps," Grüner corrected him. "It is part of the U.S. Navy."

"—excuse me, in the *Marine Corps*—if he's an Argentinean?"

"His mother was an American. He was raised there. He has dual citizenship. I have an agent in Internal Security, a Comandante—Major—Habanzo. He showed me his dossier."

"Fascinating. What did you say he's doing here?"

"No one seems to know. He came ostensibly to make sure that American petroleum is not being diverted from here to Germany."

"And obviously the Americans don't like that."

"No, of course they don't. We managed to acquire some petroleum products here at the start of the war—at a great cost, I might add. But the Americans solved that problem early on by controlling the amount of petroleum they are willing to sell Argentina, and by applying diplomatic pressure. Meanwhile, the Argentines have a growing need for oil, so there is less and less available to us, no matter what we're willing to pay for it.

"So, while it is possible that young Frade is here to make sure Germany is not buying American oil, I doubt it. That leaves several more likely possibilities. The most logical is that he is here to influence his father."

Grüner stopped, and looked at Peter.

"The only way I can explain that is to deliver a lecture on Argentinean politics. I'd planned to do so in a day or two anyway. But why not now?"

"Please do, Herr Oberst."

"Their politics are Byzantine. Or perhaps Machiavellian, or Spanish, or perhaps simply Argentinean. But certainly not democratic, as Northern Europeans understand the term. They have elections every once in a while—between takeovers of the government by military juntas. The election of the current president of Argentina was, by local standards, remarkably honest. The man's name is Castilló—and he is quite sympathetic to Germany. But he has lost favor with the people, not in small part because of British influence here. The British built the Argentine rail system and the telephone network, and they trained their Navy. The Navy is therefore sympathetic to the British. German engineers built their dams and power stations, and we trained their Army. The Army is therefore pro-German—generally speaking, with certain specific exceptions."

"I understand. I hope I understand."

"It takes some getting used to. And the British do better with propaganda, frankly, than we do. That recent declaration, for example."

"Sir?"

"Where they accused us of murdering hundreds of thousands of Jewish women and children."

"I'm afraid I don't understand, Herr Oberst."

"They put out a proclamation, in the name of the King, Stalin, the President of the United States, and even that ludicrous Frenchman, de Gaulle, charging Germany with murdering hundreds of thousands of Jews. An absolutely fantastic accusation, but one which got wide play in the local press, including, so help me, *Die Freie Presse.*" (The *Freie Presse,* a German-language newspaper, was then published daily in Buenos Aires.)

"I haven't heard anything . . ."

"You were on the ship. I have a copy in the office, and I'll let you read it. It's absolutely outrageous. I can't believe they actually thought anyone would believe a word of it, but unfortunately, many people seem to take the document seriously.

"Anyway, whether because of British propaganda or not, Castilló has lost much of his support. Thus, if the elections were held today, he would almost certainly lose. So he has naturally decided to ignore the results of the next election."

"Can he get away with that?"

"If it weren't for the G.O.U.—the Grupo de Oficiales Unidos—he probably could. But if El Presidente does not voluntarily relinquish power when he loses the election—or even if he wins it—the G.O.U. will almost certainly stage a coup d'état. And to anticipate your question, Peter, can they get away with that? Yes, I think they can. And so does the Bureau of Internal Security, I'm reasonably certain."

"And that junta would not be pro-German, but pro-Allies?"

"Not necessarily. There are both pro-German and pro-Allied factions within the G.O.U. The power within the G.O.U., however, the money and the brains, belongs to el Coronel Jorge Guillermo Frade. On the one hand, Frade is the uncle of the heroic Hauptmann Duarte, who died fighting godless communism with von Paulus at Stalingrad. And on the other, he is the father of Lieutenant Frade of the United States Marine Corps."

"I see."

"Which very possibly explains the presence of 'ex'-Lieutenant Frade, in civilian clothing, in Argentina. He has been sent here to tell his father that the Americans will help him in any way they can. And, very probably, to establish a line of communication with him."

"Yes," Peter said thoughtfully.

"Now, with Oberst Frade, there is another factor involved,"

Grüner said. "You met, I believe, Oberst Juan Domingo Perón in Germany?"

"Yes, Sir. He came as far as the Franco-Spanish border with me."

"And your relationship with Oberst Perón?"

"Actually, Sir, we got along rather well. He told me I would enjoy my time in Argentina and was quite gracious to me."

"That cordiality almost certainly will be valuable later on," Grüner said. "The point is that, despite their different backgrounds—Frade is one of the most wealthy men in Argentina, and Perón's background is simple—Perón and Frade are quite close. They became friends in the army when they were both lieutenants."

"I see what you mean, Sir, by Byzantine."

"Perón is very sympathetic to Germany, in particular with Germany's socialist political philosophy, and with Germany's demonstrated concern for the welfare of the working man.* It is to study our system that he is in Germany. And the reason he wishes to become expert, so to speak, in German socialist social policy is that, when the G.O.U. stages its coup d'état and takes over the government, Oberst Perón will become what we would call the Minister for Public Welfare."

"A military man as Minister of Social Welfare?" Peter asked, surprised.

"The military runs Argentina, Peter. You must keep that in mind. Which means that our mission is to ensure that *our* colonels, and not the British colonels, are in charge."

"I understand," Peter said.

"The third possibility is that 'ex'-Lieutenant Frade is a member of the OSS, the Office of Strategic Services, and that he is here to damage or sink a U-boat replenishment vessel we have in the River Plate."

"Really? How?"

"Good question. He probably knows no more about sinking a ship than you do.

"Now all this leads to a distasteful aspect of our duty here, one that frankly troubles me personally, but which I have come

---

*It is perhaps germane to note here that "NAZI" was the shortened form of NSDAP, Nationalsozialistische Deutsche Arbeiterparteı (National Socıalıst German Workers' Party), and that the root of Hıtler's power when he was first elected Chancellor, quite legally, was from Germany's socialısts

reluctantly to decide is essential. There is no civilized way to wage war, and we are fooling ourselves when we think there is."

"Yes, Sir. I agree."

"It is not in Germany's interests to permit a cozy relationship between Lieutenant Frade—that is to say, the American government—and Oberst Frade, who will almost certainly be a major influence on Argentine policy."

"Obviously."

"Considering the stakes—Germany needs and buys enormous quantities of Argentine wool, Argentine leather, Argentine foodstuffs—we cannot afford to have someone in a position of influence who will lead Argentina into the war on the side of the Allies . . . or stand by while our supply line is cut. Since removing Oberst Frade is obviously out of the question, that leaves 'ex'-Lieutenant Frade. The question then becomes how."

What does he mean by remove? Certainly not "assassinate"?

"Excuse me, Herr Oberst. 'Remove'?"

"There is no civilized way to wage war, and we are fooling ourselves when we think there is," Grüner quoted himself, met Peter's eyes for a moment, and then went on. "To that end, in my conversations with Major Habanzo of BIS, I have been advancing the theory that Lieutenant Frade is an OSS agent sent here to violate international law vis-à-vis the actions permitted of belligerent powers resident in a neutral country. I have suggested specifically that young Frade is here in order to cause harm to neutral vessels suspected of supplying German submarines. The BIS knows there was a team of OSS agents here with that mission."

"*Was*, Herr Oberst?"

"They disappeared. No one seems to know what happened to them. They were not successful."

"And you think that the BIS will arrange for Lieutenant Frade to similarly disappear?"

"That would be the ideal solution," Grüner said. "But in my business—in our business, Peter—one seldom finds an ideal solution. No, I don't think that the BIS will cause Lieutenant Frade to disappear. What I am hoping is that Oberst Frade will soon learn from his friends within the BIS that the BIS believes his son is an OSS agent sent here to cause damage to our replenishment vessel."

"I don't think I understand, Herr Oberst."

Grüner didn't respond to the question.

"The new replenishment vessel is here," he went on. "At anchor in the Bay of Samborombón, within Argentina's territorial waters. It arrived several days ago."

"Herr Oberst, you're moving too fast for me."

"Bear with me. It would be ideal for us if Lieutenant Frade is in fact an OSS agent. As I said, I doubt that is the case. But if he were, he would get on with his mission of trying to cause damage to our U-boat replenishment vessel. That attempt would be doomed to failure. The ship is thirty-odd kilometers offshore; and it is moved five or ten kilometers every day or so. It is armed. It is highly unlikely that Lieutenant Frade could even find it, and no way that he and his men could come close to it."

Peter was now wholly confused.

"Unfortunately, I'm afraid, the impossibility of harming our ship will be evident to him. They already lost one team trying to damage the last one. So he won't try it. And that leaves him in place to do what I believe he is really here for, to influence his father."

"May I ask a question?"

"Certainly."

"Why don't the Americans simply sink our boat with their Navy?"

"Our *ship,*" Grüner corrected him. "For propaganda purposes. When the British damaged the *Graf Spee,* they were very careful not to violate Uruguayan and Argentinean territorial waters or Uruguayan and Argentinean neutrality. This paid off in enormous goodwill for them. We Germans were regarded as the aggressors, the violators of neutrality. The Americans follow the English lead in most things diplomatic; they are not going to ignore that lesson of history."

"I understand," Peter said. "I understand *that,* Sir. But . . ."

"How do we remove Lieutenant Frade?"

"Yes, Sir."

"Speaking hypothetically, Peter. Perhaps a tragic auto accident . . . Or burglars might kill him in his home . . ."

Good God, he is *talking about having Clete assassinated!*

"Could that be accomplished without causing suspicion?"

"I'm sure it could be," Grüner said matter-of-factly. "Argentina has a criminal element who could teach our criminals a lesson or two. And they relish violence. But hypothetically speaking, of course, a lack of public interest in Lieutenant Frade's removal might not be as much in Germany's interest as widespread public attention.''

Grüner looked at Peter for his reaction, was apparently satisfied with what he saw, and went on: "For example, if on the day after tomorrow—the day after the funeral of his heroic cousin, Hauptmann Duarte—Lieutenant Frade were found in his bed, with his throat cut, with 'death to godless communists and their allies' written in soap on his dresser mirror . . .''

You're not just talking assassination, Herr Oberst. Murder. You're talking about brutal, cold-blooded murder!

''. . . that would certainly get in the newspapers. Even in the Gottverdammte *Buenos Aires Herald,''* Grüner said.

"Oberst Frade won't believe it.''

"It doesn't matter if he does or not.''

He looked at Peter, and Peter understood that he expected approval, perhaps even enthusiastic approval.

"May I ask two questions, Herr Oberst?''

"Of course.''

"Hypothetically, of course.''

"Of course.''

"If this were to happen, wouldn't Oberst Frade suspect something?''

"He is a very intelligent man. I'm sure he would.''

"And, Herr Oberst, wouldn't he hate us for killing his son?''

"Yes, of course he would hate us. And yes, he is a powerful man. But according to my information, he does not at this point absolutely control the G.O.U. And his power would be weakened when the word spread that his son was an OSS agent.''

But, goddamn you, you don't know that he is!

What's the difference? The interests of Germany require that Clete be "removed." This is simply a way of accomplishing that "removal" in the most efficacious way.

"Even though the other members of the G.O.U. would sympathize with Oberst Frade's loss, they would still question whether Frade had a connection with the Americans that he has concealed from them. Oberst Frade has too much invested in the G.O.U. to risk losing his influence there. That means he must minimize his relationship with his son . . . and thus with the Americans. Like you and me, Peter, and like Willi, he is a soldier. He knows that one most accept one's losses and get on with the mission.''

"Herr Oberst, I'm flattered, but more than a little surprised that you have taken me into your confidence."

"This was just a hypothetical discussion, Peter. And, hypothetically, don't you think that a man in my position can safely trust a man who comes from a distinguished military lineage? Who has risked his life for my son? And who wears the Knight's Cross of the Iron Cross as proof of his dedication to Germany?"

"I will try to prove myself worthy of your confidence, Herr Oberst."

I didn't get the goddamned Knight's Cross for cold-blooded murder. And part of my distinguished military heritage includes a concept of honor.

"I'm sure you will, Peter."

"May I infer, Herr Oberst—hypothetically—that Ambassador von Lutzenberger is not aware of your plans?"

"He is not. But he will approve *ex post facto*. He has nothing to lose."

But my friend Clete does.

"One final hypothetical question, Herr Oberst?"

"One final question."

"Can you trust the people you mentioned to carry out the plan?"

"To carry out my instructions? Absolutely. I pay them well, and they are violent men. Do I trust them? Absolutely not. After they do what they have been hired to do, they will leave Buenos Aires for Paraguay. I have given them the address of a hotel in Encarnación, a small town just across the border, where they expect to take a holiday until things calm down here in Buenos Aires. In fact, others will meet them there; and that is the last anyone will ever see of them."

Two more murders. Maybe three, or even four. You are a cold-blooded bastard, aren't you, Herr Oberst?

"I am really not qualified to judge a plan like this, Herr Oberst," Peter said. "But for what it's worth, it seems to me you have covered every contingency."

[TWO]
Suite 701
The Alvear Palace Hotel
Buenos Aires
0915 19 December 1942

In response to the fifteenth or twentieth ring of the telephone on
the table beside his bed, Hauptmann Freiherr Hans-Peter von
Wachtstein finally sat up abruptly and answered it.

"Buenos días, Señor," an outrageously courteous, infuriatingly
cheerful female voice came over the line. "It is nine o'clock,
Señor."

"Gracias," Peter said, picking up a stainless-steel-cased wristwatch from the bedside table and with some effort focusing his
eyes on it. It informed him that it was not nine, but 09:15:40.

"I will require immediately a pot of coffee," he ordered. The
way his tongue felt, like a North African desert, he was surprised
that he could speak at all.

"I will connect you with Room Service, Señor. Un momento,
por favor."

He looked at the watch again as he replaced it on the bedside
table. It was a U.S. government–issue Hamilton chronograph
identical to the one he had spotted on the wrist of Lieutenant
Cletus Frade of the flying service of the Corps of U.S. Marines,
who would have his throat cut tonight.

This Hamilton had been issued to the pilot of a U.S. Army Air
Corps B-26 Peter shot down over Cherbourg. An Abwehr Hauptmann showed up at the squadron's officers' mess the same night
and announced that Peter's brilliant aerial victory—having been
witnessed by three reliable spectators—was confirmed and made
a matter of official record; and the Hauptmann thought the Hauptmann Freiherr might like the watch as a souvenir (the Hauptmann
took it from the pilot during interrogation).

Peter did not immediately reply. He was a little drunk at the
time, but sober enough to recognize the foolhardiness of lecturing
an Abwehr captain—who goddamned well should have known
it—that stealing from prisoners of war was not only a violation
of the Geneva Convention, but a pretty goddamned dishonorable
thing for an officer to do.

"And where is the prisoner now, Herr Hauptmann?"

"He has been taken to the Central Detention Facility outside

Paris, Herr Hauptmann Freiherr. At Senlis.''

"And do you happen to have this officer's name, Herr Hauptmann?''

"Not at the moment, Herr Hauptmann Freiherr,'' the asshole replied, and then the confusion on his face was replaced by comprehension. "Of course, I should have thought of that myself. It will have more meaning to you if you know his name. I will find it for you.''

It will also permit me to return this officer's watch to him, preferably in person, together with an apology from one officer to another for the shameful behavior of an asshole wearing a German officer's uniform.

"I would be very grateful, Herr Hauptmann.''

"My great pleasure, Herr Hauptmann Freiherr.''

I never got the poor bastard's watch back to him. When the Abwehr asshole never sent me his name, I just kept it. Good watch. I'm glad I wasn't wearing it when I met Cletus. He wouldn't have understood.

Yeah, Cletus would have understood.

And what the hell am I going to do about Cletus? Simply sit around with my finger in my ass waiting for Herr Oberst Grüner to happily inform me that his Argentine gangsters have followed his neat little Operational Plan and cut Clete's throat?

"Buenos días, Room Service.''

"This is Señor von Wachtstein in 701. Will you send up a pot of coffee, please? Right away?'' He looked at the Hamilton chronograph again. "How long will that take?''

"I will have it there within half an hour, Señor.''

That means an hour. I don't have an hour. Goddamn it!

"Forget it, thank you just the same.''

He hung up, then walked quickly to the bathroom and stood under the cold shower for five minutes. Then he shaved, cutting himself twice in the process, put on his winter dress uniform, and left his suite.

In the elevator, he felt woozy.

I have to put something in my stomach, or I will be one of those poor bastards that fall on their face during the ceremony. Wasn't there a restaurant in the lobby?

There was, in a wide corridor to his right when he stepped off the elevator. He walked to it, found a small table, and sat down. He looked around for a waiter. Several of them were standing near a buffet table. He finally managed to attract one's attention.

"Coffee, por favor, and a pastry of some kind."

"Señor," the waiter said. "It is a buffet. Complimentary to guests of the hotel. Señor *is* a guest?"

"Yes, of course I am," Peter replied, and took a closer look at the buffet. A line of prosperous-looking people were there. A man inclined his head toward him and smiled. And another did the same.

What the hell is that all about? Oh, hell, of course. These people are here for the funeral, and they are being charming to the young man whose dress uniform and Knight's Cross of the Iron Cross tell them he is the man who brought poor Whatsisname's body home for burial.

Peter smiled and nodded back.

Do I have that goddamned thing on right?

He looked down at his chest. He didn't have the goddamned thing on at all.

"Señor," the waiter asked. "Would you be so kind as to give me your name and room number?"

Peter looked at him.

He reached in his pocket and came out with money.

"I am Hauptmann Freiherr von Wachtstein," he said. "I am now going to my room, Number 701, where I forgot something. When I return, if there is a glass of orange juice and a coffee cup with a double cognac in it on this table, this is yours."

"It will be my great pleasure," the waiter said with a smile.

Why the hell not? He works in a hotel. I am not the first painfully hung-over guest he has seen.

When he returned with his Knight's Cross of the Iron Cross in its proper place on his uniform and walked as straight as he could to the table, even more people smiled at him.

And there was a large glass of orange juice on the table, plus a glass of soda water, and a coffee cup filled to the brim with a dark substance that was not coffee.

If anyone thought it was strange that the young German officer gulped down half the orange juice, mixed the rest of it with coffee poured from his cup, gulped that down, diluted the last of the coffee with soda water, and then gulped that down, he was of course too polite to remark on it.

Three minutes after he returned to the dining room, Hauptmann Freiherr von Wachtstein marched erectly out of the dining room, through the lobby, out the door, and turned left down Avenida Alvear toward the Duarte mansion.

A long line of people sought entrance to the mansion, many with their invitations in their hands. The line stretched from the door out onto Avenida Alvear. Mounted troopers of the Husare de Pueyrredón, already showing signs of the heat, lined the driveway, while policemen—and men in civilian clothing who looked like plainclothes policemen—kept a watchful eye on those waiting to enter the mansion.

I don't have an invitation. I don't suppose I need one, but I don't think I should just go to the head of the line and announce my arrival. I'll stand in line and see what happens.

Just inside the gate, a large, smoothly shaved man in civilian clothing eyed Peter unabashedly for a full thirty seconds, then walked toward him.

"El Capitán von Wachtstein?"

"Sí."

"Let this gentleman pass," the man ordered the policemen. "He is with the family."

When Peter walked to him, he explained, "Mi Capitán, I am Enrico. If you will come with me, please, Sir, I will take you to el Coronel."

"Gracias," Peter said.

Enrico did not look entirely at ease in his blue business suit, and he had the somewhat stiff walk—as if on parade—of the long service sergeant.

Enrico was almost certainly Suboficial Mayor Enrico, Peter thought. *Clete told me about him, an old soldier who worked for el Coronel Frade from the time el Coronel was a teniente. They are a type. For twenty-five years, my father had Oberfeldwebel Manntz running his errands, taking care of him, until Manntz's luck ran out in Norway.*

Enrico marched him past the door of the house, where people were checking invitations against a typewritten list, then through the foyer, where the late Capitán Duarte's casket rested on a catafalque, and into a small sitting room.

"If the Capitán would be so good as to wait here, I will tell el Coronel that you have arrived."

Enrico headed for a man wearing an ornate uniform that looked like a costume for a Viennese light opera about shenanigans in some obscure Balkan dukedom.

Jesus Christ, he realized somewhat belatedly, *that's Cletus's father!*

Beatrice Frade de Duarte, wearing a black silk dress, a hat with

a veil, and a single strand of enormous pearls, saw him first. She
came quickly across the room, took his arm, and led him into the
presence of Cletus's father.

"Capitán von Wachtstein," she said, as if they were at a dress
ball, "may I present my brother, el Coronel Jorge Guillermo
Frade?"

"A sus órdenes, mi Coronel," Peter said, then clicked his heels
and bowed, which caused him to feel alarmingly light-headed.

"Capitán von Wachtstein is the officer who brought Jorge
home, Jorge," Señora de Duarte said.

"So I have been informed," el Coronel Frade said. "Might I
have a word with you, Capitán?"

"Of course, mi Coronel."

Frade took his arm and led him out of the foyer down a corridor
into the kitchen. He went to a refrigerator, took out a lemon,
sliced it into thirds, and handed one of the thirds to Peter.

"If you eat the whole thing, skin and all, it will probably mask
the fumes of the cognac," Frade said.

Oh, shit!

"Apologies are in order. I extend them. And I thank you,"
Peter said, and put the piece of lemon in his mouth, chewed it,
and swallowed it.

"I cannot ask an apology from you for doing exactly what I
have been doing," Frade said. Peter looked at him in surprise. "I
required the same liquid courage," Frade went on. "If I had not
arranged for the Ministry of Defense to approve my nephew's
idiot notion to go to Germany, neither of us would be here."

What an astonishing thing to say!

"Oh damn you, Jorge, you promised!" a very striking middle-
aged woman said, mingled anger and resignation in her voice.
"And don't try to tell me that lemon is for tea."

"That is exactly what it's for," Frade said. "El Capitán von
Wachtstein and I are about to have a cup of tea. And then I
thought I would offer the Capitán a little liquid courage to help
him through this . . . this obscene ceremony."

"Jorge!"

"Capitán, may I present Señora Carzino-Cormano, who has the
odd notion that she is entitled to treat me like a child."

"Encantado, Señora," Peter said, and clicked his heels and
bowed again.

"If you are visibly drunk, I will never forgive you," Claudia
said to Frade, ignoring Peter.

"I am never visibly drunk."

"Cletus just arrived," Claudia said. "Just as you came in here."

"The Señora, Capitán," Frade said, "refers to my son, late Teniente of the U.S. Corps of Marines aviation service. He served with great distinction at Guadalcanal. Presumably, you have heard of Guadalcanal?"

"Jorge, my God!" Claudia protested, and turned to Peter. "You must excuse el Coronel, Capitán. He mourns the death of his nephew more than he is willing to admit."

Alicia Carzino-Cormano walked up to them.

Remarkably beautiful young woman!

"Cletus is here," Alicia said to her mother, then turned to Frade: "I think he's looking for you."

"Captain, this is my daughter, Alicia," Claudia Carzino-Cormano said.

"Hauptmann Freiherr von Wachtstein at your service, Señorita."

Isabela Carzino-Cormano walked up and smiled dazzlingly at Peter.

"I don't believe I have the privilege of this gentleman's acquaintance," she said.

Frade, ignoring her, took Peter's arm.

"Perhaps you would like to meet my son," he said.

"Jorge, damn you!" Claudia said. "How much have you had?" Then she turned and smiled at Peter. "And my other daughter, Capitán, Isabela," Claudia said.

"Encantado, Señorita," Peter said.

Not nearly as beautiful as the sister.

Frade tugged at his arm.

"I have the privilege of the Herr Lieutenant Frade's acquaintance, mi Coronel."

"The privilege of his acquaintance?" Isabela asked incredulously. "Isn't he your enemy?"

"I met him briefly," Peter went on, "when enjoying the hospitality of your Guest House, mi Coronel."

Not briefly. We got drunk together. We were not enemies, but pilots talking about flying.

"Though el Capitán and my son, Isabela," Frade proclaimed, "are officers of opposing military services, they are first and foremost officers and gentlemen. They bear each other no personal animosity. Isn't that so, Capitán?"

"Sí, mi Coronel."

"That's outrageous!" Isabela said. "The Capitán is agreeing with you to be polite."

Frade snorted.

"Tell her, Capitán. She has her mother's inability to conceive that she could possibly be wrong."

"No tea for you," Claudia said. *"Coffee.* Several cups. Right now. You must again forgive el Coronel, Capitán. His behavior is inexcusable."

"Forgive me, Señora," Peter said. "El Coronel is quite correct. I bear Herr Lieutenant Frade no ill will. In other circumstances, I feel sure we could become friends."

On the other hand, I am obviously perfectly willing to sit here with my finger in my ass doing nothing to warn him that he's going to be murdered.

But, of course, I can't do that. From the moment Grüner told me his plans, I knew I wouldn't be able to just let things happen. I will warn him.

But how?

Perhaps if I went to von Lutzenberger and told him, he would order Grüner to call off his thugs. But Grüner would certainly work out where von Lutzenberger got his information. And if von Lutzenberger decides that Cletus is expendable, and that I should just stay out of it, then I could not warn Cletus; Grüner and von Lutzenberger would both know I told him.

And Grüner would call that "giving aid and comfort to the enemy."

Enrico appeared.

"Mi Coronel, there is a German officer looking for el Capitán. I put him in the small office off the library."

Grüner with the Knight's Cross and the goddamned pillow, Peter thought.

"I will take you to him," Frade announced.

"No, you won't," Claudia said. "You will stay here and have coffee. Alicia, would you please take el Capitán to the library?"

Alicia took von Wachtstein's arm.

"Yes, of course, Mother," she said, smiling sweetly at her sister.

XVI

Clete Howell wasn't able to get anywhere near Aunt Beatrice's house in the Buick. So he parked three blocks away. As he uneasily left the car, the maid's lecture on crime in the streets of Buenos Aires was very much on his mind. Then he stood in line. When he reached its head, he encountered a polite but firm plainclothes policeman, who seemed deeply saddened to inform him that without an invitation he could not enter the mansion.

Everything is going splendidly, Clete thought. *Getting better and better every day in every way. Not only did that bastard Nestor as much as accuse me of cowardice for telling him the truth, but now they won't let me into a funeral I don't want to go to in the first place.*

The more he thought about flying a TBF down from Brazil to torpedo the *Reine de la Mer,* the more it seemed like a good idea . . . the best he could come up with.

Or do I like it mostly because Nestor thinks it is a bad idea?

Nestor was probably right when he said that the OSS brass decided against taking out the Reine de la Mer *with a torpedo-carrying airplane . . . just as they must have turned down the idea of taking it out with a B-17 from Brazil.*

The problem with the B-17 is that it has a lousy record against shipping. And the TBF idea was rejected, in all probability, because it does not have the range to make it from wherever they are operating in Brazil to the Reine de la Mer *in Samborombón Bay.*

It doesn't. And since Uruguay is neutral, the brass obviously concluded that a TBF could not file a flight plan to an en route airport, where the pilot could sit down and tell the ground crew to top off the tanks, and then ask for the weather between there and Samborombón Bay. And the brass also understandably de-

cided that it could not sit down on a dirt road somewhere in the middle of nowhere and get refueled. The landing gear of a TBF was designed for use on the paved runways of an airfield, or else on the deck of an aircraft carrier.

But what it was designed for is not the same thing as what it is capable of doing. That was proved at Henderson Field on Guadalcanal. Henderson was a hell of a lot rougher than the dirt road where the guy put down his Piper Cub—especially after the Japanese spent all night shelling it, and the holes were quickly and not too neatly filled in by Marine bulldozers.

But the Cactus Air Force—including yours truly, on occasion— operated TBFs out of there just about every day. Even with a torpedo in its belly, I could sit a TBF down on that dirt road. Nice, long, slow approach to grease it in. And I only have to make that one landing.

Or why not? Maybe two. After I put the torpedo into the Reine de la Mer, *I could go back to the dirt strip, take on some more fuel, and fly back to Brazil. The second landing would be easier; the torpedo would be gone. God knows that would be better than jumping out over the estancia. I really don't want to do that. Tony may think that parachute jumping is the next-greatest thing to sex, but it scared the hell out of me when I bailed out.*

Could I hit the Reine de la Mer? *Why not? All you have to do is fly close enough so there's no chance to miss. You've been shot at before; you just don't pay attention to it. And I don't think that people on the Bofors and the machine guns will have had much experience. A low-flying airplane has a much better chance against them than against Japanese gunners.*

I think I could reason with Colonel Graham about this, tell him I know what I'm talking about, and convince him that my idea stands a much better chance of working than anything else I can think of.

The question then becomes, how do I get in touch with Colonel Graham? I can't use commercial, Mackay or RCA, to send him a cable. Argentine Intelligence certainly reads commercial cables. And Nestor won't let me use the Embassy's communications or codes.

That leaves the destroyer. "Good afternoon, Captain. I'm Lieutenant Frade of the Marine Corps down here on a classified mission, and I need your radios to complain about my orders."

Hell, just tell him the truth. Let him see the message to Colonel Graham. He may understand it and send it for me. Or he may think I'm some kind of lunatic and throw me off his destroyer. In which case, I'd be no worse off than I am now.

The Alfred Thomas gets here Christmas Eve. I'll be waiting for her. That's the only real option I have, convincing her captain to let me get in touch with Colonel Graham.

Do I really have the balls to fly close enough to her to make absolutely sure the torpedo strikes? Into all that antiaircraft? Watching the TBF guys do that, I was perfectly willing to admit they had much bigger balls than I do.

I don't have any choice; that's the only way...

"This is the son of el Coronel Frade," he heard Enrico indignantly announce to the plainclothes policeman who wouldn't let him in. "He does not need an invitation!"

Enrico led him into the reception hall, where an honor guard of the Husares de Pueyrredón stood guard at the corners of the casket.

His father and his aunt and uncle were nowhere in sight. They were probably in the library. He decided against trying to find them. Uncle Humberto's "why Jorge and not you" look made him very uncomfortable.

A hand touched his arm.

"Cletus!" Dorotea Mallín said.

He turned to her. She kissed his cheek, really kissed it, not the air kiss American women give to casual acquaintances. As she came close to him, her breast pressed against his arm.

Jesus Christ, don't do that! Even if you don't know what you're doing.

He next accepted a kiss from Señora Mallín, then a kiss from the Mallín boy, Enrico—an Argentinean custom that bothered him a little. And he finally shook hands with Señor Mallín himself. Mallín smiled broadly, but Clete had a strange feeling that he was not nearly as delighted to see him as he claimed he was.

"On our way here, we saw a Buick convertible," Dorotea said. "A beautiful machine. Was that yours, Cletus?"

"If it was parked three blocks away, it probably was."

"But you promised to take me for a ride just as soon as it arrived," she pouted.

"Soon, Princess," he said.

To judge by the look in his eyes, Big Ernie considers calling her "Princess" about on a par with calling her a Miña.

"Tomorrow?" the Virgin Princess pursued.

"Tomorrow, Dorotea, is out of the question," Mallín said quickly. "You know we are going to Punta del Este this afternoon."

"I loathe and detest Punta del Este," Dorotea announced.

"And Señor Frade has more important things to do than take a young girl like you riding in his car," Mallín added. "People would talk."

"Henry!" his wife protested. "What a thing to say!"

"People can talk about me all night and all day, for all I care," Dorotea said.

"Perhaps when you come back from Punta del Este, Princess," Clete said.

Why the hell did I say that?

"And I would love to have a ride in your car, Clete," Señora Mallín said.

"And myself as well," Little Henry said.

"Certainly," Clete said.

"If you will excuse us, Señor?" Mallín said. "I see your aunt. We should pay our respects."

"I will telephone the moment we come back from Uruguay," Dorotea said, and stood on her toes to kiss his cheek again, thereby once more pressing her breasts against his chest.

Oh, Jesus Christ, I wish you wouldn't do that, Princess!

"You will see, Pamela," Mallín said, "that she does no such thing."

Pamela de Mallín winked at him.

A moment later, Enrico came out of a corridor, followed by Peter von Wachtstein, with Alicia Carzino-Cormano holding his arm, an arrangement both seemed to find delightful. Isabela trailed along behind them, looking more than a little unhappy.

Unhappy, Clete thought, *as in pissed, because Alicia is on Peter's arm, where she realizes she doubtless wants to be . . . rather than playing the role she's chosen for herself as the grief-stricken near-fiancée of the late Captain Duarte.*

When Clete's eyes met his, von Wachtstein changed course.

"Buenos días, Teniente," he said.

"Mi Capitán," Clete said. "That's quite a uniform. And the Señoritas Carzino-Cormano, what a joy it is to see you again!"

Alicia smiled warmly; Isabela icily. Neither said anything.

"Your father, Teniente, has been explaining to the Señoritas Carzino-Cormano and her mother that while we are officers of opposing military forces, we bear each other no personal ill will.

I thought I would greet you to make that point."

"In other words, Señoritas," Clete said with a slow grin, "while it would give me the greatest of professional pleasure to shoot el Capitán down, I would hope to do so while smiling with warm affection at him."

"Precisely," Peter said. "But I would be unhappy in such an encounter because it would be ungentlemanly of me to take advantage of an inferior foe."

"We will have to try it sometime," Clete said. "In a spirit, of course, of friendship and professional admiration, mi Capitán."

"Teniente, I would not have it otherwise."

"El Capitán is a credit to the officer corps," Clete said.

"How kind of you, Teniente, to say so."

"De nada, mi Capitán."

It occurred to Isabela Carzino-Cormano that they both were mocking her. For a moment, Clete thought she was about to storm away angrily, but she didn't. Her smile, however, became even more icy.

"I saw your little friend around here a moment ago," she said. "I can't imagine what happened to her."

"What little friend?" Peter asked.

I think you're crocked, Peter. And now that I've thought about that, that cloud of fumes around you is not eau de cologne.

"I think, Señorita Carzino-Cormano," Clete said, "that it was time for the lady in question's bottle. But I appreciate your interest in my personal life."

Hauptmann Freiherr von Wachtstein bowed and clicked his heels.

"It has been a pleasure to see you again, Teniente," he said. "But now duty calls."

"The pleasure has been mine, mi Capitán," Clete said.

"Watch out for bandits coming out of the sun, Clete," Peter said.

He is crocked. Why else would he say something like that? And why the hell is he shitfaced now? At this hour, and with all the brass around?

"What did you say?" Isabela asked.

"I will try, mi Capitán," Clete said.

"We always say, in the Luftwaffe, that it is the ones you don't see that get you," Peter said.

"We say much the same thing in the Marine Corps," Clete said. "And that has been my personal experience."

Peter made another curt bow of his head and clicked his heels, and let Alicia lead him to the library. Clete saw Enrico waiting for them there.

[TWO]

Wearing a splendiferous uniform complete with saber, el Coronel Jorge Guillermo Frade appeared then, under the firm control of Señora Carzino-Cormano.

"Cletus, what are you doing standing out here?" Claudia demanded. "Your place is with the family."

"Probably counting his blessings," Frade said, and before Claudia could stop him, went on. "I rather hoped you would wear your uniform with your decorations."

"I don't have my uniforms with me," Clete said.

"Pity," he said. "I took the trouble to look it up in the *Encyclopaedia Britannica*. The Corps of Marines dress uniform is splendid."

He's crocked too. Is that the local custom? Is this thing going to be sort of an Argentinean Irish wake?

"Come with us, Cletus," Claudia said, taking his arm and leading them both across the room.

[THREE]
The Basilica of St. Pilar
Recoleta Square
Buenos Aires
1325 19 December 1942

In the ecumenical belief that any religion is better than none, when Martha Howell was for some reason unavailable to drag Clete and the girls to Midland's Trinity Episcopal Church, she permitted Juanita the housekeeper to drag them to the Roman Catholic parish known in Midland as the Mexican Catholic Church. Clete was therefore no stranger to a Roman Catholic mass celebrated by Spanish-speaking clergy.

It was, however, his first high requiem mass; and while he expected the ceremony to run long—the personal participation of the Cardinal Archbishop brought at least five other bishops, an abbot, and a platoon of other magnificently robed clergy to the Basilica—he never imagined it would go on as long as it did.

Everyone was seated European style on hardback chairs. He was seated in the third row from the altar. The other chairs in the first rows were occupied by the other members of the family, and by dignitaries of church and state. For the first forty minutes or so of the mass, he studied their uniforms and regalia with a mild interest, and then he wondered where the Virgin Princess was sitting.

Both Big Henry and Little Henry Mallín walked in the ranks behind the caisson after they carried Jorge's casket out of the house, but he didn't see Dorotea there or her mother.

The women bring up the rear in this society. I wonder how Claudia Carzino-Cormano puts up with that.

Answer: She gets no gold stars to take home to Mommy for perfect attendance at mass.

There was a mirror behind the choir. Its function, Clete knew from painful experience, was to permit the choir director, the organist, and the priest to observe which of the choirboys was at that moment offending the dignity of the House of God and taking that first step down the slippery path to hell.

From where he was sitting, it reflected the rows of chairs just behind his.

Reflected there, her mother beside her, sat the Virgin Princess, a black lace shawl modestly covering her head.

Just before he came to understand that she was mouthing something to him—meaning she could obviously see his reflection, too—he was enjoying an erotic fantasy in which the Virgin Princess was wearing her loosely woven shawl and nothing else.

She is obviously paying no more attention to the Cardinal Archbishop than I am, and as obviously staring directly at me as I am staring directly at her. So what the hell is she saying with those exaggerated motions of those soft beautiful lips?

"I love you" . . . ?

Oh, shit, Cletus, you're letting your imagination run wild. She wouldn't do that. You have given her no reason to believe that you consider her anything but a child. It is absolutely absurd to imagine that when she—twice—rubbed her breasts against you, it was anything but innocent. So what else could her lips be saying?

It sure looks like "I love you."

And Jesus H. Christ, even if it is—and it goddamned sure looks like it—a relationship with that girl is idiotic.

So what do I do?

Obviously, I purposefully misunderstand what she's saying.

Clete just finished giving the Virgin Princess a happy, platonic, absolutely innocent "And how are you, Little Girl?" smile and wave of the hand when everybody around him suddenly stood up.

Preceded by the Cardinal Archbishop, the casket was carried from its place in front of the altar down the aisle and out of the church, trailed by the family members and the dignitaries of church and state.

Then the people in the first chairs followed, which meant that Clete proceeded down the aisle before the Mallín family did. As he passed the Virgin Princess, she smiled at him with those goddamned fall-into-them eyes, then pursed her lips in a kiss.

Oh, shit!

Outside, the German Ambassador expressed the profound sympathy of the German *Führer und Volk* over the tragic price paid by this heroic son of Argentina in the noble war against godless communism.

Behind him, Clete saw Peter, holding a pillow.

What the hell is that? Oh, yeah. The posthumous decoration.

A German colonel stepped to the casket, read the citation, then turned to Peter and took a decoration from the pillow and pinned it to the Argentinean flag that was draped cockeyed across the casket.

He and Peter then rendered the Nazi salute.

Fuck you, Peter.

What the hell is that decoration they just gave Cousin Jorge for what amounts to gross stupidity?

It looks just like the one Peter is wearing. And the one Peter is wearing is a no-bullshit medal—I pulled that out of him during the Christmas Eve armistice. It ranks right up there with the Navy Cross, maybe even the Medal of Honor.

And Cousin Jorge gets it because he got killed flying an artillery spotter he wasn't supposed to be flying in the first place?

Bullshit!

Peter and the German colonel did an about-face and marched back behind the German Ambassador. Six large troopers of the Husares de Pueyrredón picked up the casket, and the procession started off again.

Clete watched them go, exhaled audibly, and said softly, "A

Dios, Cousin Jorge. Vaya con Dios.'' And then turned and walked
in the opposite direction.

*I don't have to watch the end of this. And I certainly don't
want to go back to the house and face Uncle Humberto's sad
eyes again. Or the Virgin Princess. . . . Did she really just tell me
she loves me?*

I will find the Buick and drive back to the house.

*And write a message that will be the sort of thing the skipper
of a U.S. Navy destroyer might accept as genuine and that will
convince Colonel Graham that letting me have a TBF is the only
way I can take out the* Reine de la Mer.

[FOUR]
4730 Avenida Libertador
Buenos Aires
1420 19 December 1942

Clete entered the house via the kitchen, after parking the car in
the basement garage.

He was a little surprised that Señora Pellano did not show up
in the basement to silently chide him for opening the garage door
himself, until he remembered that she was at the Big House. He
was surprised again that none of the maids appeared in the kitchen
while he prepared a wine cooler with two trays of ice from the
refrigerator, then stuffed it with bottles of beer.

But one did appear as he was trying without much success to
open the sliding elevator door with his elbow. His hands were
occupied with the wine cooler and the necks of two additional
bottles of beer he was taking upstairs now so he wouldn't have
to come back for them later.

She slid the door open for him.

"Gracias," he said. "And could you please fix me a sandwich?
Ham and cheese and tomato? Something like that?"

"Sí, Señor Cletus," she said, wrestling the wine cooler away
from him. "Señor, there are two norteamericanos waiting for you
in the library."

"Who are they? Did you get their names?"

"No, Señor Cletus," she said, as if this caused her great sor-
row.

When he pushed open the door to the library, Second Lieutenant Anthony J. Pelosi and Staff Sergeant David G. Ettinger, both neatly dressed in seersucker suits, quickly rose to their feet.

"Good afternoon, Sir," Tony said formally.

"Tony. David. To what do I owe the honor? Can I offer you a beer?"

"No, thank you, Sir," Tony said, and then, "Clete, I met Mr. Nestor."

"How did that happen?"

"Dave brought him to the apartment and introduced him."

"You're talking about Mr. Nestor of the Bank of Boston?"

"I know he's the OSS Station Chief," Tony said.

"He told you that?" Clete asked, looking at Ettinger for confirmation. Ettinger nodded, just perceptibly.

"And he also gave a line of bullshit that you have proved yourself . . . What did he say, Dave?"

"Unsuitable," Ettinger furnished.

"*Unsuitable* for the mission, and that he is now relying on me to carry it out. Real bullshit speech. Like in the movie where Pat O'Brien played Knute Rockne, and whatsisname, Ronald Reagan, played the football player." He stopped, then looked at Clete. "What's going on, Lieutenant?" Tony asked.

"I found the *Reine de la Mer*," Clete said. "That's the German replenishment ship."

"So did Ettinger," Tony said. "He told me on the way over here."

Clete looked at Ettinger.

"I finally found one of the Jewish refugees with some balls," Ettinger explained. "He told me that an agent of the Hamburg-Amerika Line contacted his firm—he works for a ship chandler—and asked them to furnish an extraordinary quantity of meat, fresh and frozen, plus other foodstuffs and supplies, for delivery by lighter to the *Reine de la Mer* in Samborombón Bay, where she is at anchor with 'mechanical difficulties.' The name matched the list. I figured this had to be the ship."

"It is," Clete said. "She's anchored twenty miles offshore in Samborombón Bay."

"How did you find her?" Tony asked.

"I went looking for her in my father's airplane."

"So what's this all about?" Tony asked. "If we know where it is, why don't we just go sink the sonofabitch?"

"This isn't the movies, Tony, and I'm not John Wayne, and neither are you two," Clete said.

"Well," Tony said. "Maybe Dave isn't John Wayne, but I always thought that I . . ."

"Tony," Clete said, smiling, "I got a good look at the ship. Not only is she twenty miles or so offshore, but she's equipped with searchlights and machine guns, and probably with twenty-millimeter Bofors autoloading cannon. There is no way to get near her. Or none that I can think of."

"A small boat, at night?" Ettinger suggested.

"You can hear the sound of a small boat's engine a long way off from a ship at anchor, Dave," Clete said. "And they're certainly taking at least routine precautions; I'm sure that they sweep the area with floodlights at night, post lookouts, that sort of thing."

Ettinger shrugged, accepting Clete's arguments.

"I went to see Nestor as soon as I could when I came back," Clete continued.

"You didn't say anything to us," Tony interrupted, and looked at Ettinger for confirmation.

"I didn't have anything to tell you, except that I'd found her. And that could wait until I talked to Nestor, and listened to what he had to say when I told him there was no way we could damage the ship where she lies—not with just twenty-odd pounds of explosive."

"I can do a lot with twenty pounds of explosive," Tony said.

"Presuming you can lay your charges, right? I'm telling you, there is no way to get close enough to that ship to do that."

"What about the airplane you found her with?" Ettinger asked.

"Lieutenant, I don't want to sound like I'm questioning your judgment, but I really would like to put that ship out of action."

"The airplane I found her with is my father's Beechcraft stagger-wing. It's a small civilian airplane. I couldn't carry in it more than three or four hundred-pound bombs—if I had three or four hundred-pound bombs—and I don't think I could hit . . ."

"Then what was Nestor talking about? He said you had some wild idea about torpedoing the *Reine de la Mer*."

"What I told Nestor was that if he could get me a TBF from Brazil . . ."

"A what?" Tony asked.

You don't know what a TBF is either?

"A torpedo bomber. A single-engine Navy airplane with a bomb bay that can handle a torpedo."

"They have them in Brazil?"

"We're equipping the Brazilian Navy. It seems logical to me that we'd give them TBFs."

"You could sink the ship if you had one?"

Clete nodded. "Yeah. I think the reason they haven't thought of putting out the *Reine de la Mer* with one is that they don't have the range to reach here from Brazil."

"You're thinking of refueling it where we were in Uruguay?" Tony asked.

Clete nodded and waited for his reaction.

"Where are we going to get the aviation gas for that?"

Damn, I didn't think of that!

"I don't know. But there is aviation gas in Uruguay, and so are the people who loaned us the walkie-talkies we lost. They can get avgas for me."

Tony nodded.

"Nestor didn't say anything about a torpedo bomber," Ettinger said. "Why is that a wild idea?"

"I don't know," Clete said. "He said something like that had already been considered and rejected by the OSS. I told him I wanted to appeal the order up the chain of command to Colonel Graham. I think I can convince Graham that getting me into a TBF would be the best way—hell, the only way that I can see— to put the *Reine de la Mer* out of action."

"And?" Tony asked.

"He said that was out of the question. I had my orders and I would carry them out. And then I lost my temper, told him I had no intention of committing suicide, and then, I'm sorry to say, I threw him out of the car."

"Lieutenant," Ettinger said carefully, "I can't think of a delicate way to put this. . . . Did Nestor suggest you were overly concerned with your own skin? Is that why you lost your temper?"

Clete met Ettinger's eyes, then nodded.

"What?" Tony exploded incredulously. "That sonofabitch! You've been in combat. You're an Ace, for Christ's sake, a fucking hero, and he knows that."

"Cowardice is apparently in the eyes of the beholder," Clete said.

Ettinger, recognizing the wordplay, smiled. Tony looked confused.

"Well, fuck him, and his orders," Tony fumed on.

"So what happens now, Lieutenant?" Ettinger asked.

"The only thing I can think of is to keep trying to reach Colonel Graham," Clete said.

"How are you going to do that?" Ettinger asked.

"David, would the *Alfred Thomas* have a radio capable of communicating with—hell, I don't know—some Navy radio station in Washington? Or with a station that could relay a message to Washington?"

Ettinger shrugged doubtfully, but then nodded and smiled.

"It's possible, Lieutenant," he said. "When Admiral Byrd was down in Antarctica, which isn't far from here relatively speaking, he was unable to communicate with the Navy. But there was a radio ham, an amateur in Cedar Rapids, who could talk to him— I think on the twenty-meter band. The Navy was very embarrassed—I got this story from Mr. Sarnoff at RCA—but they had to swallow their pride and go to this fellow Collins and ask him how he did it. He started a company to build his equipment for the Navy, and it seems logical to assume that the Navy would at least try to equip their vessels in the South Atlantic with such equipment. But I don't understand . . ."

"When the destroyer arrives, I'm going aboard. I'll identify myself as a Marine officer and ask her captain to send a message to Colonel Graham."

"And if he doesn't have the right kind of radios, or let you send Colonel Graham a message, then what?" Tony asked.

Clete shrugged. "If you can think of anything else, Tony, I'm wide open to suggestions," Clete said, then turned to Ettinger. "Unless you could set up a radio here?"

Ettinger shook his head no. And then explained: "I don't have the equipment. And I don't think I could find it here. I asked around. Most of their equipment is pretty primitive. And from what I remember about what this fellow Collins used, it required a hell of an antenna. Nothing we could hide; it would attract a good deal of attention. Sorry, Lieutenant."

"It never hurts to ask," Clete said.

"So what do we do now?" Tony asked. "While we're waiting for the destroyer to show up?"

"Try to think of some way to take out an armed merchantman besides using a TBF . . . or three lonely guys with twenty-odd pounds of explosive," Clete said.

"One thing we absolutely must not do," Ettinger said thoughtfully, "is tell Nestor about this little chat."

"He's the OSS Station Chief," Clete said. "I don't want to

put you in the middle of the fight between the two of us."

"I told you before, Clete, that a man can't serve two masters," Ettinger said. "And the oath I swore when I came into the Army was 'to obey the orders of the officers appointed over me.' I don't think Nestor qualifies as an officer, Lieutenant. You do. That's the philosophic argument. What Tony would call the gut reaction is: 'If Lieutenant Frade doesn't trust this man, why should we?' "

"No matter how this turns out, Clete," Tony said, "we're with you. OK? We decided that on the way over here."

Christ, I'm no better than my father. I want to cry.

"Which brings us back to Tony's question," Ettinger said. "What should we do now, Tony and I?"

"Nothing. Unless someone comes to you and tries to order you to commit suicide by trying to take out the *Reine de la Mer.* This is a direct order, Lieutenant Pelosi: I forbid you to attempt any action against the *Reine de la Mer* without my specific approval. Clear?"

"Yes, Sir," Tony said.

"If you want to get in touch with me, have David call and say he's from American Express and I have mail there. I'll then meet you at five o'clock the same afternoon. Where?"

"One of the hotel bars," Ettinger said. "That would look co-incidental."

"The bar in the Plaza," Tony decided.

"The bar in the Plaza," Clete parroted. "And now get out of here."

Pelosi and Ettinger both offered their hands.

Clete watched them as they walked to the library door.

Pelosi turned at Ettinger's arm, surprising Clete, and then surprised him even more:

"Detail, Ten-hut!" Pelosi barked.

Ettinger came to attention.

Pelosi raised his hand in a crisp salute and held it.

"Permission to return to post, Sir?"

Clete returned the salute.

"Post, Lieutenant Pelosi."

Pelosi brought his saluting hand crisply to his side, then barked, "Haa-bout, Face!" and "Faw-wud, Harch!" and marched out of the library.

Just in time. Otherwise they would have seen the tears running down my cheeks.

[FIVE]
Recoleta Cemetery
Buenos Aires, Argentina
1435 19 December 1942

As he observed the casket of el Capitán Jorge Alejandro Duarte being placed before the altar inside the Duartes' enormous marble tomb, Hauptmann Freiherr Hans-Peter von Wachtstein decided that he was honor bound to inform Lieutenant Cletus Howell Frade that an attempt would be made to murder him.

He reached this conclusion by a circuitous route, starting from a moment when he glanced down at the Knight's Cross of the Iron Cross around his neck and at the other one on the red velvet pillow.

His first thoughts were unkind: *This goddamned fool does not deserve the Knight's Cross. He got himself killed flying an airplane that he was not supposed to be flying in the first place, in a war that wasn't his.*

Other thoughts immediately followed: *Furthermore, he was probably unqualified to fly the Storch at all. It is a relatively simple, stable aircraft; but like all airplanes, it has its peculiarities. The Storche I've flown have gone from the first faint, barely detectable indication of a low-speed stall condition to a full stall in the time it takes to spit.*

Whereupon, the sonofabitch drops through the sky like a stone. Standard stall-recovery procedures work, of course, providing you have several hundred feet of altitude to play with. If not, you encounter the ground in an out-of-control attitude, and with consequent loud crashing noises.

There are two ways to enter a stall condition—in addition to on purpose, which is what the instructor pilot does to you during Transition Training, which it is safe to assume the late Capitán Duarte did not have, the Luftwaffe not being in the habit of teaching Cavalry officers from South American countries to fly its airplanes. An airplane goes into an unplanned stall either because the pilot is stupid enough to allow the airfoils to run out of lift, or because the propeller has stopped turning and pulling the airplane through the air with enough velocity for the airflow over the airfoils to provide sufficient lift. Propellers stop turning usually because the engine has stopped turning. Engines are fairly reliable. They seldom stop turning unless they are broken, as when, for example, they are hit by small-arms fire.

The rule to be drawn from this is that if you are flying a Storch near the ground someplace, you pay particular attention to airspeed and engine RPM, so that if the engine is struck by small-arms fire and shows indications of stopping, you can make a dead-stick landing someplace without stalling.

Capitán Duarte did not do this. The documents accompanying the remains gave the cause of death as "severe trauma to the body caused by sudden deceleration." If he was hit, the documents would have said so.

The late Capitán Duarte crashed the sonofabitch, because he didn't know how to fly the sonofabitch. And he took some poor bastard with him.

He therefore deserves the posthumous award of the Knight's Cross of the Iron Cross about as much as Winston S. Churchill does. And awarding it to him is a slap in the face to every pilot who has earned it, including, of course, Hauptmann Freiherr Hans-Peter von Wachtstein.

By the time the funeral procession moved from the courtyard outside the Basilica to the cemetery, Peter was having second thoughts:

Wait. Am I being fair to the poor bastard? Is the coffee cup full of brandy I had for breakfast talking? Or the monumental ego of Hauptmann von Wachtstein, fighter pilot extraordinary? Or both?

Bullshit. Clete Frade was contemptuous when he heard they were awarding this clown—his cousin, by the by—the Knight's Cross. Christ, even Oberst Grüner was disgusted.

From that point, Peter became less unkind.

On the other hand, even if he was a Hauptmann, Duarte was an inexperienced officer. Inexperienced officers do dumb things, especially before they learn that all the talk of the glory of war is pure bullshit. I did. To save Germany from godless communism, and to bring glory to the Luftwaffe and Der Führer, I did some pretty goddamn dumb things in Spain myself. And in Poland. And in France.

Cletus told me that he went on his first combat mission determined to personally avenge the humiliation the United States suffered at Pearl Harbor.

"It took about fifteen seconds with a Zero on my tail," Clete said, "to realize that all I wanted out of the war was Clete

Frade's skin in one piece; somebody else was welcome to the glory of avenging Pearl Harbor."

Clete is an honest man, more honest than I am. I would find it hard to publicly admit a sentiment like that, even though I felt it. And Clete is no coward. He told me that he thought his "chances of getting off Guadalcanal alive ranged from zero to none," but he continued to fly.

El Capitán Duarte presumably was not a stupid man. He would have learned that lesson probably as quickly as Clete, and surely more quickly than I. It's a pity he killed himself before he acquired a little wisdom.

An officer is honor bound to face whatever hazards his duty requires; not throw his life, or that of his men, away.

And that brings me back to Cletus Howell Frade.

On one hand, if Clete is in fact an OSS agent, he knows full well the risks he is running coming down here. It may not be spelled out in neat paragraphs in the Geneva Convention, but everyone understands that spies operating in neutral countries get killed by the other side's spies.

In war, the Geneva Convention permits the out-of-hand execution of spies and saboteurs. The Geneva Convention is quite clear on the subject: A soldier found out of uniform behind enemy lines loses the protection afforded a soldier in uniform. He is presumed to be a spy or saboteur.

But Grüner—he said so—doesn't know if Clete is an OSS agent or not. And even if he is, he may just be down here to influence his father, or as some kind of high-level message deliverer.

And if Clete is not a spy, where does Grüner get the authority to order his execution?

And if Clete is a spy, what then is Grüner? He is certainly not functioning as an officer of a belligerent army, facing his enemy on a battlefield. He is an agent of an intelligence service. In other words, they are both out of uniform; both are outside the protection—and the restrictions—of the Geneva Convention.

But if Grüner is caught for ordering the murder of Clete—or of his own hired assassins, for that matter—he will escape prosecution . . . not because his actions are permitted by the Rules of Land Warfare, but because he is carrying a diplomatic passport, which renders him immune to the laws of Argentina.

On the other hand, if Clete killed Grüner on his country's orders, and was caught, he would face an Argentine judge on a charge of murder. That's unfair.

Can I thus conclude that since Grüner's conduct fails to meet the small print in the Geneva Convention, as well as the German Officer's Code of Honor, I am therefore at liberty to violate the German Officer's Code of Honor and warn Clete?

By stretching the point, yes I can.

But be honest with yourself, Peter. You don't want to warn him because you have put yourself through this exercise in moral philosophy, but because you like him. We thought we were witty when we told each other we would like to shoot each other down, meanwhile smiling at each other with warm affection. But beneath the warmth there is also the cold truth. If duty requires, we would try to shoot each other down. Yet there would be no smile on the victor's face—his or mine.

I wonder which of us would be good enough to shoot down the other. I have more victories, but until recently, most of my opponents were inexperienced pilots flying inferior machines.

Clete's kills were experienced pilots, flying aircraft at least as good as his own. He's probably a damned good fighter pilot.

I like him, but I would be willing to kill him in the air; as he would me. That would be an honorable death for a warrior. And my conscience, like his, would be untroubled. But for me to stand by silently waiting to hear that his throat has been cut by Grüner's hired assassins would not be honorable, and I could never find an excuse to forgive myself.

A final thought came to him:

My father would understand my decision.

That brings me back to how do I tell him?

He will almost certainly be at the Duarte mansion for the reception after the funeral. I will somehow manage a minute alone with him.

[SIX]
1420 Avenue Alvear
Buenos Aires, Argentina
1605 19 December 1942

"I wondered what happened to you," Señorita Alicia Carzino-Cormano said, walking up to Hauptmann Freiherr von Wachtstein and smiling at him over the rim of her teacup. "Is this pretty awful for you?"

Peter bowed and clicked his heels, but there was not time for
him to reply before Señorita Isabela Carzino-Cormano walked up
to them.

"Señorita," he said.

Isabela gave him her hand to be kissed, and he kissed it.

"I was deeply moved when the decoration was given to Poor
Jorge," Isabela said.

Peter nodded.

"Isn't that decoration the one your government gave our Poor
Jorge?" she asked, touching Peter's Knight's Cross.

"Yes, it is," Peter replied. "I wondered if either of you charming ladies have seen el Teniente Frade?"

"I don't think he's here," Isabela said. "I think his father's
disgraceful behavior embarrassed him and he left."

"Excuse me?"

"Oh, for God's sake, Isabela!" Alicia protested.

"Of course," Isabela said. "You are too much of a gentleman
to have noticed him."

"Noticed him doing what?"

"Weeping in the church, like a child. And, of course, quite
drunk."

"I understand he was quite close to el Capitán Duarte," Peter
said.

And holds himself responsible for the poor bastard's death.

"If Cletus is not here, then he's probably at the Guest House,"
Alicia volunteered.

If I can get to a telephone, I can call him.

"Señorita, do you happen to know where I could find a telephone?"

"Finding the telephone is easy," she said. "There are two lines
here. But if you intend to make a call . . ."

She inclined her head. Peter saw a group of people near a
telephone set in an alcove in the wall. A gentleman was speaking
excitedly into it, and he was oblivious to the dirty looks of the
others waiting for it.

"I was thinking of calling a friend," Alicia said. "But it was
no use, so I gave up."

"Señorita, I am staying at the Alvear Palace. My call is important. Official business. Might I suggest that you walk down
there with me and make your call from one of the telephones in
the lobby?"

Inspiration! I don't know where that idea came from, but it was divinely inspired. I can walk out of here with her—if I can get rid of the older sister, that would not be a bad idea, in any case—which will satisfy Grüner's curiosity about what happened to me. And I can telephone Clete from my room.

I don't have his goddamned number! How the hell do I get the number?

"In Argentina, Capitán, young ladies of a certain position do not go to a gentleman's hotel," Isabela said.

Shit!

"Señorita, I am a stranger to your country. No offense was intended."

"And none should have been taken," Alicia said. "If you need to make a telephone call from the hotel, I'll be happy to walk there with you. It would be nice to leave here anyway."

"You are very gracious."

And you have marvelous eyes. I wonder why I never noticed that before.

"Señorita, what are the customs of Argentina? May a stranger to your country telephone a young lady of a certain class and ask her to take dinner with him?"

"If the stranger is a gentleman, and you certainly are," Alicia said, "and they have been properly introduced, and we have, in the presence of the young lady's mother, then it is acceptable."

"Wonderful! And might I presume to avail myself of this acceptable custom in the next day or two?"

"You may call, and I will see if I am free."

"You can't tell me that now?"

"You may call," Alicia teased, "and I will see if I am free."

"I will adjust my schedule to yours," Peter said. *I will, as a matter of fact, now that the subject has come up, do everything necessary, including standing on my head, to see that fantastic hair undone and spread out on my pillow.* "But for now, Señorita, may I accept your gracious offer to walk to the hotel with me, so that I can use the telephone."

"You may not care about your reputation, Alicia," Isabela said. "But I do. I can't let you go to the Alvear alone with el Capitán von Wachtstein."

"How do you propose to stop me?" Alicia said. "Wrestle me to the ground?"

She has a spark too. I like that.

"Perhaps," Isabela said, "under the circumstances—I would

have to ask Mother—we could escort an honored guest of our country to the Alvear."

"*I'll* ask Mother," Alicia said firmly, and turned to Peter. "You will wait for me?"

"With my heart beating frantically in anticipation of your return."

He watched her move across the foyer. *The curve of her hips is magnificent too, and she has a delightful walk.* When she disappeared behind a door, he turned to Isabela. "And will you excuse me a moment, Señorita?"

"Certainly," Isabela said.

And with a little bit of luck, you won't be here when I come back.

He walked quickly across the foyer toward a corridor.

One of the servants surely knows the number of the Guest House. I just hope this corridor leads me to the kitchen.

He was in luck in the kitchen, which he hoped would turn out to be an omen: The first person to notice him there was the housekeeper from the Guest House.

"May I help you, mi Capitán?" Señora Pellano asked, smiling as she walked up to him.

"I was wondering if you could give me the telephone number of the Guest House, Señora?"

"Is there anything I can do for you there. mi Capitán? I'm afraid the telephones here are all tied up. And in just a few minutes I will be returning to the house on Libertador myself. I would be happy . . ."

"Thank you, no, Señora. If you would just give me the number, please, Señora."

"I will write it down for you," Señora Pellano said.

As he came back into the foyer, Oberst Grüner was waiting for him.

"I was about to organize a search-and-rescue party for you, von Wachtstein," Grüner said. "What were you doing in the kitchen?"

"Looking for someone, Herr Oberst."

"For whom?"

Peter gestured across the foyer to where the Carzino-Cormano sisters were standing.

"For them. Or at least for the younger one. They come in pairs down here, I have just learned."

"With a little bit of skill, I'm told, they can be separated,"

Grüner said with a smile. "Which answers my second question for you."

"Which was, Herr Oberst?"

"If you would like to come by my quarters for a light supper with myself and Frau Grüner."

"Herr Oberst is most kind."

"There is always something for you to eat at my quarters, Peter," Grüner said. "But that fräulein is, I would judge, a rare opportunity. Good luck!"

"Thank you, Herr Oberst, for your understanding."

He bowed and clicked his heels and walked away, toward Isabela and Alicia Carzino-Cormano.

A little gemütlich family gathering, Herr Oberst? A little Apfelstrudel mit Schlagobers, and a little glass of schnapps, while you await word that your thugs have murdered a very decent human being? Fuck you, Herr Oberst. Willi would understand what I'm doing.

"Mother said it's all right if both of us go," Alicia reported.

"How very gracious of you to join us, Señorita Isabela," Peter said.

Shit!

[SEVEN]
Suite 701
The Alvear Palace Hotel
Buenos Aires
1705 19 December 1942

The odds are that my telephone is not tapped, Peter von Wachtstein thought as he waited for the hotel operator to connect him with the Frade Guest House. *What reason would Grüner—or anyone else—have to tap it?*

"Hola?" Cletus's voice came on the line.

Not this phone line, but his! Grüner has a man—Comandante Habanzo, or something like that—in Argentine Internal Security. And Grüner has him thinking that Clete is an American agent, which means he almost certainly will have tapped Clete's line. And if Grüner's man hears about this conversation, then Grüner will hear about it!

Shit!

"Is that Leutnant Frade?"

It's Peter. What the hell does he want?

"*Former Lieutenant* Frade, Hauptmann von Wachtstein. What can I do for you?"

"I am taking tea with two ladies, *Teniente*," Peter said. "The sisters Carzino-Cormano. At the Alvear Plaza. I thought you might care to join us."

He's drunk. What the hell is he doing with the Carzino-Cormano girls?

"The invitation is most gracious, mi Capitán, but just between us fighter pilots, Isabela Carzino-Cormano cannot be numbered among my legion of female admirers. In English we would say that my presence would piss on your parade. I'll pass, thank you, and in the morning you will be most grateful that I did."

"I would like to impose on your well-known good nature, and ask that you reconsider."

What the hell is going on? Oh, shit. He wants me to get El Bitcho off his hands; he has carnal desires for Alicia.

"Peter, I don't think you can separate them."

"Hope springs eternal in the human breast."

"What if someone sees us together, Peter? I don't think that would look wise to that boss of yours."

"We are in a neutral country. I will simply be acting as an officer and a gentleman, asking you to join us when you happen to walk in and pass our table. We're in the lobby restaurant. You know it?"

"I'll be there in fifteen minutes. I hope you know what you're doing."

"So do I, Cletus."

[EIGHT]

As soon as he was out of the garage, Clete stopped the Buick and put the top down. His uncle Jim spent a good deal of time during Clete's last year at Tulane listing the many inconveniences of owning and driving a convertible. But you could sum up his entire list under one heading: the top. The mechanism was delicate, he told Clete fifty times; and once it was out of alignment it was almost impossible to repair. That meant the roof would leak, and that meant the floor pan would rust out. And it meant that the leather upholstery would rot, or else get stiff and crack.

And if the top was wet, and you put it down before it dried, it would shrink. So when you tried to put it up, the mechanism would not be up to the strain of stretching it and would pull itself out of alignment. Whereupon the roof would leak, et cetera, et cetera, et cetera.

"Only idiots own convertibles," Uncle Jim said. "Why anybody smart enough to graduate from college would even think of wanting one, I'll never know."

That lecture came the day Uncle Jim told him to get off his lazy ass and help Martha weed the tulips by the driveway. When he got there, he found the Buick Roadmaster convertible with a large yellow bow tied to the bull's-eye hood ornament.

Clete thought of Uncle Jim every time he put the roof up or down. Now he thought of Uncle Jim and the Virgin Princess. On the one hand, she was a kid who wanted a ride in the convertible. On the other hand, she was a perfectly gorgeous woman who mouthed "I love you" to him in the Basilica of Our Lady of Pilar. And pursed her lips at him as he walked out.

What the hell am I going to do about her?

A man was standing under a tree fifty yards from the Guest House, studiously looking the other way. Twenty yards farther down Avenida Libertador, the momentary glow as he took a drag on his cigarette revealed another man sitting at the wheel of a small Mercedes sedan parked with its lights out.

If those two guys are not cops—what do they call them, "Internal Security"?—watching me, then I'm the Commandant of the Marine Corps.

I will do nothing about the Virgin Princess, except ignore her like she has hoof-and-mouth disease. As long as Internal Security is interested in me, I have to stay away from her. I certainly can't let them get interested in her.

Jesus H. Christ, she was so beautiful in the church!

When the top was down, he turned up Avenida Libertador toward the two watchers. When he was parallel with the one under the tree, he blew "Shave and a Haircut Two Bits" on the Buick's loud horn, waved cheerfully, and called out, "Buenas noches, Señor!"

Then, impulsively, he floored the accelerator and roared down Avenida Libertador. In the rearview mirror, he saw the parking lights of the Mercedes come on, and the man under the tree running toward it.

"Earn your money, fellows," he said aloud.

[NINE]

Alicia Carzino-Cormano was delighted to see Clete walking toward their table in the lobby restaurant of the Alvear Palace. Her
sister was not.

"Well, what a pleasant coincidence," Clete said. "Alicia. Isabela. Mi Capitán."

"Teniente," Peter said, standing up, bowing, and clicking his
heels. "Perhaps you would care to join us?"

"I would hate to intrude."

"Nonsense," Peter said. "I insist."

"Well, if you're sure it will be no imposition," Clete said, and
pulled up a chair.

He met Alicia's eyes as he sat down and then winked at her.
She smiled back.

"You really should be at the Duartes'," Isabela said.

"Why?" Clete asked simply.

"Jorge was your cousin. It was unseemly of you not to be there
with the family."

"Isabela, I never met the man. I didn't even know I had a
Cousin Jorge until a couple of weeks ago."

"If you had been there, your father might not have gotten so
drunk."

"Isabela!" Alicia protested.

"Well, he is," Isabela said. "Disgustingly drunk. Weeping
drunk. Telling everyone who'll listen it's his fault that Jorge is
dead. Making a spectacle of himself. Humiliating Mother."

"My father," Clete said, coldly angry, "buried his nephew
today. He loved him very much. Maybe that's why he got drunk."

"He had no right to make a spectacle of himself. To humiliate
my mother. Everyone important in Argentina was there."

Clete stared hard at her, then stood up and looked down at
Peter. "I had the feeling I shouldn't have come here."

"Oh, Clete, you're not leaving. Please don't leave!" Alicia
said.

"Alicia, it's always a pleasure to see you," he said, and smiled
at her. Then he extended a hand to Peter. "Sorry, mi Capitán,"
he said.

"Please," Alicia pleaded. "Isabela, say you're sorry!"

Clete nodded at Peter and started down the corridor toward the
lobby. As he reached the center of the lobby, Peter caught up
with him and touched his arm.

"Cletus, my friend, listen carefully to me. An attempt will be made on your life, probably tonight."

"What?" Clete asked incredulously.

"Don't go back to the Guest House tonight. Better yet, go to your father's estancia."

Clete looked into Peter's eyes.

"Jesus Christ! You're serious."

"On my word of honor."

Peter touched Clete's arm, then turned and walked back toward the restaurant in the corridor.

XVII

[ONE]
Bureau of Internal Security
Ministry of Defense
Edificio Libertador
Avenida Paseo Colón
Buenos Aires
2230 19 December 1942

Comandante Habanzo delivered the preliminary visual and communications surveillance reports ten minutes late, at 2210 hours. While he leafed through the five-inch-tall stack of papers, el Teniente Coronel Bernardo Martín kept Habanzo standing in front of his desk.

He wondered if he was doing this because Habanzo was late, or because he simply did not like the man. He decided it was the latter. He had often warned his agents that it was far better to turn in a report late than to turn it in inaccurate—but obviously not often enough, to judge by the quality of the visual surveillance reports in front of him.

The question then changed to why he disliked his deputy. First of all, obviously, because Habanzo was stupid. Stupid people did not belong in internal security. How Habanzo wound up there was one of the great mysteries of life. For a long time, he simply assumed that he never completely trusted the information Habanzo gave him because the man was so devastatingly stupid. But now vague, uncomfortable tickles in the back of his mind were suggesting other reasons as well.

Could Habanzo be taking small gifts—or large ones, for that matter—from some interested party or other? Could he be passing items of interest to them?

Could the Grupo de Oficiales Unidos, for example, have him on their payroll? The answer came swiftly: Not likely. Habanzo's limited mental abilities would be immediately apparent to the G.O.U. And they would be afraid of him, too; for they would see

him as the loose cannon that he is. He was perfectly capable of
having a sudden attack of conscience and confessing, for instance.
Or of selling out to a higher bidder.

On the other hand, in the counterintelligence business, one was
expected to consider the unlikely—even the absurdly unlikely—
as a possibility.

The communications surveillance preliminary reports were
typewritten. Almost all of the wiretappers came from Army and
Navy Signals, where they'd been radio operators. Radio operators
were trained to sit before a typewriter and almost subconsciously
transcribe Morse Code signals. Now they sat before a typewriter
in a basement somewhere, or in an office off the Main Telephone
Frame Room in the Ministry of Communications, and pecked out
a transcript of someone's telephone calls. Aside from minor cor-
rections, and the elimination of abbreviations, their final reports
would not be much different from what Martín had in front of
him.

The visual surveillance preliminary reports were something
else: They were handwritten, compiled from notes discreetly
taken on site. And predictably, the syntax in these reports was
often highly imaginative. More important, they were liberally
sprinkled with question marks. This was done in the interest of
fairness, so that El Coronel A's words would not become a matter
of official record when the agent was not absolutely positive that
it was El Coronel A who spoke them, or that these were his exact
words. The idea was that questionable items would be verified in
the final reports: that it was not El Coronel A, but in fact El
Coronel B, and that he said he was *not* going to Córdoba, rather
than that he *was* going to Córdoba.

By the time the preliminary reports were finalized, about
ninety-five percent of the information verified was no longer of
any interest whatever. It was a terrible system. But—as Winston
Churchill said about democracy—el Teniente Coronel Martín
could not think of a better one.

Nothing in the reports before him was especially interesting.
That was not surprising. Just about all of the members of the
Grupo de Oficiales Unidos attended el Capitán Duarte's funeral,
but they were all far too intelligent to reveal anything worth paying attention to anywhere they might be overheard.

And though el Coronel Jorge Guillermo Frade solaced the loss
of his nephew with a liter or so of Johnnie Walker, this did not
yield useful information . . . unless irreverent remarks about the

funeral ceremony could be considered useful.

Visual surveillance of young Frade was a little more interesting. He did not follow the casket to Recoleta Cemetery, but instead returned to the Frade Guest House on Avenida Libertador, where two American men were waiting for him.

One of them, Pelosi, Anthony J., was ostensibly an oil-industry technical expert who came to Argentina with young Frade. The other, Ettinger, David, was a newly arrived employee of the Banco de Boston.

If one accepted the theory that young Frade was an OSS agent *. . . and Habanzo is strongly convinced of this; I wonder why . . .* then Ettinger would likely be the third member of a three-man team. But on the other hand, none of these three look like men any intelligence agency in its right mind would send anywhere.

Which, of course, might be precisely what the OSS hopes someone like me will think.

Martín would have liked very much to know exactly what they talked about, but that was out of the question. At the same time, Martín was sure that his decision not to install listening devices in the house was correct. Tapping a telephone was relatively simple, and difficult to detect. Listening devices were the opposite, difficult to install and easy to detect. They were also very expensive and hard to come by. He had a budget to consider. If el Coronel Frade or his son came across a listening device—and they more than likely would—they would simply smash it. And a good deal of money, time, and effort would go down the toilet. All a listening device would accomplish would be to remind Frade and his son that they were under surveillance.

There was one anomaly in the reports, which of course Habanzo's summaries offered little to explain: Shortly after young Frade met with the two other Americans, he returned to the Duarte mansion. On the way there, he stopped for a time at the lobby restaurant in the Alvear Palace Hotel. There he encountered the young German Luftwaffe officer and the two Carzino-Cormano girls.

Habanzo did not have a man on the young German officer, pleading a shortage of available agents. And "technical difficulties" created a ten-minute loss of phone coverage at the Guest House—which meant the man tapping the Guest House line had gone either to relieve himself or to have a little snack. During that time there could possibly have been a telephone call in connection with the meeting between young Frade and the German.

According to the visual agent's report, young Frade suddenly left the Frade Guest House garage and then drove at "a high rate of speed" to the Alvear Palace. By the time the agent caught up with him, Frade was in a confrontation with the older of the Carzino-Cormano girls, Isabela. This was followed by an apparent confrontation with the young German officer, as Frade "walked angrily" out of the hotel.

Since it was reasonable to presume that the young German officer was not involved with young Frade's mission for the OSS (if indeed young Frade was actually working for the OSS), it seemed reasonably safe to presume that the confrontation had something to do with the Carzino-Cormano girl. Isabela was a beautiful young woman, and both the German and the American could easily be romantically interested in her.

Thus, a likely scenario: Young Frade slipped away from the funeral and the post-funeral reception for a meeting with his men, then telephoned the Duarte mansion (during the period of "technical difficulties" with the telephone surveillance), somehow managed to get through, and was informed that the Señorita had left with the German officer.

Thirty-two incoming calls came to the Duarte mansion during the afternoon; four of them asked for Señorita Isabela Carzino-Cormano.

Masculine ego outraged, he went looking for them in one of the very few public places where a young woman of her position could be seen, found her with the German, expressed his displeasure, and "walked angrily" out of the hotel.

He next went to the Duarte mansion and stayed there for several hours, presumably helping Señora Carzino-Cormano deal with his father, who was by then very deeply in his cups.

"And where, Habanzo, is young Frade now?"

"At the Guest House, mi Coronel."

"You're sure of that?"

"Sí, mi Coronel."

"And the agents on duty are prepared to deal with the situation if he suddenly erupts again from the garage and drives away at a high rate of speed? They will not, to rephrase the question, lose him again?"

"No, mi Coronel."

"And may we expect further 'technical difficulties' with communications surveillance of the Guest House line?"

"I have been assured, mi Coronel, that the equipment is now

working perfectly. But on the other hand, mi Coronel . . .''

"I don't wish to hear about 'on the other hand,' Habanzo."

"No, mi Coronel."

"I want enough people on the communications surveillance, and enough visual people watching the house, so that tomorrow morning I will know if there were telephone calls to him, and what was said. And I want to know who comes to visit him."

"Sí, mi Coronel."

"And if he leaves the Guest House by car—even at a 'high rate of speed'—I want to know where he goes, who he sees, and with a little bit of luck, what he says."

"Sí, mi Coronel."

"That will be all, Habanzo. I will see you here, with tonight's preliminary reports, at nine in the morning. And if there is any unforeseen problem, I expect you to telephone me at my home."

"Sí, mi Coronel. I understand."

"I devoutly hope so, Habanzo."

[TWO]
4730 Avenida Libertador
Buenos Aires
0015 20 December 1942

"I wonder," Clete Howell said aloud as he pulled off the avenue onto the driveway and stopped, "if I can get this big sonofabitch through that narrow gate."

He was driving his father's Horche, with Señora Pellano sitting next to him. He had the Horche because he took his father home from the Duartes' in it, and he needed a way back to the Guest House.

An hour earlier, though he seemed to have passed out for the evening in a leather armchair in the Duartes' upstairs sitting room, El Coronel suddenly stood up and announced that he was tired and going home.

"You are not going to drive," Señora Carzino-Cormano said. "You're drunk."

"Don't be absurd."

"Dad, you've had a couple," Clete said.

"He's had a liter!" Señora Carzino-Cormano said.

"I have never been drunk in my life."

"It is a pity, Jorge," Señora Carzino-Cormano said, "that Cletus is such a bad driver. Otherwise he could drive you home in your car."

"Cletus, you silly woman, is a splendid driver. I myself accompanied him while he was at the wheel of the Horche. He drives it nearly as well as I do." He turned to Clete. "It is settled. You will drive me home in the Horche. Then you may use the Horche as long as you like." He turned back to Señora Carzino-Cormano: "Are you satisfied, you silly woman?"

"Perfectly, my darling. You are always such a reasonable man."

Not without difficulty, El Coronel was installed in the front seat by Clete, Enrico, and Señora Pellano. And he was asleep by the time they reached the big house on Avenida Coronel Díaz. With Señora Pellano preceding them to open doors, Enrico and Clete half-carried, half-dragged him up the stairs to his bedroom, undressed him, and put him to bed. As soon as he was on his back, he started to snore.

"Will he be all right?" Clete asked Enrico.

"I will stay with him, mi Teniente, until Señora Carzino-Cormano arrives."

Clete considered waiting for Claudia, then decided to hell with it, he would take the Horche and worry about the Buick in the morning.

"Señor Clete?" Señora Pellano asked.

"I was wondering if I can get this car through the gate."

"I will guide you," she said. She stepped out of the car, opened the gate, and with great seriousness (which made him smile), used hand signals to guide him into the basement garage.

"Can I make you a little something to eat, Señor Clete?" she asked as they entered the house through the kitchen. "Perhaps a cup of coffee?"

"No, thank you, Señora Pellano. I'm beat. I'm going to bed."

"You're sure?"

"I am positive."

"Señor Clete, I have something to say," she said hesitantly.

"Say it."

"Today was a sad occasion. But it was not the burial of Jorge that made your father drink."

"Excuse me?"

"It was happiness. You are here and alive, and your war is

over. That is why your father drank. He is so relieved, so happy about that.''

She touched his face.

"¿Con su permiso?'' she asked, and before he could reply, she stood on her toes and kissed his cheek.

Without thinking, he put his arms around her and hugged her.

It was hotter than hell in Uncle Guillermo's playroom. No one had raised the vertical blinds to take advantage of the breezes coming off the Río de la Plata. *Señora Pellano would have taken care of that; but she wasn't here.*

By the time he raised them and opened the windows to the balcony, Clete was sweat-soaked. He stripped down to his undershorts and boots, then stepped onto the balcony to catch the breeze.

Who's going to see me, anyhow? And if somebody does, so what?

He relaxed for a moment on one of the six comfortable, cushioned chairs around the table, wiping the sweat from his brow as soon as he was seated. Then he stood up and went to the ice chest. *It should certainly be stocked with cold beer,* he thought with pleasure.

The beer was floating around in tepid water.

When the cat's away, the mice will play, he thought. *If Señora Pellano had not gone to the Duartes' to help out at the funeral, there would be cold beer in here.*

And then the hair on his neck curled.

Jesus Christ, if Peter was serious, I'm one hell of a target for somebody with a rifle over there in the racetrack grandstands!

He quickly returned to the bedroom and stood with his back against the wall. His heart was beating rapidly, and his sweat was now clammy.

Then he told himself he was being foolish.

It's incredible to think that someone is in the grandstands with a rifle. If there were, they would have taken a shot at me when I drove up in the Horche.

And besides, those Argentine FBI guys—the Internal Security agents—are outside on the street.

But then he remembered that he didn't see a car on the street when he drove up, and no South American Humphrey Bogart in a trench coat standing under the tree.

I probably lost them when I took the Old Man's Horche from

Uncle Humberto's. They are standing around watching for the Buick.

That made him smile. And with the smile, he lost the feeling of terror. He pushed himself off the wall.

You are a melodramatic asshole, Clete Frade!

But, shit, Peter sounded serious. Better safe than sorry.

He walked quickly around the room, turning off the lights. Then he carefully lowered the shutters.

He turned the lights on again.

As I learned as a Boy Scout, "Be Prepared!"

He went to the wardrobe where he was hiding the Argentine copy of the Colt Model 1911 .45 pistol and took it out. He removed the clip, emptied and reloaded it, dry-fired the pistol, satisfied himself that it was functioning properly, and then reinserted the clip and worked the action, chambering a round.

And then he felt a little absurd, again.

"Why don't I do this right?" he asked himself aloud. "If this is going to be a replay of the Gunfight at the OK Corral, why not do it with a Colt six-shooter?"

He went to the desk and took out the felt-lined walnut box containing the old Hog Leg, the Colt Army .44-40 revolver that his grandfather carried while commanding the Husares de Pueyrredón.

You'd be proud of me, Grandpa, sitting here with your Hog-Leg about to defend myself against the Argentine equivalent of the Apaches.

Jesus Christ, it's hot in here with those goddamned blinds closed!

He stood up and walked to the rear of the apartment, where there was a second balcony behind the elevator shaft and the steep stairway. It was barely wide enough for two simple wooden chairs with leather seats and backs. And it offered a far-from-charming view of the service entrances of other houses—and to judge from the smell of it, the Buenos Aires version of a privy.

But it was in the open, and there was a small breeze. He started to sit down, but decided a warm beer was better than no beer, and returned to Uncle Guillermo's playroom.

Feeling more than a little sheepish, he turned off the lights, opened one of the vertical blinds, and crept onto the balcony. He took two beers from the ice chest, then crept back inside. He lowered the blind again, then started back toward the other balcony.

The .45 automatic was on the desk, beside the .44-40 Hog Leg.

I should put that away before Señora Pellano comes in here with my breakfast and sees it.

Ah, to hell with it. I'll take it with me and put it away before I go to bed.

He went to the rear balcony and laid the pistol on the floor of the balcony. Then he settled himself as comfortably as he could—sitting in one of the chairs, resting his booted feet on the other—and opened one of the beers.

Warm beer is better than no beer at all.

While he sipped the beer, thoughts of the Virgin Princess passed pleasantly across his mind.

Can I tell her I love her?

Why the hell not, she already said that to me . . . probably.

And she looked at me out of those beautiful eyes and pursed her lips in a kiss. . . .

Jesus Christ, I'd give my left nut to put my arms around her and kiss her!

He heard the sound of feet on the stone stairs.

What the hell is that?

A cat or something? Rats?

What the hell is it?

He carefully lowered his booted feet to the floor and stood up. He had left the door to the rear balcony slightly ajar. He approached it, put his hand on the knob, and started to open it. Then he changed his mind, dropped to his knees, and felt around the floor until his fingers touched the Argentine .45.

He went back to the door. He heard feet on the stone stairs again, then his heart jumped as he realized someone was coming up the stairs.

No. Someone is already on the top floor; and somebody else is coming up the stairs. And it goddamned sure isn't Señora Pellano. Then who the hell is it?

He smelled a man.

A man who hasn't had a bath in a long time. Smells like an infantry Marine from the 'Canal.

The second man walked toward Uncle Guillermo's playroom.

What the hell do I do now?

Clete eased the door open. Walking on his tiptoes, he left the balcony and walked toward the playroom.

It was absolutely dark inside.

He found the light switch, closed his eyes, and turned the lights on.

He opened his eyes. In the time it took them to adjust to the sudden glare, he saw two men.

What the hell is he doing next to my bed?

The second man was closer, shielding his eyes. He held a long, curved knife. When he saw Clete, he brought the arm holding the knife up across his chest, so he could slash at Clete when he moved in.

The man next to Clete's bed turned—he had an even larger knife—and assumed a crouching position.

Clete glanced at the closer man, in time to see him start to rush at him.

Did I chamber a round in this thing?

The .45 kicked in his hand, and then again and again. The noise was deafening.

The man rushing him staggered, with a look of surprise on his face. He fell to the ground. The back of his head was a horrible, bloody mess, shattered like a watermelon.

Where the hell did I hit him? In the mouth? I had to; there's no other mark on his face.

The other man was now rushing at him with his knife held high over his shoulders.

The .45 bucked again and again and again and again. The man rushing him started to fall.

Clete pulled the trigger again. The pistol didn't fire. He checked it. The slide was locked in the rear position. He had emptied the magazine.

The man he had just hit was now screaming in agony, holding his right leg with both hands.

Jesus Christ, when Señora Pellano hears all this noise, she'll be terrified!

Señora Pellano! How did these bastards get past her?

He looked at the man screaming in pain. The way his leg was bent, it was clearly broken. Blood covered the man's hands.

I shot at him four times and only hit him once, in the lower leg?

He walked to him, kicked his knife across the room, then went to the desk. He picked up a loaded .45 magazine, ejected the empty one in the pistol, loaded the fresh one, and let the slide go forward.

He went to the stairs and started down them.

There were no lights.

He went down carefully, rubbing his back against the wall, desperately hoping he wouldn't fall.

He reached the first floor and found the handle to the kitchen door.

He raised the pistol and pushed the door open. The kitchen, too, was dark. He felt around for the switch, found it, and snapped on the lights.

Señora Pellano, in a black bathrobe, was sitting at the kitchen table. Her eyes were open and her head was thrown back.

Her throat had been cut. Through the gaping wound he could see bone and her slashed throat. Blood soaked her bathrobe and dripped onto the floor.

"You miserable sonsofbitches!" Clete said, his voice breaking.

He ran back up the stairs to Uncle Guillermo's playroom. Half-way up, he could hear the man screaming again.

"For the love of the Blessed Virgin, please help me!"

He reached the playroom. The man had crawled to the bath-room, where he had pulled a towel from the rack and was at-tempting to make a tourniquet with it.

He looked at Clete.

"Please, Señor, for the love of God, help me!"

Clete raised the pistol and shot him in his good leg. And then, when the man looked at him in surprise and terror, he shot him again, aiming between his eyes. His aim was a little off; he hit him in the center of his forehead.

[THREE]
4730 Avenida Libertador
Buenos Aires
0115 20 December 1942

El Teniente Coronel Bernardo Martín made an illegal U-turn in the middle of Avenida Libertador and pulled up behind one of the five Policía Federal police cars parked in front of the Frade Guest House.

His action attracted the attention of two uniformed Policía Fed-eral officers—the one assigned to make sure that traffic continued to flow along Avenida Libertador, and the one assigned to make sure that no unauthorized persons entered the scene of the crime.

Both greeted him as he left his car.

"Yo soy el Coronel Martín, del Servicio de Seguridad del Interior," he said. Though he was out of uniform—he was wearing only the shirt he had worn that day and a pair of casual trousers—he spoke with such authority that one of the policemen saluted and the other begged his pardon for stopping him.

He entered the foyer of the Guest House and found el Comandante Habanzo in animated conversation with several Policía Federal officers—two uniformed senior officers, one a capitán, the other a teniente, and two plainclothes detectives, most probably from the Homicide Bureau.

Habanzo looked enormously relieved to see him.

"Mi Coronel," he said.

Interesting that he is here, Martín thought as Habanzo briefly described the carnage at the Guest House. *Is this a manifestation of his devotion to duty, inspired by our little chat earlier? Or is there another reason?*

"You are?" the Capitán asked, not at all friendly, when Habanzo finished.

"Mi jefe, el Coronel Martín," Habanzo introduced him.

"¿Credenciales?"

Christ! They are in my jacket pocket.

"Capitán," Martín said. "You have two choices. You may accept the word of el Comandante Habanzo, whose credentials I presume you have seen, that I am who I say I am . . ."

"Credenciales, por favor."

". . . or we will all stand here while I telephone my office and have an agent dispatched to my home to pick up my credentials. While we are waiting, I will telephone my friend el Coronel Savia-Gonzalez, wake him from a sound sleep, and tell him that one of his capitáns is interfering with Internal Security."

"With respect, mi Coronel," the Capitán said. "We have three murders here. Murder is the responsibility of my office."

"What we have here, according to el Comandante Habanzo, is three bodies. If my investigation indicates that there were in fact three murders, and that these murders have no connection with Internal Security, then I will happily turn over the investigation to the Policía Federal."

He locked eyes with the Capitán, who after a moment backed down.

"Sí, mi Coronel."

"Where is the American?" Martín asked.

"In there, mi Coronel," Habanzo said, pointing to a closed door, before which stood a uniformed Policía Federal. "It is the library."

"Has he been interrogated?"

"No, mi Coronel. He refuses to answer any questions."

"I have placed him under arrest," the Capitán said.

"No, you haven't," Martín said. "Be good enough, Capitán, to accompany el Comandante and me on a preliminary survey of the crime scene."

"There are two," Habanzo said. "The kitchen, and the apartment on the upper floor."

"We will begin with the kitchen," Martín said. "Where is it?"

"Through that door, mi Coronel."

Martín's stomach nearly turned when he saw the body sitting at the kitchen table. There was already the sickly sweet smell of blood, and flies.

"Get a towel, or a sheet or something, and cover the body."

"Photographs have not been taken," the Capitán protested.

"If I decide photographs are in order, the sheet can be removed," Martín said, and went to the doors leading outside from the kitchen to examine them for marks of forcible entry. There were none.

Which means nothing. People will remove dead bolts and chains to open doors to complete strangers.

He turned from the door to the basement.

"Habanzo, have you examined the door from the street to the garage, and the front door, for signs of forcible entry?"

"I have," the Capitán answered for him. "Or rather, one of the Homicide Bureau investigators has," he corrected himself. "There were none."

"Thank you," Martín said. "How do we reach the—you said 'upper-floor apartment'?"

"There is a stairway and an elevator, mi Coronel," Habanzo said.

"We will use the elevator," Martín said. "It may be necessary to seek evidence on the stairway. I don't think robbers would use the elevator; they make noise." He turned to the Capitán: "To judge from the position of the woman's body, I would say that she was sitting there when her throat was cut; that she was not moved there. Would you agree?"

The Capitán nodded. "Which suggests she was taken by surprise," he said. "Which in turn suggests she knew the people who murdered her."

"Possibly," Martín agreed. "Where is the elevator?"

The smell of blood in the apartment was even stronger than in the kitchen. And there were more flies.

Martín examined both bodies, then the trail of blood leading to the bathroom, and the towel used as a tourniquet. The tiles surrounding the bathtub were shattered, as well as the tub itself, which sat inside the tile base.

He returned to the bedroom and saw the Colt single-action revolver on the desk. A holster for a .45 automatic and an empty clip lay on the table. A bowl for pencils was on the desk. Martín picked up a pencil, hooked the trigger guard of the Colt revolver, and sniffed at the barrel. It had not been fired.

"Other weapons?" he asked.

"There is a .45 automatic, mi Coronel," Habanzo said. "It has been fired. It is in my possession."

"Where did you find it?"

"When the young Norteamericano opened the door to me, he had it in his hand. He gave it to me."

"A stolen Army pistol," the Capitán said.

"Not necessarily," Martín said. "This house is owned by el Coronel Jorge Guillermo Frade. The pistol may be his. It is conceivable that he loaned it to his son for protection."

"That is illegal."

"You tell el Coronel that, Capitán," Martín said.

He looked around the room again.

"I now wish to speak to the Norteamericano," he said. "Here. Habanzo, will you bring him up?"

"You wish to talk to him here, in the scene of the murders?" the Capitán asked.

"It sometimes makes people uneasy to be brought to the scene of the crime," Martín said. "Uneasy people often say more than they wish. Habanzo, just put him on the elevator. I'd like to speak to him alone."

"I'd prefer to be here, mi Coronel, when you speak with the suspect," the Capitán said.

"First of all, he is not a suspect. Secondly, he has refused to answer your questions. Perhaps he will answer mine."

"I respectfully protest, mi Coronel."

Martín shrugged.

"And when you have put the Norteamericano on the elevator,

Habanzo, please telephone to el Coronel Savia-Gonzalez, apologize for waking him at this house, and tell him that I consider it very important, in a matter of Internal Security, that he come here immediately.''

"Sí, mi Coronel."

"Thank you, Comandante," Martín said.

He had a second thought.

"Where is the .45 automatic, did you say?"

"In my possession," Habanzo said.

"Can you give it to the Norteamericano and have him bring it up here?''

Habanzo's face registered surprise.

"Presumably you unloaded it?" Martín asked.

"Yes, mi Coronel."

"Then I don't think he will try to hold me at gunpoint, do you?''

"His fingerprints will be all over it!" the Capitán protested.

"Since el Comandante Habanzo has told us the Norteamericano was carrying the pistol when he opened the door to him, his fingerprints are already all over it," Martín said, with sarcastic patience. "Please have him bring the pistol."

"Sí, mi Coronel."

When Cletus Howell Frade stepped off the elevator, Martín was somewhat shocked at his appearance. He was naked, except for a pair of bloodstained white boxer shorts and cowboy boots. His face, chest, and legs were bloodstained, and there were finger marks where he had tried to wipe them. And he was carrying the .45 automatic by lopping a finger through the trigger guard.

"Teniente Frade, I am el Teniente Coronel Martín of Internal Security. We have met. Do you remember that?"

Clete nodded. He handed the pistol to Martín.

"This is the weapon you used to do that?" Martín asked, nodding toward the two bodies.

Clete was silent.

"We must talk seriously and quickly," Martín said. "Let me begin by saying I know you are an intelligence officer of the OSS. I am presuming that you are a very good one, or otherwise your government would not have sent you to Argentina."

Clete met his eyes but did not reply.

That was a shot in the dark, Teniente Frade. And, while I am not very good at judging reactions by watching people's eyes and other body signals, I'm not all that bad, either. I would wager three-to-one now that you are an OSS agent.

"I like to think that I am also a competent intelligence officer. A good intelligence officer does not choose sides. He simply gathers information and passes it to his superiors for their decisions. That luxury is no longer available to me. Because of who you are, I must either choose to offend your father . . . which may prove very costly to me in the future, I'm sure you know what I mean . . . or I must ally myself with him. I have decided to ally myself with your father."

Clete said nothing.

"You have no response?"

"Could I go in the bathroom and wash myself?" Clete asked.

"Not just yet," Martín said. "What I want from you now is for you to tell me what happened here tonight."

"Mi Coronel, I think I would prefer to wait until my father can find me a lawyer."

"You don't have that luxury," Martín said. "We need a credible story, and we need it before the Chief of the Policía Federal arrives. He's on his way. Just tell me what happened. We're alone, and you can deny anything you tell me now later."

Clete said nothing.

"I'm sure this doesn't frighten you, but I think I should tell you that unless we can come up with a credible story for el Coronel Savia-Gonzalez, he will insist that you be taken to police headquarters for interrogation. They won't kill you, but they will make you very uncomfortable, and it may be days before even your father can get you released."

What the hell have I got to lose?

"I was at the home of my uncle, Humberto Valdez Duarte, following the funeral of my cousin. Later, I drove my father home, then returned here with Señora Pellano. I came up to my apartment. The blinds had not been raised, and it was very hot in here. I took a beer and went out onto the servants' balcony on the rear. I heard noises, came in here to investigate, and found two men, armed with knives. They attacked me, so I shot them. I went downstairs and found Señora Pellano with her throat cut. There was a pounding at the door, and I opened it. A man who said he was Comandante Habbabo . . ."

"Habanzo," Martín corrected him.

". . . was standing there with a gun. I gave him the automatic. He tried to question me. I refused to answer until I had a lawyer,

420 W.E.B. GRIFFIN

and we argued about that awhile, until the police came. I was then locked in the library and was there until just now."

"Do you know the men whom you shot?"

Clete shook his head no.

"Do you have any idea why they wanted to kill you?"

"No."

"Where did you get that stolen .45 automatic pistol. Is it your father's?"

Clete was silent.

"All right. Now I will tell you what I believe happened," Martín said. "You returned from your uncle's home, and did not raise the blinds because you thought there might be an attempt on your life. You believed this because you earlier met the German, el Capitán von Wachtstein, at the Alvear Palace Hotel. For reasons I cannot imagine, he warned you that the Germans would try to have you killed. That also explains why you went out on the servants' balcony with a pistol.

"When the attempt was made, you killed one of the men and wounded the other. You went looking for Señora Pellano, found her with her throat cut in the kitchen, lost your professional detachment, and returned here and shot the other man, who had by then dragged himself into the bathroom. The bullets ricocheted off the tile of the bathtub, which explains the blood on your body. And the human flesh, which I think is brain tissue."

Clete said nothing.

"Killing the one and wounding the other was self-defense. Coming back here and killing the wounded man was murder . . . unless, should the matter reach trial, your lawyer pleads a crime of passion, based on your close personal affection for Señora Pellano."

"Those bastards didn't have to kill her," Clete heard himself saying. "She never hurt anybody in her life."

"I'm surprised to hear you say that," Martín said. "Of course they had to kill her. It was at no cost to them. They were going to kill you, and they can only hang you once for murder. Killing her removed a potential witness against them."

"You're a cold-blooded bastard, aren't you?"

"I am beginning to suspect that I have more experience in these matters than you do," Martín said. "Professional judgment does not make me cold-blooded."

Clete exhaled audibly.

"This is the story we will tell," Martín said. "On your return

from the Duarte mansion, you came to your apartment. You were
surprised by armed robbers. You managed to put your hands on
the old Colt and killed them both with it. Since the six-shooter
was empty, you picked up the robbers' gun, the automatic, went
downstairs, and found Señora Pellano murdered in the kitchen.
At that point, Comandante Habanzo knocked at the door. You let
him in and gave him the robbers' gun."

"There's a couple of large holes in that story," Clete said.
"For one thing, the Colt has not been fired. And what about the
automatic?"

"Anything else?"

"There's a trail of blood on the floor, leading to the bathroom."

"That robber crawled in there during the gunfight," Martín
said. "Where he threatened you with the .45. So you killed him
with the old revolver."

"The old revolver has not been fired."

Martín ignored him.

"You are more seriously injured than you think you are," he
said. "You will require immediate emergency medical treatment.
I am going to summon an ambulance from the Military Hospital,
which is nearby. You will be treated and placed under protective
custody. I doubt if the Policía Federal can gain entrance to you
in the hospital, but if they somehow manage to—I really don't
know how cooperative el Coronel Savia-Gonzalez will be in this;
he is not an admirer of your father—you will refuse to answer
any of their questions without a lawyer."

"The .44-40 hasn't been fired," Clete repeated. "The bullets
in the bodies are .45 ACP, not .44-40."

"Your professionalism, Teniente, is returning," Martín said approvingly. He went to the desk and picked up both pistols. He
went into the bathroom and pressed the .45 against the right hand
of the man with the bullet hole in his forehead, then stood up.
He took the Colt .44-40 revolver, fired two cartridges into the
body, then went to the body of the man in the bedroom and fired
two cartridges into his body. Finally he walked to the desk and
fired two cartridges into the wall, one next to the bathroom door,
the other through one of the closed blinds.

Then he laid both pistols back on the table.

"The revolver has less recoil than the automatic," he observed
calmly. "I would have thought the reverse."

A few seconds later, puffing from the exertion of running up the stairs, Comandante Habanzo rushed into the room with a .32 ACP Colt automatic in his hand.

"What are you doing with that?" Martín asked.

"I heard shots."

"You heard a car backfiring," Martín said. "Habanzo, do you remember offhand the number of the Military Hospital?"

"No, mi Coronel."

"Presumably, you have it written down somewhere?"

"Sí, mi Coronel," Habanzo said, more than a little awkwardly stuffing his small automatic back into its shoulder holster and then producing a notebook.

[FOUR]
Room 305
Dr. Cosme Argerich Military Hospital
Calle Luis María Campos
Buenos Aires
0205 20 December 1942

Siren screaming, the ambulance, a 1937 Ford station wagon, pulled up to the emergency entrance of the hospital. The driver and his assistant jumped out, walked quickly to the rear, opened the doors, and pulled out the stretcher holding First Lieutenant Cletus Howell Frade, USMCR, under a thick wool blanket.

He raised his head. A gurney was being hastily wheeled to the station wagon under the supervision of a very large and stern-faced nurse. He was moved, none too gently, from the stretcher onto the gurney. The wool blanket from the ambulance was jerked off and replaced by a thinner cotton cover.

The gurney was then wheeled into the hospital, now accompanied by a man in a business suit, who made little effort to hide the .45 automatic he carried, riding high on his hip.

The gurney was rolled onto an elevator. It rose (three floors, Clete guessed) and stopped. It was then rolled down a corridor and into an operating room, which made Clete more than a little nervous.

He was transferred to an operating table. Its cold stainless steel was cool against his back and buttocks. A short, unpleasant-looking, mustachioed doctor in a white jacket bent over him, pried his eyelids apart, and shined a small flashlight in his eyes.

"I'm all right, Doctor," Clete said.

The doctor ignored him. He made a sweeping gesture with his hands, and the nurse snatched the thin hospital blanket away and then pulled off his boxer shorts.

Jesus Christ!

As the nurse wrapped a blood-pressure collar around his arm, the doctor applied a stethoscope to his chest and then his throat. She gave him a sharp shove so he would roll onto his side; and a moment later, he felt the annoying and humiliating insertion of an anal thermometer. He watched as someone dropped his bloody shorts into a stainless-steel tray.

The anal thermometer was finally removed, his temperature announced orally, and then repeated by a woman in hospital whites holding a clipboard.

He was moved back onto his back. His blood-pressure reading was announced orally, repeated by the woman with the clipboard, and then the large nurse inserted a needle in his left arm to draw blood.

That completed, the doctor made another sweeping gesture with his hand. And the nurse, using what looked like a miniature spatula, began scraping his body.

Martín said that was probably brain tissue.

He felt slightly nauseous when she carefully scraped the brain tissue off the first spatula with a second one. The tissue was dropped into a second stainless-steel tray.

He was then given two sponge baths, first with water, then with alcohol. His face, chest, and legs stung uncomfortably. And when he moved his left leg, the large nurse firmly pushed it down against the operating table.

His chest stung, and he put his hand to it. Her hand grabbed his.

"I itch, goddamn it, take your hand off!"

She did not. There was a test of arm strength.

"Let him," the doctor said.

He scratched, and was sorry he did; he felt a sharp pain.

A tray of instruments appeared. The doctor took a scalpel in one hand and a ferocious-looking set of tweezers in the other. Starting at Clete's forehead, he began to remove tiny pieces of tile, dropping each piece into still another stainless-steel tray.

There is a moral in this, Clete thought, wincing at the pain: *When you shoot someone in the forehead, be sure of your backstop.*

He smiled at his own wit. The doctor smiled, very insincerely, back at him.

Jesus Christ, you must be losing your marbles. You killed a man, and that's nothing to smile about. Not only killed him, shot him in cold blood. Well, maybe not cold blood. You were pretty goddamned pissed after seeing what they did to Señora Pellano. But the bottom line is you killed a defenseless man.

He closed his eyes and kept them closed until he sensed the doctor stand up after he finished working his way down his body with the scalpel and tweezers.

The large nurse then appeared with a stainless-steel bowl and what looked like a small paintbrush. She carefully wiped each small wound with an alcohol towel—it stung painfully. And then she painted each wound with the purple substance that was in the stainless-steel bowl—it stung even more painfully.

The doctor looked down at him once more.

"Thank you, Doctor," Clete said.

The doctor ignored him and disappeared.

The large nurse nudged him again, and he slid off the operating table back onto the gurney. The thin cotton blanket was once more draped over him, and the gurney was wheeled out of the operating room and down the corridor.

The man with the barely concealed .45 marched alongside.

"Wait!" he ordered curtly.

"I have inspected the room, Sir," another man said.

The man with the .45 grunted, and went into a room to conduct his own inspection. He came back out, carrying a telephone.

"You inspected the room, did you?"

The second man looked sheepish. The man with the .45 shook his head at him in tolerant disgust, then motioned for the gurney attendant to push Clete into the room.

"In the bed, please, Señor," the man with the .45 said.

"I have to urinate," Clete said.

"Over there," the man said.

Clete walked naked to a small room equipped with a toilet, a bidet, and a shower.

When he returned, the room was empty.

It was also hot. The heavy vertical shutters had been lowered. When he went to them, he saw that the lowering belt had been padlocked. It could not now be moved.

Shit!

He went to the door. It was locked. He banged on it, and finally it was opened. There were two men, obviously armed, in the corridor. The man with the .45 who had been in the operating room was not there.

"I want the window open," Clete said. "It's as hot as a furnace in there."

"Sorry, Señor," the taller of the two men replied. "That is prohibited."

"By who?"

The man shrugged.

Clete went back inside, and as he walked to the bed, heard the door being locked.

He lay down on the bed, put his hands under his head, and started to wonder about what was going to happen next. Then he heard the door being unlocked again. It opened, admitting a hospital attendant who handed him a small gray paper-wrapped package and left. The door was locked again.

Clete opened the package and found it contained a tiny bar of soap, a tiny towel, shaving cream, a razor, toothbrush (no toothpaste), a glass, a hospital gown, and cotton slippers.

"To hell with it," he said aloud. "It's too hot in here to put that on."

He lay down on the bed, and again began to wonder what would happen next.

[FIVE]

Clete woke up suddenly, and with a reflex action, he looked at his Hamilton. It was eight-fifteen in the morning. On the crystal of the chronograph he noticed a small piece of whitish substance, flaked with now darkened blood. The large, unpleasant nurse did not look for brain tissue on his watch.

He left the bed, walked to the washbasin, and carefully scrubbed the watch clean. Then he glanced at himself in the mirror. His face was covered with violet patches—the disinfectant the nurse had painted him with—and so was the rest of his body.

I look like a clown. I wonder what the hell that purple stuff is.

He scrubbed at his face with no success, then tried a shower, which proved equally ineffective.

Maybe alcohol will get it off.

He went back to the bed and put on the hospital gown, then slipped his feet into the slippers. Another glance at the mirror confirmed his suspicion that his ass was hanging out.

And he was hungry. And thirsty. He banged on the door again, and in a moment it was unlocked and opened. Two strange men were in the corridor, cast from the same mold as the previous two. Though both were standing, now they had chairs. One waved a forefinger at him as if he were a small child.

"You must remain in your room."

"I'm hungry and thirsty."

Both men shrugged helplessly.

He closed the door himself, heard it being locked, and then returned to the mirror to examine himself—with mingled shock and amusement. There came the sound of the door being unlocked again.

Breakfast?

The door opened. A little pale, but otherwise showing no signs of passing out drunk eight hours before, el Coronel Jorge Guillermo Frade entered the room, freshly shaven, perfectly dressed. He was trailed by Enrico, who was carrying a small leather suitcase.

"Are you all right?" Clete's father demanded. "You are not seriously injured?"

"I'm pretty sick about what those bastards did to Señora Pellano."

His father nodded.

"I will of course help you, Cletus, any way I can. But the time has come for you to tell me what you are really doing down here."

"I'm here to make sure that Howell Petro—"

"Refuse to answer me, if you must. But don't lie to me again," his father interrupted him.

Clete met his father's eyes. His father nodded, as if he was satisfied that he had gotten through to Clete.

"The Bureau of Internal Security believes you are an agent of the OSS," he said.

"Do they?" Clete said. And then he decided he didn't want to lie to his father anymore. That did not mean telling him everything; but he wouldn't lie about what he told him.

"I'm a serving officer of the U.S. Marine Corps," he said. "I'll tell you that much."

El Coronel Frade nodded again, as if he thought he was making progress.

"And you're here to damage the German ship in Bahía Samborombón?" his father asked.

"If I were, I couldn't tell you that. You're an officer, you know what it is to be under orders."

"Or to try to influence me?" He gave Clete a hard look. "Depending on who I talk to in the BIS, I am offered both possibilities."

"I'd like to influence you," Clete said. "Your neutrality, your *alleged* neutrality, in this war makes me sick to my stomach."

"Does it indeed?" his father asked, his face tightening.

"You—and the BIS—apparently know all about the *Reine de la Mer*. You even called it a German ship just now. And you close your eyes to it. If you were really neutral, you'd have done something about it."

"You seem to know a good deal about it yourself," Frade challenged. "You know its name . . . very informative."

"If you hadn't closed your eyes to the Germans' replenishing their submarines in your sacred neutral waters, it wouldn't have been necessary for the U.S. government to send people down here to do something about it."

"Has it occurred to you that if the United States government had not sent you down here, Señora Pel—what happened to Señora Pellano would not have happened?"

Clete felt anger welling up.

"I'm as sorry as you are that Señora Pellano was killed. I was goddamned fond of her. She'll be on my conscience, all right. But not because I'm here doing what I was sent here to do, but because I forgot for a moment that the Germans have no qualms about killing innocent people. They kill innocent people by the millions. What's one more?"

"In the First World War, Allied propaganda showed German soldiers bayoneting babies in Belgium. That Allied Declaration, if that's what you're talking about, is the same sort of thing."

"If you believe that, I feel sorry for you." Clete said softly. He was aware that the flash of anger was replaced by a sad resignation, as if their roles were now reversed . . . as if he was now the parent talking to the child who would not accept the unpleasant truth.

"International law . . ." Colonel Frade began, and stopped.

"I should have protected her," Clete said, his voice calm and sad, "and I didn't. I'm ashamed of that. But I'm not ashamed of coming here to do what I was sent to do. If there's any shame, you should feel it, because Argentina is too stupid or selfish to know or care what this war is all about."

His father's face grew white. It was a moment before he spoke.

"El Almirante de Montoya believes it will be best for you, under the circumstances, to remain here in the hospital for the next few days."

"Who? Admiral who?"

"El Almirante de Montoya is Chief of the Bureau of Internal Security. He has assumed jurisdiction in your case. Fortunately, he and I are friends, because your fate is in his hands."

"And what exactly does that mean?"

"When de Montoya feels it would be safe for you to leave the hospital, you will come to the estancia, until I can arrange to send you safely out of the country."

"I'm not leaving the country," Clete said.

His father met his eyes.

"You have no choice in the matter."

"I'm not finished here. I killed the men who killed Señora Pellano," Clete said. "Now I want to get at the people who hired them. The Germans."

"You don't know for a fact that the Germans were behind this."

"Of course it was the Germans," Clete said, less angrily than sadly. "Don't tell me you closed your eyes to that too."

As if he had not heard a word, el Coronel Frade went on: "I have arranged for the release of Señora Pellano's body. I will accompany it to the estancia, where she will be buried. De Montoya has agreed to release you from here in time to attend Señora Pellano's funeral. That will provide a satisfactory reason for you to move to the estancia. You will stay there until I can make arrangements for you to leave the country. In the meantime, Enrico will stay with you."

"What? What for?"

"If one attempt to kill you was made, there will probably be another."

"But there are guards in the corridor."

"I know where Enrico's loyalties lie," Frade said simply. "Enrico will stay with you.

"You have disappointed me, Cletus," Frade went on carefully. "A good woman is dead on account of you. And you have lied to me. The estancia is large. You and I will only have to see a little of one another."

"I want very much to go to Señora Pellano's funeral, Dad,"
Clete said. "But I don't think it would be a good idea for me to
stay at the estancia."

El Coronel Jorge Guillermo Frade met his son's eyes, then
turned on his heel and walked out of the room. After he passed
through the door, Enrico locked it.

Enrico turned, met Clete's eyes for a moment, and then went
to the bed, where he unzipped the suitcase and took from it what
seemed to be a Browning twelve-bore self-loading shotgun. He
assembled it, then loaded it with five Winchester 00-buck cartridges.

"Browning?" Clete heard himself asking. "A Browning, or an
Argentine copy?"

Enrico didn't reply for a moment, then held the shotgun out to
Clete.

"A Remington Model Eleven, mi Teniente," he said.

Clete examined it and handed it back.

"Marianna was very fond of you, mi Teniente," Enrico said.
"She was always talking to me about you, like you were her
son."

*Marianna? Oh. He means Señora Pellano. I never knew her
first name. And now she's dead, because of my stupidity.*

"I was very fond of her. I am ashamed she is dead."

Enrico met his eyes again.

"I have asked the Blessed Virgin to let Marianna know that
you avenged her death, so that she may find eternal peace in the
company of the angels, knowing you are alive and they are dead."

"Until just now, I didn't know you and Señora Pellano were
close," Clete said.

"She was my sister," Enrico said simply. "I will now protect
your life, mi Teniente, with my own. But I would also very much
like to kill some Germans myself. Do you perhaps have a name?
Or names?"

*Jesus, he means all of that. If anyone tries to kill me in here,
it would have to be over his dead body. And if I gave him the
German ambassador's name, he'd kill him. Or die trying.*

Clete shook his head no.

"I'll work on this," Enrico said. "Honor demands that I also
avenge her death, even if that is against mi Coronel's wishes. I
will help you in any way I can, especially if it means I can kill
Germans."

And he means that too.

"Thank you, Enrico," Clete said.

I wonder if that means he would let me go, let me escape from my father's protection.

Having said his piece, Enrico went on to immediate, practical matters.

"Mi Teniente, where is the telephone?"

"They took it out," Clete said. And then, curiously: "Who did you want to call?"

"I thought we would have coffee, and perhaps the newspaper, mi Teniente. We will be here a long time."

"I could use something to eat."

"Bueno, I will take care of everything," Enrico said. He walked to Clete and held out the shotgun. "Mi Teniente is familiar with this shotgun?"

"Yes. I've got a Browning. They're about identical."

"It is loaded, and the safety is off, mi Teniente," Enrico said, and handed the Remington to Clete.

He walked to the door, pounded on it, and left the room.

Five minutes later, he was back.

"Coffee and some pastry is on the way," he announced. He walked to the window.

"It's locked," Clete said.

Enrico looked at him and winked.

"The clowns in the corridor asked where I was going. I told them for breakfast, a telephone, and the key to the window. They told me I could have neither the key to the window lock," he held up a small key, "or a telephone."

He removed the padlock, opened the vertical blind three feet, and then opened the window. He whistled. Moments later, a telephone appeared outside the window; it was hanging on a cord. Enrico hauled it in, untied the cord, then closed the window and the vertical blind.

He plugged the telephone in, picked up the handset, listened for a moment, nodded his head in satisfaction, then unplugged the telephone and put it in the cabinet beside the bed.

"We will keep it there until we need it, mi Teniente," he said. "In case the clowns in the corridor become curious."

"How did you do that, Enrico?"

"The Suboficial Mayor of the hospital was in the Husares de Pueyrredón when el Coronel and I were with the regiment. He was injured in a bad fall, and is on limited duty."

"He gave you the telephone?"

"Sí, mi Teniente, and he will see that we eat well, from the Sargento's mess."

"When they hear what happened on Avenida Libertador and cannot find me, my two friends will be worried about me. Can I call them, Enrico?"

Enrico met his eyes for a long moment.

He is not going to let me use the phone. All that talk about going against my father's wishes sounded great, but when push comes to shove...

"The clowns cannot listen to that line," Enrico said, pointing to the telephone wall plug. "I thought of that. But I think the clowns will be listening to the line of your friends."

"You're probably right."

Probably, shit! Of course he's right.

"It would be better to have them come here. Do you need both of them, or just one?"

"Just one. Could you do that? How would you bring him past the clowns?"

"You do not have suboficiales mayores in your army, mi Teniente?"

"I am a Marine, Sergeant Major, not a soldier. But yes, we have men like you in the Corps. They call them 'gunnys.' It means gunnery sergeant."

"And when your officers have a problem they cannot solve, do they turn to the 'gunnys'?"

"Yes, we do."

"It is the same here. This problem may take some time, but it can be solved. I suggest, mi Teniente, that you write a short note to your friend, telling him to accompany the man who gives him the note. And tell me the address."

XVIII

[ONE]
Room 305
Dr. Cosme Argerich Military Hospital
Calle Luis María Campos
Buenos Aires
1745 20 December 1942

Wearing a somewhat soiled, loose-fitting white cotton uniform of
the type issued by the Argerich Military Hospital to its maintenance personnel, Second Lieutenant Anthony J. Pelosi, CE,
USAR, moved slowly down the third-floor corridor of the hospital. He was holding a large coil of black electric wire, and
following a man moving a floor polisher in a slow sweeping motion from side to side.

The man with the floor polisher stopped in front of Room 305
and put a key to the locked door. The door was opened by a large
man; he was holding a shotgun in one hand. The muzzle was
eighteen inches from Tony's belly. The man motioned for him to
enter.

First Lieutenant Cletus H. Frade, USMCR, wearing a light-blue
hospital gown, was seated at a small table. Tony could see a pot
of coffee on it and the remnants of sandwiches and pastry.

"Jesus, what's that purple shit all over you, Lieutenant?"

"Some kind of antiseptic," Clete said, walking to Tony and
shaking his hand. "How did you get past the clowns?"

"I'm holding the cord for the guy with the floor polisher,"
Tony said. "He said we have ten minutes, and the less time I'm
in here, the better."

"That'll be enough. Tony, this is Suboficial Mayor—Sergeant
Major—Rodríguez. Enrico, el Teniente Pelosi."

"A sus órdenes, mi Teniente."

Tony shook Enrico's hand.

"What the hell happened at your house? When I went by there,
the place was surrounded by cops; I couldn't even get near. And

when I tried to telephone, I got some guy on the line who was obviously a cop, and he wouldn't tell me shit."

"The Germans sent a couple of guys to kill me; the local mafiosi."

"No shit?"

"They killed Señora Pellano," Clete said.

"And then you killed them? With your grandfather's six-shooter?" Tony asked in a combination of admiration and incredulity.

"I thought you didn't know what happened."

Pelosi hoisted the hem of his white jacket and came out with a copy of the Buenos Aires *Herald*.

"You're on the front page," he said, handing it to him. "I suppose most of the story is bullshit."

ROBBERY ATTEMPT IN BELGRANO LEAVES HOUSEKEEPER AND TWO CRIMINALS DEAD

By C. Edward Whaley
Herald Staff Writer

Buenos Aires 20 Dec—An attempted robbery of the residence at 4730 Avenida Libertador just after midnight this morning left the housekeeper, Señora Marianna Pellano, 52, and two as yet unidentified criminals dead, according to Colonel Ricardo Savia-Gonzalez, Chief of the Policía Federal.

"These criminals," Colonel Savia-Gonzalez told the Herald, "apparently in the belief the residence was not occupied, broke into the house from the rear. Surprised by Señora Pellano, they cruelly took her life, then proceeded upstairs.

"There they encountered Señor Cletus Frade, son of el Coronel Jorge Guillermo Frade, and attempted to murder him with a pistol it has been determined was stolen from the Argentine Navy.

"Señor Frade, luckily, was in the process of cleaning an historic military firearm, a Colt revolver once carried by his grandfather, El Coronel Guillermo Alejandro Frade, who carried it while commanding the Husares de Pueyrredón. Although wounded, he courageously managed to load the revolver and with it dispatched both criminals, killing both instantly.

"He then summoned the police, who upon arrival, dispatched Señor Frade to a hospital for treatment of his wounds, and began an investigation into the identity of the criminals."

The Herald has been unable to obtain any details concerning Mr. Frade's condition, but a police official who did not wish to be identified said that the scene of the shooting was bathed with blood, that "many shots were exchanged," and that Mr. Frade was "extremely lucky to have survived the encounter." The same official said that Mr. Frade, who has been living in the United States, recently returned to Argentina as General Manager of Howell Petroleum, Venezuela, and has been living in the residence temporarily.

"These were obviously brutal, hardened criminals," this official stated. "And it was only God's mercy and Señor Frade's great personal courage that saved his life. Clearly, if he had been unarmed, he would have suffered the same tragic fate as Señora Pellano."

"Everything is bullshit, except that they murdered Señora Pellano."

"The guy that came to get me said they cut her throat, practically cut her head off," Tony interrupted.

Clete saw Enrico's face darken.

"Señora Pellano was Sergeant Major Rodríguez's sister, Tony," Clete said evenly.

"Jesus! Sorry, Sergeant," Tony said. "I didn't know."

Enrico nodded: *It doesn't matter. No offense.*

"So who were these guys? I didn't think they were burglars. Real mafiosi? Italians?"

Clete nodded. "I don't know if they were Italians. But local gangsters. They were sent to kill me. Almost certainly by the Germans. So they knew about me. And if they know about me, they probably know about you. And maybe about David, too."

Tony accepted that without much surprise.

"How do you think they found out?"

"My father was here. He let it out that the BIS know we work for the OSS. There must be somebody in the BIS talking to the Germans."

"And you just got lucky when they came after you?"

"I was warned they were coming. And just in time."

That got Tony's attention.

"By who?"

"Tony, I just can't tell you that."

"Why not?"

"I just can't."

Tony considered that a moment, and drew his own conclusion, which obviously pleased him.

"We've got somebody in with the Germans?"

"I didn't say that."

Tony shrugged, signifying Clete didn't have to put it in words, that's what it had to be.

"So what happens now?"

"I don't know," Clete said. "My father's going to have me expelled from Argentina. And the destroyer will be here in a couple of days. I'm going to have to leave . . . unless, of course, I can get to use the destroyer's radios and get in touch with Colonel Graham. The best I can hope for is that my father can't have me expelled before the destroyer gets here."

"So what happens to Ettinger and me? What do you want us to do?"

"Nothing. I brought you in here to tell you what happened at the Guest House. And to tell you to watch out for yourselves. But nothing's changed about the orders I gave you. Just sit tight."

"If you say so, Lieutenant," Tony said, not liking it at all.

"Consider it an order, Lieutenant," Clete said, and then had another thought. "And speaking of orders: I told you to stay away from me. So what were you doing at the Guest House?"

Tony looked very embarrassed.

"It was a personal matter, forget it."

"I don't want to forget it, Tony. I want to know what was so important you went to the Guest House after I told you to stay away."

Tony looked even more uncomfortable. He looked at Enrico.

"Does he speak English?"

"No."

"I got a girl in trouble," Tony blurted.

Jesus Christ, is he serious?

"You did what?"

"I got a girl in trouble."

You certainly didn't waste any time, did you?
And you're really upset about it.

For the girl. This is not "Oh, shit, I knocked up a girl and her father wants me to marry her."

"Do you mean what I think you mean, Tony?"

Tony looked confused for a moment, then his expression changed to outraged innocence.

"It's nothing like that. Jesus, Clete, she's not that kind of a girl! Christ, I've never even tried to cop a feel."

"Then how is she in trouble?"

"Her boyfriend saw us in El Tigre. Or, really, some sonofabitch saw us in El Tigre, took our picture, and showed it to her boyfriend, and he's a real prick."

"Tony, I don't understand what the hell the problem is. Is the boyfriend coming after you?"

"He's not exactly her boyfriend," Tony said uncomfortably.

What the hell is he talking about?

"What exactly is he?"

"I mean, I don't think she even really likes him. He's sort of, like, supporting her."

Oh, Tony. You poor bastard. You've got yourself hooked by a clever whore who saw what a wholly decent and damned naive kid you are!

"This man is supporting her? Then she's not your girlfriend? You're not in love with her?"

"Of course not. I mean, no, I'm not in love with her . . ."

Like hell, you aren't. You just don't want to admit it to me. Or maybe even to yourself.

". . . and yeah, her boyfriend is, was, supporting her."

"I don't understand, Tony."

"I talked her into going to El Tigre. It's my fault."

"And somebody took a picture of you and showed it to her boyfriend," Clete said. "And he got sore. And dumped this girl, the one you're not in love with, and now she's telling you you're going to have to support her?"

"No," Tony said firmly. "She didn't say anything like that at all. I know what you're thinking, Clete. But she's not playing me for a sucker, Clete! Absolutely not!"

Sorry, but that's exactly what it looks like to me.

"Then what's the problem, Tony?"

"This guy guaranteed a loan for her father—her father owns a restaurant—and now he's going to the bank and telling them to cancel the guarantee. And her father'll have to pay off the loan, and he doesn't have the dough, so they'll take the restaurant. And the house upstairs."

He probably still believes in the tooth fairy!

"How much, Tony?"

"Thirteen grand. Maybe a little more."

Does he really expect me to come up with thirteen thousand dollars?

Yes, he does. He believes in both the tooth fairy and in the universal goodness of man.

"Tony," Clete said, as gently as he could. "Have you thought how this looks to me? I know, you say she's not that kind of a girl, and that you're not in love with her, but it looks to me like she's playing you like a violin."

"Forget I asked," Tony replied, with both anger and hurt in his eyes.

"Tony, have you considered that it's at least a possibility—I mean, this isn't some girl you've known for years. You just met her—that as soon as you give her the money, she says 'Muchas gracias' and goes back to her boyfriend?"

"I told you it's not like that. And she didn't ask me for a dime. I had to pull the story out of her."

Yeah, sure you did. While she looked at you with big, tearful eyes and a few well-timed sobs.

"And anyway, I wasn't going to ask you to give me the fucking money, just help me get it in a hurry down here from my bank in Chicago. I got fifty-three grand in the bank."

"Where'd you get fifty-three thousand dollars?" Clete asked in surprise.

And is the girl you don't love and is absolutely not playing you for a sucker aware you're got fifty-odd thousand dollars?

"Three of it was my college money, and my grandfather left me fifty grand when he died. I figured, since you know people here, you could help me get thirteen grand down here, maybe fifteen, just to be sure."

As sure as Christ made little apples, he's being played for a sucker; but I can't convince him of that.

So what do I tell him?

He stuck with you. Loyalty is loyalty, and it works down as well as up. This guy is on your team. So what you do is try to help him. If you can minimize the damage, fine, but you help him.

"Tony, I'll tell you what I will do. You come up with the facts.

Your girlfriend's name, her father's name, the name of the bank
. . . all the information you can get out of her. I'll check it out. If
it checks out . . ."

And I'll be goddamned surprised if it does!

"I got it right here," Tony said. He dug into his white hospital
uniform trousers and came out with a thick wad of paper.

"You can't keep those . . ." Tony said.

Why am I not surprised?

". . . because her father needs them back. He's running around
trying to get the money from other people, family mostly. I got
two grand from Ettinger, it was all he had, and he's come up with
about four. So we still need seven."

*Ettinger can't afford to lose two thousand dollars. But he
couldn't turn Tony down. And you almost did.*

Clete quickly went through the documents, more than a little
surprised to see that the mortgage, made by the Anglo-Argentine
Bank, looked legitimate. He wrote down the pertinent facts, remembering as he did so that Uncle Humberto was a banker and
that he could ask the appropriate questions.

"Mi Teniente," Enrico said, frowned, and tapped his wristwatch.

"Yeah, OK. He's going." He handed the documents back to
Pelosi. "No promises, Tony. I'll check it out."

"Thank you," Tony said. "I . . . Thanks, Clete. I really hated
to bother you with this, you being in the deep shit and all."

"It's OK, Tony. If I can help, I'll be glad to."

"Now I feel like a shit," Tony said.

"Why?"

"I lied to you. And Dave."

"About what?"

"I knew what you'd think," Tony said.

"If what, Tony?"

Jesus!

"If I told you I'm in love with her. I am, Clete."

*Either it's pure love at first sight, or you're thinking with your
dick, one or the other.*

*Who the hell are you to ridicule him for falling in love at first
sight?*

"Tony, just make sure that what you feel for this girl is the
real thing," Clete said. "We're down here alone . . ."

"Yeah. I knew that's what you'd think. But I'm glad I told
you anyway."

"You have to get out of here," Clete said.

"Yeah."

"I'll be in touch, through Enrico or one of his friends," Clete said, and put out his hand.

"Thanks, Clete."

"You and Ettinger watch your ass, Tony. These bastards are liable to come after you. They probably will."

"We'll be all right, Lieutenant."

I wonder.

[TWO]
The Office of the Military Attaché
The Embassy of the German Reich
Avenue Córdoba
Buenos Aires, Argentina
0925 21 December 1942

"You wished to see me, Herr Oberst?" Major Freiherr Hans-Peter von Wachtstein asked as he entered Oberst Karl-Heinz Grüner's office.

"The Ambassador wants to see you, Peter," Grüner said. "His secretary called here at nine oh two." Grüner waited until the young Luftwaffe officer had squirmed uncomfortably for a while, then went on. "I told her you were in the rest room."

"Thank you, Herr Oberst. I regret that I was delayed."

Smiling, Grüner held up his hand and stopped him.

"A late, romantic evening, I gather, von Wachtstein?"

"Romance is difficult, Herr Oberst, when the object of your intentions is connected like a Siamese twin to her older sister."

Grüner chuckled. "You are an enterprising young man. You'll find a solution."

"Is Ambassador von Lutzenberger waiting for me, Herr Oberst?"

"He wants to see you at 9:40. Not 9:35, not 9:45. 9:40. The Ambassador is a very precise man, von Wachtstein."

Peter looked at his wristwatch.

"We have a few minutes," Grüner said, then handed Peter a folded newspaper. Peter saw that it was the Buenos Aires *Freie Presse.* "Have you seen this, Peter?"

He pointed to a story with the headline "Murder and Robbery in Belgrano."

"Not this story, Herr Oberst. But I saw a similar one in the *Herald*. The hotel placed one before my door; I read it at breakfast."

" 'The best laid plans of mice and men,' " Grüner said. "I think it was a Scotsman who said that."

"I saw young Frade earlier in the evening," Peter said. "He came into the hotel."

"So I understand," Grüner said. "It was reported to me that you had angry words."

"He was angry with the lady, Herr Oberst."

"And she with him, I understand," Grüner said. "I don't suppose we'll ever know what went wrong, except that I violated the adage that one should never underestimate one's enemy. Leutnant Frade may not be the babe in the woods I took him to be."

"May I ask what happens now?"

"Well, first you see von Lutzenberger. I suspect there may have been a letter for you in the diplomatic pouch. There was a Condor flight this morning."

"Oh, really?"

"He will deliver the standard speech, that you are not free to use the diplomatic messenger service for personal business. That should take about three minutes. He probably has you on his schedule, 'von Wachtstein, nine-forty to nine forty-four.' "

Peter smiled, thinking it was expected of him.

"And when he turns you loose, I thought we would take a look at the advertisements in the *Freie Presse* and see about finding a suitable apartment for you. Or would that interfere with your romantic life?"

"No, Herr Oberst. Thank you very much," Peter said.

Grüner stood up.

"I noticed in the *Freie Presse* three or four apartments for rent that might be suitable for you. When von Lutzenberger is through with you, I suggest we have my driver take us past all of them. We will then wind up at my quarters, where my wife has her camera prepared to take pictures, to send to Willi. She will even feed us lunch. And afterward, if any of the apartments has taken your fancy, we can have a closer look on our way back here."

"You're very kind, Herr Oberst."

"Nonsense. Your father would do no less for Willi. But now I suggest you go to the Ambassador's office so that you will be there when the second hand on his watch indicates that it's precisely nine-forty."

"Thank you, Herr Oberst."

"Oh, one final thing."

"Yes, Herr Oberst?"

"When young Frade surfaces—Internal Security has him in the military hospital, but he should be out and about in several days—you should telephone to him and express your delight that he came through this terrible event unscathed."

"I don't think I understand, Herr Oberst."

"You know him socially. You are a German officer and a gentleman. This is a neutral country. It would be the correct thing to do. And when Oberstleutnant Martín gets the transcript of the telephone call, it will drive him mad trying to figure out the connection between you two."

"I'll call him, Herr Oberst."

Grüner, now delighted with his idea, had an even better one.

"Better yet, invite Leutnant Frade to lunch at the downtown officers' club. We'll stop in there during the apartment search and obtain a membership for you."

[THREE]

"You wished to see me, Mr. Ambassador?"

"Ah, yes, von Wachtstein," von Lutzenberger said. "I have a letter for you. There was a Condor flight this morning."

The Ambassador rose from his desk and walked to a wall safe concealed behind the official photograph of Adolf Hitler. He worked the combination, pulled the safe open, took an envelope from it, carefully closed it, and then spun the combination dial.

He handed Peter the envelope; it was sealed with green wax, in which was the impression of a signet ring. The letter was from his father. Peter recognized this, however, by the paper of the envelope and not the seal. A box of this stationery was kept in the library at Schloss Wachtstein; it was purchased in London by Peter's grandfather; and it was used up at the rate of one sheet and one envelope per year to announce births, deaths, marriages, and other significant family events to his grandfather's sister (and her descendants). She had married an Englishman and lived in Scotland.

"Thank you very much, Mr. Ambassador," Peter said.

"Read it here, von Wachtstein," the Ambassador ordered softly.

Peter looked at him in surprise.

"That came to me by hand," von Lutzenberger said. "Not in the pouch. I suspect it should not leave this room."

Peter broke the wax seal and opened the envelope.

```
                  Schloss Wachtstein
                     Pommern
Hansel—

   I have just learned that you have reached
Argentina safely, and thus it is time for
this letter.
   The most serious violation of the code of
honor by which I, and you, and your brothers
and so many of the von Wachtsteins before us
have tried to live is of course regicide. I
want you to know that before I concluded that
honor itself demands that I contribute to
such a course of action, I considered all of
the ramifications, both spiritual and practi-
cal; I am at peace with my decision.
   A soldier's duty is first to his God, and
then to his honor, and then to his country.
The Allies in recent weeks have accused the
German state of committing atrocities on
such a scale as to defy description. I must
tell you that information has come to me that
has convinced me that the accusations are not
only based on fact, but are actually worse
than alleged.
   The officer corps has failed its duty to
Germany, not so much on the field of battle,
but in pandering to the Austrian Corporal and
his cohorts. In exchange for privilege and
''honors'' the officer corps, myself in-
cluded, has closed its eyes to obscene viola-
```

tions of the Rules of Land Warfare, the Code
of Honor, and indeed most of God's Ten Commandments. I accept my share of the responsibility for this shameful behavior.

We both know the war is lost. When it is finally over, the Allies will demand a terrible
retribution from Germany.

I see it as my duty as a soldier and a
German to take whatever action is necessary
to hasten the end of the war by the only means
now available, eliminating the present head
of the government. The soldiers who will die
now, in battle, or in Russian prisoner of war
camps, will be as much victims of the officer
corps' failure to act as the people the Nazis
are slaughtering in concentration camps.

I put it to you, Hansel, that your allegiance should be no longer to the Luftwaffe,
or the German State, but to Germany, and to
the family, and to the people who have lived
on our lands for so long.

In this connection, your first duty is to
survive the war. Under no circumstances are
you to return to Germany for any purpose until the war is over. If you are ordered to return, find now some place where you can hide
safely.

Your second duty is to transfer the family
funds from Switzerland to Argentina as
quickly as possible. You have by now made
contact with our friend in Argentina, and he
will probably be able to be of help. In any
event, make sure the funds are in some safe
place. It would be better if they could be
wisely invested, but the primary concern is
to keep them safe from the Sicherheitsdienst
until the war is over.

In the chaos that will occur in Germany after the war, the only hope our people will
have, to keep them in their homes, indeed to
keep them from starvation, and the only hope
there will be for the future of the von

Wachtstein family, and the estates, will be
the money that I have placed in your care.
    I hope, one day, to be able to go with you
again to the village for a beer and a sausage. If that is not to be, I have confidence
that God in his mercy will allow us to be all
together again, your mother and your brothers, and you and I, in a better place.
    I have taken great pride in you, Hansel.
        Poppa

Major Freiherr Hans-Peter von Wachtstein turned away from
the desk of the Ambassador of the German Reich to the Republic
of Argentina and cleared his throat; and then, because it was
necessary, he took his handkerchief from his pocket and wiped
his eyes and cheeks.

"Excuse me, Mr. Ambassador."

"May I see the letter, please?"

"It is a personal letter, Mr. Ambassador."

"You either trust me or you don't, Freiherr von Wachtstein."

Peter met his eyes for a moment, then handed the letter over.
The Ambassador read it.

"Your father is eloquent, as well as a brave and honorable man,
von Wachtstein," the Ambassador said, and then added, "Hold
it over the wastebasket and burn it."

Peter met his eyes again.

"No, Sir," he said. "I don't wish to burn it."

"If Oberst Grüner finds that letter . . ."

"He will not find it, Mr. Ambassador."

The Ambassador considered that for a moment, and nodded.

"As to the other matter," he said. "Transferring the funds here
from Switzerland is a simple matter of sending a cable. Keeping
their presence here unknown, and investing them wisely, is quite
another problem."

"I understand."

"How much help do you think your friend Frade will be?"
von Lutzenberger asked. "His uncle is General Manager of the
Anglo-Argentine Bank."

"I don't think I follow you, Mr. Ambassador."

"You are beginning to frighten me, von Wachtstein, and to
annoy me," von Lutzenberger said coldly. "Please don't waste

my time by telling me you didn't warn Frade about Grüner's idiotic plan to eliminate him. Frade owes you his life. My question is how helpful you think he will be. If that young Duarte fool hadn't gotten himself killed at Stalingrad, the Anglo-Argentine Bank would have been a helpful connection."

"I hadn't thought about . . ."

"Start thinking, von Wachtstein. Otherwise we'll both be dead."

[FOUR]
Room 305
Dr. Cosme Argerich Military Hospital
Calle Luis María Campos
Buenos Aires
0905 22 December 1942

Clete was lying on the bed, reading *La Nación* and sipping at a cup of coffee, when he heard the locked door being opened. Enrico, whom he thought was sound asleep, was instantly awake, with the Remington in his hands.

El Teniente Coronel Bernardo Martín stepped into the room, carrying a small suitcase. After a moment, Clete recognized it; it was his. Martín looked at Enrico and his ready shotgun with approval.

"Buenos días, Suboficial Mayor," Martín said dryly, then switched to English. "How are you this morning, Mr. Frade?"

"I'm fine, thank you. A little bored."

"Well, the doctors tell me that you can leave the hospital," Martín said.

What doctors? I haven't seen a doctor since the one who hacked away at me when I got here.

"So I have taken the liberty of bringing you some of your things from the Guest House."

He laid the suitcase on the bed.

"Thank you," Clete said. "You mean, I'm free to go?"

Martín ignored the question. "I hope that you will report to the man from your embassy that you have been well-treated here."

"What man from the embassy?"

"Your embassy seems extraordinarily concerned with your

welfare," Martín said. "As soon as the story of your encounter with the burglars appeared in the *Herald,* they started making quite a nuisance of themselves, first at the Policía Federal, and lately at the Foreign Ministry."

"Is that so?"

"There's a Consular Officer, a man named Spiers, waiting downstairs to see you now. He was told you're being given a final physical examination, which should be over about half past nine. Will that give you time for a shower and a shave? Or shall I have him told you'll be a little longer?"

"You didn't answer my question. Am I free to go?"

"Certainly, now that we are sure you are in the best of health, and the Policía Federal have concluded their investigation of the unfortunate incident on Avenida Libertador."

"Thank you."

"Thank you for your cooperation," Martín said. "You might be interested to know that the criminals have been identified. Both of them have long criminal records, including a history of armed robbery. The Policía Federal will not miss them."

"Thank you again."

"May I make a suggestion?"

"Of course."

"Your Consular Officer might misinterpret Sergeant Major Rodríguez's shotgun. Would you feel comfortable if he put it away? I assure you that adequate protection for you is in place."

Clete shrugged his shoulders.

"Here and at your home. The Policía Federal are more than a little embarrassed that such a terrible incident could have happened on Avenida Libertador at the home of one of our more prominent citizens. I feel sure that for the next month, at least, the area will be heavily patrolled."

"You think it will take that long for my father to arrange to have me expelled?"

"This is Argentina. Even under these circumstances, any administrative procedure takes a long time."

Martín put out his hand.

"While I regret the circumstances, Mr. Frade, it has been a pleasure meeting you. Perhaps we will see one another again in the future."

Clete shook Martín's hand.

"Thank you," he said.

"Take care of yourself, Mr. Frade," Martín said. He smiled at

Enrico, offered him his hand, and then left the room. This time there was no sound of a key being turned in the lock.

"Is it permitted to ask what that was all about?" Enrico asked.

"Put the shotgun away, Enrico," Clete said. "I'm about to be visited by an American diplomat, and it would frighten him. After that, we can leave."

Enrico nodded.

"Out of sight," he said. "Not away."

He moved his chair beside the bed, then slipped the shotgun under the sheet.

"I'm going to take a shower and a shave," Clete said. "If someone knocks, let him in."

[FIVE]

"Mr. Frade, I'm H. Ronald Spiers, Vice Consul of the United States here in Buenos Aires."

He was a slightly built, thickly spectacled, somewhat hunch-shouldered man in his late twenties. He was wearing a seersucker suit and carrying a stiff-brimmed straw hat and a briefcase. He gave Clete a calling card.

"How do you do?" Clete asked.

He saw a question in Enrico's eyes and nodded reassuringly at him.

"I'm really sorry it took so long for me to visit you," Spiers said. "Please believe me, we have been trying since the story appeared in the *Herald.*"

"I appreciate your concern," Clete said.

"Frankly, you're sort of a special case," Spiers said.

"How's that?"

"Senator Brewer sent a cable asking us to keep an eye on you," Spiers said. "And to notify him immediately if you encountered any problems down here."

After a moment Clete remembered Senator Brewer. He was the senior senator from the state of Louisiana. *"He is a pompous windbag of incredible stupidity,"* Cletus Marcus Howell called him. *"But he's surprisingly useful to me if I have the time to explain in excruciating detail what I want done."*

Just like the Old Man, Clete thought, smiling, *having a word with the Senator, telling him to make sure the embassy looks out for me down here.*

And then another thought:

I don't think this Spiers guy has any idea what's really going on.

"Well, you can cable the Senator that I'm fine," Clete said. "They have given me the best of treatment, and I have been told that the investigation is over. The people who robbed the house have been identified as known criminals."

"I'm delighted to hear that," Spiers said. "And I'm sure the Ambassador will be."

"I was just about to leave, as a matter of fact."

"Could I drop you off?" Spiers asked. "I have a car and driver."

"I'd appreciate that," Clete said. "Are you sure it's no imposition?"

"Not at all. My pleasure."

Clete turned to Enrico.

"We're leaving," he said in Spanish. "What are you going do about the shotgun?"

"The shotgun?" Spiers asked, visibly surprised.

Shit, he speaks Spanish. I should have thought of that. Diplomats aren't very useful if they can't speak the language.

"Señor Rodríguez is my father's gamekeeper," Clete continued in Spanish. "We were looking at a shotgun—we're going to my father's estancia this afternoon—and we sort of hid it when we heard you were coming."

"The bird shooting here is supposed to be magnificent," Spiers said. "I myself don't hunt, but I have friends who do."

"You don't hunt?"

"I just can't stand the thought of killing anything," Spiers said.

[SIX]
4730 Avenida Libertador
Buenos Aires
1105 22 December 1942

Two policemen were strolling down the sidewalk in front of the Guest House, and Clete saw a car that was almost certainly an unmarked police car parked farther down the street.

Clete thanked Spiers for the ride, and for his concern, then passed through the gate and up to the door.

A maid he didn't recognize, a middle-aged woman, opened the door and looked at him dubiously.

Señora Pellano will never open the door to me again. Shit!

"This is Señor Frade," Enrico said behind him.

The woman stepped out of the way.

Now that he was here, Clete was sorry he had come.

"I don't think I want to stay here," he said to Enrico. "I think I'll put some clothes in a bag and check into a hotel."

"It is better that you stay here," Enrico said. "I can protect you better, and this is your home, mi Teniente."

"OK," Clete said, deciding he was being a little overemotional.

"Mi Teniente, when do you plan to go to Estancia San Pedro y San Pablo? I must see that we have petrol, the air in the tires . . ."

Christ, Señora Pellano's funeral!

I have to go. If I don't, he won't go with me. And he has the right to be at his sister's funeral.

"Let me put some things in a bag, Enrico. We might as well go now. There's no point in hanging around here."

"Sí, mi Teniente."

[SEVEN]
Estancia San Pedro y San Pablo
Near Pila, Buenos Aires Province
1615 22 December 1942

El Coronel Jorge Guillermo Frade was sitting on the verandah of the ranch house with Señora Carzino-Cormano and her daughters, when Clete drove up in the Horche.

When he saw Clete at the wheel, he quickly stood up and went inside the house.

Señora Carzino-Cormano, shaking her head sadly, moved off the porch and up to Clete and kissed his cheek.

"Are you all right?" she asked. "You weren't seriously injured?"

"I'm fine."

"Your father wasn't expecting you. You and he had words?"

"Yes," Clete said simply. "We did. I'm here for Señora Pellano's funeral."

"And you stay angry, don't you, like him? Is that why you drove his car here . . . you know how he is about that damned automobile . . . to make him angry?"

"My car is at the Duartes', and when I telephoned to ask about it, there was no answer. I had the Old Man's car, so I drove it."

" 'The Old Man'? Is that what you call him? To his face, I hope not."

They smiled at each other.

"Is there a hotel, or somewhere else I can stay?"

"Where? The hotel in Pila is . . ." She raised her hands helplessly. "You're determined to go to the funeral?"

"Yes, of course."

"Good for you," she said, and turned to Enrico. "Enrico, put Señor Cletus's things in my car. He will be staying at my estancia for the night."

"Mi Teniente," Enrico asked uncomfortably, "may I have an hour?"

"I don't understand, Enrico," Claudia said.

"I would like an hour with my family, Señora," Enrico said.

"Señor Cletus is going to my estancia, Enrico. Not you."

"With respect, Señora, where el Teniente goes, I go."

"I will speak to el Coronel about that, Enrico. It will be all right with him."

"With respect, Señora, this has nothing to do with el Coronel."

She stuck her tongue in her cheek thoughtfully.

"Very well, Enrico," she said. "You go to your family. Take all the time you need. When you are finished, Señor Cletus will be here on the verandah, and then you can drive him and the señoritas to my home."

"Gracias, Señora," Enrico said.

"And for the next hour," Claudia said, "the Old Man can sulk in the house while we have a coffee. Or perhaps something stronger, Cletus?"

"Nothing, thank you," he said.

[EIGHT]
Estancia Santa Catharina
Buenos Aires Province
2145 22 December 1942

Clete was startled when he became aware of the human form standing next to him. A female human form, to judge by the perfume.

He was lying on a chaise longue, examining the heavens with a pair of Zeiss 7 × 50 binoculars that he found in his bedroom. The room—actually an apartment—obviously served as the last repository of the personal property of the late Señor Carzino-Cormano; there were riding boots and a photo album and other things he suspected Claudia was unable to part with, even though her husband was long dead and she was in everything but law now married to his father.

After dinner, a magnificent entire lomo, roasted whole with red sweet peppers, mushrooms, and two magnificent bottles of vino tinto, Clete went to his room and to its chaise longue for a look at the stars.

He sat up. Enrico, the Remington on his lap, was about to allow himself to doze off again, satisfied that the visitor, whom Clete now recognized, posed no threat to Clete.

"I am not disturbing you?" Alicia Carzino-Cormano asked.

"Of course not."

"Is he . . . is that, necessary?" Alicia asked, nodding at Enrico and his shotgun.

"He thinks so."

"And do you?"

"I don't know," Clete said. "I am willing to defer to his professional judgment."

"May I ask you a question?"

"As long as it does not involve my love life. I am an officer and a gentleman, and officers and gentlemen do not kiss and tell."

"I heard my mother and your father talking."

"Eavesdropping on Mama and the Old Man? I am shocked, Alicia."

She smiled at him.

"El Coronel said there is no doubt that the Germans were behind what happened at the Guest House."

"I'm sure they were," Clete said.

"Why did they kill Señora Pellano?"

"Straight answer, Alicia? Because they are no-good sonsof-bitches who are perfectly willing to kill innocent people to get what they want."

"There was a story in *La Nación*," Alicia said, "which said that the English and the Norteamericanos . . . which accuses the Germans of killing thousands of innocent people. You believe that too?"

"Yes, I do," Clete said, now seriously. "I'm afraid it's even worse than that. That they have killed more than thousands. I think they've probably killed millions."

"It is impossible to believe!" she said, and made a strange noise. After a moment he recognized it was a stifled sob. She turned and walked—almost ran—away from him. The sudden motion woke Enrico from his doze. He jumped to his feet with the Remington at the ready.

Suddenly understanding why she was doing that, Clete jumped off the chaise longue and ran after her and caught her arm.

"Listen to me, honey," Clete said. "I don't believe for a minute that Peter von Wachtstein had anything at all to do with killing Señora Pellano, or with what they tried to do to me. And I know him well enough to be certain that if he was aware of what was going on in Germany, he would do anything he could to stop it."

She looked up at him. He could smell her breath.

"Is that true?" she asked, just barely audibly.

"Yeah, honey, it's true. Ol' Hans-Peter is an officer and a gentleman and a fighter pilot. We officers and gentlemen and fighter pilots don't do things like that."

Alicia Carzino-Cormano then threw her arms around him, hugged him tightly, put her face on his chest, and said, "Oh, Cletus, thank you very much!"

Then she kissed him square on the lips and ran from the room.

[NINE]
La Capilla de Nuestra Señora de los Milagros
Estancia San Pedro y San Pablo
Near Pila, Buenos Aires Province
1105 23 December 1942

The Chapel of Our Lady of the Miracles seems to be a wholly owned subsidiary of Saints Peter and Paul Ranch, thought First

Lieutenant Cletus H. Frade, USMCR, onetime acolyte of Trinity Protestant Episcopal Church, Midland, Texas.

Until he walked into this one, he assumed that a "chapel" was sort of an altar off to the side of the main part of the church. The chapel at Trinity, for example, was in fact a small church within a church used mostly by a small group of the unusually devout for the celebration of seven A.M. Sunday Morning Prayer before they hit the links of the Midland Country Club.

Or once in a while, he thought, remembering two specific incidents, *for the quiet, family-members-only marriage of a bride who wanted a church wedding but was reluctant to march down the main aisle to the strains of "Here Comes the Bride" in a white dress which could not entirely conceal the fact that she was about to add to the world's population.*

La Capilla de Nuestra Señora de los Milagros was a large religious edifice, seating normally maybe three hundred people (it was almost as large as Trinity Episcopal, and a hell of a lot more ornate). Today it held more than that. It came fully equipped with an organ, a choir loft, a cemetery, and a rectory. And two priests in absolutely stunning vestments heavy with golden thread, one a doddering old man who seemed to have trouble staying awake, and the other who looked as if he was ordained last week.

And there were three social classes of worshipers: First, there were two kinds of pews in the church itself. All but the first three rows were simple wooden benches. The first three rows were softly upholstered in red velvet.

These were reserved for important worshipers, which today meant the family of the late Señora Marianna Maria Dolores Rodríguez de Pellano, whose beautifully carved solid cedar casket now rested just before the communion rail. And today, at the invitation of Suboficial Mayor Enrico Rodríguez, Cavalry, Argentine Army, Retired, included First Lieutenant Cletus H. Frade, USMCR.

The Old Man, Señora Carzino-Cormano, the Carzino-Cormano girls, Uncle Humberto and Aunt Beatrice, and some people Clete did not recognize were seated in the VIP section of La Capilla de Nuestra Señora de los Milagros, a wing off the main body of the church, where there were individual prie-dieux and nicely upholstered chairs with arms.

The healthy-looking young priest delivered an angry homily, promising eternal damnation for those who lived by the sword. Clete suspected that the homily was directed mostly at him and

Enrico, who had his Remington with him, not at all well-concealed in a poncho.

Just for the record, Padre, I didn't come down here because I wanted to. I didn't go in the goddamned Marine Corps because I get my rocks off shooting people. I would even have obeyed Christ's "turn the other cheek" rule if those two bastards hadn't come at me with knives.

But what about the one I shot in the forehead while he was actually screaming, "Please, Señor, for the love of God. help me!"?

Martín was right: That was murder, Cletus Frade. You didn't have to kill that sonofabitch. You shouldn't have killed him.

Familiar words from the 1928 Book of Common Prayer came into his mind: *"I have done those things that I ought not to have done, and I have not done those things I ought to have done, and there is no help in me."*

Come to think of it, Cletus, the only thing you have done lately that you ought to have done is to keep your hands off the Virgin Princess. You get a small gold star for that.

His meditation on his own guilt and innocence was interrupted when Enrico nudged him. And then he saw that Enrico had not nudged him, and was in fact completely unaware of him. Enrico was weeping.

More than a little awkwardly, Clete put his arm around him and held him comfortingly.

[TEN]
The Ranch House
Estancia San Pedro y San Pablo
Near Pila, Buenos Aires Province
1425 23 December 1942

There was a knock at the door.

"Come in," Clete called. He was lying on the bed.

El Coronel Jorge Guillermo Frade entered the room and stared at Clete without speaking.

"Claudia called the Duarte house," Clete said without getting up, "and arranged for my car to be driven to her estancia. In an unusual manifestation of Argentine efficiency, it was actually sent there. So she's having it brought here. I'll be out of here just as soon as it arrives."

"It's here," Frade said.

Clete rose to his feet. "Thank you," he said. "I'll be on my way."

"Do you think we could have a small talk, as officers and gentlemen?"

"We could have a shot at it. What's on your mind?"

"Enrico, leave us, please," Frade ordered.

"Mi Teniente, should I put your bags in the Buick?"

"Please, Enrico. I'll be right out."

Frade waited until Enrico picked up the bags and left the room. Then he checked to make sure the door was closed, and finally turned to Clete.

"You are planning to leave without greeting your aunt Beatrice and your uncle Humberto?"

"Well, I thought I would avoid a—a what?—a possibly awkward situation."

"I see."

"And the truth is, now that I think about it, blood aside, the two of them don't really feel like my aunt and uncle. They're just two nice people I feel sorry for because they lost their son. I just met them; I hardly know them."

"I had trouble with that too," Frade said.

"With what?"

"Realizing, blood aside, that you are really my son. A flesh-and-blood creature . . . not a dream."

Clete could think of no reply to make.

"After you arrived yesterday," Frade said, "Enrico came to see me. He told me that honor requires that he leave my service."

"I had nothing to do with that," Clete said.

"Enrico left Estancia San Pedro y San Pablo to enlist in the Army shortly before I was to be commissioned. That way he could complete his training by the time I became an officer, and he could be my batman."

"Your what?"

"My personal servant. Officers in the Corps of Marines do not have servants?"

"No, we don't," Clete said, chuckling. "I thought he was a Suboficial Mayor?"

"He was, of course, much more than a servant. As long as I can remember, back to when we were boys on the estancia, he has been my friend. So I saw to it that he became a soldier, not a servant in uniform. He ultimately became a Suboficial Mayor, and a very good one.''

"I understand, I think."

"When I retired from the Army, he retired with me. And when he came to me yesterday and told me he must leave my service, I told him to do what he wished, but that he was never to visit San Pedro y San Pablo again, after today."

"You're a real friend, Dad," Clete said, angrily sarcastic. "I'd hate to think how you treat people you don't like."

His father did not reply, but Clete saw the immense pain in his eyes.

"I'll talk to him, try to patch it up between you," Clete said. "If that's what you want me to do."

"Thank you, but that will be unnecessary," Frade said.

"Your pride, of course, your Argentinean pride, won't permit you to do that, right?"

"I will go to him and beg his pardon. But before that, I wanted to come to you . . ."

"You don't need my permission to talk to Enrico."

". . . to ask your pardon as well, and to tell you that I will do whatever I can to help you against the Germans."

That's a switch. A one-eighty-degree turn. What brought that about?

"Because of what they did to Señora Pellano?"

"Partly, and partly because you are my son and need my help."

I'll be damned, Clete thought as he felt his throat tighten painfully, *he means that.*

"Before the funeral, I called el Almirante de Montoya, the Chief of the Bureau of Internal Security, and told him that the price of your expulsion from Argentina would be the loss of my friendship," Frade said. "He told me I was a fool—and I have known him since we were at the university—but you will not be expelled."

"Thank you," Clete said.

"You are determined to go through with whatever it is you intend to do to the German ship?"

"I intend to carry out my orders."

Frade shook his head, started to say something, stopped, and then said, "Presumably you have a plan?"

Clete's hesitation was evident.

"You don't know if you can trust me?" his father asked. "Is that it?"

Clete's face gave him his answer.

"No matter what you think of me personally, Cletus, I am a man of honor. Would you take my word as an officer and a gentleman that I am prepared to help you?"

I'm not sure.

But my only other option is the vague hope that the destroyer will have radios capable of communicating with Colonel Graham in the States, and that they will give me access to them.

"I don't have a plan," Clete said. And when he saw his father's face, he added, "Really, I don't. I'm not just saying that."

"But I don't understand."

"Harming the *Reine de la Mer* is impossible with what they have given me to work with."

"Which is?"

"A radio expert and an explosives expert. And a small quantity of explosives. Even if we could get to the *Reine de la Mer*—"

"You have explosives?" his father interrupted him. "Where?"

"About twenty pounds, ten kilos. In the Guest House."

"You *had* explosives. If they were in the Guest House, Martín found them. He's very good at his job, and I'm sure he thoroughly searched the house when you were in the hospital. And if he didn't mention to me that he found them, then he has them. He will be cooperative, but only to a point."

"They're there. I checked. I was at the Guest House before I came here."

"Then I'm wrong. El Coronel Martín closed his eyes."

"No. I'm sure he didn't know what he was looking at. It's a new kind of explosive, called C4. You can mold it like putty. What I have looks like pieces of a wooden crate."

"Apparently, you too are very good at your job."

"There is no way to get close to the *Reine de la Mer*. She has floodlights, .50-caliber machine guns, and I think a couple of twenty-millimeter automatic cannon. And even if we somehow could get to her and attach the explosives, I don't think we have enough C4 to do real damage."

His father looked thoughtful, as if considering the problem.

In for a penny, in for a pound. I don't have any other options.

"And that isn't the only problem," Clete went on. "When I tried to explain to the OSS man here, my commanding officer, so to speak . . ."

"Mr. Nestor, of the Banco de Boston," his father said. "El Coronel Martín told me who he is."

Acknowledging that would be admitting he's right, and I don't want to do that. I guess I don't trust him.

". . . when I told him I could see of no way to carry out my orders, I was relieved."

"Relieved?" his father asked, and his face lit up.

"He as much as accused me of cowardice."

"Cowardice?"

"Cowardice."

"But you've already proven your courage. In the war in the Pacific, and at the Guest House."

Clete met his father's eyes and shrugged, then went on:

"The destroyer may have the ability to communicate with the United States. If it does, then I'll try to go aboard. If they will let me use their radio, I'll try to get in touch with the man who sent me down here and give him my side of the story."

"And if that is impossible? I believe the radios of warships are put under a seal when they enter our waters."

"I don't know," Clete said, smiling. "I'm fresh out of clever ideas. I'm determined to have a shot at that damned ship."

His father nodded, as if he had expected that answer. He pursed his lips for a moment, then asked, "Tell me about the destroyer. For one thing, if your government has a destroyer here, and if they are willing to send an OSS team down here . . . why doesn't the destroyer sink the *Reine de la Mer*?"

"I think they don't want to commit an act of war within your waters."

"That's splitting hairs," Frade said. "What's the difference between you destroying this vessel and one of your warships destroying it?"

"None that I can see," Clete said. "I'm going to make that argument again to Colonel Graham when I get in touch with him. *If* I can get in touch with him."

"Who is Graham?"

"Colonel Graham. The officer in overall charge of this mission."

"He's here?"

"In Washington. I hope he's in Washington. The last time I saw him, he was on his way to Australia."

"If he's in Washington, why don't you go there?"

"How?"

"The same way you came here. By Pan American. Do you still have your passport? I can arrange for an exit visa."

"I didn't think about the exit visa, but I called Pan American. They told me they give seats only to Americans who have a priority from the U.S. Embassy. Obviously, they're not going to give me one."

"I know the Pan American–Grace General Manager. I can get you a seat."

"I don't think so, Dad."

"I think so. I own ten percent of the shares in Panagra-Argentina. I'm on the board of directors."

"What's Panagra-Argentina?"

"Panagra stands for Pan American–Grace. It's a partnership between Pan American Airways and Grace Shipping. Panagra is in partnership with an Argentine company, Panagra-Argentina, to operate here."

"Jesus, could you?"

"It will take a few days, but it can be done."

"How can you be so sure?"

"Because Mr. Trippe and Mr. Grace have told Panagra to give me anything I want. You know who those men are?" Juan Trippe was President of Pan American Airways, and William R. Grace was President of Grace Shipping Corporation.

Clete nodded. "Sure. But why did they do that?" he asked, confused. "You can throw a lot of business their way?"

His father looked at him for a long moment, and Clete sensed that he was debating telling him something. Then he smiled, just a little sadly.

"I think it would be reasonable to assume that Señores Trippe and Grace have considered that a President of Argentina could, as you put it, 'throw a lot of business their way.' "

"My God!" Clete asked incredulously, even as he realized his father was telling the truth, "Are you going to be President of Argentina?"

"That was a strong possibility," el Coronel Jorge Guillermo Frade said quietly, "before I realized that I must be involved in your affairs."

"Graham didn't tell me that," Clete said thoughtfully, and then anger swept through him, quickly and bitterly. "But he knew. That sonofabitch knew—of course he knew—and didn't tell me. That devious bastard! He sent me down here to get close to you! It had nothing to do with this goddamned ship!"

"That outburst becomes you. I can't tell you how happy I am to see that you were unaware of such things," el Coronel said.

"But I think the ship was an integral part of his plan."

That surprised Clete. It showed on his face.

"I don't understand . . ."

"Have you considered that it would be in their interest if you had attacked the *Reine de la Mer* and were killed in the process?"

"Jesus Christ!"

"Even if we had remained estranged," Clete's father went on, "you are my son. If the Germans killed you, my honor as well as my heart would demand revenge. I am an influential Argentinean. I may perhaps even become President."

"Goddamn!"

"They had an officer of the Corps of Marines, who proved his courage in battle . . ."

"And they almost hoped I would get killed!"

"Almost?" his father said, dryly sarcastic, and then went on, ". . . and who could be expected to carry out his orders, regardless of the risk."

"It's hard for me to believe that Graham would be capable of that kind of scheme," Clete thought aloud. "I liked him. He's the sort of man you instinctively trust. The sonofabitch!"

"In war, decent men are often forced to do dishonorable things," Frade said. "What went wrong with his plan was he did not take into account your loyalty to your men. You might be willing to give your life, but you would not sacrifice the lives of your men."

"I thought about flying that goddamned Beechcraft right into the sonofabitch," Clete blurted. "But I didn't think it would be any more effective than the lousy twenty pounds of C4 they gave me."

"I am very glad you reached that decision, Cletus," his father said.

Clete looked at him. Tears were running down his father's cheeks. Their eyes met.

"Would it be a great embarrassment to you if I put my arms around you?" el Coronel Jorge Guillermo Frade asked.

"No, Sir," Clete said, his voice breaking. He went to his father and they wrapped their arms around each other.

Finally, they broke apart.

"Well," his father said, "at least we know where things stand."

"Do we? I don't know what the hell to do now. Right now, I am having some very unpatriotic thoughts. If the OSS doesn't really give a damn about the *Reine de la Mer,* why should I?"

His father didn't respond for a long moment, but then said, "Because you have been ordered to destroy it. Your admirable concern for your men doesn't change that. So long as the *Reine de la Mer* is in the Bahía Samborombón, you are obliged to do your best to destroy it. Honor requires that you do anything you can—short of suicide—to carry out your orders."

"You said you would help?"

"I have a suggestion," Frade said. "I will call el Almirante de Montoya again and tell him that I have changed my mind, and that he should expel you from Argentina."

"What good would that do?"

"And then I will get you a seat on the Pan American flight to Miami. You will go to Washington and tell this Colonel Graham to his face . . ."

"Doing that won't—"

"Hear me out."

Clete shrugged.

"You will tell Colonel Graham that I deduced the real reason he assigned this mission to you, and that I had you expelled to save your life. That has the great benefit of being the truth."

"I don't want to be expelled."

"You have no choice in the matter. If you feel that you should, you can tell your Colonel Graham that you are willing to come back secretly to sink the *Reine de la Mer*—you can be put ashore from a U.S. submarine, or come from Brazil via Uruguay. If you return, you will of course have my assistance."

El Coronel let that sink in for a moment, and then went on.

"You have no options, Cletus. Without my assistance, there is no way you can harm the *Reine de la Mer*. And if, for example, you try to hide yourself in Argentina, el Almirante would learn of it, and there would be nothing I could do for you. El Coronel Martín's men, believe me, would find you in a matter of days. You would then be imprisoned. Possibly for a long time. There are a number of people in this country who would like to hold that sword at my throat—the sword of my son in an Argentine prison."

"If I came back, you would help me?" Clete asked.

"I give you my word."

"Why?"

"To try to save your life."

Christ, he's got me. I don't have any other option.

"I think it would be best for you to stay here at the estancia, until your expulsion can be arranged, and until I can get you on the Pan American flight to Miami."

Clete accepted the inevitable.

"I have to go to Buenos Aires," he said. "I have to explain all this to Ettinger and Pelosi."

His father considered that.

"Very well. I think you'll be safe. Enrico will of course go with you, and Martín's Internal Security people will be watching Uncle Guillermo's house."

Clete nodded.

"I'll be all right."

"And I will go to the city too. Perhaps we could even have dinner together or . . ."

"Why not?" Clete chuckled.

Now that the decision had been made, he felt an enormous sense of relief.

It troubled him.

"Can you think of anything else?" his father asked.

No. Not a thing.

Oh, yeah!

Clete smiled. His father looked at him curiously.

"Dad, how would you like to loan me thirteen thousand dollars?"

"Excuse me?"

"I need to borrow thirteen thousand dollars," Clete asked. "Will you loan it to me?"

"Of course. But why?"

"It involves a Miña," Clete said.

"You have become involved with a Miña?" Frade asked, disappointment all over his face.

"One of my men has," Clete said. "And her Argentine boyfriend found out about it, and is being a real bastard to the girl and her family."

"I thought for a moment . . ."

"One of my men, Dad, not me. I can get in enough romantic trouble without paying for it."

"I never took a Miña," Frade announced righteously. "Never. Not even in the long, lonely years."

"Before you met Claudia, you mean?"

His father ignored him. "A man who has to pay a woman is not really a man. I find the custom disgusting."

"Well, this guy, the Argentine, is apparently a real bastard. He co-signed a mortgage, and when he found out that the girl was seeing one of my officers, he told the bank he would no longer guarantee payment."

"I am not surprised. A man who would pay for sex . . ."

Clete dug in his pocket and came out with the notes he took when Tony came to see him at the hospital.

"The mortgage is with the Anglo-Argentine Bank. The father's name is Alberghoni."

"And the man's name?"

Clete shrugged helplessly.

"It will be no problem," he said. "Your uncle Humberto is managing director of the Anglo-Argentine Bank. You and I will go to the library now and have a quiet word with him. And he and I will take personal pleasure in frustrating this man's ungentlemanly behavior. The mortgage will be paid in full by tomorrow."

"Thank you."

"It is my pleasure," el Coronel said. "And now, to restore my relationship with Señora Carzino-Cormano, may I suggest we go see her?"

"*Restore* your relationship?"

"Señora Carzino-Cormano told me that unless I made my peace with you before you left today, she would never forgive me. I think she meant it."

"Your relationship with Claudia is important to you?"

"Obviously."

"Then why don't you marry her?"

"Why I don't marry her is none of your business. How dare you ask a question like that?"

"Because I'm concerned with your welfare," Clete said.

"Are you indeed?" el Coronel replied, and marched out of the room.

XIX

[ONE]
4730 Avenida Libertador
Buenos Aires
1330 24 December 1942

A thunderstorm that threatened most of the way on the drive to Buenos Aires struck minutes before Clete and Enrico arrived at Uncle Guillermo's house. The rain drummed on the Buick's canvas roof and almost overwhelmed the windshield wipers; the thunder and lightning were as awesome as they were in West Texas.

Attired in undershorts and Sullivan's boots, Clete lay with his back propped up against the elaborately carved headboard of Granduncle Guillermo's bed. As he watched the lightning flash on the River Plate, he sipped an early Christmas Eve beer, or a pre-luncheon beer, whatever you want to call it.

He remembered that he also had had a Christmas Eve, pre-luncheon beer the year before, aboard USS *Saratoga*. It had also been raining heavily, he recalled, a sudden rain squall that had come up quickly, and from which he had found shelter under the wing of one of the F2A-3 Brewster Buffaloes lashed to the *Saratoga*'s flight deck.

Schultz, Second Lieutenant Charles A., USMCR, inevitably called "Dutch," had suddenly appeared beside him, his khakis drenched by the rain. He was clutching something lumpy wrapped in a flight suit to his chest, and happily proclaimed, "Who says there's no Santa Claus?"

The lumps turned out to be two quart bottles of Budweiser beer, smuggled aboard at Pearl Harbor in defiance of Navy regulations.

"Merry Christmas, Clete," Dutch had said, handing him one of the bottles. They had pried the tops off on the undercarriage of the Buffalo.

But it was beer, and even warm, proof that there was indeed a Santa Claus, for those who really believed.

"Next year," Dutch had said, raising his bottle in a toast, "Cold beer, at home!"

It didn't turn out that way, did it, Dutch?

The next day, Christmas Day, we flew those outdated god-damned Buffaloes off the Saratoga onto Midway Island. And then we flew them against the Japs. A Buffalo was no match against a Zero. Every goddamned one of us was shot down.

You never will get to go home, will you, Dutch? I got picked up, and you didn't. The Secretary of the Navy regrets to inform you that your son, Second Lieutenant Charles A. Schultz, USMCR . . .

And the circumstances under which I am "at home" are not quite the ones we had in mind when we had that fantasy, are they, Dutch?

But this beer is cold, and this is a marvelously comfortable bed with clean sheets, and when, in the inevitable course of human events, I will have to let the beer out, it will be into a porcelain fixture in a marble floored bathroom, not into a foul smelling opening in a stinking compartment labelled, probably with un-intentional humor, "Officer's Head."

And I am alive, and in one piece, and there is a good deal to be said for that.

At least, so far, I am alive and in one piece.

And, in the sense that I am going to have a little Christmas Eve supper with my father, I am home.

That little supper will probably consist of no more than eight or nine courses, served on fine china and dissected with mono-grammed sterling silver. Last year, it was sort of turkey chop-suey, eaten off a stainless steel tray, with cranberry sauce atop the mashed potatoes. Or was it mashed potatoes dumped over the cranberry sauce?

And if that sounds awful, I wonder what the boys on the 'Canal are having for Christmas this year?

Stop being maudin, Clete, things are getting better.

Without much effort, he thought of two prime examples:

On the way to Buenos Aires, Enrico, literally riding shotgun beside him in the front seat of the Buick, worked out how to meet Pelosi and Ettinger without broadcasting everything they said to one another to Internal Security or the Germans.

"Your problem, mi Teniente, is keeping the clowns and the Germans from hearing you. The clowns will of course be follow-ing you, and them, and they will have telephone surveillance on your line and theirs."

"So what do I do?"

"Mi Teniente, you take them for a ride in your automobile. The clowns will not be able to hear what you say, and it will embarrass them to have to be so obvious about following you."

"Just telephone them and say I'll pick them up?"

"No. Just set a time and place to meet them. The man who brings daily deliveries of *agua mineral,* vegetables, and meat to the house is a friend. He will carry messages safely past the clowns."

"When does he make his next delivery?"

"Starting at three o'clock this afternoon. Three times a day."

"This is Christmas Eve."

"People need food and *agua mineral* on Christmas Eve," Enrico said with a shrug.

"You've got everything laid out, right? You're pretty good at this, Enrico."

"I have learned much from your father, mi Teniente."

And then Clete himself worked out a temporary, partial solution to the problem of the Virgin Princess: At Clete's suggestion, his father agreed to invite the Mallíns and their children to dinner at the big house on Avenida Coronel Díaz in Palermo.

"After Christmas, of course, and before New Year's. As an expression of my gratitude to them for their hospitality when you first arrived."

"Thank you."

"You will be able to see Dorotea before you go to Miami."

"It's nothing like that, Dad," Clete said, aware that he didn't sound at all convincing. "They were just very kind to me."

"I understand completely," his father said, and winked at him, man-to-man. "Get one young, and train her right."

Somehow—he wasn't sure how—he would take the Virgin Princess aside for a few minutes and talk to her. He wasn't sure yet what exactly he would say, but the gist of his words would be that there was a great difference in their ages, that she was really too young to know her own emotions, that while he held her in the highest possible regard, et cetera, et cetera, et cetera.

He would at least have a chance to be with her one last time before he left. That was very important to him.

He was considering that the real, as opposed to the wishful thinking, chances were that somewhere down the pike . . . *If I even come back to Argentina at all, if I survive the war, if she doesn't just dismiss me from her mind when I'm away from Argentina, I might be able tell her how I really feel about her—*

Christ, ask her to marry me! . . . when he heard the whine of the elevator motor, and then the sound of the door sliding open.

He didn't even turn to see who it was. The bad guys stood little chance of getting past Enrico, who had stationed himself and his Remington in an armchair in the foyer. And in any event, bad guys would not take the elevator. It was either Enrico checking on him, or one of the maids, here to clean the bath, make the bed, or do something else useful.

It was much more pleasant to fantasize about the Virgin Princess in a white dress in a church somewhere smiling at him as he lifted her veil and the priest saying, "You may now kiss the bride."

"You bah-stud!" the Virgin Princess said loudly, indignantly, and quite clearly, in perfect Oxford English.

He jerked his head toward the elevator. The Virgin Princess was walking angrily across the room toward him. She was rain-soaked. Her hair hung wetly down her cheeks. Her blouse and skirt were plastered to her body.

"Well, look what the cat dragged in! Been out in the rain, have you, Princess?"

"You despicable bah-stud! I utterly loathe you!"

Clete laughed.

"I have been out of my mind with worry about you!"

And then she was on him. He quickly put his hand up to thwart her obvious intention, which was to slap him. He missed her wrist, and she punched him in the face.

Or, precisely, she connected with his nose.

"Hey, Jesus Christ! Take it easy! That hurt!"

She then slapped him, open-handed, on the head. The blow landed on his ear. It hurt even more than the punch in the nose. When he put his hand to his ear, she punched him in the face again.

He grabbed her. It took much more effort than he expected to hold her hands, then pin her to the bed. During this defensive tactic, she managed to kick his legs, his ankles, and his lower abdomen. She missed the symbol of his gender by no more than an inch.

But finally she was immobile under him.

"You didn't even call me to tell me you weren't dead!" the Virgin Princess said, and tears started down her cheeks. "On Christmas Eve, goddamn you!"

And then he was kissing her.

A minute later, when he felt her go limp, he rolled off her onto his back, breathing very heavily. After a moment he looked at her. Her nipples were clearly visible, standing erect against her rain-sodden blouse and thin brassiere.

He raised his eyes to hers. She was also breathing heavily. Eyes locked with his, she put her hand to her blouse, tore the buttons open, then freed her breasts from the confinement of the brassiere.

He put his mouth on the one closest to him.

"Cletus!" she said. "Oh, Cletus!"

"You were a virgin," he said.

"I wasn't aware it was a sin to be a virgin."

"Oh, for Christ's sake, Princess."

" 'Oh, for Christ's sake, Princess,' " she mocked him, then rolled over on top of him.

"Princess!"

"I wanted to kill you," she said. "I have never been so furious with anyone in my life."

"Princess . . ."

"I thought the first time would be dreadful," she said. "It was actually rather nice."

" 'Rather nice'?"

"Was it nice for you too?"

"Oh, Jesus Christ!"

"Was it?"

"What do you think?" he asked. His hand seemed to find her breast as if it had a mind of its own.

"I don't know what to think, having no experience in this sort of thing to speak of."

He kissed the top of her head and said, "It was very nice, Princess."

"I'm glad," she said.

And then he was kissing her forehead and her eyes and then her mouth again.

The elevator whined.

"Somebody pushed the elevator button."

"So?" she asked, pulling his face to hers again.

"That means somebody is coming up here."

"Don't let them! Not now, Cletus!"

He freed himself, stepped out of the bed, and walked naked to the elevator.

Christ, I didn't even take my boots off!

He looked back at the bed. She was propped up on one elbow.

That has to be the most beautiful female in the world.

"Pull the sheet over you," he ordered.

"Oh, my!" she said, and reached for the sheet.

It was Enrico.

"I didn't think the lady posed a threat, mi Teniente," Enrico said, his eyes carefully raised to the ceiling, "so I let her up."

"What the hell do you want?"

"There is a Norteamericano downstairs, mi Teniente. A coronel."

"A colonel?"

"Si, mi Teniente."

Who the hell can that be? A Norteamericano *colonel?*

"I'll be right down, Enrico."

He walked to the bed. She was prone under a sheet.

"I have to go downstairs a minute."

"I heard. Damn!"

"I'll be right back. We have to talk."

She sat up. The sheet was dislodged.

He kissed her forehead, then walked to the wardrobe, took out his bathrobe and put it on, and walked to the elevator.

"Cletus, if you're wearing that, what am I to wear? My clothing is soaked!" the no-longer-Virgin Princess demanded indignantly from the bed.

"Take one of my shirts," Clete said. "They're in the wardrobe."

He stepped into the elevator beside Enrico. As it started to descend, she was walking naked to the wardrobe.

When he opened the elevator door, he saw the Norteamericano coronel sitting in one of the armchairs in the foyer. He was in civilian clothing. He rose and smiled at Clete.

"Merry Christmas, Tex," Colonel A. F. Graham said, then asked, "Did you really threaten to punch Nestor into next week?"

"What are you doing here?" Clete asked coldly.

"Right now, I'm hoping that you will tell your friend to point that shotgun in another direction."

"I should tell him to blow your ass away with it," Clete said. "You sent me down here hoping that I'd be killed."

Graham stopped smiling.

"That was one of the scenarios, Clete," he said. "But it wasn't mine."

"Bullshit!"

"If were I in your shoes, I suppose I wouldn't believe me either."

"Why the hell should I?"

"Because it happens to be the truth, Clete," Graham said.

Why do I believe him?

"What are you doing down here?" Clete asked.

"Despite the reports to the contrary I've been getting, when I heard the Germans tried to kill you, I decided you must be doing something right, so I decided to come see for myself what's going on down here. I mentioned this at lunch to Newton-Haddle, and he somewhat—"

"Newton-Haddle?" Clete interrupted.

"Colonel Baxter F. Newton-Haddle. That's right. You never met him, did you? He's the Army Colonel who ran the Country Club."

"I don't know him," Clete said coldly.

"Anyway, when I told Newton-Haddle I was coming down here, he told me, in the strictest confidence, that that would interfere with the scenario he and General Donovan were running. And he more or less politely told me to butt out. I went to Donovan to find out what that scenario was. And he had never heard of it, Clete. It was a solo operation cooked up by Newton-Haddle and Nestor."

"You expect me to swallow that whole?"

Graham did not respond directly. "I have my own most likely scenario about how this happened," he said.

"I'll bet you do."

"Nestor got close to Newton-Haddle when he went through the Country Club."

"Nestor went through the Country Club?" Clete interrupted incredulously. It was difficult to imagine the banker running around the woods of Virginia with his face painted black, learning fine points of hand-to-hand combat and throat cutting.

Graham nodded. "And the two Brahmins of course found each other," he said. "Nestor saw in Newton-Haddle a powerful spy-master with access to Donovan—an obvious avenue to enhancing his own career. Newton-Haddle saw in Nestor a chance to prove he could do something more worthy of his talents than teaching people how to stab each other with daggers. When Nestor discovered that your father had an American son, he thought he hit his payload. He would be the man responsible for getting Argentina into the war. So he went to Newton-Haddle with his scenario; and Newton-Haddle thought it was a splendid idea. It wasn't difficult for him to find out where you were, and he managed to bring that information to my attention."

"We're back to question one," Clete said. "Why should I believe that?"

"We're back to answer one," Graham said. "Because it's the truth. If it makes you feel any better, Newton-Haddle is now at Fort Benning, Georgia, teaching knife fighting to parachutists; and Jasper Nestor has by now received a radiogram from the Bank of Boston ordering him home by the first ship. Donovan recruited him from the Bank of Boston. I don't think he'll send him back with a glowing letter of recommendation and appreciation. He—both of them—violated the First and Great Commandment of the OSS: Thou Shalt Not Deceive the Director."

Despite himself, Clete was aware that he was smiling.

"That's the truth, Clete," Graham said. "And essentially all of it."

" 'Essentially all of it'? What's the rest of it?"

"Donovan sent me down here to salvage what can be salvaged. I think he expects me to see that the *Reine de la Mer* is taken out of action."

"She's anchored twenty, twenty-five miles offshore, in the Bay of Samborombón," Clete said. "She's equipped with searchlights, heavy machine guns, almost certainly a couple of 20-mm Bofors automatic cannon, and probably has a five-inch cannon concealed in her superstructure. There's no way anybody can get near her."

He was surprised when he sensed Graham accepting his assessment without question.

"If you were God, how would you take her out?" Graham asked.

"With a B-17 from Brazil. But I'll settle for a TBF from Brazil."

"Both ideas went on the table and were shot down. Politically impossible."

"Colonel, if you can find me a TBF in Brazil, I can refuel it in Uruguay. That'll give me enough range to make the Bay of Samborombón. And then, after I put a torpedo in the *Reine de la Mer,* I'll have enough range to fly over my father's estancia. I'll put the TBF on a heading that will take her out over the Atlantic and bail out." He paused for a moment, thoughtful. Then he went on, "I could also take her back to Uruguay and refuel there again, if people want the TBF back."

"You can fly a TBF? That wasn't in your records."

"And it's official doctrine that a TBF needs a paved runway. And I've flown one a dozen times off Henderson Field, which is a lot rougher than the dirt road we used as a drop zone in Uruguay."

"That may be interesting information for the future. But using a TBF—or any warplane—has been decided against. The political price is considered too high."

"What are the Argentines going to do, bomb Miami?"

"No, but if we bombed a neutral ship in Argentine waters, that would blow your father's chances of becoming President of Argentina out of the water. The President says we can't do that."

"The President?" Clete asked incredulously. "President Roosevelt?"

Graham nodded. "Newton-Haddle went to him—they were at Harvard together—and complained about being relieved. The President called Donovan in for an explanation. The result was a compromise. They sent Newton-Haddle to Fort Benning instead of home, and Donovan was ordered to take out the replenishment ship by any means short of overt act of war. For this mission, an overt act of war has been defined as the use of military aircraft."

"What about the destroyer that's . . ."

"The *Alfred Thomas*? Same answer. No overt act of war within Argentine waters, and no board-and-search of neutral vessels on the high seas."

"Then what?" Clete asked in frustration. "We're ordered to do something; and in the next breath we're told we can't carry out the orders. We're told we can't use anything that would actually get the job done."

"The President is the Commander in Chief," Graham said. "He gives the orders, we obey them. And the only thing he'll let us use now is a submarine, but how we'd use it God only knows . . ."

"I thought submarines were on the forbidden-to-use list too. I asked Nestor why they didn't sink the *Reine de la Mer* in the middle of the Atlantic, and—"

"In the middle of the Atlantic," Graham interrupted, "the *Reine de la Mer* was a peaceful merchant ship flying the flag of a neutral country. It's not against international law for a neutral ship to carry anything it wants to—fuel, torpedoes, anything. It is only when it uses its cargo to the benefit of a belligerent power that it loses its neutral status."

"I don't quite follow that."

"We routinely intercept radio messages between U-boats and the Oberkommando of the Kriegsmarine," Graham explained. "Not without difficulty—a lot of difficulty, I was there—Donovan managed to convince the President that the *Reine de la Mer* has already begun to replenish German U-boats, and in so doing has lost its neutral protection."

"The President says the Navy can send a submarine?"

"Yes. But don't get your hopes up high. We are still forbidden to attack replenishment vessels until we have convincing proof they have supplied at least one submarine, which means they can't be sunk on the high seas on the way here. And so far as sinking the *Reine de la Mer* in Samborombón Bay is concerned, the Navy says submarines can't operate in Samborombón Bay. It's too shallow."

"Submarines operated in some pretty shallow waters off Guadalcanal," Clete thought aloud. "Without *any* charts."

"That's what Admiral Leahy said," Graham said.

"Who?"

"The President's Chief of Staff," Graham said. "I think what we should do now, Clete, is go take a look at the charts."

"Where are we going to get charts?"

"According to the Navy, the *Alfred Thomas* has the most recent charts available."

"She was supposed to arrive here today," Clete said.

"She arrived at 0500 this morning," Graham said.

Clete's eyebrows rose, but he didn't say anything.

"She has, under the Geneva Convention, seventy-two hours to refuel and leave Argentinean waters. If she leaves slowly, maybe she can take soundings of the Bay of Samborombón that will answer the question of whether we can bring a submarine in there or not. A submarine is on the way."

"Jesus!"

"Is there any reason you can't come with me to the *Alfred Thomas*?"

"Give me ten minutes to get dressed."

His conversation with Colonel A. J. Graham, USMCR, so distracted First Lieutenant Cletus H. Frade, USMCR, that he completely forgot the visitor in his apartment. When he returned to his apartment and found the visitor—clad only in one of his shirts, mostly unbuttoned—sitting on his bed combing her hair, he thereupon became so distracted that he completely forgot Colonel Graham was in the foyer, expecting his momentary return. Consequently, Colonel Graham was forced to cool his heels for thirty-five minutes before Lieutenant Frade returned to the foyer, neatly dressed, though bearing on his neck what looked to Colonel Graham like the teeth marks of another human being. This is sometimes called a "love hickey."

[TWO]
Dársena "B"
Puerto de Buenos Aires
1715 24 December 1942

Getting past the Armada Argentina and Policía Federal guards to
Dársena "B"—Wharf "B"—where the USS *Alfred Thomas,*
DD-107, was docked proved considerably easier than getting past
the two U.S. Marines, in dress uniform, stationed on the wharf
barring access to her gangplank.

"I'm sorry, Señores," the Marine buck sergeant said, politely
but firmly, in not bad Spanish, "but the vessel is not open to
visitors."

"It's all right, son," Graham said, producing an ID card. "I'm
Colonel Graham, and this is Lieutenant Frade."

"Sir, I'm sorry, but my orders are that no visitors are allowed
aboard."

"Your orders from whom, Sergeant?"

"From the officer of the deck, Sir," the Marine said, nodding
his head toward an ensign in dress whites standing by the gang-
way.

"Son, you think about this. Who would you rather have pissed
at you? A wet-behind-the-ears ensign or a Marine colonel?"

"If the Colonel will tell the sergeant where he wishes to go
aboard the vessel, Sir, the sergeant will be happy to escort him."

"We're here to see the Captain, Sergeant."

"If the Colonel will follow me, Sir? The Captain is on the
bridge, Sir."

The Marine walked up the gangplank. An ensign in dress
whites and a sailor stood by a table.

"Sir," the Marine barked, "a colonel, United States Marine
Corps, and a lieutenant, United States Marine Corps, request permission to come aboard, Sir."

The Ensign looked baffled, and made no reply.

"You're not considering withholding that permission, are you,
Mister?" Graham asked.

By God, Clete thought admiringly, *that sounded like a Marine
colonel.*

"No, Sir. Permission granted."

Graham stepped onto the deck. The Ensign saluted him. Graham returned the salute, then faced aft and saluted the national
colors.

I don't think you're supposed to do that in civilian clothing, Clete thought. *But what the hell!*

He stepped aboard, saluted the Ensign, and then, facing aft, the national colors. He was surprised at his emotional reaction.

"How may I help the Colonel, Sir?"

"We want to see the Captain," Graham said.

"Sir, the Captain is on the bridge. I will escort you. You may return to your post, Sergeant."

"Aye, aye, Sir."

The Ensign led them to the bridge. A lieutenant commander, in a sleeveless white shirt and shorts, was seated in a nicely upholstered chair mounted on a pedestal, drinking a cup of coffee.

"Sir," the Ensign said, "these officers wish to see you."

"Good morning, Captain. I am Colonel A. F. Graham, USMC," Graham said.

The Captain got out of his chair. "I'm Commander Jernigan," the Captain said. "How may I help you, Sir?"

"Captain, as I understand your orders, you were, Direction of the President, ordered to proceed to Buenos Aires at maximum speed consistent with fuel exhaustion, there to hold yourself prepared to receive further orders, to be delivered by an individual who would identify himself by uttering a certain phrase."

"The Colonel will understand that I cannot comment on a classified order."

"Complete cooperation, Captain."

The Captain smiled.

"That's the phrase. I'm at your disposal, Colonel. What can the *Alfred Thomas* do for you?"

"I chose the phrase." Graham smiled back. "I thought it would remove any possible misunderstanding."

"The orders, Sir, would be hard to misunderstand. What you want, you get."

"Captain, this is Lieutenant Cletus H. Frade, USMCR. He flew Buffaloes at Midway and Wildcats from Guadalcanal. He is down here on a mission of great importance, and our mission is to help him accomplish this. Do you understand?"

"Aye, aye, Sir."

"Is there somewhere we can talk?"

"My cabin, Sir. But in this weather, may I suggest the chart room? My cabin is stifling."

"The chart room is fine," Graham said.

* * *

"Let me recap all this," Graham said. "You can, Captain, as you exit the Río de la Plata estuary, take soundings of Samborombón Bay. But, in your professional judgment, these won't be of much use to the skipper of the . . . What's the name again?"

"The *Devil Fish,* Sir."

". . . of the submarine *Devil Fish,* because the bay is so enormous, and the *Reine de la Mer* can be expected to move every day or so. So we won't know where she is."

"Yes, Sir. I'm sorry, but that's the way I see it. If I had a couple of weeks, I could take soundings of the whole damned bay and come up with some decent charts. But I'll have no more than six or eight hours, and if I start maneuvering all over the bay, it will be damned obvious what I'm doing."

"Sir," Clete asked, "can you find someplace out there, within, say, a fifty-mile circle of the last known sighting of the *Reine de la Mer*—someplace that the sub could more or less easily find, deep enough for her to lie on the bottom?"

"Frade, you probably know more about submarines than I do."

"I know nothing about submarines, Captain, except that I'm glad I don't have to serve on one."

"What are you thinking, Clete?" Graham asked.

"If the Captain can find such a place, and give its location to the skipper of the submarine—"

"That won't be a problem. I've made rendezvous at sea with the *Devil Fish* before," the Captain interrupted.

"Then the sub could move close to the *Reine de la Mer,*" Clete went on, "lie on the bottom, and surface, periscope depth only, at a specified time. If we can establish radio contact with the sub—"

"And we don't know that we can," Graham interrupted.

"If we can get a decent transmitter and a decent receiver from Captain Jernigan, and get it off the ship and to my father's estancia, Ettinger will be able to talk to the submarine. All he'll need is the frequency and the schedule."

"My orders are to give you whatever you ask for," Captain Jernigan said. "But—and this is probably none of my business—how are you going to operate a transmitter without being caught at it? The minute we entered Samborombón Bay, *la Armada Argentina* came aboard from a pilot boat and sealed our radios. I'm sure they monitor the frequencies you'll have to use, and they'll start looking for the transmitter. What do they call it, 'triangulation'?"

"We'll keep moving the transmitter," Clete said. "Ettinger will know how to deal with that. OK, for the sake of argument. We find someplace the sub can hide on the bottom. Captain Jernigan gives the sub the precise location, plus the frequencies, the times, and the codes, when he makes the rendezvous at sea. The sub comes into Samborombón Bay, finds the place it can hide, hides, and then, at the scheduled time, surfaces to periscope depth and tells us she's arrived.

"The next night, I go find the *Reine de la Mer,* radio its position to Ettinger, who relays that position to the sub. The sub goes after the *Reine de la Mer* either submerged or on the surface."

"Again, I don't know a hell of a lot about submarines," Captain Jernigan protested, "but I don't think it's as easy as they make it in the movies for a submarine to hit a ship at night. I think they need more to aim at than running lights."

"It has to be at night," Graham said. "During the day the Argentine Coast Guard patrols the Bay, and the Air Service of the Argentine Army routinely overflies it."

"Ships don't enter the Bay at night?" Captain Jernigan asked.

"The channel-marking buoys are not illuminated," Graham said. "I don't know what they do in an emergency."

"Put a Coast Guardsman on the buoys with a lantern?" Jernigan asked facetiously.

"So I'll get them to light it up, turn their floodlights on," Clete said.

"How?"

"I'll buzz the *Reine de la Mer,*" Clete said. "That'll make them turn their lights on to look for me."

"Or off," Graham said softly. "How about it, Captain? If you were anchored out there and heard an airplane engine, what about the lights?"

"Off," Captain Jernigan said without hesitation. "If they can't see you they can't bomb you."

"Sir, what if you were attacked by an airplane, strafed by a light airplane?" Clete asked. "Even strafed ineffectually," he added.

"What do you mean, 'ineffectually'?" Graham asked.

"Say with a .30-caliber Browning. That's about all I could get into the Beechcraft."

"One plane, even a fighter plane?" Jernigan said. "I'd try to fight. The natural instinct would be to fight."

"And to turn on good floodlights, if you had them, right?"

"Yes," Jernigan agreed.

"OK," Clete said.

"It's occurred to you, no doubt," Graham said, "that if they put their floodlights on you, they will get the Bofors on you seconds later?"

"And if they have their floodlights on, the submarine will have a better target than running lights."

There was no response from anyone.

"Has anybody got a better idea?" Clete said.

"I'm not sure if it's a better idea," Graham said, "but it's another idea. What about a boat? If there was a boat, I'm talking about a small boat, say, twenty-five feet, running around out there."

"The last three guys who tried that disappeared," Clete said. "No way. They would just blow it out of the water. I'll find the ship with the airplane and get them to turn their lights on."

There was silence for a moment, then Graham said, "OK. The first priority is to take the transmitter and the receiver ashore. I'll go to the U.S. Embassy and have them bring them ashore under diplomatic immunity."

"That should be no problem, Sir," Commander Jernigan said. "I have some crates for the Embassy. I'll just crate up some radios and send them ashore with the other diplomatic cargo."

"Clete, what about putting Captain Jernigan's communications officer together with Sergeant Ettinger?"

"That would depend on the communications officer," Clete said without thinking, then added, "Sir, no disrespect intended. But does your communications officer know radios, or is he just filling the billet?"

"I've got a chief radioman who knows all there is to know about radios," Captain Jernigan said.

"Then he's the man, Sir, who should get together with Sergeant Ettinger," Clete said.

"Then that's our first order of business," Graham said. "Getting the Chief in here, telling him what we need, and then getting him ashore to meet Ettinger."

"I think our first order of business is to see my father," Clete said.

Captain Jernigan's eyebrows rose in question, but he didn't put the question in words.

"Do you know where he is?" Graham asked.

"By now, he should be at his house, here in Buenos Aires."

"OK. We'll go face the lion in his den," Graham said. "Captain, you have my authority to make your Chief privy to your orders. When I visit the Embassy, I'll arrange for him to call on the Naval attaché."

[THREE]
1728 Avenida Coronel Díaz
Buenos Aires
2005 24 December 1942

"I will listen to your plans, Colonel," el Coronel Jorge Guillermo Frade said to Colonel A. F. Graham, USMCR, "and you have my word as an officer that they will not go further than this room. But I must tell you, Sir, that I do not share my son's confidence that you are now telling him, or me, the truth."

They were seated around a large table in the library. A silver coffee service had just been delivered, together with a walnut cigar humidor. Having dismissed the servants, el Coronel Frade ceremoniously served the coffee and offered the cigars.

Frade was seated at the head of the table, with Clete and Graham facing each other across it. Enrico had pulled a chair up from another table, and was sitting with the Remington in his lap, five feet behind el Coronel Frade. He had declined coffee, but he now held a large, thick, black cigar in his teeth.

"If I were in your position, mi Coronel, I would feel exactly the same way," Graham said calmly, lighting a cigar.

Frade nodded. "Proceed, Colonel. I will listen."

"A United States submarine, the *Devil Fish*, which has been on patrol off the coast of Africa, has been ordered, at best speed, to rendezvous with the destroyer *Alfred Thomas*, which is here in Buenos Aires. The rendezvous will take place at a point one hundred nautical miles off Punta del Este, Uruguay. Her estimated time of arrival . . ."

Frade held up his hand. Graham stopped.

"Two things, Colonel Graham."

"Sir?"

"I hope you are providing exact details, not details altered sufficiently to be useless in case you don't trust me to keep them within this room."

"You have my word as an officer, mi Coronel, that I am giving you the facts exactly as I know them."

"Then please proceed in Spanish, mi Coronel, so that Suboficial Mayor Rodríguez may hear what you have to say. He has a nose for—to use the delightful phrase I have learned from my son—bullshit."

Graham smiled, and went on in Spanish. "The estimated time of arrival of the *Devil Fish* is 0900 29 December. A U.S. Navy fleet tanker has been ordered from Panama to rendezvous as quickly as possible with the *Devil Fish* on her course from the African coast. Once that rendezvous has been made, and there is some question when or if this can be accomplished, the submarine can proceed without consideration of fuel exhaustion—at full speed, in other words. So her estimated time of arrival may be as much as twenty-four hours sooner. The tanker is faster than the submarine; it will accompany her to Punta del Este and refuel her again there."

"And if the rendezvous proves impossible?"

"Then we fall back to the 0900 29 December arrival time. The submarine can make that time with available fuel on board, and be refueled by the *Alfred Thomas.*"

"You are confident you can accomplish this without the Germans becoming aware of it?"

"So far as we know, mi Coronel, our communications are secure."

"As far as you know," Frade said. "Have you considered, mi Coronel, that vessels of the Armada Argentina will almost certainly accompany your destroyer, for several hundred miles at least, when she sails from Buenos Aires?"

"The *Thomas* will engage in certain maneuvers, mi Coronel, to 'test her engines and steering apparatus,' while she is passing through the Bay of Samborombón."

"Taking soundings?"

"Yes. Following these maneuvers, she will then test her engines in a high-speed run. She is capable of making at least thirty-five knots. The fastest vessel in the Armada Argentina, the Corvette *San Martin,* has a top speed of twenty-four, for limited periods. It will be difficult for the Armada Argentina to accompany the *Thomas* very far."

"I am impressed with your intimate knowledge of the capabilities—or should I say limitations?—of our Armada, mi Coronel." El Coronel Frade nodded, and there was the suggestion of a smile.

"Insofar as getting the radio equipment off your destroyer, mi Coronel," Frade said. "The vessel will be taking aboard foodstuffs, fresh meat, vegetables?"

"Yes, I'm sure it will," Graham said.

"The contract to victual foreign warships has been granted to Servicios de Proveedores Asociados by the Armada Argentina. I doubt very much if the Armada Argentina would question what the people from S.P.A. took off your destroyer after they had delivered the victuals. Or if the S.P.A. refrigerator truck went from the wharf to the Frigorífico del Norte slaughterhouse. And there certainly would be nothing suspicious about a Frigorífico del Norte truck going to Estancia San Pedro y San Pablo."

"Can you arrange that?" Graham asked. "That would be more efficient than funneling the equipment through the Embassy."

"Enrico?" el Coronel asked in turn.

"No problem, mi Coronel. It is done."

"That was easy," Graham said.

"I own S.P.A. and Frigorífico del Norte," Frade said, "and Enrico has many trustworthy friends."

There was a knock at the door, and then it opened. A maid, looking more than a little nervous, stepped inside.

"We require nothing," Frade snapped.

"Mi Coronel, there is a telephone call for Señor Cletus."

Christ! The Virgin Princess. Worried about me.

"It is a Comandante von Wachtstein, Señor Cletus."

Frade looked at Clete, his eyebrows raised in question.

"I'll take it, thank you," Clete said.

Curiosity overwhelmed El Coronel Frade. "The German officer? What does he want?"

"I'm about to find out," Clete said, rising to go to the telephone.

"He is a Luftwaffe officer," he heard his father explain to Colonel Graham. "He accompanied the remains of my nephew, who was killed at Stalingrad, here for burial."

"He's also the fellow who warned me those bastards were going to try to kill me," Clete said as he picked up the telephone. "¿Hola?"

"Señor Frade? This is el Comandante von Wachtstein."

"Comandante?"

"Yes. Somewhat belatedly recognizing my extraordinary talents, the Oberkommando der Luftwaffe has promoted me."

"How wise of them. And how nice to hear your voice, mi *Comandante.*"

"How nice to hear yours, Señor Frade, especially after your unfortunate encounter, which I read about in the newspaper. I called to let you know how pleased I was to hear that you're all right."

"Unfortunately, mi Comandante, Señora Pellano is not all right."

"The world seems to be full of vicious bastards, doesn't it, Señor Frade?"

"It certainly does."

"But life goes on, Señor Frade. I had another reason to call."

"And what was that, mi Comandante?"

"The day after Christmas, I am having luncheon at the Centro Naval. The Officers' Club, downtown. They have honored me with a guest membership."

"How nice for you, mi Comandante."

"It's a pity you are no longer a serving officer, Señor Frade. Perhaps, if you were, your father could arrange such a membership for you. It's a lovely place."

"My father is an amazing man, mi Comandante. Perhaps he can arrange a membership for me anyway. Do I understand you are inviting me to lunch?"

"Actually, it was Señorita Carzino-Cormano's idea. And with your approval, she suggests we ask Señorita Mallín to make it a foursome."

Clete saw that El Coronel Frade and Colonel Graham were shamelessly eavesdropping on the conversation. He smiled warmly at both.

"Under that circumstance, mi Comandante, I gratefully accept your kind invitation."

"Splendid. We will look forward to seeing you at two at the Centro Naval."

"I'll be there, mi Comandante," Clete said, and hung up.

"Isn't your friend sticking his neck way out having lunch with you?" Graham asked.

"Whatever he is, Peter von Wachtstein is no fool," Clete said.

"And don't turn your imagination on, Colonel," Clete continued. "Don't even start to dream up one of your goddamned scenarios if it involves von Wachtstein."

Graham held his hands up in innocence.

"It never entered my mind, Clete."

"Bullshit, Colonel. Just forget it."

"Dorotea?" his father asked.

"Our relationship has changed, Dad."

"Now, Cletus? Under these circumstances?"

"Why not? And anyway, it's out of my control."

His father met his eyes, then smiled and shrugged.

"Shall we continue with the business at hand?" he asked.

[FOUR]
4730 Avenida Libertador
Buenos Aires
1205 25 December 1942

When Chief Radioman Oscar J. Schultz, USN, arrived at the Guest House in the back of a truck, wearing civilian work clothes and carrying a case of mineral water, he looked more than a little dubious about the whole operation.

He set the case of mineral water on the kitchen table and glanced around.

"Mr. Frade?"

Clete nodded.

"I'm Chief Schultz."

"This is Lieutenant Pelosi and Staff Sergeant Ettinger."

"Who's the character with the shotgun? Is he in on this?"

"¿Señor?" Enrico asked.

"Chief Schultz, this is Suboficial Mayor—Sergeant Major—Rodríguez, Argentine Cavalry, Retired," Clete said.

"No shit?" Chief Schultz replied, examined Enrico more carefully, and then offered his hand to him.

"Chief Radioman Schultz, Suboficial Mayor," he said in Spanish. "I'm damned glad to see you here. I was afraid I was going to be the only professional involved in this nutty business."

"Where'd you learn to speak Spanish, Chief?" Clete asked.

"I did two hitches at Cavite, in the Philippines," Schultz replied, winked, and added, "I had what we called a sleeping dictionary."

"Perhaps you would like a beer?" Enrico asked.

"I've never been known to turn one down," Chief Schultz said.

Three bottles of cerveza and a perfectly cooked T-bone steak later, Chief Schultz turned to Staff Sergeant Ettinger.

"You're the radio guy, Sergeant, right?"

Ettinger nodded.

"What do you know about nighttime radiation in the twenty-meter band?"

"A little."

"I don't suppose you've ever heard of a Collins Model Six?"

"I had a look at the schematics," Ettinger said. "It has a very interesting secondary exciter."

"How 'interesting'?"

"The *theory* is interesting," Ettinger said. "But I wondered about harmonic synchronization before crystal temperature stabilization."

"The way it comes from the factory, harmonic synchronization's not worth a shit," Chief Schultz said, the tone of his voice making clear his relief at finding a peer on whom he would not be wasting his valuable time, effort, and knowledge. "Somebody get me a sheet of paper and a pencil, and I'll show you the fix I come up with."

From that point onward, Clete and Tony understood not one word of their conversation. Chief Schultz and Staff Sergeant Ettinger, talking in tongues, filled sheet after sheet of paper with esoteric schematic drawings of radio circuitry and mathematical formulae, determining among other things the optimum length and orientation of the antennae that would be erected on Estancia San Pedro y San Pablo.

At twenty past one, one of the maids came into the kitchen and handed Clete a large, well-sealed envelope, bearing the return address of the Anglo-Argentine Bank on Calle San Martín.

"A messenger brought this for you, Señor Frade," the maid said.

Clete opened the envelope. It contained documents, each stamped, embossed, and signed with flowing signatures in several places by various functionaries. These documents stated that the financial obligations incurred by one Señor Francisco Manuel Alberghoni in connection with the Ristorante Napoli and associated property in the District of Boca, Buenos Aires, to the Anglo-Argentine Bank, S.A., had been satisfied in full by the transfer this date of certain funds to the Anglo-Argentine Bank, S.A., from the funds held by the Anglo-Argentine Bank, S.A., in trust for one Señor Cletus Howell Frade, of Estancia San Pedro y San

Pablo, Pila, Province of Buenos Aires, thus relieving the original guarantor of the aforementioned financial obligations of the aforementioned Señor Alberghoni, one Señor Enrico Mallín, of the Sociedad Mercantil de Importación Productos Petrolíferos, Edificio Kavanagh, Buenos Aires, of any further financial liability of any kind with regard to the Anglo-American Bank, S.A.

"I'll be damned!" Clete said.

"What is that?"

"You owe me thirteen grand, Tony," Clete said. "Your girlfriend's father is off the hook."

"Jesus, Clete," Tony said. "Thanks. Can I see that?"

Clete hesitated, then remembering Tony's very poor Spanish, handed it to him.

"I can't read this," Tony said after a moment.

"Don't bother," Clete said. "Take my word for it."

Tony looked at him curiously.

"Sometimes when you turn over a rock," Clete said, "slimy things crawl out. It's all done, Tony. All you have to do is come up with the thirteen grand to pay me back." He retrieved the stack of paper from Tony and smiled at him.

Tony looked distressed.

"Something else on your mind?" Clete asked. "Don't tell me you've had second thoughts about your lady friend?"

"No," Tony said quickly. "Nothing like that. Jesus! She's really a nice girl, Clete."

"But?"

"Lieutenant, I've been thinking," Tony said uncomfortably.

"Lieutenant"? We're back to "Lieutenant"?

"Second Lieutenants are not expected to think, Lieutenant," Clete said. "I thought you knew that."

"I don't want to sound like a wiseass."

"Out with it, Tony."

"I don't think your idea of making that fucking ship turn on its searchlights by shooting at it with a .30-caliber Browning makes a whole lot of sense, Lieutenant, is what I've been thinking."

Clete made a "come, let's have it" gesture with his hands.

"For one thing, you're going to have to get pretty close to it to hit it, and I don't know how the hell you plan to mount a machine gun in that little airplane, but it's not going to be easy."

That problem is actually Number Two, or maybe even Number One, on my list of Problems to Be Resolved.

"And you said the *Reine de la Mer* has .50s, and probably twenty-millimeter Bofors. All you're going to do is make a god-damned target out of us."

That thought, Lieutenant Pelosi, has run through my mind once or twice.

"Us?" Clete asked.

"I figured I'd be working the machine gun," Tony said.

Actually, I was thinking Enrico would.

Clete said that aloud: "Tony, I thought I'd take Enrico with me. I haven't figured out how to mount a machine gun in the Beechcraft. The .30 Browning may not work. We may have to use a BAR"—a Browning Automatic Rifle, a fully automatic shoulder weapon. "Enrico's a BAR expert; they've had in them in the Argentinean Army for years."

"And what am I supposed to do," Tony asked indignantly, "sit around somewhere with my thumb up my ass while you're off in the airplane?"

"I was thinking you could back up Dave," Clete said, aware that it was a lame reply. "You were going to tell me what you were thinking, Tony."

"Why do we have to fuck around making the ship illuminate herself? Why don't we illuminate the sonofabitch ourselves?"

"How?"

"I don't know. But I figured I'd ask the Chief here. Maybe they've got something like an illuminating round."

"How would we fire it?" Clete asked. "You need a cannon to fire an illuminating round."

"We have Very pistols," Chief Schultz said, turning from the table to join the conversation. Clete was surprised. He'd thought Schultz was deep in technical conversation with Ettinger.

"They're signaling devices," Clete argued. "Flares. The submarine'll need more than that kind of light."

"The five-inch rifles have an illuminating round," Chief Schultz said.

"How does it work?" Tony asked.

"Time fuse. You set it. You fire the round. So many seconds later, a charge in the projectile detonates, shattering the shell casing. That releases the flare, which is on a parachute. I don't know if the timing fuse sets off the magnesium, or what."

"Can you take one of the rounds apart?" Tony asked. "Just get me the parachute and the magnesium flare?"

"I don't see why not," Chief Schultz said. "But you would

need something to light the magnesium. You're thinking of throwing it out of the airplane?''

Tony nodded.

"You'd have to figure out some way to ignite the magnesium,'' Chief Schultz said. "Some kind of a detonator. And it would be touchy. If a magnesium flare went off inside the airplane, you'd really be in the deep shit.''

"I know about detonators,'' Tony said. "What I need to know is whether the temperature and duration of burn of the detonators I have would be enough to set off the magnesium. Or maybe I could somehow rig the Navy detonator, the one inside the shell . . . or maybe set that off with one of my detonators.''

"When I finish with Dave here,'' Chief Schultz said, "coming up with a list of what we need for the transmitter site, I'm going back aboard the *Thomas*. I could ask the Chief Ordnanceman.''

"It would be better if Tony talked to him, Chief,'' Clete said. He looked at Enrico and switched to Spanish. "Without the clowns knowing of it, we'll either have to take el Teniente Pelosi onto and then off the American destroyer, or bring one of Chief Schultz's friends from the destroyer here and then back to the destroyer. Can you do that?''

"Sí, mi Teniente.''

[FIVE]
Centro Naval
Avenida Florida y Avenida Córdoba
Buenos Aires
1415 26 December 1942

Clete had to impatiently circle the block twice before he found a place to park the Buick. As he was putting the roof up, he saw the car which had followed him from Avenida Libertador drive up on the sidewalk at the next intersection. A furious policeman stalked over to it, and didn't seem to be very appeased by the documents the driver showed him.

I wonder if they will follow me into the officers' club, or just hang around outside?

He walked quickly through the entrance of the Centro Naval, then took the wide marble stairs to the second-floor dining room two at a time.

Peter von Wachtstein, Alicia Carzino-Cormano, and Dorotea Mallín were at a table at the far side of the room. Peter rose and waved his hand when he saw Clete.

The Virgin Princess smiled at him. His heart jumped.

"Ah, Señor Frade," von Wachtstein said. "We were growing concerned."

"Sorry to be late, mi Comandante. I had trouble finding a place to park."

"Cletus, we were worried," Dorotea said.

"Nothing to worry about, Princess."

"Princess?" Alicia Carzino-Cormano said. "How sweet!"

No longer the Virgin Princess, but still the Princess, Clete thought as he kissed Dorotea's extended cheek. He walked around the table, kissed Alicia's extended cheek, then sat down beside Dorotea. Her knee immediately found his.

"I took the liberty of ordering champagne," von Wachtstein said. "But perhaps you would prefer corn whiskey?"

"Champagne will be fine, mi Comandante," Clete said.

"I heard Americans prefer corn whiskey to everything else," Peter said.

"And I heard that Germans preferred peppermint schnapps to all else," Clete replied with an equally broad smile.

"You are, I hope, fully recovered from your injuries?" Peter asked. But before Clete could reply, a waiter appeared with a bottle of champagne in a cooler.

"I was not aware that Germans drink champagne in the middle of the day," Clete said. "I would have thought beer."

"Only fighter pilots," Peter said. "Bomber pilots and other lesser mortals drink beer. Or peppermint schnapps."

"Ah ha!"

"I have the feeling that you two are about to say something rude to each other that will ruin our lunch," Alicia said.

"You have no cause for concern, my dear Alicia," Peter said. "I am here under orders to be charming to Señor Frade."

"Under orders, did you say, mi Comandante?" Clete asked.

"The orders of my superior, el Coronel Grüner, the Military Attaché, Señor Frade."

"How extraordinary!" Clete replied as the waiter finished pouring the wine. "I can't imagine why he would do that, mi Comandante."

"I think he wants to make the point that we Germans had

nothing to do with the unfortunate business at your home," Peter said.

Clete felt a shoe push against his. He moved his foot. A moment later he felt Dorotea's leg pressing against the back of his calf. He looked at her, then decided that he did not want to look at her.

"Apparently, your Colonel has not read Shakespeare, mi Comandante."

"Shakespeare?"

" 'Methinks thy Colonel dost protest too much,' " Clete quoted.

"There is another line, Señor Frade," Peter said. "I don't know who wrote it, some Englishman probably. It had to do with the charge of the light brigade at Balaclava: 'Theirs not to reason why, theirs but to ride...' et cetera."

"I believe it ends, 'into the valley of death,' mi Comandante," Clete said.

"I don't like this conversation at all," Alicia said.

"Neither do I," the Princess said.

"This is a friendly conversation, with literary overtones, between friends. Isn't that right, Señor Frade?"

"Absolutely, mi Comandante."

"If you're friends," the Princess said with surprising firmness, "then you should stop that ridiculous 'mi Comandante' and 'Señor Frade' business."

"Princess, there is nothing that makes a brand-new comandante happier than to hear himself called 'Comandante,' " Clete said, laughing.

Alicia gave him a dirty look. Peter laughed.

"We have a saying in the Luftwaffe that there is nothing faster than a brand-new Unterfeldwebel—I think you say 'Corporal'—rushing to his first noncommissioned officers' meeting," Peter said. "But may I suggest we indulge the ladies? May I call you 'Cletus'?"

"You may call me 'Clete,' my friend. It's 'Hans-Peter,' right? Do I call you 'Hans' or 'Peter'?"

"Peter, if you please," von Wachtstein said.

"Tell me, Peter," Clete asked mischievously, "when you were a little boy, did they call you 'Hansel'?"

"Hansel?" the Princess asked.

"As in Hansel and Gretel," Clete explained. "The fairy tale."

"Oh, yes," the Princess said. "Of course."

"Yes, they did," Peter said. "My parents called me Hansel until . . . I guess until I went off to the university. And sometimes afterward."

There was something in his tone, something artificially bright, that made Clete look at him. And then he saw that his eyes were very thoughtful. Sadly thoughtful.

Well, what the hell. He's a long way from home, too, and it's the day after Christmas. And home for him is not somewhere safe like the States. We're bombing hell out of Germany.

"Clete," Peter said, "before I forget it. I don't want to bore the ladies with business, but I need a service, a favor. Could I call on you?"

"I owe you," Clete said. "You've got a blank check, Peter."

"Excuse me?"

"You name it, you've got it, my friend."

"Thank you," Peter said. "I understand."

The Princess's hand patted Clete's leg under the table.

"That's much nicer," she said. "Thank you."

If she doesn't take that hand away, I'm going to get a hard-on to end all hard-ons.

She didn't, and he did. And she moved her hand so there could be absolutely no doubt in his mind that she was aware of his physiological transformation and had a possessive interest in it.

He looked at her face. Total innocence.

"What are you thinking, Clete?" the Princess asked.

"I was thinking we should drink to Peter's promotion," Clete said.

"Oh, yes," the Princess said, and after sort of a farewell squeeze, removed her hand from beneath the table and picked up her champagne glass.

[SIX]
The Embassy of the German Reich
Avenue Córdoba
Buenos Aires, Argentina
1630 26 December 1942

Major Freiherr Hans-Peter von Wachtstein took a long, effusive time to thank Señor Cletus H. Frade and the ladies for the pleasure of their company at luncheon.

He's doing that, Clete reasoned, *so he will be seen. I wonder what the hell kind of a favor he wants? Or whether he is the one who wants the favor, or his Colonel, with some scenario à la Graham and company in mind?*

"And we will be in touch soon, Señor Frade?"

"Like I said, Hansel, anything but my toothbrush or my girl."

"You should stop calling him that," Alicia protested. "He is not a child."

"My friends can call me Hansel," Peter said. "You may call me Hansel, Alicia, if you like."

"All right," Alicia said. "I think I will. I like 'Hansel.' "

Peter shook Clete's hand a second time, then walked through the gate in the fence onto the embassy grounds. A large, brilliant red flag with the Nazi swastika hung limply from a flagpole on the lawn.

"Can we drop you at my father's place, Alicia?" Clete asked, turning to face her in the backseat.

"Please," she said.

"This is not the way to your house," the Princess accused ten minutes later, somewhat indignantly turning on the seat of the Buick to look at him.

"This is the way to your house," Clete said.

"We are not going to your house?"

"No."

"I have somehow offended you?"

"I have some stuff to do."

"I thought you would like my little caress," the Princess said. "All the boys here beg me to do that to them."

"And do you?"

"All the time," she said. "But I will never do it again to you if you don't like it. And besides, we can't go to my house. Mother thinks I am having luncheon and then bridge at the Belgrano Athletic Club. I can't go home before eight-thirty."

"What if your mother finds out you were with me?"

"Mother would understand, I think," she said. "My father . . ."

"He will find out," Clete said. "Then what?"

"I'll tell him we are in love," she said. "But I would rather not face that today. Is there some reason I can't wait at your house, while you do—what was it you said—your 'stuff'?"

"Why don't I drop you at the Belgrano Club?"

"If you did that, my parents would hear about it within the hour. You'll have to think of something else."

I already have. I put you in a taxi and send you to the Club. That would solve the problem neatly.

What the hell. There's nobody in the house.

You're thinking with your dick, pal.

You look for the first taxi and put her in it.

"My father's having you, your whole family, to dinner on Tuesday," he said.

The Princess shrugged.

"I didn't say I didn't like it," he said. "Jesus, I loved it."

The Princess shrugged again.

"If you liked it, we would be going to your house."

The Buick entered a wide, sweeping, tires-screaming U-turn.

"If you think I am going to move next to you and do it now, you are mistaken."

"How about when we get to the house?"

"Perhaps," the Princess said. "Perhaps not."

She resolved her indecision in the affirmative the moment they were in the basement garage of Granduncle Guillermo's house.

First Lieutenant Cletus H. Frade, USMCR, was therefore in an understandable state of excitement when—his arm around the Princess, her arm around him, his face smeared with her lipstick—he walked into the kitchen and found Chief Radioman Oscar J. Schultz, USN, in full dress-white uniform, gold hash marks from sleeve cuff to elbow, gleaming, full-sized medals dangling from his breast, sitting at the table drinking a beer with Suboficial Mayor Enrico Rodríguez, Argentine Cavalry, Retired; Second Lieutenant Anthony J. Pelosi, CE, USAR; and Staff Sergeant David G. Ettinger, AUS, all of whom were in civilian clothing.

"We got a problem, Mr. Frade," Chief Schultz said. "Dave here, it turns out, can't take code worth a shit. And Chief Daniels, the Ordnanceman, says Mr. Pelosi's going to blow hisself up if he tries to take apart an illuminating round by hisself."

"What is he talking about?" the Princess asked. "Darling, who are these people?"

"Jesus, Mr. Frade, I didn't think she'd speak English," Chief Schultz said, sounding genuinely contrite.

"You didn't see the lady, understand?"

"Aye, aye, Sir."

"I'll be with you in a minute," Clete said.

"Take your time, Mr. Frade," Chief Schultz said understandingly.

Clete led the Princess from the dining room to the foyer. As he boarded the elevator, he heard Chief Schultz's somewhat gravelly voice pass on a bit of Naval lore to Lieutenant Pelosi and Staff Sergeant Ettinger.

"Them Marines are all like that. They don't let nothing get between them and their squeezes. Not a goddamn thing."

He had, Clete thought, a certain touch of admiration in his voice.

XX

[ONE]
4730 Avenida Libertador
Buenos Aires
1735 26 December 1942

"Sorry to keep you waiting," Clete said, thirty-five minutes later, as he walked into the kitchen.

Chief Schultz held up both hands in a "no explanation necessary; I know how it is" gesture.

"It's OK, Mr. Frade," he said. He winked, and then offered Clete the bottle of beer he had been in the process of opening.

"No, thank you," Clete said. "Enrico, would you take the Señorita to the Belgrano Athletic Club, please?"

"Sí, mi Teniente."

"Honey!" Clete called.

The Princess marched through the kitchen and out the door to the garage without looking left or right. Enrico followed her.

"Maybe you'd want to rub your neck, Clete," Lieutenant Pelosi said. "Up under the chin."

Clete took out his handkerchief and rubbed his neck, up under the chin. He was not surprised when the handkerchief showed a red smear.

"I didn't think you guys would still be here," he said. "What's going on?"

"Well," Chief Schultz replied, pausing to take a pull at the neck of his beer bottle, "when we went aboard the *Thomas,* the Skipper was waiting for me. The local chiefs are throwing a reception for the chiefs at the Escuela de Guerra Naval"—the School of Naval Warfare—"and he thought it would look strange if I didn't go. I'm the senior chief aboard; they would wonder where I was. So the Skipper and Mr. Pelosi talked it over, and I put on my dress whites, and at half past seven I'm gonna be at the reception."

"What's this about Dave not being able to take code?"

"That's one of the two problems we have, Mr. Frade: Dave

here, and Mr. Pelosi, which is why I come here.''

"Tell me about Dave first," Clete said.

"I'm not very good at Morse code," Ettinger confessed. "I can send maybe ten or twelve words a minute, and I'm even worse at taking it."

"Christ, you are supposed to be a radio expert!" Clete said.

He remembered his own experience with Morse Code training. It was a required course in ground school, and he had a hell of a time acquiring the absolute minimum proficiency: sending and receiving twelve words a minute, with a ninety-percent accuracy.

"He knows *radios*," Chief Schultz came to Ettinger's defense. "With the fixes we worked out, he could probably set up the transmitter without a damn bit of trouble. But working the *Thomas* and the *Devil Fish*? With his hand? Forget it."

"Explain that to me," Clete said.

"You'll be using one of the Contingency Codes," Chief Schultz said. "There's maybe a dozen of them in the Captain's safe. Just for some screwy operation like this one. They're all numbers. Numbers, for somebody like Dave, is the hardest to transmit and receive. And you get a couple of numbers wrong, maybe just one number wrong, you're all fucked up. The codes are numerical nonrandom sequential, you know what I mean? There's phase shift built in . . .''

Clete held up his hand.

"I haven't the faintest idea what you're talking about, Chief."

Chief Schultz did not seem at all surprised.

"Take my word for it, Mr. Frade," he said. "What you need with codes like this is an operator with a pretty good hand, thirty-five, forty words a minute, with a zero error rate."

"Like you, for example, Chief?"

"That's what I was thinking, Mr. Frade," Schultz said. "I wouldn't be the first sailor in the history of the Navy to get hooked up with some local lollypop and miss his ship . . ." He stopped. "I didn't mean nothing by that, Mr. Frade. I could tell right off that the one you had in here was a nice girl."

"No offense taken, Chief," Clete said.

"And, Dave told me something about the walkie-talkies he's been working on," Chief Schultz went on quickly, obviously relieved that he had gotten himself off the lollypop hook. "I think we can probably rig them, work on them a little more, so that we can have our own air-to-ground link."

"What?" Clete interrupted.

"You use the aircraft radios, Mr. Frade," Chief Schultz explained patiently. "There's sure to be someone monitoring those frequencies. And you'll be using voice . . ."

"I didn't think of that," Clete said.

"And as far as communicating with the submarine, Clete," Ettinger interjected, "the longer we're on the air, the more time the Argentines will have to triangulate the transmitter. We'll be on three or four times as long if I try to key code than if the Chief does it."

"How does that work?" Clete asked.

"Two, preferably three receivers with directional antennae," Ettinger explained. "They know their precise location on a map. They get a bearing on the transmitter from their receivers. They draw straight lines. Where the lines intercept, there's the transmitter. Very simple. We need the Chief."

"What happens to a sailor, Chief, who gets hooked up with a local lollypop and misses his ship?"

"In the States, or someplace like Cavite in the Philippines, Guantánamo, someplace where there's a Navy shore installation, they toss them in the brig with lost time."

"What's lost time?"

"They count from the time you miss the ship until you get back aboard as lost time. You don't get paid for it, they add it to the end of your enlistment, and the next time you get paid, they deduct the cost of your rations. Depending on the skipper, you get captain's mast or a court-martial."

"You really wouldn't be jumping ship," Clete said. "That would be for public consumption, that's all."

"I figured that."

"When this is over, you could be placed in the custody of the Naval Attaché, maybe, until we could get you back to your ship," Clete said. "Let me think about this, Chief. I'll have to ask my boss, too."

"We don't have much time, Mr. Frade."

"I know. Now tell me about this Ordnanceman—Chief Daniels, you said?"

"Well, he don't know shit about what's going on here. All he knows is that I brung Mr. Pelosi on board. And I told him that this guy that's wearing butcher clothes with blood all over them is an Army officer, and that he needs to know about taking a five-inch illuminating-round shell apart, and to keep his mouth shut."

"I didn't know how much I was authorized to tell him about

why I needed the flares and parachutes,'' Tony Pelosi explained.

"So you told him nothing?'' Clete asked.

Tony nodded.

"So what happened?''

"Chief Daniels,'' Chief Schultz answered for him, "said Mr. Pelosi is going to blow hisself up if he tries taking one of them rounds apart.''

"Tony?''

"I know explosives. No problem.''

"With respect, Mr. Pelosi,'' Chief Schultz said, "you don't know diddly-shit about Naval Ordnance.''

Clete looked at Schultz. The old Chief was obviously right.

"Chief, do you think Chief Daniels could be talked into missing the ship too?''

"I don't know, Mr. Frade. Maybe, if he knew what this screwy operation is supposed to be all about.''

"You think you or Mr. Pelosi should have told him?''

"No. He's not cleared. Shit, the Skipper had ants in his pants when he told me about it, and I already knew, 'cause I decoded the Direction of the President order. That's a pretty heavy security classification.''

"When are you going to see Chief Daniels?''

"At the Chief's Reception.''

"You have my authority, Chief, to inform Chief Daniels of the nature of this mission, and then to ask him if that changes his mind, under the circumstances, about the risk of Lieutenant Pelosi working on the five-inch rounds. If he still thinks Mr. Pelosi can't handle it, approach him about missing the ship. Tell him not to worry about any real charges being placed against him.''

"You have that kind of authority, Mr. Frade?''

Do I?

"Tell the Captain that we will require as many five-inch illuminating rounds as Mr. Pelosi thinks we'll need, plus some spares for testing,'' Clete said, hoping his voice reflected more confidence than he felt. "When Enrico comes back, we'll decide how to get them, and you, and maybe Chief Daniels from here to Estancia San Pedro y San Pablo.''

"Aye, aye, Sir,'' Chief Schultz said.

[TWO]
Bureau of Internal Security
Ministry of Defense
Edificio Libertador
Avenida Paseo Colón
Buenos Aires
0905 28 December 1942

"The American battleship *Thomas* sailed at three-thirty P.M. yesterday, mi Coronel," el Comandante Carlos Habanzo reported, reading from a manila folder. "It dropped the Armada Argentine pilot—"

"A question of precise terminology, Habanzo," el Teniente Coronel Bernardo Martín interrupted.

"¿Sí, mi Coronel?"

"While the *Thomas* is in fact a battleship, a warship, it is not a *battleship,* but a destroyer. A battleship is much larger. You remember the *Graf Spee*?"

"Of course, mi Coronel."

"The *Graf Spee* was much larger than the American destroyer *Thomas,* no?"

"It was enormous, mi Coronel."

"The *Graf Spee,* Habanzo, was a battleship. It was a warship and a battleship."

"I understand, mi Coronel."

"Actually, it was a 'pocket battleship,' " Martín said, "implying that it was not quite as large or as powerful as other warships called battleships."

"I see, mi Coronel."

"For your general fund of naval information, Habanzo, there are 'battleships'; then, somewhat smaller, 'cruisers'; then, smaller still, 'destroyers'; and finally, generally speaking, 'corvettes,' which are even smaller than destroyers. The vessel you are talking about, Habanzo, is a United States warship, the destroyer *Thomas.*"

"I understand the distinction now, mi Coronel," Habanzo said. "Thank you."

"Proceed."

"The American *destroyer,* the *Thomas,* sailed at three-thirty P.M. yesterday, dropped the Armada Argentina pilot immediately outside the port, then proceeded down the Río de la Plata accompanied by the Armada Argentina battleship—'' He stopped and quickly corrected himself: *"Warship,* the corvette *San Martín.* Upon entering the upper limits of Samborombón Bay, the destroyer engaged in a series of slow-speed maneuvers, the purpose of which is not clear . . .''

I don't suppose the notion that they were taking soundings of the Bay ever entered your mind; but since I am not in a mood to deliver another lecture, "The Importance of Accurate Charts to Naval Operations," I will let that pass without comment.

''. . . these maneuvers lasting until the lower limits of Samborombón Bay, and thus Argentinean waters, were reached. Whereupon, the American *destroyer* headed on a due east course into the Atlantic Ocean at a high rate of speed. The corvette *San Martín* lost sight of her approximately thirty minutes later.''

Which means what? That the American Captain wanted to rub in the face of the Captain of the San Martín *the overall technical superiority of a U.S. Navy destroyer over an Armada Argentina corvette? Or that he didn't wish the* San Martín *to guess which course he assumed when he reached the Atlantic Ocean? Or that he had a schedule to keep, a rendezvous with another vessel?*

"Habanzo, I presume the Armada was monitoring the radio frequencies the American warship was likely to use?''

"Of course, mi Coronel.''

"And did the American warship use its radios?''

"Twice, mi Coronel. First, there was a message to the Captain of the *San Martín,* just before he left Argentinean waters. I have it here.''

He handed Martín a sheet of typewriter paper:

```
FROM: CAPTAIN USS ALFRED THOMAS DD-107
TO: CAPTAIN ARMADA ARGENTINA VESSEL SAN
MARTIN
THANK YOU FOR YOUR ASSISTANCE, COURTESY AND
COOPERATION.
COME SEE US SOMETIME
JERNIGAN, LIEUTENANT COMMANDER, USN
```

"And shortly after they began to move at a high rate of speed, there was another message,'' Habanzo reported, handing Martín another sheet of typewriter paper.

```
OPERATIONAL IMMEDIATE
FROM: USS ALFRED THOMAS DD-107
TO: CHIEF OF NAVAL OPERATIONS WASHDC
ALL RECEIVING USN VESSELS AND SHORE STATIONS
TO RELAY
USS ALFRED THOMAS DD-107 LEFT ARGENTINE
WATERS 0125 GREENWICH 28DEC42. RECEIVED
COMPLETE COOPERATION IN ARGENTINA.
PROCEEDING.
JERNIGAN, LTCOM USN COMMANDING
```

This was sent in the clear. As a courtesy? Or because they wanted to lull us into thinking that they have no other intentions in this area?

"Was there anything else of interest, Habanzo?"

El Teniente Coronel Habanzo smiled.

"Some of the destroyer's men found Argentina, or perhaps Argentinean woman, impossible to leave, mi Coronel."

"What, precisely, does that mean, Habanzo?"

"Several of the destroyer's sailors missed the sailing of their ship, mi Coronel," Habanzo said. "Just before the pilot left the vessel, the Captain gave their names to the pilot, together with a letter to the American Ambassador, asking him to inform the proper Argentine authorities, and to arrange for the men to be held in custody when they finally turn up."

"Let's see the names," Martín said.

There were three names on the list: Chief Radioman Oscar J. Schultz, USN; Chief Ordnanceman Kenneth B. Daniels, USN; and Seaman Second Class Horace K. Williams, USNR.

"We have no idea where these people are?"

"I have checked with the various police agencies, mi Coronel. No."

"No idea at all?"

"The Chief Petty Officers attended a reception given for them at the Escuela de Guerra Naval, mi Coronel. They were last seen there entering a taxi, presumably to return to their ship."

Martín turned in his chair and took out his English-Spanish dictionary and looked up the word "ordnance." He found what he expected to find, but it never hurt to be sure.

"Habanzo, I want you to meet with el Coronel Savia-Gonzalez and tell him that I consider this a matter of the greatest importance. I want the Policía Federal to find these sailors, if it means they have to visit every brothel in Buenos Aires, every bar, and the residence of every woman who has a reputation for not keeping her knees together in the presence of an American dollar bill."

"Sí, mi Coronel. You suspect they missed their ship on purpose, mi Coronel?"

"I do not know that, of course, Habanzo, but I think we should err on the side of caution, don't you?"

"Of course, mi Coronel."

"Assign as many of our men as you think appropriate to assist the Policía Federal, Habanzo."

"Sí, mi Coronel."

"And I am to be notified, no matter the hour, when any one of them is located."

"Sí, mi Coronel."

By now, Martín thought, *all three of these American sailors are at Estancia San Pedro y San Pablo, doing for young Frade and his men whatever they are unable to do by themselves.*

And Señor A. F. Graham will doubtless be there too. That "Vice-President of Howell Petroleum"—according to his visa and passport—who has not once visited the offices of Sociedad Mercantil de Importación Productos Petrolíferos. But who has visited both the American Embassy and the Destroyer Thomas, *where he was saluted by the Officer of the Deck as he went aboard. And who was last seen in el Coronel Frade's Buick station wagon on the road to Pila and Estancia San Pedro y San Pablo.*

But no one will be able to accuse me of closing my eyes if the sailors who "missed their ship" are caught trying to sink the Reine de la Mer—*possibly by affixing a mine to her hull; a chief ordnanceman works with explosives—or if they disappear after doing something else in violation of Argentine neutrality; or if such an act causes one or more of their bodies to wash up on the beach. I might be looking in the wrong direction, possibly, but not closing my eyes.*

"That will be all, Habanzo. The sooner we find these sailors, and find out what they're up to, the better."

"Sí, mi Coronel."

[THREE]
Estancia San Pedro y San Pablo
Near Pila, Buenos Aires Province
1315 29 December 1942

Second Lieutenant Anthony J. Pelosi, CE, AUS, was alone when he drove a Ford Model T pickup truck up to the ranch house.

First Lieutenant Cletus H. Frade, USMCR, Colonel A. J. Graham, USMCR, Suboficial Mayor Enrico Rodríguez, Argentine Cavalry, Retired, and Staff Sergeant David G. Ettinger, USAR, were sitting on the verandah.

"That truck is older than he is," Colonel Graham observed.

"Where's Chief Daniels?" Clete asked when Tony walked onto the verandah.

"Taking five-inch rounds apart."

"Still? How many flare assemblies will we need?" Clete asked.

"Twenty-four," Tony replied, his tone of voice suggesting he was puzzled by the question. That number was agreed to after much discussion and a few practical experiments, and Clete knew that.

"How many do we have? Now?"

"We had eighteen, maybe nineteen this morning, that we can trust."

"How long does it take to take five or six more apart?"

"That depends on who's doing it. Chief Daniels is taking his time. He doesn't like the look of the explosive charge," Tony said. "The goddamned shells were loaded in 1935, can you believe that?"

"The powder's old?" Graham asked.

"Yeah, and it's sort of like TNT, which is trinitrotoluene. It gets unstable if it settles—the nitro sort of leaks out of the fuller's earth—and then you've got nitroglycerin, which is unstable as hell."

"Out of the what?" Clete asked.

"Think of dirt mixed with sand," Tony explained. "This is special stuff. I don't know what the Navy calls theirs; but in commercial TNT, it's fuller's earth. It's uniformly porous, so it absorbs the nitroglycerin evenly. You understand?"

Clete nodded.

"OK. That makes it stable. And when it burns, it burns uniformly. So when it's improperly stored—in too much heat, for example; or for too long, like these shells, loaded seven years ago—the nitro seeps out, and you have nitroglycerin again."

"And you didn't think you could help Chief Daniels?" Colonel Graham asked.

Tony didn't like the question.

"Yes, Sir, I could have helped him. But he said there was no point in both of us getting blown up; and he ran me off."

"You're an officer," Graham said, not pleasantly. "Daniels is a chief."

"Just a minute, Colonel!" Clete protested angrily. "You're talking to somebody who was willing to make his own magnetic mine and stick it on the goddamned *Reine de la Mer*."

Graham looked coldly at Clete, then said, "No offense, Pelosi."

Pelosi, perhaps encouraged by Clete's defense, had a reply of his own.

"The way it works when you're fucking around with high explosives, Colonel, when you have a fuck-up like this one, is make the guy responsible fix it. The Navy fucked these shells up, let a sailor fix them. If he blows himself up, don't worry. If I have to, I can go into those ancient shells and get out what I need, and I know I won't blow myself up."

"Señor Cletus," the housekeeper announced behind him. "If it is convenient, luncheon is served."

"Saved by the bell, Colonel," Clete said.

"You look as if you belong there, Clete," Colonel Graham said a minute or so after they took their seats at the dining room table.

"Excuse me?"

"At the head of the table, in the Royal Chair, approving the wine."

What is he trying to do, charm me?

"Do I?"

"Have you ever considered that it will be yours one day—the Royal Chair, the whole estancia?"

"No, as a matter of fact, I haven't."

"The law is quite clear. Unless your father marries, when he dies, it's yours—lock, stock, and barrel."

"Is that so?"

"You're the only child. They consider you an Argentine national. That's it."

"How will that Argentine national business affect me if they find out I helped sink the *Reine de la Mer*?''

"Interesting question," Graham said matter-of-factly. "I don't know." He looked at Clete and smiled. "Don't get caught."

The housekeeper brought in a telephone, set it on the table beside Clete, and then plugged it into the wall. She then took the handset from the cradle, handed it to Clete, and announced, "El Coronel, Señor Cletus."

"Cletus? This is your father."

"Hola, Papá," Clete said, smiling.

"Papá?" el Coronel repeated incredulously, then went on: "The reason I called, Cletus, is about tonight."

Tonight? What the hell is he talking about?

"I wanted to make sure you asked Señor Graham to join us, in case you have not already done so."

Jesus, I asked him to have the Princess and her family to dinner. And that's tonight.

"I just about forgot about tonight, to tell you the truth."

There was ample justification for forgetting a dinner. A hell of a lot was going on at the estancia. There was far more involved in setting things up—*secretly*—than Clete expected when he started.

Setting up a high-powered radio transmitter and receiving station, Clete learned, was not simply a matter of erecting a couple of towers and stringing a piece of wire between them.

To begin with, there was no topographical map of the estancia and its surrounding areas, something that Chief Schultz considered a necessity for locating the transmitter site.

In the absence of a good map, finding a transmitter site entailed several hour-long flights in the Beechcraft, mostly at fifty feet off the ground, so that Schultz could find suitable high ground. They found several possibilities, but these had to be narrowed down, taking into account that the site had to be easily accessible to transport. That was because the material to erect the towers, a gasoline generator to power the radios, the radios themselves, and a small building to house everything had to be transported there. And then there had to be an emergency exit route to move the radios quickly away, in case of an invasion by Argentines who had triangulated the antenna location.

They'd have ample warning of such an invasion. There already was an in-place system of what the Marine Corps would call perimeter patrols. Every possible access route to the interior of Estancia San Pedro y San Pablo was watched around the clock by gauchos working (and sleeping) on the pampas, or else by the proprietors of small *cantinas* (small general stores which also serve food) and *pulperías* (male-only bars). These businesses operated at the pleasure of el Coronel Frade; they were happy to keep him advised of strangers.

The warning system had to do with Clete's father's involvement with the Grupo de Oficiales Unidos, which in turn had something to do with what his father said about deposing the current President of Argentina. His father and his G.O.U. associates obviously didn't want people snooping around Estancia San Pedro y San Pablo. Hence the in-place perimeter security operation.

There was no way to avoid, however, having the takeoffs and landings of the Beechcraft witnessed by a very curious el Capitán Gonzalo Delgano, Argentine Army Air Service, Retired, and other members of what Clete came to think of as the San Pedro y San Pablo Air Force. In addition to the Beechcraft, there were five Piper Cubs based at the estancia. Three belonged to el Coronel, and two to Señora Carzino-Cormano. These were for use on her estancia, but they were based for convenience at Estancia San Pedro y San Pablo.

Delgano and the other pilots lived on the estancia in what amounted to a small village not far from the ranch house. The village housed the estancia's professional staff: the estancia manager; a doctor; a veterinarian; the schoolmaster; a resident engineer, and so on.

"They are my people; they can be trusted to do what they are told without asking questions," Clete's father told him when that question came up during a meeting with Graham.

Apparently operating on the theory that if orders came via Suboficial Mayor Rodríguez they came from el Coronel, the estancia manager and the resident engineer provided anything asked of them without argument or question. Delgano was not so agreeable. Probably because he regarded the Beechcraft as his personal property before the arrival of el Coronel's son from the Estados Unidos, he was visibly petulant when Clete politely told him he would not need his services to fly the Beech.

But when the petulance was replaced by a suspicious anxiety to be as helpful as possible, Clete and Graham decided that whether Delgano could be completely trusted or not, a little deception seemed called for when it came time to make the in-flight tests of Tony's and Chief Daniels's flares.

The tests were conducted in two phases: First they used inert charges (the magnesium of the flares replaced with sand)—to test the opening of the parachute and the timing of Tony's homemade detonating devices. And finally they tried fully functioning flares.

Dropping them required removing the door of the Beechcraft. Unfortunately, this could not be done in flight. And it couldn't be done at the estancia's airstrip, either: Clete and Graham knew that Delgano's curiosity—as would their own, in similar circumstances—would shift into high gear if he saw them taking the door off, loading mysterious packages into the plane, and then taking off.

The solution they came up with was to use a landing strip—a straight stretch of dirt road with a wind sock—in a remote corner of Señora Carzino-Cormano's Estancia Santa Catharina. They sent Tony there in the Buick with the flares. Then they flew the Beech there with Chief Daniels as a passenger. They took off the door, loaded the flares, went up and dropped them, landed on the dirt strip to drop Tony off and put the door back on, and then flew back to the field at Estancia San Pedro y San Pablo

When they were in the air over Estancia Santa Catharina, Capitán Delgano twice "happened" to be making a routine flight in one of the estancia's Piper Cubs. But the Beechcraft was so much faster than a Cub, losing him was no problem.

Neither Graham nor Clete was happy with el Coronel's confidence in el Capitán Delgano, but there was nothing they could do about it.

"And if you forgot dinner with the Mallíns," el Coronel said, sounding annoyed, "it would follow that you forgot to ask Señor Graham for the pleasure of his company. I think that good manners requires that you—we—do so."

Why is it important to my father that Graham come to dinner? Because he wants a report of our activities out here, and he wants to be able to look at Graham's face when he delivers the report.

"Señor Graham is here with me. We're having lunch. Hold on a minute and I'll ask him if he is free to accept your kind invitation."

"Tell him that I would consider it a great favor."

Clete put his hand over the telephone receiver, then changed his mind.

"It is my father, mi Coronel," he said in Spanish, loudly enough for his father to hear. "My father asks me to tell you that he would consider it a great favor if you would take dinner with us tonight in Buenos Aires."

Also in Spanish, Graham replied, loud enough to be heard over the telephone: "Please tell your father that I would be delighted to accept his kind invitation."

"Papá," Clete said, "Señor Graham says he would be honored to accept your kind invitation."

"I heard, and I don't think you are amusing," el Coronel Frade said. Then he added, "Early. Nine-thirty," and hung up.

"Mi Coronel," Clete said. "Mi Papá, el Coronel . . ."

"I heard, and I don't think you're amusing either. What's this dinner all about?"

"He's having the Mallíns to dinner, to thank them for putting me up when I first got here."

"Mallín, as in Sociedad Mercantil de Importación de Productos Petrolíferos?"

Clete nodded.

"I should have gone to see Mallín, and I didn't," Graham said. "There might be questions about that. Do you think your father thought of that?"

"I think Papá wants to know what's been going on out here."

"That, too, certainly. Well, I suggest we finish our lunch, then go see Chief Schultz, tell him we're going into town, and then go."

"Dinner isn't until nine-thirty."

"I will pay a call on Señor Mallín before I meet him socially tonight," Graham said.

"Schultz is at the transmitter site. We'll have to drive a Model T out there—the Buick would get stuck—and then come back here for the Buick."

"OK," Graham said. "I just want to make sure that Schultz is on schedule."

Chief Radioman Oscar J. Schultz walked up to the Model T sedan at the transmitter site. He was wearing the familiar strained smile of a Chief who knows what he's doing when he sees the brass, who cannot find their asses with both hands, coming to inspect his work.

As they bounced over the pampas in the Model T, it was difficult to pick him out from among the twenty-odd gauchos working in the area. He was dressed as they were, in a flowing shirt, billowing black trousers drawn together at the tops of his boots, a wide leather belt around his waist (complete to a menacing-looking knife with a foot-long blade), and a large, floppy beret on his head.

"You really ought to learn how to ride, Chief," Graham said. "You're already in uniform."

"The Colonel, Sir, is dressed as if he and Mr. Frade are going somewhere," Schultz replied, not amused.

He and Chief Daniels had arrived at Estancia San Pedro y San Pablo in their dress-white uniforms. The gauchos' clothing was the only solution to the clothing problem. Chief Schultz didn't mind much—Clete observed him examining himself in a mirror with approval. But Chief Daniels was uncomfortable in the gaucho costume; he was in fact heard mentioning to Chief Schultz that they both looked like Mexican pimps.

On the other hand, while there were only a few actions that Chief Radioman Oscar J. Schultz, USN, was unwilling to undertake in the service of his country, high on that short list was approaching closer to large animals—such as horses or cattle—than was absolutely necessary. That he might actually climb on a horse and use it as a means of transportation was absolutely out of the question.

Enrico solved that problem by obtaining for him the keys to one of the estancia's dozen or so ancient, but perfectly maintained Model T pickups from the estancia manager. They were nearly as good off-the-road, or through-the-mud, as a jeep.

"We're going into Buenos Aires for dinner, Chief," Graham said to Schultz. "We'll be back in the morning. You have things under control here? You need anything from the city?"

"I'm going to hang the antennae in the morning," Schultz answered. "We've got everything we need. Maybe, with a little luck, we can get on the air tomorrow afternoon. What's going on in Buenos Aires?"

"I think Mr. Frade's father wants to know what we're doing out here," Graham said.

"With you two gone, that'll mean only Ettinger and me are left who speak Spanish," Chief Schultz said.

"That'll pose a problem?"

"It will if Enrico goes with you."

"He and Mr. Frade are like Siamese twins, but if you think it's important, Chief . . ."

"He's the only guy around here who knows how to make these people jump, Colonel."

Ten minutes later, a visibly reluctant Suboficial Mayor Rodríguez—having been convinced that he could contribute to killing Germans by remaining at the estancia to help Chiefs Daniels and Schultz and Staff Sergeant Ettinger—handed his Remington Model 11 to Colonel A. F. Graham.

"With respect, mi Coronel, be very alert."

"You have my word of honor, Suboficial Mayor," Graham replied solemnly.

"I will pray for God to protect you."

When they returned to the ranch house to pick up the Buick, el Capitán Delgano, attired in a natty suit, was waiting for them on the verandah with a suitcase. So was Second Lieutenant Anthony J. Pelosi, wearing a dress shirt with the sleeves rolled up. His seersucker jacket was lying on the verandah rail.

Delgano walked off the verandah and was approaching the Buick when Clete got there.

"Señor Cletus," he said. "I overheard the housekeeper say you and Señor Graham are going to Buenos Aires. I wondered if I could join you."

"It would be my pleasure, mi Capitán," Clete said.

Delgano turned and started quickly toward the verandah to retrieve his bag. Tony picked up his coat and walked to the car.

"I wonder," Graham said softly, "what el Capitán's plans are in Buenos Aires."

"I couldn't tell him no, could I?"

Graham shook his head.

"Lieutenant," Tony said. "I checked with Daniels. He'll have twenty-four flares and a couple of spares in an hour or so. Is there any reason I couldn't go into Buenos Aires with you?"

"I'm not so sure that's a good idea, Pelosi," Graham said.

"The condemned man wants a last meal—a last Italian meal? Peppers and sausage, maybe?" Clete replied.

"I was thinking of maybe some veal parmigiana," Tony said, smiling shyly.

After a long moment, Graham shrugged.

"I left that damned shotgun in the Model T," he remembered. "What do I do with it?"

"I think you better bring it with you, mi Coronel," Clete said. "I wouldn't want to be you if Enrico came here and found it."

Delgano came up with his suitcase.

"Put it in the trunk, mi Capitán," Clete said. "Get in, Tony."

[FOUR]
Ristorante Napoli
La Boca, Buenos Aires
1815 29 December 1942

"They serve pretty good food in there, Tony?" First Lieutenant
Cletus H. Frade, USMCR, asked of Second Lieutenant Anthony
J. Pelosi as Tony crawled out of the backseat of the Buick.

"As a matter of fact, it's pretty good," Tony replied.

"Well, eat a lot. And don't complain about the prices. I want
them to be successful. They owe me money."

"They don't owe you the money, I owe you the money," Tony
said, and then changed the subject. "How are we going to get
together?"

"If you think you'll be through *dinner* by then, I'll pick you
up at your apartment at eight in the morning."

"Very funny," Tony said, nodded at Graham, and walked into
the restaurant.

"What's that all about?" Graham asked as Clete pulled away
from the curb.

"True love. Tony met a girl. An Italian girl. Her father owns
that restaurant."

"And the crack about the money?"

"*That's* personal."

"It would have been better if you weren't so considerate of
his love life," Graham said. "I don't think Internal Security is
going to pick you up—or me—and take us someplace to work
us over with a rubber hose, but I'm not so sure about Pelosi."

Clete looked at him but didn't reply.

"At least we got rid of el Capitán Delgano before we dropped
him off. Unless, of course, they already know about his girlfriend."

"They meaning Internal Security?"

"He's either headed right for Internal Security or to someone
else who'll be grateful for a report on the interesting things we've
been doing on your father's estancia. I thought about blowing the
sonofabitch away on the drive here. Now I'm sorry I didn't."

"It would have gotten blood all over my nice leather seats,"
Clete said, not willing to accept that Graham was serious.

"Disposing of the body would have been the problem, and I
didn't know how you two would react."

My God, he's serious.

"My father doesn't seem worried about Delgano."

"I am," Graham said simply.

"Well, what the hell, Colonel. Eat, drink, and be merry, for tomorrow . . . or a day or two later . . . we probably die."

"Good God!" Graham said, his voice falling into a groan.

"Do you want me to take you to your hotel? Or the Edificio Kavanagh?"

"What's that? Oh, Mallín's office?"

Clete nodded.

"I better go there," Graham said.

There was a large, sharp-pointed grain of truth in Clete's flippant remark.

Based on his professional experience as a Naval Aviator while operating from Henderson Field on Guadalcanal, First Lieutenant Cletus H. Frade, USMCR, was possessed of knowledge that he did not elect to share with anyone but Second Lieutenant Anthony J. Pelosi, CE, AUS.

While he was confident that their system to illuminate the *Reine de la Mer* by means of parachute flares would probably illuminate the *Reine de la Mer* enough to permit whoever was firing the torpedoes from the submarine to see the sonofabitch well enough to aim accurately, the chances of the aircraft coming out of the encounter intact were practically nonexistent.

The odds of the crew of the aircraft surviving the encounter intact were somewhat less. For a number of reasons: The crew would not have parachutes, for instance. Nor would they have life belts that Clete had any confidence in. After an extensive search, he found the ones they were using in a warehouse at the estancia. They looked as if they had floated off the *Lusitania* when she sank and were dry-rotting away ever since.

While there was an element of risk in actually dropping the flares, that operation was simplicity itself. A chute had been constructed of wood. This fit in the door of the aircraft, and was long enough to hold six flare assemblies in a row. There was room for two rows, for a total of a dozen flares.

On the command "Get Ready," the flare dropper—Pelosi— would elevate the interior end of the chute by propping it up with legs mounted to its sides. He would then remove a board at the exterior end of the chute, which held the rows of flares in place.

On the command "Go," the flare dropper would simultaneously activate two detonators, each with a five-second delay, and immediately shove all twelve flares off the chute using a built-in pusher.

Five seconds later, approximately two to three seconds after leaving the aircraft, the detonators would function, in turn igniting a length of primercord (which bound the six-flare bundles together) and the detonators which would ignite the magnesium. Once freed of bundling, the flare assemblies would separate, and their parachutes would deploy, a second or two before the magnesium in each reached full burn.

It sounded like a Mickey Mouse rig, especially to Chief Daniels, but to Clete and Graham as well (especially since the primercord was locally manufactured by Lieutenant Pelosi). But it worked from the first test, and they tested it twice.

According to the plan, the flare dropper would then reload the chute with a second dozen flare assemblies and stand by for the "Get Ready" and "Go" orders in case a second run over the *Reine de la Mer* proved necessary.

The odds that a second run over the *Reine de la Mer* would not be necessary were, in Lieutenant Frade's judgment, approximately one hundred to one.

His reasoning was that even with the *Reine de la Mer* in plain sight, permitting a perfect overtarget run, he would have absolutely no idea, when they began their descent, how the slipstream and other factors like winds aloft would affect the flares' position in relation to the *Reine de la Mer*, and thus how they were illuminating it.

The illumination pattern could of course be perfect for the torpedo aimer in the submarine. This was highly unlikely, but possible.

At this point, there entered another messy question: Would the submarine be in position to fire its torpedoes once the target was bathed in the light of the magnesium flares?

Submarines firing torpedoes are not like warships firing their cannon, or hunters shooting ducks. Cannons can be traversed, moved from side to side, just as a hunter can turn to move his shotgun. But torpedoes fire in a straight line in the direction the submarine is pointed. While it is possible to adjust the course of a torpedo—turning it left or right off a dead-ahead course—that can only be adjusted so much.

Presuming the submarine got a good look at the *Reine de la Mer* in the light of the first flare run, it was very probable that it would be necessary to move the direction of her bow ten, twenty, maybe thirty degrees to the right or left.

But when the flare run began, the *Devil Fish* would not be moving. Or if it was moving, it would only be just fast enough to maintain steering way. Turning would take time, more time than the duration of the flare burn.

And after the first flare run, meanwhile, the crew of the *Reine de la Mer* would not only be alerted but would have time to man the heavy machine guns and the Bofors cannon—if they weren't already manned.

And there would be enough light from the first-run flares to illuminate the Beechcraft. When the second flare run started, the *Reine de la Mer* would be prepared for it.

It was unpleasant enough to dwell upon what heavy machine bullets would do to the fuselage, wings, and gas tanks of the Beechcraft without considering what would happen inside the aircraft if 40-mm exploding projectiles struck it and sympathetically detonated Tony's homemade (quarter-inch cotton rope impregnated with nitroglycerine) primercord, and thus set off a dozen flares.

"Well, what the hell, Clete," Tony said. "It will be a spectacular way to go."

[FIVE]

Maria-Teresa's father almost ran to greet Tony when he stepped inside the Ristorante Napoli; and he treated Tony like royalty when he bowed and scraped him to a table.

"I'm profoundly sorry, Señor Pelosi, that Maria-Teresa is away at the moment," Señor Alberghoni announced in a rush to Tony, once he was seated. "She certainly would have been here for you if she had known you were coming. But she has gone to confession at the Church of San Juan Evangelista. That's not far away, as you know. She'll certainly return shortly, and she'll be delighted to see you. And remorseful that she was not here when you were kind enough to call at the restaurant.

"In the meantime, would Señor Pelosi like a glass of wine and a little something to eat?"

The "Señor Pelosi" business made Tony uncomfortable, and so did the bowing and the scraping, but that wasn't as bad as when Maria-Teresa's father wept and kissed his hands after

Maria-Teresa gave him the paid-off mortgage.

"Grazie," Tony said. "I'd like a glass of wine."

Half a bottle of vino tinto and a huge platter of vermicelli with a mushroom-tomato sauce later, Maria-Teresa still hadn't shown up. So Tony decided to walk over to San Juan Evangelista and wait for her. He didn't want to say what he had to say to her with her father hanging over him anyway. Maybe he would meet her on the street.

But he didn't meet her on the street. And when he went inside the baroque church, he didn't see her there either. Maybe she took a back alley or something on her way back to the ristorante.

A priest was sitting outside one of the confession stalls. It wasn't that way at home. When you went to confession there, you couldn't see the priest. Maybe you could recognize his voice, or he could recognize yours; but you couldn't see him and he couldn't see you.

What the hell, he doesn't know who I am.

He entered the confession stall and dropped to his knees.

"Bless me, Father, for I have sinned."

"Habla español? Italiano?"

Tony switched to Italian.

Aside from not going to mass, the only sin he could think of was one that had been troubling him since he was thirteen years old.

"Father, I have been having impure thoughts. About a specific girl."

Priestly interrogation brought out that he had also been guilty of the sin of Onanism in connection with his impure thoughts about the specific girl. He received a brief lecture on forcing impure thoughts from his mind and the harm that self-abuse inflicts on the body and the soul; and then he was given absolution and a relatively minor penance.

He left the confession stall and dropped to his knees before a larger than life-size statue of Saint John the Baptist, lit a votive candle, and asked God to make it easy for his mother and his father and his brothers to understand if he didn't come through the business with the *Reine de la Mer*. And he asked Him not to let them mourn so badly. And then he stood up.

When he turned around, he saw Maria-Teresa standing by one of the enormous pillars. Her head was covered with a shawl.

Jesus Christ, she's beautiful!

"I saw you come in," she said.

"I was looking for you."

"What are you doing here?"

"I told you, I was looking for you. Then I went to confession."

"I thought you would come," Maria-Teresa said. "But not here."

"Excuse me?"

"What do you want, Anthony?"

"I want to talk to you for a minute. Can we go get a cup of coffee or something?"

"To the ristorante?"

"Not to the ristorante."

"There is a café near here."

He took her arm on the street. She didn't shrug it away, but she didn't seem to like it much, either.

They took a tiny table in a small, crowded café, and a waiter came and took their order. Tony was going to order coffee, but changed his mind and asked for a glass of vino tinto. He asked Maria-Teresa if she wanted a cake or a dish of ice cream or something, but she said no thank you, all she wanted was coffee.

"Do you want me to come with you, Anthony?" Maria-Teresa asked.

"Come with me where?"

She shrugged. He understood.

"Jesus Christ, no! Nothing like that."

"Then what do you want?"

He reached inside his jacket, came up with an envelope, and handed it to her.

```
2nd Lt A.J. Pelosi, 0-538677, CE
Army Detachment
Office of Strategic Services
National Institutes of Health Building
Washington, D.C.

                    Military Attaché
                    U.S. Embassy
                    Buenos Aires
                    Argentina
```

"What's this?"

"If you don't see me again in a week," Tony said, "I want

you to take that to the U.S. Embassy. You know where that is?"

Maria-Teresa shook her head no.

"What is this?"

"It's in the Bank of Boston Building," Tony said. "There will be a Marine guard."

"A what?"

"A Marine guard. Sort of a soldier. You tell him you want to see the Military Attaché. He'll probably ask you why, and you tell him that it's about an American Army officer."

"An American Army officer?" Maria-Teresa asked, now wholly confused.

"Yeah. Look here." He pointed at the envelope. "That's me, up in the corner."

"That's you? I don't understand."

"Maria-Teresa, for Christ's sake, just listen to me. You give this to the guard and tell him you want to see the Military Attaché."

"Why don't you just give him this letter yourself?"

"I may not be here."

"You're leaving Argentina?"

"Yeah. Maybe."

"And not coming back?"

"If I leave, I won't be coming back."

"Where are you going? Back to the United States?"

"Something like that."

"What's in the envelope?"

"A couple of letters."

"What kind of letters?"

"That's what I wanted to talk to you about. If I don't come back, there will be some money for you. But to get the money, you have to take this letter to the Military Attaché."

"I don't want any more of your money. What are you talking about, giving me more money? This is crazy."

"Goddamn it, if I go away, I won't need any money, and I want you to have it."

"I want to know what's in this envelope," Maria-Teresa said firmly.

"Help yourself. They're in English; you won't know what you're reading."

She opened the envelope and took from it two sheets of paper.

Tony was right. She couldn't understand much of either of them.

Buenos Aires, Argentina
28 December 1942

To Whom It May Concern:

Through: The Military Attaché
          U.S. Embassy
          Buenos Aires, Argentina
I desire to change the beneficiary of my
National Service Insurance from Mrs.
Pasquale Pelosi, 818 Elm Street, Cicero,
Illinois USA, to Miss Maria-Teresa
Alberghoni, c/o Ristorante Napoli, Boca,
Buenos Aires, Argentina.

                Anthony J. Pelosi 0-538677
                2nd Lieut CE, AUS

(On TDY from Army Detachment
Office of Strategic Services
National Institutes of Health Building
Washington, D.C.)

December 28, 1942
Somewhere in Argentina

PLEASE FORWARD TO:
Mr. Pasquale Pelosi
818 Elm Street
Cicero, Illinois

Dear Pop:

  If you get this, I will have done what you
always said I was going to do, test the
detonator after I hooked up the charge.
  Maybe after the war, somebody will tell you

what I was doing down here, but right now
it's classified, and all I can tell you is
that it was important, and I volunteered to
do it.

What comes next is probably going to upset
you a little.

I fell in love down here. Her name is
Maria-Teresa Alberghoni, and she is a nice
Italian girl whose family comes from around
Naples someplace. Pop, she and her family
don't have a dime. They work hard, but
they're really poor.

So what I've done is make her the beneficiary
of the ten thousand dollar GI insurance policy
I get from the Army, and I want you to somehow
arrange to get her the money I inherited from
Grandpa, less thirteen thousand dollars I owe
First Lieutenant C.H. Frade, USMCR, c/o OSS.
If he doesn't come through this either, the OSS
can get you the name of his family in New
Orleans.

Since I can't use it, I think Grandpa would
like what I want to do with his money. If he
told me once he told me a hundred times how he
came from Italy with sixteen dollars and the
clothes on his back. You don't need the money
and it will help Maria-Teresa get a start on
life here in Argentina.

Kiss Mamma, those ugly brothers of mine,
and maybe light a candle for me every once in
a while.

                         Love, your son
                              Anthony

"This is a letter to your father?"

"Right."

"What does it say?"

"It says that if something happens to me, I have some money
I want him to send to you."

"What's going to happen to you?"

"Maybe nothing."

"And maybe what?"

"Maybe I'll get killed."

"How?"

"I can't tell you about that."

"Why not?"

"I just can't tell you, that's all."

"It has to do with the war?"

Tony nodded.

"I thought so," she said. "I knew you were doing something. You told me you were an American, and you told my father you were from the North of Italy. You lied."

"I had to."

"Are you lying to me now?"

"About what? No, I'm not lying to you."

"Señor Mallín said you would come to me."

"Mallín? You saw that sonofabitch? What did he want?"

"He came and said that he would forgive me if I promised not to see you again."

"And?"

"I told him that I did not want to be with him anymore, and he said that you would come to see me, and want to be with me."

"Not like that, I don't want to be with you."

"When I saw you go in the restaurant, I thought that was what you wanted."

"Look, Maria-Teresa, just take the goddamned envelope to the U.S. Embassy if I don't come back, all right?"

"If you wish," she said, and stuffed it in her purse.

He drained his wineglass, looked around for the waiter to order another, changed his mind, stood up, and fished in his pocket for money.

"You're going?"

"Right."

"Where?"

"I don't know. To my apartment, I guess."

Maria-Teresa stood up, and he followed her out of the café.

She stopped and waited for him, and put her hand on his arm.

"You want me to walk you back to the ristorante?"

"No."

"Then what?"

"Is there anyone at your apartment?"

"No."

"Then we will go there," Maria-Teresa said.

"I told you, I didn't come here for anything like that."

"I want to go with you to your apartment."

"Why?"

"It will be an interesting experience," Maria-Teresa said matter-of-factly. "I have never made love before because I wanted to."

XXI

[ONE]
Bureau of Internal Security
Ministry of Defense
Edificio Libertador
Avenida Paseo Colón
Buenos Aires
1905 29 December 1942

"Would you wait outside, please, gentlemen, to give Coronel Martín and myself a word alone?" el Almirante Francisco de Montoya, Chief of the Bureau of Internal Security, Ministry of National Defense, said to el Comandante Carlos Habanzo, of the Bureau of National Security, and el Capitán Gonzalo Delgano, Air Service, Argentine Army, Retired, who stood before his desk, their hands folded on the smalls of their backs. El Teniente Coronel Bernardo Martín sat slumped on a leather couch at one side of the room.

The two left the office, wearing looks of self-approval. After they were gone, Martín leaned forward, picked up a small cup of coffee, and took a sip. When he set it down, he saw that el Almirante de Montoya had left his desk and assumed what Martín thought of as his Deep-In-Thought position: He was standing in front of his window, staring out over the Río de la Plata. His hands were behind his back, his fingers were moving nervously, and he was rocking slightly from side to side.

Finally, he snorted and turned to face Martín.

"I am curious, Martín, why I was not aware until just now that you had this man Delgano reporting on el Coronel Frade."

"I was aware, mi Almirante, of your friendship with el Coronel Frade . . ."

"Friendship is not the point, Martín. Friendship is friendship; information is information."

". . . and if Delgano went to Frade and informed him of his relationship with me, I wished to leave you in a position where you could truthfully tell el Coronel Frade that you knew nothing about that . . . that you stopped the surveillance the instant you did hear about it; and that you are dealing harshly with the man who ordered it."

"I am touched by your loyalty to me, and your willingness to sacrifice your career to protect me," de Montoya said.

"I am loyal to you, mi Almirante," Martín said. "And I feel I can serve you best by not sacrificing my career unless absolutely necessary."

El Almirante de Montoya looked at Martín with a frown, then he slowly smiled.

"El Comandante Habanzo is the officer who put his career at risk by enlisting Delgano," Martín said.

"You are a devious fellow, Bernardo," el Almirante de Montoya said approvingly. "I'm sure this was a painful decision for you to make."

"At first, it was. And then I began to develop suspicions about el Comandante Habanzo."

"And have these suspicions been confirmed?"

"Let me say this, mi Almirante: If sacrificing el Comandante Habanzo's career for the greater good of the BIS becomes necessary, I will not consider it a particularly heavy loss."

"There is such a thing as being too discreet, Bernardo."

"Nevertheless, I am not completely sure of my facts. It seemed odd to me, however, after I personally charged Habanzo to surveil young Frade, and to use any assets and personnel he considered necessary, that the men who tried to kill young Frade, and who murdered that poor housekeeper, were able to gain access to the house without being seen."

"But you did not pursue this line of thought?"

"Young Frade made that impossible, mi Almirante. It's difficult to interrogate dead men."

"Yes, you're right, Bernardo," el Almirante said thoughtfully. "Curious. And what do you conclude?"

"That it's quite likely that Habanzo has a relationship with the Germans."

"Quite possible," el Almirante said, pausing for a moment to stare out over the river. Then he went on, "Let me say, Bernardo, *ex post facto*, that you handled the situation at el Coronel Frade's guest house as I would have handled it myself. That required both imagination and a willingness to assume responsibility."

"Thank you, mi Almirante. I did what I thought you would

want me to do in those circumstances.''

De Montoya smiled and nodded: ''So then we must consider the motives of the Germans, mustn't we? Is this replenishment vessel of theirs so important to their submarine operations that they would be willing to alienate a man who may well become President of Argentina to preserve it?''

''If you would permit me to express my thoughts—not conclusions—about that, and then tell me where I may have gone wrong?''

''Please do.''

''Possibility One is that their replenishment vessel is in fact so important that they would be willing to pay any price to ensure that it remains operational—even if that means earning el Coronel Frade's hatred by killing his son . . . and/or the embarrassment of being caught by us.''

El Almirante de Montoya grunted, accepting that theory.

''Possibility Two,'' Martín went on, ''is that they wished to demonstrate both to the Americans, and in particular to el Coronel Frade—and the Grupo de Oficiales Unidos—that they are so powerful that they can do whatever they wish with impunity. They caused the disappearance of the first OSS team that was sent here to deal with the replenishment vessel. By eliminating the head of the second OSS team—''

''Let me interrupt for a moment,'' de Montoya said. ''What about young Frade? Is he a professional intelligence officer, or was he sent down here because he is his father's son?''

''I at first thought the latter,'' Martín replied. ''Now I am having second thoughts. It seems certain that the OSS sent him here to deal with the *Reine de la Mer*.''

''You think they can sink her?''

''No, Sir. I don't think that will happen. The man I had on the pilot's boat when the *Reine de la Mer* entered our waters reported—I sent you his report, mi Almirante—that she is heavily armed for a merchant vessel, with what we believe are two dual forty-millimeter Bofors cannon, plus heavy machine guns, and what is very likely a radar antenna.''

''A what?''

''A device that uses radio waves to detect other vessels, or boats, within a ten-to-twenty-mile range.''

''I've heard that both the Germans and the English have such devices, but I was not aware they were commonly available.''

''The replenishment vessel is tremendously important to the

Germans. It would follow she would have the best available equipment."

"So young Frade's mission is doomed to failure?"

"That is my belief, mi Almirante. If we are to believe everything Delgano said about the current activities at Estancia San Pedro y San Pablo, Frade intends to bomb the *Reine de la Mer* with incendiary devices, apparently designed to explode her fuel tanks, or at least set them on fire. And all he has to do this with is his father's airplane, which is, as you know . . ."

"I know," de Montoya said impatiently. "I've flown in it. It is not a warplane."

"As I was saying a moment ago, mi Almirante, my second theory vis-à-vis the motives of the Germans is that killing young Frade would send the message that they have the better intelligence operation; that they are so powerful that they don't care if they enrage a possible President of Argentina; and, as a secondary benefit, they protect the *Reine de la Mer*."

"In either case, young Frade dies?"

"I'm afraid so, mi Almirante."

"Pity. It will be difficult for his father personally, and difficult for us, my friend, if we have a President who hates the Germans."

"I don't see how it can be avoided. The Americans are apparently determined to make the attempt against the odds."

"And what, in your opinion, should our course of action be?"

"What I have been thinking—what I would like to present for your concurrence, mi Almirante—is that we do nothing, simply let happen what happens."

"Based on what reasoning?"

"We are a neutral power. We don't *know* that the *Reine de la Mer* is in fact a replenishment vessel in our waters, thus violating our neutrality; and we don't *know* that young Frade is in fact an OSS agent sent here to sink her, thus violating our neutrality. Consequently, however the attempt to sink the *Reine de la Mer* turns out, we can express surprise, regret, anger, whatever would be appropriate. But to repeat, I think young Frade will fail."

"And die in the attempt?"

"Regrettably, mi Almirante."

"If your suspicions that that fool Habanzo has been dealing with the Germans are justified, they will know within a half hour of his leaving this building—if they don't already know—everything that's going on at Estancia San Pedro y San Pablo."

"Delgano came directly here to report to Habanzo," Martín

said. "And I haven't let either of them out of my sight since Habanzo brought Delgano to me. I don't think Delgano knows Habanzo has a German connection. And in any event, I don't think that even Habanzo would be fool enough to try to telephone the Germans from this building. So I am assuming that the Germans know nothing about the activities at Estancia San Pedro y San Pablo."

El Almirante de Montoya grunted again, accepting that.

"How will you deal with those two?" he asked after a moment.

"With your concurrence, mi Almirante, I'll have Habanzo send Delgano back to Estancia San Pedro y San Pablo, with orders to keep his mouth shut and his eyes open until he hears from Habanzo. And then I'll send Habanzo to Uruguay with several men—including a young Capitán, Oswaldo Storrer, in whom I have complete confidence. His orders will be to detect and interrupt the American supply line from Brazil through Uruguay to Argentina. Storrer's orders will be to not let Habanzo out of his sight or near a telephone."

"And then?"

"When this whole business is over, mi Almirante, I suggest that you approach el Coronel Frade and tell him that you have just learned from me that an officer in the BIS—whom you have transferred from BIS to an obscure post—had the effrontery to recruit el Capitán Delgano."

De Montoya thought about that for a long moment.

"He knows, of course, that you cleaned up the mess at his Guest House, so he will trust you. But of course, Martín, that means that you have chosen sides—and he will know it."

"I see no alternative, mi Almirante. El Coronel Frade has reached the stage where anyone who does not support him is against him."

El Almirante de Montoya grunted again, turned to his window, and assumed his Deep-In-Thought position, and remained in it for over a minute.

Finally he turned.

"When the opportunity presents itself, I will have a word with el Coronel Frade. And, in the meantime, you will keep me informed?"

"Of course, mi Almirante."

"For the present, do what you think should be done about those two," el Almirante said, gesturing toward the closed door.

"Sí, mi Almirante," Martín replied. "Con permiso, mi Almirante?"

With an impatient gesture of his hand, el Almirante de Montoya dismissed him.

[TWO]
1728 Avenida Coronel Díaz
Buenos Aires
1925 29 December 1942

Like Tony Pelosi, Clete Frade also decided to write farewell letters—to his grandfather and his aunt Martha, and to Señorita Dorotea Mallín.

He spent the better part of an hour at the desk in Granduncle Guillermo's playroom working on them, with absolutely no success. With regard to his grandfather and aunt Martha, he finally concluded that letters would be counterproductive. They would arrive several weeks after the notification of his death, and would only tear away the scab from that emotional wound.

He was glad that he told Martha at Uncle Jim's grave that he loved her. And he was sorry he had not put the same thought in words to the Old Man.

Who probably would have responded by announcing something like "people who can't handle alcohol should leave it alone," or "only fools and drunks wear their emotions on their sleeve."

So far as the No-Longer-Virgin Princess was concerned, perhaps there would be time tonight at the *en famille* dinner to have a private word with her—*a private one-way word; I certainly can't let her know that I think I'm about to get my ass blown away*—during which he could try again to point out that she was much too young to know what love was all about, and that she had an exciting period of her life before her, during which she would meet a number of young men.

The problem of farewell letters resolved, it occurred to him that he hadn't had anything to eat lately. He could, of course, push the call button and have them rustle up something in the kitchen.

What I really want—God knows what the Old Man will serve tonight, but it certainly won't be simple—is a hot dog with onions and a beer. And there's a place a couple of blocks down Libertador where I can get one.

He was in his underwear, because of the heat. He went to the wardrobe, took out a red polo shirt, a pair of khaki pants, a cotton blazer, and Sullivan's boots. When dressed, he examined himself in the mirror and was satisfied that he was wearing the right thing—that he actually looked rather spiffy—for an *en famille* dinner.

Then he went down and backed the Buick out of the basement, drove half a dozen blocks down Avenida Libertador until he found the small sidewalk restaurant he was looking for, and went in.

He had a private chat with the man tending the *carbón parrilla* (a wood-fired barbecue grill), finally convincing him that he really wanted the hot dogs grilled and not boiled, and served with chopped raw onions on French bread. Then he took a table, ordered cervezas, and watched the people walk by.

Three grilled hot dogs with raw onion and a pair of liter bottles of beer later, he glanced at his watch. It was nine o'clock. He would just have time to drive to the house on Avenida Coronel Díaz and arrive at the socially accepted time—fifteen minutes late.

[THREE]
1728 Avenida Coronel Díaz
Buenos Aires
2115 29 December 1942

A butler in a tailcoat opened the door to his knock.

"Buenas noches, Señor Frade," he said, straight-faced. "El Coronel and his guests are in the first-floor reception room."

The first floor, the way the Argentines count, is really the second floor, Clete was pleased to remember.

He went up the curving, wide staircase two steps at a time, in happy anticipation of seeing the No-Longer-Virgin Princess, only halfway up remembering that if the opportunity presented itself to kiss her, he would reek of beer and raw onions.

He entered the reception room. The first person he saw was Major Freiherr Hans-Peter von Wachtstein, resplendent in a white Luftwaffe summer uniform, with his Knight's Cross of the Iron Cross dangling over his chest. He was chatting with Señorita Alicia Carzino-Cormano, who was in a floor-length white dress cut so that not only a strand of pearls but a wide expanse of bosom—both magnificent—were on prominent display.

Also present in the room were Señorita Carzino-Cormano's mother and sister, also wearing shades of white; Uncle Humberto and Aunt Beatrice, she in a floor-length black gown, he in a white dinner jacket; half a dozen other people, including an Argentine admiral and the fat colonel of the Husares de Pueyrredón in mess dress; and their ladies; Señor A. F. Graham, in a white dinner jacket; and of course the Mallín family, Mamá, Papá, the No-Longer-Virgin Princess, and even Little Enrico, all done up in a dinner jacket.

Plus, of course, the host, el Coronel Jorge Guillermo Frade, in a white dinner jacket.

The No-Longer-Virgin Princess, when she saw him in the red polo shirt and blue blazer, smiled warmly and then giggled. Though they didn't giggle, Señor Graham's and Major Freiherr von Wachtstein's faces reflected a certain amusement at Clete's discomfort, and then at the sight of his father stalking across the room to greet him.

"At least you managed to arrive," Clete's father said as he took his arm and led him out of the room, "at the dinner I gave at your request. I suppose that's something."

"What I had in mind was just the Mallíns," Clete said. "Sorry."

"You should be glad that didn't happen."

"Excuse me?"

"Mallín came early," his father said as he led him down a wide corridor and then through a double door. "I have some clothing in here that should fit you."

"I don't think so," Clete said. His father was forty pounds heavier than he was. "Mallín came early and . . . ?"

"I bought much of this when I was your age," his father said, throwing open a closet that looked like a rack in a formal clothing store. "There's a dinner jacket in here from Close and Marsh in London that should do."

He found what he was looking for and thrust it at Clete.

"I don't know about a shirt," he said. "But there's a drawer of them over there, and you'll find studs and so on on my dresser. And now, the entertainment of the evening finished, I will return to *your* guests."

Clete put his hand on his father's arm and stopped him.

"Answer the question. Mallín was here, and . . . ?"

"He wished to talk to me privately, man-to-man, as one father to another," Frade said. "About your relationship with his daughter. While he assured me that he felt you were a fine young man of sterling character, who would never take advantage of an innocent young girl, as men of the world, we both knew that when two young people fancy themselves in love . . . et cetera, et cetera . . . and that he hoped I would be good enough to have a word with you. I told him that you are a man, and that I have no control over your romantic life."

"That's it?"

"I also told him that I rather understood your interest in his innocent young daughter. I suggested that you perhaps acquired your interest in young girls in the bar at the Plaza Hotel, watching middle-aged men fawning over Minas young enough to be their daughters."

"You didn't!"

Frade nodded. "And I also told him that he should be glad that you are both my son and an officer and a gentleman, who therefore can be expected to do the right thing by his innocent daughter, rather than one of the middle-aged men in the Plaza bar who behave despicably toward their young women."

"He took this?"

"He seemed rather discomfited," Frade said, obviously pleased with himself. Then his tone changed. "Cletus, I looked at Dorotea tonight for the first time as a young woman, not as a girl."

"I'm in love with her, Dad."

"To look at your faces when you greeted one another, I would never have guessed," Frade said. "But the way you said that makes the other things I intended to say to you unnecessary." He paused. "You will be taking Dorotea into dinner—sitting with her. I had the butler rearrange the seating arrangements."

Frade looked at his watch.

"Dress quickly; your odd Norteamericano notion of appropriate dinner dress is delaying the serving of dinner."

"Sorry about that."

"You should be," Clete's father said, and walked out of the room.

Clete was at the bathroom mirror tying his bow tie, when he heard the door to his father's apartment creak open. He'd had his choice among dress shirts—too large or too small. He opted for a loose collar. After he adjusted the tie as best he could, he returned to the bedroom, expecting to see his father, or maybe the butler, sent to help him dress.

He found instead Major Freiherr Hans-Peter von Wachtstein, leaning on the closed door, holding a bottle of champagne in one hand and two glasses in the other. Peter held out the glasses to him.

"Hold these," he ordered, "while I open the bottle."

"I'm grateful, mi Comandante, especially since this act of Christian charity obviously tore you away from the magnificent Alicia ... and her magnificent ..." He made a curving motion above his chest to indicate what he meant.

Peter popped the cork.

"If you were a real officer and gentleman, which fortunately you are not," Peter said as he poured the champagne, "I would be forced to challenge you to a duel for insulting the lady with whom I intend to share my life."

"I'll be goddamned, you sound serious."

"The duel, no. The lady, possibly. She has, certainly, a splendid body. But she also has qualities I've never encountered before."

"I'll be damned," Clete said.

Peter raised his glass.

"Fighter pilots," he said.

"Fighter pilots," Clete replied, tapping Peter's glass with his. "And their ladies."

"Since I *am* an officer and a gentleman, I will refrain from commenting that yours has a rather attractive mammary development herself, even if she is so recently out of the cradle."

"Go fuck yourself, Peter."

"I had an ulterior motive in bringing the wine to you," Peter said. "Actually, several of them."

Now he wants the favor.

"I'm not surprised."

"Oberst Grüner called me into his office this afternoon."

"The military attaché?"

Peter nodded. "He wanted to make sure that everyone here tonight sees that we have become friends ..."

"And the champagne is intended to do that?"

"... because he has good reason to believe you will not be among us much longer."

"Really?"

What the hell is this all about?

"He has learned from a reliable source in Internal Security that you are about to engage in a very foolish, amateurish operation . . . and that it is doomed to failure."

"I can't imagine what he's talking about."

"If his information is correct, you are about to use your father's airplane to make a bombing run on a neutral ship in the Bay of Samborombón, with the hope of igniting her fuel tanks with homemade incendiary bombs."

Shit, if Oberst Whatsisname knows, they'll be waiting for us.
That miserable sonofabitch Delgano!
What is this "homemade incendiary bomb" bullshit?
Christ, they mean the flares. Which means they haven't thought of a submarine!

"I think your Oberst Whatsisname has been at the schnapps," Clete said.

"Oberst Grüner went on to say that the ship, the *Reine de la Mer*, is armed with two dual forty-millimeter Bofors and some heavy machine guns. It will have no trouble at all shooting you down."

Clete met Peter's eyes but said nothing.

"Now I personally felt that the Oberst's information was wrong," Peter went on. "For one thing, a pilot with your experience would know that if the pilot on such a mission were actually lucky enough to hit the ship with an incendiary bomb, the only thing the bomb would do is lie around on thick steel plates and burn itself out."

"I never gave the subject much thought," Clete said. "But now that you mention it, I think you're right."

"I did not offer my opinion on the subject to Oberst Grüner," Peter said. "I suppose that I should have. And I daresay in some quarters that my failure to do so would constitute treason."

"Why are you telling me all this, Peter?" Clete asked.

"Treason is a subject I've given a good deal of thought to, lately," Peter said.

"Where are we going with this conversation?" Clete asked.

"That remains to be seen," Peter said. "Did you mean what you said?"

"Said about what?"

"You said, if memory serves, that I have 'a blank check' with you."

"As long as it has nothing to do with the . . . idiotic notion your Oberst Whatsisname has, you do."

"I need your help."

"Anything I can do, you've got it."

"When I give you this, I'm putting my father's and several other people's lives in your hands," Peter said. He took his father's letter from his pocket and handed it to him.

Clete glanced at it.

"I don't speak German, Peter. You're going to have to translate this."

"Yes, of course, I didn't think about that," Peter said, and took the letter back and read it aloud, translating it with some effort into Spanish.

Toward the end, through eyes themselves bleared with tears, Clete saw that Peter's eyes, too, were teary. And his voice was breaking.

"I think I need a little more champagne," Clete said, picking up the bottle and filling their glasses.

"Can you help me?" Peter asked.

"I can't help you," Clete said. "I'll have to go to my father. He'll have to hear what this letter says."

Peter nodded.

Clete went to the bedside and pushed the servant call button.

"You're doing what?" Peter asked.

"I'm sending for my father."

"I didn't mean tonight."

"That's all the time we have."

"Grüner was right?"

There was a knock at the door, so quickly that Clete was surprised. It was a maid.

"Señor Cletus?"

"How did you get here so quickly?"

"El Coronel told me to wait in the upstairs pantry in case you needed something, Señor Cletus."

"Please tell el Coronel that I need him here immediately; that it is something you can't do for me."

"Sí, Señor," the maid said, and quickly left the room.

"Grüner was right?" Peter repeated. "Clete, you don't stand a chance."

"I am not going to bomb anything with incendiary bombs, OK? Now leave that alone, Peter, for Christ's sake!"

Peter met Clete's eyes again.

"As you wish, my friend," he said.

*   *   *

"What now?" el Coronel demanded as he came in the room. "Your guests will start eating the furniture."

He saw the look on Clete's face and stopped.

"What is it?"

"You know I owe Peter my life," Clete said. "It's payback time. Or partial payback time."

"A debt of honor?" Frade asked. "What is it?"

"Peter has a letter from his father. It's in German. He'll have to translate it for you."

"Let's have the letter. I speak German. Among other things you don't know about me, I'm a graduate of the Kriegsschule."

Peter handed Clete's father the letter.

When he finished reading the letter, it took el Coronel Frade a long moment before he trusted his voice enough to speak.

"I can only hope, my friend," he said finally, "that one day my son will have reason to be half as proud of me as you must be of your father."

"Danke schön, Herr Oberst."

"Perhaps you will be able to find time in your busy schedule to spend a few days at Estancia San Pedro y San Pablo in the very near future. I will ask my brother-in-law, who is Managing Director of the Anglo-Argentine Bank, to join us for a private conversation."

"That's very kind of you, Herr Oberst."

"That business concluded, can we finally join Cletus's guests?"

The No-Longer-Virgin Princess' knee found Clete's knee within thirty seconds of their taking their seats at the dinner table. Her hand followed a moment later.

Anticipating this move, Clete caught it with his own hand and held it.

She turned to him in surprise.

"You look very nice in your dinner jacket," she said innocently.

"And you are the most beautiful thing I have ever seen in my life," Clete said.

[FOUR]
Radio Room
USS *Alfred Thomas,* DD-107
100 Nautical Miles Due East of Punta del Este,
Uruguay
0615 30 December 1942

Ensign Richard C. Lacey, USNR, the Communications Officer of
the *Thomas,* a short, somewhat pudgy twenty-two-year-old, had
spent most of the night trying to familiarize himself with the
intricacies of the ship's cryptographic machine. Though all of his
effort had resulted in virtually no success, he was hoping he'd be
able to muddle through when he had to.

When Chief Schultz was still aboard, he politely suggested
more than once that while only the *supervision* of shipboard cryptographic activity was among the communication officer's duties,
not the actual *operation* of the equipment, it might be a good idea
for him to show Mr. Lacey how the equipment actually worked.

Lacey declined the Chief's offer, thinking that as long as the
Chief was aboard, the Chief could handle the decryption operations. And he would of course supervise them.

Captain Jernigan himself made it crystal clear that Chief
Schultz would remain aboard. "When you get a good chief, Mr.
Lacey," Captain Jernigan said, "any good chief, but in particular
a good Chief Radioman, you do what you can to keep him. Chief
Schultz will leave the *Thomas* only over my dead body."

Captain Jernigan was still alive. But Chief Schultz was gone,
replaced by Radioman First Class Henry Clatterman, who was
younger than Ensign Lacey. Clatterman promptly announced that
he really didn't know diddly-shit about the cryptographic machine
when he came aboard, and that despite Chief Schultz's on-the-
job training on the voyage, he was still baffled by most of what
he was supposed to do.

With a little bit of luck, however, Mr. Lacey felt that the professional inadequacies of the communications section might not
be brought to Captain Jernigan's attention. Or at least delayed:
The first attempt to communicate with the *Devil Fish* was scheduled for 0615. At this hour, the Captain, following his routine
inspection of the ship after rising, normally took his breakfast.

At 0612, Captain Jernigan entered the radio room.

"We all set up, Mr. Lacey?"

"Yes, Sir."

"Clatterman?"

"We're ready, Sir."

Precisely at 0615, Clatterman started pounding his key in an attempt to communicate with the US submarine *Devil Fish*, which was somewhere on the high seas between the coast of Africa and the coast of South America.

There was no reply after three attempts.

Mr. Lacey was enormously relieved. They would try again, according to the schedule, at six-hour intervals hereafter—at 1215, 1815, 0015, and 0615. Eventually communication would be established. Between each try, there would be an additional six hours for him to learn how to operate the cryptographic machine.

"Clatterman, try to contact the *Nantucket*," Captain Jernigan ordered. "They should be monitoring the frequency. If you reach them, send Contingency Code Six in the clear, and then stand by for a crypted reply."

"The *Nantucket*, Sir?"

"The *Devil Fish*, I hope, has by now made a rendezvous with, and is being accompanied by, a fleet tanker," the Captain explained. "I only know the names of two fleet tankers operating out of Panama, the *Nantucket* and the *Biloxi*. We'll try both of them; a fleet tanker will have better communications than a submarine. What have we got to lose?"

"The call sign, Sir?"

"It's in the book," Captain Jernigan said, a touch of annoyance in his voice. "You mean you don't have the book out?"

"No, Sir," Clatterman replied. "Mr. Lacey didn't tell me to, Sir."

"My God, Lacey!" Captain Jernigan said, went to the safe, worked the combination, opened the safe, and removed a notebook.

He looked at Mr. Lacey.

"You *did* remember to take the contingency codes out of the safe, Mr. Lacey?"

"I thought I would wait until we established contact with the *Devil Fish*, Sir. I don't like TOP SECRET material lying around the radio room."

"Mr. Lacey, go find the Exec. Tell him I'll be here for a while, and would he please remain on the bridge. And then see if you can make yourself useful to him."

"Aye, aye, Sir. Do you mean you don't want me to return here?"

"That is correct, Mr. Lacey," Captain Jernigan said. He turned to Radioman First Class Clatterman. "GHR, Clatterman. See if you can raise them, please."

"Aye, aye, Sir."

Clatterman put his hand on his key.

GHR, DSI, GHR, DSI.

There was no response from the Fleet Tanker *Nantucket*, call sign GHR.

"Try HJI," Captain Jernigan ordered. "That's the *Biloxi*."

Clatterman turned to his key.

This time there was a reply:

GHR, HJI, GA GHR, HJI, GA.

"Send them, in the clear, Contingency Code Six," Captain Jernigan ordered, and headed for the cryptographic machine.

Radioman First Class Clatterman heard the Captain mutter, "Now if I can only remember how to operate this sonofabitch."

Twenty minutes later, Captain Jernigan examined a decrypted message from the Fleet Tanker USS *Biloxi,* which advised that she and the *Devil Fish* were proceeding according to orders, and that they expected to reach Point J at 0345 Greenwich time 1 January.

"Send them in the clear: "We will maintain established radio schedule and will monitor frequency,' " Captain Jernigan ordered.

"Aye, aye, Sir," Clatterman responded.

The Captain waited until there was acknowledgment from the *Biloxi,* then ordered: "Now try HKG. If they respond, send Contingency Code Six, and if they reply, relay the *Biloxi*'s radio to us."

There was no response in four tries from HKG.

"Try HKG at hourly intervals," Captain Jernigan ordered. "If they respond, send them Contingency Code Six, then relay the last radio from the *Biloxi*. Notify me at any hour when you establish contact."

"Aye, aye, Sir."

Captain Jernigan then left the radio room for the bridge, where he asked Mr. Lacey to join him in the chart room. He delivered there a five-minute lecture to Mr. Lacey, whom he caused to stand to attention. During the lecture Mr. Lacey was advised that his performance of duty in the radio room half an hour before was

below his expectations of his communications officer, and that if
Mr. Lacey did not wish to spend the balance of the war serving
as a permanent ensign and a venereal-disease-control officer
aboard a yard tug operating in the Aleutian Islands, it would well
behoove him to learn how to do what was expected of him, and
then to demonstrate his ability to perform his duties when called
upon to do so.

[FIVE]
Radio Room
USS *Alfred Thomas*, DD-107
100 Nautical Miles Due East of Punta del Este,
Uruguay
2220 30 December 1942

"What have you got, Sparks?" Captain Jernigan inquired as he
entered the radio room. He was attired in his underwear, his bathrobe, and the somewhat battered brimmed cap with its somewhat
moldy insignia and gold strap he customarily wore at sea.

Radioman First Class Clatterman was at the radio console. Ensign Lacey, in a crisp cotton uniform, showing evidence that he
had recently shaved and was in need of sleep, sat before the
cryptographic machine.

"HKG, Captain," Ensign Lacey replied. "We have . . ."

"I was speaking to Clatterman, Mr. Lacey, if you don't mind.
Sparks?"

"HKG, Sir. They're coming in five-by-five. It's Chief Schultz,
Captain. I recognize his hand."

"Did you relay the *Biloxi*'s last radio?"

"Yes, Sir."

"Send, 'Well done,' Sparks," Captain Jernigan ordered. "And
then advise HKG that we will be monitoring the frequency."

"Aye, aye, Sir."

"I'll be in my cabin. Call me if we hear from anyone."

"Aye, aye, Sir."

[SIX]
Estancia San Pedro y San Pablo
Near Pila, Buenos Aires Province
0740 1 January 1943

The chief operator of Navy Radio Station HKG tore the sheet of paper from the typewriter on his makeshift desk and turned around, taking off his headset as he did so.

"That has to be the oldest fucking typewriter in the world," he announced.

"Beggars, Chief Schultz," First Lieutenant C. H. Frade, USMCR, replied, somewhat unctuously, "cannot be choosers."

"Up yours, Mr. Frade," Chief Schultz said, adding, "it'll take me fifteen, twenty minutes to decode this; without a machine, it's a pain in the ass. Whatever it is, it's not just one of them 'standing by' messages. It's too long for that, and they said switch to Contingency Code Eleven."

"I don't have anyplace to go, Chief."

"You want to hand me one of them beers? It's hotter than hell in here."

Eighteen minutes later, Chief Schultz handed Lieutenant Frade a sheet of typewriter paper.

"It's two messages, Mr. Frade," he said.

Clete read the messages, then passed the sheet of paper to Second Lieutenant Pelosi, who read it and handed it to Staff Sergeant Ettinger.

```
TOP SECRET
OPERATIONAL IMMEDIATE
FROM: ALFRED THOMAS DD107 0320 GREENWICH
1JAN43
TO: CHIEF OF NAVAL OPERATIONS WASH DC
ALL USNAVY VESSELS AND SHORE STATIONS RELAY

1. RENDEZVOUS WITH BILOXI AND DEVIL FISH MADE
AT POINT J 0310 1JAN43.
2. REFUELING WILL TAKE PLACE AT FIRST LIGHT.
3. IN CONTACT WITH PETER.
4. PROCEEDING ACCORDING TO ORDERS.

JERNIGAN, LTCOM USN COMMANDING.
```

> FROM THOMAS TO PETER
> REF OPERATIONAL IMMEDIATE FROM THOMAS TO CNO
> 0320 GREENWICH 1JAN43.
>
>
> 1. ESTIMATE COMPLETION REFUELING 0930 GREEN-
> WICH 1JAN43.
> 2. ESTIMATE ARRIVAL DEVILFISH POINT M REPEAT
> POINT M 2300 GREENWICH 1JAN43.
> 3. ESTIMATE DEPARTURE DEVILFISH POINT M RE-
> PEAT POINT M 0200 GREENWICH 2JAN43. SHE WILL
> ATTEMPT ADVISE ACTUAL DEPARTURE TIME PRIOR
> DEPARTURE.
> 4. ESTIMATE ARRIVAL DEVILFISH POINT O REPEAT
> POINT O 0400 GREENWICH 2JAN43. SHE WILL REPORT
> ACTUAL ARRIVAL TIME.
> 5. GODSPEED AND GOOD LUCK.
>
> JERNIGAN, LTCOM USN COMMANDING

"Chief," Clete said, "since you're dealing with a bunch of amateur sailors, maybe you'd better translate all that for us."

"You mean that, Mr. Frade?" Chief Schultz asked.

"Each tiny little detail, each tiny little step," Clete said.

"OK," Schultz said. "OK. For openers, all these times are Greenwich times, which is a place in England. There's four hours' difference. When it's noon here, it's four in the afternoon there. Got it?" He looked at his wristwatch. "It's quarter after eight. That's 1215 Greenwich. Got it?"

Clete nodded.

Tony said, "Got it, Chief."

"So, let's talk about our time," Chief Schultz went on: "The tanker, the *Biloxi,* and the *Devil Fish* rendezvoused-up with the *Thomas* off Punta del Este about eleven-ten last night. What I'm guessing is that Captain Jernigan decided there wasn't much point in starting the refueling in the dark. If things fucked up—laying alongside another ship on the high seas isn't easy in the first place, and at night it's a bitch—forget the whole operation. So he waited until it was light to start the refueling.

"Only ten minutes later, he sent that Operation Immediate to the Chief of Naval Operations. That seems pretty dumb, but maybe when you're operating DP you have to do it.''

'' 'DP,' Oscar?'' Ettinger asked.

They must have a mutual admiration society, Clete thought. *It would never have entered my mind to call Chief Schultz by his first name.*

''It means 'Direction of the President,' Dave,'' Schultz explained patiently. ''Really big-time stuff. There's probably six admirals sitting on their ass in the Navy Department, waiting to hear that you guys carried this off. Praying they don't have to go to the CNO hisself and tell him he has to go to the President and tell him this got fucked up somehow.''

''Interesting,'' Ettinger said.

''Anyway, to go through this, when Captain Jernigan sent that Operational Immediate at 2320 our time, it was not light.

''As soon as she's fueled, which would be right about now, in another fifteen or twenty minutes, the *Devil Fish* will take off for Point J—which is probably just outside the twelve-mile line, just outside Argentine waters, off the Bay of Samborombón. She'll try to contact us just before she leaves. We've been talking to the *Biloxi* and the *Thomas,* not the *Devil Fish.* They want to know if we can communicate with her. We'll probably hear from her in the next couple of minutes.''

He turned around in his chair, picked up the headset, and put it on so that one speaker was on his left ear and the other was resting against his forehead.

''The *Devil Fish*'ll probably run on the surface for a while, but then she'll run submerged, which is slower, to make sure nobody sees her. Then, when she's at Point M, which she estimates at 1900 our time, she'll surface, just far enough out of the water to get air to run her diesels and recharge her batteries, and then lay on the bottom until maybe 2300, when she will stick her antenna out of the water long enough to contact us and tell us she's leaving.''

He turned suddenly in his chair, put both cans over his ears, and after tapping his key briefly, began to type on the typewriter. Finally he turned again.

''I'll have to decode this to be sure, but I'll bet—it's short and right on time—that it's the *Devil Fish* telling us she's leaving for Río de la Plata. You want me to go on, or decode it?''

''Decode it, please, Chief,'' Clete ordered.

It was in fact a message from the *Devil Fish,* reporting that she was departing Point J for Point M.

"Which proves our radio works," Chief Schultz said. "Even with the shitty antennas on a submarine. Where was I?"

"The *Devil Fish* contacts us when she's leaving for Point O," Clete furnished.

"Not exactly," Chief Schultz said. "She contacts us to find out where the *Reine de la Mer* is, so from the charts Captain Jernigan gave her, she can pick the best spot for her to lay on the bottom of Samborombón Bay."

"I stand corrected," Clete said.

"Then the *Devil Fish* goes submerged to Point O, sticks her antenna out of the water, and tells us where she is. Then Mr. Frade here tells her where the *Reine de la Mer* is, and asks when he should drop the flares."

"And if the *Reine de la Mer* moves after Lieutenant Frade gives her position to the *Devil Fish?*" Ettinger asked.

"Then we start all over again, finding the sonofabitch, and then waiting for the *Devil Fish* to get close enough to her to get a shot at her."

"Is there enough moonlight for you to find her, Lieutenant?" Ettinger pursued.

"It depends on the cloud cover, and how much light I have. But I'll find her. I'm going to keep tabs on her all day, starting now. You want to come with me, Tony?"

"Yeah, sure."

[SEVEN]
Samborombón Bay
0940 1 January 1943

Clete tapped Tony's shoulder and gestured toward the water 10,000 feet below them.

"You're sure that's her?" Tony asked.

"Yeah, that's her."

He consulted his Hamilton chronograph and the compass, made some quick computations, and then marked the position of the *Reine de la Mer,* sixteen miles off the coast, on the chart he had in his lap.

"Now we're going back?" Tony asked.

"Now we're going to go back and figure out some way to rig the chute so that I can operate it from up here," Clete said.

"It can't be done," Tony said. "I thought about it."

"Think some more."

"Hey, I'm going. First: There's no way you can drop the flares by yourself. And second: I'm going. And anyway, even if you could drop the first dozen by yourself, you'd have no way to reload the chute for a second run."

"I'll be very surprised if there will be a second run," Clete said. "They expect us down there."

He looked at Tony, who obviously believed him. There was fear in his eyes.

"They even know about the flares," Clete added. "They think we're going to try to set the sonofabitch on fire."

"How do you know that?"

"I have a reliable source of information. He also tells me there are two Bofors dual forty-millimeter cannon on board."

"I say again, repeat, first: There's no way you can drop the flares from up here," Tony said. "And second: I'm going."

"I say again, repeat, that when we get back we're going to see if there is a way I can do this myself."

"If they have Bofors forty-millimeters down there shooting at us, you won't have time to even think about dropping the flares yourself. Don't try to be a fucking hero."

Clete looked at Tony for a moment, then said, "Put the wire out the tail, and we'll see if the walkie-talkies work."

"Flyey-talkies?" Tony responded. "About the only thing left of the walkie-talkies after Ettinger and the Chief finished fucking with them is the nameplate."

"Let the wire out, Lieutenant Pelosi," Clete said.

"Yes, Sir, Mr. Frade, Lieutenant, Sir," Tony said.

Tony went into the now-stripped cabin of the Beechcraft and dropped to his knees near the open doorway. He put on a pair of heavy leather work gloves, then picked up a tiny parachute—a drogue chute—and carefully held the tiny chute out into the slip-stream.

It was immediately snatched from his hand; and the wire it was attached to moved so quickly over the gloves that they smoked. When all the wire, which had been carefully coiled in a wooden box, was deployed outside the Beech, he carefully looked out of the door. He could see the wire, but not the drogue chute.

He smiled with satisfaction. This idea of his had worked too. When the wire was fully extended, the force exerted by moving through the air at 120 miles per hour was enough to tear off the drogue chute. Otherwise, what Chief Schultz referred to as "the straight-wire antenna" would have gyrated wildly, and would not have been a "straight wire."

He had also solved the problem of dealing with the wire before landing, during which it would have posed problems. After Chief Schultz and the Argentine ex–Sergeant Major spent hours trying to come up with a crank to pull it back inside, he suggested they "just cut the sonofabitch; we have plenty of wire."

The suggestion earned him the highest possible praise from Chief Schultz: "Coming from a second lieutenant, that ain't too dumb an idea, Mr. Pelosi."

Tony went back through the cabin to the cockpit.

"You couldn't put the straight wire out by yourself, either, Clete," he said.

"Where there's a will, there's a way, Lieutenant Pelosi," Clete replied, and picked up a microphone.

"Peter, this is Paul. How do you read? Over."

"Paul, Peter," Chief Schultz's voice came back immediately. "Five-by-five."

"Peter, Paul, out," Clete said, set the microphone down, and turned to Tony.

"Be so good, Lieutenant Pelosi, as to cut the wire. Then we'll go home."

"Yes, Sir," Tony said.

[EIGHT]
Samborombón Bay
0325 2 January 1943

"Put the wire out, Tony," Clete ordered. "There's just enough light for us to find the sonofabitch."

"Ain't we lucky?" Tony said, and got up from the co-pilot's seat and went into the cabin.

Two minutes later he was back. He nodded at Clete, who picked up the microphone.

"Peter, Paul. How do you read?"

"Paul, Peter, five-by-five."

"Peter clear."

"Paul standing by."

"That was Ettinger," Tony observed. "I wonder where the Chief is."

"I know where he is, he went for a cerveza."

Tony laughed out loud, and Clete joined him. The laughter was contagious and hysterical.

A manifestation, Clete thought, *of extreme stress.*

He consulted his Hamilton and his chart, and then five minutes later consulted them again.

"That's where the sonofabitch was," Clete said. "Where did you go, you sonofabitch?"

"There it is," Tony said, pointing downward.

Clete looked. He could make out the shape of ship. There were no running lights or other visible activity. But it was the *Reine de la Mer.*

"I wonder why they didn't move," Clete said, and the answer came, but he kept it to himself.

They didn't move because they're not at all afraid of a single-engine civilian aircraft about to drop incendiaries on them. Or at them.

They're getting ready for a little target practice.

There's probably some sonofabitch down there with binoculars looking for us. "Ach du lieber, I hope he hasn't changed his mind and doesn't come. I was so looking forward to a little sport!"

He picked up the microphone.

"Peter, Paul."

"Go," Ettinger's voice came back immediately.

"Position unchanged."

"Hold one."

The holding took three minutes, before Ettinger's voice came over the radio.

"Paul, Peter, they want fifteen minutes."

"Understand fifteen, repeat, fifteen minutes."

"Right."

"Paul clear and standing by."

Clete pushed the button on the Hamilton that started the stopwatch function.

"We have fifteen minutes," he said.

"I heard."

"You know what I was thinking, Clete?"

"I'm afraid to ask."

"I was thinking that maybe this would be a good place—Argentina, I mean—to live."

"Right now, Mr. Pelosi, I am of the belief that practically anywhere would be a good place to live. Considering the alternatives, of course.''

"No. I mean it. I was thinking that they probably don't have a good demolitions company down here.''

"You want to blow up Buenos Aires, Mr. Pelosi? Is that what you're saying?''

"There's a lot of old buildings here that have to come down. They probably take them down the way they put them up, one brick at a time.''

"And you could improve on that system?''

"I'm pretty good at what I do, as a matter of fact,'' Tony said.

"Yes, Tony, you are.''

"What the hell, it don't cost to dream, does it?''

"Not a dime.''

"I'm really stuck on Maria-Teresa, Clete. It's not her fault she had to do what she did with that bastard Mallín.''

"You are speaking of my future father-in-law, Mr. Pelosi.''

"No shit? You're really going to marry that girl?''

"That thought has been running through my mind.''

"What the hell, why not? If you love her, that's all that really matters, right?''

"My sentiments exactly, Mr. Pelosi.''

"You be my best man, and I'll be yours, deal?'' Tony said cheerfully, and put out his hand.

Clete shook it.

"Deal.''

After a moment, Tony said, "So we're pissing in the wind. So what?''

They did not exchange another word for another twelve minutes, when Clete said, "I think you better go get set up, Tony.''

"Yeah, right.''

The first antiaircraft weapon on the *Reine de la Mer* to come into action was a heavy machine gun mounted above her bridge. It was firing one-in-five tracers. These arched through the sky and then seemed to die a hundred yards or so below the Beechcraft.

After the tracer charge burns out, Clete thought, *the projectile—plus, of course, the projectiles that don't contain a tracer element, four times as many of those—continue on their trajectory.*

Clete waited as long as he could after two other machine guns opened fire, and after first one and then the other of the Bofors 40-mm cannon began to fire, before calling, "GO!"

He held the Beechcraft as steady as he could for fifteen seconds, then turned to look over his shoulder at Tony.

Tony was reloading the chute with the second dozen flares.

I can't believe we haven't been hit!

There was a faint but perceptible yellow brightness, reflected off the underside of the upper wing, and then a much brighter glow as the magnesium of the flares ignited.

He dropped his eyes in ritual habit to the control panel. There were red lights all over it, OIL PRESSURE FAILURE being the most significant of them.

The engine coughed and died.

The wind whistling through the guy wires of the wings was eerie.

"Tony!" Clete called. "Dump the flares, we have engine failure."

"What?"

"Dump the goddamned flares, and put your goddamned life jacket on!"

He made a shallow turn to the left, away from the *Reine de la Mer* and its cannon and machine guns.

The engine nacelle suddenly glowed and then there were flames licking out its rear.

Tony came and stood behind him, trying to tie the cords of the ancient, cork-filled life jacket.

"Jesus!"

"I'm going to have to put it in the water," Clete said. "If those flames reach the fuel tanks, we're fucked."

He pushed the nose over and watched the airspeed indicator climb to the red mark and then beyond.

He was hoping that the rush of air would extinguish the blazing engine. It didn't. The fuel lines were apparently ruptured and feeding the fire.

"There was a submarine down there," Tony said.

"There was supposed to be," Clete said.

"I mean one of theirs, alongside that fucker."

"Go back and brace your back against my seat," Clete ordered.

Clete brought the Beechcraft out of its dive. If the wings came off, there would be no chance for them at all. As opposed to one chance in, say, two million.

The flame from the engine now licked at the windshield, black-

ening it, distorting it, finally burning through in front of the co-
pilot's seat.

"Shit!"

The altimeter showed three hundred feet.

He pushed the nose down, watched the water approach, and
praying that he had judged the distance with some accuracy,
pulled the nose up and waited for it to stall.

Just as he noticed that the flames from the engine were playing
less fiercely than before against the windshield, the Beechcraft
stopped flying. It fell to the left, and a second later the left wingtip
struck the water and the plane cartwheeled.

It stopped upside down, then started to sink by the nose.

He tore himself free of the lap belt, aware that he had cut
himself somewhere, fell from the seat, and made his way back to
Tony. Tony was groggy, but awake enough to be trying to make
his way to the open door.

Clete followed him, deciding that wherever the *Lusitania* life
belt he'd stored behind the co-pilot's seat was now, he had no
chance of finding it. He went through the door as the fuselage
turned upward, then settled into the water.

His first thought was that he was alive, that they were alive.
But this was quickly replaced by the thought that without a life
belt, there was no way he could swim for much more than thirty
minutes; and thirty minutes wasn't going to get him anywhere
near the shore.

He didn't think they could both be supported by Tony's life
belt. And then he realized that, too, was a moot question. Even
if they could stay afloat, they would be swept out to sea.

*It would have been better, neater, easier, if the fucking thing
had blown up in the air.*

He saw Tony bobbing around in his life vest at the same moment Tony saw him. They started to swim—Tony to paddle awkwardly—toward one another.

There was a far-off explosion, followed by a dull flash of yellow light, and then a second explosion, and a second flash of
light, and then a third.

"We got the sonofabitch!" Tony said.

"The Navy got the sonofabitch."

"Yeah, where the fuck was the Navy before . . ."

There was a final explosion, a spectacular series of explosions,
accompanied by brilliant fire rising high in the sky.

The light died quickly, and then all that they could see was burning fuel floating on the surface.

Then there was a series of splashes.

Christ, that blew pieces of the ship all the way over here!

And then there was silence.

"Put your life belt on," Tony said.

"I don't have it."

"I've got it."

With a good deal of effort—it was unbelievably difficult to manage in the water—Clete finally got the life belt on.

And now we get swept out to sea by the waters of the beautiful Río de la Plata.

"There's a light," Tony said.

Clete looked around. A searchlight was sweeping the sea. He could hear the sound of a marine engine.

"Over here!" he shouted.

"It may be from that fucking ship!" Tony said.

"And it may not be. I'll take my chances."

The spotlight found them, blinding them.

Two minutes later a boat hook caught Clete by the collar of his life jacket. He felt himself being dragged to the boat.

"Señor Cletus," Enrico's voice said. "If you would turn around, it would be easier to lift you in the boat."

Clete turned and found himself facing a polished mahogany hull. A moment later, he was jerked into the boat, falling flat on his face. He raised his head and saw another familiar face, this one at the controls.

"Where'd you get the boat, Chief?"

"Same place we got everything else," Schultz said. "From your father. Enrico and I didn't want to say anything, but we figured you was going to go in the water, and we figured we'd be here to fish you out. You all right, Mr. Frade?"

"I'm fine. Where's Mr. Pelosi?"

"Aft," Schultz said, and Clete looked. Tony, dazed but smiling, was sitting in the rear cockpit of what looked to be a Chris-Craft speedboat.

"Did you see that sonofabitch blow?" Chief Schultz asked as he spun the wheel and pushed the throttle forward. "It blew pieces of that sonofabitch to Africa."

[NINE]
Café Paris
Recoleta
Buenos Aires
1425 5 January 1943

Dorotea Mallín, wearing a pink cotton dress, removed her hand from that of First Lieutenant Cletus H. Frade, USMCR, and smiled over his shoulder.

"Hello, Señor Graham," she said.

"Miss Mallín," Graham said. "How nice to see you. Clete, you're a hard man to find."

"Not by accident," Clete said.

"Miss Mallín, I have a few things to say to Clete before I leave."

"I was afraid of that," Clete interrupted.

"Do you suppose I could have a few minutes alone with Clete?" Graham concluded.

"Princess, would you take a walk around the park, please?"

"Of course," she said, smiling and not liking it a bit.

"Beautiful girl," Graham said, watching Dorotea walk away.

"What's on your mind?"

"Well, there are some choices you have to make."

"Such as?"

"What you do next."

"I'm being given a choice?"

"On the one hand, the Marine Corps is perfectly willing to have you back—you're a major, by the way, congratulations."

"What the hell are you talking about?"

"Well, you were promoted captain the day after we met in San Francisco. I didn't tell you because it would have started you thinking about getting your own squadron."

"Thanks a lot, Colonel. Are you saying I can go back to the Corps and get a squadron?"

"No, I'm not. You're not listening. You can go back to the Corps, but they won't give you a squadron because majors don't command squadrons. You know that."

"What's this major business?"

"You were promoted major as of the day the President heard of the mysterious maritime incident in the Bay of Samborombón. For exceptionally meritorious leadership of an unspecified nature."

"I almost believe you."

"Your second option is to remain here."

"Doing what?"

"Ostensibly as Assistant Naval Attaché."

"And non-ostensibly?"

"Working for us. The Naval Attaché will be advised that his only role in your regard will be to assign you no duties and to ask you no questions."

"You want me here because of my father," Clete said bluntly.

"Obviously. Your father thinks he lost his chance to become President. I don't think so. But whatever his role will be down here, it will be important to us. If nothing else, you'll have his ear."

"How are you going to tell whose side I'm on?"

"You proved your loyalty beyond any reasonable doubt a couple of days ago."

"And the Argentines know how. They'll know I'm a spy, or whatever."

"As a general rule of thumb, all military attachés are spies. Some of them are better at it than others. Think it through, Clete. It makes a good deal of sense."

"What about Pelosi and Ettinger?"

"Ettinger came to me. He wants to stay here. He thinks he can get interesting information from the Jews coming from Europe. I don't know about Pelosi."

"Pelosi wants to stay."

"No problem, we assign him as an assistant to the Army Attaché."

"Chief Schultz?"

"I thought you might want him. Sure."

"There's probably a hook in here somewhere, even if I can't see it. I don't trust you as far as I can throw you."

"Good first rule for an intelligence officer. Trust nobody. Can I take it you'll stay?"

Clete looked out the window. The No-Longer-Virgin Princess had taken a very quick walk around the park and was now standing outside the café, smiling somewhat nervously.

"Only a fool would leave, Colonel. And I'm not a fool."

He raised his hand to the No-Longer-Virgin Princess.

Smiling happily, she walked quickly toward him.